THE COMPLETE SERIES
BOOKS 1-3

SECRETS TRILOGY

MELISSA LAM

12Bunnies
Publishing

Developmental editing by: R. D. Langr
Editing, proofreading, blurb, cover design, and edges design by: Enchanted Ink Publishing
Author photo by: AB-Photography.us
Logo and line art by: A. Krause Studio
Edges embedded by: PrintedEdges.com

www.authormelissalam.com

CONTENT WARNING

This trilogy is not:
- a cozy story that leaves you feeling safe and wholesome
- plotless smut
- a dense high fantasy with maps, glossaries, and complex world-building
If that's what you're in the mood for, this ain't it.

But if you're craving:
- an emotional roller coaster that will make you laugh, cry, swoon, lose sleep, and possibly yeet this book across the room
- a mash-up of the author's favorite tropes (slow burn, forbidden love, forced proximity, a protective hero, and some lady-nabbing)
- messy characters who face real-life trauma, like death, violence, domestic abuse, attempted rape, and pregnancy loss
- a foul-mouthed biker in a leather jacket who battles with addiction, bad decisions, and the occasional suicidal thought
- an intense plot laced with open-door spice (for readers 18+)
- a contemporary romance sprinkled with fantasy and pronounceable words
Then buckle up for this chaos and turn the page.

PART ONE
ORDINARY SECRETS

PLAYLIST

1

TREY

It's easy for me to screw things up. I've done it countless times. From little things like saying the wrong thing at the wrong moment, to big things like not saving my parents from getting blown up. Today is a day I'm determined to get right.

I can do this. I can do this, I chant in my head over and over, as if the more I lie to myself, the more I'll believe it.

I continue internally chanting as I pull my car up behind a white Honda Civic parked on the side of a busy highway. The car's hazard lights flash as I idle my car about two truck lengths behind it and pop my door open.

Sand and gravel crunch beneath my shoes as I head toward the Civic. Rumbling car engines whiz past me, blowing my dark hair around. I drag a shaky palm through the longer strands at the top, trying to make it all stay in place, but my attempts are useless. The second a semitruck flies by, my hair is ruined again. *I guess the messy look will have to do.*

Off in the distance, the burning California sun blurs the air. It's warm on my skin. It would feel much warmer if my body's natural equilibrium wasn't working to cool me down. I'm grateful for this bodily function that all Zordinary humans have, because the last thing I want is to look like a sweating pig the first time I meet this special woman.

As an effort to keep my hands from jittering, I shove them into my jeans pockets and keep crunching the gravel.

Just don't mess up, I tell myself. Easier said than done.

Things have to go well today, because if they don't, that's it.

The end.

My life will be meaningless.

Liz usually smacks my arm whenever I'm being "dramatic," but it's true. My success today will be the beginning of making my parents' deaths count for something. If I can continue and *finish* the work they left behind, I'll be able to say that I did something they can be proud of. I'll be able to say that I brought something of value to this world. Whereas right now, I'm just the pitiful son of two Zordinary researchers who hasn't done anything nearly as impactful as his parents did before they died in a "house fire."

For years, I've lived with that story.

Today, I have a chance to change the ending—and it all starts with getting this special woman to tell me everything about her. To do that, I need to gain her trust. To do that, I need to get close to her. But first, she needs to know that I exist.

Over the last month, I've written out tons of plans outlining how I can stumble into her at a grocery store or strike up a conversation with her at a coffee shop. Unfortunately, all of those ideas went straight into the trash.

Now, I'm not gonna say this meeting her on the side of a busy highway idea is any better, but this is the most promising, so I'm hoping this works. This *has* to work.

Then again, a thousand things could go wrong. I could trip and fall and make a fool of myself. She could shoo me off. She could—*Oh no.* A mess of tight black curls peeks out from the front passenger seat.

She could have a friend with her. *Dammit!* Of all the things I planned for, not once did I think she'd have company. She's never had a friend with her on the way home from work before. Why does she now?

Abort! Abort! Abort! my brain shouts. My feet don't listen. They keep moving. I've already reached the trunk of her car, and the women have probably already seen me. I can't stop now, or I'll look like a crazy person.

That is how I feel though—crazy.

What makes me think I can pull this off? Or that this will work at all? When I got assigned this mission, I was told my objective is to get close to this woman so I can find out what makes her immune to Zordi powers. Considering she's an Ordinary and doesn't know that people with powers exist, she doesn't even know she's immune.

So, I'm supposed to ask her lots of questions to learn as much about her as possible. Sounds simple enough, but what if she doesn't have the answers I'm looking for? And if she does, what if she isn't willing to share them?

Only one way to find out.

I step up to the passenger-side window with my hands still hiding in my pockets. In the seconds it takes for the glass to roll down, I pathetically forget all the lines I rehearsed this morning.

Maybe my uncle is right. Maybe I'm not cut out for this field-agent thing. Although, this *is* my first mission. I could go easier on myself.

Nah. This'll be my first and *last* mission if I fail. *I have to do this right.*

Bending at the hip, I offer my friendliest of smiles. "Hey. Need some help?"

My attention locks onto the beauty behind the wheel. When her gaze meets mine, my heart drops. Her round coffee-colored eyes are more captivating in person than they are in the pictures I've been studying. I knew she was gorgeous, but *damn!*

"Flat tire," she says, telling me information I already know.

"Want me to take a look at it?" I ask.

Her friend arches an eyebrow. "Do you know how to bring tires back from the dead?"

"How 'bout I assess the damage, then we can go from there?"

The friend gestures a pink-nail-polished hand out the window. "Be our guest."

Both women climb out of the car and meet me at the back right tire. I've seen these two together before. Since they hang out pretty often, I'm assuming they're good friends. I don't know the Black woman's name or anything about her. She looks around the same age as the brunette—twenty-two-ish, only four years younger than me.

I kneel and pretend to inspect the blown rubber. What I'm actually doing is trying to process the strange sensation of *knowing* there are two women behind me yet sensing only one.

Excitement radiates off the Black woman in waves, colliding into my head. I wish I knew what was lighting her up so much. That's the downfall of my gift—it only tells me *how* a person feels, never why.

"What happened?" I ask, even though I know damn well what happened. Still kneeling, I twist around to face the ladies. The sun almost blinds me, so I cup my hands above my forehead and squint. Within seconds, my Zordi eyes adjust and the women become crystal clear in my vision.

"We don't know." The one I can't take my focus away from moves all of her long waves to rest over one shoulder. "We heard a loud pop, then the car swerved a little."

I don't have to pretend to sound concerned. "Did you hit anything?"

"Thankfully, no. I pulled over right away, and we were about to call for a service when you showed up."

Thank fuck. The device I planted into her tire last night was supposed to leak the air out *slowly* and *safely*, not pop it. Some gadget that was. The point of my mission is to get information. I can't do that if this woman gets hurt. From now on, I'll make sure all my mission plans put her safety first.

With a hand against her car, I stand and lightly kick the blown tire. "Bad news, ladies. Doesn't look like you'll make it anywhere with this." I know the answer but ask anyway. "You got a spare?"

They shake their heads.

"I could take you to get a new tire. I'll even help you put it on."

"That's very nice of you, but"—the brunette hooks a thumb toward her curly-haired friend —"her brother's a mechanic. We'll be okay."

My hopes deflate like a thumbtacked balloon as I rub a hand over my stubble. What are the odds that she'd have a friend in the car with a brother who's a mechanic?

"He hasn't responded to my calls or texts yet," the friend says. "Maybe we should accept the help from . . ." She circles a hand in the air.

I thrust my palm out. "Trey Grant."

With a sharp gasp, the friend's mouth pops open. Her excitement from earlier that merely waved through my head now smacks me in the face. "See? I knew it! I freaking knew it! I told you it was him! You're in that pop rock band that plays at the Soul House, right?"

I try not to show how thrilled I am that she's recognized me. Not because I like the attention, but because this could work in my favor. I flash her a giant grin. "Yep, that's me. And your name?"

"Javina Abrams." Finally, she shakes my hand, which has been outstretched and waiting. "I went to one of your shows a few months ago. I bought your band's album that night, and I've been watching all your music videos on YouTube ever since." More elation comes from her. It's so strong, it's drowning out the emotions of all the people driving by.

"Thank you. That means a lot to me." And I mean it. I get compliments on my band often, but when it comes from someone who seems as genuine as Javina, the words carry more weight. I offer my palm to the woman I came to meet. "And your name?"

"Ari," she says, lightly returning my handshake.

This isn't the first time I've touched her. The first time was two weeks ago when I "accidentally" bumped into her at a restaurant. I made sure our bare arms brushed as much as possible while keeping it brief. I don't normally need to touch someone to sense their emotions, but since I can't sense this woman at all, I thought maybe the physical contact would help. It didn't then, and it's not now either. *How is she doing that?*

As if my hand is scorching hers, she tugs her arm back, then her gaze falls to the grass. *Whoops.* I definitely didn't mean to hold on to her for longer than socially acceptable.

Finally, her name registers in my brain. *Ari? That's not right.* "What's that short for?"

"Arella, but everyone just calls me Ari."

"Arella is a beautiful name. It suits you."

She smiles bashfully, and I can't tell if it's because she liked the compliment or because she hated it and is simply being nice. I've never had to guess how people feel before—ever.

"Anyway, could I help you get a new tire?"

"I don't want to inconvenience you." Arella fidgets with the bottom of her yellow T-shirt. The logo on the front reads *Sunrise Daycare*. Javina's wearing a matching shirt. Seeing them in their work attire makes it easier to not get caught already knowing that they work together.

"It's not an inconvenience at all," I say with a bright smile. *It's the very reason I'm here.*

"Well, I wouldn't want to inconvenience your friends." Arella gestures toward my car.

Fuck. I was hoping she wouldn't notice my friends. Like how I didn't plan for Javina to be here, I didn't plan for my friends to tag along either. I meant to come *alone* during this part of my assignment. The only reason I didn't was because Liz guilt-tripped me into having dinner with her and Kevin.

During band rehearsal earlier, I refused dinner three times, until Liz whispered, "We need to cheer him up. You know his mom just got diagnosed with breast cancer. He's worried about losing her."

I would've been a dick to say no. How could I? I'd lost my mother too. If taking Kevin out for sushi would help take his mind off his mom for a while, I'd comply. As long as my friends didn't interfere with my plan today.

Just as Arella mentions my friends, my car doors swing open, then Liz and Kevin step out. *Dammit.* My friends' energies float toward me, all light and curious. They have the right to be curious. After I agreed to dinner, I volunteered to drive without telling them we'd be taking a detour.

"What's the holdup?" Kevin shouts on his way over. His jet-black hair is so gelled up, the wind from the passing cars isn't affecting it at all.

Next to him comes Liz with a peppy bounce in her step. "Everything okay?"

"Just a flat," I say as a semitruck zips by us.

Liz stops at my side. Her nearness causes the Zordi sense in my chest to tingle. It reminds me that Liz and I are the kind of humans who are born with powers and the people around us are not.

Like I did earlier, Liz squats to examine the busted tire. "There's no fixing this. The hole's too big."

"You ladies need a ride to a tire shop?" Kevin asks. "We could take ya, right, Trey?"

"Yeah," Liz adds through a yawn, covering her mouth with a satin-gloved hand. "There's probably one not too far from here."

Why did I think for even a second that my friends would be an interference? Of course they'd want to help. They're good people like that. Now that I think about it, having a woman with me could increase my chances of getting Arella to accept my help. Women are more likely to trust other women than a man they've never met. If I had been smart, I would have planned for Liz to be here from the beginning.

"See?" I beam with a renewed sense of hope. "You're not an inconvenience at all."

Arella turns to her friend. "Why don't you call your brother again?"

Javina rolls her eyes. "I could, but I ain't seein' the point of that when we've got three perfectly capable helpers standing right here."

I hold back a grin. Javina just made it to the top of my *befriend now* list.

Arella thinks, then nods. "Okay. Let's grab our things."

On the inside, I jump up and down like a giddy child in a toy store. On the outside, I play it cool. "We'll be in my car."

Liz claims the front seat like she always does as Kevin plops into the back behind me. I don't take my eyes off Arella while she and Javina saunter over with their purses in hand.

Arella slips in first, settling on the middle seat next to Kevin. I'm gifted with a perfect view of her in my rearview mirror. Our eyes lock for half a second before she turns to click her seat belt in. I'm still staring at her as she sets her little purse on her lap and Javina climbs in.

Once everyone is buckled, I force my eyes back onto the busy highway. When I get an opening, I join the flow of traffic.

Liz wastes no time twisting around to wave a gloved hand at our new additions. "Hi, I'm Liz."

"I know!" Javina's exhilaration rushes through my head again. "You're one of the two girls in the band, right? The soprano and dancer?"

"Yep!" Liz's lips curve upward. Her spirit does the same. Out of everyone in the band, Liz enjoys meeting our fans the most.

Javina leans forward to lock eyes with Kevin. "And you're the bass guitarist, right?"

He nods with a closed-mouth smile. "Mm-hmm."

"Don't you play the guitar too?"

"Yeah. I'm not as good as Trey though."

"Lies!" Liz reaches back to slap Kevin's boney knee. "Kevin's just being humble. He's amazing on guitar. He's also our tenor and does most of the creative video editing for our YouTube channel."

"Impressive! I'm Javina." She points a finger at her chest, then places a light palm over Arella's thigh. "This is my bestie, Ari."

That nickname is still confusing me, because I've been referring to her in my head as Arella. I never knew she went by anything else. There are just some things a manila folder can't tell me—hence why I'm here.

"Are you two from the Los Angeles area?" Liz asks.

"I'm originally from Chicago," Javina says.

Liz's jaw drops with a little gasp. "I'm from Chicago too! What about you, Ari?"

"I've lived almost everywhere in Cali," Arella says, all soft and sweet.

"How long have you been in LA?"

"About four years."

I've never been more grateful for Liz. Not only am I learning things about Arella that aren't in her limited file, but I'm also not doing the work. Liz doesn't know about my mission. If she did, she'd be doing a hell of a job assisting me. Apparently, I need the help, because I can barely think with this beautiful mystery in my back seat. All the free space in my brain is consumed with trying to sense her.

"So what cover song is gonna be your next single?" Javina asks.

Liz puts on her thinking face. "It's an acoustic rendition of a Backstreet Boys hit, right, Kev? Are we allowed to tell them which one?"

Kevin shrugs a shoulder. "Why not? It releases tonight for Throwback Thursday. It's 'Show Me the Meaning of Being Lonely.' "

Javina gasps. "I love that one!"

After she gushes about the Backstreet Boys for a minute, she spits out a long string of questions. When is the next original music video coming out? What's the craziest fan encounter you've ever had? Do you normally get recognized everywhere you go?

Liz and Kevin do a great job answering everything while I contribute nothing. Actually, I stop listening after a while. My mind is buzzing with all the puzzling thoughts I have about the quiet woman behind me.

Is Liz's mind power working on Arella? I want to ask, but I can't do that in a car full of Ordinaries. That would break the number-one Zordi law: Never reveal anything from the Zordinary world to an Ordinary. Maybe after sushi tonight, Liz and I can—

"T?" A gloved finger taps my shoulder.

I jolt, and the car goes quiet. "Hmm?"

Liz dips her eyebrows at me. "I asked if you know where we're going."

"Oh." I clear my throat. "Yep. There's a tire place just off the next exit." *The one I Googled last week when I came up with this plan.*

"Anyway," Javina says, stealing the attention back, and I'm happy for it. "How far have you guys gotten on your next original album?"

Perking up, Liz shares some general details about our band's second original album, which we've been working on since we released the first one. Liz's details aren't anything our band manager doesn't want us to reveal.

The whole time, Arella stares out the windshield with a blank look on her face. One would think that after observing her for the last four weeks, I'd be sick of looking at her, but I'm not. It's not only because she's stunning, either. I'm desperate to know how she's deflecting my gift and if she knows she's doing it at all.

If I shut my eyelids, I wouldn't even know she was in this car. I sense that Liz is happy. Javina is still exhilarated out of her mind. While Kevin's got a content look on his face, he's a little anxious on the inside. As for Arella . . . nothing.

When we arrive at the tire shop, Liz and Kevin opt to stay in the comfort of my car's air conditioning. I gladly leave the engine running for them, then volunteer to escort Arella and Javina inside.

"Well, aren't you a gentleman?" Javina says when I hold the door open for them.

I return her smile with my own.

Besides a gray-haired man reading a magazine in the waiting room, the lobby is empty. The scent of fresh rubber fills the air. At the same time a burst of joy rushes through my head, a round of laughter comes from the other side of the glass wall where three cars are raised on lifts. A group of eight-ish people in red polo shirts surround the vehicles with various power tools.

From behind me, something vibrates. Javina digs through her purse before pulling a phone out.

"Ooh! I gotta take this!" She rushes back outside with her phone pressed to an ear as her excitement spikes again. I'm getting the impression that she's easily excitable.

For the first time ever, I have Arella to myself. This is my chance to say something—to find out something valuable about her. Sooo, what do I say, and how do I say it? It figures that it'd be *now* when my brain decides to shut down. No words—at least none that form intelligent sentences—come to mind.

Like a sheltered teenage boy in the presence of an attractive female, I fidget with the zipper of my black leather jacket. I pull it halfway up my chest.

Then down.

Up again.

Stop it!

I shove my hands into my jeans pockets.

Then I take them out.

In once more.

What should I say?

Hey, Arella, you come here often? Dumb question. She's only here because of me.

Sooo, you work at a daycare. You like kids? Another stupid question. Why would she work at a daycare if she despised children?

How 'bout that heat, huh?

A glass door slides open, releasing me from my inner torture.

"Hi there!" says the cute blonde woman with a black smear of oil running down the front of her polo. "How can I help?"

Arella steps up to the counter while I stand off to the side, pretending to be interested in a chart on the wall that asks, "When do you need new tires?"

It's strange. Even without Arella's emotions hovering in my head, I still feel extremely aware of her presence, her every move. Usually, I know exactly how far someone is from me by how strong their emotions come through my head. With Arella, I sense nothing, yet there she is, existing merely ten steps over.

As discreetly as possible, I lock my gaze onto her back and focus my gift on her. The only thing that comes is the emotions of the blonde behind the counter. It's as if Arella isn't there at all.

For the last month, I've kept my distance. Now that I'm here, I don't know what to do with myself. I need to touch her again. The brush of our arms and our little handshake isn't enough to confirm if physical contact can or can't break down her immunity walls. I was told that if I can find a way to break through her invisible shield, it might help us figure out how she's immune. Do I have the first clue how to do that? Nope. Not one bit.

As Arella finalizes the payment, I make a mental note to pay her back for this. There's no reason she has to spend her hard-earned money on something I caused. I'll be sure to get her something she needs but can't afford for herself. Something at least triple the price. It's the least I can do.

Within no time, we've got a new tire in my trunk and our seat belts secured again. Liz and Javina dominate most of the conversation on our way back. They talk like they're old friends who haven't seen each other in months. I don't mind. It gives me a chance to regain myself. I don't normally get nervous around women. Apparently when it matters, I lose all sense of control.

Back at Arella's car, I grab some tools and get straight to work. Before today, I have changed a tire all of two times, with the sole purpose of practicing for this moment. I didn't wanna look stupid.

"Can I help?" Arella drops to her knees at my side.

I startle, falling backward onto my tailbone. My ass lands on the jack. A few curse words—all beginning with *F*—fly through my head. I'm not used to people sneaking up on me without me sensing them first.

"Sorry. I didn't mean to scare you." She lets out an adorable laugh, making goose bumps run up the back of my neck.

"It's all right." I chuckle lightly as I pull the jack out from under me and hand it to her. "Could you turn this little knob to lower it enough so we can fit it under your car?"

"Sure." Arella sets the jack down, then gathers all her hair toward the top of her head. I'm mesmerized by the way she swiftly ties it up within seconds. Once she's done, her eyes meet mine and she flashes me a tender smile.

Shit. I've been gaping at her with my mouth slightly open. *Way to play it cool.* Tearing my attention off her, I go back to loosening the lug nuts.

As Arella lowers the jack, I feel the need to make conversation with her, except I can't think of anything to say. *Do I even know how to talk to women anymore?*

Behind us, in the grassy ditch, Liz, Kevin, and Javina seem to have no problem making conversation. With all the noisy cars passing us, I can't make out every word they're saying, but from the little I can catch, it sounds like they're still talking about music. *Would Arella like it if I talk to her about music?*

"Done." As she leans over to set the jack near my feet, I catch a whiff of her light floral scent—lavender and springtime.

Does her scent have anything to do with her immunity? Probably not, although I've been told not to rule anything out. It could be *anything* that shields her from Zordi powers.

When I finish loosening all the lug nuts, I push the jack under her car and twist the knob. After a few turns, the car lifts off the ground.

I continue twisting it up. "Do you know where to get rid of this blown tire?"

"Where?"

I banked on her not knowing. "I can take care of it for you."

"No way. You're already helping plenty."

"It'll be my pleasure. One less thing for you to worry about."

She opens her mouth, seemingly about to object, then stops. "Thank you, Trey. Seriously. You're doing so much for me, and I don't even know you."

"Let's get to know each other, then." *Wow!* Those words weren't practiced, yet they sounded right. *Gold star for me!*

The air stands still as I wait for Arella's response. Seconds pass as I keep working the jack up. Her reply never comes.

Good going, dumbass. What kind of pickup line was that? I sounded way too forward. Might as well have used the "Hey, did it hurt when you fell from heaven, 'cause you look like an angel" line.

"Sorry," I say because I don't know what else to say.

"For what?"

"Trying to flirt with you. I'll assume your silence means it's unwelcome." I've had her semi-alone for all of two minutes, and I've already fucked up. *Figures.*

"Oh. It's okay. I mean, um . . ." She's struggling to find her words, and I wish I knew why.

Am I making her nervous? That's not my intent at all. If anything, I *need* her to be comfortable with me.

"Honestly," she says gently, "I'm not used to men trying to flirt with me. I didn't realize that's what you were doing."

I freeze to gape at her. "What? You're gorgeous. Do you really expect me to believe that guys don't hit on you *all* the time?"

At first, she blushes, then her head droops. "They don't."

"Well, good." I return to working on her car. "That gives me more of a chance with you."

She shakes her head, rolling her eyes. "Don't waste your time on me."

"You wouldn't be a waste of time." I almost scowl at her for thinking that of herself. "Are you single?" I already know the answer. Unless she's got a boyfriend she hasn't seen for a month, this woman is very available.

"I . . . am . . . single," Arella says slowly as if giving herself time to think. "That doesn't mean I'm looking though."

I don't like that answer, so I take that information, crumple it up, and toss it into the recycling bin in the back of my head.

Once the car is lifted off the ground enough, I twist off the first lug nut and hold it out to her. "You mind hangin' on to these so we don't lose 'em?"

She flips her palm open, and I drop the first one in, making sure to brush my fingers against hers. The physical contact does nothing. She's still blank.

We work together until the old rubber's off. When I'm home later, I'll dispose of the tiny device that's probably still stuck in that rubber somewhere.

After the new tire is on, I lower Arella's car to the ground, then slide the jack out. With a grunt, I push myself up and slap my dirty palms on my thighs. "You're all good now."

"Thank you. Here, let me pay you." She digs out her wallet from the purse hanging by a strap across her body.

I slash a hand through the air. "Don't worry 'bout it."

Not listening, she holds out three twenties. "Seriously, take it. Calling a professional would have easily been four times this."

"It's okay, really." I push her cash away, then give her hand a gentle squeeze. "I'm just happy to help."

She flinches, and the color washes from her face. A woman has never reacted to my touch that way before. Instantly, I let her go and step back. Within seconds, the tension in her shoulders releases and she lets out a breath.

Glancing up at me with those big brown eyes, she forces a tiny smile. I know that smile. It's the same one I use whenever I'm trying to hide my pain. *What pain is she trying to hide? And does it have anything to do with her immunity?*

Arella stuffs her cash back into her purse, then hugs herself, looking anywhere but at me. "Thanks again."

Perking up, I pretend that my next idea is a spur-of-the-moment one. "Hey, so, my band is performing a show tomorrow. Would you wanna come out to support us?"

"I can't," she says way too quickly. "I work tomorrow."

"Our set starts at eight. You work that late?" If she says yes, she's lying.

"I don't. Where is it?"

"It's a cool music bar downtown called the Soul House. Great food, great service, and I hear the entertainment's not too bad either." I wink and immediately regret it. *Why did I do that? I'm so lame.*

"Um . . ." she says, biting her lip. Not the reaction I expected. "How much are tickets?"

"For you? Nothin'. I'll put your name on a special VIP list so you can walk right in. It's last minute, so you'd probably have to sit at the bar, but it's still a good spot."

"Oh. Um . . ."

Javina materializes at Arella's side, gripping her arm. "Ari, this kind man just helped us out, then offered to put you on a VIP list to see his show tomorrow. Do you understand that their tickets are hard to get last minute? They're usually sold out for weeks in advance. *Weeks*, Ari. Weeks. If you don't go, I will."

And that's the reaction I was hoping for.

Arella straightens her back. "I'll come if Javina can come too."

If that's what it would take to get this woman back into my space, done. "Great. I'll put you both on the list for tomorrow. Javina Abrams and Arella . . . Sorry, I never got your last name." I already know it, but it's important to hear it from her.

"Rance."

"Perfect. I'll see you tomorrow, then."

While this didn't go exactly the way I had imagined it, I still accomplished what I needed to, and that's what matters.

Phase one—complete.

Now on to phase two.

2

ARELLA

The gratitude I have for Javina will never end.

Tonight is our monthly movie night. Since we also happened to be scheduled for the same shift, we carpooled, and I'm glad for it. If it wasn't for her recognizing those people, I wouldn't have accepted their help. I know better than to get into a car with three strangers. What if they were serial killers? Since we're still alive, I'm going to assume they aren't.

I can't believe I agreed to go to their band's show tomorrow. Bars aren't my thing, but it's Javina's thing, especially the music ones. So I'm happy to go if it'll make Javina happy.

She's practically dancing in my passenger seat. "All right, babes, you're never gonna guess who called while you were getting a new tire."

I merge my car into the leftmost lane. "Your brother?"

"Nah. Still haven't heard from him. I'll give you a hint. We should stop somewhere for a celebration cake."

I knit my eyebrows together, then my jaw drops. "You and Rachel got approved for the apartment?"

Her face falls. "I wish. We should find that out next week."

Javina and her girlfriend have been apartment hunting for almost three months. Every place they've toured is either a dump or the rent is too high. Last week, when I found out that my upstairs neighbor was moving, I texted Javina and told her to apply for it.

"Okay, I'm just gonna tell you." She grins with all her teeth. "I got the promotion!"

"What!" I squeal. "I knew you'd get it!"

"Thanks. I wasn't confident. I was up against Carrie, who has been at the daycare for, like, three years longer than me."

"Yeah, but you work harder than Carrie does."

"If there's anyone who works the hardest, it's you. You always do all the extra shit nobody else wants to. I still think you should have applied."

Our director hinted to me that if I applied, I was guaranteed the position. I didn't apply because I knew Javina really wanted the job. I also knew that if our director didn't promote me, she'd pick Javina.

She'll be better at it, anyway. My strengths reside in handling the kids. Javina is better at all that leadership, organization, and technology stuff—all the skills she'll need to be the best assistant director Sunrise Daycare has ever had.

In the grocery store, Javina stares at the cake options for way too long. Nothing fits her expectations for the "perfect celebration cake," so we get popcorn instead.

The sun sits along the horizon in hues of pinks and purples as we arrive at my apartment in Culver City. Out of habit, I step out of my car and scan the lot to see if *his* car is around.

When my tire blew, I thought the source of my problems was *him* again. *He* has been messing with my life for years. It wouldn't have been the first time he'd sabotaged my vehicle either. Thankfully, my flat today was just an accident.

When I finish doing a quick eye sweep of the area and don't see his car, I let out a breath.

"Don't sweat it, babes." Javina throws up a closed fist. "If he was here, we both woulda taken him. He'd be leavin' with a bloody nose and a limp."

I offer Javina the biggest smile I can manage. *I love this woman.*

The first thing we do when we enter my apartment is kick our shoes off, then drop our grocery bags onto my kitchen counter. Javina takes the liberty of rummaging through my fridge for a can of root beer. I'm not a fan of root beer. I only stock my fridge with it for her.

"Did you tell Rachel about the promotion yet?" I slide my finger under the flap of the popcorn box. It tears open easily.

"Yeah. I texted her as soon as I got off that call." Javina takes a long chug from her can. "We're celebrating on Sunday."

"Why Sunday?" Today is Thursday. It's rare for Javina to go more than a day without seeing Rachel.

"She's on a business trip and won't be flying back until late Saturday night."

I unwrap the plastic off the popcorn. "How are you guys going to celebrate?"

"Probs go out for dinner and get drunk on wine."

I chuckle. "Nothing like living your best life."

Minutes later, we've got a bowl of yummy, extra-buttery goodness in hand as we head to my living room.

"Pick out somethin' good for us," Javina says as she shuffles down the hall. "I'll be right back."

My butt makes a light *thud* as I flop onto my worn garage-sale couch. The TV brightens to life with the hit of a button. I scroll through our entertainment options, logging some choices into a mental list. Most are true-crime related. Javina and I like to judge the way murderers get caught and discuss how we could have done it better.

"Yo!" Javina calls from the bathroom. "When are you planning to fix this gaping hole in your wall?"

I still have nightmares about that fist flying at my face. When I ducked, his fist ran straight into the drywall with a *crack!* He bled quite a bit. While I bandaged him up, I secretly wished he had broken something. That was the moment I knew I had to get out.

A week later, I was busy packing a bag when he arrived home early from work. Getting caught trying to leave only made a bad situation worse. For weeks, he barely let me out of his sight. He stole my car keys and hid them. Every day, he'd drop me off at work and pick me back up. The daycare became my safe haven, and I'd dread whenever my shift ended.

When I wasn't working, he'd lock me up in our apartment and try to brainwash me into believing that I was nothing without him. Sometimes, it worked. Other times, I wished for him to get hit by a bus.

During those dark days, whenever Javina asked if we could hang out, I'd lie and tell her I already had plans. Eventually, she caught on. The day she pulled me aside during our lunch break and vocalized her suspicions, I burst into tears. It didn't take me long to confess how I'd got the marks on my face that I'd been hiding under layers of foundation and concealer.

That night, Javina showed up with her buff dad, her athletic brother, and her two heavily tattooed uncles. All of them had broad shoulders and stood to at least six three. While one guarded me, the others threw all of my ex's things out the door—literally. Socks were scattered across the grass, and his can of shaving cream exploded all over the sidewalk.

For the next few weeks, Javina's family took turns camping outside my place to ensure he stayed away. Javina still talks about how much she loved seeing the fear in my ex's eyes when four large Black men showed up and wouldn't take *no* for an answer.

"I'll do it eventually," I say, hoping I'm speaking loudly enough for Javina to hear. "I haven't found the motivation yet."

"Want my help? I can't imagine staring at a hole in the wall every day while I do my business."

I've thought about patching it up, but then I'd need to patch up the three holes in the bedroom. In the middle of our fights, he used to point at those holes and say, "*That* is what happens when you disobey me and try to fight back. Just do what I say, when I say it." That normally scared me into submission because he was right. Fighting back only ever made him more violent. It was always easier to just give him what he wanted. Now, I hide those holes behind artwork and framed photos. If I only had one hole to fix, it'd probably be done already. Four is a daunting project.

I would cover the hole in the bathroom with a picture if it wasn't in such an awkward place—right below the towel bar, slightly to the left. My bath towel usually hides it, and nobody except Javina ever comes over anyway, so why bother?

Besides, whenever I see that hole now, I'm reminded of the naïve, trusting person I used to be. I'm reminded that I don't need a man or his money to make it. Over the past eight months, I've picked up a weekend nanny job to cover his part of the rent. I've learned the difference between real love and the love to control. I've even learned that I can make jokes and laugh out loud without his permission. Seeing this hole now reminds me that I'm stronger today than I was before, and it encourages me to continue to be strong.

The toilet flushes, and the sink runs, then Javina reappears in the living room. "Sorry, babes. Didn't mean to bring him up again."

"It's fine." I force a smile—something I've learned to do well. Yeah, I'm getting better, but time hasn't completely healed me yet. There are still things that shut me down. Like whenever I see or hear his name. Whenever I catch a whiff of alcohol. Whenever a man gets too close.

I've been relearning that not every man who touches me wants to bruise me. My brain knows it, but it's harder to convince my body to know it. I still tense up whenever I'm touched by a man, which is progress from eight months ago, when I'd practically break down in tears.

In the beginning, my ex's touches were loving and didn't leave bruises. The first time he slapped me, we were in a heated argument over something I can't even remember. He promised it would never happen again. And it didn't . . . not for another four months. Eventually, his slaps turned into punches, his promises turned into begging, and the months between those fights became weeks or days.

He spent a lot of nights conditioning me into believing his behavior was my fault and that

I deserved it. Apparently, I didn't listen, I was too defiant, and I questioned him too often. After a while, I just obeyed. Whenever he talked, I listened. Whenever he told me not to wear something, I didn't. Whenever he came home late, I stopped asking where he had been. I know now that his actions were not my fault and that I never deserved it.

Javina plops beside me and digs her hand into our popcorn bowl. "One last question, then we can be done talking about him."

"Okay?" I keep scrolling through the movies, even though my brain isn't registering any of the titles. I'm too focused on what Javina has to say next.

"When's the last time you saw that low-life bitch face?"

"A month, I think."

Thirty-seven days, to be exact. And yes, I keep count because thirty-seven is a record—a *huge* record.

Unfortunately, that means he's bound to reappear soon.

3

TREY

In the back lot of the Soul House, I pull my car up next to Kevin's.

"Thanks again for taking me out for sushi, guys," Kevin says as he pops his door open. "I really appreciate it."

"You're welcome, Kev," Liz says, waving one of her gloved hands. "See ya tomorrow."

I wave too. "See ya, bro."

The second Kevin is in his car and has driven away, Liz turns in her seat to face me. I already know what she's gonna say. "Oh my god, T. Please tell me you got a reading off that Ari girl."

"Nope. Did you?" I know this answer too. Why else would she be asking?

"I couldn't smell her at all!" Liz clasps a hand against her temple.

The way she describes her mind power, the first of three powers all Zordis are born with, is weird. I guess, simply put, "smelling people's souls" is exactly what her mind power does.

Whenever Liz gets within an arm's reach of a person, her mind senses the quality of their soul and interprets it into a scent. If a person's soul is good, they could smell like freshly baked muffins or blooming flowers in a field. If a person's soul is bad, they could smell like sewage or a two-week-old corpse.

"I feel better now that I know it wasn't just me. Pense que me estaba volviendo loca." *I thought I was going crazy.*

"You're not going crazy," I say, underutilizing my conversational Spanish skills. I don't practice the language enough with her. The only time I speak Spanish to Liz is when I want to say something I don't want the rest of the band knowing.

I press the button to turn my engine off since it seems like Liz and I might be here for a while. "If you could smell her soul, what do you think it would smell like?"

"She seemed like a good person, so probably something like an apple cinnamon pie straight out of the oven, or maybe some flowers."

Liz is probably right about the flowers. Maybe Arella's soul would smell like lavender. I guess we'll never know.

Liz says that my soul smells like roasted marshmallows on a campfire and the wick of a burning candle. What's interesting about her mind power is that it gives her the ability to guess a Zordi's elemental power, our second gift. Within seconds of meeting me, she knew my element was Fire.

"Do you think it's possible she doesn't have a scent?" I ask.

"Do you think it's possible she doesn't have any emotions?" Liz makes a good point. "Everyone's got a soul, T. Unless they're dead, and Ari looked very much alive to me. I thought about it during dinner and thought maybe her soul is neutral. Now that I know you couldn't sense her either, I don't think that's the case." With a jolt, Liz gasps. "What if she's a robot?"

Not missing a beat, I fake the same big gasp. "What if she's part of an alien invasion team that's scoping out our planet to strategize the best time to attack? You can't smell alien souls, can you?"

With an eye roll, she smacks my arm.

I rub the spot she hit, pretending like it stung. "In all seriousness, do you think if you took your gloves off and shook hands with her, you'd catch a memory?"

"I dunno, but I'm not willing to test that."

A body power is the third and final gift every Zordi is born with. Liz's allows her to see people's memories. She calls this gift more of a curse because she can only see a person's most painful memory—the one that haunts them and tears them apart inside.

Thankfully, her gloves act like a barrier, but they don't keep the terrible memories she's already caught from replaying in her head at night. Because of that, Liz can't stay asleep for long. She always lurches awake, screaming from the scenes playing out on the back of her eyelids like a private horror movie.

If given the opportunity to trade my body power of telekinesis with Liz's of memory catching, I'd do it. I wouldn't even think twice about it. Liz deserves to be saved from the agony of living through everyone else's suffering night after night, and I'd gladly volunteer.

Unfortunately, trading powers isn't a thing, so I do my best to help Liz feel comfortable in other ways—everything from letting her cry on my shoulder to shutting people down whenever they get a little too curious about her gloves.

When I first met Liz four years ago, she claimed she wore gloves because she's a germaphobe. I knew it was a lie, but I didn't care enough to interrogate her. It didn't change that she needed a dance partner to enter a competition with. I was taking dance lessons at the studio Liz still works at when my instructor recommended me to her.

For the next few months after that, I met with Liz at the studio to help her choreograph a winning routine. One day, she hadn't put her gloves on yet, and I accidentally grazed my hand against hers. She froze, and her terror shot through my body like an arrow through the heart.

It all happened so fast. One second, her eyes were screwed shut with a pained look on her face. The next, she let out a sharp gasp and erupted into tears.

Because many mind and body powers are viewed as intrusive or dangerous, it's part of Zordi culture to keep that information private. Elemental powers are widely discussed, though, since everyone has one of four: Fire, Water, Earth or Air. That's why I didn't know that Liz was a Memory Catcher. It's also why I didn't understand her suddenly crying for no reason.

My uncomfortable response was "You okay?"

"Trey . . . you—you were there."

"I was where?"

Without hesitation, she explained what her hands could do. "You told me your parents died. You didn't tell me that it was because of something traumatic or that you witnessed the whole thing happen."

I blew up at her. "You crossed a fucking line! Using your body power on me like that? Really? Find yourself a new dance partner for your stupid competition. I quit!"

I hurled all my things back into my backpack and stormed out of that studio without any intention of ever returning.

Liz ran after me, unwilling to let me leave. I was unwilling to hear her out.

"I'm so sorry, Trey. I didn't mean to. Your memory came to me when our hands touched. I can't control it. Trust me, if I could choose, I'd rather be an Ordinary."

I was already halfway to my car when I froze right there in the parking lot. I understand what it's like to not have control of your powers. Often, I've wished to be an Ordinary too. It's common for Zordis to long for better powers. What's uncommon is for us to long to be completely powerless. The moment Liz said those words through tears, it hit me that maybe, just maybe, I wasn't alone.

Fuming a little less, I allowed her to talk me into staying. That night, instead of dancing, we had a lengthy heart-to-heart conversation—a form of torture for me.

"I'm sorry I got angry," I said, apologizing for the tenth time. I felt like an asshole for yelling at her the way I had. "It's just that . . ."

"You don't have to explain," Liz said when I couldn't find the words. "I'm glad I saw your memory—for your sake."

"How's that for *my* sake?"

"It'll be good for you to have someone to confide in. Someone who understands you. Now I know why you're so closed off."

That last comment didn't make me feel any better. I am fully aware that I shut down the second anyone asks me a personal question, but to hear Liz verbalize it? I felt called out. I had half a mind to walk out again.

"I'll make it even with you," she said. "I can tell you about something that kills me deeply too."

So, she did, even after I told her it wasn't necessary. She told me all about the most disturbing memories she'd caught over the years and how they still affect her. She even shared some of her own dark memories—of things she's experienced herself.

I listened in awe of her every word, mostly in awe of her. I'd had no idea how much agony hid behind those bright smiles and cheery hugs. Liz had fooled me into thinking her happiness came easy.

Looking back on it now, I realize that Liz told me all those dark things because she needed someone to confide in too. Before me, she never had anyone she could share that pain with. No one had ever wanted to share it, especially not her family. There she was, carrying the weight of all those distressing memories on her own two shoulders, and I was more than happy to help her carry that burden. I still am.

If everyone knew all the shit Liz has been through, they'd have as much respect for her as I do. Liz has the kindest, most caring and understanding soul I've ever known. For that, I will protect her at all costs.

"Why do you think our gifts didn't work on Ari?" Liz asks, drawing my attention back to her.

"I'm not sure," I say. *But I'm gonna find out.*

4

TREY

The second Liz gets into her car and drives away, I reach back to feel around the fabric of my back seats. It doesn't take me long to find what I'm looking for. When I do, I carefully fold the strands between a napkin from my center console; then I drag my phone out to call Victor.

"What?" my uncle answers, all clipped as if I'm interrupting a meeting with the fucking president.

"I got the sample."

"Good. Come to Shadow Ridge. Now."

I pull my phone from my ear to glance at the screen. "Now? It's really late."

"And?"

I should just do whatever he wants. It's easier that way. "All right. I'm coming."

Zordis only need to sleep half as often as Ordis. Lucky for me, I slept last night—not that Victor knows that. What if tonight was my night to rest?

"Can you send a Teleporter?" I ask.

"I only have one Porter right now. He's busy, so you're on your own. Don't dawdle." *Click.*

Huffing, I shove my phone back into my pocket. With a Teleporter, I could be at the Ridge within seconds. Now, I have a three-hour road trip ahead of me and another three hours back.

Whatever, I guess.

I start my engine, then head toward my house. Once there, I switch my car out for my motorcycle. Riding it will make this last-minute errand feel less daunting.

Going with Liz would make it feel less daunting too, but she doesn't know that I'm a Zordinary Innovations Research and Development Agency agent. It's better that I keep that information from her, too. She wouldn't approve of me working for a group of Zordis who operate outside the zovernment on their own terms. Besides, it's against ZIRDA policy to tell people in our personal lives that we're ZIRDA agents.

While ZIRDA does good things, the secret organization has a reputation for being a group of vigilantes. Like how we're working to discover what makes some rare Ordinaries immune to our powers. After that, we'll figure out how to replicate their immunity, then ZIRDA will be able to overpower and take down the people who killed my parents. As for me, I'll sleep better knowing that the people who destroyed my family never get the chance to hurt another little boy ever again.

Three hours later, I'm near my hometown, about halfway up the dark mountain. On the side of the road, I cut the engine and dismount my bike. A refreshing breeze grazes my cheeks as I yank off my helmet.

Since there's a shortage of parking lots in the middle of nowhere, I flick my wrist, and my Harley lifts off the ground. It floats in front of me as I tuck my helmet under my arm and hike off the road, through some tall grass.

I trek through the woods until I can't see the road anymore. In the air, my bike follows my hand movements, maneuvering around every tree in its path. As I lower my hand, it eases to the ground behind two thick tree trunks, where it'll stay with my helmet until I return.

On foot, I march deeper through the forest in search of the perfect hover-log. The denser the woods get, the more I lose the moonlight, so I open my hand and imagine fire. A glowing ball of red and orange appears in my palm. Its warmth on my skin offers me a tiny sense of comfort between the dread and loathing of coming back to this place. I use the volleyball-size fireball to illuminate the ground until I spot a piece of wood about the size of a skateboard.

With a turn of my wrist, the log glides through the air toward my ankles. I knock on it a couple times to make sure it's sturdy enough to hold my weight. It is, so I step onto it and kill my flames. As I lift my hand, I'm carried into the air above the trees.

I fly so fast that the wind whips across my face like I'm in a speeding car with my head out the window. Below me, the treetops are a dark trap waiting to swallow me whole if I fall. Of all the times I've flown above this forest, I've never fallen.

I used to hover-log over this area every day just to get to school, and I despised every minute of it. Doing this again reminds me that I didn't grow up in a normal house like normal kids with a normal family.

I tilt my head back to gaze at the stars. Maybe my parents are up there somewhere, watching me. Does knowing that I'm working on the research they started make them proud of me? Or do I need to *complete* their research for that to happen? Either way, I'm going to finish this for them—no matter what it takes.

By the time the familiar peak of a mountain appears, my throat is dry. The still and silent mountain seems to say, "What are you doing back here?"

Trust me. I'm not happy about this, either.

Even though I lived at the Ridge from the age of seven to eighteen, I never called it my home. All of my memories here are of bloody noses and nights spent locked alone in my bedroom. I can't count how many times I planned to run away, or how many times I was told to leave and never come back. In a way, staying was rebelling. Also, I had nowhere else to go.

The closer I get to my destination, the closer I hover near the treetops. I'm not ready to land yet though. Up here, I don't have to watch for booby traps. If I had to hike this, like many do, I'd have to study where the traps are. I don't come around often enough to do that. The only other time I've been back here since I moved out was last month when Victor called to assign me this mission. Otherwise, I wouldn't have come back at all.

I used to watch the weekly footage of wayward hikers tripping the traps. Some traps release snakes. Others release swarms of hornets or fire ants. Anything that keeps people from getting too close to this ZIRDA base.

In addition to the animal deterrents, small speakers are hidden in the trees that play bird sounds all day and crickets chirping all night. The extra noise masks the sounds of the waterfall that veils the entrance to Shadow Ridge.

Since I'm up in the air, the sounds of the waterfall reach my ears before it comes into view. The base's entrance hides beneath strategically grown trees that blend in with the rest of the forest. Through a slight break in the treetops, I dip my hover-log down and stop just above the grass. Then I step off and drop my hand, making my hover-log return to its former useless state on the ground.

A towering waterfall stretches before me, cascading into a small lake. I used to spend hours swimming in that water, mostly because there isn't much else for children to do around a secret hideout. Cable couldn't have been installed out here even if I'd wanted it. As for the Internet, Victor made it a rule that children aren't allowed to use the Ridge's satellite. Since I was the one and only child who lived here, it was obvious who he made that rule for.

Trickles of cold liquid splash onto me as I enter the cavern behind the waterfall. My footsteps echo in the darkness. I open my hand and imagine fire until warm flames appear. I throw my fireball into the air and keep it floating a few feet ahead of me as I trudge deeper into the hollow.

Tiny cameras embedded into the rock wall follow my movements. I know where most of them are hidden. As I look for them, I spot more cameras that weren't there before. They seem to have doubled.

Waving, I wink into one of the thumbtack-size lenses I've never seen before. The security guards hate it when I do that. They think their camera-concealing skills are top-notch. For the untrained eye, they probably are.

After a couple minutes, my fireball illuminates the Ridge's entrance—a wide door that looks like any other part of the cave. With my hands flat, I feel around the rocks for the little hole. Once I find it, I stick my index finger in and press it against a fingerprint scanner.

Beep! Beep! Beep! With a mechanical screech, a ten-foot section of the rock wall retreats inward, then slides to the left.

Two men in security guard uniforms greet me with unwavering frowns. The zense in my chest spikes, confirming what I already know. Their aggravated energy seeps into my head, bringing my already shitty mood down more.

" 'Sup, Carlos," I say to the older one. He's been working here for as long as I can remember.

"Don't think I missed that wink," he growls.

The younger, more muscular guard hooks his thumb toward me. "Who's he?"

"Big V's annoying nephew. He used to live here and liked to play practical jokes on me."

I played jokes on Carlos because he was an easy target. This other guy though . . . He must be new, because I've never seen him before. He's got a scar down his left eyebrow and looks like he lifts trains for fun. As a kid, I wouldn't have played jokes on him. I wouldn't have even considered it.

"You know the drill," Carlos says. "Arms up."

After being frisked, I take the elevator down from the sixth floor to the fourth. When the elevator opens again, I find two more guards waiting for me with stony expressions. The bulkier one gestures for me to follow him.

Based on their fancy suits in place of security uniforms, I'm gonna assume these men are Victor's personal guards. Each of them has a wired device in his ear. If they were standing next to the president, they wouldn't look out of place. The only difference is that they aren't carrying any weapons. As trained ZIRDA agents, *they are* the weapons.

The bulkier guard stomps ahead of me while the skinny one trails behind. Our footsteps echo loudly against the walls of the wide hallways. As we turn the corners, I catch glimpses of more uniformed guards. When I lived here, it was never this packed with security. *What changed?*

We arrive at a locked door, where the bulkier guard holds his ID card up to a black device on the wall. A tiny light flashes green with a soft *beep*, and then the door unlocks. On the other side is another long hallway with more doors. At the end stand two guards posted outside a set of double doors. One of them scans their ID card and gestures for me to step into Victor's office—alone.

Chilly air nips at my skin as the door shuts. My body's equilibrium immediately works to warm me. Victor's office feels cold because it's huge for no goddamn reason. There's barely anything in it. A giant desk sits smack-dab in the middle, and behind that are a bunch of filing cabinets. Otherwise, there's so much open floor space that he could fit at least four king-size beds in here.

Victor, in a brown tailored suit, scowls at me from his colossal office chair behind the U-shaped desk. His emotions slap me in the face, somewhere between frustrated and angry. It's nothing new. I wish I could say his hostility is because of the stress from being the head of a ZIRDA base. I'm sure he's got lots on his plate, but Victor's hostility is only ever directed at me. Whenever he talks to other people, he's always firm but never demeaning.

"What took you so long?" Victor turns his finger in a circle above his mug. His wind power spins the metal spoon around.

I want to say that if he had sent a Porter like I asked, I would have been here hours ago. Since that'll only piss him off, I say, "Traffic."

My uncle flashes me a foul look. We both know there's no traffic at three in the morning.

"What's with all the extra guards?" I ask, desperate to change the subject. I take a seat in the small wooden chair on the other side of Victor's desk.

Every little movement sounds like nails on a chalkboard. The chair creaking beneath me. Each clink of Victor's spoon against the side of his mug. The cold air blowing in from the vents.

Silence always irks me. It makes me feel lonelier than I already am, so I usually play music around my house to cover it up. Ever since Aunt Jodi left him, Victor's opinion of music is that it's "for the weak." To him, my career choice is simply a "pathetic grab for attention."

"We've discovered moles," Victor says, scratching his forehead.

"Moles?"

"Yes, as in double agents. Royals."

My heart shrivels up at the mention of Royals. "How many have you found?"

"Two, and we took care of them appropriately."

I know exactly what that means and feel no remorse. The Royals deserve that fate for all the innocent lives they've stolen—especially my parents'. Instead of fighting for the development and growth of Zordis like ZIRDA does, the Royals would rather cause chaos and destroy any sense of peace in the world.

ZIRDA has been around since before the Grand Separation in 1326. Before that, Zordinary humans lived in harmony with Ordinary humans. Besides being born with powers and different bodies, we're all the same. Everyone just wants to be happy.

Unfortunately, some Ordinaries didn't see it that way. They felt threatened by anyone with gifts, so they manufactured a poison that affected only Zordis and distributed it through alcohol. Two million of us dropped dead within a year.

After that, it was clear that Zordis weren't safe anymore. Our choices were to either eliminate all the Ordis who wanted us dead, or go into hiding. So the zovernment recruited eighty-nine of the world's most powerful Scrubbers to alter the memories of all Ordis at once, erasing our existence from their minds. Sadly, not all Zordis agreed with this decision, and they came together to establish the Royals.

They're the Zordis who believe that we were robbed of our freedom. They believe that because we are born with powers, we are entitled to power over Ordinaries, a mindset I can never understand. Some Royals go as far as believing that Ordinaries don't have a place in this world at all. Those are the people who scare me the most.

The Royals want to control all governments and be treated like kings, hence why they named themselves *Royals*. They will stop at nothing to get what they think they deserve. They have gotten and will get rid of anyone who stands in their way. Unfortunately, while in the middle of working their Immunes project, my parents learned what happens when you stand in the way of the Royals.

Now, ZIRDA doesn't work only on the development of Zordis but has also established an anti-Royals department. The department that I'm now a part of. The department that I've wanted to be a part of since I was seven and was told the truth about who caused the explosion that killed my parents.

Victor stops spinning his finger over his mug, and the spoon goes still. "Where's the sample?"

From the inner pocket of my leather jacket, I pull out the folded napkin holding the three strands of Arella's long hair. The woman has so much of it, I'm surprised I didn't find more lying around on my back seat.

Victor accepts the napkin from me, setting it on his desk. "I'll have our lab techs run their tests on this right away."

"What are you looking for in her DNA?" I ask.

"Defects. Anything abnormal for an Ordi. We'll also see if there are any matches to the other two Immunes we have DNA from."

"How are those missions going?"

When Victor gave me this assignment, he told me that there are two other agents doing the same thing I am. Even though I've experienced being around an Immune myself, it's still hard to imagine that there are other Ordinaries out there like Arella. How many more? I have no idea, because according to my extensive research on the z-net over the last month, being immune to Zordi powers isn't possible.

Victor shoots me a venomous look. "You know the rules. Missions are not to be spoken about between agents."

I know that. I was just trying to make conversation, but whatever.

"Are you making any progress with the girl?"

He's not gonna like my answer, but it's the only one I have. "This might take more time than we thought."

Originally, Victor and I estimated that this mission would take about two months. Three, max. I spent the entire first month observing Arella from afar. Now I'm almost through week five, and all I've got is some hair in a napkin.

I continue, "She seems reserved. Not quick to trust people."

"Work around it!" Victor snaps. The long horizontal scar on his neck shifts as he swallows with anger. The scar reminds me that a Royal almost took his life too—on the same night my parents died.

"You need to think more like a woman," Victor says. "If you were in her shoes, what would make you trust someone enough to spill every little detail about yourself?"

I think about that for a moment. The only person I've ever trusted enough to tell almost everything to is Liz, and that's only because she's seen the worst of my memories. Otherwise, I would always keep my lips sealed around her. Even now, I still don't tell her everything.

Apparently, I've taken too long to think, because Victor scowls at me. "It's simple. To get, you need to give. If you tell her personal things about yourself, she'll return the favor."

"Tell her personal things? Like what?"

Victor bends back in his chair. "I don't fuckin' know. This is *your* mission, so *you've* gotta figure it out."

With a nod, I say, "Fine, but I still need more time."

"The longer you take, the longer you're postponing the process of figuring out how to reproduce her immunity. We need this to have an advantage over the Royals. Can you imagine how much easier it would be for us to overpower them if their gifts can't affect us? The sooner we can destroy all their bases and capture their leaders, the sooner we can stop them from killing more innocent people. So stop wasting time, and go get the information we need."

Ever since a Royal tried to kill him, Victor has dedicated his life to eradicating the Royals. Over the years, he's gotten more and more bitter about how they're still a thriving organization of violent criminals. He'll probably stop at nothing to take them down.

What Victor doesn't realize is that I feel the same. I want the answer to Arella's immunity just as much as he does. I want to take down the people who killed his brother—my father— just as much as he does.

That's why when I arrive back home, the first thing I do is grab my laptop and log in to the z-net. A few thoughts occurred to me during my three-hour ride home, and I'm itching to do some research.

In the search bar, I type, *Is it possible for an Ordinary to be part Zordinary?*

My theory is that maybe, by some fluke in the biological laws of reproduction, Arella could be half or even part Zordi. If so, maybe immunity is her gift.

After reading many articles written by reputable professors and medical zoctors, I conclude that the answer is no—being part Zordi is impossible. The Ordinary egg isn't strong enough to hold a Zordi sperm. The aggressive Zordi sperm always destroys the Ordinary egg upon impact. On the other hand, Ordinary sperm isn't strong enough to penetrate the cell walls of a Zordi egg. Most of the time, a Zordi woman's body kills off the Ordinary sperm before it can reach the egg, anyway.

So I ask the search bar another question: *Is it possible to block the zense?*

Since it's not possible for a person to be part Zordi, maybe Arella is full Zordi. Maybe her immunity can block that tingle we get in our chests whenever we get near one another.

After some reading, I conclude that it's also impossible to block the zense. Even Zordis with dormant powers will still activate the tingle in other Zordis.

Back at the search bar, I type, *What can make a person immune to Zordi powers?*

I get the same information I got all the other times I researched this question weeks ago, which is nothing. The bottom line is that since people don't know that Immunes exist, there's no information about them.

But if Immunes have existed since before my parents were killed, how is there not a single article about them? ZIRDA can't be the only people who know about Immunes. The zovernment has to know they exist too, right? So why isn't there any information anywhere?

5

TREY

I sense it before it comes. From behind, Liz's bubbly energy fires through my head like little pellets. Her heels clack rapidly across the backstage floor until her front slams against my back. The zense in my chest tingles as I fall forward off my barstool and catch myself right before the guitar in my lap hits the carpet.

Not even for a second does Liz release her arms from my torso. "Hey there, T-Bear!"

"Seriously, Liz? You act like you didn't just see me all day yesterday." *And every other day.* Dramatically, I pry myself out of her grasp, pretending she's a slimy slug.

With a huff, I plant my ass back onto the barstool. Once Kevin's guitar is repositioned over my thighs, I go back to changing the strings for him. He's been saying that he needs new strings, but he hasn't had the time to do it with all the stuff going on with his mom, so I figured I could help.

I twist the knob for the E string a few times. "You still trying to get that T-Bear thing to stick?"

Liz has been calling me that for the last few weeks. "I'm not trying. It's already stuck."

I throw my head back and groan.

"Ya know," she sings in her soprano voice, "I only call you that because ya hate it."

"I don't hate it," I grumble. "I just don't prefer it."

"Whatever." She narrows her eyes playfully. "You secretly like it."

"Do not." I do, not that I'll admit it out loud.

Liz is the only person I allow to call me silly names. She wears yellow every day of her life while she struts around the Earth spreading joy to everyone in sight. Even the people who don't deserve it—like me. For that, she can call me any stupid name in the book.

With a swoop, Liz flings her purse onto the sectional couch shoved against the wall, then heads to the mini bar for a bottle of water.

Our backstage area is one big room with our instruments lining the perimeter. In the middle sits a large open space where we like to rehearse. Down the hall in the back are some bathrooms. Across from those is our recording studio, where I've occasionally brought women in for a good time. I haven't done that for a while, because the last time I did, the redhead I invited in used teeth. My dick was sore for a week. Never again.

Liz claims a spot on the couch and pulls her yellow satin gloves off by the fingertips. The gloves flop onto the coffee table. I've come to appreciate the short moments when Liz's hands are bare. It doesn't happen often—only when it's just us.

It takes me another minute to finish tuning Kevin's guitar. With a flick of my wrist, the instrument hovers through the air, back to its stand. Then I join Liz on the sectional, resting an arm across the back.

She tucks one of her cherry-brown curls behind an ear. "Sooo, I read some of the comments on last week's music video."

"I thought we decided you weren't gonna read online comments anymore?"

"I didn't wear gloves for that video shoot," she says a little defensively. "I wanted to see what the fans' theories were."

"And?"

She chuckles. "The best theory was that I've been replaced by an alien clone and aliens are allergic to gloves."

I let out a loud *ha!* "Yep. That makes way more sense than the fact that you did your scenes alone, so you didn't need hand protection."

"I know, right?"

Over our four years as a band, our fans have drummed up hundreds of wild theories as to why Liz always wears gloves. While most people accept her excuse of being a germaphobe, many others like to spread theories about her having robotic hands or that she's hiding Hispanic gang tattoos.

It used to bother Liz. Now she owns it as her thing. Our sassy band manager, Monique, says that having a "thing" is great for branding. It gives people something to recognize Liz by. It's endearing when our hardcore fans come to our shows wearing satin gloves of their own. Monique has suggested that we slap our band logo onto some gloves and sell them as merchandise, but Liz refuses to monetize her curse, fearing that if she does, it'll get worse. I don't blame her. I'd feel the same.

"I sense three people coming." I point at Liz's gloves. They fly off the coffee table and land in her lap.

"Thanks, T." She doesn't hesitate to slip into them as Kevin swings the back door open. Sunlight radiates into the room while he holds the door wide for Marcus and Emmy to enter.

"Grant!" Marcus shouts. Our fans have labeled our drummer as the tough guy of our band because he's a tall, broad-shouldered Black man with a "Come at me, bruh!" resting face. On the inside, though, he's a softy, especially when it comes to his girlfriend. "Lemme ask you somethin'. If, before you walk into a gas station, you ask your girl if she wants a snack and she says *no*, can she get mad at you for not buyin' her a snack?"

I cock my eyebrows up. "No?"

Marcus turns to Emmy, who's barely a step behind him. "See, babe?"

Emmy, our band's pianist and alto, scowls at him. "Liz! If your man comes out of a gas station with three snacks for himself and none for you, then refuses to share *one* potato chip, do you have a right to get pissed?"

Liz laughs, pushing herself off the couch. "I mean, I'd be a little ticked."

With a flash of red curls, Emmy turns to slap her boyfriend's arm. "See?"

"It's never just *one* chip!" Marcus says. "One always turns into the whole goddamn bag."

Kevin makes a few *tsk tsk tsk* sounds as he wiggles a finger back and forth. "Word of advice, man: Always get your girl a snack."

"Whose side are you on, Chan?" Marcus gapes at Kevin. "She told me she didn't want nothin'!"

"Nah, bro." Kevin shakes his head. "They *always* want somethin'. And if they don't, now you got an extra snack."

Marcus glances at me with a *back me up* look.

The most I can offer him is a shrug. "Kevin knows what's up."

Knowing he's lost this one, Marcus mutters something under his breath as he takes his spot behind the drum set.

We're able to rehearse a few songs before the opening band arrives. Around that time, our crew members trickle into the room.

By seven, our openers are on stage while my band is backstage with Monique, talking through our upcoming filming schedule. I'm barely paying attention, for two reasons. First: I don't have anything going on in my life, so whatever dates work for them work for me. Second: I keep checking the time every two minutes. Arella should be here soon, and the clock on my phone seems to get slower with each glance.

Forty long minutes later, our security manager peeks his head backstage and motions for me. Earlier, I asked him to come find me whenever Arella got here.

Emmy is in mid-sentence when I shoot off the couch.

"Be right back," I say.

"What?" Marcus says as I rush away. "We're goin' up in like fifteen minutes."

I ignore him as I exit through a door and come out at the side of the stage. I scan the crowded restaurant for her face but don't find it.

"Where is she?" I ask.

Our security manager points with one of his thick tattooed fingers. "At the far end of bar."

Even through the dim lighting and all the people surrounding her, my eyes pin onto her immediately. She's got her back facing me, with all her wavy chestnut locks pulled into a long braid hanging over one shoulder.

The openers are in the middle of performing their closing song as I make my way toward Arella. Occupied tables of all sizes cover the floor from the stage to the back wall. From a side table, a pair of young women shout my name over the music. I flash them a smile and a quick wave. Instant giddiness flies through my head. Then comes their disappointment when I don't stop to chat with them. *Sorry, ladies, but I've got more important things on my plate.*

Tonight, for phase two, I have two objectives. First is to ask Arella out on a date. I need to keep seeing her until I find out what makes her immune. Since it could be *anything* that causes it, I need to learn as much about her past, her family history, her genetics, and whatever else as possible.

My second objective is to get her to tell me all the basic information I already know about her. I would hate to slip up and mention something I know that she hasn't told me yet.

Arella, looking as stunning as yesterday, has her phone pressed to her ear as I approach her from behind.

"What do you mean, you're not coming?" A pause. "You're kidding . . . No. I can't be here without you, Javie." Silence, then she groans. "All right, fine. No, it's okay. Yes, really. Mm-hmm. I'll see you tomorrow." With a deep sigh, she sets her phone onto the bar counter.

Now's my chance.

"Hey." I slide onto the empty barstool next to her.

Arella jumps back a little, clasping a hand against her chest. "Ah! You scared me."

"Now we're even."

She crumples her eyebrows together before making an *oh!* face. "That's right. I scared you yesterday while you were fixing my tire. Thanks again for that."

"No problem. Where's your friend?"

Arella rolls her eyes, but her irritation doesn't shoot through my mind like it should. "Javina's girlfriend flew back from a work trip early as a surprise. Apparently, that means Javina needs to go to the airport and ditch me here by myself."

"You're not by yourself. You've got me."

"But won't you be up there?" She points at the stage, just as the opening band's final song ends.

The floor vibrates with an eruption of cheers as the lead singer waves at the crowd. The lights go wild with bright neon colors flashing back and forth. The singer says his last thank-yous, then vanishes behind the black curtain with the rest of his band. Slowly, the stage lights dim out as the cheering fades and transforms into a loud hum of conversation.

I have little time left, so I throw a hand up to get one of the four bartenders' attention. The guy with an eyebrow piercing spots me right away and offers me a curt nod as he finishes the drink he's making.

After he sets two drinks in front of a young Asian couple, he approaches me. The name tag pinned to his upper chest reads MITCH. I've never seen him before, so he must be new.

"What can I get for you?" Frustration simmers in Mitch's gut. I wonder what from.

"I've got my card on file under Trey Grant." I gesture to Arella. "Anything she wants is on me tonight."

Mitch squints his eyes. "Huh? What d'you mean you've got your card on file?"

"Just tell Sophie I'm covering her bill."

The guy scoffs. "And you are?"

I don't expect the new guy to know who I am. Still, he doesn't have to come at me with that snippy attitude. Twisting on my seat, I hop off and head toward the nearest table.

"Excuse me," I say to the group of men shoving onion rings into their mouths. I grab the little acrylic sign off their table. "I'm just gonna borrow this for a sec."

I hand the sign to the bartender, then point at my face. "That's me. Tell Sophie this guy is getting this girl's bill, 'kay?"

"Cool." Mitch tosses the sign back to me, and I catch it easily. He's lucky I've got good reflexes, or I would have dropped it from his shit throw. From under the bar counter, he pulls out a laminated menu and shoves it at Arella. "Be back in a jiff."

I should speak to Sophie about Mr. Rude and Unfriendly later. He's not someone I'd want bartending at my joint. No doubt, Sophie doesn't want him either.

After I return the sign to its original table, I reclaim my place next to Arella, who's reading the menu. "What're you in the mood for?"

"Thank you, but you don't have to pay for me."

"No worries. Sophie gives the entire band and crew a huge discount. She says we help bring in most of her income."

I check the time on my phone. Monique is probably freaking out right now about me not getting mic'd up. I'm gonna hear it from her later about how I purposely do things just to piss her off, even though that's never my goal. If Arella wasn't such a vital puzzle piece to finishing my parents' research, I'd be back there already.

While Arella focuses on the menu, I focus on her as if staring longer will make my mind power kick in. So far, nothing. *Damn, she's beautiful though.* Undoubtedly the prettiest Ordinary I've ever laid eyes on. Strands of wavy locks fall out of her braid, framing her rosy cheeks. Long black lashes surround her hypnotizing brown eyes, and her nose has that delicate small and rounded shape about it. All her features fit with her sweet and gentle demeanor.

Arella sets the menu down and turns to me with a shy smile. "Am I that interesting to watch?"

I smile back sheepishly. "A little."

Mitch returns with that same snippy tone. "You decide on somethin' yet, sweet cakes?"

Sweet cakes? I can't stop myself from shooting him a dirty look. Mitch pretends like he doesn't see it, but I sense it when he does, the moment his nerves spike. Subtly, I give him my best *I'm this close to hitting you* face.

"I'll have some water and the chicken nachos, please," Arella says, never acknowledging Mitch's stupid pet name. Maybe she doesn't care that he called her *sweet cakes*, but I do.

"Cool." Mitch snatches the menu from her, then leaves.

Now that he's gone, it's time for me to make good on my mission. "So, Arella, do you work anywhere besides Sunrise Daycare?"

Her shoulders stiffen. "How do you know where I work?"

"You and Javina were wearing the same T-shirt yesterday. I just assumed . . ."

"Oh, right." She relaxes. "I'm also a nanny over the weekends. How about you? What do you do?"

"You know what I do. I'm a musician." I nod my head toward the stage I'm supposed to be behind right now.

"Do you do anything else?"

"Just this."

Her fingers play with the end of her long braid. I can't tell if she's doing it out of habit or because she's nervous. Here I am, playing that guessing game again.

"If you don't have another job, what do you do in your free time?" she asks.

This is supposed to be me learning about her, not the other way around. I answer anyway. "Doing what I do keeps me busy enough. We film videos at least once a week and rehearse a lot. Then there's all our writing and recording sessions. I also do a lot of the background work like song arrangements and producing. When I have free time, I like to ride my Harley around the suburbs, read, work out, you know."

"Sounds like you've got it good."

I purse my lips together into a thin line. "Sure."

Something I've learned about life is that the way things look on the outside isn't always what they are on the inside. I would trade away the Internet fame and everything I have if it meant I could live the life I would have if my parents had never been murdered.

"What do you do in your free time?" I ask.

"Um, are they looking for you?" Arella points toward the stage. I turn at the hip to find two crew members up there, cupping hands to their eyebrows and surveying the crowd.

Dammit. I've never been this late. Monique is gonna kill me.

"You're staying for the whole set, right?" I force my ass to slide off my seat.

"How long does it go 'til?"

"Ten."

"Oh, that's kind of late." She tugs at the bottom of her shirt. "I'll stick around for as long as I can."

"It'd mean a lot to me if you stayed. I'd like to know what you think of our music." I *need* her to stay. If she leaves, I'll have to plan another run-in with her. At that point, it might look suspicious.

I see the battle she's having with herself in her head, even though I can't sense it. I've gotta get her to stay, so, with the sweetest puppy-dog eyes I can muster, I add, "Please?"

After a moment, she lets out a breath and smiles sweetly. "All right. I'll stay for your whole set."

Thank fuck. "Great. I'll come find ya when I'm done."

Backstage, the openers are getting their instruments packed up as I beeline past them to my electric guitar. Liz and Emmy each have a microphone in their hand, flashing me a *what the hell* look. Kevin, with his bass guitar strapped over a shoulder, taps the invisible watch on his wrist. Marcus spins his drumsticks around his fingers, shaking his head at me. The crew members are all in position, ready to roll. The only person not in sight is Monique, and I count it as a W.

I'm about to swing my guitar strap over my head when a large hand shoves me so hard, I'm launched forward a step. It's Marcus, and his mood swarms around me like angry bees. "Bro, you missed our entire pre-show routine. I was 'bout to send out a search party."

I throw both hands up in surrender. "I'm here now. No need for the helicopters."

"I had ten dollars on you hiding in the bathroom, whackin' one off." Marcus huffs as he makes his way back to join the rest of our band near the stage door.

Our gray-haired sound manager replaces him. "I bet twenty dollars." He hands me my earpiece.

I shove it into my ear, then hook the mic pack to the back of my jeans.

Our sound manager marches away as his voice bellows through my earpiece. "Found Grant. He's ready."

Monique growls my name through the device. I know it's her from the same exasperated tone she always says my name in. "Trey Grant, I swear to Lord Jesus, you be givin' me more aneurysms than all six of my children put together."

I ignore her. She says that about me at least once a week.

Our sound manager responds with a chuckle. "Monique, you say that about him every week, yet ya still like the kid."

"I'd like him more if he didn't purposely try to make my job harder."

I chuckle to myself, then press a button on my mic pack. "Monique, we all know you enjoy yelling at me as much as I enjoy making you yell at me."

She growls again. "Get to your position, Grant."

I rarely get nervous before a show., but tonight, my mind feels chaotic. My body's here, about to perform, but my mind's still with Arella, trying to figure her out.

Focus! I order myself as my bandmates and I step out onto the stage, still hidden behind the giant black curtain. On the other side, the audience is screaming at the top of their lungs. I allow their intense energy to rush through me and take control. Hopefully, it'll drown out the tension in my stomach.

The crowd gets louder when the lights flash and our intro music drops over the speakers. A heavy drum beat with a guitar riff plays, then comes Liz's recorded voice.

"Like a sunrise on the darkest day or a shining star within the black sky, you'll always see us because we are . . . Flames in the Night!"

The crowd chants along with the countdown. "Five. Four. Three. Two. ONE!"

As my bandmates march out from behind the curtain, the rumble of screams pulsates through my veins. I'm always the last to come out. When I do, I lift my guitar into the air, and the crowd gets wilder. Their rush of exhilaration slams into my head so hard, I almost lose my balance.

With my Empath powers having the range of a quarter mile, I can sense hundreds to thousands of people at once. Usually, I'm able to minimize my range to only those within a few steps of me. It makes the emotions of everyone else in the distance feel like a low hum—still present, just not as loud.

On stage, I like to expand my range to everyone in the audience. Being able to sense every single person as I perform is one of the few perks of this empathy gift—a gift I never would have chosen. Not that anybody gets to choose.

Marcus ticks off four beats on his drumsticks before going into his drum solo. After eight measures, I enter with my guitar. After that, the rest of the band joins in, and we play our usual opening song, "Fired Up!"

The more I sing and play, the more I lose myself in the moment. Music has always been my escape. It helps me forget about my bullshit childhood and seeing my parents die in front of me.

6

TREY

I'M ABOUT TO FINISH BUILDING THE FIRST WALL OF MY LEGO CASTLE WHEN MAMA COMES INTO MY bedroom and sits on the floor with me.

"Hey, honey." She grabs my teddy bear and puts it in my lap, then drags her fingers through my hair. I usually love it when she does that. Tonight, I know she's only doing it to distract me from how she feels. I can't ignore it. Her heartache is making my heart ache.

"What's wrong, Mama?" I rub the wetness off her cheek with my fingers. *Did I do something wrong?*

"Nothing's wrong."

"Then why are you crying?"

She wipes her tears off on her sleeve, then pats her lap. "Come here, baby."

I listen to my mama and crawl onto her legs.

"Let's sing our song together," she says.

Last year, Mama wrote a song for me. She said that whenever I'm sad, I should sing the song and it'll remind me that everything will be okay. I love the song, and we've been singing it together every day.

I pull Andy, the bear I named after Daddy, closer to my chest as Mama and I sing.

When you're lost without me,
you'll always have Andy.
When you feel you don't belong,
hug this bear and sing this song.
Look to the sky when you feel down.
Know that things will turn around.
Work twice as hard to the finish line.
Now it's your time to shine.

Mama kisses my forehead. "I love you so much, honey."

"I love you too, Mama."

Daddy's footsteps thump down the hall, stopping outside my bedroom door. "It's time to go."

Mama doesn't move. She keeps running her hands through my hair.

"Suzie . . ." Daddy says as his tense feelings rush through my mind.

I think of earlier that day when my parents made my favorite pancakes with strawberries and whipped cream. I turned my entire plate into a tower of white fluff. Mama and Daddy couldn't even tell there were pancakes underneath. I think about how happy I felt while eating it. Any cheerful thought will work as long as I think about it hard enough, then push it into Mama's head.

She smiles, squeezing my hand. "Thank you, but you know I don't like it when you do that."

"I just want you to be happy," I say as she pushes off the carpet.

I slide out of her lap and look up at her. She wipes more tears off her face, and it makes me want to push more happiness into her.

Daddy always says there isn't a point to having powers if we don't use them. Mama always says it's okay to use my powers as long as I don't hurt anyone. *Does making people happy hurt them?*

"Listen to me, son." Daddy kneels at my side and points at the clock hanging on my wall. "You see that shorter arrow pointing at the nine?"

I already know how to tell time. The clock says it's nine thirty-six.

"When that short arrow reaches the twelve, if Mama and I aren't back yet, run to one of the neighbors' houses, okay? And take Andy with you."

"What time will you be back if you're not home by midnight?"

Daddy swallows, looks up at Mama, then back at me. "If you get hungry, there are some leftovers in the fridge." He stands and pats my shoulder. "Be a good boy now."

Something bad is happening. I know it. I can *feel* it. Maybe if I cry and tell them I don't want them to go to work, they'll stay.

No. They'll still go. They always do. Besides, I'm seven now. Seven-year-olds don't cry.

"Goodbye, honey." Mama leans down to kiss my forehead.

"Wait. You said to never say goodbye. Goodbye means forever."

"I'm sorry, baby. I meant bye for now."

Outside the living room window, my parents run through the rain, get into their car, and drive away into the darkness. I drag my feet back to my room and slump over my bed, waiting for the short arrow to tick away from the nine.

Usually whenever my parents get called in to work, Aunt Debbie comes over to watch me. Earlier, Mama told me that Aunt Debbie couldn't come. Mama asked if I could stay home by myself. I told her that I'm old enough. Besides, I've stayed home by myself before. Most of the time, it's only for a few minutes while my parents run to the store.

Vroom! Every time I hear a car, I rush back to the living room window. The cars never stop, and there have been at least six cars now.

When the short arrow points at the ten, water pours onto the house. It's so loud, it sounds like all the kids at my school are stomping on the roof. To try to block out the noise, I point at the TV. It turns on with a bright screen that hurts my eyes for a second. Once my eyes are clear again, I sit in my spot on the couch. I always get the middle cushion because I like to be right between Mama and Daddy.

I wiggle my fingers at the TV, pressing buttons until *The Lion King* plays. With another wave of my hand, a blanket floats off the floor and drapes over my legs.

My eyes get sleepy as Simba and Scar battle on top of Pride Rock. I shove Andy behind my head to use as a pillow. His fur is soft and—

BOOM!

The front door bursts open.

I yelp and fall to the floor, getting tangled in the blanket.

"What was that?" a deep voice asks.

I peek my head out from under the fleece. Two tall people are standing in my living room. *Who are they?*

With heavy footsteps, two more people rush into my house.

The biggest guy points at me. "It's their kid! Get him!"

I toss the blanket over my shoulder. A fireball the size of a baseball appears in my hand. My fireballs aren't as big as Daddy's, and I've never cared—until now. I throw my fireball at the biggest guy and don't even wait to see if I hit or missed. The second I let it go, I run.

The carpet rumbles beneath me like I'm standing on train tracks with a moving train coming right at me. I fall and hit my face on the corner of a table. I cry as I rub the pain in my cheek.

"Come here, you little shit," a big man says from behind me.

I twist around, then scream as I crawl backward away from him. Behind him, a fireball shoots through the open door. It sets one of the bad guys on fire. My skin burns, even though it's not *my* body on fire.

Two more people run through the door. It's too dark to see who they are, especially when they're moving so fast. One of them throws a fireball at the bad guys. If they're fighting the people who are trying to hurt me, that means they're good, right?

I don't stick around to find out. On my hands and knees, I crawl away. I'm about to turn in to the kitchen when a fireball lands right in front of me. I scream with my arms over my face. The flames burst upward, blocking my way.

Hide! I need to hide! I crawl until I've shoved myself into a corner behind an end table. Hopefully, no one can see me here. More fireballs fly around the room. I can't tell who they're coming from or who they're aimed at.

A woman screams as something sharp jabs into my side. I pull my shirt up to check my skin. Nothing's there. My face burns like someone's thrown a fireball at my head. My body's going numb, and I think I'm going to puke. I haven't learned how to stop my body from feeling other people's physical pain yet. Daddy says I should be able to once I'm older, but I want to be able to do it now.

More flames consume my house, destroying everything. All the people are screaming and shouting at each other as my body continues to ache. A chair cracks into pieces against the wall by the TV. I dare one look up, only to find a vase flying at me. It shatters right above my head. I throw my arms up as the glass falls over me, and liquid drenches my shirt.

"Honey?" Someone shakes my shoulder.

"Mama?" I open my eyes.

A long cut runs along her bottom lip to her chin. Blood drips from it. She's got another cut on her forehead, with even more blood running from that. Suddenly, my head and lip hurt too.

"Run outside!" Mama shouts over the crash of someone being thrown against the floor.

She yelps as she's jerked away from me by her hair.

"Mama!" I shriek, reaching for her.

The big man who yanked her climbs on top of her and punches her in the face. I feel it in my cheek.

Then again.

And again.

And again.

The man shocks her with a lightning ball. She cries out as my body shakes.

"No!" I throw my unsteady hand up and launch a fireball at the guy.

He only flinches as it hits his arm, falls to the floor, and rolls away. The tall guy behind him flicks his wrist in circles. A tornado appears in front of me, sucking me into it. The air leaves my lungs as I spin until my back slams against the wall. I fall to my knees and gasp for a breath.

I'm still dizzy as someone lifts me into their arms. I'm about to blast them with a fireball until I see his face. It's Daddy—with a gash in his cheek. It's so deep, it looks like part of his face is falling off. Red streaks pour from his wound, all the way down to his chest.

"Outside! Now!" Daddy points at the coffee table. It flies up and crashes through the big living room window, landing in the front yard. Glass falls everywhere.

My back hits the couch. I scream and grip the cushions as Daddy waves his hand, and I'm flown out the window on the couch.

It crashes next to the coffee table, bounces once, then tips over, dumping me onto the muddy ground. Water pelts my eyes. I can't see. I can't—

BOOM!

My house explodes into a giant mushroom of fire. It throws me backward. Heat pricks my skin as I fall to the ground. Pain bursts into the side of my head. A high-pitched ringing sound pierces my ears. I can't hear anything else.

I wipe the water from my face. It feels weird. I glance at my hands. They're red. Why is the water red?

I have to get up. I have to help my mama and daddy.

I try to push off the grass, but my arms don't work. I collapse into the mud, and then darkness takes over.

7

ARELLA

I'm totally going to kill Javina. While I'm at it, I'm going to kill Rachel too. If it weren't for them, I wouldn't be sitting at a bar by myself.

Once Javina told me that she wasn't coming—last minute, I might add—I figured I could stay for a few songs, then leave. Screw Trey and his show-stopping smile and those puppy dog eyes.

"It'd mean a lot to me if you stayed." How is a woman supposed to say no to that?

I munch on a cheesy chip off my plate of nachos as Trey effortlessly performs a guitar solo on stage, his second of the evening. There's no denying that he's talented. His fingers slide up and down the guitar as if it's a part of him. I can't imagine how many long hours it took him to learn how to play that fast and make it sound good.

While everyone in the band has singing parts, Trey seems to have the most. It doesn't seem like anyone's disappointed about it, either. When he's not singing or playing the guitar, he's behind the drum set, banging some drumsticks all over it. When he's not doing that, he's behind the piano, delivering a perfect tune. If the crowd isn't impressed by how many instruments he can play, it's probably because they're too busy gawking at his arm muscles straining the sleeves of his leather jacket.

Midway through the show, the rest of the band disappears behind the curtain and Trey performs by himself from the piano. He sings with his eyes closed and his lips practically making out with the microphone. I wouldn't be surprised if all the women here wished they were that microphone right now.

After he finishes the song, he thanks everyone, and the lights go dark. A second later, the spotlight returns as Liz, Kevin, and the other female band member take the stage. The women perform a perfectly harmonized song with Kevin on the guitar. I'm just as mesmerized by their voices as I was by Trey's.

From behind a ketchup bottle, I find one of those table signs displaying the band's picture. All five of them look like models, with their flawless faces and matching outfits. Trey's in the middle, wearing the same thing he wore yesterday and is wearing today: a black leather jacket over a plain black V-neck that hugs his torso. In the picture, he's got the same styled hair and stubbly beard. The only difference is that he looks slightly younger in the picture, but not by much.

"That picture is over a year old," someone says from behind me. "We're getting them updated soon."

I twist on my barstool to find the dazzling man I was just admiring. When our eyes lock, my heart kicks up a notch. My body reacted like this around him yesterday, too. It's not like me to get this excited around men. Usually, I'm trying to escape as fast as my legs will carry me. Right now, that urge is absent. If anything, I'm a little drawn to him, and I can't figure out why. It's not like Trey's the only attractive man in this city. A cute guy made conversation with me at a gas station this morning, and not once did he make my stomach flutter the way Trey is.

I pretend like his presence doesn't affect me as I tilt my head toward the stage. "Aren't you supposed to be over there?"

"Nah. It's solo time. Everyone gets to show off their individual talents for a while and give the others a break."

I do my best not to stare at his can't-help-but-gawk-at-them features. "It's fun to watch your band perform. I didn't know you played so many things. Which instrument did you learn first?"

"Guitar. I first picked one up when I was—" Trey catches that my attention has slipped to the two ladies with eager smiles standing behind him. He flips around.

The one with teal blue tips in her blonde hair perks up. "Hi, Trey. Can we get a picture with you?"

"Oh, sure." He drapes an arm around the blonde's shoulder and flashes his pearly whites. Her friend snaps a few photos, and then they alternate.

"We've both been huge fans ever since your first YouTube video went viral," Blue Tips says. She goes on and on about how much she loves his music and, more so, how much she loves *him*. Her friend adds to the conversation by asking him question after question. They sound as fangirly as Javina did yesterday, except I'm bothered by them and not by Javina.

They steal Trey away from me for so long, it's Kevin who's got the stage to himself now.

"Thanks again, ladies," Trey says halfway through Kevin's solo. "I appreciate the support."

It's obvious that he's trying to close the conversation, but the ladies don't take the hint. They keep fawning over him and praising *him*, not his music. I can't tell if he likes it or not.

Patiently, I wait until Trey presses a finger against his earpiece. The fangirls are still blabbing as he listens to whatever is being said on the other end.

With a groan, he takes a step backward toward the stage. "Sorry, ladies. I gotta go before my manager chews my head off. It was great to meet you both."

Finally, the ladies say their goodbyes, then depart into the sea of people around us.

Trey turns back to me. "I'm really sorry 'bout that. I gotta go back up. We've got a meet and greet right after this. Would you mind coming to that for a bit? I won't make you stay long. I promise."

I don't know what possesses me to do it. Maybe it's because I know the answer he wants to hear, or because I'm a people pleaser. Maybe it's because throughout the show, I've been in awe of him and I want to keep being awed. But I say, "I'd love to."

The bright smile that spreads across his cheeks makes my heart swoon and confirms my decision. After he thanks me, he sprints off behind a door marked BACKSTAGE. AUTHORIZED PERSONNEL ONLY.

The moment he's gone, those two fangirls materialize on either side of me.

Blue Tips speaks first. "Do you know Trey Grant? Like, personally?"

"Uh . . ." I don't *know* him. Not really.

The other girl doesn't wait for me to respond before she asks, "What's he like in real life? Is he like what they say online?"

"Um, what do they say online?"

"You know, that he's charming, mysterious, and really good in bed."

"Oh. I—I suppose I don't know him like *that*."

"Does that mean you're not on his list?"

I scrunch my face together. "His VIP list?"

"No. His *list*. You know . . ." Blue Tips nudges my arm with her elbow and waggles her eyebrows up and down. "Of people he's fucked. I've heard he's into doing it with his fans."

"And sometimes with multiple at the same time," the other girl adds.

Are these ladies trying to have a threesome with him? *Wait . . .* Is that why Trey invited Javina and me here tonight? Was he trying to entice us into his bed? If so, he chose the wrong woman. I'm not interested in being anyone's plaything.

"No," I say firmly. "I'm not on his list."

"In that case," Blue Tips says, grinning, "can you get us into the meet and greet tonight? Tickets were sold out, and we really wanna go."

"Uh . . ." I don't know how to respond. Thankfully, I don't have to, because a thick guy with a long scruffy beard comes up behind the girls and speaks for me.

"Ladies, leave her alone. If you wanna bang the guy, find your own way. You're making her uncomfortable."

That's putting it lightly.

Blue Tips shoots Scruffy Guy a dirty look. "Mind your own business."

The man uses his large body to stand in front of me protectively. "Walk."

The girls glance at each other, then silently agree to leave. They mutter foul words under their breath as they slither away.

"Thanks for that," I say once they're gone.

"No worries." The towering man sticks out a hand with a smile. "I'm Dex."

"Ari." I shake his thick palm. That's two days in a row now that I've shaken hands with a man and didn't feel violated by it. I'm making wonderful progress.

Dex slides onto the empty barstool next to me and takes a swig of his beer. "Pretty name. Where ya from?"

"Around here," I say vaguely. While I'm grateful he told those girls off, it wasn't an open invitation to befriend me. He seems to think it was though.

As Kevin leaves the stage and is replaced by Trey and Liz, Dex asks about my age and what I do for a living. I give him undetailed answers like "A woman never shares her age" and "I work with kids." Then I move the subject back to him. I've learned that most men like talking about themselves more than they like listening to women talk, and Dex is no exception.

My nachos are gone by the time I've heard all about Dex's plan to get rich as a travel agent. I fake laugh and nod whenever appropriate. Listening to him go on and on about himself reminds me of why I don't enjoy first dates. I have yet to go out with a man who genuinely wants to know more about me than he wants to brag about himself, though I've only been on three first dates, so I don't have the best pool of results.

"And I got this one after I moved to San Fran." Dex points at his huge upper forearm where a detailed dragon is inked into his skin. He's been yammering on about his tattoos and love for dragons for about fifteen minutes now. Judging by the way he talks about dragons, their diets, and what their scales feel like, I'd say he thinks they're real.

Mitch, the rude bartender, interrupts Dex's tattoo-flaunting session. "Another beer?"

Dex hands Mitch his empty bottle. "Yeah, and how about a cocktail for this pretty lady?"

I shake my head. "No, thanks."

"You sure?"

I'm positive. "Thank you, though."

"It's my treat."

"No, really. I don't drink." That's not something I usually tell people right away, but I don't want to seem impolite.

"How 'bout a lemonade, then?"

I shrug a shoulder, giving in. "Sure."

Mitch departs, then comes back with a glass of icy lemonade and another beer for Dex. I take a sip of my drink. It's sweet and tangy, exactly the way I like it.

Once the bartender takes off to help the next customer, Dex goes back to mansplaining dragons to me. I thought turning my entire body away from him would indicate that I have no interest in dragons, but nope. He's too self-absorbed to pick up on any of my social cues.

Thankfully, the entertainment is a good distraction. Trey's now playing an acoustic guitar and singing a duet with Kevin. For a second, Trey locks eyes with me, and my heart skips a beat. I must have imagined it though. There's no way he can see me from all the way up there with all those bright stage li—

Someone taps my arm. "Ari?"

I flinch, jerking my arm back.

Dex puts a hand up, palm forward. "Sorry. Think I lost you there. You didn't answer my question."

I take a well-needed sip of my lemonade, holding back a groan. "What was your question?"

"I asked if you've ever been to Europe."

"No."

"Well, as I was saying . . ." and he goes on yapping.

The more he talks, the less I pretend to listen. I nod occasionally while keeping my eyes on the amazing entertainment.

After a few more songs, my lemonade is gone and Dex is *still* talking. About what? I have no idea. My grandparents taught me to always be nice to people, but I'm losing my patience with this guy. Also, my head feels hazy. I'm hot, I'm sweaty, and the room is swaying.

"You all right?" Dex asks. At least, I think it's him. I've shut my eyes to block out the flashing lights that are suddenly way too bright.

"I'm getting a headache." Placing my elbows on the bar, I dump my head into my hands. The music's way too loud. Every bass drop feels like it's rattling my brain.

"You wanna go home?"

"I'm fine."

"You're turning red." Dex catches me with his enormous hand as the room tilts to the side. "And now you're falling . . ."

I understand that he's only trying to stop me from crashing to the floor, but him grabbing me like that makes me want to recoil into myself. I'm close to shoving him away. I don't because I don't want to be like that anymore. It's exhausting to be scared all the time and to wonder if the hand on my body will leave another bruise. I want to be a normal person—someone who can be touched by a man without dying on the inside.

"I'm gonna get some fresh air." I toss the long strap of my purse over my shoulder, then get to my feet.

Dex puts his beer down. "I'll come make sure you don't fall over."

"No, thanks. I'll be fine." The room wavers as I navigate through the crowd from my seat to the door.

Fog settles into my brain as I stumble into the warm night air. The massive line of people waiting to get inside earlier has disappeared. It's quieter out here than in there, which helps me feel a tiny bit better—right until a car drives by with lights as bright as the sun.

"Be careful." Someone steadies me with an arm on my waist.

I flinch as my eyes meet with Dex's. I thought I'd told him I'd be fine, but apparently I'm not if I can't even walk straight.

Dex keeps me upright as I shuffle behind the restaurant to sit on a patch of grass under a looming palm tree. I pretzel my legs together and throw my head into my hands.

What's going on? Why does my head hurt so much? Was it something I ate? *Wait . . .* Did someone drug me? My head springs up.

"You okay?" Dex squats in front of me with concern etched into his face.

I peer over Dex's broad shoulders to scan the area for my ex's car. I wouldn't put it past him to slip some money to the bartender to drop something into my lemonade, and then when I come outside, he attacks me.

My vision is blurry, but from what I can tell, his car isn't here. *Maybe he parked it in a parking garage?*

"Looking for someone?" Dex asks, glancing back.

Was it . . . ? No. It couldn't have been Dex. I kept my hands and eyes on my drink the whole time, and not once did he reach for my lemonade.

Rummaging through my purse, I pull out my phone. The brightness of the screen makes me screw my eyes shut again. "I'm going to call my friend to pick me up."

"I could take you home?" he offers gently.

Yeah, right. "No, thanks," I say kindly yet firmly.

"I don't mind."

I mind. "I appreciate the thought, but I—"

The world tips upside down. All I can see is the back of Dex's jeans. His hard shoulder digs into my stomach, and my purse flops against him as he steadily carries me across the parking lot.

"Hey!" I shout. The word barely comes out. "Put me down."

I struggle to raise my arms. My attempt at punching the guy looks like my hand twitched. My leg doesn't lift when I tell it to. Neither does my head.

No! I scream at the top of my lungs, but it doesn't reach my ears.

A car beeps, then a door opens. I can't pry my eyelids apart. Warm leather presses against my cheek. My mind races to all those kidnapped, raped, and murdered women I watch true crime shows about. *Am I about to become one of them?*

I try to scream again. Nothing comes out. I try to move but fail. My legs are moving, but that's because Dex is pushing them into the car. I tell my legs to kick him. They don't.

The door slams shut as a deep voice bellows, "Step. Away. From. The girl."

"Don't worry, man. She's my girlfriend. She's just had too much to drink."

"Get away from her," the other man growls.

"Fuck off."

I wrench my eyes open just enough to see Dex's giant frame bend forward as he grunts. His head snaps back as the other guy punches him again. With a growl, Dex swings his fist at the smaller man, who ducks and strikes Dex in his jaw.

Vomit is coming. It's slowly creeping up my throat.

Someone lets out an ear-piercing scream, then wails. I think it's Dex. At least, I *hope* it's him.

The door flies open. Someone's warm palm cups my cheek. "Are you okay?"

I try to force my eyelids open, but they don't budge.

8

ARELLA

The blinding sunrise shines through my tinted windows. I drag my blanket over my face. *Why does my blanket smell like a man? And since when are my windows tinted?*

I jolt upright. The blanket I don't recognize slides down my front.

Whose bed is this? It's king-size, I think. I can't tell for sure; I've never been on one. The sheets are gray and silky, not purple and cotton like the ones at home.

I'm alone. *Is that a good thing?*

The denim shorts I wore last night are still on. As is my shirt. *Good sign.*

The other side of the bed looks slightly made. *Another good sign.*

On the nightstand are three bottles of cologne, a lamp, and a book with a dragon on the cover. Visions of a scruffy-bearded guy sipping beer zip across my mind like flashing lights. He went on and on about his dragon tattoo.

What happened last night? I try to remember, but my memory fails me. Everything beyond dragon talk is a blur. Am I at that guy's house? *Oh, god. I hope not.*

This bedroom is twice the size of mine. Maybe triple. The white walls are bare. *How am I supposed to figure out whose house I'm in if they don't have any personal pictures hanging up?*

After scooting off the gigantic mattress, I peer into the walk-in closet. Dark jeans and plain T-shirts are hung in neat rows. Whoever's closet this is doesn't wear any color.

The master bathroom is complete with a jacuzzi and a shower as big as my entire bathroom. This house belongs to someone with money, that's for sure.

I press my ear against the bedroom door. Silence. No movement, either. After taking the lampshade off the lamp, I unplug the lamp and grip it tightly. Anyone I feel threatened by is about to become a victim of my lamp bat.

As softly as I can, I open the door and tread down the hall with sloth-like footsteps. Maybe I'm in *his* house. Then again, he could never afford something this nice. Not without Daddy's money. Nor does he read.

I keep tiptoeing over the soft carpet. Sunlight gleams from the other end of the hall. A familiar scent floats up my nose. I'd know that smell anywhere. *Bacon.*

When I round the corner to where the sizzling is coming from, I raise my lamp bat, ready to strike.

The tall man in front of the stove jumps. "Shit!" His spatula somersaults onto the hardwood floor with a clank.

I freeze with my weapon up. It's not the man I was expecting.

Trey scoops up the spatula, then wipes the floor with a towel. "Dammit. You've really gotta stop scaring me."

Trey Grant? That's who lives here?

"What's with the lamp?" he asks. I'd like to think he feels intimidated, but the knitted brows and hint of a smirk on his lips tell me he's more amused than anything.

I keep my lamp bat held high and muster up the sternest voice I can. "What happened?"

Nonchalantly, Trey slides two slices of bread into a toaster. "How do you like your eggs?"

My eggs? What? He's asking me that as if I casually stay overnight at his house all the time. Maybe he's used to women waking up here, but I'm not used to waking up anywhere except in my own bed.

"What happened?" I ask more firmly this time.

"I'll tell you once you put my lamp down."

If Trey wanted to hurt me, he would have already, right? Sighing, I set his lamp onto the island.

"Is scrambled okay?" Trey asks, all light and gentle.

"Um, sure."

From the refrigerator, he pulls out a carton of eggs. "What do you remember?"

"I remember being at the Soul House. I was watching your band play and . . ." Then I was thrown over the shoulder of a giant man like a sack of potatoes.

"Did you know that dirty-mouthed motherfucker?" Trey's tone has lost all his earlier gentleness. It's ironic that he's calling Dex dirty-mouthed when he's no better.

"No."

"He drugged you."

My jaw drops. "How? I nursed my lemonade the entire night."

"I know. I was watching you. More specifically, him. You kept talking to him, so I thought maybe you knew each other. I never saw him put anything into your drink, so I called Sophie. She owns the bar. I told her what happened. On a hunch, I asked her to check out the new bartender. She found drugs on him. Lots of 'em. The cops were called. Got a text from Sophie this morning. Apparently, Mitch and Dexter were in on it together, and this wasn't their first time."

A shudder runs down my spine. If I'm not the first, what happened to the others? I don't think I want to know.

"What now?" I ask.

Trey turns back to the stove and flips over the sizzling bacon. "They're both arrested and are probably gonna go away for a while. Sophie is gonna do a better job at performing background checks before she hires. I get that she's short-staffed, but she can't just take in anyone off the street."

"Was that you who beat up Dex?"

"Once I saw him take you outside, I jumped off the stage to make sure you were safe. At first, I couldn't find you. I was really worried, Arella."

The idea that Trey was worried about me stirs a little flutter in my belly. Just another one of the many uncontrollable reactions my body has to him. Like the way my heart jumps through my shirt every time he says my name.

"Thanks for coming after me. I'm very grateful."

"Me too, Arella. You have no idea."

There he goes saying my name again, making my insides leap. No one ever calls me Arella, not even my grandparents. I've been going by Ari since kindergarten, when none of the other kids could remember how to say ah-rel-lah, so my teacher suggested that we shorten it. I liked it so much that now, barely anyone even knows that Arella is my real name. Most people think Ari is short for Ariana, and I don't care enough to correct them.

The toaster pops up with some perfectly browned bread.

"Butter?" Trey asks as he grabs a ceramic dish from the cabinet.

My stomach rumbles. "Yes, please. And thank you, Trey, for everything."

"No problem." He smiles sweetly, then gestures toward the row of barstools on the other side of the massive island. "Take a seat."

I claim the rightmost stool, leaving the other three empty. Trey's back faces me as he cracks a few eggs into a buttered pan. No complaints about the view. His rippling muscles are practically bursting out of his white T-shirt. His dark-chocolate hair is tousled in that just-out-of-bed sort of way. Last night, he had a dreamy, superstar aura about him. Now, in gray sweatpants, tossing eggs around in a pan, he looks . . . normal. Or as normal as men with model-like faces can look.

From the fridge, he grabs two cartons of juice and holds them up. "Apple or orange?"

"Apple, please."

He pours me a glass, then one for himself. I accept it and take a sip, shivering a little.

"You cold?" he asks.

"Kind of." Although I do get chilly easily, it feels like Trey's got his air conditioning extremely high. I suppose he can afford it. I mean, look at this place.

He shuts the stove off, moves the pan off the heat, then pads down the hall. Within seconds, the air conditioning stops humming.

"You didn't have to turn the air off just for me," I say when he comes back. In his arms is a throw blanket, which he drapes around my shoulders. My body betrays me again as my heart dances around from his nearness. I'm beginning to think it's impossible for a woman not to react like this around him.

"I wouldn't want you to turn into a popsicle," Trey says, and his tender smile makes me smile back.

"You're probably the only person in California who just turned off their air conditioning in the middle of summer."

He chuckles and nods. "Probably. I can turn it back on later."

Concentration is painted over his face as he arranges our food onto square white plates. He sets one in front of me, then one in front of the chair directly on my left. Then he sits there. Oddly, I'm okay with it. A year ago, I would have freaked out. He's so close that I can smell him. His scent reminds me of the bedsheets I woke up in this morning.

Wait a second . . . "Hey, if I slept in your bed last night, where did *you* sleep?"

"The couch."

Behind us sits a long couch in the massive living room. It faces the huge tinted windows looking out into a cul-de-sac. *Why are all his windows tinted?*

Maybe Trey's a drug dealer. He doesn't want people to be able to look in and see him making his deals. It would explain how he's got such a nice place. He can't afford all this on a musician's salary, can he?

Something about his living room feels off. All he's got are end tables with lamps on them. No messes of any kind. No clutter. No pictures on the walls. His place looks like a page out of a home décor magazine.

"How many bedrooms do you have?" I ask, then take my first bite of bacon. *Mmm.* It's perfect. Soft yet crunchy.

"Four. One master and one music room. Upstairs is my workout room, and the other room sits empty."

"This seems like a lot of space for one guy."

"It is. If I could, I'd probably just rent a one-bedroom apartment near a gym. I only bought this house because when we started the band, we needed a place to play, and I figured this was more economical than renting an apartment *and* rehearsal space. Then a year later, we got in at the Soul House, and now, I'm stuck with this."

I glance behind me into his living room again. It hits me why it looks odd. "Where's your TV?"

"Don't have one."

I consume the rest of my delicious bacon strip in one breath. Apparently, I have no self-control. *Is there such a thing as self-control when it comes to bacon?* "Are you not a TV person?"

"I didn't have a TV growing up." His face falls for a second before he flashes me a fake smile. "Anyway, your car is in my driveway. Our security manager drove it here for you last night."

"Really?" I hop off my seat to look out the window. Sure enough, there's my white Civic next to Trey's black Lexus—another item that seems outside of his musician salary. He can't be getting paid *that* much, can he? He has to be doing something else.

I return to my chair and readjust the blanket over my shoulders. "Thanks, Trey. Seriously."

"Like I said, no problem." He continues eating his eggs as if helping me with a flat tire, saving me from getting kidnapped, then making me breakfast—all within three days—is nothing.

"Is there anything I can do for you in return?"

"Nah." He waves a hand through the air. "It's all good."

I feel like I owe him, although I don't know what I can get for a guy who seems to have everything yet nothing at the same time. If I could, I'd get him some pictures of his family to hang on the walls. It would add some life to this place.

"Do you have any siblings?" I ask, then take a bite of my toast.

"Nope. You?"

"Me neither. I'd probably have siblings if my parents didn't pass away so young."

Trey stops eating to stare at me.

I know the question he wants to ask, so I answer it. "Car accident."

"Oh."

Whenever I tell people that my parents are gone, they usually say they're "sorry" out of politeness. Trey doesn't do that, but the sympathetic look on his face feels more genuine than any sorry I've ever received.

I have a bite of my scrambled eggs. "It's okay. I don't remember them. I grew up with my grandparents."

"Are they still around?"

"Yeah. I'll probably go visit them soon. How about you? Do you see your family a lot?"

Trey clears his throat and gazes aimlessly at his half-eaten plate. "Not really."

Judging from the desolate look in his eyes, he doesn't like talking about his family. Maybe they don't get along. That would explain why he doesn't have any pictures of them.

I should change the subject. "This breakfast is amazing. Are you normally a good cook?"

"Eh. I wouldn't classify myself as good. I'm decent. I only started cooking this year."

"What made you start?"

"Liz. She was sick of me ordering pizza whenever she came over."

I laugh, admiring his blunt honesty. "Does she come over a lot?"

He nods, scoff-chuckling under his breath. "Enough to drive me crazy."

"Do you not like when she comes over?"

"Eh. Depends on what I'm doing."

Playfully, I narrow my eyes. "In other words, if you're in the middle of something with another woman, you don't want her barging in."

Trey laughs, and the sound of it lights a spark in my chest. "Thankfully, that's never happened, and I hope it never does."

"Would Liz freak out and get all jealous?"

"Nah. She's not like that. *We* are not like that."

Ever since I saw Trey and Liz sing their duets last night, I've been a little jealous of her. The way they looked at each other, danced together, and held hands seemed to be on a level of comfort above friendship. I thought maybe there was something between them. *Maybe not?* Or maybe that's what Trey wants me to think.

"Are you like that with anyone?" I ask, and I'm not sure why. His relationship status shouldn't matter to me. Still, I'm curious.

"Nah, I'm not seein' anyone."

I let out a *pfft*. "I find that hard to believe."

"I could say the same about you, Arella. You really expect me to think that a woman as stunning as you is actually single and not looking? Come on."

"It's true. I *am* single, and I'm *not* looking." Suddenly, I'm no longer convinced by that last part. The way Trey just called me "stunning" has my lips curved into an immovable grin.

I picture the two of us together, holding hands, kissing, spending our nights cuddled up watching movies . . . The vivid images come to my head too easily.

"Why aren't you looking?" he asks.

Because I'm too busy still trying to get rid of the last boyfriend. "I'm happy being single." Not completely a lie. I'm very happy. Although I am comparing my current level of happiness to my level of sadness when I was with an abusive man.

"Everyone says that until the right person comes along," Trey says with a smirk. "Maybe yours came along on the side of a highway."

I knit my eyebrows together. "I've barely spoken two words to Kevin. I highly doubt he's right for me."

Dramatically, Trey slumps his shoulders. We both know I knew what he meant. "I wasn't talking about Kevin," he says.

"So, what? You were talking about yourself?" I try not to show how much that piques my interest, because again, I'm not looking . . . right?

"Is it out of the realm of possibilities for that to be true?"

"You barely know me."

"You're right. How 'bout we get to know each other over dinner?"

Dinner? With this guy? A man who looks like he just walked off the cover of a magazine?

"Uh, you're not really my type," I lie because I can't have dinner with him. Getting involved with me is a whole can of worms he doesn't want to open. Until my ex is officially out of my life, I can't start something new. Especially not after what happened with the last guy I had dinner with. I can't put anyone else in danger like that.

"Not your type?" Trey jerks his head back like he's offended. He probably is. I'm sure he's used to being everyone's type. Women probably throw themselves at him left and right. I witnessed it firsthand when those fangirls were practically begging me to help them get into his pants.

"Yeah." I avoid his eyes by playing with the bits of egg still on my plate. "I'm not really into guys like you."

"Guys like me?" He sets his fork down and twists on his stool to fully face me. His tone goes from sounding offended to slightly hurt. "And what exactly is the type of guy you think I am, that I'm not good enough for you?"

"Oh no! I didn't mean it like that. I just . . . Oh, never mind." I slash a hand through the air, trying to end this conversation before I dig myself into a deeper hole.

"No, no," he chuckles, not because anything is funny. He's chuckling to hide how much my rejection is damaging his ego. "Please, do explain. Don't leave me hangin'."

"Come on, Trey," I say, smiling as an attempt to keep things lighthearted. I don't mean to hurt him. This is for his own good. "You've got a long line of women who'd love to have your attention. Don't waste your time on me."

He leans over to look out the living room window. With a hand cupped to his forehead, he squints as if trying to see better. "Hmm . . . Where is this *long line* of women you speak of?"

I giggle at his overdramatic silliness. "I didn't mean literally. Just that there's plenty of women out there who'd want to date you."

"Who says I want to date any of them?"

"Don't you?"

"Only if *you're* in that line."

I can't see it, but I know my cheeks are turning red.

How can I tell Trey that this is for his sake without explaining the situation with my ex? Would anything I say stop him from having an interest in me? I don't even know why he's interested at all. We just met, and he knows nothing about me, yet I've caught him staring at me more times than not.

I can't think straight. There's no denying that I'm attracted to this man. Who wouldn't be? Stunning blue-gray eyes. A handsome smile. *And those arms* . . . The fangirls last night were right about his charming personality. It must be working, because I'm actually considering accepting this dinner thing.

"Arella . . ."

My name sounds so sweet coming from his lips. I want to keep hearing him say it.

"Could you give me a chance?"

I ponder it for a moment, even though I already know which way I'm leaning. "How about this? We can go out for dinner, but not as a date. Could we go as a couple of new friends grabbing a bite to eat?"

He flashes me the biggest grin. "I'll take what I can get."

9

TREY

P hase two: complete. Not without a mishap though. I don't feel bad for breaking that crooked-teethed goat-fucker's ankle last night. Sex predators don't deserve sympathy. Honestly, he's lucky I didn't break more. I wanted to, especially after Arella passed out.

For a moment there, I thought she died. I checked her pulse at least seventeen times before I was satisfied. I almost took her to the hospital, until I figured that Healing Water would work better than any medicines the Ordinary doctors would give her.

While she slept, I sponged Healing Water into her mouth. It didn't hit me until three sponges in that the Healing Water might not work on her since it derives from Zordi powers. Once the color returned to her face, I knew it was working. I don't know how it worked, but I'm glad it did.

Am I allowed to use Zordi products on Ordinaries? *Nope.*

Could I get into deep trouble if anyone ever finds out that I did? *Abso-fucking-lutely.*

Do I care? *Hell no.*

All I care about is making sure that Arella is okay.

I stare at the taillights of her car leaving my street as I call my uncle to give him the update he asked for.

"Find out anything yet, kid?" Victor says when he answers. No *hello*. No *hey, how ya doin'*? I don't know why I'm surprised.

"Nothing out of the norm so far," I say as I pace my living room with the phone pressed to my ear.

"What have you learned about her childhood?"

"Not much. I've barely been able to talk to her." *Fuck.* Why did I just say that?

As the CEO of ZIRDA California, Victor assigned me this mission. As my uncle, he threatened to beat me up if I fail. I don't mean in the philosophical sense, either. He will actually bloody me up. I should be more careful of what I say and only tell him things that will make him think I'm accomplishing something.

Victor's tone turns icy. "Isn't that the fucking point of your mission? To talk to her?"

"I was planning to last night, but some bastard at the bar drugged her and—"

"Well, make sure it doesn't happen again! If you don't have any progress to share, why the fuck are you calling?"

Um, because you asked for an update? I can't say that. Instead, I say, "I do have progress to share. She finally agreed to go out on a date with me." Technically, she agreed to dinner as *friends*, but Victor doesn't need to know that.

"Wait a fuckin' minute. You haven't even been on a date yet?"

Shit. "Like I told you, she's reserved and—"

"Don't call again until you have something good to say!" *Click.*

Really? Sometimes I wonder why I give a damn about getting Victor's approval. He's an asshole to me more days than not. Most of all, he's not my dad. I can't even say Victor's *like* a dad to me. Sure, he took me in after my parents died, but it's not like he actually took care of me. At a young age, I was forced to learn how to fend for myself.

Sadly, Victor wasn't always like this. He used to be that fun uncle who came over with new toys—just because. We used to play basketball in the driveway for hours. He'd take me out for ice cream after dinner, and we'd go for walks around the park. Many of my weekends were spent at his house, where we'd stay up all night eating spray cheese straight from the can.

Then one day, out of the blue, Aunt Jodi left him. I guess coming home to a half-empty house and a note about her finally finding her soul mate is awful. But I don't understand how Victor's personality took a complete one-eighty after that. All of a sudden, he was always angry and hated my guts.

It was normally Aunt Jodi who hated me, not Uncle Victor. She used to push me out of her way and call me a "piece of shit" under her breath. She'd take my favorite toys and shove them down the garbage disposal in front of me. Once, she kicked me down a full flight of stairs and claimed it was an accident. Since she never acted that way in front of my parents or Victor, no one believed me when I told them.

After she ran off with another man, it was like Victor felt the need to replace her—as if there always had to be someone who bullied me. I used to overhear my parents talk about Victor's overnight attitude change. They were just as confused as I was.

I would give anything to not only have my parents back but also have my loving uncle back. That's partly why I want to succeed in this mission so much. This is the first time he's ever trusted me with anything important. If I can do something he'll be proud of, perhaps our relationship can be better. No, I don't expect us to have sleepovers with spray cheese again, but it'd be nice to finally have a conversation with him without all the animosity.

I spend the rest of my morning planning out my "dinner as friends" with Arella.

After lunch, I head to the Soul House for band rehearsal. By the time I'm done with that, performing our two-hour show, and doing our lengthy meet and greet, I'm exhausted.

Back in my dark garage, I park my Harley next to my car, then kill the engine. Still on the bike, I drag out my phone to do the one thing I've been thinking about doing all day: text Arella.

Before she left this morning, she entered her number into my contacts. I wanted to text her earlier but didn't because I didn't want to seem desperate.

The screen glows in my face as I search for her contact and send her a text.

> Hey gorgeous! Thanks for putting your name into my phone as Arella. It made it easy for me to find you. 😊

Now comes the waiting game.

I stare at the screen for a full minute to see if the little dots will start jumping around. Nothing happens. She's probably not by her phone. Or worse, she read my text and ignored it. Or maybe she's already sleeping? *Dammit, I'm being pathetic.* I've never sat around waiting for a text from a girl before.

The moment I hop off my bike, I freeze. Someone's emotions hover toward me—coming from *inside* my house. *What the fuck?*

I tiptoe through the door, being as quiet as possible. No lights are on. I don't hear anything either.

Whoever's here probably didn't hear my garage door open, because the emotions I'm sensing from them are content, not scared, and, oddly, a little horny.

I tread down the hall to where my gift leads me. It's not until I'm near the bedroom that my chest tingles, and suddenly, I know exactly who's here.

I stomp through the door. "Get out."

Jess doesn't even bother looking up at me. "Is that any way to greet a person?"

She's lying on my bed with her ankles crossed over each other. The lamp's on, and she has one of my naughty magazines flipped open over her thighs. Her low-cut pink tank top gives me a full view down her shirt, leaving nothing to the imagination. Based on the wrappers on the floor, I'm gonna say she's been in my pantry.

"How did you get in my house?"

Keeping her attention on the photo of the topless woman, she gestures toward a key on my nightstand. "I know where you leave it outside."

"Good. That means you know where to put it back." I lift my finger, and the key flies into the air. When I drop my finger, the key falls into Jess's lap. I wave at the door, and it swings wide open, coming to a halt just before it hits the wall.

Finally, Jess looks my way and tosses the magazine and key over her shoulder. They land on the carpet with light thuds. "You haven't seen me in months, and you're kicking me out already?"

Jess is never an easy person to get rid of. Maybe if I'm nice to her, she'll leave faster. I soften my tone. "What's up, Jess?"

She pouts. "My boyfriend dumped me."

"The Teleporter?"

"Yeah."

Jess and I used to have an on-and-off relationship. I haven't seen her since she started getting serious with her boyfriend—ex-boyfriend now.

"I went to see him today." Her sadness drenches me like heavy rain from a gray cloud right above my head. "I thought maybe we could work things out. He doesn't want anything to do with me anymore."

I sigh, plopping next to her on the edge of my bed. I have no idea what to say to make her feel better. Thinking of a happy time and pushing those feelings into her might work.

She continues talking before I can think of anything happy. "I thought maybe if I showed him that I want him back, he'd want me too. But all he said was—" Jess's skin bubbles as her shoulder-length blonde hair transforms into curly black dreads. Her skin fades from a California tan to a deep bronze until there's a brawny Black man wearing a pink tank top next to me.

Jess drops her voice into a deep, husky tone. "You're too fucked-up for me. Go get your shit together."

Her skin bubbles again and her hair grows, turning blonde until the real version of Jess is back.

"Sorry," I say because I suck at pep talks. Also, her ex is right. She does need to get her shit together, and that's coming from me, a man who never has his shit together.

She stares at me with a dark expression in her eyes. I know that look. Before she can say anything, I'm back on my feet with my hands in my pockets. "Not tonight, Jess."

"What? Why not?"

Because I have important shit to do. Besides, even if I wasn't in the middle of something, I still wouldn't want to have sex with her. This woman only ever shows up when she needs a rebound fuck. Yes, I've always allowed her to use me, but I've been getting sick of our relationship existing on only *her* terms. She's never here when *I* need her.

Five months ago, when I was going through a rough patch, she wouldn't even answer my texts. Now that I think about it, I'm still fuckin' pissed.

I hook my thumb toward the door. "So, you gonna leave, or what?"

"Seriously?" She gives me a look like I've just smeared mud all over her shirt. "Can't you *feel* my pain? I thought *you*, of all people, would understand."

Of course I can feel her pain, and it's exactly why I don't want her here.

"I want to get fucked like an animal, Trey. And you're the only man who's ever rough enough with me to do it right."

"Jess, you can't just break into my house and demand that I fuck you. Especially when you haven't spoken to me in over five months. Plus, you went through my shit." I point a stern finger at the empty chips bags on the floor.

"I'm sorry, okay? I couldn't talk to you back then because of my boyfriend. He didn't like me talking to any of my exes. As for tonight, I didn't want to be alone. It's not my fault you weren't home when I arrived. I didn't think you'd care as long as I made it up to you . . ."

With her best *screw me now* face, she hooks her fingers through my belt loops and yanks me in. As soon as she flips her emotions to make me feel what she wants me to feel, I'm a goner. Within seconds, my energy feeds off hers, and it's not long before she's won the fight. Her erotic emotions take over my mind, and the next thing I know, she's beneath me—topless.

As I kiss her neck, I wonder if I would still want this if I weren't feeling what she's feeling. It's hard to know. While I rip my shirt over my head, I decide it doesn't matter. As long as she wants this, that's all that matters.

It doesn't take me long to finish. It's been at least a month. I lie on my back, panting as I pull the rubber off and toss it into the air. When I point a finger at it, it flies across my bedroom, landing into a little trash bin in the corner.

Jess scoots toward me and props her head on my shoulder. Then she rests a hand over my chest as she lets out a little exhale. My body stiffens. She knows how much I hate cuddling, yet she does it to me anyway. I know how much she hates when I shove her away, so I make sure to do it extra rough this time.

On my way to the bathroom, in the corner of my eye, I see her roll her eyes like she's disappointed. Call me an ass, but it's not like I've never warned her. As if it'll make things better, I offer her a little shrug. "You know I don't like cud—"

"Yeah, yeah," she says. "I know."

After we're both cleaned off and dressed, Jess asks for a loan. Without hesitation, I grab my wallet and offer her two thousand dollars, knowing I'll never get it back. We've gotten to the point in our relationship that when she asks to "borrow" money, we both know it's a gift. I've never asked for the money back, and she's never offered. I wouldn't accept it anyway.

Jess struggles a lot financially. Her father walked away before she was born, and her mother died of a z-drug overdose before her second birthday. The way she grew up consisted of hopping around from foster home to foster home where nobody wanted her and even fewer people cared.

I'd probably be in the same financial situation if my parents weren't the researchers who discovered how to turn Healers' tears into usable products that keep their healing abilities. Royalties for Healing Water, Healing Goo, and Healing Spray are like a never-ending gold mine. Lucky for me, I'm the main person reaping the benefits.

Jess waves to me from the Uber as it drives away. I'm not even back in my house before I've got my phone out.

Yes! I've got a text from the woman I've been waiting to hear from.

> I figured if I added myself into your phone as Ari, you'd get confused.

I smile. A *real* smile. Not one of those fake ones I use out in public.

> I am a man. We are easily confused creatures.

My phone buzzes within seconds. I'd like to think she was on the other end, waiting for me to text back.

> I'm very familiar with your kind. 😌

> You excited for dinner tomorrow?

> Yes. Dinner. With a new FRIEND.

> OK, friend. Let's carpool. I'll come pick you up. 😊

> I can meet you at the restaurant. Thanks tho.

> You don't even know where we're going.

> I would if you told me.

> It's a surprise! What's your address?

I've been to her apartment before—plenty of times. I'm always parked on the street, hunched in my car, studying her routine. I've never been *inside* her apartment though, and that's where I need to get. Seeing her living space might help me know her better. There's only so much a background check and Google searches can tell me, which is nothing of value. Her background check was pretty blank, and all I got from Google were pictures of people who weren't her. She doesn't have any social media for me to scroll through, either. It's like she's purposely making this harder for me.

My phone buzzes.

> Okay, we can carpool.

Her next text includes her address.
Then my phone vibrates again.

> You know, one of these days, you'll learn that you can't always get your way. 😊

I snort. Funny that she thinks I always get my way. I figured out as a child that life will hand me rotten lemons and there's nothing I can do about it.

Some might say that living with Victor wasn't *that* bad. A kid can survive demeaning comments and some violent outbursts here and there. A few smacks to the face usually shut me up. Nothing I couldn't handle. To make myself feel better, I always compared every hurtful thing Victor said or did to seeing my parents get blown up. After that, taking a few hits was nothing.

10

ARELLA

At exactly six o'clock, someone lightly thumps their knuckles against my apartment door. I jump in front of the mirror to inspect myself one last time. The extra minutes I spent on my makeup paid off. I look like I'm glowing. My lacy plum-colored dress falls just above my knees, and my hair features more defined waves, thanks to my curling wand.

I know, I know, tonight's not a date. That doesn't mean I can't look cute though. I was never allowed to wear anything like this around my ex. He would yell at me for dressing like a "slut." To him, showing legs is "asking for it." Now that I'm done living by his rules, I'm going to wear whatever I please.

The second I open the door, Trey whistles through his teeth. "Damn. If I knew I was gonna have competition, I would have tried harder."

I almost laugh. There is no competition, and if there was, he'd win. Trey looks more gorgeous than the last time I saw him. I'm not even sure how that's possible. Hair fluffed up, perfectly trimmed stubble, and an irresistible smile to top it all off.

He's in his usual black V-neck that hugs his broad shoulders and a pair of jeans that hangs a little low on his narrow hips. If he raised his arms up, I'd probably get a glimpse of those defined abs Google images showed me earlier.

"Ready?" he asks with the sunlight hitting him in just the right way for me to see how smooth his skin is. I'm jealous. I want skin like that. I'll bet he's never had a blemish.

I nod eagerly, yet not as eagerly as I feel. "Ready."

As he leads me to his car, my eyes scan the parking lot. I think we're in the clear. If my ex was here, we would have known by now. He would have picked a fight with Trey the moment Trey knocked on my door.

How embarrassing would that have been? Now that I think about it, maybe this dinner thing isn't a good idea. What if, when Trey drops me off later—

"I've been looking forward to this all day," Trey says, cutting into my thoughts.

I fake a smile, pretending that I wasn't thinking up ways to end the evening right now. "Me too. Where are we going?"

"It's a surprise, remember?" Trey opens the passenger door for me—like a gentleman. "Hop in."

I don't move, even though I appreciate his kind gesture. "This isn't a date, remember?"

He rolls his eyes and chuckles. "Just get in."

Once we're on the road, Trey turns the radio down. "How was your nannying job today?"

"Wonderful." I tell him about the four kids I spend every weekend with and how we finger-painted dinosaurs on canvases. "How about you? What did you do today?"

"Sunday is the band's day off. I literally just sat around until it was time to pick you up." His tone is gloomy, like he wishes he had other things he could have been doing. I imagine him in his big living room, all by himself, aimlessly staring at a clock. Surely, he was more productive than that.

Trey flicks his blinker on and speeds to pass a slow car. "So, you told Liz that you've lived everywhere in Cali. Where'd you live before you moved to LA?"

I can't believe he remembers that. I didn't think he was paying attention to anything that was said in the car the day we met. He seemed so out of it. "I moved here from Brawley. It's a small town about three hours south of here."

"Where'd you grow up?"

"My grandparents and I have moved around every year since I was little, so I kind of grew up everywhere."

Trey merges between two trucks, then into the left lane. "I see. What are your grandparents' names?"

"Phil and Roxy."

"Last name?"

I'm not sure why their last name matters. I tell him anyway. "Ward. How about you? Where did you grow up?"

"Three Rivers. It's near Fresno."

"Did you go to college there?"

He keeps his gaze aimed out the windshield. "Nah. I never went to college. You?"

"I studied early childhood education at UCLA. Originally, I wanted to be a kindergarten teacher. Then I realized my passion is baking. I want to have my own bakery someday. I already have a name picked out."

"Which is?"

"A Slice A Day." Just saying it out loud gets me excited, even though the reality of that dream is so far away.

"What do you like to bake?"

I can't believe he's actually asking questions about me right now. More so, I can't believe he's not trying to tell me stuff about himself that he thinks will impress me. I thought that was a first-date standard for men. "I do it all. Mostly cakes and cupcakes, because I love to decorate."

"I'd love to see some of your work."

I perk up. "I've got a blog you could check out."

"That's cool. Could you send me the link? I can take a look later."

"Sure." I'll text him my link, but I have no confidence that he'll ever enter my website. Trey doesn't strike me as a man with an interest in cake decorating.

"When did you start baking?"

I spiral into my story of getting my first Easy-Bake Oven and always helping Grammy in the kitchen. Trey listens with nods, asking the occasional follow-up question. I can't remember the last time I spoke this long without a man interrupting me. Usually, I don't even talk this much. With Trey, I can't stop. Although I could go on and on about baking.

"Enough about me," I say a while later. "Tell me about your hobbies."

"I don't have any."

I eye him. "You play music."

"Yeah, but it's also my career, so does it still count as a hobby?"

"What about your nonprofit organization? Is that a hobby for you?"

Trey turns his head to stare at me. "How do you know I have one?"

"Oh, I—um, I might have . . . Googled you."

Chuckling, he shakes his head at me. "Don't believe half the shit you read."

"You don't have a nonprofit?"

"I do, but the rest is trash."

I twist at the hip to face him. "Like what?"

"Tell me what you read, and I'll tell you if it's true."

"You can play over twenty-five instruments?" I've already seen him play three. Twenty-five blows my mind. I can't even play one.

He pauses with a thinking face on. "True, probably. I haven't really counted."

"You produce all of your band's work?"

"Half true. I do most of it, but it's not all me."

"I read something about how you broke someone's car window while filming one of your music videos."

"Hey." He lifts his pointer finger, laughing. "It was an accident, and they weren't supposed to be parked there."

I tap my chin. "Seems like my research has been accurate so far. What about the Liz rumors?"

Trey groans as his hands slide down the steering wheel. "Which ones?"

"The ones about how you two date on and off, and you're always leaving her for other women."

He laughs, and it eases the pang of jealousy in my belly. "Liz told me about that one. Those people twisted my interview into something it wasn't. They asked me about my relationship with her, since our fans are always pinning us together. I told them that Liz means a great deal to me but I'd never make her my girlfriend. They reworded it, saying that I was sleeping with her but refused to commit." He sighs deeply. "Media these days."

Why does it thrill me so much to hear that he doesn't have a thing with Liz? I mean, he's already said it before, but hearing it again feels more validating. *This is not a date*, I remind myself. *This is not a date.*

"Anything else you read about me?" he asks.

I read that his parents were killed in a house fire. It made me feel bad for asking if he saw his family often. I can't believe he didn't mention that his parents were gone when I told him about mine. Anyone else would have. Not many people lose both parents to tragic accidents as young kids. Why didn't he want to tell me that we have that in common? Maybe it's still hard for him to talk about it. Either way, I'll try not to mention that I already know, since he obviously didn't want to tell me, but maybe he needs a little push.

"I read a little about your foundation and how it supports school-aged kids with deceased parents. Tell me more about that."

Trey goes back to gripping the steering wheel at the top. "Not much to tell. We just offer free mentors, tutors, and funding for therapy and after-school activities. Whatever keeps the kids busy."

"That's wonderful of you." I gave him the perfect opening to tell me about his parents, and he didn't take it.

"Eh. Don't give me too much credit. It wasn't my idea. It was my friend Sharon's. I agreed to finance it with the expectation that I wouldn't have to get too involved. The extent of my duties is transferring a chunk of my bank account over each month and signing a few papers here and there."

"Oh, I'm sure you do more than that."

"I really don't. I used to mentor one of the kids. I stopped once . . ." His face falls.

"Once what?"

He rakes a hand through his dark locks, keeping his eyes glued to the road. "Uh, about five months ago, my mentee kid—he, um, he . . . passed away."

The car goes silent as Trey swallows his pain, and it makes my heart ache for him. "That must have been really hard."

"Yeah, well, I never wanted to be a mentor. I got guilt-tripped into it. Once Elliott was gone, I decided getting close to the kids wasn't for me, so I quit." He clears his throat. "Anyway, do you like pasta?"

I take the hint. "I *love* pasta."

"Good. We're going to my favorite pasta place in Long Beach."

"Long Beach?" I didn't realize how long we'd been driving for and in what direction. I assumed Trey was taking me somewhere in LA.

He must see the discomfort on my face. "Is that okay?"

"Isn't it too late to change plans now?"

"I can turn around and we can go somewhere else, if that's what you want."

Do I want that? If we're going to Long Beach, the likelihood of us running into my ex is low. One would think that with living in a big city like Los Angeles, he'd be harder to run into, right?

Wrong.

Living on the other side of the city doesn't stop him from showing up behind me at the grocery store. Or getting gas at the same time and station I'm at. Or "coincidentally" going to the dentist at the same time too. Yes, I can't even get my teeth cleaned without him following me there.

"Actually, Trey, I think Long Beach sounds wonderful!"

11

TREY

The restaurant host leads us toward an outdoor corner table under some twinkling string lights. The other tables are occupied by people sipping from wineglasses. From a small stage at the front of the patio area, a violinist in a flowy dress plays an enchanting upbeat melody. Couples dance together in the grass, their energies full of warmth and lust.

"Your waitress will be here shortly," the host says as she sets two menus onto our table, then leaves.

Almost everyone here is horny. I sense it from most of the men and plenty of the women. I need to be careful about not letting their emotions control me. If Victor was here, he'd tell me to embrace it. He seems to think that having sex with Arella as soon as possible will get her to trust me faster, which will get her to tell me her secrets. I don't know Arella very well yet, but I know her well enough to know that Victor's method is more likely to scare her away.

"Wow," Arella says with her jaw slack. I pull out her chair, and she accepts it without making another comment about how tonight *isn't* a date. "This place looks way too romantic for a *friendly* dinner."

And there it is. After draping my leather jacket over the back of my chair, I sit on the other side of our cozy table. Whether she considers this a date or not, I've already told Victor it is.

"You've been here before?" she asks.

"Yep. This was one of the first places our band played at. We did acoustic covers of lovey-dovey songs all night."

"Hi." Our waitress sets two glasses of water onto our table. Her exasperated energy shoots at me while her cheerful tone comes out through a smile. "Would you like to try our house wine?"

I turn to the exquisite woman sitting across from me. Before I can ask her if she prefers red or white, she smiles and says, "Water's fine. Thank you."

I guess getting her tipsy to talk is out of the equation. "Me too, thanks."

"Awesome. I'll give you a moment."

Once the waitress leaves, I take the silverware out of my cloth napkin and drape the napkin over my thighs. Liz taught me to do this the first time I ever ate at a fancy place. I hope it makes Arella think that I'm a proper guy and that I know shit.

I pick up my menu and pretend to read it. "Are you sure you don't want any wine? I'm treating."

Arella responds sweetly yet firmly. "I'm sure. And no, you're not treating. I don't want this to be a date, remember?"

Of course I remember. She's reminded me so many times now, I'm beginning to think she's trying to convince herself, not me. "Friends are allowed to treat each other."

Ignoring me, Arella flips over her menu to read the other side. I already know what I'm getting, so while she chooses what she wants, I keep my menu in my hands and concentrate on trying to sense her. With all my might, I narrow my eyes on her and fire every ounce of my mind power her way. My energy tightens in on her body, straining to latch onto something, *anything.* The only thing I get is the sexual tension of the man behind her.

After a full minute, all I've accomplished is a headache.

"Do I have something on my face?" Arella asks when she sets her menu down.

"No. You're just beautiful and easy to stare at."

"So . . . you admit you were staring?"

I chuckle, nodding. "You'd do the same if you were in my shoes."

We make small talk for a bit before our waitress comes back. Whatever upset her before is passing, because her mood is calmer now. Arella and I place our orders, then the waitress takes our menus away.

Leaning forward, I rest my arms on the table. "So, tell me more about your grandparents."

Arella unfolds her cloth napkin, then sets it onto her lap the way I did. "What would you like to know?"

"You mentioned that you guys moved around every year. Where do they live now?"

"They're still in Brawley. After I graduated high school and came to LA, they decided to stay."

"Are they retired?"

She takes a sip of her water. "Yeah. Gramps was a mechanic. Grammy stayed home with me."

How odd. What kind of mechanic gets a new job in a different town every year? It's not a career that requires traveling. That makes me think he was running from something. Question is: What and why? Then, once Arella moves out, all of a sudden, he's done running? Something's not adding up.

"If they liked moving around so much," I say, "why aren't they anymore?"

Arella shrugs like there isn't anything more to this. "It's not the moving they loved. It's the living in different places. The adventures. The new experiences. Since I was in school, they didn't get to explore the world like they wanted to. Moving around the state was a good second option until I graduated. Now that I'm not around, they travel all the time. They're currently in Alaska until tomorrow. In two weeks, they're off to Brazil."

I guess that's a possible explanation. Still, I think there's more to it. Either that or I want there to be more, so I'm looking for it.

Arella continues, "They get antsy when they stay in the same place for too long."

I can relate to that. The minute I graduated, my uncle told me to get out and "find my place in the world." I packed up the little I had, bought a car, and went wherever life took me. I'd stay in one city for as long as it suited me, then I'd pack up and do it again.

The longest I've lived anywhere since I left home is LA, and that's only because of my band. I'd like to think I've found my place here, but if that's the case, why do I always feel like I don't belong?

The violinist finishes her piece, and the crowd erupts with applause. In the grass, a few couples swaying together mosey back to their seats. After some thank-yous, the violinist turns a page in her book, then returns the instrument to her shoulder.

"What about you?" Arella asks as another tune fills the air. "Do you like to travel?"

I'm not a fan of how she keeps spinning our conversations back to me. Talking about myself depresses me. Plus, that's not the point of this dinner. "I do. I've been to lots of different places. How 'bout you?"

"I haven't gone anywhere outside of California."

That's odd. How has a girl whose family loves to travel not been anywhere except this one state?

"What's been your favorite place to visit so far?" Arella asks.

"Besides here, I lived in Spain and France the longest, so maybe those two."

"Did you pick up the languages there?"

"Only conversationally."

Her face lights up. "Have you ever been to Paris?"

"Of course."

"Ah!" She throws her head back, swooning. "I've always wanted to go there. I've heard they have the best bakeries."

Although I can't sense it, I can *see* her strong desire for Paris. *Seeing* her feelings but not *feeling* them is like I'm watching TV, where people are expressing emotions I can't sense.

"Trey?"

My head jerks up. "Huh?"

"You got quiet all of a sudden."

"Sorry. I was thinking."

"About?"

I clear my throat, trying to think of a lie. Nothing comes to me, so I go with the truth. "You. Just wondering what you're feeling."

As impassive as ever, she says, "I feel fine."

Well, I've accomplished nothing. All I've got is more questions. How do I ask her if her grandpa was running from something, without sounding like a psycho?

"House salad with the dressing on the side," our waitress says, placing it in front of Arella. "Caesar for the gentleman."

While we indulge in our salads, I ask Arella about what her favorite movies and books are, because it'll help make my questions about her family and childhood less suspicious. Victor wants me to rule out that her immunity is caused by something that happened to her as a kid. Besides the annual move and being raised by her grandparents, she seems to have had a normal upbringing.

One of Victor's many theories to explain Arella's immunity is that she was experimented on in a lab as a baby. By the way she talks about how much her grandparents love her, I doubt they would have allowed that to happen.

Another one of Victor's theories is that Arella possesses some kind of gene defect. To me, she looks, sounds, and acts like any other twenty-two-year-old Ordi woman.

The most ridiculous theory Victor had is that Arella came from another planet. It's only the first date, but I'm pretty sure I can rule that one out. Arella seems as human as anyone else.

"Wow," she says, wiping her lips off on her napkin. Two empty pasta plates sit between us. So far, I've learned a lot about her, yet nothing at all. "That was the best Alfredo I've ever had."

"I'm happy you think so." I clean off my hands and nod toward the grass. "Now that we're done eating, do you wanna dance?"

Dancing is the main reason I chose this place. While we slow-dance, I'll have permission to touch her for an extended period of time. This will be a great opportunity for me to continue my physical research because, sadly, the verbal kind is getting me nowhere.

Unfortunately, Arella shakes her head. "I can't dance."

"It's easy." I stand and hold my palm out to her. "I'll teach you."

"Um, you go. I'll watch."

I make a crumpled face at her. "I'll look like an idiot slow-dancing by myself. Is that what you want?"

Grinning, she nods eagerly.

She thinks I won't do it. Clearly, she doesn't know anything about me.

Challenge accepted. "All right. I'll dance solo."

Arella's eyes go wide as I saunter away. She whisper-yells, "Trey! I was kidding!"

I wasn't. I stop at the top of the patio steps and say over the heads of couples eating, "You gonna come dance with me?"

Her head shakes again.

Without another word, I hop down the steps and join the sea of couples swaying to the melodic notes. With gusto, I put my hand on the waist of an invisible woman and pull her close. My other hand holds her invisible palm up, then I twirl her around the grass.

The more dramatic my turns are, the more Arella loses it. She laughs so hard, she's slapping her knee. I don't care that other people are staring at me like I'm stupid and ridiculous. I know I am, and that's the point.

"Okay, Trey," Arella says through giggles over the railing. "You can stop now."

"Nah. Miss Invisible and I are enjoying ourselves." I continue for another minute before the song ends. To finish my performance strong, I spin my lovely dance partner twice, then dip her for a solid beat. Only once the crowd claps for the violinist do I make my way back to the table.

"Oh. My. God." Arella's still giggling. "I can't believe you did that. Aren't you embarrassed?"

I plop back into my chair, unashamed. "It made you laugh. The embarrassment is worth it."

Arella's cheeks fade into the most adorable shade of pink as she giggles some more. Whatever I'm doing, it's working. She's becoming more comfortable with me. Soon, she'll be comfortable enough to tell me the information I need.

12

ARELLA

"The Big Ka-booms?" My stomach aches from all the laughing.

Ever since Trey stopped frolicking around the grass like he's a cartoon character, he's been telling me funny stories about the early days of his band.

"Yep, that was our first unofficial band name. Kevin and Marcus came up with it. They were arguing over whose dick was bigger. Marcus said, and I quote, 'Bro, I'm Black. When I take mine out, it falls and goes ka-boom.' "

I could sit here all night listening to this man tell me stories. "How did you end up becoming Flames in the Night?"

"The brains of the band, of course. Liz and Emmy were our final additions. They wanted a name that represented our band's diversity. Kevin is half Chinese, and Liz is half Hispanic. Marcus is Black, and Emmy's family is from the UK. Liz said that our diversity makes us stand out. What stands out better than fire in darkness?"

"You boys are so lucky you have Liz and Emmy around."

"No kidding. Without them, we're a—" Trey's head snaps to the right. A frown replaces his smile as he glares off into the trees.

I glance that way but don't see anything to be frowning about. "Everything okay?"

His head whips back to me. "Uh, yeah." Forcing a half smile, he says, "What were you saying?"

"I wasn't. You were."

"Oh, right. I was saying that without the girls, we're a mess." His head snaps to the right again. This time, his face twists like there's something sour in the air. Under his breath, he grumbles something. It's so quiet, the only words I catch are "ignore it."

Ignore what?

For a moment, we sit in silence. Trey glares at his water glass with a crumpled look on his face like he's contemplating life—hard. He must come to some sort of decision, because with a creak of the wicker, he's out of his chair with his wallet out.

After tossing three hundred-dollar bills onto the table, he says, "Stay here. I'll be right back."

And just like that, he's gone. He doesn't even grab his jacket before sprinting away as if the restaurant is on fire.

Where is he going? Curiosity takes me over as I grab my purse and his jacket and run after him. It probably looks like we're pulling a dine-and-dash, but I'm confident those three bills will cover double what we ordered and a hefty tip.

When I catch up to Trey on the sidewalk, he's glowering at the groups of people strolling the busy street.

"Are you okay?"

He jumps and flips around. "I thought I said to stay at the table."

"Yeah, but—"

He doesn't let me finish. Roughly, he snatches his jacket from me and shoves his arms into it. "Stay here. Please. I'll be right back."

Without waiting for me to respond, he runs off again, zigzagging around pedestrians with the speed of a wild animal chasing its prey. I run behind him, a little less aggressively, spitting out apologies to the people with crooked faces left behind in his path.

I almost lose him when he turns a corner down a backstreet. At the end of the alley is shouting and laughing. Three teenage boys stand over a smaller teenage boy on the ground, kicking him. Before I can process anything else, a loud voice yells, "Stop!"

The three teenagers jerk their heads up. The bulkiest one steps forward with his hands up in surrender. "Chill. We're just playin' a game."

Trey gestures toward the boy on the ground. "It doesn't look like *he's* having fun."

"No worries, dude," the tallest teenager says. "We're all friends."

Trey turns to the boy, who's still covering his face with his arms. "You okay, buddy?"

The boy sits up, making a movement with his hands, and mouths something.

"He's fine," the bulky teenager says. "It's just a game."

Trey scowls, then moves his hands around too. The kid on the ground widens his eyes as he picks himself up. He rubs his ribs a little, then moves his hands again. It takes me a moment to realize that he's using sign language.

When Trey communicates back the same way, the three bullies drop their jaws. I do too. I had no idea Trey knew sign language.

After he signs back and forth with the boy for a moment, he turns to the bullies with a grimace. "Get outta here."

"Look, dude, you don't understa—"

"Go!"

It doesn't take more than a second for the teenagers to realize that they don't have a choice. Their shoes stomp against the pavement as they dash off. Trey's gaze follows them until his eyes land on me. His expression turns stony. I wish I would have stayed at the restaurant, if only to have avoided that look.

The Deaf boy plucks the lid off a garbage can and chucks it. It clanks to the ground with an echo. After some digging, he wrestles out a backpack from the trash, pats it off, then throws a strap over his shoulder.

Turning to Trey, he signs something. I don't know anything more than the ASL alphabet and baby signs from working at the daycare. All I catch is the boy saying thank you. The rest is lost on me.

As I approach Trey's side, he gestures at me and signs my name in letters. He does it so fast, I barely catch that it was my name.

"Arella, this is . . ." Trey pauses and signs as he says, "Sorry, what's your name?"

The boy moves his fingers so fast, I can't understand.

"Lucas," Trey says.

I wave. "Hi, Lucas."

The boy waves back and signs to me.

"Nice to meet you," Trey interprets. "You have a beautiful name."

"Thank you," I say and sign.

Trey turns to the boy as he signs, "Don't allow those boys to haze you anymore. It's not worth it, okay? Do you need a ride home?"

With a shake of his head and another thank-you, Lucas limps out of the alley.

Once he's gone, Trey shoves his hands into his pockets. "You ready to go, babe?"

My insides dance at the sound of him calling me *babe*. I used to cringe whenever my ex called me that. He only used pet names when he wanted something. Or when we were around other men. Or when he was apologizing for the night before. Hearing Trey call me *babe* doesn't elicit that fight-or-flight reaction from my core. I actually like the sound of it.

As we speed back to LA, Trey talks my ear off about everything except what just happened. This entire evening, he's been asking me buttloads of questions about me and barely talked about himself unless I asked a question first. Now that he's suddenly openly sharing, it makes me think he's filling the silence just to ensure I don't have a chance to ask him about Lucas.

I'm barely paying attention to his words. My mind is reeling about how he knew a teenage boy was getting beat up in an alley—from the restaurant.

"How do you know sign language?" I ask, interjecting into whatever story he's telling me about a time he used to live in Georgia. Or maybe it was Oregon.

Trey clears his throat. "Uh, Elliott, the kid I used to mentor . . . He was Deaf. I took private lessons so I could communicate with him."

"How did you know Lucas was in trouble?"

His fingers curl tighter around the steering wheel as he swallows. "I thought I asked you to stay at the restaurant."

"Sorry, I didn't listen."

He scoffs loudly. "I see that. I asked you to stay because I didn't want you to get hurt."

"I didn't."

"That's not the point." He breathes out, all exasperated. "Can we just forget that ever happened?"

Moments like these with my ex always turned into fights, until eventually, my choices were to keep quiet or get smacked. I really don't want to fight with Trey. I don't think he'd hit me, but I miss the lighthearted conversations we've been having all night.

Playfully, I lower my voice to a whisper. "You can just admit that you're Superman. I can keep a secret."

My tactic works, because Trey perks up, laughing. "I'm not Superman."

"So, you're Spider-Man, then? You've got Spidey senses that tell you when someone's in trouble?"

He chuckles lightly. "Not even close."

For the rest of the car ride, I don't mention Lucas again, even though I want to, because knowing things like that isn't normal.

As Trey pulls into the parking lot of my apartment, I subtly glance around for *his* car. When I don't see it, I let out a breath of relief. Day forty and counting. *Maybe he's done stalking me . . .*

"Did you have a good time?" Trey asks after he parks his vehicle.

I offer him a genuine smile. "I did."

That was the best dinner I've had in a long time. Plus, I haven't laughed that much since, well . . . before my ex. I hate that I allowed him to take away my happiness for so long.

"Thanks again, Trey. Tonight was fun." It was so fun that a part of me doesn't want to leave. I'm enjoying his presence, and the way he looks at me like I'm the only person in the room who matters. Unfortunately, this was a one-time thing, and as much as I don't want to go, I have to.

I'm about to grip the door handle when a firm palm on my shoulder pulls me back.

"Hold on a sec. I didn't get a chance to ask you out again."

All the air leaves my lungs as I screw my eyes shut. The world around me stills. The hand gripping my shoulder is the one that used to bruise my face. It's the one that used to control me in ways that still haunt me.

He yells at me. "You can't wear dresses like this, you whore!"

I try to get away, but his fingers claw into me like talons wrapped around a mouse.

"Don't you dare walk away when I'm talking to you! We're not done!"

"Arella?" Trey's gentle voice pulls me back. His hand is gone. It's in his lap now, away from me, not hurting me. "You okay?"

Nodding, I force a smile.

Judging by the way Trey crinkles his forehead together, he's not buying it. "You sure?"

"I'm fine." My voice shrinks so much, even I don't believe it.

Slowly, he leans into me, and I catch a whiff of his scent. He's wearing a sweet cologne that smells nothing like Nathan. Usually, my ex smells of gin and cigarettes.

In almost a whisper, Trey asks, "Do you wanna talk about it?"

I glue my lips together and shake my head. I can't talk about it. Not with him. I'll start crying. Talking about it is like reliving it, and I've already lived it for enough years to never want to do it again.

I feel him staring at me. He's probably debating whether or not to push this subject further. Like how he didn't want to explain Lucas, I don't want to explain this.

Finally, Trey leans back and smiles warmly. "I'd love to see you again."

My voice comes out soft. "I don't know if that's a good idea."

His face drops. I wait for him to lash out at me and yell at me for not giving him his way. I wait for him to call me a bitch because I'm being "disobedient."

Instead, he tenderly asks, "Can you explain why?"

Because I'm starting to like you. I can't admit that.

Because my ex-boyfriend is a psycho and will scare you off like he did the last guy—with a knife. Telling Trey that will prompt more questions.

Because Nathan is still under the impression that he can control my life. That will make me sound pathetic. I hate acknowledging that my three-year mistake still has power over me. Not as much as he used to—just enough to keep me fearful.

I've been doing everything I can to cut ties with him. Telling him off has only made things worse. Never leaving my apartment isn't feasible, and never coming home is the same. I've tried looking for a new place to live. Unfortunately, all the other apartments I've toured are smaller for twice the rent. He'd find me anyway. Filing a restraining order did nothing more than get his deputy chief father involved. After that, it's like the entire police force was on his side.

Am I ever going to get my life back? I hate that I can't spend one night out with a guy without my past huffing down my neck. Tonight was the first time in a while that I've felt some peace. I felt *safe*. Being in Long Beach made me feel like Nathan couldn't find me. Being with Trey made me forget about him altogether. I can't allow my ex to keep doing this to me.

Eventually, things need to change. I just wish I knew how to make it happen.

13

TREY

It's been two days since I had dinner with Arella. We've been texting back and forth so much that my phone is almost always in my hands, but I have yet to see her again. She has yet to mention it, either. Two days is long enough to wait before giving it another shot.

> Hey beautiful! My band and crew are coming over tonight for a little get together at my place. You wanna come? Javina and her girlfriend are welcome too.

> Hey pretty boy! It's Javina. Ari and I will be there. What time? 😑

I grin at the text. I purposely waited until I knew Arella was at work with Javina before texting her. I figured that if Javina knew she was invited, she'd convince Arella to come.

> How about seven?

I text her my address.

> Thanks, hot stuff. We'll see ya then! 🌝

> Sorry, you'll have to excuse Javina and do the same tonight too. She has no boundaries. I'll see you tonight.

> Can't wait!

Fuck yeah. Now all I've gotta do is convince people to come over.

When I arrive at the Soul House for rehearsal in the afternoon, the backstage area is empty. After my bandmates show up, I mention the idea of having a little get-together. Marcus and Emmy are the first to jump in.

"I'll bring some snacks!" Emmy says.

"I'll get the drinks," Marcus adds.

"I'll provide the pizza," I say, glancing at Kevin, who looks hesitant. "And we can set up a poker table."

He flashes me a *you know me so well* grin. "Pizza? Poker? I'm down!"

By the time we're done working and everyone's in my backyard, my "little get-together" has turned into a huge party. I figured that since it was last minute, only a few people would show up.

And I thought wrong.

Not only is most of the crew here, Kevin's two older brothers are too. Like Kevin, they heard *poker* and couldn't resist.

Upbeat music blasts over my speakers. Cardboard boxes of pepperoni pizzas decorate a long fold-up table. A few crew members have brought their dogs and are chatting by the fire pit. Everyone else is scattered around playing card games, mixing drinks, or telling stories on my patio.

Arella and Javina are the last to show up. Javina struts through the wooden gate first. Behind her comes Arella in a flowy white sundress that shows just enough cleavage to get my dick to harden. My gaze skates down her slender legs. My hands twitch from wanting to run my palms up and down her skin. I know I'm supposed to only get information from her, and I shouldn't be as attracted to her as I am, but damn, she's fucking gorgeous.

I wave from the pizza table, hoping my boner isn't noticeable. "Hey, ladies! Thanks for comin'." In my head, I thank Javina profusely for being here. I doubt Arella would have come on her own.

"Thanks for the invite!" Javina says.

"Wow. There's a lot of people here." Arella has all her hair tied into a braid falling over one shoulder. Wisps of wavy curls frame her face as she eyes the crowd.

"Apparently our team didn't have much else going on tonight," I say.

"T!" Liz calls from a distance. "Come! Monique wants us to take a quick band pic for the socials."

I groan out loud. These "quick band pics" are never quick. Monique usually makes us pose for a few minutes so she has enough content to work with. While I'm glad she takes care of our band's social media, I'd rather not have to take pictures all the time. But I've learned it's easier to comply than to resist, so I take a step backward, away from the only reason I have all these damn people at my house.

"Help yourself!" I gesture toward the food. "I'll be right back."

For longer than necessary, I smile, I pose, and I put my hands where I'm told. The second Monique says, "Awesome job, everyone!" I beeline back to Arella, who's quietly nibbling on some pizza crust.

Unsurprisingly, Javina has inserted herself into a game of poker. Arella looks like Javina's plus-one as she stands behind her friend's chair, watching the card game.

"You look beautiful," I say once I'm back at her side. Under the sun and in this dress, she looks like she's a glowing angel sent from the heavens.

Arella glances up at me with a sweet smile. "Thanks. You don't look too bad yourself."

I receive compliments all the time, but they never feel the way it does when Arella says it. When other girls tell me I'm hot, it's because they want me to fuck 'em, and it feels like a transaction. When Arella says that I "don't look too bad," I believe her.

I tilt my head to the side. "You wanna go for a walk?"

She gives me a look like I've just stumped her with a riddle. "Um, shouldn't you stick around? It's *your* party."

"Nah. Nobody'll miss me."

"Um, I don't know if I should leave Javina here alone."

Without taking her eyes off the poker table, Javina speaks over her shoulder. "Go for a walk with the man, Ari! I'll still be here when you get back. Except I'll have double the money in my pocket."

The boys around the card table erupt into laughter.

"Yeah, right." Kevin chuckles. "Start weeping!" He throws his cards down, face up. It's a full house. Three queens, two jacks. Kevin's brothers groan, chucking their cards at the table. Laughing, Kevin snatches the chips from the middle.

I'm not a poker person. My ability to read emotions tells me exactly when someone's bluffing. It's not fun when I'm basically cheating.

Arella pops the last bit of pizza crust into her mouth, then throws away her paper plate. "Okay, I'm ready."

We're just through the wooden gate when Liz shouts at me. "T!"

I twist on my heel with an exasperated "Whaaat?"

"Where ya goin'?"

"For a walk."

She flashes me the same look Arella did when I suggested that we ditch my own party. "Okay . . . ? Don't be long."

"I won't, Mom."

Liz responds with an eyeroll, then goes back to her conversation with Emmy.

When Arella and I make it to the sidewalk, I shove my hands into my pockets. I have the urge to offer her my arm to hook hers through, but I'm pretty certain she won't accept it.

I've got a hunch as to why Arella's so jumpy whenever I touch her. I think she's been abused. I used to be jumpy, too, whenever Victor raised a hand around me. Once I got as tall as him, he stopped hitting me like that, and I stopped being jumpy.

Considering Arella is all of five-two, with skinny arms that resemble tree branches, whoever abused her is probably *still* bigger than her. I doubt it was her grandparents, since she seems to adore them and vice versa. If I had to put money on it, I'd say it was an ex-boyfriend.

"I'm glad Javina forced you to come out tonight," I say as I shift to walk on Arella's side closer to the street.

"She didn't force me. When I saw your message at work, I mentioned it to her. I'm not really a party person, so she thought I was going to say no, which is why she stole my phone and texted you."

I raise my eyebrows with a smile. "So . . . you wanted to come?"

"Mm-hmm."

Hearing that makes me feel like I'm doing something right. "Javina seems like a good friend."

"She's my bestest friend." After a few steps, Arella asks, "Who's your best friend?"

My answer comes easily. "Liz."

"Does she always keep tabs on you?"

"Sometimes. She thinks I'll get into trouble if she doesn't."

"Is she right?"

I purse my lips together, tilting my head from side to side. "Kinda."

"What kind of trouble do you usually get into?"

"Fights, mostly. When I was in school, I'd get sent home early for fighting in class. My teachers suggested that I join after-school programs as a way to help me control my anger, or some bullshit like that."

"Did you?"

"Yep. Theater, art, football, soccer, basketball. None of them worked."

After-school programs work for most kids, like the ones my foundation supports. Being able to do something fun outside of their depressing homes helps them forget about their dead parents. I only wish it had worked for me.

"It sounds like your bad-boy phase started young," Arella says.

This isn't the first time someone's called me a bad boy. I wouldn't say I'm a bad person. It's not like I purposely tried to pick fights with the other boys at school. It's that when they didn't stop bullying me for wearing the same three outfits, I couldn't stop my fists from pounding into their faces.

Three outfits were all I had. Victor didn't care enough to provide anything more. The only reason he paid for me to join all those after-school activities was because it kept me away from him.

"You seem to be more tamed now," Arella says. It warms me a little because "tamed" seems to be something she wants. I'll be tamed or whatever else if it means she'll tell me if she's ever been experimented on in a lab. "I mean, you might try to *look* like a bad boy some-times, but I think that's just a defense mechanism."

"Defense mechanism?"

She narrows her eyes at me, smug. "Don't act like you don't know."

"I don't."

"If Liz keeps tabs on you, that means the fighting didn't stop once you got older, right? I'm guessing bars or clubs? Maybe both?"

"Right . . ." I don't like where this is going.

"I'm also going to assume you have a history of drugs, drinking, and sleeping around. Maybe you still do. Either way, I think you like to *look* like a bad-boy because you think it keeps people away. You probably think that's easier than actually letting people in, because the fewer people you get close to, the fewer people you have to lose."

I freeze to gape at her. I've never thought about the reason why I keep people at a distance. In school, people were either afraid of me or pitied me, and I didn't want to be friends with either. Even now, I see my bandmates all the time, and besides Liz, they don't know that much about me. What Arella said has some truth to it. Letting fewer people in does mean I have fewer people to lose.

Her dress twirls around her thighs as she turns to face me. "I'm sorry if I'm wrong. I'm just saying this because of the way you talked about losing Elliott and how it made you never want to mentor another kid."

I clear my throat and resume our walk. "So, um, anyway . . . Tell me about your plans for the weekend."

She offers me an understanding smile as she returns to a steady pace at my side. "I'm going to visit my grandparents."

Last night, I did some digging into Phillip and Roxanne Ward. Roxy's background check came back mostly empty, which checks out because she was a stay-at-home grandma.

As for Phil, his background information is fishy as hell. A few auto shops came up as past employers, but I didn't see a new employer every year like Arella claims happened. Either he was getting paid under the table or someone has tampered with his records. In addition, neither of her grandparents' information revealed past addresses. It's like someone went through and deleted as much as they could. Question is: Who and why?

"Are you staying there for the whole weekend?" I ask as we wait on a curb for a car to pass before crossing the street.

"I'll leave Friday after work and come back Sunday evening."

I guess I won't be able to see her this weekend . . . "What do you guys usually do?"

"Sometimes we go out to eat. For sure we'll play board games, and I'll bake something with Grammy."

"Did you play a lot of board games growing up?"

"Mm-hmm. You?"

"Not really." By that, I mean none at all. The idea of Victor breaking out Candy Land with me is unimaginable.

"If you didn't watch TV and you didn't play board games, how did you spend your childhood?"

If I tell her how I spent my childhood, she won't believe me. Hell, *I* wouldn't believe me.

She'll think I'm joking if I tell her I grew up under a mountain in a secret compound. She'll think I'm insane if I tell her that a few weeks after I moved in, I discovered that burning down trees with the fire that comes out of my hands made me feel better.

At the age of eight, I spent most of my after-school hours trying to make money to buy myself new clothes and shoes.

At nine, I was put into training with the new ZIRDA agents to learn how to fight properly. Victor allowed me to learn in hopes that it would help me control my gifts better. Either that or he got off on seeing me get beat up. Whichever it was, it didn't change that whenever I got too upset, my powers would get out of hand. My room used to light up in flames almost once a week, and things would fly all over the place.

How I spent my time as a kid isn't something I want to share with Arella.

"I went for a lot of walks," I say, thinking about all the times I hiked the forest for a good tree to burn. It's the truth, just not the specific truth. "And I worked out a lot."

"Were you a chubby kid?"

"No, but I enjoyed exercising." *If getting beat up by people twice my age counts as exercising . . .*

Victor didn't tell the adults I trained with to go easy on me. They were told to fight hard, and they did. The worst part is that along with my own pain, I could feel theirs too. It made me twice as weak.

It wasn't until I hit puberty and finally learned how to block other people's physical emotions from mirroring onto me that I began winning fights. Otherwise, I was basically used as a punching bag.

Arella and I loop around the sidewalk to head back toward my house. Before we arrive there, I need to ask her out again. I just don't know how.

"I checked out your blog last night," I say.

Her eyes widen. "You did?"

"Yeah. You make cakes look like works of art displayed in a museum."

"Wow. I didn't think you'd actually look at it."

With any other girl, I wouldn't have. But this is Arella, and I need to learn everything about her. I hoped that going through her website would give me some insight on who she is. All I got out of it was a craving for baked goods.

"Do you make money on your site?" I ask.

"Some. Not enough to live off of. It's based on ad clicks and how high the traffic is."

"That's how my band makes money on YouTube, too. Ad partners and brand deals. The more clicks and views, the bigger the paycheck."

Arella steps over a large crack in the sidewalk. "You must make a ton of money on YouTube if you're able to split it between the band, hire a crew, and still have enough to afford a four-bedroom house in Brentwood on your own."

"Most of the band's income comes from tickets to our live shows, meet and greets, and merch. Also, I didn't buy my house with the band's earnings. I bought my house *because* of the band, remember? We needed a place to play, so I provided it."

"Then, I'm curious . . . How are you able to afford your house? And afford to travel internationally? And start a foundation?"

The only people I've ever told about my inheritance are Liz and Jess. Whenever people ask, I usually tell them I have a lot of investments and leave it there. While that's true, the money I invested with came from my inheritance. I don't like telling people exactly where my money comes from. It usually leads to them asking how my parents died. I hate having to retell the fake story, so the less I have to talk about it, the better.

Maybe because Arella understands what it's like to be parentless, I can tell her that I lost mine too—without all the meaningless *I'm sorry*s and pity looks. She probably knows how useless those are.

"My parents were wealthy," I say as a way to imply that they're gone without actually saying it. "They left me everything they had."

"What did they do for a living?" she asks without a hint of surprise.

Did she already know that they died? How? I haven't said anything to suggest that my parents are dead until now.

"They were researchers." Technically, that's true. My parents were researchers . . . for ZIRDA. They were the ones who spent years in a lab, working to uncover if it was possible to create a usable product from Healers' tears that kept its healing abilities.

Now that we know it's possible, who's to say we can't discover the source of an Ordinary's immunity, reproduce it, and create a pill, or a liquid, or anything that will give ZIRDA agents immunity over the Royals?

I swallow hard before asking, "How did you know my parents are gone?"

She looks away from me as she plays with the end of her long braid. "Um, I read about it when I Googled you. Your Wiki page mentions it briefly."

"I see," I say to the sidewalk. It's been years since I looked myself up. I didn't realize my Wikipedia page included that information.

A moment passes before Arella breaks the silence. "Do you wish I didn't know?"

"Nah, it's fine. I just don't like to talk about it."

"We can talk about something else," she says cheerfully, and I appreciate her attempt at bringing the mood back up. "What are *your* plans this weekend?"

I don't miss a beat. "Thinking up ways to win you over."

The mood officially changes the second Arella bursts into laughter. A hint of pink forms on her cheeks. "Is that so?"

"Yeah, and if you tell me how to do that, it'll make my job a lot easier."

It takes a few heartbeats before she says, "Maybe I'm not something you can win, Trey."

I narrow my eyes at her. "Are you saying that you're not an option at all? Or that I gotta work to *earn* you, not win you?"

She pauses to think. "Um, maybe I'm just not in the right place right now to start something new."

"Bullshit. Not buyin' that. I think that if a person, especially a woman, *really* wants something, she'll make it happen. So, that means you don't want me enough, and I'm gonna change that. You just gotta tell me how."

"Shouldn't that be something you figure out on your own?"

I theatrically slump my shoulders. "But I'm impatient. It'd be much easier if you just tell me. If you don't, I'll have to resort to my own dumb ideas."

"Which are?"

"Doing lots of cheesy romantic things until you're swept off your feet and want me more than you want to bake. If that doesn't work, I'll try plan B."

"Which is?"

I grin. "Pulling my pants down."

Arella laughs again, covering her mouth with a palm in the most adorable way. "Does that usually work for you?"

"Hasn't failed me yet. Typically, that's plan A, but I figured you're not the type to fall for that."

She's still laughing, and I love the sound of it. Her laugh means I'm making progress. "Do you have a plan C?"

"Nah. I'm hoping I won't need one."

Her laughter fades as she rolls her eyes. "I still don't understand why you're trying so hard to date me. If you want something easy, you should look through that long line of women ready to throw themselves at you."

"You're different, Arella. I don't know why, but you've captured my attention." That's a lie. I do know why. Arella is the most unique person I've ever met. She's literally one of three people in the entire world that I know of who are immune to Zordi powers.

"Why do you always call me Arella?"

I press my brows together. "Because that's your name?"

"But everyone calls me Ari."

"Would you rather I call you that?" I call her Arella because for four weeks before I met her, I referred to her in my head as Arella. Calling her *Ari* now would sound weird. But if that's what she wants . . .

"I don't mind," she says. "I actually kind of like it."

I'm going to take her "kind of" as that she *really* likes it.

We talk easily until we arrive back in my driveway. One of my band's songs is playing from the backyard speakers. My time alone with Arella is almost up, and I haven't thought of a way to ask her out yet. I still get the feeling that she'll reject me.

When I asked her out before, she only agreed on the premise that we'd be going as friends. Victor made it clear that being friends isn't good enough and that getting intimate with her will encourage her to tell me secretive things about herself. How can I get her to date me if—

That's it! I can't present the date as a date. I've gotta make it sound casual. That's how I got her to come out to my show. That's how I got her out for dinner. And that's how I got her here tonight.

If I had texted her saying, "Hey, wanna come to a party as my date?" she absolutely would have turned me down. I informally invited her, nonchalantly asked her to bring Javina, and it got her to show up.

"What're you doin' tomorrow?" I ask with a newfound vigor.

"Work."

I don't hide my disappointment as I grunt. "Nanny or daycare?"

"Daycare. I only nanny over the weekends. Except this weekend because the family I nanny for is going on vacation. That's why I'm going to see my grandparents."

"Do you have a day off next week?"

She nods. "Monday."

Make it sound casual . . . "You wanna hang out?"

At the closed gate to my backyard, Arella stops and turns to me, tilting her head back a little to meet my eyes. "What do you have in mind?"

Thank fuck she didn't immediately say no. "I've got a video shoot in the morning. How 'bout something fun in the afternoon, and then we can get dinner afterward?"

She squints at me with a smile. "Is this your sly way of asking me out on a date?"

Abso-fucking-lutely. "Nah. We can just hang out as friends, if that's what you want."

Spending time with her as *friends* is the same as dating, just without the label. I don't need the label to work my mission, especially if it's the one thing holding her back.

Making our time together sound casual must be working, because Arella perks up. "Okay. Let's hang out on Monday."

14

TREY

M onday

It doesn't take me long to finish filming my solo scenes. While the rest of the band films their scenes outside the Soul House, I head inside, backstage. I've just started messing around on a loop station when Liz strolls in and stops at my side.

She has tense energy. "Hey, T-Bear."

I press my foot against the loop pedal to stop the beat. "What?"

She feigns innocence. "What, what?"

"You're all nervous and shit."

Liz knows how much I hate playing mind games, so she gets straight to the point. "She seems sweet."

"Who?" I ask, even though I know exactly who.

After Arella and I returned to my backyard party, I refused to leave her side. I felt Liz's glare on me the entire time. Every time I made Arella laugh, Liz didn't miss it. Anyone who noticed that probably thought Liz was jealous, but I know better.

She doesn't approve of me flirting with Ordi women, which I'll admit I tend to do sometimes just to get them into bed with me. She probably thinks that's all I'm trying to do with Arella, when that's not the case at all. Would Liz approve of me befriending Arella if I told her that this woman could be the key to saving innocent lives from the Royals' violence? I'm not sure.

Liz calls me out on my bullshit. "You know who I'm talking about. Ari. You seem really into her."

"Sure." I try to sound nonchalant. The last thing I need is for Liz to lecture me about women again.

"How into her are you?"

With a long sigh, I set my guitar down. "Are you about to reprimand me? 'Cause if so, we should go sit on the couch. It's comfier."

Liz heads there, and I follow her.

"You know what I'm about to say," she says, plopping onto the cushions.

I do the same. "What? That I shouldn't be fucking around with Ordi women?"

"Yes!" She gives me a *duh* face. "You're the only Zordi I know who actually finds Ordinaries attractive. They're meant to be our friends, not our partners. Plus, it's breaking the second most important Zordi law."

That second law was only established to enforce the first one. Since we aren't allowed to reveal anything from the Zordi world to an Ordinary, we're not allowed to engage in sexual or romantic relationships with them, either. Getting too close to them means there's a higher chance of exposure. Exposure means a scrub for the Ordi and z-prison for the Zordi. Depending on how bad the exposure is, sometimes it means death.

There aren't a lot of Zordis who like sex with Ordis. Most people think it's bizarre. Like as strange as it is to chew on glass or to purposely burn your own hair off. To me, sex with Ordinaries feels just as good. Better, actually, because it's risk-free. Zordis can't catch Ordinary illnesses, and they can't catch ours either, meaning we can't transfer STDs. And since we can't reproduce with them, why not take advantage of the pregnancy-free sex?

"You're lucky you've never been caught doing it with an Ordi," Liz says as she leans back against the couch.

"The only way for me to get caught is for another Zordi to report me," I say. "Since you're the only one I see regularly, I think I'm fine."

"Either way, Ari's sweet and innocent, and that's dangerous for a guy like you."

My face screws together. "A guy like me?"

"You know I think you're a great man." She chuckles lightly and cocks her head to the side. "Complicated, but still great."

"Why do I feel another *but* coming?"

"But . . . as soon as a girl starts to have *real* feelings for you, you always drop them like they're lethal."

"Do not."

"Do too."

"Hey," I say with a finger up, "the last Zordi I dated used me to make her ex-fiancé jealous."

"What about the girl before that? The really busty Black one." Liz puts on her thinking face. "Kelly?"

"Keelah."

"Yeah. What happened to her?"

"She cheated on me, got pregnant, and tried to tell me I was the father."

Liz's jaw drops. "Were you?"

"Hell no. She's an Ordinary and a gold digger. She demanded money from me until I asked her to take a DNA test. I even offered to pay for it. Haven't heard from her since."

That woman ran straight back to the guy she cheated on me with. I can only assume they're still together. At the time, I was pissed, but I wasn't too broken up about it. We'd only been sleeping together for a month.

"Rodrigo and I have been together for almost a year now," Liz says. "We met on Glimmer, that dating app for Zordis. Maybe you should try that. With your face, I'm sure you'll land a date in a snap. Even for our kind, you're one of the better-looking ones."

Zordis naturally have big eyes, clear skin, straight teeth, and healthy bodies. Because of that, we're seen as more desirable by Ordinaries. By Zordi standards, I think I'm average, but Liz always tells me otherwise.

"Thanks for the advice, Mom. I'll try that dating app sometime."

She backhands my chest, scolding me. "Look, I understand that you have a wall up against our kind because with your gift, it makes it hard for you to know if you truly like someone or if you're just mirroring their feelings. You stick to Ordis because it's easier. Legally and biologically, it won't work. There's no real commitment and no harm when you fuck it up. Because when you do fuck it up, which you will because you're a man, instead of taking responsibility for it, you can easily brush it off because, no matter what, that relationship wasn't bound to work anyway. However, that doesn't mean you should cut Zordi women off forever. Eventually, you'll get tired of this and want to find your soul mate."

What is this? Call-Trey-out-on-his-shit day? I've never thought about any of that as reasons why I steer clear of Zordi women, but when Liz puts it that way . . .

"Come on, Liz. You don't really believe in that soul mate bullshit, do you?"

"Of course I do!" She gapes at me like I'm insane for not believing it.

Besides our differences in bodily functions, another thing that makes Zordis unique from Ordis is that we have strong connections with our soul mates—or so people say. Apparently, there are ways to know when someone is your soul mate. Tons of books have been written about it. It's even taught in Zordi school, but it's all nonsense.

My belief is that when people claim to have found their soul mate, it's just a ploy to either steal someone else's girl or to justify adultery. Aunt Jodi used the soul mate excuse to rationalize leaving Victor out of the blue, turning him into the petulant asshole he is today. So yeah, soul mates are dumb.

"Please, Trey. Could you just leave Ari alone and give someone legal a chance?"

I toss my arms into the air, letting them fall back into my lap. "It's not like I haven't given Zordis a shot. All the ones I've been with have only wanted me for money."

"Well, you're not gonna find someone who wants you for *you* while fishing in the ocean of Ordinaries."

AFTER WORK, I HEAD STRAIGHT TO ARELLA'S APARTMENT TO PICK HER UP FOR OUR DATE. WE'RE only halfway into it when I decide we need to get out of the public. Two ladies recognized me while we were go-karting. A group of guys bombarded me at the bowling alley. Another girl recognized me when I was about to beat Arella at air hockey. I lost concentration, then the game. I'm supposed to be spending time with her and building a connection—not making her wait around for me to finish taking pictures with strangers.

"Do you mind if we cook dinner instead of going out?" I ask as we head back to my car.

"I thought you said you wanted to get Mexican?" Arella says.

"I did . . . until we kept getting interrupted."

"Do you normally get recognized everywhere you go?"

"Typically, but put me in a crowd with those over thirty-five, and I guarantee you I'm a nobody." After we climb into my car and buckle ourselves in, I say, "How 'bout we make tacos at your place? That way I won't have to drive you back."

"That sounds wonderful."

Perfect! I'll finally get to see the inside of her apartment.

At the grocery store, nobody recognizes me. We're able to get in and out within five minutes.

As I pull up to Arella's apartment complex, she gazes intently out the window.

"Whatcha lookin' for?" I ask, putting the car into park.

Her back snaps straight. "Nothing."

Bull. She does this every time she comes home, and I don't know why. I exit the car and skim my eyes across the parking lot. Nothing looks out of the norm, so I follow her inside.

Arella's little apartment smells like a bakery—sugar, bread, and frosting. There's stuff everywhere. Assorted trinkets litter the tops of her tables. Framed floral artwork covers the walls. All that can possibly be purple is purple. Violet curtains. Lavender pillows. Lilac throw blankets. Even her lampshades are purple.

She kicks her sandals off by the door, and I do the same with my shoes.

"Would you like something to drink?" she asks as she heads into her postage stamp of a kitchen.

I trail her. "How 'bout some coffee?"

"It's almost seven."

"And?" Caffeine doesn't affect Zordis the way it does Ordis. Our bodies absorb and filter the caffeine way too fast for it to give us any energy. It's the same reason why Zordis can't take Ordinary medicines and drugs. Our bodies need stronger remedies. I still like the taste of Ordinary coffee though.

"Sorry," Arella says. "I don't drink coffee, so I don't have any. I could make you some tea?"

"Tea sounds great."

From the cabinet, Arella pulls down a mug, fills it with water from the fridge, then sticks it into the microwave. Since I don't wanna be the one to tell her that's not how you make tea, I keep my mouth shut. Next, she grabs a large pan from under the stove and starts heating it up with some oil.

"What can I help with?" I ask as I slip out of my jacket and drape it over the back of a worn dining chair.

"You can just set the table while I do all the cooking." She points at a drawer. "Place mats are here. Silverware is right above it."

The tiny thing she calls a table looks like it belongs in an office with a printer on it—a *small* printer. Her apartment couldn't handle anything bigger anyway. I decorate the table with plum-colored place mats, then set down some napkins and silverware.

Since I can't be of more help, I casually saunter the two steps it takes to get to her living room. Off an end table, I pick up a framed photo of Arella standing next to an old couple. The man is tall and lean, with salt-and-pepper hair. The woman has wavy hair like Arella's, except it's shoulder-length with silver streaks.

"Are these your grandparents?"

Arella peeks her head out of the kitchen as I hold up the frame. "Yeah. That's them."

I set the frame down, then pick up another one. It features a kid version of Arella behind a cake with a 7 candle on top. Something drags the corners of my mouth down.

That was the last age I had a birthday cake. It's also the last age I celebrated a holiday, or had a family dinner of any kind—up until I met Liz.

She makes it a point to celebrate every holiday with me, which is good for her, too, considering her family has basically deserted her. For my birthday, she always gives me two gifts: one for that year and a second to make up for a past year. She does the same for Christmas. For Thanksgiving, she cooks me a huge meal with at least six sides, even though it's always just us. *What did I ever do to deserve Liz?*

The rest of the photos in Arella's living room all tell me the same thing: She lived a good childhood with two people who love her. There are pictures of her as a kid on rides at the fair, petting animals at the zoo, and getting piggyback rides from her grandpa at a playground. I've never gone to a fair or a zoo. Maybe my parents took me before they died, but I don't remember. *It woulda been nice to be able to do stuff like that . . .*

With a heavy heart, I plant myself onto the chair holding my jacket. The wood creaks under my weight. "How did your weekend go with your grandparents?"

Arella sets a steaming mug in front of me with a tea bag already in it. After I thank her, she goes back to the stove. "It was wonderful. Grammy and I baked some cookies, and we ate them while we played Scrabble."

"You any good at Scrabble?"

"I'm decent. Grammy is the best though. I swear she makes up words, but when I check them online, they're legal. Like, do you even know what a Q-A-T is?"

"Not a goddamn clue."

"Exactly. It's a legal word though."

While Arella cooks the taco meat, I focus on her emotions—or lack thereof. I concentrate as hard as I can, but nothing comes. I'm still sensing all the people from the surrounding apartments.

After a few deep breaths, I try again. This time, I close my eyes and imagine myself touching her heart. I do that for a few seconds before a sharp pain pinches my temples, then a headache eases into me. It's the same type of headache I get whenever I don't consciously dial back my Empath power all the time and I'm sensing too many people at once.

"You're quiet today," Arella says as she cuts up some lettuce.

"Just thinkin'." I take my first sip of the warm tea. *Mmm. Earl Grey.*

"About?"

The last thing I'm gonna tell her is the truth. *Oh, I was just thinkin' about how, for some mysterious reason, I can sense everyone's emotions but yours.* She would question the fact that I have the ability to sense emotions more than the fact that I can sense everyone but her.

"I was just wonderin' if you think your grandparents would like me or not."

Arella throws her head back, laughing so hard, she has to set the knife down on the counter.

"What's so funny?"

She continues to giggle. "Don't take this the wrong way, but they wouldn't like you. They wouldn't like anyone who shows interest in me. They're super-protective. When I told them I wanted to move to LA, they fought me on it for months."

"Why are they so protective?"

"I'm their only grandkid. It's expected." With a wooden spoon, Arella stirs around the taco meat. "Since my mom passed away so young, they treated me like their own child instead of a grandbaby."

Here's my chance! Make it sound unintentional. "What was your mom's name?"

"Bella."

"And your dad?"

"Aries."

I make a mental note to dig up everything I can on Bella and Aries Rance tonight. "What did they do for a living?"

"Dad was an accountant. Mom was his secretary."

"Sounds kinky." I wiggle my eyebrows, and it makes Arella chuckle.

"It's exactly what you think it is. Grammy said they hit it off during the job interview. Apparently, my dad only hired my mom because he wanted to date her."

"And you said they passed away in a car accident?"

"Yeah. They were driving home on a rainy night in September of '95. It was dark, and they went right over a cliff."

A rainy night? In September of '95? My heart stills, and my back straightens like a rod. No way in hell. It'd be too much of a coincidence.

But I have to ask . . . "What day was it in September?"

She pauses to think. "Um, I'm not sure."

I'm barely breathing as more words spew from my lips. "Where was the cliff?"

"Don't know." Arella shrugs nonchalantly as she goes back to stirring. I can't tell if she actually doesn't know or if she's trying to hide information. Seriously, what a time to not be able to sense someone! If I could sense her, maybe I could tell if she's lying or not. But what reason would she have to lie?

I try to keep my voice from shaking. "Do you remember where you lived when you were that age?"

She shakes her head. "I was three. I barely remember what I ate yesterday."

Since she doesn't seem to have the answers I'm looking for, I stop asking questions.

Eventually, dinner is ready. I'm quiet as we consume our meal, because my brain is too busy thinking up an excuse to leave.

When we finally finish the tacos, I say, "Hey, I just got a text from Liz. She needs me for somethin'. You mind if I head out?"

If she's disappointed about me leaving, she doesn't show it. I hate having to rely on someone's facial expressions to know how they feel.

"Don't worry about the dishes," she says as I'm about to pick up my plate. "I'll get it."

I'm halfway home when I realize I forgot to make plans with Arella to see her again. I'll have to text her tomorrow. Right now, my mind's a mess. The only thing I can think about is going home to research Arella's parents. I almost stop on the side of the road to do it. I don't though, because I know if whatever information I find jumbles my mind even more, I won't be able to get home safely.

I run into my house so fast that I trip over some shoes I apparently left lying in the middle of the entrance. In my bedroom, I wave a hand at my burner laptop. It flies toward me at full speed, and I catch it in midair. With it propped open on my mattress, I type, *Bella and Aries Rance.*

What comes up is a bunch of romance novels. Definitely not what I'm looking for.

I try searching for each of her parents' names on their own and find nothing useful. On a whim, I type, *Isabella Rance.* A lady from the 1200s shows up for that. Not Arella's mother.

Finally, I try *deaths in September 1995.*

It's too broad. What comes up is a bunch of dead famous people.

So I try again: *deaths in September 1995 California.*

I gasp when my parents' names pop up first. I don't know why I'm surprised. I already knew it was the same month. I click the first link and read it.

The article doesn't state anything I didn't already know about the tampered story. It highlights some details about a few propane tanks exploding, causing the immediate death of a thirty-three-year-old couple. There's only one line about me, the "seven-year-old son of the deceased," and I'm labeled as "the lucky survivor."

The article doesn't mention the body parts that were found that didn't belong to my parents. It says nothing about the intruders' car that was still parked in the driveway when the cops came, and nothing about how that car mysteriously disappeared after the cops left. The article is so fabricated that if someone read it to me with different names, I wouldn't even know it's my family's story.

The Royals have people everywhere. I wouldn't be surprised if all the cops that came that night were Royals. I wouldn't be surprised if this article's author was a Royal either. If not that, the Royals probably threatened the writer into telling these lies to cover up their crimes.

Back in the search bar, I try being even more specific: *deaths in September 1995 California down a cliff.*

The first article is about Arella's parents. At least, I *think* it's Arella's parents. The article states that a couple was driving when the rain and darkness made them lose control of their car and they went right over the cliff.

A few things are fishy about the article.

First, the couple's names are Stanley and Robyn Calder, not Aries and Bella Rance. Second, they weren't the only ones who died in the car that night. Apparently, their three-year-old daughter, Hannah, died with them. Third, this happened in Three Rivers, near the same mountain that Shadow Ridge is hidden under, and it happened on the *exact same night* my parents died.

Coincidence? I think not.

I came to the Internet for answers, and all I've got are more questions. Why would Arella lie about her parents' names? Or did someone lie to *her* about her parents' names? If that's the case, who and why? It's possible that the article printed false names to cover something up. If so, that begs the question: Who was trying to cover up what?

Next, why would the article state that the couple's daughter died with them? Arella—or should I say *Hannah*?—is very much alive. I'm certain this article is about her parents, because I spend the next hour scouring the Internet, and there isn't any other report of a couple driving off a cliff to their death in September of 1995.

It's too much of a coincidence that Arella's parents died on the same night that mine did in the same town. There's a connection here, and I'm determined to find it.

15

ARELLA

I t's beginning to turn into something.

Three days have passed since Trey and I hung out, and every morning since, I have woken up to his text that says, *Good morning, beautiful.*

Whenever his name pops up on my phone, the corners of my lips get yanked upward. They stay that way while I read his message and giggle at all the funny things he says.

He has asked if we could hang out again this week, but our schedules didn't match up. While he's free during the day, I'm at work. While I'm free in the evenings, he's at work. I didn't realize how much goes into what he does. Everything from rehearsals to recording sessions to writing sessions to planning out their videos and filming them. Then there's all the meetings they have with their manager and potential collaborators. It all sounds complicated, but he seems to enjoy it.

When I'm not actively texting him, I'm on YouTube, watching as many of his band's videos as possible. I knew they were good after seeing them perform the one time, but I didn't know they were *this* good. The production value and creativity of their music videos are impressive. Their millions of subscribers and even more millions of views tells me I'm not the only one who's impressed.

On my lunch break today, the first thing I do is check my phone, hoping Trey has texted me. I can't hold back my smile when I see his name.

> Hey! You free tonight? My manager rescheduled my band's social media meeting to next week, so I'm open.

I'm flattered that his first thought after finding out he has some free time was to ask if I'm available.

> Sorry. 🙁 I have a movie date with Javina.

I feel the same, but I won't ditch my best friend to hang out with him, no matter how badly I want to.

Will I ever get to see you again?

I'm free tomorrow night?

I play a show every Friday and Saturday, then I've got meet and greets afterward. I won't be able to have alone time with you. How about Sunday?

My heart does backflips in my chest. He wants *alone time* with me. Why does that excite me so much?

Sure! We can hang out after I'm done nannying at five.

I'll take it!

LATER THAT EVENING, IT'S LATE AND DARK ON MY DRIVE HOME FROM THE THEATER—SO DARK THAT I don't see the shattered glass outside my door until it crunches beneath my shoes. It's everywhere. My first thought is that someone broke my window, except I don't have a window by the door.

Crushed purple flowers are scattered all over my front stoop. Ripped into fourths is a little card. Careful not to touch any glass, I pick up the card pieces and hold them together like a puzzle. In all caps handwriting, it reads:

FILLING OUR TIME APART WITH PLAN A
—T.G.

A wide, ridiculous smile spreads across my face. When Trey said he was going to do cheesy romantic things to win me over, he wasn't kidding. It's kind of working.

After shoving the ripped card into my purse, I scowl at the mess. *Who would do something like this?*

Suddenly, it clicks. There's only one person I know who's low enough to trash someone else's property—especially *my* property. It only takes me a second to wrench my keys out of my purse, but it's too late. The sound of his heavy footsteps rushing from around the corner sends a chill down my spine. Before I can do anything else, he slaps a palm over my shoulder and flips me to face him.

"Wish you coulda seen how big that vase was. Seems like that guy was tryna compensate for somethin'." Nathan's slurred words make the little hairs on my arm stick up.

My ex looks different from the last time I saw him. Now he's got a buzz cut, which is a huge upgrade from the long, greasy mop he used to have. Even with the upgrade, he still looks as cold and callous as ever.

"Who's T.G.?" Nathan towers over me, speaking so close to my face that his gin-and-cigarette breath poisons my air.

"None of your business." My voice comes out smaller than I wanted it to. I can't stand how much this man affects me. Within seconds, he's already turned me into the scared little girl I was when I was with him. All that progress I've made over the past eight months, gone.

"Ari, Ari, Ari." Each time he says my name, a nasty bite nips at my skin. "Everything you do is my business."

I try to sound more firm this time. "Leave, or I'm calling the cops."

"Right." He chuckles low in his throat. "How many times has that helped you before?"

None . . . "I'm serious," I say, my voice growing stronger as I channel whatever confidence Javina always has. "If I keep calling about you, *someone* will figure it out eventually."

Nathan rips my purse from me. It falls to the ground behind him with a thud. Then he seizes me by my shoulders and yanks me toward him until his nose touches mine. I cringe, trying to push him back. It does nothing.

He's bigger. Taller. Stronger. And he's angry. "You won't be calling anyone about me."

I don't know what gives me the courage to do it, but I hack one back and spit it into his face. He releases me with a growl.

"You little bitch!" He swipes at the loogie dripping down his eye, then smacks me in the face. My head whips to the side as I yelp.

Ignoring the pain, I jab my keys into his stomach.

"Fuck!" He groans and keels over, grabbing his torso.

I take advantage of his temporary weak state by bashing my knee between his legs where it hurts. He cries out as I shove him to the ground.

After thrusting my key into the doorknob, I stumble inside. A hand clutches my ankle, and I fall face first against my living room carpet. My head bounces back as pain erupts up my jaw. I taste blood where my tongue got caught between my teeth.

"Let go!" I jerk my leg back and forth until he loses his grip. Then I kick him in the face, and I'm not even sorry.

Nathan's head snaps back as he roars, "FUCK!"

Finding my balance, I pick myself up and slam the door shut. Then I click the bolt lock in place and sink to the carpet with my back against the door. My chest heaves for air as my eyes water.

I knew it. It was only a matter of time before he showed up again. For a while there, I thought he had finally forgotten about me.

Not a chance.

He probably did that on purpose—gave me time so I'd think I was safe and lower my defenses before he came back to haunt me.

A fist bangs against my door three times. "You little bitch. My fuckin' nose is bleeding."

Good! I need to call the cops. This time, he didn't just verbally harass me. He *hit* me. The police have to do something about him. They just have to.

Now, where's my pho—I almost face-palm myself. My phone is in my purse. The one that Nathan chucked to the ground on the other side of this door.

With my heart still pounding and my tongue throbbing, I steal a look through the peephole. It's too dark to see anything, so I flip the light on. A dim yellow glow illuminates my front stoop.

Nathan's not there. Neither is my purse. *Did he take it?*

I don't dare twist the lock open to check. Not yet. Not until I know he's gone. Knowing him, he's probably hiding around the corner, waiting for me to come out.

"I asked you first!" Nathan barks.

Who's he yelling at? As if he can hear me, I tiptoe toward the living room window and peer out between a small opening in the blinds. Sure enough, there's that lame excuse for a human standing on the sidewalk with a phone pressed to his ear.

But not just any phone. *My* phone.

"Who are you? Why are you calling my girlfriend?"

Is he seriously still calling me that?

"She's not available right now. How 'bout you give me a message, and I'll relay it to her?"

Who's on the other line? No one ever calls me besides Javina and my grandparents, and Nathan's not brave enough to talk to any of them that way. My grandparents don't even know he's abusive. They think we broke up because he met someone else.

As he treads farther from my window, he says words I can't make out. All I can see is the side of his face when it twists from anger to something dark and dangerous.

With the bottom of his shirt, he wipes off the blood trickling down his nose. He's back to yelling again. "The fuck did you just say?" A short pause. "You listen here, douchebag. If you think you can come here and kick my ass—"

I don't stay to listen to the rest because it finally clicks who has called me. Within seconds, I'm out the door, because the last thing I want is for Trey to be involved in this.

"Nathan! Stop!" I run to him, reaching for my phone.

Big mistake.

He backhands my face with so much vigor that I plummet to the ground. Before I can even think about standing, he grabs me by my hair and jerks me up. I scream and punch at him, but it does nothing.

"Are you seein' this Trey guy?" Nathan holds my phone out to me. Trey's name appears on the screen, the call still in progress.

"Arella?"

"Let go of me!"

Nathan tightens his grip on my hair. "What did I say about seeing other men? I'll show you what happens when you disobey me."

16

TREY

I'm on my way home from dinner with Liz when I call Arella. I'm excited to ask her if she likes the flowers I sent—until a man answers her phone.

At first, I play it cool and ask who he is. Once he gets angry at me for no goddamn reason and calls Arella his girlfriend, things aren't cool anymore.

"Could I speak to Arella, please?" I try to keep my tone patient but fail. One hand is on the wheel while my other presses the phone to my ear.

"She's not available right now. How 'bout you give me a message, and I'll relay it to her?" Whoever this guy is, he must be drunk, because he's slurring his words. My best guess is that this is the abusive ex. He's the reason why Arella jolts whenever I touch her. The reason why she looks over her shoulder all the time. The reason why she's so hesitant to move forward.

I despise him. Any man who makes a woman that fearful doesn't deserve to breathe.

I'm about twenty minutes from Arella's apartment. Fifteen if I don't get stopped by any lights. Ten if I drive like a maniac. So I stomp my foot against the gas.

"Where is she?" I'm still flooring it as I weave around some cars that honk at me.

"She's busy," the asshole says.

"Doing what?"

"Suckin' my dick." The man laughs as if he's just told the funniest joke in history.

I'm done being nice. "Tell her I'll be there soon to save her from your pencil dick. I'll bet yours resembles an overly sharpened pencil that's more eraser than anything."

His laughing stops. "The fuck did you just say?"

"I said give Arella her phone back, or I'll come do it for you." A truck angrily honks at me as I swerve around it. I don't blame him. I'm going at least double the speed limit.

"You listen here, douchebag. If you think you can come here and kick my ass, then come. I'll show you what I'm fuckin' capable of."

"Nathan! Stop!" Arella shouts in the background. I didn't realize she was in the room with him.

My heart drops when I hear a smack and a scream. *Arella's* scream.

Shit. Did he just hit her?

"Are you seein' this Trey guy?" Nathan yells.

"Arella?" I say, as if it'll help.

"Let go of me!" she shrieks.

Dammit. I pissed him off, and now he's gonna take it out on her.

Cars honk at me left and right. I ignore them, focusing on the only goal I have: protecting Arella.

"What did I say about seeing other men? I'll show you what happens when you disobey me."

More shouting comes from Arella and her drunk ex. I put my phone on speaker, drop it into my lap, then grip the wheel with both hands. Only a few miles to go.

Every car on the road drives at a snail's pace as Arella screams. Every yelp she makes tightens a knot in my chest.

"Shout all you want, Ari. I want him to hear you."

Next comes some grunting and struggling, then something heavy topples to the floor. Nathan groans, yelling out swear words.

"Get out of my apartment!"

"You bitch! How dare you hit me again!"

Yes! She's fighting back!

The line goes dead. *No!*

My wheels squeal as I whip around a turn. Going over sixty down a thirty is bound to get me arrested, but I don't care.

Eventually, Arella's apartment complex comes into sight. My tires squeal again as I jerk my car into park behind her car. I don't even bother shutting my door as I bolt out.

I'm about to fly into Arella's apartment when my body slams against her locked door. *Fuck exposure.* I wave a hand at the doorknob. The bolt lock clicks open, and I run inside.

A lanky guy with an ugly buzz cut straddles Arella on her living room floor. They're between the couch and her tipped-over coffee table. She struggles with him as he attempts to rip her pants off. Thank fuck I got here when I did. The man's rage storms through my head, mixing with my already boiling anger.

I don't think as I seize the guy's shoulder, twist him to face me, then hurl a fist into his already bloody nose. It's nice to know that Arella did some damage before I arrived. I'm so fucking proud of her.

A dull ache explodes into the middle of my face, exactly where I punched her ex. It makes my eyes water. Feeling other people's pain never stopped me from fighting before, and it sure as hell isn't gonna stop me now. I expand my mind power outward, because sensing more people will help me sense less of the piece of shit in front of me.

I draw my elbow back and punch him again. With a yelp, Nathan topples backward, trips over the coffee table, then tumbles to the floor. Like a spring, he jumps back up and charges at me. I leap around the table, getting as far away from Arella as possible.

Nathan swings at my head, and I almost laugh. Based on the way he stands and throws his fist, this guy doesn't know what he's doing. He's no match for my many years of training in hand-to-hand combat. It's too easy for me to duck and strike him in the gut. He collapses to his knees with a moan.

I think he's done for.

And I think wrong.

I'll give him some credit because he stands up again and moves so fast, he knocks the wind out of me with a kick to my stomach. I hunch over with a groan. Unfiltered agony shatters through my face when he slams his fist against my upper cheek. For a lanky guy, he sure does punch hard.

When I regain my composure, I pound my fist straight into his ribs, making him fall to his knees again. Then I grab his head and smash it against my knee. His head whips backward with a *crunch!* as his back slams against the carpet. I hope I broke something. I think I did, by the way my nose feels like it's twisted to the side.

Again, I'll give the guy credit, because somehow, he still has enough strength to roll onto his hands and knees. Blood pours from his nose onto Arella's beige carpet as he coughs. I feel worse about dirtying up her carpet than I do about beating up this man I don't know.

Kneeling, he wipes his nose off on the bottom of his shirt. Then he looks up at Arella, who's standing a ways behind me. I almost kick him for thinking he has the right to look at her.

Nathan smirks. Laughs even.

What the hell is so funny?

"You're lucky this bastard showed up," Nathan says. "I was about to fuck you like the dirty little whore you are."

That's it. No more holding back. I yank him up by his shirt and punch him again. Agony tears through my jaw. I ignore it as I hit him again—harder.

Then again.

And again.

And—

"Stop!" Arella shouts from behind me.

My balled-up fist freezes barely a finger from the asshole's face. I don't dare take my eyes off him as I speak through gritted teeth. "You want me to stop?"

"Yes," Arella says firmly. "Let him go."

It takes everything in me to release Nathan's shirt. He thumps to the floor.

I still don't take my eyes off him, nor do I unclench my fist. "Arella, please tell me you have a good reason for stopping me from hurting the man who was hurting you."

Her voice goes soft. "He'll press charges if you keep going."

"And you're going to press charges against him for assaulting you!"

"I'd like to see you try," Nathan snickers as he stares up at the ceiling. His face is bright red, already swelling up in the areas I hit him the most.

I resist the urge to break his teeth in. "Babe, go call the cops."

In the corner of my eye, she snatches her phone off the floor. Nathan laughs as he finds enough strength to stand and hold the bottom of his shirt to his nose. Obviously, I haven't wounded him enough to keep him down. That can easily be changed though.

"Go ahead and call, Ari. When they get here, I'll explain that you and I were hooking up when your side toy walked in on us and attacked me."

"We're over!" Arella shouts, and it surprises me. I never pictured her as a shouter, especially not with such venom. "Why can't you get that through your head?"

Nathan continues as if she hasn't said a word. "I'll tell them that we have our moments here and there. I've been telling them that anyway, so they'll believe me. Everyone thinks you call me up weekly because you can't stay away. You know they'll listen to me with my dad there. Then I can press charges against this fuckwad."

The flames in my palms flicker. Heat forms between my fingertips. If I don't control myself, this entire apartment will go up in flames. If this guy knows what's good for him, he'll shut the fuck up.

I don't take my focus off his bloody face. "Call the cops, Arella."

In the corner of my eye, she sets her phone down. "No."

Finally, I look at her. "What?"

"He's right, Trey."

"Again—what?"

"I'm not going to risk him getting you in trouble."

"And I'm not going to let him get away with hurting you!"

Arella squares her shoulders. "You can, and you will. We're letting him go. We can talk once he leaves, then decide if we'll call the cops or not."

I shake my head. "Let's skip the talking part and call now."

"Trust me, Trey. Just let him go."

She's asking me to trust her—the one thing I've been trying to get her to do with me since we met. Victor's words echo in my head.

"To get, you need to give."

I'll trust that Arella has a good reason why she doesn't want to call the cops. But I still can't let Pencil Dick walk away freely.

With a grunt, I grab the shithead by his shirt and drag him down the hall.

"Let go!" He claws at my hand.

In Arella's bathroom, I shove him into the tub, where he can bleed some more without getting it all over the carpet. He stumbles backward, landing on his ass.

I point a stern finger at him. "Stay here, asshole. You open this door, and I'll cave your face in so hard, a bat will make you its home. Got it?"

"Fuck you!"

I can't control myself. My balled fist strikes him in the gut. Twice. "Got it?"

The troll-faced jerk off curls into himself, gasping for air as he nods.

"Good." Shutting the door behind me, I make my way back into the living room. Arella is in the same place I left her. "All right, babe. Let's talk."

She hooks a thumb toward the front door, raising her eyebrows with a wordless question.

I nod, then follow her out.

A yellowy moon hangs above us in the black sky as we face each other on the front lawn of her apartment complex. Arella hugs herself as if she's freezing. She's not. It's June in California.

I think about holding her, but I don't know if that would comfort her or make her tense, so I decide against it. Quietly, I wait for her to explain. To tell me why we aren't calling the cops. Why we're standing outside instead of in there, making sure her ex knows he's never allowed to breathe around her again. Instead, she just stares at the grass.

"Arella?" My voice is calm, even though I'm fuming. "You know, I don't care about him pressing charges against me. I want him behind bars and away from you."

"Me too," she says softly.

"Then why aren't we calling the police?"

"Nathan's dad is the LAPD deputy chief. They'll twist this into something it's not. They'll make *you* look like the bad guy."

I'm not sure how else to say it to make her understand how serious this situation is, so I tell it how it is. "Arella, he tried to *rape* you."

The way she doesn't flinch at the R-word tells me this isn't the first time he's forced himself on her. I'm gonna punch one of his teeth out for that.

"Do you have a record?" she asks.

Is that a trick question? I'm not sure what answer she wants, so I go with the truth. "Yeah . . ." When she doesn't respond, I feel the need to explain. "Two counts of disorderly conduct and another charge for attempting to run from the police. And maybe a parking ticket or two." *Or twelve . . .*

"I figured you had something."

"Look, I don't care about keeping my record clean. It's already dirty."

"It's not about that. It's that Nathan and his dad will dig up everything they have on you and turn it around to use to their advantage."

I only met Nathan a few minutes ago, and I've never met his dad, but they've both made it to the top of my shit list.

Arella continues, "With your record like that, they'll have no problem getting an attorney to make it sound like you attacked him first, which technically, you did. Think about your career, Trey. If this gets out, how will this affect your band?"

I didn't even think about how this would look for me. Social media would have a fit. So would Monique. And Liz. Honestly, Liz's opinion is the only one I care about.

"I'm willing to risk all that if it means you're safe." And I mean that with all my heart.

"I'm not."

With a heavy sigh, I accept that she's made up her mind. If this is what she wants, so be it. Just in case, though, I ask one more time. "Are you sure you don't wanna call the cops?"

A firm nod. "I'm sure."

"All righty, then. Stay here. I'ma go take care of Pencil Dick lying in your bathtub." My Empath power tells me that he hasn't moved from where I left him and he's angrier than he was before. He's about to be even angrier when he sees my fist again.

An instant smile appears on Arella's face. It eases all the tension in my gut. "Pencil Dick?"

"You got a better name for him?"

"Nope. Pencil Dick is perfect."

"Great. Don't come in 'til I say so, 'kay?"

Once she nods, I head back inside and shrug my jacket off. With balled fists, I march toward the bathroom.

17

ARELLA

I sit on the curb and pick at my nails for a while before my door finally opens.

Trey has Nathan in his grasp. My ex's face is swollen red. On his bare chest, written in big black letters, are the words I ASSAULT WOMEN.

That should be a tattoo.

"Hey, angel," Trey says tenderly. "Thanks for waiting. Come on in."

After I step inside, Trey shoves Nathan out the door. Dramatically, my ex collapses to the ground. Trey hadn't pushed him *that* hard. The same message on his chest is written on his back. That's not coming off easily.

When Nathan doesn't get back up, I ask Trey, "Is he alive?"

"He's just puttin' on a show." Trey scoffs. "I only hit him one more time, and only 'cause he wouldn't sit still."

"Not true," Nathan says from the ground. "You hit me twice."

"Okay, fine. When I finished my artwork, he swung at me, calling me every nasty name in the book. So I might have punched him once more."

I don't feel sorry for Nathan. None of the things Trey did to him tonight will ever compare to the many bruises I endured. This doesn't make up for all the days I missed work because I was too weak to move, or the times I cried all night because I was scared I wouldn't wake up in the morning.

Nathan pushes himself up and wipes the blood off his mouth with the back of his hand. "Where's my shirt?"

"Fuck off," Trey says.

"I'm not leavin' without my—"

With a cheesy smile and a wave goodbye, Trey slams the door and locks it. I wait a second and am pleasantly surprised when I don't hear any pounding.

A moment later, I catch a good view of Nathan stumbling past my living room window and around the corner. He must have parked his car on the street where I wouldn't see it. I shudder with the thought of what he planned to do if Trey hadn't shown up. Would I have been able to fight him off? *I was never able to before.*

"Sorry for taking so long," Trey says. "It took me a while to find a Sharpie around here. He won't ever bother you again."

"How are you so sure?"

"Because I threatened to slice off his micropenis if he does."

No words come to me. I'm still trying to process everything. It all happened so fast. My heart is still racing from when Nathan climbed on top of me and held my arms down.

A trickle of blood dripping down Trey's hand makes me gasp. "Oh no!"

He flexes his bloody knuckles, then shrugs. "I think that's mostly his."

"I'll go get the first aid kit." I rush away to rummage under the bathroom sink for my big red box.

When I return to the living room, Trey is in the kitchen, washing off. His right hand looks drastically less gory as he dries off on a paper towel. He's got some gashes, but they aren't too deep. Still, another man got hurt because of me. This is exactly what I was trying to avoid.

The first and only guy I've been on a date with since leaving Nathan got chased off by drunk Nathan with a knife. My date ran away and tripped on the curb, spraining his ankle. Then he hobbled to his car and drove away. I haven't heard from that guy since, no matter how many apology voicemails I've left.

Trey takes the first aid kit from my grasp. "I've got this, babe. Why don't you go sit down while I wrap up my hand?"

"I'd like to do it for you, if that's okay." I need to feel helpful.

He thinks for a second, then sticks his hand out to me. "Have at it."

After applying the ointment, I wrap some gauze around his knuckles. There's still blood oozing from the small gashes. Just looking at it makes me squirmy. There's a difference between seeing it on TV and seeing it in real life.

Trey doesn't seem to mind the blood. If anything, the expression on his face tells me he's proud of himself.

"I could get used to you being my doctor," he says, smiling at me all handsomely.

I don't respond. I feel terrible that I have to be doing this at all.

With his other hand, he tilts my chin up. "Don't look so sad, baby. It's not your fault."

I force a smile. He can tell me all night that it's not my fault, but I know it is. If I had gotten rid of Nathan years ago, when all the red flags started waving, I wouldn't still be dealing with him today. I allowed things to get too far. Now, I have to deal with the aftermath. I just wish the people around me didn't have to deal with it too.

"Now I understand why you freeze up whenever I touch you."

"It's not just you," I say faintly. "It's *all* men."

Trey's fingertips graze my jawline. I wince when he lightly brushes against the spot I fell on when Nathan grabbed my ankle.

Trey's mouth turns into a grimace. "He used to do this a lot, didn't he? Mark you up."

I nod, unable to respond any other way.

Leaning in to me, he gently says, "I will never hurt you the way he did. You have the power to stop me from touching you if you ever don't want it, okay? Just say *no* or *stop*, and I will."

I gape into his eyes, trying to make sense of his confusing words. What does he mean that I can just say *no* and he'll actually stop? *Is that even a thing?*

I finish wrapping his hand, then pack up the first aid kit.

"Thank you, Doctor Rance," Trey says, offering me a honeyed smile.

I smile back, and it's not forced this time. "You're welcome. I'll bill you next week."

"Can I pay you in the form of a dinner date?"

I don't miss a beat. "It's against the official doctor code for me to date my patients."

"Hmm. That leaves us two options, then. Either you quit your job or I will find a new doctor."

I'm not sure what comes over me. One second, I'm chuckling, and the next, I'm throwing myself into his chest. Trey doesn't hesitate to circle his muscular arms around me as I bury my face into his shirt. The longer he holds me, the more warmth washes through me.

"Thank you," I breathe as a tear drips down my cheek. It's more from relief than anything. "You have no idea how long I've been trying to cut him out of my life."

My throat closes up as I remember the threats Nathan used to hiss at me for saying I wanted out. He used to tell me he'd kill me before I could get away.

Trey draws back to look at me. "He's out of your life now, baby. And I'll be right here to make sure it stays that way."

Because I don't have the words to express my immense gratitude, I just smile at him. He smiles back, then pulls me closer against his hard body and holds me. Nothing else.

He doesn't talk.

He doesn't move.

He just holds me.

For the first time in years, I feel safe in a man's arms.

18

TREY

I've got two options.

One: Don't show up.

Two: Play it off like it's no big deal.

I'd get more shit for ditching, so I text Liz and ask her to come to rehearsal early with her makeup bag. Then I suck it up and drive to the Soul House.

The second I enter the back door, Liz takes one look at me and plants a firm hand on her hip. "You know we have a show tonight, right? Like, in front of people?"

"Did you bring your makeup bag?"

She groans, glaring at me. "Sit your ass down so I can fix your face before the rest of the band comes, or more importantly, Monique."

On the sectional, Liz slips off her gloves, then unrolls a bag with a collection of items I have no idea what to do with.

Liz remains quiet while she applies skin-colored goop to my purple cheek.

When I can't take the silent treatment anymore, I say, "Please don't be mad."

"I'm not mad, T. I'm disappointed."

"Goddammit, Liz. I'd rather you be mad." Even though she is three years younger than me, Liz is obviously the more mature one in this relationship.

"I'm disappointed because you were going so strong. It's been, what, two years since you got into a fight?"

"I had a justified reason this time." The reasons I fought before weren't justified in Liz's eyes. I, for damn sure, think they were justified.

She stops applying the makeup to lean back and scowl at me. "Were any drugs or alcohol involved with this one?"

"Nope. I was completely sober last night," I say proudly, like I should receive a gold medal for not shooting poison up my bloodstream anymore. "I was at dinner with you right beforehand."

"Did you try sleeping to speed up the healing process?"

"No." Zordi bodies naturally heal faster than Ordinary bodies, and even faster when we sleep. If I had slept last night, I probably would have woken up with a clear face. Unfortunately, my adrenaline was still pumping after I left Arella's apartment, so I couldn't sleep at all. It wasn't my night to, anyway.

Liz resumes covering up my bruise. "It doesn't look like you drank any Healing Water either."

"I didn't." I used my last bottle of Healing Water on Arella the night she was drugged—something I can't tell Liz. Using Zordi products on an Ordi is just another thing she'll scold me for.

"Don't you find it ironic that you're the son of the inventors of healing products but you had none when you needed it?"

"Sure." I wince when she presses a makeup sponge a little too hard against my cheek. I think she's doing it on purpose.

Liz yawns, covering her mouth with a hand. "So, what was this fight about?"

"Arella's ex-boyfriend attacked her."

With a gasp, Liz stops what she's doing. "Is she okay?"

"Yeah. She's a really strong person. Probably as strong as you."

My compliment works to ease Liz, because she's gentler with me as she pats some powdery stuff onto my face. "I've been thinking about you and Ari. Or Arella, as you call her."

I'm not sure why, but my heart rate kicks up a notch. "Okay?"

"I've been thinking about how perfect she is for you, except that she's an Ordi, of course."

Of all the things Liz could have said, I wouldn't have guessed it'd be that. "Perfect for me? How so?"

She leans back to look at me. "You really haven't figured it out?"

My tone goes dry. "Enlighten me, Liz. I'm an Empath, not a Mind Reader."

"Sometimes your gift makes it hard for you to know which of your emotions are real and which aren't. For some strange reason, Ari's invulnerable to our gifts. Whatever feelings you might have for her aren't muddled by what you'd be sensing from her if you could. Ari could be the first *real* relationship you ever have."

"I have a real relationship with you, don't I?"

Liz huffs. "You know what I mean. Like a real *romantic* relationship. Not what we have."

I swallow thickly. The idea of having a *real* relationship, the kind of *real* Liz is referring to, makes my stomach churn. Especially if it's with Arella. Not only is she an Ordinary; she's just a mission. Once I get the information from her that I need, we'll go our separate ways. I'll move on to helping ZIRDA figure out how we can replicate her immunity and use it against the Royals. She'll move on to having a real relationship with someone else. Someone who's capable of having real relationships. Someone who actually deserves her.

Liz finishes with my face, then tosses everything back into her makeup bag. "Don't you think that *my* feelings for you play a big part in what our relationship has become? Don't you think that because I care about you as much as I do that it makes you reciprocate it for me?"

I pause to think about that. I can't say it does, and I can't say it doesn't. I adore Liz—more than I adore anyone else in this world. Actually, she's the only person I adore at all. I would do anything for her. Do I only feel this way about her because she feels it for me? Would Liz and I be this close if I could separate my feelings from everyone else's? I'd like to think the answer is yes, only because that means I have control over my decisions. I hate thinking that I'm living my life based on how other people's feelings affect me.

Wait . . . What if that's all my life has ever been? The last time I slept with Jess was because she projected her desires onto me. Would I have done it otherwise? Maybe this is why I jumped on the idea of starting a band with Kevin. When we met, he got excited about the possibility, so I did too. Maybe this is how I got roped into becoming Elliott's mentor. Sharon brought up the idea of me mentoring a Deaf kid no one else wanted. She felt determined to include him, so I did too.

Have any of my life decisions been my own?

19

ARELLA

Trey's bruises sure healed quickly. When he comes to pick me up, the shiner on his face is gone. The gashes on his knuckles have disappeared, too. His injuries were worse than mine, yet my face is *still* purple. It's only been three days. *How did he heal so fast?*

"Did you drink some magic potion or something?" I joke as he ushers me into his kitchen with a hand on the small of my back. I barely flinched when he placed his hand there, and I'm pretty proud of myself for it.

"Magic potion?" He drops his hand from my back, and I kind of wish he hadn't.

"Yeah, to heal your knuckles."

He flexes his fingers, staring at the places where the gashes used to be. "They weren't that bad."

Maybe, but his hand looks brand-new . . .

With a waggle of his eyebrows, he says, "So, am I allowed to classify tonight as a date?"

"Is that what you want?" I smile back and set my purse on his black countertop.

"I only want to call this a date if *you* want to call this a date."

I nod a little too eagerly. "I'd like that."

"Great!" He flashes me one of the biggest grins I've ever seen on a man. "For our date, do you wanna teach me how to bake?"

I perk up. "Really?"

We spend some time picking out a recipe online. After we decide on something easy, I teach him how to correctly measure out flour.

"When baking," I say as I dump the spooned white fluff into a mixing bowl, "you usually want to put the dry ingredients into the bowl first. Then you add the wet ingredients after you make a well."

"Make a what?" He's cute when he doesn't have any idea what he's doing.

"Here, I'll show you." After I measure out a few more dry ingredients into the bowl, I show him how to make a well.

He scoffs. "That's it? It's just a hole in the middle with a fancy name."

I laugh as I pour in the wet ingredients, and then I gesture for him to mix it all together. "You don't bake very often, do you?"

He takes the bowl. "I've never baked anything at all."

"Um . . ." I gesture at all the baking supplies scattered across his countertop. "You sure have a lot of baking tools for someone who never bakes."

"I just bought all this shit last night."

"Why?"

"Because I read on Google that baking can be a fun date activity. You love baking, so I figured you'd like this."

I laugh, slapping my palm against the counter. "Wait! You *Googled* date ideas?"

"Yeah . . ." He looks away sheepishly. "I've never done this before. I'm clueless, and Professor Google has never let me down."

"You've never done what before?"

"Date."

That can't be true. "How many girlfriends have you had?"

"Eh. Let's not talk about that." Trey passes me the bowl, then picks up his phone and pretends to read the snickerdoodle recipe.

"That many, huh?" The dough isn't completely incorporated yet, so I resume mixing it.

"No. I just didn't invite you over to talk about other women."

"Sorry, I was just curious."

Trey steps around to the other side of the island and takes a seat on one of the barstools. "How 'bout this? For every personal question you ask me, I get to ask you one."

"Deal. I'll start. How many girlfriends have you had?"

"Just one."

That's it? One seems low for a guy with a face like his. Although, to him, women he's slept with and women he's called his girlfriend are probably two different things.

"How long did that relationship last?"

"Nuh-uh." He wiggles a finger. "You're jumping ahead of the game here, Miss Rance. I believe it's my turn." He thinks while I line the baking sheet with some parchment paper. "Did you take your mom's last name or your dad's?"

"They got married before I was born, so technically, I have both their last names." Between my palms, I roll some dough into an inch-wide ball, dip it into the cinnamon sugar, then place it onto the parchment. "So how long did your relationship last?"

Trey digs his fingers into the dough and repeats my process. "Shit, I dunno. I think Jess and I made it, like, three months."

"Do you still talk to her?"

"Not really. And now, I get two questions. First: You mentioned that your parents worked together. Do you know which company they worked for?"

"No . . ." I don't understand why Trey is so interested in my family. I suppose since he doesn't have a family of his own, it's reasonable to be curious about mine, but he asks about my family a lot.

"Second question: Have you ever Googled your parents?"

"No . . ." I narrow my eyes. "Should I?"

"Nah." He rolls out another dough ball. "I was just wondering 'cause I Googled mine recently."

"Did you find anything interesting?"

"Not really, and now it's your turn."

"Okay." I've been thinking about this topic a lot, so the question comes easily. "Your bad-boy habits. All the fighting, drugs, and girls, and stuff . . . has it stopped?"

"That's a hard question. If you wanna know when I stopped doing drugs, it was about two years ago. The fighting stopped around then, I think. As for the girls, I'll still occasionally enjoy a good time here and there. I mean, if the opportunity presents itself."

It makes me happy to know he's been clean for two years. I'm not happy to know he still sleeps around, although I'm not surprised. "What changed you?"

We roll out a few more snickerdoodle balls before Trey finally looks at me. "Two things. First: music. The first time I picked up a guitar, I was hooked. Whenever I play, my mind feels less . . . chaotic. When I moved out of my hometown, I left my guitar behind, and it all went downhill from there.

"A few years later, I came to LA and met Kevin in a guitar store. We got to talking, and he told me about his dream to play in a band. I said I wanted to help him live his dream. So we started our band, picking up Marcus, Emmy, and Liz along the way. Once everything took off for us, I decided it was what I wanted to focus on, so I dropped the bad habits."

I finish rolling out the last doughball, then turn on the sink to wash my hands. Trey comes up beside me, running his palms under the faucet too.

"What was the second thing that changed you?"

"Liz." He doesn't offer any further explanation, and it makes the jealous green monster awaken inside me. Liz seems to be important to him. I know they're close. I just wish I knew exactly how close.

Are they the type of friends who come with benefits? Judging from the way the Internet talks about them, yes. Liz kept glaring at him for talking to me and not her at his house party, so I wouldn't be surprised if they have a past.

Trey dries his hands off on a towel, then leans his back against the counter. "Liz taught me that shit happens and you've got two choices. You can either let it bring you down or build you up. While the things she and I went through are completely different, they are equally as shitty, yet there I was, getting high and drunk and fucking faceless women, while Liz moved halfway across the country by herself to pursue her dreams in dance. If Liz can go through her battles and still make something of herself, why can't I?"

I stick the baking sheet into the preheated oven, then set the oven timer. "It sounds like she made a huge impact on you."

"Yeah, but don't tell her that. She'll get all mushy, and I hate it."

With a chuckle, I toss all the dirty baking supplies into the sink. "*Sure* you do. I bet on the inside, you secretly like it."

"I plead the fifth." His tiny smile confirms that I'm right. Then his smile dips into a light scowl as he gestures at his black countertops sprinkled in flour. "Damn, babe. You really know how to make a mess 'round here."

I run the dough-covered rubber spatula under the water. "It's baking. Messes are necessary."

"Maybe this is why I don't bake."

I don't even think about it. My hand simply digs itself into the bag of flour and plops it onto his countertop.

Trey's mouth pops open. "Oh, hell no!" In one swift motion, his hand flies into the flour, and he throws a handful onto my chest.

I gasp, jumping back as white dust flutters to my feet. "Hey!"

I reach for the flour again, but he snatches it first. With a sly look, he dashes around the other side of the island.

I chase him, giggling. "Give that back!"

"Not a chance. If you wanna make a mess in my kitchen, then baby, we will make a mess."

He flings another handful of flour across the island at me. I put my hands up to block, but I'm too late. Flour lands all over my hair and dress. More of it flurries onto the floor.

I cross my arms over my chest with a pout. "I'm covered in it."

It only takes him a second to cave. Instantly, he's back at my side, setting the flour bag down. "I'm sorry, babe. I'll help you get it out." Gently, he shakes some of the white powder off my dress.

Too easy. My hand goes straight into the bag, and flour flies into his face. "Ha! Gotcha!"

A slow grin spreads across his lips as his tongue runs along the inside of his mouth. "Damn. I shoulda seen that comin'."

As he wipes the flour off his face, I laugh hysterically. "I can't believe you fell for that."

Trey goes motionless, staring at me. I see it in his eyes—the moment his willpower snaps. Before I can get a word out, he shoves the hair from my face, and then his lips devour mine.

20

TREY

She tenses at first.

I don't stop. I don't want to stop. If someone tried to pry me away from her, I'd blast them with a fireball.

My lips massage hers open until she melts into me. Her body relaxes in my arms as her hands circle the back of my neck. I draw her in by her waist, needing every part of her body to be touching mine. At the sound of her breathless moan, my cock hardens.

I kiss her as if I'm starving—because I am—for her.

I've been waiting to do this for what feels like months. I told myself I wouldn't kiss her until she told me she was ready. After seeing her so playful and laughing all adorably, I couldn't stop myself.

She tastes amazing—like honeyed watermelon on a warm summer day. My tongue explores her mouth as desire pumps inside my jeans. I desperately want to be inside her. Gently, I shove her back against the island, clawing at her dress. I want it gone. Anywhere but on her.

I grip the back of her thighs, lifting her onto the counter. We separate for barely a second before she pulls my face back to hers. I pant as I take her in. All of her. The feel of her tongue between my lips. The sweet way she smells. How she's making me lose my mind with each little moan she lets out. I draw back a little so I can take a breath, but a forceful tug of my shirt yanks me right back to her.

Fuuuck . . . Screw breathing. Who needs to do that, anyway? I consume her, taking all I can get. My hands travel everywhere on her, up and down her back and from her head to her thighs. Her fingers splay over my pecs, sending tingles down to my toes. When she pulls on my hair, my dick almost explodes.

I thought I was the one calling the shots.

Nope.

It's her. She's destroying me, and I want her to keep doing it.

I'm not sure how long it is before she finally releases me. With our foreheads pressed together, we pant—hard. My heart beats so fast, I'm pretty certain it's about to give out. My lips feel cold without her. I need to kiss her again.

So I do.

I ease her lips back open with mine, and she lets me. After pulling her hair to one side, I leave her lips to kiss her neck. She arches her head back, giving me full access. I savor her delicious skin, nipping at the tender spot behind her ear as I breathe in her inebriating scent. Sweet lavender, springtime and . . . Arella. Her scent is familiar to me now. If I could only smell her for the rest of my life, I wouldn't mind.

"Trey," she moans in a whisper, and damn if it doesn't make me weak in the knees. She could tell me to jump off a bridge, and I'd do it. No questions asked.

Finally, I lean back and breathe. If we continue this any longer, I might die from the lack of oxygen.

In a whisper, I say, "You wanna take a shower?"

"No," she answers sharply.

I laugh, realizing how that sounded. "I didn't mean together. We're covered in flour. I figured you'd want to wash off, but you don't have to if you don't want to."

Her cheeks turn rosy. "What will I wear?"

"My clothes. They'll be big on you, but you'll look great." I've never let anyone wear my clothes before. It feels too intimate. But the idea of Arella in my shirt makes me more eager to get her into the shower.

"We should finish the cookies first."

Right on cue, the timer beeps.

With some oven mitts on, I pull the baking sheet out and place it onto my new cooling rack. Then I offer Arella my hand. She takes it and allows me to help her hop off the counter. I like that she didn't hesitate. She took my hand as if we hold hands all the time, except this is the first time. *And it feels so . . . normal.*

I don't let go of her until we reach my bedroom. There, I point at my drawers. "Dig through these 'til you find something that fits. Bathroom is through there."

After returning to the kitchen, I wave my hands back and forth, making damp towels slide up and down the countertops. The towels erase the evidence of our flour fight. I've still got a semi under my belt, and it's super uncomfortable. *Saggy grandmas, foot fungus, math problems . . .*

"Trey?" Arella calls out.

Shit. My hands fall to my sides, and the towels freeze where they are. I glance up, but she's not there. I breathe out a sigh of relief. I never know where she is.

I peek my head around the corner. "Yeah?"

Her voice comes from inside my bedroom. "Could you show me how to turn your shower on? I can't figure it out."

After instructing her on how to work the nozzles, I go back to cleaning the kitchen. Once that's done, I grab some clean clothes, then run upstairs to my other shower.

By the time I'm out, Arella's still showering. It's no big deal, because I can start on dinner without her. This time, she's going to sit around while *I* do all the cooking.

At the fridge, I rummage around for some steaks and a do-it-yourself salad kit. When I close the fridge door, Arella's standing right there.

I jump back. This time, I don't drop anything. "Goddammit. You gotta quit doin' that."

"You didn't hear me coming?"

"No." I've always relied on my Empath powers to tell me when someone's near. Guess I'll have to start training my ears. It doesn't help that Arella's so fucking quiet.

I step back to get a better look at her. Long wet strands of hair drip water down my white T-shirt that dwarfs her. No makeup. Flushed cheeks. *And those lips!* I want to kiss her again.

Finally, my eyes make it down to her legs, and I laugh. "Are those my boxers?"

"Yeah. It was the only thing that would stay up on my waist. Do you mind?"

I'm about to say "of course not," then I stop. Instead, I grin like a mischievous little puppy. "Actually, I do mind. You should take my boxers off right now and just lounge in your underwear."

"I might have . . . if I was wearing any."

My dick turns rock solid again. "Say *whaaa*? You're not wearing any underwear?"

"Well, I was, but they got wet."

"How did they get wet?"

She bites her lip, smirking at me. Finally, I get it.

"Fuck." I throw the steaks and salad onto the counter, then stomp down the hall.

Arella giggles, and it only makes my cock twitch more. "Where are you going?"

"You're driving me crazy, babe," I say over my shoulder. "I can't stand to be in the same room with you right now."

Any longer and I'll lose what little control I have, put her over my shoulder, and strip her naked in my bedroom. She's not ready for that . . . yet.

"Okay," Arella calls after me. "I'll start seasoning the steaks."

HALF AN HOUR LATER

"Would you like some wine?" I ask, gesturing toward the three bottles on the shelf behind me. In addition to all the baking supplies, I also purchased these last night, just for her. I hope I got something she'll like.

"No, thank you," she says, and I have to keep from frowning. "Water's fine."

I'm curious to see how or if alcohol affects her immunity, but I can't do that if she doesn't accept the damn wine. If a little alcohol can break down her immunity walls and let me sense her, that might be the breakthrough I need to figure this out. *Maybe next time.*

I'm about to sit in front of my warm plate when I sense someone approaching my house. Their depressing energy weighs me down like bricks tied to my arms. Heavy emotions like that always come at me stronger. The more the energy seeps into me, the more I've got a hunch as to who it is. The curtains in the living room are drawn shut, so I can't peek outside to confirm, but nobody ever comes over unannounced with emotions like that—except one.

Jess is the last person I want to see right now, especially with Arella here. When the doorbell rings, I make no effort to stand.

"Aren't you going to get that?" Arella asks.

"Eh. It's probably just UPS."

The doorbell rings again.

Arella glances that way. "Maybe they need a signature."

Groaning, I get up. *At least she didn't barge in this time.*

When I open the door, my heart plummets. Liz has puffy eyes, red cheeks, and messy hair. My irritation from five seconds ago instantly melts into concern.

Liz runs her face into my chest, sniffling. I wrap a protective arm around her and slam the door shut. She quietly sobs as I hold her. Usually, crying makes me cringe, but this is Liz.

She's the one who can turn any storm into sunshine. If she's crying, something is seriously wrong.

My tone comes out rough. "What happened?"

She lifts her head and wipes away some tears with her gloved fingertips. She's careful, as if not to ruin her makeup, but it's too late for that.

"I—" Liz catches a glimpse of Arella at the dinner table. "Oh, sorry. I didn't mean to impose on—"

"Stop." I grab her face with both hands, forcing her to look at me. "What happened?"

She breathes in heavily, not answering. Maybe this isn't a conversation we should have in front of an Ordinary. Taking her hand, I drag her toward my music room.

"I'll be right back, babe," I call over my shoulder. No reply comes.

Five guitars, a drum set, and various other instruments are scattered around the perimeter of my music room. Gently, I click the door shut. With a flick of my wrist, the curtains glide open to let some sun in. Liz loves the sunshine. Maybe it'll help lift her mood.

I sit on my long keyboard bench, then pat the empty space next to me. Liz plants herself at my side as she slips out of her satin gloves and drops them onto the carpet. Then she dabs her face off with the bottom of her shirt. Tenderly, I pull her against me, and her head falls onto my shoulder.

"Did I interrupt something?" Liz's voice comes out as broken as her energy feels.

"No." I could be in the middle of getting heart surgery, and Liz would have my full permission to interrupt. Sensing her pain makes me want to hit someone. Preferably the mouth-breathing toe-licker who upset her. "What happened?"

"Rodrigo broke up with me." Liz sniffles as her sadness rains over my head.

"Why?" I try to keep my voice steady. I need to control my emotions so she doesn't cry any more.

"He can't get over that I'm a Hydro and he's a Pyro. He's got issues with being with someone who's got a dominant power over his."

Having a best friend with the dominant element over mine has never bothered me. Liz has always been the stronger one in more ways than that anyway, and I admire that about her. Why can't Rodrigo see it that way?

I'm at a loss as to what to say because I suck at pep talks. Instead, I close my eyes and think of my happy place: my little cabin out in the Colorado mountains. I imagine the flowy trees and the scenic flowers. The peace and quiet. The calm of being alone in my own head since there isn't anyone else around for miles. Being there soothes me.

As soon as my emotions are controlled, I project them into Liz.

She immediately straightens up, breathing easier. "Whatever you're thinking about, it's working."

Growing up, I used to get beat for using my mind power to make Victor feel calmer and happier—two things he never felt after Aunt Jodi left. I thought I was being helpful. Turns out, Victor didn't want to be helped. Being able to use my gift on Liz, knowing that she *wants* me to, is freeing.

"You want me to kick his ass?" I'm mostly asking to get her to smile, but if she says yes, I'll leave right now.

"No." She doesn't smile.

"How 'bout I go over there and show him how dominant *my* Pyro power can be?"

"No." She still gazes somberly at the floor.

"How 'bout we sit outside his place and I'll wiggle my fingers around until all his furniture is upside down?" I motion toward a small table in the corner and theatrically circle my wrist. My songwriting notebook on top falls to the carpet as the table rotates and then drops back down with its legs sticking up.

Finally, Liz laughs and I get a sense of relief. "That'd be funny, but no."

I pull Liz up with me as I stand. Naturally, our hands intertwine. I'm the only person in the world she can hold hands with—bare.

After Liz saw my worst memory for the first time, any time our hands touched, she saw it again: my mother getting shocked with a lightning ball, my father's bloody face, the explosion, all of it. This went on until last November when I was at her place for Thanksgiving. As we both reached for the plates, our hands touched and she saw nothing. It's been that way ever since, and neither of us knows how.

Liz doesn't question it. She embraces it, holding my hand as often as possible. Like when we watch movies together or when we're just sitting around talking. I let her. Not just for her benefit, but for mine too.

I won't admit it out loud, but Liz makes me feel like I'm worth something. Like I'm more than just a body taking up space, breathing someone else's air, using up other people's precious resources. Sometimes, she even makes me feel like I have a purpose: to be the person who'll always be there for her because nobody else is.

I just wish that was enough for me. Enough for me to feel like I actually belong in this world. For me to feel like my life isn't pointless. To make me stop wishing I had died in that explosion too.

Liz tells me that surviving it wasn't luck. She says that I survived because I was *meant* to, but I can't have survived just to be her support person. There has to be something else, something more that I'm meant to do, and I think this mission is it. This is what the universe kept me around for.

"How 'bout we go out with the band after recording tomorrow?" I say, pulling Liz in for a tight hug. "You'll forget all about what's-his-nuts by the end of the night."

"I'd love that." Liz squeezes me back so hard, the air leaves my lungs. "Thanks, T. I knew coming here would help me feel better."

She's starting to get sappy, so I need to counteract it. "My offer to kick his ass still stands."

Liz leans back, rolling her eyes at me. "Your fists can't solve every problem, T. In fact, they never solve *any* problems."

That's not true. My fists solved Arella's Pencil Dick problem in one night. "What kind of best friend would I be if I didn't at least offer?"

"Speaking of being best friends, as your best friend, I gotta talk to you about Ari again."

I don't miss a beat. "Uhh, my dinner's gettin' cold." I'm about to open the door when Liz pulls me back.

"Just hear me out, okay?"

With a slump of my shoulders, I remain where I am. "Fine. What?"

"Remember how I said that I think Ari's perfect for you?"

"Yeah?"

"Well, it doesn't change that she's an Ordinary. If you get caught doing things with her you shouldn't be, it'll affect more than just you. You're no A-lister, but people still recognize you on the street. I'm not gonna report you, but what if someone else does? If the Enforcers take you away, what happens to the band?"

A chill creeps up my spine at the mention of the Enforcers. Keepers are the ones who make Zordi laws. Enforcers are the ones who, well . . . enforce them. Together, they make up the

Superiors, Supes for short, otherwise known as the zovernment, otherwise known as pieces of shit.

Enforcers are known to be tough and unrelenting. Zordi parents like to use Enforcers as a threat to get their kids to behave. Now Liz is using them to try to get me to behave.

Nonchalantly, I wave a hand through the air. "Don't worry 'bout it."

"I can't not worry. I just read an article on the z-net yesterday about some guy who got arrested for kissing an Ordinary behind a mall. He's probably gonna get at least ten years, and that's just for *kissing* an Ordinary. Imagine how much time you'd get for having an ongoing sexual relationship with one. We can't hold our band rehearsals from inside a z-prison."

"And we won't," I say reassuringly. "I'm being careful."

"If you say so. Either way, I'm worried about Ari too."

"Why?"

"Because when you break things off with her, it'll break her heart. She's really sweet, T. I don't like the idea of you hurting her."

"We're just friends hangin' out," I say with a shrug. "It's not serious."

Liz arches an eyebrow. "You hate cooking, and you cooked dinner for her. When have you ever done that for a girl?"

"I've done that for you."

"I don't count."

I fake a gasp. "Liz! Is this how you tell me you've got a wiener?"

She backhands my chest so hard, it stings. "You're not taking this seriously!"

I rub the spot she hit. "Ow! You and Marcus should have an arm-wrestling match. I think you'd win."

"Trey Andrew Grant!" She scowls at me so hard, I'm afraid her face will stay like that.

I'm still rubbing my chest because, damn, that shit hurt. "All right. I get it. Be careful with the Ordinary. Can we be done now?"

"Fine," Liz says with a roll of her eyes.

Together, we head to the dining table to find Arella almost finished with her steak. I feel like a dick for leaving her to eat by herself.

"Sorry, babe," I say. "Thanks for waiting."

"That's okay." Arella shivers, and her teeth clack together.

"I'll be right back." I go down the hall to kick up the temp, then set it to stay in the mid-seventies from now on. It won't affect me, but it'll make Arella feel more comfortable whenever she's here.

I hear Liz talking to Arella, but I can't make out the words as I disappear into my bedroom.

When I return to the table, Liz is sitting in the chair next to Arella's. I interrupt Arella's explanation about why she's wearing my boxers to hand her my black hoodie.

"Thanks." She slips into it immediately, looking so adorable, I could kiss her. I'll wait until Liz leaves though.

"You hungry, Liz?" I ask.

She shakes her head. "Don't fuss about me. I'll grab something on the way home. I just wanted to say hi to Ari before I left, and tell her why I was upset earlier, and apologize for crashing your night."

"You don't have to stop anywhere. Here, you can have my steak. I'll reheat it for you." I pick up my plate and head toward the kitchen.

"What are *you* gonna eat?"

"We've got more food."

Liz's chair slides back as she stands. "No, really. I'll just—"

Turning on my heel, I glare at her. "Sit your ass down." I point at her, then at the empty chair. She just got dumped. There's no way in hell I'm letting her go home to eat by herself.

Liz raises her hands in surrender. "Okay. I'll stay."

A minute later, I return with a warm plate and clean silverware. I set it all in front of Liz with a fresh napkin, then leave to find myself something to eat.

In the freezer, there's some frozen mac and cheese and a frozen pizza. The mac and cheese won't take as long, so I choose that. Once it's heated, I join the girls with it.

"Damn you, T," Liz says, dropping her fork. "Now I feel bad. Are you sure you don't want this?"

"I'm sure. Now, you're gonna eat that piece of cow, and you're gonna like it." I take a bite of my highly processed pitiful excuse for nutrition, pretending to love it. "So, what were you ladies talking about?"

"Ari asked what I was doing this weekend. I told her that we're having an appreciation party on July Fourth for the crew and their families." Liz turns her attention to Arella. "As I was saying, Trey rents out the park, and the rest of the band brings all the food and drinks. This is our third year hosting an appreciation party, and we've decided to make it an annual thing."

I butt in. "We?"

Liz rolls her eyes. "Okay, *I* decided to make it an annual thing. Everyone loves it except you."

"And you know why," I mutter under my breath.

Liz shrugs nonchalantly as she shovels some mashed potatoes into her mouth. "Come up with a good excuse this year."

Arella's face crumples together. "Excuse for what?"

Liz and I glance at each other, then at Arella. I know Liz is gonna hate this, but I do it anyway because I just realized that my excuse this year is sitting right here.

"Hey, babe, you wanna come to the party with me?" If Arella's there, she can be my reason to leave early that people can't judge me for.

After Arella happily agrees to attend the party, we finish our meals, and then Liz heads home with a lighter spirit.

For the rest of the evening, Arella and I lounge on my couch and talk. Honestly, we kiss more than we talk, but I'm not complaining. I try asking more questions about her family until she asks me, "Why do you want to know so much about them?"

I give her a long-winded explanation about wanting to know everything about her because I really like her, then I go back to kissing her and stop with the questions.

Eventually, when my lips are numb, I lie back and motion for her to lie with me. Without hesitation, she does, nuzzling her head into the crook of my shoulder. She places a palm over my abs while I drape my arm around her back, resting it over her hip. Our bodies fit together as if they were made to.

It takes me a few minutes before I realize that I'm cuddling. *I*, of all people, am *cuddling*. And enjoying it! It feels so natural that it didn't occur to me that I was even doing it. Maybe this cuddling thing I've been avoiding isn't so bad after all.

Ultimately, our time together ends. Since her clothes haven't finished washing yet, I tell Arella she can wear my shirt and boxers home. It'll also be a good excuse to see her again.

When we arrive at her apartment, I walk her to the door like a fucking gentleman. Once our lips meet again, the gentleman in me is lost. Roughly, I shove her back against her door and pin her arms above her head. I kiss her until she's moaned my name at least three times.

"I can't get enough of you," I say. Based on the way she keeps tugging on my shirt to pull me closer, she hasn't gotten enough of me, either.

"I really should go now," Arella pants as I pepper kisses down her neck.

"Five more seconds," I beg. I count to five in my head about twenty times before I finally gather enough willpower to let her go. "When can I see you again?"

"I get off at four tomorrow?" She looks up at me all hopeful. It's cute.

"We've got a recording session from three to seven; then we're probably going out for dinner afterward."

"How about the next day?"

I sigh deeply. "We have a video shoot all day. I might be done by seven or eight. Would you wanna hang out for a bit after that?"

"Our schedules don't match up very well, do they?"

"Nope." I lean in to kiss her, and she opens her mouth for me willingly. "I'll text you, okay? We'll figure somethin' out."

With a dazed smile, she says, "Mm-kay."

I take a step backward toward my car. "Sleep well, angel." That name fits her perfectly. It embodies all of her innocence and beauty in one word.

"You too, Trey," she says with a wave. "Goodbye."

My body freezes in mid-step. I swallow hard as my words come out sharply. "Please don't say that."

Arella is just getting her door open when she turns to me. "Say what?"

"Goodbye. I'm not fond of that word." *An understatement.*

"Oh. Why's that?"

Because my mother said it to me the last time I ever saw her. I try to sound as nonchalant as possible, acting like all the chaos from that night isn't suddenly eating me alive. "There's just . . . a kind of finality to it, ya know? It makes me feel like I'll never see you again. I was taught that goodbye means forever. *Bye* is just for now."

Arella must see the distress on my face, because she comes to me, plants her hands on either side of my face, and brings me down to meet her lips. Our kiss is short but still satisfying. "Bye for now, then."

As she releases me, the pain instantly melts away.

21

TREY

I wake up to my phone buzzing on my nightstand. The name on the screen makes me groan.

When I tell Victor why I haven't seen Arella for five days, the truth isn't acceptable. Apparently, I need to drop everything in my life, including my "dead-end career," and dedicate myself to this mission until it's finished. He's delusional if he thinks I'm gonna do that. Finishing my parents' mission is important, but my band is important too. I can't just drop them.

"Tell me you have something of value." Victor growls into my ear. "Something that can give us a direction."

"Not yet," I lie.

"Wow, you really are useless." *Click.*

Victor can call me whatever he wants, but without a clear answer as to why or how Arella's parents died the same night mine did, I'm not telling him about it. The last thing I need is another reason for him to hound me, when besides that, all I know is what Victor told me when he assigned me this mission.

"Before your parents were killed," he said, "they were working on discovering how some rare Ordinaries could be immune to Zordi powers. They pretended to be part of the government and told the research subjects they were needed for a top-secret medical study.

"Every week, the subjects would come to Shadow Ridge to be analyzed, and ZIRDA paid them well for their time—until one day, the Royals found out about the Immunes project and tried to take it over.

"They stormed my house, demanding that I take them to ZIRDA California's hideout. And when I refused, they sliced my throat and left me for dead."

Since missions aren't to be spoken about between agents, Victor doesn't know anything else beyond that. At least, that's what he said. I wouldn't be surprised if he's keeping vital information from me.

Either way, I've come up with my own theory. My explanation for Arella and her parents being near Shadow Ridge that night is that three-year-old Arella—I mean *Hannah*—was one of my parents' research subjects. Maybe my parents were about to meet with them to take them to the base when Arella's parents got attacked by the Royals. I'd bet anything the Royals killed the Calders so they could take Hannah for themselves. Then somehow, my parents were able to save Hannah and get her somewhere safe.

I have a feeling that the same Royals who sliced Victor's throat are the ones who came crashing into my home, probably looking for Hannah. That would also explain how my mom's lip and my dad's face got slashed so badly—a sight I have yet to forget.

While this is a possible theory, I'm missing significant pieces to the puzzle. Like, how did the Royals find out about the Immunes project? Were there moles back then like the ones Victor discovered recently? Is that how they knew Victor was a ZIRDA agent and where he lived? Is that how they knew where my parents lived, too?

Also, how did my parents know where and when the Royals were attacking Arella's parents? And if Arella was one of my parents' research subjects, does Victor know that the little girl back then is the same one he found and assigned me to? If so, why wouldn't he tell me that? Most importantly, why would my parents leave the house that night feeling anxious if they thought they were simply meeting with Arella's parents for another research session?

There's too much here that doesn't add up, and sadly, the person this entire thing revolves around seems to know the least. Based on the way she talks about it, Arella thinks her parents' car accident was exactly that—a car accident. She has no reason to think otherwise.

Do her grandparents know the truth? If my theory is correct, the ZIRDA agent who delivered Arella to her grandparents probably said nothing more than "Her parents were found in a car wreck at the bottom of a cliff, but this little girl survived." If that's the case, why is Hannah's name now Arella? And why would her grandparents move her around California annually if it wasn't to make her harder to find?

Her grandparents have to know something, which is why the next phase of my mission is to get Arella to introduce me to them. Maybe the more I know about them, the more answers I'll have.

It's just past noon when my phone buzzes again. I haven't eaten or done much beyond lie on my couch, trying to decipher my thoughts. My phone flashes with a picture of Jess. I almost let it go to voicemail but don't because I don't want her to take my silence as an invitation to show up.

"Happy Fourth!" Jess says. "You wanna get lunch?"

"Can't. Busy."

She snorts. "Doin' what?"

"Workin' on stuff." I'm playing with a little stress ball, throwing it into the air and catching it with my telekinesis before it lands on my face. The goal is to stop the ball as close to my nose as possible without the ball actually touching me. *Real important stuff.*

"Take a break."

"Can't. I've got a lot of work to do." I throw the ball up and stop it with my Kinetic power about a fingertip from my nose. *Eh. I can do better.*

"You really can't take off, like, a half hour? Not even for me?"

I know what that means, and I'm not interested. I'm not dating Arella for real, but having another woman over just to fuck still feels weird. Besides, I'm in the middle of trying to figure out a gift to get for Arella.

Earlier, Victor suggested that, to speed things up, I should shower Arella with gifts. The only problem is that I don't think she's easily impressed by material things. If I'm gonna get her something, which I fully intend to, it has to be something meaningful to her. I just don't know what that would be.

Jess isn't used to hearing *no* from me. After I keep denying her, she calls me nasty names and hangs up. I think about texting her that I'm sorry, but it'd be a lie. She's not my priority right now. Arella is.

The rest of the afternoon drags on. By the time I've thrown the stress ball into the air another hundred times, I still don't know what Arella's perfect gift is. I think about asking Liz for advice, then realize it's a dumb idea.

If Arella was a Zordi, Liz would probably have the perfect suggestion. Because Arella's an Ordinary, the only advice Liz'll give me is that I need to quit before Arella gets hurt. Little does Liz know, I don't plan on hurting this woman. When the time comes, I'll get *her* to break up with *me*. Problem solved.

I'm still thinking about a gift idea as I pull up to Arella's apartment. When she steps out of her home, I hop out of my car to greet her properly. Before she can say anything, I scoop her up, press her back against my car, and plant a heavy kiss over her lips. It's a full minute before I release her.

"Your kisses are getting addicting," I pant.

She's got a dazed expression as she responds with a breathy "Yours are too."

"You didn't stiffen up when I lifted you."

Her brows crumple together as she thinks. A second later, she leans back, and her eyes light up. "Wow. I didn't."

Gently, I pull her in for a hug. "You're so strong; you know that?"

Besides Liz, Arella is the strongest woman I know. For three years, a weak man stole that strength from her. It took a lot of courage for her to walk away, and not only did she do that, but she was brave enough to fight back.

On the night I kicked her ex's ass, she told me she used to always fight back until doing so only made him hit her harder. Eventually, she learned that taking it resulted in less bruises. I'm glad that she's finally done with his shit. Now she can live her life the way she wants. If only I could find the strength to fight my battles the way she has.

Beautiful waves of red and orange paint the sky as Arella and I arrive at the park. Vehicles of all colors and sizes are scattered around the lot. We find a parking spot toward the back; then I cut the engine.

"Babe . . ." I say, placing a hand over her knee. She doesn't flinch, and it makes my insides throw confetti into the air. "I'd like to leave before the fireworks start. Is that okay?"

"What? Aren't fireworks, like, the main part of a July Fourth party?"

I swallow hard and turn toward my window. "I guess."

"You don't like fireworks?"

It's not that I don't like them. I think they *look* cool. It's the bomb-like noises they make that I don't like.

"How 'bout I come back to pick you up after the fireworks?" I say to the steering wheel. "That way, you can still see 'em."

Arella's tender hand cups my face. She trails light fingertips along my stubble before turning me to look at her. I go willingly. Her calming eyes and tender smile send a wave of comfort through me. It's as if she has her own body power of easing my anxiety and it works by touching my face.

"I'll be happy to leave with you, Trey."

I place my hand over hers, pressing it harder against my cheek. I'm grateful that she didn't ask for an explanation, because I'm not ready to give her one.

With Arella's arm looped through mine, we join the party. Looming trees surround the park. A sand volleyball court already has a team on each side, with a ball in the air. Kids scream at the top of their lungs as they race around the playground. Most of the people are gathered at the pavilion where all the food is. More are down by the small pond, singing around a fire with Kevin on a guitar and Marcus on a box drum. The upbeat energy emitting from everyone lifts my spirits.

Arella and I head toward the pavilion where a couple of teenage boys are going through the buffet line. They pile food onto their plates as if they haven't eaten in days.

I grab a beer from a cooler and hold it out to Arella. "Want one?"

"No, thanks."

"How 'bout a hard lemonade?"

Between her fingers, she twists the ends of her hair. "I'll just have a soda."

I'm about to tell her that she should let loose and have fun when it hits me that I've never seen her drink alcohol. Not once during those four weeks I studied her. Not during these last few weeks since we've met, either.

I place the beer back into the cooler, then take her hand and give it a squeeze. "You don't drink, do you?"

She doesn't pull her hand away. She doesn't squeeze my hand back either. "Not really."

"Sorry, babe. I didn't know." Which is stupid, because I'm supposed to know everything about this woman. How could I have missed this? What other details have I missed?

"That's okay. I never told you."

"Can I ask why you don't drink?" *Maybe this has something to do with her immunity . . .*

She keeps her eyes anywhere but on me as she, aggressively now, rubs more hair between her fingers. The distress on her face tells me all I need to know.

Instinctively, I pull her close and whisper into her ear, "I won't let him hurt you ever again."

She melts into me, circling her arms around my back. "He was always worse when he was drunk. Everything about it reminds me of him. Seeing it, tasting it, smelling it. Everything."

I know all about avoiding things that bring up bad memories. Alcohol to her is like fireworks to me.

After shutting the beer cooler, I open the one labeled NONALCOHOLIC, all while keeping Arella's fingers intertwined with mine. She plucks a Sprite off the top, and I grab one for myself too.

"Trey, you don't have to drink soda just because I am."

"Didn't you just say that the smell of alcohol makes you think of Pencil Dick?"

She nods slightly.

"Are you gonna make out with me later if I smell like beer?"

"Probably not, but—"

"Hey, if my choices are to taste you or some stupid beer, I'd rather have you."

I don't see it coming. She throws herself at me, kissing me like she's never kissed me before. Urgent, passionate, and needy. The Sprite slips from my hands. It falls, pops, and sprays everywhere, but I don't care. I need my hands free to take in as much of this woman as possible. Even with her breasts pressed up against my chest and my hands all over her back, she still isn't close enough.

Something hard hits my back, then thumps to the ground and rolls away. I don't let it stop me, because tonight is proof that I'm making progress. Arella initiated this kiss, and that's a huge step for her. I'm not planning to release her until she pulls back first.

My powers tell me that two people are approaching us from behind—probably the same people who just threw something at me. When the two stop at my heels, one of them clears their throat.

Only then does Arella draw back, and it takes a lot of willpower for me to let her. When I open my eyes, I find that hers have that dazed look again. Her flushed cheeks and plump lips are already begging for me to come back. *I will, baby. Later.*

Without looking, I already know who's behind me. No other two people would ever throw shit at me. I flip around to greet Liz and Emmy with a scowl.

"There are children here," Liz says, returning my scowl. Her dirty look has nothing to do with the kids. After her warning about getting caught with an Ordinary and how it could affect the band, it's probably not the smartest idea to kiss one in public. The Enforcers won't accept "This is all part of my top-secret ZIRDA mission" as a reason not to send me to z-prison. I'm fine though. Everyone in our crew is an Ordinary.

Emmy laughs, picking up a partly eaten apple off the ground. "Even my apple didn't stop him."

"Do you mind if we steal Ari from you, T?"

"Of course not." I need to show my face around the party before I dip out early, anyway. Having Arella at my side will force me to introduce her to everyone, and I'm pretty sure she would hate that. "Just make sure you feed her before you convert her to the dark side."

"We won't convert her into anything," Emmy says. "We're just gonna tell her all of your dirty little secrets."

I play along with her joke. With two fingers, I point at my eyes, then at my friends. "I'm watching you. If I catch my girl running outta here screaming, I'll—"

"Your girl?" Liz says, arching her eyebrows.

Arella gapes up at me with the same wide-eyed expression.

"What?" I feign innocence.

"Ari's *your girl* now?" Liz asks.

I nod confidently. "Yes, she is."

"I am?" Arella says, jerking her head back. Not the reaction I was hoping for.

Emmy chuckles, shoving me in the shoulder. "Most men *ask* the lady before they start telling people. Ya know, in case she declines."

I gaze into Arella's eyes. "What do you say, babe? You wanna be my girlfriend?"

Her cheeks fade to a light pink. "Um, I . . . I'll think about it."

My mouth drops. In my head, I shout some F-words to the sky. I thought for sure that if I asked her in front of Liz, she'd not only say yes but it'd help her feel better about Liz being my best friend. *Guess I was wrong.*

Arella's lips curve upward into a smile that she was holding back. "It's way too easy to mess with you."

I slap a hand over my chest, letting out a breath of relief. "Don't do that to me."

The women laugh, and it eases my tension.

"So, is that a yes?" I ask, because I need verbal confirmation.

Arella pretends to think for a second before grinning up at me. "Yeah. I'd love to be *your girl*."

Disappointment slams into my gut from Liz's direction. In the corner of my eye, she huffs out a frustrated breath and shakes her head slightly. Maybe one day, I'll be able to explain to her why I'm doing this. Why I'm risking going to z-prison. Why, one day, hopefully soon, I'll be able to stop the Royals from hurting more people like me.

22

TREY

I wanted to make things "official" with Arella because I thought it'd be a good reason for her to introduce me to her grandparents.

I was wrong.

It's been over a week, and every time I mention the possibility of us paying her family a visit, she says things like "It's too early for that" or "They're traveling right now."

I call bullshit. I think there's a family secret she's afraid I'll uncover, and it'll be the exact answers I'm looking for—answers that Victor won't stop hounding me about. He calls every other day to check in—or should I say to give me shit for being "worthless." He thinks I'm going too slow.

Sadly, he's right. I'm not utilizing my time well enough. If I keep going days between seeing Arella, it'll take me forever to finish this. That's why, for the last week and a half, I've made it a point to see her every single day, even if it's only for an hour. Either I drop by for breakfast in the morning before she heads to work or she meets up with me at the Soul House whenever she gets off.

So far, it's been working. I can feel her trust in me growing with each lingering hug, each prolonged kiss, and each time she lets me touch her somewhere new. I haven't seen her naked yet, and although I crave to, I don't push her. The last thing I want is to ruin all the progress I've made just because I wanna get my dick wet.

Yeah, this is the slowest I've ever gone with a woman. And yeah, the blue balls every night is torture. But in the end, when she trusts me enough to tell me everything about herself, it'll be worth it.

I've got two things with me when I arrive at Arella's apartment on Sunday evening: a backpack full of goodies and an extra helmet. I'm in the middle of admiring the beautiful sunset when she steps out, looking like a fucking snack. It takes everything in me not to drag her back inside and lick every inch of her delicious skin.

Instead, I take her in by the waist and spin her around before I plant my mouth over hers. Once I've had my fill of her lips, I hand her the extra helmet. *Her* helmet. The one I purchased today in her size, just for this. I help her strap it on, and she looks so adorable in it that I kiss her again.

When I let her go, I hand her the backpack.

She slides her arms through the straps. "It's heavy. What's in here?"

"Stuff."

"For what?"

I mount my bike, then gesture for her to hop on. "Stargazing."

"Oh!" A bright smile spreads across her face. "Where?"

"Uh, I haven't figured that part out yet. I thought we'd ride away from the city until we find a place that's secluded enough."

She perks up. "I know a place."

"You do?"

"Yeah, it's about an hour and a half away though."

"Perfect. Let's go."

The sun is almost gone by the time Arella tells me to park my bike on the side of a gravel road. When she said this place was secluded, she wasn't lying. I haven't seen another car in a while.

In my head, the low hum of other people's emotions is gone. A place like this is hard to find in California. I'm impressed.

I cut my Harley's engine, and the air goes still. Crickets chirp around us.

"I usually park my car right here," Arella says as she dismounts the motorcycle.

"Where is *here*, exactly?" I lift my helmet off, then a light breeze blows through my hair.

"You'll see."

We hang our helmets on the handlebars, then I steal the backpack from Arella so she doesn't have to carry it. From the side pocket, I pluck out a flashlight—another thing I bought today because I'd probably scare Arella off if I whipped out a fireball.

With my Ordinary torch in one hand and my girl in the other, I let her lead me down the ditch, then back up through some trees.

We hike through the woods for a while. It's a beautiful night. The air feels warm against my skin, and I can already see some stars above. I couldn't have asked for anything better.

Eventually, Arella leads me to a trail . . . sort of. It's more like a path of dirt, barely wide enough for one person. Our hands let go, and I offer her the flashlight, then follow her up the steep hill.

I duck under a tree branch. "This seems like a place where you'd take someone to kill 'em."

"Relax. I've only ever killed two people here. The third one got away."

A dry stick cracks beneath my feet as I stop to gape at her.

Giggling, she turns around and grabs my arm. "I'm kidding. Now, come on! We're almost there."

A few minutes later, we're out of the woods and the ground levels out into a grassy meadow. In the middle of it, slightly to the left, is a lone oak tree. The breeze is a little stronger up here, and it smells of ripe nature.

I follow Arella to the oak, then we stop under all of its long branches. Dark green leaves stretch out in all directions like an umbrella protecting us from whatever may fall from the darkening sky.

Arella opens her arms out wide and does a spin. "Welcome to my *thinking spot*."

"I like it." My backpack drops to the grass with a thump. "How did you find this place?"

"I found it by accident. Sometimes when Nathan—"

"Pencil Dick."

She laughs and rolls her eyes. "Yes, him. Sometimes when we got into a fight, I'd go for a drive. One night, I ended up here. I liked the atmosphere and the quiet. Later, I started coming back whenever our fights got really bad, because you know . . . he couldn't find me here."

With a hand splayed over the small of her back, I pull her toward me until her entire body is flush against mine. Tenderly, I place a little kiss on her forehead. I don't know why. I just feel the need to comfort her.

"He hasn't been coming around or contacting you at all, has he?"

She shakes her head.

"You'd tell me if he does, right?"

"You'd be the first to know."

"Good." I have a strong feeling that Nathan's out of her life now. That night, after Arella convinced me not to call the cops, I needed insurance that he'd stay away. Taking pictures of him with the words I ASSAULT WOMEN written across his body was my way of gaining that insurance. I made it clear that if he ever as much as looked at her again, I would post the pictures everywhere for the world to see.

From the backpack, I yank out a violet blanket. I spread it out under the tree, then bring out the meats, cheeses, crackers, and water bottles. Then I sit and pat the empty space next to me.

Arella smiles down at me. "You're adorable, you know that?"

"Hmm. Can't say I've ever been called that before."

"Well, it's true." She sits and helps me unwrap our snacks. "You come up with the most romantic things for us to do."

"I wish I could take the credit, but this was another idea I stole from Professor Google."

"What did you type in?"

"Um." I clear my throat as I tell her the truth. "Romantic things to do with a pretty girl."

"Really?" She laughs, and it sends a spark through my chest. I like hearing her laugh and seeing it too. Since I can't sense her happiness, seeing it is important.

"Yeah, really." I run my palm across the blanket. "This is for you, by the way. I bought it for you 'cause you're always cold at my house. You can leave it there to keep you warm."

Her bottom lip puckers out into a pout. "But I like wearing your hoodie."

"Oh! That reminds me." I dig toward the bottom of the backpack to find my black hoodie. The one Arella has been wearing every time she comes over. The one she looks irresistible in. "This is for you too."

Her eyes widen as she accepts it. "To keep?"

"Yep. I figured since you like it so much, you should just wear it all the time."

She lunges at me. Her kiss is quick—too quick. When she draws back, my hands instinctively reach for her. She comes willingly, and I get to kiss her for a little longer. I could probably kiss her all night.

Sometimes, it's hard for me to let her go. A few nights ago, when she came to my place and we were up talking past two in the morning, I almost asked her to stay the night. The only reason I didn't was because I had a feeling she wasn't ready for that step yet, and I didn't want to make her feel obligated to stay.

"Thank you, Trey," she says when I finally release her lips. "I love them both. Your hoodie more, but I love the blanket too."

It took me a while to decide on a good gift for her. I had already bought her this blanket when I realized that the perfect gift had been in my house the whole time. My goal was to give Arella something that would be meaningful to her. Based on her reaction, I'm gonna say I nailed it.

To Victor's knowledge, I bought Arella an expensive bracelet. He thinks I gave it to her last week and that she loved it so much, she cried. I'm glad I went with my hoodie instead, because I doubt a stupid bracelet would have elicited such a happy reaction from her.

We talk easily while we munch on our cheese and crackers. With passion, Arella tells me about her dream bakery. Everything from the paint color on the walls to what kinds of sugary treats she wants to have on display. It doesn't take long for me to get lost in the sound of her voice. It's so soft and sweet. She could be talking about a bloody massacre, and it would still sound like a lullaby to me.

Eventually, we finish snacking and find other things to do with our mouths. Mine starts at her lips before it maneuvers down her neck and behind her ear. She lets out breathy moans as I travel down her chest.

Panting against her cleavage, I ask, "Can I take your shirt off?"

I expect her to say *no* like she has every time I ask. Instead, she surprises me by nodding and lifting her arms up. My heart thrashes against my ribs as I drag her little shirt over her head and toss it behind me.

I barely have time to admire her lacy white bra before she climbs on top of me, straddling my lap. I feel like her prisoner. She's captured me, and I can't escape. I don't even want to.

My hands grip her plump ass as I jerk her body closer to me. With a grunt, I press my stiff cock against her inner thigh. She lets out a sexy moan that makes my arms go weak.

Our breaths are heavy as I pepper kisses along her collarbone. When she arches her head back, I take the hint. I nip, suck, and bite at every inch of her neck until I'm ready to go back to her lips.

When our mouths meet again, it feels like coming home. This is where my lips are supposed to be. Kissing her forehead is great, her neck is like heaven, and I love kissing her everywhere else, but *this* . . . This right here. This is where it's at.

With a finger, I pull the strap of her bra down her shoulder. When she doesn't stop me, I leave home to trail kisses down her chest. I suck a little bit of her cleavage into my mouth and wait for her to tell me *no*. Hope sparks inside me when she doesn't.

"Babe?" I say like a plea.

"Mm?" she moans.

"Stop me."

She shakes her head as she whispers, "I don't want to."

At that, my cock hardens so much, it's painful. Within a flash, I've got her breast out and her nipple in my mouth. She gasps as she arches her head back and grips my hair. While I suck on one nipple, I roll the other between my fingertips. It drives her insane. I know not because I sense it but because she writhes on top of me.

Before tonight, I thought the reason I always have great sex is because I can feel the woman's pleasure on top of my own. It never occurred to me that someday, I'd be going to second base with a woman I can't sense at all. If someone had asked me if I thought it'd be as good, I would have said *no*.

And I would have been wrong.

All I've done is touch and kiss Arella, and now I'm sucking on her breasts for the first time, and it already feels better than sex with any woman I've ever been with.

My fingertips graze against the button of her jeans for only a second before she grabs my wrist. I take that as a sign that I've reached her limit. Instead of tearing her pants off the way I want to, I fist her hair, yank her head back, and return to sucking on her neck.

It takes a lot of willpower, but eventually, I find Arella's shirt in the grass and help her put it back on. With a hand behind my head, I lie back on the blanket and motion for her to join me. Naturally, she rests her head over my shoulder, and I pull her close until there isn't a sliver of space between us.

For a long time, neither of us says anything. I appreciate the way we can be with each other and not have to fill the silence. Usually, quietness irks me because I hate being alone with my thoughts, but whenever I'm with Arella, my thoughts aren't that hard to handle. They aren't dark or depressing or what Liz calls self-degrading. When I'm with Arella, my thoughts are about her, which are light and cheerful.

I listen to the sounds of her easy breaths as I stare up at the black sky, where a few stars are shining. *Would my parents have liked Arella?* I bet they would have, only because there's nothing about her not to like. She's kind, beautiful, and she's got a great sense of humor. Her immunity is just the cherry on top of all that.

Suddenly, it hits me how special this moment is. For the first time ever, I'm alone in my head—and someone is right here! To be truly alone, I typically have to travel to my secluded cabin in Colorado. When Elliott died, I hid there for a month.

When I finally came back, I explained to a furious Liz that I had disappeared because I'd needed to clear my head. Getting everyone else out of it is the only way to do that. Yeah, it's lonely, but until now, I've never had another choice. Never did I imagine that it'd be possible to have a clear head minus the loneliness. Arella has made that possible. Here she is, cuddled in my arms, and the only emotions I feel are my own. It's amazing!

Now I'm more in awe of her than ever. She's so fucking special, and she doesn't even know it. Leaning down, I plant a hard kiss against her temple, but it's not nearly enough to fully express how much I enjoy being here with her. I wish I could tell her with words, but I don't know how. Not that I could explain it to her anyway. I'd have to tell her that I have an ability she doesn't know exists.

I kiss her temple again, harder this time, because I want to show her how grateful I am for her. I hope she can feel my gratitude through my lips.

"What're you thinking about?" she asks softly as she continues caressing little figure eights over my abs.

It takes me a second to gather myself with all the overwhelming fluttery thoughts I'm having. "You. I think my parents would have liked you."

"You think so?"

"Yeah. They probably would have loved to hang out here with us, too. When I was little, my parents took me hiking a lot. Our favorite spot was near this small town a few hours south of LA. We'd hike to this big rock, and they'd bring snacks like I brought for you tonight. The three of us would lay out on a blanket under the stars, just talking."

"That sounds wonderful. My grandparents never took me hiking. They like to do more indoor things."

"Like meet your new boyfriend? That's indoors."

She chuckles, and I'm not fond of how it comes out with a hint of annoyance. With a deep sigh, she pushes herself up and sits with her legs in a pretzel.

"What?" I say and follow suit. My body feels a little cold where hers used to be.

"Nothing. I just feel like you're obsessed with meeting my grandparents. That's the third time you've brought it up this week."

"You're counting?"

She ignores my question. "What's up with you wanting to meet them so bad?"

"What's up with you *not* wanting me to meet them?"

"Like I said before, I think it's too early for that."

"Did Nathan get to meet them?"

She nods.

"How long did he have to wait?"

"About six months."

Six months? I don't have time for that.

"And," Arella continues, "I didn't introduce him to my grandparents until I felt like he and I had really connected, like on a level deeper than just two people dating. I don't think you and I are there yet."

"Okay . . . How can we get there?" *And fast* . . . I'm running low on time, and Victor's running out of patience—that is, if he had any at all.

She lets out a small laugh and shakes her head. "That's not how it works, Trey. A deep relationship takes time."

"How will I know when we've reached that point?"

"I think you'll just know."

Playfully, I narrow my eyes at her. "You're giving me too much credit, babe. I'm clueless about this stuff, remember? You're gonna have to give me more details. Like . . . what will it look like?"

"What does a deep relationship look like?" She shrugs and thinks. "I suppose the biggest factor is that we'll be in love."

"In love?" Just saying that word out loud makes my throat dry. *Me? In love?* Is that possible? Probably, but not with an Ordinary. I could pretend though. "What does being in love look like?"

"You've never been in love?"

"Don't think so." I have an idea of what it looks like from hanging around Marcus and Emmy. They're always touchy-feely with each other, and they do everything together. Whenever one walks into the room, I sense the other's happiness spike upward. I assume that means they're in love.

"Love looks different between everyone, but I think the one thing that's constant is what my grammy always tells me. She says that when you love someone, you put their happiness before your own."

I think about that for a moment, racking my brain for anyone I've ever felt that way about. Sadly, I can't think of anyone. Even sadder, no one has ever felt that way for me. At least, not romantically.

I know my parents loved me—before they were murdered.

Victor *used to* love me. Maybe he still does . . . in his own sick, twisted way. If he ever verbalized it now, I'd be certain he's been replaced by a Shifter or a Mind Swapper.

I think I loved Elliott. Why else would I have taken his death so hard? I would have done anything to protect that child or to have saved him from the cancer.

Now that I think about it, I think I love Liz. I one hundred percent would put her happiness before mine, but I don't think the way I feel about her is the same kind of love Arella's talking about.

"How do you know the difference between regular love and romantic love? Like, I think I love Liz, but I don't wanna make out with her. At the same time, I'd do anything to make that woman happy."

Arella purses her lips together in thought. "My grandpa says that he knew he loved my grandma when, one day, he looked at her and couldn't picture the rest of his life without her."

"Hmm. If that's the case, then I might love Liz romantically. I can't imagine my life without her. Who will be there to yell at me for making dumb decisions?"

Arella bursts into a light chuckle. "Maybe if you stop making dumb decisions, she won't have to yell at you."

"That's impossible. I'm a man. It's what we do." I'm glad that Arella didn't take my loving Liz romantically comment seriously. I only said it to be funny.

"You don't have to be *romantically* in love with someone to want them around for the rest of your life. You can feel that way about Liz and still love her as a friend."

"Good, 'cause that's exactly how I feel about her."

Between a few fingers, Arella plucks a blade of grass and plays with it. Without looking up at me, she asks, "Do you ever think that Liz is secretly in love with you? Like, as more than a friend?"

Confidently, I shake my head. "Never."

"How are you so sure?"

"Trust me, baby. I, of all people, am sure." I can sense the way Liz feels about me, and it's never anything close to the way Marcus and Emmy feel about each other. Unfortunately, I can't tell Arella that.

"Then how can you say that you don't know what a deep relationship looks like, when it's exactly what you have with Liz?"

Good point. "I guess I didn't think about my relationship with Liz being that deep until now."

"How did you guys build such a strong connection?"

I know exactly how. Liz brings it up all the time. She even knows the exact date and calls it our friendiversary. It was the day our hands first touched. The day we shared about our pasts.

Would sharing about my past with Arella get her to share everything about herself with me? Possibly, and I'm willing to do that . . . *I think.* Maybe I don't have to share every little detail, but I could tell her that my parents didn't actually die in a house fire.

An idea pops into my head, and suddenly, I'm ready to leave.

I toss our stuff back into my backpack. "Let's go, babe. I need to show you something."

23

TREY

I t's well past midnight when we finally arrive at my place. On my bed, Arella's next to me wearing my hoodie—her hoodie now. Her new blanket is draped over her lap, keeping her legs warm. Between us, I have my most valuable possession: a shoebox-size wooden box.

"Please tell me there aren't any human body parts in there," Arella says.

I laugh a little. How does she know exactly what to say to ease the tension in my gut?

I've never shown this box to anyone before. My heart thrashes because I'm about to now. "Why would you think I'd keep body parts in a box?"

"I watch a lot of true crime shows with Javina. A big wooden box with a lock? Total grounds for a collection of eyeballs."

I make an *ick* face. "Gross, babe. No, I don't have any eyeballs in here."

"Wonderful. In that case, please proceed with showing me what's in this mysterious box."

I suck in a deep breath before sticking a little metal key into the lock. With a twist, it opens, and I flip the lid. The first thing I pull out is a small framed picture.

Arella takes the scorched item as I hand it to her. "Are these your parents?"

"Yep, and that's me when I was four." I point at the little blonde boy with the shit-eating grin on his face. "This was the only picture I was able to recover from the fire. It was saved by this heavy-duty frame."

"You were adorable! I mean, you still are, just with darker hair. And you look exactly like your father."

"Everyone said that." The next thing I pull out is a small chain with a circle pendant hanging from it. On the pendant are three birthstones. "This was my mom's necklace."

"Do these colors represent you and your parents?"

"Yep." Next, I pick up a worn baseball. "I found this in the backyard the morning after they died. My dad and I went to baseball games pretty often. Whenever we played catch in the yard, he'd tell me that I'd play for the Dodgers someday."

"Do you think about them a lot?"

"Occasionally." *An understatement.* I think about my parents all the time.

Whenever I see people at the grocery store with their kids, I think about how my parents

125

used to let me pick out what we got for dinner. The three of us would cook it all up, even if it didn't go together.

I usually think of my mom whenever I see flowers. She used to always have a vase of freshly cut ones sitting on the dining table.

Yesterday, I saw a kid with his dad in a big blue truck, jamming out to music while they played the air drums. My dad and I did that plenty. He's part of the reason why I love music so much.

My heart aches the more I think about my parents. This is usually when I distract myself with sex or music. Before Liz encouraged me to be sober, this was also when I'd get high. Thanks to her, now, I just live through the pain.

From the box, Arella grabs a small wad of cash paperclipped together. "What's up with this?"

I take it from her and slide the paperclip off. A ten, two fives, and four ones. "Twenty-four dollars. Back then, this used to be a lot to me."

"I thought you said your parents left you everything they had."

"They did, but my uncle didn't share that information with me until I turned eighteen. At first, I was ecstatic that my parents left me with money. Then, after reading through the paperwork, I learned that I could have been using it the whole time. My uncle purposely hid it from me."

Arella's face crumples. "Why?"

"Because he's a dick. When I first moved in with him, all I had were the things in this box and the clothes on my back. He provided me with two shirts, two pairs of pants, some underwear, and that was it.

"I went to school rotating through those same three outfits. Eventually, the other kids noticed, and that's when the fights started. I begged my uncle over and over to buy me more clothes, but he never did.

"Ultimately, I did what I could to make my own money. When I wasn't in school, I was with him at work. He ran a big business with lots of employees. I did small jobs for them around the office, like making coffee or cleaning their shoes. I'd earn a few quarters here and there. Depending on the job, sometimes they'd pay me a whole dollar. Eventually, I saved up enough cash to make a trip to a store.

"I was so excited to buy myself a new shirt, pants, and socks. I still remember how the cashier looked at me funny, and I don't blame her. I was an eight-year-old boy shopping by himself. I told her that my uncle was just down the road at a different store. Eventually, he noticed that I was wearing new clothes. When I told him I bought them myself, he didn't believe me. I was beaten that night for lying."

Arella's eyes water, and she uses the sleeve of her hoodie to wipe the tear away. I debate on ending the story there but feel the need to finish it.

"I didn't tell my uncle that his employees had been paying me to do stuff for them. I knew he wouldn't like it and would make me stop. Somehow, he found out and threatened to fire anyone who continued to pay me. Not only that, but he took what cash I had at the time and forced me to burn it."

The memory of that night flashes across my mind. Victor slapped my face and yelled at me until I did what he demanded. A fireball appeared in my palm, and I threw it at all my hard-earned cash. I cried as I watched it burn until every last flame had flickered out. I think it was only fifty-some dollars, but at the time, that could have been new shoes.

Arella places a hand over her chest as another tear rolls down her face. Usually, crying makes me uncomfortable. With Arella, all I want is to comfort her, so I take her hand in mine and kiss her knuckles.

She wipes at her damp face with her other hand, then squeezes mine in a way that offers me comfort back. "I'm so sorry that happened to you."

"Don't sweat it, babe. It turned out okay. In the end, I actually made more money. It'd been going on for so long that his employees were kinda dependent on me to do things for them. They got sneakier about paying me. Some of them even tipped me more because they heard about what my uncle did and felt bad."

"Weren't they afraid of getting fired?"

"Nah. If he was gonna fire one, he'd have to fire 'em all. I had a hand in almost every department. Everything from cleaning bathrooms to hauling boxes around to bringing people lunch."

She gives my hand another comforting squeeze. "I can't believe your uncle treated you that way."

"That's not even the half of it."

"Would you like to tell me more?"

Surprisingly, I do. Sharing deep stuff isn't easy for me usually, but with Arella, it's not only easy, it's soothing. I like how she listens without pity in her eyes. I hate when people look at me like that. I don't want pity. I want what Arella and Liz have given me—understanding. Except, Arella's version of it feels different. She doesn't look at me like I'm damaged the way Liz does.

"I would like to tell you one more thing." I've never said what I'm about to say out loud before. Liz only knows through seeing my memory. If it wasn't for that, she wouldn't know anything.

Do I really want to do this? I only think for a second before coming to the conclusion that yes, I do. I *need* to. If I share this piece of myself with Arella, maybe she'll want to share pieces of herself with me. *I can do this.*

"My parents didn't die in a house fire." The second those words leave my mouth, I almost wish for them to come back.

Arella cocks her head to the side. "What do you mean?"

"I just tell people that because it's easier than explaining the truth."

"Which is?"

"They were . . . murdered." That last word comes out cracked and broken. "And—I . . . I saw it happen."

"What?"

"I was home when . . . you know, the people came. They blew up my house with my parents still in it. I only survived because my dad threw me out the window just before the explosion."

Arella's warm hand cups my stubbly cheek. Like it has before, her gentle touch eases the pain. I press my hand over hers to make sure she doesn't pull away. I'm not ready for her to yet.

"Sometimes," I whisper, "I wonder how things would have turned out if I had done something to save them."

"You can't blame yourself, honey."

I don't . . . much. Mostly, I blame the Royals, which is why I'm working so hard on this mission.

Wait . . . Did she just call me *honey*? She's never called me a pet name before. I like the sound of it. It's the same name my mother used to call me.

With her fingertips, Arella caresses the spot behind my ear. No one's ever touched me like this before. So comforting and nontransactional. "Now I understand why you don't like fireworks."

"Yep. Hate 'em."

"Maybe this is a weird question, but why would someone want to harm your parents?"

"I dunno." It's not entirely a lie. I have theories, but nothing's confirmed. I've already accepted that I may never know.

"Can I see the rest of your box?" Arella asks.

With a nod, I draw out the last few items. Everything is either half-burned or got lucky in the explosion. My dad's green tie, a piece of my mom's floral dress, a chunk of her favorite vase, and my old teddy bear.

This is the luckiest stuffed animal in the world. It was on the couch when my dad threw me on it and tossed me out the window. Besides getting drenched in the rain, it never saw damage. "This is Andy."

Arella takes the bear from me and pets the top of its head. "He doesn't look like he was used much."

"He wasn't. I've barely touched him since I threw him into this box."

She squeezes the bear's paws. "Does it sing or anything?"

"Nah, it's just a regular ol'—"

Something mechanical clicks. A robotic voice comes out of nowhere. "Password?"

Arella perks up. "Oh, it talks!"

"What?" I snatch the bear from her and crush it against my ear. The bear goes silent. Frantically, I press the bear's stomach, willing it to speak again. "How did you do that?"

"Incorrect password," the bear says, making my heart pound.

Arella shrugs. "I just felt something hard inside and pressed it."

I shove the bear back into her hands. "Do it again."

After giving me a sideways glance, she presses on the bear all over. It takes her a moment to find the sweet spot again. When she does, something clicks, and that same robotic voice chimes. "Password?"

"Uh, Trey Grant," I say.

"Incorrect password."

Arella eyes me through a skeptical gaze. "You didn't know it did that?"

"No." Hastily, I toss everything back into the wooden box and lock it up. My chest is heavy, and my lungs feel tight. I can barely breathe as I say, "Let's get you home."

After dropping Arella off with a promise to see her in the morning, I'm back in my bedroom, staring at my old teddy bear. I've got a kitchen knife in my hands, hovering over the stuffed animal like I'm about to perform surgery.

"Sorry, Andy."

Carefully, I slice into the bear's back. White stuffing spills out of the hole. I dig most of it out before finding a black button-shaped object. I press it.

"Password?"

"Trey Andrew Grant," I say in a clear, crisp voice.

"Incorrect password."

I press the button again. "Andrew James Grant."

"Incorrect password."

"Suzie Marie Grant."

"Incorrect password."

Dammit.

It had to have been my parents who hid this device inside my bear. What password would they have chosen?

I try my birthdate in every combination I can think of. I try their wedding date. Our old home phone number. The name of my pet fish who died in the explosion. The name of my bear. Nothing works.

Defeated, I sink to the floor. *What could it be?*

An hour passes before Arella's words echo in my head. *"Does it sing or anything?"*

That's it! It seems obvious now that I think about it. My mom's song. The one she wrote just for me. The one I occasionally sing to myself whenever I'm sad. That's gotta be it.

I press the button again.

"Password?"

I sing each word clearly, "When you're lost without me, you'll always have Andy. When you feel you don't belong, hug this bear and sing this song. Look to the sky when you feel down. Know that things will turn around. Work twice as hard to the finish line. Now it's your time to shine."

I expect the device to reject me again. This time, my mother speaks.

"Hi, honey." I've forgotten what her voice sounds like. Hearing it makes me choke up.

I shoot off the floor and shove the device against my ear.

"If you're listening to this, it's probably because our plan didn't go as planned and something bad has happened. You're most likely with Aunt Debbie right now. We told her that if anything were to happen to us that she should tell you to hug your bear really tight and sing our song."

The next voice is my father's. "Son, your mama and I wanted to make sure that you'd be safe and taken care of. That's why everything we have is now yours, including a safe house by our secret rock. Aunt Debbie is the only person you should trust, and the only person you should take with you."

The only person I should trust? Why is the only person I should trust a woman who over-dosed on z-drugs the morning my parents were killed?

I still remember the first thing I said when I arrived at Shadow Ridge and a grumpy Victor showed me to my new bedroom. "Why can't I go live with Aunt Debbie?"

He laughed, then said something people shouldn't say to seven-year-olds. "That bitch was found dead in her home yesterday with a syringe still in her hands."

That was how I found out that I hadn't lost only my parents the day before but also my only aunt. It clicked then why Aunt Debbie hadn't come to babysit me when she was supposed to. How could she, when she was dead? As I've grown older, I've come to realize that Aunt Debbie's death probably wasn't an overdose.

My mother continues talking on the recording. "When you get to the rock, take a hundred steps away from Cheesy. There, you'll find the safe house. You're the only one who can get into it. Remember that Trackers can't sense you once you're inside and underground."

"Take care, son," my father says.

"And don't ever forget that we love you."

The recording stops.

I stare at the small device with my mouth open. *That's it?* Who leaves a message for a child that basically says, "Hey, we're dead. Here's some money and a safe house. The only person you can trust is also dead, but have a good time at our rock!"

What bullshit! I've got half a mind to toss this stupid thing at the wall. I don't, only because I'm afraid I'll break it.

My whole life, I thought my parents just happened to cross the wrong Royals at the wrong time. Now it's obvious that they knew the Royals were after them. Why else would they have prepared a safe house for me?

If they knew something would happen to them, why not run and take me with them? Why stay in the danger zone? Could finishing their mission really have been that important? More important than me, their son? They knew they were risking their lives, risking leaving me to grow up alone, and they went on anyway. *They abandoned me on purpose!*

I wipe away the one tear rolling down my cheek. After regaining my composure, I drag my phone out of my pocket and open the GPS app.

I can't recall the exact town my parents used to take me to stargaze. It's been so long. All I remember is that it was a town named after a person with a name starting with a J. My parents used to make up stories about whoever it was named after, saying they were probably a janitor, or a journalist, or a jewelry maker.

Now that I think about it, maybe my parents made up stories on purpose to help my young mind remember the right town. If that's the case, that means they were putting things into place for over a year to keep me safe. Which would have been plenty of time for them to pack up and move away with me if they'd wanted to.

I scan the GPS for any J-named towns in California. Was it Jason? Jacob? Julie? Once I catch sight of the town Julian on the map, it clicks. Within a minute, I've got my helmet on and I'm mounting my bike.

Three hours later, my headlight illuminates a green sign that reads JULIAN 1 MILE.

It's been almost nineteen years since I've been around this area. Everything looks the same. Quiet roads, quieter woods, mountain peaks in the distance.

Just before the main town is a single-lane road that leads me to the woods where my parents used to take me. I recognize the spot where we used to park the car. My mother would always say we had to park by the huge Y-shaped tree. Now I'm certain she made those comments on purpose. There's no way in hell a seven-year-old would have remembered where any of this was without her repetitive hints.

I cut my engine, then slide off my bike. After making sure no one's around, I wave a hand at my Harley. It floats through the air at my side as I step into the dark woods. Once the road is out of view, I leave my bike and helmet behind a cluster of trees.

With a little fireball hovering in front of me, I hike deeper through the woods. My ears catch sounds of small animals scurrying around, but they're gone before my eyes can spot them.

I step over a few fallen trees that I remember as bigger obstacles. My parents used to offer to lift me over them. Being the strong-willed kid I was, I insisted on climbing over them myself, without the help of a hover-log.

It feels like forever before I reach the big rock—or should I say biggish rock. *Do I have the right one?* I wave a hand to push my fireball closer to it. Like the fallen trees, it looks smaller than I remember.

My flame follows me as I head in the direction of Cheesy. It's a tree I named for all the holes in its bark. I find it about six trees away from the rock.

"When you get to the rock, take a hundred steps away from Cheesy. There you'll find the safe house."

At the rock, with the holey tree behind me, I begin counting.

One. Two. Three.

Ninety-eight . . . ninety-nine . . . one hundred. I glance around. There's nothing here. It's just more trees, bushes, and dirt. *Where's the safe house?*

The message said something about it being underground. I spend some time scouring the area but don't find anything that would take me underground.

Maybe I should try again. Back at the rock, I count another hundred steps. This time, I take kid-size steps. I end up about twenty paces back from where I was before. It's the same story though. Nothing's here.

With a fireball floating nearby the whole time, I spend the next several hours combing the area. My efforts are useless.

I can't find what I'm looking for, and it doesn't help that I don't even know what I'm looking for. A tunnel? A hidden passageway? A trapdoor? How about a sign that reads SAFE HOUSE HERE with a big fat arrow?

24

TREY

I'm pretty sure my parents hid this so-called safe house on another planet. I've gone back to Julian several times over the last two weeks. With all the holes I've dug, earth I've moved, and for as many times as I've stomped on the ground looking for a trapdoor, I haven't found anything that remotely suggests there's a safe house nearby.

I'm in the middle of doing research on underground living spaces when my phone buzzes. It's a text from Arella that makes my face contort.

> I'm not sure if you should come over today. I'm sick. 😟

What? Her daily texts usually start with "Good morning, honey!" and "Did you have sweet dreams?" Even though Zordis can't dream, I always say that I dreamt of her. Where are those texts?

> I'm coming over anyway.

> Are you sure? I have the flu. It's highly contagious.

> Positive. I'll see you soon.

The Ordinary flu isn't gonna stop me from seeing my girl, especially not on a Sunday. I don't get to see Arella for long on Fridays or Saturdays due to the nature of my work. Last night, she, Javina, and Javina's girlfriend came out to my band's show. I got to see them during the meet and greet for a bit, but I didn't get to have Arella alone. Sundays are precious to me.

I've got grocery bags dangling from my arms as I knock on Arella's door. She answers in pajama shorts and a baggy hoodie—*my* hoodie. Seeing her in it will never get old.

"Morning, angel," I say with a smile. "I brought you stuff to make you feel better."

"Yay!" She props the door open for me to enter.

For a while there, I thought maybe she was using the sick thing as an excuse not to see me. Now that I've seen her smile, it's clear she secretly wanted me to come over.

I rush in and place the bags on her kitchen counter. Then I hurry to greet my girl properly. Taking her by the waist, I lean in to kiss her.

She turns away, covering her mouth with a palm. "I have the flu!"

"Does it look like I give two shits?" I peck her forehead, then leave her to unpack the bags.

For the rest of the day, I make her soup, and we keep busy with card games and movies. During the second movie, I get her down to her panties as I massage her back, and well . . . we end up doing other things.

Even with her stuffy nose, the way she moans as I suck her nipples makes my cock hard. She clenches her hands in my hair as I kiss my way down her belly. Because my shirt is some- where on the floor, I get the pleasure of feeling her skin on mine.

She's been good about stopping me whenever she feels like we're going outside of her comfort zone. I've been good about not pressuring her. The second she says *stop*, I stop. It's not only because I don't want to ruin this mission by breaking her trust, either. I have this deep need to show her that a man can be good to her. Arella deserves to be treated like a queen, and I'm enjoying being the one to do it.

With a finger hooked through her panties, I slowly tug them down, waiting for her to stop me. Instead of grabbing my wrist like she has been, she pulls her legs out of the fabric. I don't let the shock stop me as I marvel at the sight of her fully naked for the first time. It takes everything in me to not collapse my mouth against her clit and lap my tongue over it right now. I don't, because I'm afraid that if I go too fast, she'll shut down. If I take things slowly, she'll have the opportunity to stop me if she wants to. *Hopefully, she doesn't want to.*

Tenderly, I kiss her inner thighs. She squirms and runs her fingers through my hair. I get harder as her nails dig into my scalp and I take two perfect handfuls of her breasts. Between my thumbs and index fingers, I roll her nipples around. She tells me she likes this by arching her head back with a sexy moan. I need to hear her make more of those sounds.

On my way up her thighs, I pepper lingering kisses until I reach what I'm after. I hover there for a second to see if she'll stop me. When she doesn't, I go for it. She gasps sharply when my mouth presses against her clit. At first, I go slow, taking in how soft she feels against my tongue. I go in circles, then side to side. Once she gets used to me, her body melts beneath me.

I wish I could sense her. I wish I could feel everything she's feeling right now. I want to know how good it is for her without having to focus on her moans and watch her every move. Without my gift, I'm constantly second-guessing myself.

I keep asking for verbal confirmation. "How's that, baby? Do you like it better like this? Want it harder?"

Her answers come out in breathy yeses and a guttural "Just keep going."

I do. I lick and suck her clit until she cries out my name, and I watch her fall apart with a scream. I don't even know she's coming until I see it on her face. I've never not known before. Every time I've made a woman orgasm, I could always sense it building inside her.

Not sensing Arella's climax but seeing it happen is surprisingly still as hot. Maybe a little hotter, because now, I know I can do that to a woman without the help of my gift. Plus, it's Arella. She's the hottest woman I know. My mind can't even comprehend it because she's an Ordi. I shouldn't be this attracted to her, yet here I am, craving to kiss every part of her body.

Lately, Arella's been consuming my thoughts. She's the first thing I think of when I wake up and the last thing on my mind when I fall asleep. During the long boring hours when I'm not with her, I wish I were, and it's not because I *should* be for the mission. I just miss her company. Her presence eases me in ways I can't explain.

When I feel anxious, her touch settles it. If a bad memory creeps through my mind, her smile erases it. I always feel lonely in my big empty house, but when she's around, my house feels full and lively.

When I'm with her, I don't feel like I have to put on a show like I do with other people. I don't have to act tough or pretend like I know everything, because Arella's not the type who likes that shit. Around her, I can simply be me.

I told her that I saw my parents get blown up, and not once did she give me a look of pity. I like how she treats me like I'm strong instead of someone who needs to be fixed. I know I need fixing. Liz has made that clear. The difference is that Arella seems to be fixing me without making me feel like I'm broken. She's doing it simply by the way she laughs at my lame jokes and the way she spends time with me without expecting anything in return.

Not sex.

Not money.

Not a performance.

Not a "better version of me" that she knows "exists under the fistfights."

Arella just wants me, and that seems to be enough for her. I've never had that before.

"Your turn," she says, still panting from her climax.

I chuckle, then hop off the bed in search of my shirt. I find it on the floor across her bedroom and slip it over my head.

Arella dips her eyebrows at me. "What?"

"What, what?"

"I said it's your turn."

I give her a firm shake of my head. "Don't think so, babe."

"Why not?"

"Are you ready for me to be inside you?"

The way she hesitates tells me all I need to know. "We don't have to do that. I can just do to you what you did to me."

"Nope. Can't. Thanks for the offer though." I can't remember the last time I turned down a blow job—don't think I ever have.

She side-eyes me, smirking. "Are you afraid that I'll see how small you are and break up with you?"

I let out a loud *ha!* and laugh deep from my chest. "Is that what you think?"

"Why else would a man who's had a plethora of one-night stands refuse to let me into his pants three weeks into the relationship?"

Three weeks? Is that it? It feels like I've been with her longer. She's probably counting it from the night we made things official, not the day we met six weeks ago.

"Trust me, baby. I want nothing more than for your lips to be around my cock, but I can't because it won't be enough. I'll want to fuck you properly, which means you'll be sore and screaming my name. You're not ready for that yet, so it's better if we play it safe. I can take care of myself when I get home, where I won't be tempted to cross any lines."

She gets this look on her face that I don't recognize. It's a mix of astonishment and something else. Before I know it, she's got me pinned to the bed and is attacking me with kisses. I'm a willing victim.

A feeling of warmth and light fills my chest. The only word I can think of to describe it is *happiness.* That's only half of it though. There's something else there that's making my stomach tighten into knots of bliss and panic all at the same time.

Arella pants as she draws back. "You're the best boyfriend ever, you know that?"

Her compliment warms and breaks me. I'm enjoying being her boyfriend. Unfortunately, this boyfriend-girlfriend thing is only temporary. In time, our relationship will come to an end. What then? Will she find a new boyfriend? Will she tell him that he's the best, too?

What happens to me? What will I do without her? What did I ever do before Arella? Lounge around? Drink excessively? Have meaningless sex? None of that sounds appealing anymore.

The idea of Arella with someone else sounds even more unappealing. I want her to be with *me.* I want her best to be *me.*

Internally, I slap myself. Things between Arella and me can't be like this forever. At the end of the day, she's still an Ordinary and it's illegal for me to be with her.

Besides, this relationship isn't real. Arella doesn't know that though, so of course, to her, this *is* real. To me, even though I know it's not, it *feels* real. Like when we hold hands and I get a sense of ease and joy. That feels real. The way she cups my face and makes the pain wash away. That feels real. How hard it is to let her go when we have our late evenings, making out against her apartment door. That feels real.

Does that mean what we have is . . . real? How is that possible? Maybe pretending to want her has tricked my mind into actually wanting her. Even so, that doesn't change that my body physically yearns for her whenever we're apart.

"Can I ask you something?" Arella asks as she slides off the bed to retrieve her clothes.

I would help, but all of a sudden, my mind feels foggy, and it's getting hard to breathe. My thoughts are consuming me.

"Trey?"

Shit. I haven't answered her yet. "Yeah, babe, what's up?"

"Maybe this is something we should have established three weeks ago, but I've been wondering . . . what do you want to get out of this relationship?"

"What do *you* want to get?"

Dressed now, she blows her runny nose into a tissue as she scowls at me. "I hate when you do that."

"Do what?"

"Answer a question with a question. You do it whenever you don't want to give someone a straight answer."

I won't deny that the second she asked that question, my throat closed up. My gut reaction was to ask her the same thing to avoid answering it.

I repeat her question in my head and actually think about it this time. What *do* I want to get out of this relationship?

A month ago, my answer would have been simple: I want information about her that will explain her immunity. Now, I think I want more, but I can't have that. We're from two separate worlds. Worlds that coexist but aren't meant to fully intertwine.

I stand to hug her because it'll ease the heaviness growing in my chest. Also, I can't take her looking into my eyes anymore.

I plant a soft kiss against her forehead. "What I want is more time with you."

It's the most honest answer I can give her because I'm so torn. We're like different species of the same animal family. Like how lions and cheetahs are felines with different genetic makeups. They aren't meant to be together, and neither are Zordinaries and Ordinaries. It's unnatural. Except, the way Arella and I are together feels more natural than blinking. Everything from the way she fits against my body to the way she looks at me to the way she says my name.

The more I think about it, the more my feelings get jumbled up.

Feelings . . . something I know so much about, yet so little.

25

TREY

I didn't intend to stay the night. I've never stayed the night at a woman's place before. I've never wanted to. With Arella, it was too hard to leave. We tried to say bye. I even got my shoes on at one point. When we kissed at her door, somehow, my shoes came off and we ended up back in her bed. Then I just . . . never left. How could I when she fell asleep in my arms, looking so peaceful? It would have taken a bomb threat to move me.

My beautiful angel wakes up with a sleepy smile plastered over her face. She gives me a look that says, *I'm happy you're still here.*

I am too, baby. I spent the whole night admiring how at peace she looks when she's asleep, and I'll happily do it again.

"How did you sleep?" Arella asks after we brush our teeth. I'm grateful that she had one of those free toothbrushes from her dentist for me to use.

"I slept well," I lie. "Dreamt of you," I lie again. It's not like I can tell her that I didn't sleep at all. I'd have to explain that I have a special body that doesn't need as much rest as hers does. That will lead to explaining that I have other special characteristics and abilities she's only seen in movies. Then she'll run away screaming, and I'll go to z-prison for exposure.

Five minutes later, I'm slouched at Arella's kitchen table with a plate of waffles in front of me as she flips some eggs over in a pan.

"Are you okay?" she asks.

"Yep," I lie for the third time this morning, and I hate myself for it.

When can I stop lying to her? I'm not okay. Not even a little bit. My mind is racing with thoughts I can't reel in. I've been having breakfast with Arella almost every morning lately. But today, it feels . . . different. It's hard to put into words. The only way I can describe it is that I want to do this today, tomorrow, the next day, and every day after that. Knowing that I can't crushes me.

"You've been quiet this morning," she says.

I have to think about my response because I want whatever I say to her to be the truth. "I've just got a lot on my mind."

"Do you want to talk about it?"

"Not really. We don't have time, anyway. I have to be at a video shoot at nine. I also need to run home to grab some clothes first."

With the hot pan in hand, she scoops an over-easy egg onto my plate. Then she continues cooking her egg. I've never told her that I prefer my eggs runny. Throughout our many mornings together, she's figured it out. She's been making eggs for me like this ever since.

"What's the video for today?" she asks as the toaster pops.

"It's a cover of a Justin Timberlake song. This shoot was supposed to be a while ago. It's been rescheduled twice."

Arella slides a piece of toast onto each of our plates. Then she gives me three pieces of bacon and two for herself. Once she settles across the table from me, she says, "Should we leave right after breakfast?"

I pick up my fork but don't poke anything with it. "Actually, babe, I was thinkin' you should stay home."

"What? Why?"

"Because you were sick yesterday. Don't you wanna rest?" I hate myself. I can't stop lying. Her being sick has nothing to do with why I think she should stay home.

"I'm recovered now. Besides, I always go to your band stuff with you on my days off."

And I've been thoroughly enjoying it. During band rehearsal, she usually lounges on the sectional, working on her baking blog while I work. During video shoots, she helps out the crew any way she can. At our shows, she's in the crowd, singing along to the words. I like having her around, and people ask about her whenever she's not.

Besides me, the person who misses Arella the most when she's gone is Liz. Those two get along like fuzz on a peach. Once they're together, it's hard to separate them. They're constantly bonding over their mutual love of boy bands.

Last week, I caught them laughing hysterically about something. When I went over to ask what was so funny, neither of them would tell me. They were probably making fun of me, but I don't care. It made me happy to see my two favorite people laughing together.

I don't know what happened after I left Arella with Liz and Emmy at the July Fourth party, but ever since, Liz hasn't made a peep about my strange attachment to this Ordinary. If anything, she's been encouraging it by inviting Arella out to everything our band does. I wonder what changed Liz's mind. I'm sure she still thinks that having a relationship like this with an Ordinary is bizarre. Hell, *I* think it's bizarre.

Throughout history, Zordis have always been friends with Ordis, but never lovers. It's not that we see them as less than. It's that since we can't reproduce with them, we just biologically don't see Ordis that way. At least, we *shouldn't*. So, why do I? Is there something wrong with me?

I finally stick my fork into my perfectly cooked egg. "How 'bout I come over tonight after the shoot? If you want, I could stay the night again?" Hearing those words come out of my mouth sounds as unnatural as it feels to say them. Typically, I'm packing Arella's laptop for her because I can't get her to come to work with me fast enough.

My girl is too smart for her own good. She narrows her eyes at me. "What's the *real* reason you don't want me to come? Yesterday, you didn't care that I was contagious, and now that my symptoms are gone, you're insisting that I stay home?"

I sigh as I set my fork down. Neither of us has eaten a thing yet. "The treatment for this video was written way before we met. There's stuff I'm gonna be doing today that I think would be better if you didn't see."

"Oh . . . like, what kind of stuff?" The way she hesitantly asks that question tells me she already knows.

"Like, you know . . . stuff—with another girl."

She hides her discomfort behind biting into her toast. "Who?"

"She's an actress. Bailey. I've never met her."

Arella ponders that for a moment, then relaxes her shoulders as if to say, *This is no big deal.* Her eyes tell me otherwise. "Wouldn't I see the video later on YouTube anyway?"

"That's true." Selfishly, I want her to come. I don't like being away from her. I guess she could go into another room while we film the intimate scenes. So, if she's up for it . . .

I HIKE MY DUFFEL BAG FULL OF OUTFITS FOR THE DAY HIGHER UP MY SHOULDER AS WE CLIMB THE front steps of a little house in East LA. Whoever picked this spot as our filming location did a great job. The house looks beautiful. Colorful flowers line the walkway, and a cute floral welcome sign hangs on the front door.

Arella stops on the porch and fidgets with the ends of her hair. I grab her hand to make her stop, then kiss her knuckles. My duffel bag falls to my feet with a thud as I turn to face her.

"It's not too late to leave, babe. If you don't think you can handle what I told you is gonna happen today . . ."

"Technically, you haven't told me." She cups her sweaty forehead to shield her eyes from the sun. My Zordi eyes have already adjusted to the brightness. "All you said was that you'll be doing *stuff* with another girl. What, exactly, is *stuff*?"

I grip the back of her thighs and lift her onto the porch ledge. Naturally, she spreads her legs for me to slide between them. I hold her tight to make sure she doesn't fall.

"This video is about a girl who's been hurt so much that she's too afraid to get into another relationship. Throughout the song, I do things to show her that it's okay to fall in love again. We'll be cuddling. There are kissing parts. We'll be half naked. If you still want to stay, remember that it's just acting. It doesn't mean anything. At the end of the day, it's *you* I'll be going home with."

She doesn't hesitate to smile. "Okay. Just promise me you'll kiss me tons when you're done tonight."

"Deal. I'll even start now." My intent is to give her a short, soft kiss, but as soon as our mouths collide, I can't pull away. *She tastes so good . . .* My cock hardens as her fingers trail through my hair. I press my dick against her inner thigh, and she giggles adorably.

She's the first to lean back. "Should we go inside now?"

"In a sec. I need to calm down first." After a few cars pass, I readjust myself. " 'Kay. I'm good now."

The crew is scattered around the house, setting up lights and tripods, while others are standing around chatting. Everyone's emotions jump at me from all directions, so I rake my mind power into a three-foot circle. As soon as I do that, someone enters that circle. Their energy is upbeat.

"Ey! There he is!" It's Mateo, a Hispanic man in his late twenties wearing a Giants baseball cap over his thick curly hair. The top of his cap comes up to my nipples at best.

"Mateo!" I let go of Arella's hand to give him a man hug with a quick thump on the back.

As usual, he gets right to business. "We're gonna start with them performance shots first. We won't need the rest of the band after that, so they can leave early. As for you, you be stuck with me all day."

"I'm pretty sure it's *you* who's stuck with me."

Playfully, he punches my shoulder. "Ey, you ain't too bad to look at." He turns to Arella, whose hand I've returned to holding. "Who's this?"

"This is my girlfriend, Ari. Babe, this is Mateo, my favorite video director. He's got a knack for getting some unique shots."

"Ah, don't play me up too much. Good to meet you, pretty girl."

I don't miss the way Mateo's eyes skate up and down my girl's body. As he shakes her hand, I have to hold myself back from shoving him away. I know I shouldn't be this possessive of her, but knowing it doesn't stop me from feeling it.

"Nice to meet you too," Arella says with a smile that would send most men to their knees. No wonder Mateo's still staring at her.

"Where can I change?" I point at my duffel bag.

Mateo finally peels his eyes off what's not his and hooks a thumb behind him. "There's a bedroom back there."

I practically drag Arella with me as I head that way.

In the small bedroom, I dig through my duffel to find a purple dress shirt and black dress pants. Arella's planted on the end of the bed while I change my clothes and finish my outfit with a black tie. At the mirror, I'm rolling the sleeves up to my elbows when Arella's mouth parts behind me. The look in her eyes is all desire and something else I don't recognize.

I flip around with my arms out. "How do I look?"

"Yummy," she says breathlessly.

As if she's magnetizing me, I feel a pull to her. My feet move toward her before I even process that I'm doing it. I slip a knee between her legs, spreading them apart. I have every intention of giving her a light kiss until she yanks my tie and falls back onto the mattress, forcing me on top of her. I catch myself with a hand on either side of her head. I don't kiss her lightly after that. I kiss her hard, while clawing at her body to come closer to mine. I can't get enough of—

Knock-knock.

Arella freezes beneath me. I debate ignoring the intrusion until I sense that the person isn't moving from the door. Reluctantly, I stand.

"I'm not done with you yet," I whisper.

After adjusting my hard-on, I open the door to reveal a woman I've never seen before. She's pretty for an Ordinary. Nothing compared to Arella though.

"Hi." She hooks a finger behind an ear to pull back her long blonde hair. "I wanted to introduce myself. I'm Bailey."

"Trey." We shake hands. "This is my girl, Ari."

Arella still looks flushed from our kiss as she offers Bailey a small wave. "Hello."

I can't tell how she feels. Her face gives nothing away. *Is she uncomfortable? Jealous?* I want to tell her she has no reason to be. This would be a great time to be a Telepath instead of an Empath, except neither works on her anyway.

I grab Arella's hand and give it a squeeze. It's my silent way of telling her that I'm not attracted to Bailey at all. When I look at Bailey, I just see a person. That's it.

And that's what Zordis *should* see when they look at an Ordi. They shouldn't see anything sexual. They shouldn't see someone they want to devour all the time. Most of all, they shouldn't see someone who makes their heart race as much as Arella makes mine.

There's gotta be something wrong with me. In the past, I've read articles on the z-net about Zordis with mental conditions that cause them to have Ordi fetishes. They're put in rehab and therapy to correct it. *Do I have one of those conditions?* I don't know. Either way, it's not something I can think about right now. It's time for take one.

I make my way to the backyard, where the crew has set up a gazebo in the garden decorated with flowers. As we film, Arella lounges on a lawn chair, watching us. I'm glad she came to work with me today. I always perform better when she's around.

Fifteen takes later, Mateo calls out, "Cut! That's a wrap for the full band scenes!"

Without wasting a second, Arella hops out of her chair and begins helping the crew haul stuff back inside. I'm about to go to her when a hand on my forearm stops me.

"Ey, man. You nervous 'bout your scenes with Blondie?" Mateo nods his head toward Bailey, who's chatting in a triangle with Liz and Emmy.

"No. Why?"

"Of course you ain't. You're prolly used to kissin' strangers all the time. Bailey's not though, so I was hopin' you'd go break the ice with her."

"What do you mean?" I already know what Mateo means. He's not the first director to ask this of me. Typically, I'm down for it. Today, I'm not.

"You know, just make her feel comfortable with smacking lips with you before the cameras roll. It'll make the shots look more natural."

"She's an actress." I wave a nonchalant hand through the air. "She'll be fine."

"Even actresses get nervous, lover boy. Just go ease her nerves a bit, 'ight?"

With that, Mateo twists on his heel and heads inside. I have no intention of breaking the ice with Bailey. If she's nervous, she's just gonna have to get over it.

I glance to where Arella was earlier. She's gone now. I scan the rest of the backyard. No Arella. She's probably back inside.

I'm about to yank the back door open when someone calls my name.

I turn around with a fake smile on my face. "Oh, hey, Bailey."

"Mateo said you wanted to talk to me about somethin'?"

Damn you, Mateo. "Uh, yeah," I say, going along with it. *Might as well get this over with.* The faster we can get past her nerves, the faster we can film, the faster I can go home with my girl. "Let's talk over here."

Bailey follows me to the side of the house.

I stop under the shade of a tree and rub a hand behind my neck. "So, uh, I figured . . . um, that we'd kinda get used to kissing each other before the cameras roll."

Bailey's explosion of nerves fireworks through my head.

Great. Now she's making *me* nervous. "You cool with that?"

She nods eagerly. "Sure."

Taking her face into my hands, I press my lips against hers. She tastes like mint gum and not like Arella at all. Well, she's not Arella, so what did I expect?

Bailey's not a terrible kisser. She's just . . . different. I prefer the way Arella runs her fingers through my hair. And the way she lets out those soft breathy moans. And how her kisses always give me tingles that shoot down to my toes. The worst part is that Bailey doesn't smell like lavender and springtime. She smells of vanilla and coconuts. *Gross.*

Feelings of desire rush through me, but they aren't mine. I expand my powers to latch onto someone—*anyone*—else. Within seconds, it masks Bailey's emotions from my head. I don't want to want Bailey, and I especially don't want her emotions to control how I feel.

Disgusted, I pull back and drop my arms to my sides.

"Wow," Bailey says breathlessly.

At least one of us enjoyed it.

Without a word, I rush inside to go find my girl. Call me a dick for leaving Bailey like that, but I don't care. I need Arella.

She's not in the kitchen. She's not in the living room either. My chest gets heavier with each step I take throughout the house without seeing her. *Where is she?* I need to hold her to feel like the world is right again, and it needs to happen within the next five seconds.

Oh, fuck. What the hell am I gonna do once I complete my mission? Will my world ever feel right if she's not in it? Will I ever be able to kiss another woman without thinking of her? I know the answer, and it makes my lungs tight.

Maybe once I complete my mission, I can continue my relationship with her. I'll just have to hide her from the zovernment and make sure that she never finds out about my powers. I could stop using them, couldn't I? I'll do anything if it means I can keep her.

Then again, how will I explain to Arella that we can never get married? The Supes monitor all marriage licenses to ensure that our Zordi laws are followed. Maybe I can forge marriage papers to make her *think* they're official.

I'll also have to come up with an explanation as to why we can't have children. Telling her that I'm of a different human species with the inability to mate with her won't go over well. I could tell her that I'm infertile or we could adopt. How hard can it be to forge adoption papers?

Then again, what would happen to Arella and our fake family if I'm caught and taken away? How long will I go to z-prison for? Actually, having a secret Ordinary family with forged papers is totally grounds for a death sentence.

My chest aches as I continue my frantic search for her. When I finally find her, it's in an upstairs bedroom with Liz and Emmy. She's stationed on an accent chair, about to say something, when I drop to my knees in front of her. Desperately, I clutch her face and press my lips against hers.

It takes her a second, but eventually, she eases into me and kisses me back. Our embrace is rough and intense. Still, it feels like coming home.

I slide my tongue into her mouth and bask in the familiar taste of her. The familiar scent of her. The familiar way she feels against me. The more we kiss, the more my anxiety flushes away.

Finally, after who knows how long, I pull back. We gasp for air as I press my forehead against hers and brace my arms on the chair.

When I open my eyes, her brown ones are looking back at me. That deep bliss and panic in my chest returns, rushing through me like a hurricane. It washes away the unease while also drenching me with pain.

I can't live the rest of my life without this girl.

I can't.

I won't.

26

TREY

The next day, my mind is a clusterfuck. Kissing Bailey made me realize that I never want to kiss anyone but Arella—ever. Now I just have to figure out how to make that happen.

On my way to pick up my girl for dinner, a wave of nausea hits me. My gut feels like someone's jabbing it with a wrench, so I drink the warm water from a half-empty plastic bottle that's been stewing in my car for a week. It does nothing to ease the tornado in my stomach.

This better go away soon, because I've got special plans to take Arella back to Long Beach, where we had our first date. I'm hoping that since she's more comfortable with me touching her now, she'll actually dance with me this time. I'm also hoping that being around her will help me figure out a plan as to how I'm going to keep her.

I'm about ten blocks away from Arella's apartment when my chest tightens like someone's got a tight grip on my heart and they're squeezing the life out of it. I white-knuckle the steering wheel as my lungs lose air. The dry-ass desert in my throat makes me cough, and I swear heavy sandbags have been dropped onto my chest and have made my lungs their home.

As my car pulls up to Arella's place, I tell myself the pain will pass. I'm still coughing as I knock on her door. A faint sound comes from inside. I press my ear against the door, wishing I was an Eavesdropper with enhanced hearing like Jess. I'm not, so all I hear is . . . screaming?

I try to turn the doorknob. Locked. With the wave of a hand, I fix that, and the door flies open.

My heart plummets. The sound I heard was definitely screaming. Arella's screams. And now, I know why.

Spiders.

Hundreds—no, *thousands* of little black spiders are crawling all over Arella's apartment. Some are so big, I can see the little hairs on their legs. The flames between my fingers flicker as I resist throwing fireballs at them and dash toward the screaming.

Arella's on her bed, screeching and flailing her arms. Spiders cover everything: the walls, the floor, the bed, *my girl*. I dart to her and wave a hand over her body, thinking it'll make the spiders fly off her. They don't.

In a panic, I've forgotten that my telekinesis doesn't work on living things. So with my bare hands, I swat the creatures away. Then I lift Arella into my arms and rush her out of the apartment.

She's still screaming when I set her bare feet down and flick away the last remaining spiders still crawling over her. They fall to the ground and scurry away.

"It's okay, baby," I say as calmly as I can, yet loud enough so she can hear me over her screams. It doesn't quiet her. With my thumb, I wipe away the tears running down her cheeks. "It's okay. It's okay."

I'm lying to her again. It's not okay. I'm freaking out too. It breaks me to see her like this. Roughly, I pull her against me and hold her like she's going to evaporate into thin air if I don't. I let her scream into my chest, and I clutch her until the screaming subsides. Eventually, all she does is tremble in my arms, hyperventilating.

I kiss the top of her hair. "It's all right, baby. I'm here."

I spot her phone on the ground. She must have been holding it, then dropped it on our way out. The urge to pick it up isn't as big as my need to comfort her. On the small of her back, I caress my fingertips in little circles, silently telling her that she's safe now.

"Don't worry, angel. I won't let anything hurt you."

I lean back to look at her. Her whole body is stiff. Her eyes are screwed shut, and she's still panting. I lift her and cradle her in my arms as I march to my car. She doesn't wrap her arms around my neck the way she usually does. She's just rigid and quivering, and it's scaring me.

Once I get her into the passenger seat, I lean in to examine her. Her eyes are still shut, and her hands are in tight, shaky fists.

"Babe?" I say tenderly.

She doesn't respond. I shrug my jacket off and drape it around her front. Then I click her seat belt in.

With a kiss on her forehead, I caress her cheek. "You're safe now."

She's still shuddering.

What do I do?

After closing her door, I fetch her phone off the ground. Then I round the front of my car and plop behind the wheel. I don't start the engine. I just stare at her.

"Angel?" I wait for her to say something.

She doesn't, and my throat closes up.

What's wrong? Why isn't she responding?

"Arella? Please say something." My voice breaks. I'm barely getting the words out.

She doesn't even stir. It's like she didn't hear me at all.

"Fuck." I punch the steering wheel. What the fuck is going on?

Breathe, I command myself, because I can't lose it right now. Arella needs me to be strong. I suck in a deep breath through my nose, then slowly blow it out through my lips.

I know what I have to do. I just don't want to do it. I hate hospitals. I avoid them at all costs. Sensing the emotions of dying patients, people in pain, and overworked nurses always makes me nauseous. Still, I start the car because I can't think of another option.

Arella barely moves as I pull up to the nearest hospital.

She's still unresponsive as I carry her out of the car and rush her into the building.

Her eyes still haven't opened by the time I burst through the doors of the Emergency Department.

All eyes fall on me. Sick women, irritated grandpas in wheelchairs, families in despair, and a guy holding a wad of red-soaked gauze against his eye. The cloud of depressing emotions forms a migraine in my temples. I just got here, and I already need to leave.

I rush to the front desk, ignoring the long line. "You need to see her right away."

A plump woman in her fifties glares at me from behind a pair of rectangular glasses. "Sir, you need to get to the back of the line."

"No. Someone needs to see her *now*."

She glares at me—harder this time. "Is anything broken, bleeding profusely, dying, or on the pain scale of nine or higher?"

"What? No?"

She seizes a clipboard with paperwork already on it, thrusting it toward me. "Fill out this form. Someone will see you shortly."

I glance down at the sweet girl in my arms. Her face is pale. Her breathing is shallow. She's not shaking anymore, but that doesn't change how much I'm fucking losing it. I glance back up at the receptionist. "I need that someone *now*."

"You need to fill out the forms, sir. And get to the back of the line."

"Fuck. The. Forms! Don't you see she's not responding?"

Dramatically, the lady yanks her glasses off and leans on her elbows. "You need to calm down, sir."

"I can't calm down. My *heart* is on the pain scale of nine or higher. Please! Help her!"

I feel like pulling out all my hair. I probably would if my arms weren't full of the one and only person who means everything to me. My lungs won't stop contracting, because I can still hear her screams. I can still feel her crying and trembling against my chest.

"Please," I beg. "Get someone to take her in."

The lady sighs, preparing to tell me some scripted rejection when a tan-skinned Indian woman wearing scrubs appears by the double doors. "I'll take her in."

Finally!

27

TREY

Doctor's orders. I'm doing everything she told me to. *Take her home. Help her relax. Comfort her. Don't leave her alone unless she asks to be.* No problem.

The whole car ride home, I never let go of Arella's hand once. Not until I parked in my garage and cut the engine.

Now, she's in my Jacuzzi. I thought a warm bath might help her relax. Sometimes it does the trick for me. I sit on the edge, gently rubbing a bar of soap up and down her back and around her shoulders.

I'm half expecting Arella to jump up and scream at any moment. The doctor said it's a common side effect of post-traumatic stress. The moment she explained Arella's shakiness and unresponsiveness with the word *trauma*, the blood drained from my body.

My chest has been feeling lighter ever since the color has been returning to Arella's face. Now, I just need to hear that sweet voice of hers tell me she's okay.

I don't know if she wants me to kiss her, nor do I ask. I just do it. Not for her. For me. It soothes me to kiss her shoulders, her forehead, and her cheeks. She hasn't told me not to, so I guess that's a good sign. I hope it's as comforting to her as it is to me.

After about twenty minutes, I drain the tub and assist her out of it. Then I dry her off with a towel and dress her in a pair of my boxers and a T-shirt. It takes me a few tries to get all her hair out of the messy ponytail I put it in earlier. Once I do, I kiss her forehead and pull her close.

The feel of her body against mine immediately alleviates the churning in my gut. I'm not sure why *I'm* the one who needs consolation. It's *her* who was attacked by hairy eight-legged monsters.

Where the fuck did they come from? And how were there so many? And so big? I'll have to do some research later. For now, I just want to focus on making Arella feel safe.

We stand in the middle of my bedroom, holding each other for a while, never saying anything. I don't know what I could say to make things better. All I know is that after a few minutes, her arms rise to hug me back, and my insides throw a mini party.

"Trey?" She tilts her head back to look at me. The sound of her voice makes me tear up.

"Yeah, baby?"

"Thank you for taking care of me."

I can't help myself. I seize her face and glue my mouth to hers. She doesn't hesitate to kiss me back. For me, it's more of a need than a want. It's full of anxiety, and relief, and pain, and desire all at once.

I only let go of her when my stomach rumbles. The whole hospital fiasco took several hours. I haven't eaten a single thing. Neither has Arella.

With her hand in mine, I lead her to the kitchen. She sits silently at the island while I whip up something for us to eat.

Ten minutes later, I place two plates onto the counter. They're full of pancakes, bacon, eggs, and some fresh-cut strawberries. I inhale my food like a starving animal.

I'm almost done when Arella speaks again.

"This was the first meal we ever had together. Breakfast. Right here."

That day feels like forever ago. So much has changed since the moment I met this puzzling brunette on the side of a highway. In only six and a half weeks, I've grown to adore this woman. I care more about her than I do my own limbs.

Like an annoying little alarm, my brain chimes in to remind me how ridiculous it is that I feel this way about her. It keeps reminding me that what we have is wrong. My heart though . . . It tells me that Arella is right. She's everything I want and need in ways I never imagined could exist. She understands me in ways even Liz doesn't. She doesn't make me feel like I have to fake happiness either. With her, I am genuinely happy.

I know this relationship isn't sustainable, but when it comes down to it, when my mission ends, can I really just walk away?

I already know the answer to that without having to think about it.

It's hitting me now that I haven't been actively trying to complete my mission for a while. The more time I spend with Arella, the less I've been asking to meet her grandparents. I haven't been pursuing answers about her parents, her genetics, or anything else either.

Maybe subconsciously, I haven't wanted my mission to end. This incomplete assignment is the only reason I have to stay with her. Until I find a better one, I'm gonna cling onto that for as long as possible.

"The doctor said you can't go to work for a week." Yeah, I'm a piece of shit, but I'm not ready for Arella to leave my side yet. What if something happens? I can't protect her if I'm not near her.

"I can't miss work for that long," she says defiantly.

"Doctor's orders. You're in recovery."

For the next twenty minutes, Arella argues with me about being "fine" and how she "can't go that long without getting a paycheck." The more I offer to help her, the more she argues with me. I can't comprehend it. Jess and just about any other woman I know would love to hear that I'll pay for anything she wants for the rest of her life. When Arella says something about wanting to be able to buy things without having to ask me, I offer to transfer her ten thousand dollars. She still says no. *Seriously?*

"You can buy whatever you want, babe. No need to tell me what it's for, and no need to pay me back. Whenever you run out, just let me know, and I'll transfer you more."

She groans, throwing her head back. "You don't get it."

I raise my arms up and drop them to my sides. "You're right. I don't. It still doesn't change that the doctor said you can't go to work for a week."

Eventually, she stomps away to call her bosses.

When she comes back, I'm in the middle of loading the dishwasher.

"My nanny family is going to get a backup nanny lined up. As for the daycare, my director is not happy. We're already short-staffed, and she thinks I made up the whole spider thing."

I shrug as I insert a dirty plate into the dishwasher. "Fuck her."

Arella glowers at me, crossing her arms over her luscious breasts. She's braless, and I've been staring at her nipples peeking out of my T-shirt all morning.

I feign innocence. "What?"

"Have you ever had a job?"

"I once worked on a cruise ship as a musician."

She rolls her eyes. "Like a *normal* job."

"Um, the guy who owned the music store in my hometown used to pay me under the table to help around. Does that count?"

"No. My director said that I need a doctor's note if I'll be out for more than three days in a row. Company policy."

"No problem. I can write you one." I stick another plate into the dishwasher.

"No! I need a *real* doctor's note. Do you even care that I could lose my job?"

"You won't get fired, babe." Even if she did, I'd take care of her. She has nothing to worry about.

While Arella goes off to make a few more calls, I head upstairs to work out. I'm in the middle of my weight-lifting routine when Arella peeks her head through the door. I pause the rap music that's blasting over my speakers.

"My landlord said she'll get it taken care of immediately."

"Perfect." The weights clank as I set them back onto the rack.

Arella hugs herself, staring at the carpet. "Sooo . . . where do you think all those spiders came from?"

I did some research last night, while she was asleep. According to the Internet, it was either an infestation through a hole in the wall or a spider egg sac that hatched inside her apartment. What confuses me, though, is the number of spiders. The infestations I saw online were much smaller. More like ten to twenty at most. If a spider egg had hatched inside her place, it would have only been a few hundred little baby spiders. What I saw looked like thousands, and those fuckers weren't babies.

"Have you ever seen *Charlotte's Web*?" I ask. "There's a scene in the movie when Charlotte's egg sac hatches and all her little babies come crawling out."

"Those things were too big to be babies," Arella says. "Is it possible that this was Nathan's way of getting back at me for you beating him up?"

I pause to think about that. Is that hairy-balls-eating douchebag capable of pulling off a spider infestation that big? Maybe, but would he do it knowing I have those reputation-destroying photos of him? Perhaps he thinks we can't prove he did this. Arella has mentioned that his dad's got money. For the right price, you can hire someone to do anything.

I make a mental note to look into it later. Maybe I'll pay Pencil Dick a visit. With my mind power, I can usually tell if people are lying. In the meantime, I'll keep focusing on taking Arella's mind off the whole thing. Last night, she woke up from a nightmare about being attacked by furry arachnids the size of her face. It broke my heart to see her cry like that.

After I finish my workout, I rummage through my drawers to find the clothes Arella left here that night we threw flour on each other—the night we had our first kiss. I still think about that heated moment whenever I have a date with my right hand.

Once Arella's dressed, we climb into the car to go run some errands.

As I back out of my garage, Arella asks, "Do you think there's a chance all the spiders have left?"

"I think there's a higher chance that by tonight, you'll be shooting webs out of your wrists."

She chuckles, shaking her head at me. "If I were to have superpowers, Spidey webs would not be my first choice. Now where are we going?"

"Target."

"What for?"

I press a button to shut my garage as we pull out onto the street. "To get some things you said you need—clothes, shampoo, makeup . . . a flamethrower."

Her mouth pops open with a gasp. "Flamethrower? We're not setting my apartment on fire!"

With a wink, I say, "At least you wouldn't have to pay rent anymore."

28

ARELLA

I've got a full belly as we leave the restaurant in Long Beach where Trey took me the first time we had dinner together. We slow-danced as a female duo sang perfectly harmonized love songs accompanied by their keyboard.

A dark sky stretches above us as we head to my thinking spot for another evening of stargazing. It was Trey's idea, and I didn't hesitate to say yes. I love being able to share the place that used to be my safe haven with my new safe haven.

"I liked waking up next to you this morning," I say with his hand in mine. It's rare for us to be in the car without holding hands.

A quick "same" is his response. He doesn't even look away from the road.

"I can see us having more mornings like that."

He answers with a slight nod and a somber "Me too."

He's been somber a lot today. Always staring off into space with a pained look in his eyes. Whenever I ask what he's thinking about, I get the feeling he only tells me a version of the truth.

My truth is that I can see Trey and me having more than just mornings where we wake up together. I can see us spending more days together like we did today, barely leaving each other's side. I can see me going on tour with him and his band after they finish their album. I can see him helping me paint the walls of my future bakery and him being there when I sell my first cake. I can see us having it all together. Only problem is . . . I'm not confident if *he* sees all that.

Whenever I bring up the topic of our future together, he avoids it. Earlier today, I casually asked if he ever wants kids. His answer was a gloomy "Yes, but I'm not sure if that's in the cards for me."

"Why is that?" I asked.

Instead of answering, he changed the subject.

Besides owning a bakery, my other dream is to be a mom. I love children, and working with other people's kids every day isn't enough. Someday, I want my own. If Trey doesn't ever want kids, I'm not sure if this can work.

My quiet man parks his car on the side of the gravel road where I normally do. Together, we grab our things and head into the woods. At the top of the narrow trail is that same giant oak tree that's always provided me comfort whenever I needed it. A slight breeze blows my hair around as Trey lays out a blanket for us.

"You're gonna do great," he says as he unpacks his guitar from its hard case. He thought it'd be fun to teach me some simple chords. I don't even know the difference between a simple chord and a not-simple chord. Still, I'm willing to learn because it'll make him happy.

We're about an hour into my first guitar lesson when I'm finally getting the hang of it. So far, Trey has taught me four chords. Learning to play guitar isn't as easy as he makes it look. I can barely remember where to put my fingers, let alone switch between chords fast enough to play a song.

"That's perfect!" He flashes me one of his panty-wetting smiles. "Now play a D."

I glance at my numb fingers with the string indents in them. "But it hurts."

"That's normal. Once you play enough, you'll build up some calluses, then it won't hurt anymore. See?" He shows me his hard fingertips.

"How long will that take?"

"Depends on how often you play. Maybe a few weeks. Maybe months."

"Months?" I grip the neck of his guitar and hand it back to him. "Thanks for the lesson, Mr. Grant. Now, how about you serenade me instead?"

Through dazed eyes, he runs his tongue along his bottom lip. "Don't say my name like that. It does things to me."

I narrow my eyes and smirk. "Oh? What kinds of things?"

"The bad kind."

I like the sound of that. "Tell me, Mr. Grant. What are these bad things you speak of?"

His expression darkens. "I mean it."

"Mean what, Mr. Grant?"

His guitar gets thrown to the side with a loud *clank!* The next thing I know, he's launched himself at me, pinning my back to the blanket. Our lips meet roughly. His sweet scent drapes over me like warm air on a chilly day. He fixes my wrists above my head with one hand while his other hand cups my neck to hold me in place. He doesn't need to cement me down like this. I'm an enthusiastic captive.

Eventually, our kiss turns into a clothes-clawing, lip-biting, beautiful mess. As I slide his shirt up, I run my fingertips along every hard dip of his abs. Our mouths part for the split second it requires me to tear the fabric over his head, and then we're back to kissing in a frenzy.

"I can never get enough of you," he groans.

"Take more, then."

Every part of me craves to feel his hands on my bare skin. I rip my dress off to reveal the new matching bra and lacy panties I got today. Trey attacks me with his mouth. He goes for my neck first before sliding his lips down my chest. He scratches at my bra hooks and unhooks them within seconds. The lace gets thrown behind him. I arch my head back as his mouth latches onto one of my nipples.

"Trey," I moan toward the stars.

I grip his hair, heaving him closer as my other hand clutches the blanket beneath us. He hooks a finger through my panties and drags them down. They get tossed behind him too. They haven't even touched the grass before his tongue is lapping me up. I grab a handful of his hair as a tingling pleasure shoots up my body and down my legs.

With the perfect pressure, he circles his fingers over my clit. I squirm beneath him as he slides a finger inside me, then two. The entire time he moves them back and forth, he never stops licking me. My hands claw at his shoulders, begging for him to suck me harder. He must hear my silent plea, because he does, and I let out a whimpering moan.

His wet lips pepper kisses up my belly until he reaches my nipples again. He sucks on one while his fingers keep hammering inside me.

"You like that, baby?"

My response is an animalistic "Mmm."

That encourages him to keep going.

My fingertips graze his muscular chest and abs, all the way down to his zipper. I've barely gotten his jeans unbuttoned when he snatches my wrist and slams it above my head. Then he continues to lick my breast as if he didn't just deny me.

My other hand tugs at his messy hair to pull him back to look at me. "I want to touch you."

"If you touch me, I'll need to own your body."

"Then own me."

He groans, biting his lip. "Don't tease me, baby."

"I'm not. I want you."

He freezes. "Really?"

I take in the beautiful sight of him. His gorgeous face that I love to kiss. His defined arms that hold me tight. And his eyes. Those beautiful blue-gray eyes that always stare at me with desire and admiration. I nod firmly. "Yes. Own me."

His lips smash against mine again. He holds himself up with one hand while the other drags his zipper down. I shove the denim off his hips as he nips at my neck.

Soon, his jeans are thrown onto the grass too. Kneeling next to me, he hooks his thumbs behind the elastic of his boxers, then stops. I gape at him, urging him to shed the fabric, but he hesitates.

"You sure about this, babe?"

I nod eagerly. *Will you just get naked already?*

Finally, his boxers come down and his thick, hard erection springs up. It bounces a few times as I lose my breath and marvel at his size. Before I can touch him, he pins my arms down and kisses my neck. I moan and wrap my legs around him, desperate for him to enter me. He presses his erection against my inner thigh as he sucks my bottom lip into his mouth.

Panting, he releases my arms to grab his cock. With a dazed look in his eyes, he slides the tip up and down over my wet clit.

He's right outside my opening when I push him away. "Wait."

He stills above me. Then suddenly, he's off me, lying on his side, roughly dragging a hand through his hair.

"I'm sorry," he whispers, shaking his head at himself. "I shouldn't have pushed you this far. I knew you weren't ready."

What is he talking about? "I'm more than ready, Trey. Having you inside me is all I can think about right now. I just want you inside my mouth first."

All the worry dissipates from his eyes as his breath hitches. I climb on top of him and take his throbbing length into my hands. I wrap my fingers around his base, then stroke him up and down. His massive cock pulses and jumps between my palms. It's everything I imagined it would be. Firm, full, and satisfying.

Impatiently, I take him into my mouth, and he lets out a deep, guttural growl.

"Oh, baby." His hand grips the hair at the back of my head, guiding me into a rhythm as my head bobs up and down. "That feels so good."

That motivates me. I take him deeper and harder, changing pace from fast to slow, then fast again.

His breaths grow heavy and short. "Shit. Babe. Stop."

I don't.

"Please. I can't hold back any longer."

When I still don't stop, he forces me to. In a single motion, he flips me onto my back and straddles me.

"Do you want me?" he asks, his nose barely a hair from mine.

Each pound of my heart against my chest screams, *Yes, yes, yes!*

This man has done things to me. He's made me feel safe again when I wasn't sure I ever could. He's healed me. He's made me feel like I deserve to be with a man who touches me with affection, not abuse. He's made me feel like I'm me again. The me I was before I was made to feel weak and scared all the time.

Do I want him? Yes. More than anything.

"Own me, Trey."

That is all the permission he needs to press his cock against my opening and push inside.

I whimper, gasping as he fills me. Pain and pleasure ripple between my legs. He goes slow at first, allowing me to stretch and get used to his size. Each time he draws back and pushes in again, he goes deeper. I moan beneath him, arching my head back as I take his cock the way I'm meant to.

With a grunt, he plunges into me all the way.

An uncontrollable wail escapes me as my fingernails dig into his back.

He stills. "Am I hurting you?"

"No," I pant. Total lie, but I don't want him to stop.

He kisses my forehead as he moves inside me. Soon, the soft pain turns into pure pleasure as all the protective walls I've spent years building up come crashing down.

Her light chestnut waves are sprawled out all over the grass. Her hands are clenched in the blanket beneath us. Her eyes are rolled back as her body trembles, taking every inch of me. This woman has never looked more irresistible.

She wraps around me perfectly—tight and dripping wet. Every time I thrust into her, she lets out the sexiest of moans. Arella could ask me to do anything for her right now, and I'd do it, no questions asked.

Every emotion running through me as I pump inside her is mine. The desire that shoots through my veins, the yearning in my heart, the need I feel to keep thrusting—all mine.

I'm close to the edge, but ending this too soon would be a tragedy. I've been waiting to have this moment with her for too long, and I'm not gonna ruin it by coming this fast. *She feels so good though . . .*

When my arms get tired of holding myself up, I lie on my side, facing her, and pull her leg over my shoulder. Easily, I find her damp opening again and slip back in. As every inch of me pushes its way through, my lungs lose air.

"Don't stop," she moans.

No worries, baby. I wasn't planning to.

She arches her head back. "Yes. Harder."

I obey, giving her what she wants. She screams as I thrust deeper into her, relentlessly rubbing her at the same time.

Harder.

Faster.

Harder.

Faster.

"Trey!"

I love hearing her scream my name as I watch myself disappear and reappear inside of her. Her breathless moans, her quivering hands, her curled toes. This is all I want to do—forever.

My will to hold back is dwindling. I need to release soon. I pull out to take a mini break, but Arella's not having it.

She grabs my cock and strokes me into submission. "Come back."

Breathlessly, I obey, climbing back on top of her, but I'm done being gentle. I drive into her so hard, she screams out. She keeps screaming as I pump, and pump, and pump.

"Come for me, baby," I beg.

"I'm so close," she half gasps, half moans.

That makes me almost erupt. I circle my fingers around her swollen clit over and over until, finally, her nails dig into my forearm and she shrieks. The sound of her orgasm is my sweet release. She pulsates around me as I pour into her.

Suddenly, it comes to me, clear as day. All her emotions rush through my mind. Arousal, gratification, relief. I sense her feelings for me, all desire, and need, and . . . something else. I drink in every second of it as I thrust one more time, groaning as I hammer every last drop inside her.

Then, as quickly as it came, it's gone.

I collapse over her with an arm on either side of her face, careful not to crush her. My ear presses against her thrashing heart. A thin layer of sweat coats her body, sticking to my dry skin. Together, we pant hard, and we stay like this until our breaths slow.

She lets out a little gasp as I pull out. Flopping next to her, I stare up at the stars with my mind in disarray. I *sensed* her. Only for a few seconds, but I sensed her! *How?*

I gape at her, searching for an explanation. I will my mind power to work on her again. It doesn't. She's blank, like always, except . . . *not* always. *How did that happen?*

However it happened, I can't try to figure it out now. My brain can't process anything—not after that. It was crazy. The best I've ever had. Uncontrollable passion. It unearthed a deep intensity in my soul that I don't know how to explain. All I know is that I was meant to be inside this woman.

"You didn't pull out," Arella says, interrupting my thoughts.

I pat my chest and gesture for her to scoot toward me. She does, nuzzling her head into the crook of my shoulder.

"You're on birth control, right?" I don't even pretend to sound concerned.

"Yeah."

"And you're consistent with it?"

"I have the implant."

I give her a look that says, *What the hell is that?* I know nothing about Ordinary birth control options, except that they have pills and backup pills.

"It's a little rod they stick into your arm, and it works for three years."

There's a Zordi version of that. I'm pretty sure Jess has it. "Is your three years up?"

"Not yet."

"And the success rate is . . . ?"

"Over ninety-nine percent."

"Sounds like we're good."

She makes a *pfft* sound. "That's not the point."

"Then what is?"

"The point is that you just came inside me, and you didn't even know if I was on birth control or not. You've never even asked. What if I wasn't?"

I've always been careful to use protection with Zordi women. Once, Jess tried to get me to fuck her without a condom. I'm a risk taker, but I'm not *that* much of a risk taker. One percent is still too high, and with my luck, I'd be part of that tiny statistic.

With Ordis, though, there's no risk. I couldn't have a baby with Arella even if the Zordinary fertility gods floated down from the fucking sky and sprinkled us with their golden baby dust.

I have no concerns, but if it'll make Arella feel better . . . "How 'bout we get you some Plan B pills tomorrow?"

She nods firmly. "That would be great. And next time, let's use a condom, just to be safe."

"Okay." I grin. "That means there's a next time."

THE NEXT MORNING, I WAKE WITH MY LIMBS TANGLED AROUND ARELLA'S BODY. IT'S AS IF throughout my sleep, I wouldn't allow her to get more than a breath away from me.

I still feel high from last night. When we got home, we had sex two more times before we finally passed out from exhaustion. I'm rested now, and more than ready for my next dose of her.

"Morning, angel," I say when she stirs. Even when she's rubbing the crust out of her eyes, she's the most gorgeous woman I've ever seen.

"Morning, honey."

For a few minutes, we cuddle as we go over the things we need to do today. Our two priorities are getting the backup pills and dropping off a "doctor's note" for Arella's daycare director. When Arella asks why we aren't getting a *real* note, I make up some excuse about how the doctor had already written one but I misplaced it in the shuffle of getting her home from the ER.

"I suppose I wouldn't want to bother that doctor again," Arella says with her head over my shoulder.

"I'll write you something that's official-looking," I say, still holding her close. "Besides, it's not like your boss is gonna check up on it. If she does, there's a medical record of you being at the hospital."

Arella trails a finger down my abs, making my morning wood harder for her. "I suppose you have a point."

"I've got an afternoon photo shoot with the band at a park, then rehearsal after that. You're cool to come with me?"

"I'd love to."

"Good. Now, before we start our day, I need to have you again." My hands, which were caressing her shoulder, trail down to her luscious breasts.

"So have me."

Those three little words are all I need to break through the ropes that were tying back my inner beast—the part of me that wants to tear her clothes apart and eat her up. My mouth doesn't waste a second to suck in her nipple, and once again, we become a tangle of arms and legs.

Right before I'm about to enter her, she stops me and asks for one of those stupid condoms. I comply because I can't stand to be outside her for much longer. Once I roll the rubber on, I return to where I belong—on top of her.

When she orgasms, her emotions rush through me the same way they did our three times last night. I soak up every second of it until it disappears.

Out of breath, I collapse at her side, gaping at her. Whatever immunity walls she keeps up somehow come tumbling down when I make her come. Is it only possible when she orgasms, or can this happen another way? What about the orgasm makes it possible for me to sense her? Why did this only start *after* we had sex? I've made her come before, and her emotions didn't rush into my mind until last night. Is it only me this can happen with, or would it work with someone else?

I don't know the answers to any of those questions or the other ninety-some racing through my mind. The only thing I know is that when my mission ends, there is no way in hell I'm letting her go.

30

TREY

I can see why Arella and Javina are best friends. They complement each other well. When Javina talks, Arella listens. When Javina says something negative about herself, Arella corrects her by turning it into something positive. They laugh at the same things and know how to speak to each other without saying anything at all. It's fascinating to watch.

We're having lunch together at a restaurant near the park my band just finished our photo shoot at. Arella and Javina are deep in a conversation about work. Neither Javina's girlfriend nor I have said a word in almost ten minutes.

I turn to Rachel, who's across the high-top table from me. In a low voice, I say, "Do you think they'll notice if we just leave?"

Rachel giggles. "Doubt it. These two can go on forever. Speaking from experience."

After another minute, Arella hops off her seat. "I have to use the potty. I'll be quick."

Rachel follows her. "Me too."

As Arella saunters away, I only have one thought: *That ass is mine.* Mine to touch, to slap, to squeeze, and—

A hand smacks my arm. "Hello?"

"Huh?" My attention snaps up to Javina.

"I said, don't hurt her." She flashes me an icy glare. "That girl's been through a lot, and she deserves the best. So, I'm warning you, don't hurt her. If you do, I'll hunt you down and rip your balls off with my bare hands. Ari and I watch enough true crime shows for me to know how to hide the evidence and make it look like the fucking Easter Bunny did it."

The idea of hurting Arella scares me more than Javina's threat. Actually, it scares the fuck outta me. My original plan was to get Arella to break up with me. Now I'm not so sure she will. I also don't want her to. Besides, Javina is right. Arella does deserve the best. Unfortunately, this achy feeling in my chest tells me that I'm not it.

For the rest of the weekend, I push all thoughts of my unpredictable future with Arella aside. In the little free time we have between my band activities, I perform many satisfying, mind-boggling experiments with her in my bed.

By Sunday evening, I conclude that as long as I'm touching Arella as she orgasms, my mind power works on her. By touch, I mean any skin on skin works. My hands, my tongue, my dick, anything. When I wear a condom and I'm not touching her anywhere else, she's blank. If she comes while I'm licking her, the second I pull away and that physical contact is lost, so are her emotions. One hundred percent of the time, though, as long as we're touching, my mind power works. *How?*

I try to figure out if she's aware of what she's doing. After I ask some awkward questions like "What do you think about when you're coming?" it's obvious that she has no clue she's doing anything at all. It only further confirms that her immunity to Zordi powers is outside of her knowledge.

We're about to head to bed when my phone vibrates in my pocket. It's Victor. Since Arella's been staying with me, I've been ignoring his calls during the day and only answering them at night. Since this is the second time he's called today, I should probably answer it.

I head toward the backyard. "Why don't you climb into bed first, babe? I'll be right there."

Arella nods, then she shuffles down the hall. After I close the sliding glass door behind me, I answer the phone.

"Bring her to me," Victor says.

I stiffen in mid-step. "What?"

"This project is taking too long. It's been almost three months since I assigned you this mission, and you have nothing to show for it."

Actually, I have lots to show. I've found out that even though Arella's immune to Zordi powers, Healing Water works on her. I've discovered that her parents died on the same night mine did and that she wasn't born with the name she has now. I've found out that her grandparents have background checks that come up mostly blank. And then there's this whole thing where I can sense her emotions under certain circumstances. I haven't told Victor about any of this, and I don't think I want to.

My parents' secret message in my old teddy bear stated that the only person I should trust was Aunt Debbie. Why isn't Victor on that short list? He and my dad were very close before Aunt Jodi left. They did everything together, from things like playing in bowling leagues to drinking beers on the deck over the weekends. Lots of people even got them mixed up because they looked and talked so much alike.

Lately, I've been getting the feeling that Victor knows more than he's letting on. How is it that he knows so little about my parents' mission? Yes, there's that secrecy rule between agents, but he's the head of ZIRDA California now. Doesn't he have access to those files? Doesn't he have the power to order someone to tell him what happened the night his little brother died?

I've considered questioning him about this, but I already know the outcome of that. Victor will turn it around on me, like "How about you stop being concerned about past missions you weren't a part of and start focusing on the one you've got?"

Besides, if Victor is up to something and I start snooping around, he'll get suspicious. He might take me off this assignment and give it to someone else. I won't be forced to sit on the sidelines while Arella falls for the next guy Victor sends to her. For now, I need to act as if everything is okay.

I drag a hand through my hair as I pace my backyard. "What makes you think this is something we can crack within the span of a few months? What if we're close and we just need to give it more time?"

"We don't have time, kid. Who knows what the Royals are doing while we aren't?"

That's true. While I'm over here fucking around with Arella, the Royals are probably out there murdering innocent children. All I've ever wanted is to make the Royals pay for what they did to my parents and to stop them from ever doing something like that again. Now, I'm acting as if it doesn't matter.

"I'm making some progress. I just need more time to see it through."

"Did something happen to her at birth?" Victor snaps.

"Not that I know of."

"Did she fall into some chemicals? Get attacked by a mutant animal? Was she dropped off here by aliens? Goddammit, kid. Find out."

"I will. Just give me more time." I'm almost begging.

"No. I want her here within the week."

"What am I supposed to tell her?" My palms shake. Somehow, my voice remains steady.

"Tell her you wanna go on a road trip, get her in the car, and drive over. I'll take care of the rest."

I don't like the sound of that. "What are you gonna do once she's there?"

"We'll run tests on her like we did with the other two Immunes."

I still don't like the sound of that. "Did the tests on the other Immunes come up with anything?"

"No, and we couldn't find any matches in their DNA either. That's why we need her here to perform more tests."

"What kinds of tests?"

"Nothin' too fancy. Physical, mental, intellectual."

I *really* don't like the sound of that. "You can't just send those tests to me, and I can do them with her myself?"

Victor clears his throat impatiently. "We have an entire team of people here to perform the tests and to monitor her health during the process because we need to be extremely careful with this one. We can't lose her too."

I stop pacing. "What?"

"The other two couldn't handle the pressure of the physical tests. Sadly, we lost them."

What? I was already having trouble breathing during this conversation. Now I'm suffocating. The other two Immunes are *dead*? And it's ZIRDA's fault? Since when do we ever put Ordinaries in danger? ZIRDA has a history of taking measures to the extreme for a greater cause, but killing innocent Ordinaries?

"It didn't happen on purpose," Victor says defensively. "How are we supposed to know how much they can handle until they can't handle any more? Besides, losing two Ordinaries to save the other billions of people will be worth it. Once we've got the upper hand over the Royals . . ."

The man keeps going, but I stop listening. I don't care what he's got to say, because nothing—I repeat, *nothing*—justifies killing innocent people. The anti-Royals department was created to help *save* Ordinaries, not hurt them. I thought that's why Victor came up with this grand plan for our agents to date the Immunes to learn about them without causing any harm. Now he's performing deadly tests on them? *Is he fucking serious?*

Victor refuses to let me off the phone until I agree to have Arella at Shadow Ridge within a week. I agree without any intention of ever doing so. If there's a chance that Victor's brutal tests will harm my sweet girl, fuck that. I don't care if the results from those tests are the key to taking down the Royals. I cannot and will not allow anyone to hurt my girl.

That's when it hits me.

It's over.

My mission is over.

If finding out what makes Arella immune puts her life at risk, I'd rather never know at all. Keeping Arella safe is more important to me than defeating the Royals. Yes, I still want to see them gone, but that's somebody else's job now. As for me, I'm shifting my focus from understanding Arella's immunity to protecting it.

31

TREY

The next morning, Arella and I arrive backstage at the Soul House fifteen minutes late. It took her a while to orgasm, and I refused to let her leave my bed until she did.

The entire band and our manager are all crowded around the sectional. I sense the heart-warming energy before I hear the synchronized *aws*. Once my eyes land on the photographer from our photo shoot at the park, I get a good feeling that I know what everyone's looking at.

"This one's my favorite!" Emmy says, handing a 4x6 print to Arella.

I glance over my girl's shoulder at the breathtaking photo. There I am, holding the most precious woman in the world, kissing her cheek. I get lost in Arella's sweet smile as I recall all the fuzzy feelings I got during that shoot.

Emmy had convinced Arella and me to take couples photos after she and Marcus did theirs. I'm amazed by how good the pictures turned out. *Do Arella and I always look that happy together?*

"I like this one the most," Liz says, handing Arella another 4x6 print.

I agree. It was one of our last shots, where Arella and I had our faces in each other's hands, looking deep into the other's eyes. The photo looks like it belongs on the cover of a sappy romance novel. With anyone else, I might have gagged and made jokes. Because it's Arella, I can't stop staring. The knot in my chest tightens. Any day now, I could lose all this.

When did things get so fucking complicated? This mission was supposed to be simple: Find out what makes this Ordinary immune, duplicate it, and move on. I knew I was gonna fuck this up. I just didn't think it'd be because I fell for my assignment.

"Could I get a copy of this picture?" I ask the photographer, pointing to the photo in Arella's hands.

"Sure," she says. "You can take that one, or I have a wallet size here."

I accept the wallet size. "Thank you."

"Could I get a wallet size too?" Arella asks.

"I only have one wallet of that photo, but I have many others you can choose from."

Beaming, Arella searches through the options and picks one out.

"Oh!" Emmy perks up. "You guys should do what Liz and I do with our pictures."

"Which is . . . ?" I ask with a feeling that it's something super girly.

"We write a cute note on the back for each other."

Yep. Super girly.

"Let's do it," Arella says, handing me her picture.

I trade photos with her and roll my eyes, even though I kinda like the idea. "I'll come up with a cute note to write later."

"Me too."

After we're done going through the photos, the band and I sit down with our manager to go over social-media shit for a couple of hours. Monique spends at least half the time urging me to get "more connected" with our fans through my personal accounts. As always, I refuse. I don't care that it'll help "sell more tickets" or "gain viewers." I play music because I love to, not for the money or the fame.

Once the torture is over, I grip Arella by her hand and we leave for lunch.

"I've got a surprise for you," I say a while later as I push my empty bowl aside. We've just finished eating at a nice ramen place in Chinatown.

Arella wipes her lips with a napkin, then straightens up. "What is it?"

"If I told you, then it wouldn't be a surprise."

Forty-some minutes later, we pull up to an extravagant spa with fancy lights running along the frame of the gold-painted door. Arella's jaw drops, but it's not the place she's astonished by. It's her best friend waiting for us on the golden chairs outside.

I've barely shifted the car into park when Arella runs out to greet Javina with a giant hug. "What are you doing here?"

Javina shrugs. "Dunno. I got a text from pretty boy this morning to meet y'all here at two, so I'm here."

"I'm treating you both to a spa day," I say.

Javina's excitement blasts through my head. "No way! For real?"

"Yep. You're both booked to get your nails done, have an hour-long facial, and a hot-rock massage."

Javina shrieks, then turns to Arella, patting my shoulder. "This one has my official stamp of approval."

My girl laughs. "Thanks."

I peck Arella on her cheek and give her a quick hug. "I'll come pick you up around six."

Now that Arella's preoccupied with getting pampered, I'm free to prepare the rest of my "preserve Arella's immunity" plan.

My first stop is at a jewelry store. I walk in without any idea of what I'm looking for. All I've got is one request: same-day engraving. It takes me a while to decide on a piece to purchase. When I finally do, the woman behind the counter rings me up, and I'm off to my next destination.

At a floral shop, I ask for enough rose petals to fill a swimming pool. The lady tells me she can do three dozen at most, and I accept that.

With a velvet jewelry box, a bag of rose petals, and an arrangement of flowers in hand, I head home. There, I set up the bedroom the way I want it and shut the door.

In the living room, I plant myself on the couch with a pen and Arella's photo. I write up at least fifteen drafts in a notebook before finally deciding on the right words. In my best handwriting possible, I transfer my draft to the back of our picture.

Once I'm done, I read it over a few times. It's the realest thing I've ever written. No song I've ever penned can compare. I hope Arella likes it.

A little after six, I'm waiting in my car outside the spa when Arella and Javina come out, practically glowing. I step out to greet them.

"How was it, ladies?" I hold my arms out for Arella to embrace me.

She does, giving me a hard kiss on the lips too. "Amazing! Look at my nails!"

I once-over her outstretched fingers. They're cleaned up nicely, finished with a lavender-colored polish. "Looks great, babe."

"That massage was exactly what I needed," Javina says. "Thanks, handsome. Out of Ari's two boyfriends so far, you're definitely my fave."

I chuckle lightly. "Not hard to be the favorite when the bar was set so low."

Back at home, while I make dinner, Arella interrogates me on why she's not allowed in the bedroom.

"You're not hiding any dead bodies in there, are you?" she asks playfully.

I shake my head with a chuckle. It's always dead people with her. Maybe she should lay off the true crime shows for a while.

"It's a surprise," I say for the tenth time.

"You can't give me a hint?" She puckers her bottom lip out.

"Nope, and you can pout all you want, but I'm not giving in. You'll find out as soon as we finish eating."

Arella is quick to inhale her pork chop and vegetables. If I could sense her excitement, I'm sure it'd be on the same level as Javina's was earlier outside the spa. Apparently, my girl has no patience, and neither do I, because I finish my meal within minutes of her.

My gut churns as I lead her down the hall and stop outside my bedroom. "Wait here while I put on the final touches."

She nods, then I slip inside, shutting the door behind me.

First, I turn the nozzles to fill the Jacuzzi with warm water. Then I press play on my speakers, and the bathroom fills with soothing piano music. After that, I float a little fireball around to light the wicks of the many candles I've already placed around the tub and bed. The last thing I do is position the velvet box behind some strategically stacked candles on the edge of the Jacuzzi. Finally, I open the door.

Arella clasps a palm against her face as her jaw drops. "Wow . . ."

Rose petals cover everything from the bed to the floor. The candlelight sways to the soft music, inviting her in.

I intertwine my fingers with hers and lead her to the bathroom, where more rose petals are sprinkled everywhere. "You like it?"

She attacks me with a kiss. "I love it!"

Internally, I do a happy dance. There's no way she'll say no.

A minute later, we're naked in the tub. Arella sits between my legs with her back against my front and her head leaned against my shoulder. I wouldn't have it any other way. As I caress her arm, I tenderly kiss up and down her neck.

"My apartment will be ready for me this weekend," Arella says, bursting my bubble of peace.

I scowl, even though she can't see it. I don't want her apartment to be ready. That means she won't sleep here anymore. Well, if she says yes, neither of us will be sleeping here anymore.

It's time . . .

"I have another surprise for you." From behind me, I grab the jewelry box and hold it out in front of her.

"Another? How many do you have tonight?"

Oh, just you wait . . . "Open it."

She dries her wet hands on a towel, then accepts the box from me. It's so big, it's almost double the size of her palms. Slowly, she flips the lid.

"Aw, it's our picture." She takes the photo out of the box, then gasps. "Wow! Honey! It's . . . wow!"

The flickers of candlelight reflect over a gold pendant necklace hanging from a dainty gold chain. The pendant's angel wings are spread, with a two-carat diamond heart in the middle.

"Read the back of the picture."

She does aloud. "Arella, you are my angel. You're the purpose in life I've been searching for. I want to spend eternity with you by my side. We belong together. —Trey."

The next moments of silence tear at me. The expression on her face is unreadable. Does she think it's cheesy? Does she not feel the same way? *Fuck.* I should have written something better.

She tilts her head back and grabs my face, then we embrace in a long kiss. It relaxes the nerves simmering in my gut . . . kinda.

"This is so sweet, honey," she says after she pulls away. "I love it. All of it. The surprise spa date with Javina. The delicious dinner. This candlelit Jacuzzi bath with rose petals. This beautiful necklace. Your wonderful note. Thank you so much."

"Anything for you, baby. Now, turn the necklace over."

"Let me put this down first." She leaves the tub to set the picture on the bathroom counter, where it will stay dry. When she returns, she sits in the spot next to me and flips the necklace over to read the engraving.

"Paris? T.G." Her face crinkles. "Paris? What about it?"

"I wanna take you there."

Her face goes blank. "Seriously?"

"Seriously."

She's quiet. This would be a great time to be able to project some excitement into her or, at the very least, know how she's feeling.

"Trey! That's amazing!" Her giant smile relieves me. That was the easy part. Next is the hard part. As if on cue, she asks, "When do you want to go?"

"As soon as possible," I say, then lower my voice. "Preferably . . . tomorrow."

"Tomorrow? I have to go back to work in three days."

"You don't have to work anymore. I'll take care of you."

She makes a *that's ridiculous* face. "I can't do that."

I take the jewelry box from her and set it aside. Then I squeeze her hands in mine and look straight into her eyes.

"Arella, you are the greatest thing that's ever happened to me. You make me feel happy and full and . . . well, a bunch of other things I can't put into words right now. You deserve way more than what I can give you, but I want to try, and it starts with taking you to Paris. You mentioned that you've always wanted to go there."

"I do. Not tomorrow though. Maybe in a few weeks, after I can make sure I've got the time off. How long do you want to go for?"

I swallow thickly. My answer is going to freak her out. I say it anyway because I want to be as honest with her as I can. "Forever."

"Forever? What do you mean, *forever*?"

I run my wet fingers through my hair, staring at the rose petals floating in the water. "Like, as in, we won't be coming back."

As expected, her face screws together. "What?"

"You said you've always wanted to go to Paris, right?" My tone is nonchalant, as if it's normal to ask your girlfriend to run away to another country with you.

"Yes, to visit. Not to live. You haven't even asked me to move in with you, and now you're asking me to move to Paris? Haven't you ever heard of baby steps?"

I'm not fond of how quickly she's turning me down. "Can't you at least *entertain* the idea?"

"Okay, sure. Where will we live?"

"I'll buy us a nice place there. Any place you want." I've already got options saved on my phone for her to look at. Everything from cute little apartments to fancy mansions.

"What about my grandparents?"

"We can take them with."

She shakes her head with a face that says, *You can't be serious.* "They're not going to want to move to Europe."

"Didn't you say they love traveling?"

The way she rolls her eyes at me drives me crazy. "That's different. Besides, what about your band?"

"They'll be fine without me."

"So, you're just going to abandon them?" I don't like the accusative tone in her voice or that she used the word *abandon*.

"No band stays together forever."

"But you're working on a second album together and planning to go on tour after that."

I stare at the water again because the bewildered look in her eyes tells me I'm not winning this. "We can tour in Europe."

"Okay, sure. Where will I work?"

"You won't need to."

In the corner of my eye, the face she gives me makes me feel like I'm an ignorant child. "How will I pay for things?"

"I'll pay for everything."

"Right, so you're going to quit your current source of income here and get a job in Europe?"

"I could, but I have more than enough money for us to live on for the rest of our lives." Even if I didn't, I'd make sure she was taken care of. Whether that means I'd be waiting tables or going back to school, I'd do it for her.

"You do not." The way her eyes narrow irks me. I haven't told her how much money I have, but for her to be so skeptical . . . ?

"Don't underestimate what I have in the bank."

"This is insane." She rolls her eyes again. I wish she'd stop doing that.

I lean back and drape an arm over the edge of the Jacuzzi. "It is, but I want this more than anything."

"*You're* insane."

"Only a little." This idea sounds crazier out loud than it did in my head. There, it sounded reasonable, like I'm offering her an all-expenses paid vacation . . . for life. Who wouldn't want that? To never have to worry about paying bills, and her only concern would be whether she wants to visit the Louvre or the Gardens of Versailles for the tenth time.

"Why do you want to move to a whole different country?" she asks. "No, sorry, a whole different *continent*?"

"Don't you think it'd be a fun experience?"

"Yeah, for a few days, or even a couple of weeks, but for life?" The tops of her tits keep peeking up above the water, distracting me from our serious conversation.

I lean back with my best *I promise I'm not losing my mind* face. "If you don't like Paris, we could go to any other place in Europe."

"Why Europe?"

"If you don't like Europe, we can move to Australia, China, or Africa. Whatever you'd like."

Trackers sense other Zordis by the use of their elemental and body powers, but it doesn't work underground or overseas. Since I'd rather not live in a hole, Arella and I have to move.

To be safe, I plan to live out the rest of my life without ever using my powers, in case Victor decides to send someone overseas to locate us. Hopefully, he doesn't have connections with any of the ZIRDA bases abroad. The idea that he could have a bunch of people there on the lookout for me is terrifying.

"Trey, I don't want to move at all."

"Can't you at least think about it?" I don't give a shit that I sound desperate. At this point, I'm willing to get on my hands and knees and beg if it means she'll say yes.

Frowning, she crosses her arms over her chest. "What's the *real* reason you want to move? For a 'fun experience' is not going to cut it."

Coming clean about everything was on the list of options I came up with to get us outta this mess. It didn't take me long to decide against it. If I tell Arella the truth, she's gonna run, and I'll lose her. Then she'll definitely be in danger. I've got a feeling that if I'm not the one who takes Arella to Victor within the week, he'll send someone to replace me, and I doubt that person would hesitate like I am.

Arella lowers her tone and cups my cheek. It only settles half the anxiety swirling inside me. "Honey, are you in some kind of trouble?"

"I can explain everything once we get to Paris."

She drops her hand from my face. "Why not now?"

"Because . . . then you might not come with me." I hang my head low. "Actually, you might never want to see me again."

A loud *pfft* echoes throughout the bathroom. "Well, that just makes me want to pack up and head out right now, doesn't it?"

Once it's safe to, I have full intention of telling Arella everything. How the way we met wasn't an accident, how the Royals faked her death when she was three, and everything about the Zordi world. Is it a huge risk? Of course, but I want to be done lying to her. My gut tells me she'll be mad at first but, in the end, she will understand. *She has to . . .*

With her damp hands, she rubs her face and lets out a little groan. "So, let me get this straight. You're saying that whatever secret you're hiding from me might make me leave you, but you want me to move across the world with you before you tell me?"

I guess when she puts it that way, it sounds bad. I'd tell her now if I had a guarantee that she wouldn't freak out and run away. I can't keep her safe if she leaves me. If we're in another country, at least she'll be safe while she processes all the stuff I have to tell her.

I nod firmly. "Yes."

She throws her hands up. "That makes zero sense!"

"I know, babe, but that's just the way it is." I reach for her, but she shoves me away, stinging me deeply. Then she stands and exits the Jacuzzi, grabbing a towel to wrap around herself as she storms out.

I'm left feeling like my entire world is crumbling.

32

TREY

Throughout the night, I think it over. Maybe asking her to move to Europe with me was a little rash. I should have come up with something better. Sadly, with my limited time, it was the best solution I could think of. I just need to get Arella somewhere safe, and Paris seemed like my highest chance of getting her to say yes. My other idea was to ask her to bunker down with me in my parents' invisible safe house, but since I still can't find it, I tossed that idea right out the window.

In the morning, the air between us feels stale. The rose petals sprawled out all over the carpet are a reminder of a night gone wrong. Neither of us mentions Paris during breakfast. I doubt bringing it up again this soon will benefit me anyway. As for Arella, she acts as if last night never happened.

As I place our dirty dishes into the dishwasher, Arella mentions going back to her apartment for the weekend. The thought makes me grind my teeth.

"Babe, I still want you to stay the night with me—every night."

With a smile, she cocks her head to the side. "Are you asking me to move in with you?"

I nod, trying not to look too eager in case she declines my request.

"I don't know. You're kind of hard to live with."

I jerk back a step, my hands still wet. "How so?"

"You're messy. You leave your dirty dishes in the bedroom. You toss your smelly socks all over the house. You make too much noise, and there's just not enough space for me here."

What? "I don't do any of the bullshit you just listed. If anything, I'm tidier than you!"

The corners of her mouth curve upward.

I roll my head back, half grunting, half relieved. "I never know when you're fucking with me."

She laughs adorably. "It's too easy."

When I finish with the dishes, I pull Arella into the bedroom with me. Then I make a big show of emptying a drawer, tossing all my stuff to the floor. "See? There's tons of space for you here." I head into the walk-in closet and move all my clothes to one side, then gesture toward the empty space. "See? This whole side can be yours."

She grins as she runs a hand along the bare hanger rod. "You really want me to move in that bad?"

"Yes, baby. I do." What I actually want is for her to move to Paris with me, but this is a good start.

"Okay, then I will."

My eyes widen. "Seriously?"

"Yeah, seriously."

In the middle of the closet, I pick her up and spin her around. I plant a heavy kiss on her lips as she giggles.

"You know," she says when I release her, "it wouldn't kill you to put some color into your wardrobe."

"You don't like what I wear?"

"All you've got are jeans and plain T-shirts. Don't you ever get sick of wearing the same thing over and over?"

Suddenly, I'm flashed back to elementary school, where the kids made fun of me for wearing that same striped shirt every three days. "It's what I'm used to . . ."

Arella slumps her shoulders. "Oh, honey. I'm sorry. I didn't mean it like that."

I know she didn't. "It's okay, babe."

With a seductive look in her eyes, she drops to her knees. "Here, I'll make it up to you."

There's no need to make up anything, but I allow her to anyway. Within seconds, she's got my zipper down, then my jeans. I'm rock hard before she's even wrapped her hand around my dick.

When I get my fill of her mouth on me, I pump into her against the closet wall until the pleasure ripples through me, and I jerk myself empty into a clean shirt I tear off a hanger.

"Did you come?" I ask, even though I know the answer. Her emotions didn't course through my head.

"No, but that's okay."

"The hell it is." I take her hand and lead her to the bed. "Lie down, baby. Let me take care of you."

It takes her a while to get there. Eventually, she does, and her release sends a wave of her emotions through my head.

I could get used to this.

"Do you mind if I get a workout in before lunch?" I ask as Arella gets washed up.

"Sure. I have to get some work done on my blog anyway."

An hour later, I saunter downstairs from my workout room to find Arella on the couch, typing away on her laptop.

She looks up from her screen, then frowns. "Did you work out?"

"Yeah, why?"

"You didn't even break a sweat."

"I only weight lifted," I lie because any Ordinary would be sweating through their clothes after the fifteen-mile run I just completed on the treadmill.

Arella knows I'm fibbing, because she gives me a fishy look.

I turn my back to her and head to the bedroom. "I'ma get cleaned up, then I'll make us lunch."

When I come back out, Arella is in the same spot, still working. In my palm is her diamond necklace. Sadly, I found it still in its box, where it doesn't belong.

Standing behind her, I hook the diamond around her neck, then gently pull her long waves out of the loop.

"Trey . . ." she says uneasily.

I knew she'd protest. "I want you to wear it, babe."

"But I didn't agree to the Paris thing."

"Doesn't matter. I got this for you, and it's yours whether you agree to the Paris thing or not."

"I'm never going to agree though."

Those words tear at me. They hold so much conviction. Gracefully, I flip my legs over the back of the couch and plop at her side. I take her laptop and set it onto the coffee table. Then I squeeze her hands in mine. "Could you at least think about it? Please?"

I hate how quickly she shakes her head. "There's nothing to think about. I'm not moving to Paris."

I swallow the dry lump in my throat. "Baby, I swear, with anyone else, I wouldn't give a damn. But it's you. I *really* need you to come with me."

"If you can help me understand why, I'll consider it."

I want to tell her everything. I really do, but I need to get her somewhere safe before I tell her that there are people out there who possess powers she doesn't know exist, and that I'm one of them. And that for some strange reason I still don't know, she's immune to those powers. And that my uncle wants me to bring her to him so he can perform deadly tests on her because I'm doing a shit job at solving the mystery myself. In Paris, she can get mad at me for as long as she wants, but at least she'll be away from Victor.

I sigh heavily. "I promise you, baby. I'll explain everything in Paris."

She yanks her hands out of mine, only to toss them into the air. "This is ridiculous. No, I can't wait until we're on another continent to hear why you've shipped me away from home. I want to know why now."

Don't get me wrong. I love seeing the side of her that's strong, defiant, and stands up for herself, but does she really have to choose *now* for it to come out?

With a huff, she folds her arms together. "You know, Liz told me that you like to run when the going gets tough. Whatever happened, Trey, you can't just run from it and drag me with you."

"Why the hell is Liz telling you shit like that?"

"It's not shit if it's true." That's the first time Arella's ever sworn in front of me. It sounds odd coming from her. "Liz told me what happened after Elliott passed away. About how you ran off to some cabin in Colorado for a month. Did something happen, Trey? Did you get into legal trouble or something? What's making you want to run again?"

"This isn't the same as what happened with Elliott." I choke up a little. It still hurts to say his name. "This is about you and me."

"Then why are *you* the only one who's clued in on the details?"

"I told you. I'll tell you once we get to Paris. Once we're safe."

"Safe from what?"

My eyes fall to my hands. "I can't say."

She groans and gets to her feet. "This conversation is getting us nowhere. If you want to move to Paris so bad, then why don't you just go yourself?"

The words leave my mouth before I can stop them. "Because I wouldn't be able to breathe without you."

33

TREY

A yellow Sunrise Daycare T-shirt and the angel-wings necklace—that's what Arella wore when she left for work earlier. It's her first day back to work since the spider incident. No matter what I said to encourage her to stay, she wasn't having it.

When she said she needed to work so she could make rent, I offered her triple the money. She still wasn't having it. Leave it to me to find the most difficult woman in the world to fall for. Any other person would have accepted that offer in a heartbeat. Not Arella. I guess I got my wish when I told Liz that I wanted someone to want me for something other than my money.

The only reason I didn't keep pushing Arella to stay was because she told me that Nathan used to use money to control her. He'd make her dependent on him and his daddy's money as a way to hold power over her. That's nowhere near why I'm offering her money, but I can understand why she feels the need to make her own. So, that's why I'm heading to work today—alone.

"You 'ight, bro?" Marcus slaps a palm over my shoulder in the middle of our writing session. "You been quiet, and now you be hella red in the face."

The rest of our band turns their attention to me, and their concern soars through my mind. I must look sick. I definitely feel it. A minute ago, my chest started burning out of nowhere. Now I'm getting nauseous and my arms feel numb.

"I'm fine," I lie.

I push through another two minutes before the dizziness takes over. As the room spins, my guitar slides off my lap and clanks to the floor. Emmy shrieks, and it makes the migraine in my head blister.

"You wanna lay down, man?" Kevin asks, picking up the guitar for me.

Nausea rises up my throat. *Am I about to . . . Yep, I am.* I rush behind the mini bar and find a trash can just in time to heave into it. I cough as the vomit leaves my throat. Then I heave again. I feel everyone's eyes on me as I throw up my lunch.

When I think it's done, I tie a knot into the trash bag and replace it with a new one. Then I rinse my mouth out under the sink faucet. I was right. My bandmates are gaping at me.

"Are you guys cool with finishing this song without me?" I ask. "I'ma head home."

"Of course, T," Liz says.

"Yeah, go get some rest," Emmy adds.

As I mount my motorcycle, I check the time. Arella got off work twenty minutes ago, and she planned to meet me here. She's probably already on her way, so I call her. The phone rings to her voicemail. I end the call and shoot her a text.

> Hey, babe. I'm not feeling well, so I'm leaving work early. Can you meet me at home instead?

I ride for about fifteen minutes with a splitting headache before I pull over to call her again. I end up at her voicemail . . . again. This time, I leave a message.

"Hey, angel. I'm heading home because I don't feel well. Just letting you know so you don't go to the Soul House and expect me there. I'll see you at home, 'kay?"

I wish there was a way to know if someone's listened to your voicemail. I check my messages again to see if Arella has read my text. It still says *delivered*, not *read*.

In my missed-calls log is a call from Victor from five minutes ago. Whatever he's got to say can wait, because right now, I'm too focused on figuring out where Arella is. I know we didn't leave things on the best note this morning, but she wouldn't ghost me, would she?

I ride for another ten minutes before I get impatient and pull off to the shoulder again. After I yank my helmet off, I Google the number for Sunrise Daycare. Someone picks up on the third ring.

"Sunrise. Javina speaking."

"Javina, it's Trey. Is Arella there?" I don't know what I'm hoping for. Maybe for her to tell me that Arella got held up and she's just finishing up work. Maybe that one of the kids is pulling a bad prank on her by hiding her phone, and she's running around looking for it as we speak. I would have accepted anything except the answer I actually get.

"Sorry, pretty boy. Ari left when her shift ended."

"Thanks." I hang up.

I call Liz, and she picks up right away. "Hey, T-Bear. You okay?"

Not really . . . My nausea has gotten worse, and it's not like Arella to not answer her phone. "Is Arella there?"

"Nope, why?"

"Dammit." I slap a hand against my handlebars as I hang up. *Where is she?*

A thought stops my heart. What if this is her way of leaving me? She's had enough of me hiding shit from her, and she's probably at my house, packing her stuff up right now. When I get home, her drawer will be empty, her side of the closet will be too, and I'll never see her again.

Please don't let that be it . . .

With my helmet back on, I race home. Her car isn't in my driveway. As I dismount my bike, my heart pounds against my lungs like fists against a sandbag. *Thump, thump, thump.* I rush inside, shouting for her.

"Babe? You here?"

Silence.

I wrench her drawer open so hard, it comes out of the nightstand. My nausea settles a tiny bit when I find her things still here. I don't even bother putting the drawer back in. I've got more important things to do—like find my girl.

Maybe she's at her apartment. Maybe she's surprising me by packing up her things to bring here. Even as I think that, I know it's unlikely. Still, I climb back onto my bike and head to her place.

It feels like forever getting through traffic. When I finally arrive at Arella's apartment complex, her car is missing from the parking lot.

I knock on her door and wait all of two seconds before I point a finger at the lock and let myself in. The place smells of ripe chemicals and cleaning supplies. At least it's spider-less. Unfortunately, it's also Arella-less.

"Babe?" I yell, just in case.

Nobody answers.

I head into her bedroom and find zero signs that she's been around. *Where could she be?*

I jump when my phone buzzes in my pocket. It's a number I don't recognize. Usually, I don't answer unknown numbers, but . . . "Hello?"

"Hi, is this Trey Grant?" asks a calm female voice I've never heard before.

"Who's this?"

"I'm Sara Benson, a nurse at the LA Community Hospital. I'm calling on behalf of Miss Arella Rance. She wanted me to tell you where she is."

My lungs tighten. "Why couldn't she call me herself?"

"I'm afraid she's in no condition to—"

"What happened?"

"I . . . I, um, can't tell you exactly."

"Why not?" I shout, and I don't care that it's rude.

Sara is unfazed. She replies in the same calm tone. "Because I don't know all the details. I wasn't here when she was admitted up from the ER. I was just told to call you."

"The ER?" I shout again. "What?"

"Look, all I know is that she was brought in by ambulance."

"Ambulance?" I can't breathe.

"She's on floor two. You're welcome to come here and speak to the doctor in charge of—"

"I'll be there in fifteen minutes."

34

TREY

To my ears, the hospital is quiet. To my head, it's a madhouse of insanity. Sadness, fear, anxiety, dread—it's all here, clawing at me to feel what everyone else feels. I can't shut it off. I can't even tone it down. I'm too tense to control my mind power.

"Where is she?" I ask the woman stationed behind the first desk I can find on floor two.

She looks up at me from behind a pair of sparkly pink eyeglasses. The name badge clipped to her chest reads: Sara Benson, RN.

"You must be Trey Grant."

"Yes. Where is she?" I sound rude and impatient, but I can't help it. I won't be okay until I see Arella again.

The woman doesn't seem to care that I'm on a one-track train going three hundred miles an hour toward one goal and one goal only. "Wow. You got here quick. Do you live nearby?"

Not at all. I probably broke at least sixteen laws with my motorcycle coming here as I weaved between cars and ran stop lights. "Where. Is. She?" That's the third time I've asked, and I'm not asking again.

"Look, I understand you're probably scared right now, but don't worry. She's fine." Sara smiles as if to soothe me. "Just calm down, and take a deep breath."

I hate when people tell me to calm down. It only irritates me more. Still, I obey her and suck in a deep breath. It does nothing to settle me.

"Great. I'll go grab Dr. Jordan. He'll meet you in the family waiting room." She points toward an open room down the hall with a kiddie table and chairs. "In the meantime, could you check in?" She hands me a clipboard.

I sign the damn paper, then slap a sticker with my name on it against my upper chest. Then I force my body into the family waiting room. It's small and smells of musty carpet and old shoes. In the corner, a little TV plays an animated movie at a low volume. A large round table sits in the opposite corner with an unfinished puzzle scattered on top.

My phone buzzes in my pocket. It's Victor again. I don't want to be in the middle of a conversation with him when the doctor comes, so I let it go to voicemail.

All my nails are chewed down when I finally hear, "Mr. Grant?"

A tall man with rich bronze skin and graying hair appears in the doorway. My zense activates as he offers me the knowing smile that Zordis do whenever we first meet another of our kind. "I'm Doctor Jordan. Thanks for coming so quickly."

I don't return his smile. "What happened?"

The doctor places a pen into the chest pocket of his scrubs, sighing. "Miss Rance was in a car accident."

My knees almost give out. *A car accident?*

The doctor throws his palms up. "She's fine. Just whiplash, a few stitches, and some bruises."

Whiplash? Stitches? Bruises? My brain can't comprehend what any of those words mean when it comes to Arella. How can this man talk about all of that as if it's normal?

"Can I see her?" My voice comes out broken like the way my chest feels.

"I'm sorry. You'll need to wait until she's done testing."

"I can't just *see* her?"

"Not while she's going through an MRI."

The little patience I have left snaps as I growl, "How long is that gonna take?"

"Maybe an hour. Two at most."

Two hours? My heart can't take another minute of this. "What caused the accident?"

"A car T-boned her at an intersection and fled the scene."

I plop into the closest chair. The doctor continues, but my mind doesn't process it. All I hear is *blah, blah, blah.*

When Dr. Jordan leaves, the tingling in my chest leaves with him. I barely get a moment to myself before that same nurse knocks on the doorframe.

"Could I get you anything? Coffee? Tea? A snack?" Sara's got that pointless smile glued to her face again.

"No, thank you," I reply blankly as I stare aimlessly at the TV.

"If you wanna pass some time, there's a gift shop downstairs."

"Thanks."

Twenty minutes later, I pace the hospital with a large gift bag in hand, trying to pull myself together. They said she's fine. I shouldn't be so worried. But if she's fine, why does she need MRI scans? And stitches? What if she's not fine, and they lied to me to prevent me from freaking the fuck out and tearing this place apart until I find her? If I don't see my girl soon, I might do just that.

A person in the room at the end of the hall has five miserable people surrounding them. All their feelings of despair are drowning out the emotions of everyone else in the hospital. I do my best to channel my mind power toward Sara, who seems to be the only one around who's spirit isn't dying inside. The most that does is lower everyone else's murky energy to a constant whisper—a loud whisper.

Eventually, I hide in the stairwell to call Liz. She'll have something good to say. She always does.

Liz answers on the first ring. "What's wrong?"

"What? Are you a Seer now too?"

"You never call me, and this is the second time you've called me today after you abruptly left our writing session looking like you caught a zirus. So, what's wrong?"

I pound my forehead against the wall. It echoes in the stairwell. "It's Arella. She . . ." I can't even say it without choking up. "She was in a car accident."

Liz gasps. "How bad is the damage? To her, obviously, not the car."

"The doctor said she's okay. I haven't confirmed it yet since I haven't seen her. She's going through some bullshit MRI thing that takes forever." I still don't understand what the point of an MRI is when she's "fine."

"Oh, T. I'm so sorry. What can I do for you?"

I sigh deeply, trying my best not to lose it. "Just talk to me. I hate hospitals."

"Yeah, that's not the best place for you, is it?"

"I'm getting a headache." Actually, my head pounds as if little elves are chopping wood in my brain while listening to heavy metal. The only good thing is that the nausea has simmered down and my arms don't feel numb anymore. *Which reminds me . . .* "Liz, I need to tell you something, and it's gonna sound crazy."

"Okay?"

"I—I felt it."

There's a long pause, and I picture Liz's eyebrows creasing together. "Felt what?"

"That sensation Zordis talk about. I knew that something was wrong with Arella. My *body* knew. My stomach wouldn't stop whipping around, and there's this constant burning in my chest."

"That's not possible, T. We only feel the glimmer with our soul mates."

I know that. That's why this doesn't make any sense. "Well . . . maybe, I dunno. Maybe Arella—"

"Stop. I know what you're about to say, and there's no chance. She's an Ordi."

"I know, but here's the thing. Today is not the first time I felt it. It happened last week too. I thought it was just a coincidence, so I brushed it off. I've always thought the glimmer was just some stupid thing Zordis made up to put claim on each other—until I felt it *again* today. I mean, I dunno. Maybe it was a coincidence, but it doesn't feel like it."

"Hmm . . ." is all Liz says. The call goes silent for a moment before she continues, "Ya know, if you think Ari could be your soul mate, that means you're in love with her."

I don't respond. I don't know how to.

Liz presses on. "Are you?"

In the depths of my soul, I know the answer. I inhale a few breaths of courage before I'm able to admit it out loud. "Yes, I am."

Liz perks up, and I hear her grinning through the phone. "Ah! I've been waiting for you to fall in love for years. I never thought it'd be with an Ordi though. I mean, do you know how outrageous that sounds?"

I slump onto the bottom step of the stairs and shove my face into my hand. "I know it's bizarre, but it doesn't feel that way."

"I agree."

I don't hide my shock. "You do?"

"Yeah. I've said it before, T. That girl is perfect for you, except for the one thing. If you haven't noticed, I've stopped giving you shit for being with her, 'cause you light up whenever she's around. Lately, the lyrics you've been writing aren't as dark, and your smiles look genuine. I've never seen you so happy. I wasn't about to keep nagging at you for being happy, no matter how strange and illegal it is."

As always, Liz is right. Arella does make me the happiest I've ever been. For my best friend to have recognized that and encouraged it, even when she believes it's wrong, means a ton. I already thought Liz deserves the world. Now I think she deserves the entire universe.

"What should I do?" I ask, unsure what exactly I'm referring to. I need advice on a lot of things right now.

"Have you told her?"

"Told her what?"

Liz scoffs with a *duh* tone. "That you're in love with her."

"Considering how I only admitted it to myself for the first time just now, no."

"Do you know if she feels the same?"

"I can't sense her, so I dunno." I'm still trying to process the idea that I'm in love with someone. The concept that someone might feel the same for me is even harder to swallow.

"Seriously, T? You rely on your Empath power way too much. You need to tell her."

"How?"

"I dunno. Just tell her."

Admitting that I'm in love with Arella is one thing. Now I have to tell her, too? *Since when was that a rule?* "What will that accomplish?"

"I dunno. I just think it's important for you to verbalize this to her."

"Okay, then what?"

"Then, well . . . that's where it gets difficult, doesn't it? It's not like the Superiors are gonna allow you to have this relationship just 'cause you're in love. They'll still lock you up if they find out. In court, they'll ask you about intent to determine if they should put you behind bars or in an asylum.

"In your case, I'ma guess the asylum. The second you tell 'em you felt the glimmer with an Ordinary, it'll be case closed. *Bam!* Next thing you know, you're sitting in a room with a bunch of weirdos who eat their own toenails and—"

"Liz."

"Oh, sorry. I'm not helping, am I?"

Not a fucking bit. "Not really . . ."

"Okay, how 'bout I stop over at the hospital? Would that help?"

"Yes, actually. If they discharge Arella tonight, could you drive her to my place? I rode the bike here."

"Sure. Text me the address. I'll come now."

Almost an hour later, Liz strolls through the sliding glass doors with a brown paper bag.

"What's that?" I ask as my chest tingles.

"Tacos!" She beams. "Grabbed some on the way over. I figured you probably hadn't eaten yet."

My belly rumbles from the delicious scent of food wafting from the bag. I don't know what to say. This woman never stops wowing me. I heave her in by the shoulder and snake my arms around her. Then I squeeze her as hard as I can. Her warmth washes away a bit of the stress I've been carrying.

Liz coughs. "Stop, T. I'm gonna drop these tacos if you keep suffocating me."

I release her. "Sorry. I'm just so fucking grateful for you."

"As you should be. No one else would ever put up with your shit." She leans into me and lowers her voice. "I mean, seriously, any other Zordi would be calling to get you into rehab right now. Your obsession with Ari is still a little wacky to me, but I trust that you, of all people, know that your feelings for her are real."

"They are," I say with full conviction. "Speaking of other Zordis, her doctor is one."

Liz clasps a gloved hand to her mouth. "Oh no. Does he know you're dating Ari?"

I shrug.

"Do you think he's gonna call the Supes?"

Another shrug. "I hope not. I've been too worried about Arella to even think about that."

"I'll back you up. I'll say you two are just friends."

I let out a light scoff. "Like they're gonna listen to you."

She puts a fist up. "I'll make 'em!"

Liz checks in and gets a name sticker from Sara, and then we head into the waiting room. There's a different kid's movie playing on the TV now. On the table, I push the unfinished puzzle aside to give us space to eat our tacos.

Between bites, Liz asks, "Do you think it's possible that she's one of us?"

With my mouth full, I say, "No, why?"

"Because I don't think you have a mental condition. Crazy people don't think they're crazy, and you've admitted that this thing you have for Ari is bizarre. Yeah, you like to sleep around with Ordis, but I think that has more to do with your past and your gifts than having an actual attraction to them. But to fall in love with one? And to experience the glimmer? I doubt that's stemming from your trauma. There's gotta be another explanation, and the only one I can think of is that Ari's one of us. What if immunity is her power? What if her immunity is what blocks us from feeling the zense around her?"

Wow. That's a lot to take in. "First off, my past? My trauma? How does that have anything to do with why I'm willing to sleep with Ordinaries?"

Liz eyes me, lifting an eyebrow. "Do you really wanna unpack that right now?"

I'm about to say yes because I want to hear her explanation, but now, I'm not so sure. I've got a feeling she's gonna say things I won't like.

"I'll give you a hint. It has to do with your low self-worth, what you think you deserve, and how your past affects that."

Yeah, I don't wanna hear any more. I clear my throat. "Moving on . . ."

After I chew down the rest of my first taco, I lean back in my chair. "The idea that Arella is a Zordi has crossed my mind. I did some research on it over the z-net a while ago, and the closest ability I could find to her immunity is force fields. Even then, Blockers can only block *external* powers, and Arella's immunity seems to only block the *internal* ones.

"Also, those Zordis can't block the zense. According to the z-net, nothing can. If Arella was a Zordi and didn't know it, she'd feel the tingle around us, and I don't think she does. Plus, she doesn't have any other powers."

Liz finishes the taco she's working on as she thinks. "Maybe she's defective, and that's what causes her body to not feel the zense or have any other powers?" Liz is doing what I did before: looking for any possible cause that could explain the anomaly that is Arella. I've stopped trying to explain the unexplainable. It didn't amount to anything.

I pick up another taco and bite into it. "The correct term is *restricted*, not defective. Zordis with complications in their gifts get offended when people call them defective."

"I know, but my family calls me defective all the time, and it's true, so why correct them?"

This isn't the first time Liz has called herself defective, and I hate it. In the Zordi world where everyone's born with three powerful gifts and natural beauty, having anything wrong with you results in immediate disownment. Liz's family is no exception, and it's part of the reason why I will forever stick by this woman's side.

I scowl at her. "You're not defective. Your body power works—just not in a way you'd like it to."

"You know, you're the only one who ever gets mad at me for calling myself defective. Everyone else just agrees."

I shake my head, sighing. The Zordi community needs to do better. "Anyway, if Arella is one of us, then explain how she gets cold all the time? Or how she sweats when she's hot?"

Liz bites into her second taco. "Hmm. Good point. With our bodies' natural equilibrium, it's not possible for us to sweat."

"Exactly. Also, Arella sleeps every night. She even has dreams and nightmares. She doesn't heal as fast as we can. She can't see as far as we can, either. The other day, while in the car, I asked her if she could read a sign way down the road. While I could read it perfectly, she could barely see it."

After wiping her mouth off with a napkin, Liz says, "Ya know, I've always wondered what it'd be like to have dreams or Ordinary vision. Once, I Googled what Ordinaries see when they take off their glasses. Did you know that some of their eyes are so bad, they can barely make out shapes or colors?"

"Yeah, I knew that."

A knock on the doorframe causes Liz to jolt.

"Sorry!" Sara giggles. "Just wanted to let you know she's done. You're welcome to see her now."

I shoot out of my chair before the nurse even finishes her sentence. Liz and I follow her down the hall and around a corner before stopping at a closed door. I don't sense anyone on the other side, so it must be Arella.

Sara turns to us. "Maybe just one at a time?"

Liz steps back and gestures for me to go first. With my giant gift bag in hand, I enter the small hospital room. Sara quietly shuts the door behind me.

The square room is dimly lit and smells of disinfectant. My girl is propped up on the bed in a light-blue gown, wearing a neck brace that looks like it's suffocating her. Cords are tangled around her body in every direction, hooked up to machines that do who knows what.

I'd do anything to take her place. I'd go through a thousand car accidents if it means she'd never have to go through another one again.

"Trey." Her voice cracks, sounding weak and fragile. I want so badly to hold her until the pain is gone.

After setting the gift bag down, I slide a chair closer to her bedside and sit. Then I take her hand and squeeze it between both of mine. Once again, I draw strength from her touch. A tiny beam of light shines into me, erasing some of the darkness in my chest.

"Hey, beautiful."

She lets out a little *pfft*. "I doubt I look that beautiful right now."

"You'll always look beautiful to me." I mean that with all my heart.

This catastrophe only confirms how much of a wreck I'd be if something ever happened to her. Silently, I vow to myself to never let anything else happen.

With a smile, Arella turns her head to fully face me. The stitches on her lip flash me back to when my mother's lip was cut. She had blood dripping down every curve of her face. Her screams echo in my mind as that big man drags her away from me to pound his fist into her head. I should have protected her, like I should have protected Arella.

A pang of nausea hits me hard, except this time, it's not from the glimmer. I swallow thickly, trying to keep it down.

"What's in the bag?" Arella asks.

"Something for you." The bag crinkles as I pull out a big purple teddy bear.

Her eyes light up as she accepts it from me. "Awe. It's adorable! Thank you."

My phone vibrates in my jeans. It's Victor—again. What the fuck does he need so badly?

This is the worst time to be calling. I don't want to leave Arella, but in all my twenty-six years, Victor has never been this insistent about reaching me.

"I'll be back, angel," I say as I step away. I gesture for Liz to enter the room as I head down the hall to answer my phone. "Hello?"

As always, Victor sounds snippy. "Are you with the girl?"

"Yeah, why?"

"Any updates?"

"No." I could tell him that the very person we need alive for any of this to work almost died today, but she didn't, so that information isn't relevant.

"Seriously? Have you been able to sense *any* emotions from her?"

"Nope," I lie again.

"Not a single one?"

"Nope."

"Hmm. We'll have to try something else."

I enter the stairwell as my heart clenches. "What do you mean?"

"These tests aren't working."

Something inside me flips into panic mode. Careful to keep my tone steady, I ask, "What tests?"

"You know . . . the flu, the spiders, the truck."

I stop breathing as everything clicks together. I try to sound less angry and more surprised. "Wait, all of those things happened to her . . . because of you?"

"Weakening her immune system. Invoking trauma, then a near-death experience. Since you're taking so long to get results, I thought we'd do some testing in the meantime. Our team thought lowering her natural defenses or raising an extreme emotion in her would do the trick. If we can get you to sense her when she's most vulnerable or when her emotions are at their highest, maybe we can find out the source of her im—"

"Why wasn't I informed of this?" I can barely contain myself through gritted teeth. "You could have killed her."

"Are you questioning my methods? Everything was highly controlled. The flu was a minor one, those spiders weren't poisonous, and the accident was thoroughly organized. I wouldn't risk her life without having our best agents on it. Also, I made sure she was sent to a hospital where one of our ZIRDA doctors is stationed. He's already sent me the reports from her MRI scan, and we'll cross-reference it with the others. She's completely safe."

Safe? Is he fucking kidding? I just saw her in a neck brace. It takes everything in me not to curse at him. I need to get off this call before I say something I shouldn't.

"Do you have any other tests planned?" I ask, trying my hardest to keep my tone stable.

"Yes, actually, and they involve you, but they need to be performed here. When can you bring her in?"

Never! He's insane if he thinks I'm going to allow him to breathe around Arella after he killed the last two Immunes. *Over my dead body.* "I can't convince her into a road trip now that she's in a neck brace."

"Why not?"

"Trust me. I know this woman. She's gonna wanna rest up. If I push her into it, she'll be more hesitant to do it. How about we wait until she's fully healed first?"

In the background, a spoon clinks against a mug. Victor takes a sip of the liquid. "When will she be out of the neck brace? A week?"

"At least two." I have no idea how long it'll be. I just need to buy some time. "Also, it'll be important for me to meet her grandparents first. They could give me some insight into something that may have happened to her when she was young that she doesn't remember."

"Fine. Meet them within the week and report back." *Click.*

Pulling at my hair, I collapse to the dusty floor.

This can't be happening.

35

ARELLA

The doctor said my lip would heal within a week. After two days, my lip was fully healed without even a scar to show for it.

The doctor said my body would be sore for two weeks. It's been a week now, and my body feels like it's functioning at one hundred percent again.

I'm not wearing the neck brace anymore, despite what Trey wants. He thinks I should follow the doctor's orders and wear it for the full fourteen days, but why wear something that's awkward and itchy when I don't need to?

Ever since the accident, Trey's been intense. Even when we're home, not really doing anything, he insists on being next to me at all times. If I leave the room, he comes with. I understand that I was injured, and that's been hard on him, but nothing is going to happen to me in the safety of his house. The more I remind him of that, the more protective he gets.

Lately, his eyes have been swimming with anxiety. I wish he'd open up to me and explain what's bothering him. Despite what he says, it's not only the car accident that's eating at him. However, the more I ask about it, the more he shuts down, so I let it go.

Something he *won't* let go is the Paris thing. He brings it up every day—sometimes multiple times a day. He's shown me housing options and talked my ear off about the wonderful sights. He even looked up storefronts where I can start my dream bakery. It's enticing, but at the end of the day, I'm not willing to move to Paris on the promise that he'll tell me why once we get there. No way. Whenever I urge him to tell me the reason, he refuses.

I'm climbing into bed when I ask, "Are you trying to get away from the feds?"

It's the only thing I can think of as to why he wants to flee the country. While I'm flattered that he's so into me that he won't move without me, I'm not trying to live a life on the run. He mentioned that he's got lots of investments. Maybe some are illegal and it's finally catching up to him.

"No, baby," he says somberly, sliding under the covers with me. "I'm not running from the feds."

The sincere look on his face makes me believe him, so I throw out other guesses. "Did you mess with the wrong mob boss? Is someone after your money? Did you find out you have a child somewhere, and you don't want me to find out about it?"

He pulls my back against his front. "No, baby. It's none of those."

I'm out of guesses. "And this is something that might make me break up with you?"

"Maybe, but I hope not. I'm one hundred percent sure you'll be freaked out at first, but I also have faith that you'll understand and forgive me."

I am a forgiving person—sometimes too forgiving. "Can you give me a hint?"

"No, but what I can tell you is that I care about you more than anything in this world and I hope that's enough to earn your forgiveness. It doesn't even have to be right away, just eventually. And I'll do everything in my power to make sure you'll never regret it."

He didn't have to tell me that he cares about me for me to know it. I *feel* it through the little things he does. Like the way he always brings me a fresh glass of water before bed and the way he holds me *so* tight until I fall asleep.

I'm torn. I'm nowhere closer to knowing what he's hiding from me, yet I trust that whatever it is won't change my feelings about him. This last week of watching him cook for me, clean for me, and treat me like a queen has made me realize that I'm in love with this man. While he hasn't said it, I think he's in love with me too. I can see it in his eyes every time he stares at me.

"Good night, baby." Trey wraps his arms around me tighter, then kisses my neck the gentle way he has been since the accident. While it does send a spark down my body, I miss the way he kissed me before—long, hard, and passionate.

He's the same when we make love too. He thrusts inside me like he's afraid he'll break me. I prefer the rough, animalistic way he pounded into me before. Yesterday, when I told him that, he said, "I don't wanna hurt you." No matter what I said, I couldn't convince him that my body can take it.

The other thing I couldn't convince him of is going to meet my grandparents. For weeks, he practically begged to meet them. Now he suddenly doesn't want to anymore? What changed? I'm off work, with a *real* doctor's note this time, so this is a great opportunity for us to go. Trey's excuse is that he's not ready for me to be in a car yet, but that's not true. He's been dragging me with him to work every day.

Either way, arguing with him is pointless—like the argument we've been having about my car. Since my Civic is totaled, I've been online shopping for a new vehicle. It's been hard to find something that I like and can afford. Trey keeps telling me to pick out whatever I want with any price tag because he'll get it for me, but I refuse to allow that.

Nathan used to buy things for me so he could use them against me later. Whenever we fought, he'd say things like "You wouldn't even have that if it wasn't for me." I recognize now that it was just another one of his many ways to guilt me into doing whatever he wanted. While I don't think that's Trey's intent, I still don't want to feel like I owe him.

Two weeks after the accident, I'm finally able to convince Trey to leave my side for the first time. His band has an all-day video shoot, and I want to stay home to bake. Lately, my blog hasn't seen much new content, which has been affecting my traffic, which affects my paycheck.

"I'm staying home," I say firmly. "Being out of work for the past two weeks means I need the extra money now more than usual. I promise you, honey, I'll be fine by myself."

"You're so goddamn difficult," Trey says with a huff, before getting into his car and driving away. It'll do him some good to have a few hours away from me. He needs to relearn that in life, things will happen, and he can't take me everywhere with him just to ensure I'm okay.

I'm in the middle of grabbing flour out of his cabinet when the doorbell rings. I expect it to be the mailman or someone trying to convert me into their religion, so I'm pleasantly surprised when it's neither.

"If you don't marry him, I will," Javina says when I open the door.

"What are you doing here?"

"That man of yours called me—at work, mind you, because I wasn't answering my cell, because ya know, I was *working*—just to ask me to hang out with you today. When I told him I couldn't, he offered me another spa day to get me to fake a family emergency."

My jaw drops. "Did you?"

Dramatically, Javina slaps a hand over her chest. "Please pray for my mother, who broke her ankle from falling down a ladder. She's in desperate need of my care right now."

With an eye roll coupled with a light chuckle, I gesture for Javina to step inside. "Aren't we short-staffed?"

Javina kicks her shoes off. "Yeah, but luckily, we're down five kids today, and I was able to call in Carrie last minute. So, it's all good. Besides, I wasn't gonna turn down another spa day. Also, he Venmoed me five hundred dollars after I agreed to his terms. The note said, "for missing a day of work.' " She scoffs. "As if I get paid that much to watch over children."

"Wait . . ." I lead Javina into Trey's kitchen. "What were his *terms*?"

"He just asked that I don't let you out of my sight. For five hundred dollars a day, tell that boy I'll babysit you whenever he wants!"

I roll my eyes again. "He's been overprotective lately."

"Girl, I am too. First a spider invasion, now a car accident? What's next? A building falling over you? A stampede of hyenas? If I could, I'd shrink you and put you into a padded box. Then I'd carry you around in my pocket to make sure nothing can harm you."

On the spectrum of overprotectiveness, it goes Javina, then Trey, then my grandparents. Growing up, Gramps and Grammy rarely let me out of their sight. Even when we were doing simple things like hanging out at a playground, my grandparents were always one step behind me.

I'm used to people being overprotective of me. It's part of the reason why I didn't pick up on Nathan's red flags for so long. I've since learned that there's a difference between being overprotective and being controlling. Javina, Trey, and my grandparents keep me close because they genuinely care about me. Nathan kept me close because he needed to exert power over me.

Thankfully, Trey hasn't done or said anything that's felt controlling. Yes, he's a little possessive sometimes—like the other day, when his security manager made me laugh and touched my arm, Trey stormed over within seconds to pull me away. Still, he has yet to tell me what I can and cannot wear. Not once has he tried to read my text messages over my shoulder, or suggest that I'm not allowed to see or call Javina. The second he does, I'm out. I don't care how much joy this man brings into my life. I'm not going through another three years of abuse, gaslighting, and feeling unwanted. If anything, Trey has been making me feel overly wanted.

WHEN MY MAN RETURNS HOME FROM HIS VIDEO SHOOT, HE SHOWS UP IN A CAR I'VE NEVER SEEN before. Javina and I step outside to greet him in the driveway, where a brand-new white crossover is sitting.

Javina whistles through her teeth. "Damn, pretty boy. Lexus ain't doin' it for ya no more?"

Trey flaunts a megawatt smile from the driver's seat with the door open. "I'm good with my car. This one's for Arella."

In sync, Javina and I gasp. For the first time ever, my talkative friend is out of words.

I'm not. "Honey, you didn't . . ."

"I did." He beams and even has the nerve to do it proudly.

I'm not sure if I should be mad, glad, frustrated, or thrilled. I'm a little of all. It's the anger that comes out though. "Why would you do this? After all the reasons I told you not to?"

Javina flashes me a *What the hell?* look. "Ari! Ungrateful much?"

Trey hops out of the car with his arms up in surrender. "I bought the car under your name. It's all yours. Fully paid for. No strings attached."

I pretzel my arms together. "I'm not accepting it."

Trey sighs heavily. "How 'bout you get in and drive it around before you make that decision?"

I'm about to protest again when Javina shoots her arm up. "Shotgun!"

Later that evening, Javina's gone, and Trey and I are still arguing about the car thing.

I'm heated. "You know I have a meeting with a guy tomorrow to talk about buying his used car."

"Exactly. I overheard you on the phone with him, and his car sounds as shitty as your ex. He said it's missing a side mirror. What's wrong with me buying you a nice car with *all* the mirrors and extra safety features?"

"Because you got me a car I can't afford!" I'm shouting, and I don't want to be. I'm not a shouter, but Trey's turning me into one.

He replies calmly, and it only pisses me off more. "Did you miss when I said that it's *fully* paid for?"

"I'm gonna have to pay you back."

"No, you will not." It's the firmest and loudest thing he's ever said to me.

I return the conviction. "Yes, I will."

Things between us feel tense as we get ready for bed. We've stopped talking about the car, only because neither of us will back down. He's told me that I'm "so goddamn difficult" at least four times now. Eventually, I get tired of arguing with him, and I fall asleep.

The need to pee stirs me awake. Blackness engulfs the room. I flip the lamp on to discover that Trey is missing. *Of course.*

Typically when I wake up in the middle of the night, he's gone, doing who knows what around the house. Typically, it doesn't bother me. And typically, I just go back to sleep and wake up in the morning with him here. Tonight, though, I'm not feeling typical, and I want to know what's so important at three in the morning.

I shuffle down the quiet hall toward the living room. My feet stop when Trey's voice comes from around the corner. His tone is low and laced with frustration.

"Not yet. She's still recovering." A pause. "It's a three-hour drive and—" It goes silent as he listens to whoever is on the phone. "Maybe it wouldn't take this long if she wasn't hospitalized."

This isn't the first time I've heard Trey on the phone at this odd hour. However, this is the first time I've caught this much of the conversation. Where is a three-hour drive, and who is he talking to?

"All right. Just give me more time," he says, then there's a clatter. It sounds like he chucked his phone onto the coffee table. As he lets out a long, aggravated groan, I tiptoe back to bed.

A few minutes later, my bladder is empty and I'm cuddled up in bed with my teddy bear from the hospital. Trey is quiet as he slowly slips back under the covers.

"Who was that?" I ask with my back facing him.

"Shit." He bounces backward. "I thought you were sleeping."

I turn to face him, and it goes quiet as I wait for him to answer my question.

"Sorry, babe. I didn't mean to wake you."

"Who were you on the phone with?"

"Nobody important." He said that the last three times I asked him this question.

Trey gestures for me to scoot closer, then pats his shoulder for me to lay my head on. Usually, I would. This time, I don't budge.

"What's wrong, angel?" Whenever he calls me that, I think about the necklace I haven't taken off since he hooked it around my neck. It's the most beautiful piece of jewelry anyone's ever given me.

I sit up, hugging the bear to my chest, then click the lamp on. Trey does the same on his side. For a moment, I only stare at him, admiring his adorably messy hair, sexy stubble, and those blue-gray eyes. Something in them is deeply sad. I wish I knew why, and if it has anything to do with what he's hiding or what's strange about him. Maybe it's both.

I draw in a breath and slowly let it out as I think of how to ask the question that's been burning in my mind since our first night together in Long Beach. "Is there something I don't know about you? Like, besides whatever mysterious reason you want to flee the country?"

In the time it takes for him to answer, I could have walked to Paris. His face says he's impassive, but his eyes tell me he's torn. "What makes you think there is?"

There he goes . . . answering a question with a question. "You're just different sometimes."

"Different how?"

I was hoping you'd tell me. "There are little things I've noticed about you. Things that don't make sense."

"Like?"

"Well, first, let's talk about your late-night phone calls, and how you never want to tell me who it is."

"It's not your business," he says, a little clipped.

"It is if you're talking about me."

His eyes go wide. "What did you hear?"

"Who were you talking to?"

With a heavy sigh, he gives in. "It was my uncle. He wants to meet you. I told him you need to recover first."

Reasonable, I suppose. His uncle lives in Three Rivers, which is three hours away. If that's the case, why all the secrecy? And why did he sound so exasperated? "Why is your uncle calling you at three in the morning?"

"He's not much of a sleeper."

"What about you? Do *you* ever sleep?"

"Of course."

I arch my eyebrows. "*Every* night?"

"I sleep with you every night, don't I?"

"Not really. Some nights, I feel like you're just laying there."

His eyes fall to his hands, speechless. I'll assume that means I'm right.

"Are you afraid of anything?"

"Everyone has fears, babe."

"Not you. You walked into an apartment crawling with spiders and carried me out like it was nothing."

He shrugs a shoulder. "Spiders don't scare me."

"Why do you tint your windows?"

Silence.

"Why don't you ever sweat during your workouts?"

No answer.

"How does your body heal so fast? You had a bruise on your face and gashes in your knuckles that were gone within days."

Still no answer.

"What was up with your old teddy bear asking for a password?"

Nothing.

"How did you know Lucas was in trouble?"

Finally, he looks at me. "Who's Lucas?"

"That teenager getting beat up in Long Beach."

"Oh."

"You knew something was wrong from all the way at the restaurant. How?"

Trey drags a hand through his hair, letting out a huffy breath. "I can't explain how. I want to. I just can't. And for the record, I tried to ignore it. It wasn't until I realized it was three against one that I assumed it was a girl getting raped or something. I couldn't live with myself if I allowed that to happen. I didn't want it to turn into something like this for us. That's why I asked you to stay at the damn restaurant."

"If I had, I wouldn't have known there's something unusual about you, and I think it's time you tell me what."

"I can't."

I hug my teddy bear tighter to my chest. "Are you an alien?"

His face screws together. "What? No."

"Are you a superhero?"

"No."

"Are you from the future?"

"No."

Well, that's the last of my theories. "Does anyone know your secret?"

"No."

That's a total lie. Somebody knows, and I'd put money on that somebody being Liz. "Are you dangerous?"

"No," he answers easily. "Not to you."

"Who are you dangerous to?"

"Anyone who tries to hurt you."

That makes my heart swoon until a thought hits me: Is there more to why he's been so overprotective lately? "Is there someone out there trying to hurt me?"

He swallows thickly. "Kinda."

"Were you, like, sent from another world to protect me?"

"Something like that." His gaze softens as he takes my hands into his. Instant warmth washes over me. "You asked if I have any fears, and I do have one. I'm afraid of losing you."

That's heartwarming and scary at the same time, because if he's lost me, that means I've lost him too.

36

TREY

Last month, I made a special trip into Chinatown to purchase more healing products, and I'm so glad I did. I'm surprised by how well Healing Water and Healing Goo work on Arella. It works like it does on any other person. It only took two days of light application for that cut on her lip to disappear. As for the rest of her body, it took a week of me sneaking doses of Healing Water into her system.

I offered her "Sprite" with all of her meals, because lemon-lime flavored Healing Water tastes just like Sprite. Whenever she said *no*, I filled her glass with regular Healing Water instead. Since it looks, tastes, and smells the same as filtered water, she didn't notice a difference.

I've stopped giving her Healing Water now that it's been over two weeks since the car accident. Thankfully, Victor hasn't pulled any more stunts since then. Not for a lack of begging.

Lately, our phone calls have been conversations where I'll spit out any excuse in the book to keep Arella away from him. Something's been bugging me about Victor, and it's not just that he purposely crashed a truck into Arella's car.

It's that he said he wanted to see if causing her to feel an "extreme emotion" would get me to sense her. If that's the case, why did he cause a car accident when I was nowhere near Arella at the time? Wouldn't it have made more sense to do it while I was *in* the car with her? I'd like to think he didn't want to risk my life, but let's be real—he doesn't give a shit about me. So why did he lie? What's he up to?

I don't know the answers. What I do know is that it's my job to keep Arella away from him. That's why as she leaves for work in her new car for the first time after the accident, I call her so we can talk on her drive. This way, I'll know immediately if Victor pulls another car crash. On her way home, I call her again, and we talk until she pulls into the driveway.

I do this every day for a week.

All is well until the next Monday. On Arella's way home from work, I call her three times. Each time, it goes straight to voicemail. I'm at home, staring at my phone, waiting for either the glimmer to hit me or another call from the hospital with bad news. I swear, if that happens again, I'll rush to Shadow Ridge myself just so I can punch Victor in the face.

I keep staring at my phone, willing for Arella to call me back.

She must hear my silent plea, because finally, her name and picture pop up on my screen.

"Where are you?" I ask.

"I just got to my apartment." She sounds hesitant, and I don't like it.

"Okay?" Woulda been nice if she had told me she was going there, but whatever. "When are you gonna be home?"

"Actually, I was thinking about having a night to myself."

I shoot up from the couch. "What?"

"I haven't spent a night in my own place for a while. I'm still paying rent on this, ya know?"

"Then stop paying rent and move in completely."

"I can't. My lease isn't up."

I pace toward my kitchen. My hands are jittery, antsy to hold her. "I'll pay whatever fee your landlord wants."

"Honey," she says slowly, "I just want a night to myself, okay?"

"What for?"

"I . . . I need some time to think."

"About?"

I wait for what feels like a whole minute before she finally says, "I don't know. Everything."

"Cool. We can think together. I'll be there soon." I'm done with this shit, and I need to see her. Now.

"Nooo, Tr—"

I'm already out the door by the time I hang up. *What the hell does she need to think about?*

I'VE ONLY BEEN IN HER APARTMENT FOR FIVE MINUTES, AND OUR CONVERSATION HAS ALREADY turned into a heated argument. I want to know why she's pushing me away, and she keeps giving me vague answers. She's hiding something from me. I can feel it.

I'm the first to raise my voice. "What the fuck does that mean?"

"It means that I wanted to be alone tonight. Is that too much to ask?" She's planted on the edge of her mattress as I pace her bedroom floor. My hair is all messy from how many times I've run my hands through it.

"Did I do something wrong?"

She groans, exasperated. "For the third time, no."

My knees thump onto the carpet as I kneel in front of her. In my sweetest voice possible, I say, "Tell me what's on your mind, baby."

She rubs her long hair between her fingers, looking anywhere but at me.

I grab her hand to stop her from fidgeting. "Babe, please. What's wrong?"

"I . . . I've been having doubts . . . about us."

I shoot up onto my feet. "What?" I've never been so sure of anything in my life, and here she is questioning it? "Why?"

"I dunno. I feel like lately, we've been having too much sex. I feel like it's all you want me for. You want it all the time. When we wake up. After lunch. After dinner. Before bed. It's just a lot."

"First off," I say, scoffing because my ego is slightly bruised, "sex is not the only thing I want you for. And second, I didn't realize you weren't enjoying it. I can tone it down."

"I *do* enjoy it, Trey."

"Then what's the problem?" This isn't the real issue. There's something else. Is it because of all those things she listed off that's weird about me? Last week, I made it a point to stay in bed with her throughout the night, and I haven't been working out lately, to avoid her questions about how I don't sweat.

"I . . ." Her tone softens. "I don't want to end up as a part of your list."

"My list?"

"Yeah. You know. The list of girls you've fucked and forget about later."

List of girls I've fucked? What? Obviously, she doesn't understand how special she is to me, probably because I haven't told her that I love her. I want to say those words, but I don't know how. And now isn't the right time.

I kneel in front of her again, taking her hands into mine. "Arella, you are *not* a part of any list. Don't ever think that. You mean so much more to me than that. You have no fucking clue how broken I'd be without you. Honestly, I don't think I'd be able to function." Those are the realest words I've ever said to anyone, and I mean all of it.

Her voice gets small, and she places a hand over her heart. "I didn't know you felt that way about me."

"I've been asking you to move to Paris with me. How else would I feel about you?"

She rolls her head back, yanking her hands away. "Ugh! Paris!"

"What?" I hate the way she says *Paris* like it's a poisonous word.

"You keep bringing it up."

"And?"

"Trey, I'm not moving to Paris!" Now, it's her who's shouting.

"Why not?"

"Oh my god." She clasps her hands against her face. "I cannot keep having this same conversation with you over and over."

I throw my arms up in surrender. "Just hear me out, okay? Picture this. You. Me. In a villa. Every day, we wake up to a beautiful sunrise. Every night, we fall asleep together with our little puppy. We could even travel for a while before settling into a place. Eventually, you could own your own bakery down the road. I could help you run it. It'll be perfect."

"What about my grandparents?"

"I'll buy them a villa too. Just as long as it's not right next to ours. At least down the road or something. Don't want 'em to hear you screaming my name all the time." I smirk, waggling my eyebrows up and down. She doesn't take the bait. She remains serious.

"What if they don't want to move?"

"Then they're just a plane ride away."

"Where will we get the money to fly back and forth all the time? Plane tickets around the world aren't cheap, ya know."

"Arella . . ." I say with a groan. "I have plenty of money."

"You keep saying that. How much money do you actually have?"

I shrug. "Enough."

"Care to put a number on that?"

"Millions."

She slumps her head to the side. "Yeah, right."

Why does she have to say it like that? Like it's too impossible to believe. Like I'm embellishing it. She doesn't even stop to consider that I could be telling the truth.

"I could prove it to you. Just need to log into my online bank accounts."

She presses her eyebrows together. "You don't *act* like you have millions of dollars. I mean, sure, you have nice things, but millions? What did your parents research that you inherited that much?"

Exasperated, I stand, crossing my arms over my chest. I'm not here to try to convince her that I could buy her a private island if she wanted it. I'm here because for some odd reason, she's pulling away, and I'm not going to allow it. "Look, the way I see it, you've got two choices. You can either come to Paris willingly, or tied up and duct-taped."

"Would you *really* do that?"

"Pretty close to it." I'm dead serious. We're running out of time.

Arella glares at me. "Kidnapping is a federal crime, Trey Grant."

I roll my eyes. I'm not *actually* gonna kidnap her—unless it's absolutely necessary for her safety.

She pushes off the bed to open a drawer. A shirt and a pair of boxers fly at my head.

I catch them against my face. "What the—"

"It's the clothes you let me wear home that day we threw flour at each other. I keep forgetting to give them back to you."

My heart drops. "Why are you doing so now?"

"Trey." She sighs. "I just need some time to myself, okay? Please, just take your things and leave. We can talk more tomorrow."

My mouth pops open, but no words come out. It takes me a moment to gather myself. "Why does it feel like you're breaking up with me?"

"I'm not," she says, and it only makes me feel a sliver better. "But I still need you to go. And take your belongings."

In a single motion, I scoop her into my arms and storm out of her bedroom.

She squirms, smacking my chest. "Put me down!"

"No," I say firmly. "You said to go and to take my belongings, so I am."

She goes limp, slapping a hand over her forehead, but with a hint of a smile. "And you say *I'm* the difficult one."

In the living room, I set her back onto her feet before firmly taking her face into my palms. I stare straight into her eyes, silently pleading for her to hear my next words with her whole heart.

"You belong with me, Arella, and I belong with you. I'm not leaving here without you, and if you're not leaving, then I'm staying."

She blinks up at me with her long black lashes. Before I can take another breath, she crashes her lips against mine, stealing all the air from my lungs.

37

ARELLA

"Arella, get up." Trey shakes me awake.

I jerk out of my slumber. "Huh? Where's the fire?"

"No fire. I just need to talk to you." The panic in his tone lurches me upright.

He flips the bedroom lights on, making my eyes burn. I sit up, rub my eyes, then squint to see him. He's got an expression on his face like he just witnessed someone jump off a skyscraper.

"Is everything okay?"

"Not really." His voice sounds deep and husky.

I'm still naked from our before-bed activities. Trey has finally stopped treating me like I'm made of porcelain, and he's gone back to being rough. Earlier, I was so exhausted from how good it was, I couldn't even get up to get dressed. Instead, he wiped me off with a wet towel and I passed out.

"What time is it?" I ask.

"Two thirty-ish."

In the morning?

Trey climbs into bed and sits an arm's length away. He doesn't usually sit that far from me. "I have a question to ask you, and I can't wait until the morning for an answer."

"Okay?" What could possibly be this urgent?

"Is there anything you're hiding from me?"

I freeze with the blanket held to my chest. There's only one thing I've been hiding from him, but how could he know? I haven't told anyone, not even Javina. Did his weird intuitive sixth sense tell him?

I play dumb. "What're you talking about?"

"Just answer the question."

"I . . . um, I dunno what you're talking about."

"This! I'm talking about this!" From his back pocket, he yanks out some folded papers and tosses them onto the sheets between us. I recognize them immediately.

My eyes go wide. "Where did you get those?"

"From your purse."

"What were you doing in my purse?"

"I was cleaning the kitchen. Your purse fell onto the floor, and all your shit spilled out—including these." He points a hard finger at the pregnancy brochures I got when I stopped into the doctor's office to take a test. "Just tell me it's nothing and that I'm freaking out for no reason."

I lower my head because this reaction is exactly what I was afraid of. Three nights ago, when I told him that I think we have too much sex, I didn't mean it. We have the perfect amount of sex. That night, I wanted to be alone because I was panicking for other reasons—reasons I've been keeping from him because there hasn't been a good time to tell him.

At least, that's the lie I've been telling myself. Really, I'm just scared. What will he say? How will he react? Will he take it better than I did? It's been three days, and I'm still trying to process it. How long will it take him?

When that test came back positive, my first fear was that he's not ready to be a father and that he doesn't want to be yet. Right now, he's validating that fear.

My voice comes out soft and breathy. "I'm sorry. I didn't know how to tell you."

"No!" He shoots off the bed and paces the floor. "No! No! No!"

Suddenly, I feel more naked than I already am. I clutch the blanket closer to my body, wishing a shirt was within reach.

Trey rakes both hands through his hair. "How long have you known?"

I strain to keep my voice steady. "Three days."

"*Three days*? You've known for three fucking days, and you didn't think to mention it to me? Were you ever planning to let me in on your little secret?"

I shoot dagger eyes at him. "You should not be the one to lecture about secrets. I don't think I have enough fingers to count how many you're keeping from me."

His face turns pale as his chest moves up and down in short breaths. "Who is he?"

"Huh?"

"Who's the father?"

I tilt my head to the side. "What do you mean?"

"I mean, who did you sleep with?"

"You . . ." *Why would he even ask that?*

He chuckles low in his throat, shaking his head. "Unbelievable."

"Trey, I didn't sleep with anyone else."

For a split second, his expression falters. He heard the conviction in my tone. Then he glares at me. "Don't lie."

"I'm not."

"You're not pregnant with my baby," he says with just as much conviction.

"How are you so sure?"

He crosses his arms together. "Because I'm infertile."

"What?"

"You heard me. I can't have children."

I gasp, and my head lurches back. Is this what he meant when he said he wanted kids but that it wasn't "in the cards" for him? Is this why he wasn't the least bit concerned about whether I was on birth control or not? "When were you planning on telling me that?"

"I—I didn't think it was important." Here's another secret to add to his long list.

"Obviously, you're not infertile, because I'm pregnant."

"With who?"

"With you!"

He clenches his fists together. "Goddammit, Arella. Quit lying to me."

"I'm not!" I shout.

"Bullshit!" he shouts back.

That's it. I've had enough. I'm not going to sit here and be accused of lying and cheating when I haven't.

I slide off the bed and shove my limbs into the closest shirt and pair of pants I can find. I feel Trey's eyes on me the whole time. The lump in my throat grows with each wordless second that passes between us. Tears well into the corners of my eyes. I snatch my phone off the charger and storm down the hall.

Trey follows me. "What are you doing?"

I don't answer him. Speaking feels like it'll break me, and it's taking all my strength to keep myself from crying right now. On the kitchen floor is my purse with all my things still scattered everywhere. Frantically, I thrust everything back where it belongs, then I dig my keys out as I rush to the front door.

Trey grabs me by my waist the second I touch the doorknob. He spins me around. "Where are you going?"

I knock his arms away. "Home."

"You *are* home," he says so firmly, it almost makes the hurt evaporate. *Almost.* His house feels more like home than my own apartment—only because he's here. It doesn't feel like home right now though. Not when he's looking at me like I've betrayed him. If he really thinks I'd do such a thing, he doesn't know me at all.

"I'm leaving, Trey. Call me when you—"

He snatches the keys from me and shoves them into his pocket. "No."

Oh, god. It's like I'm watching a rerun of my episodes with Nathan. When I wasn't marked up, he'd let me leave, knowing I'd come back eventually. When I was bruised, he'd take my car keys and lock me in the bedroom like a prisoner.

On the outside, this may look like the same situation, but on the inside, it doesn't feel the same. Nathan forced me to stay because he was afraid someone would see the fresh wounds. Trey wants me to stay because . . . well, I don't know. The anguish in his eyes tells me he's hurt, but I did nothing to hurt him.

Okay, maybe I should have told him the moment I found out, but that was my only mistake. I don't even understand how this happened. Trey only came inside me once, I'm on birth control, I took a Plan B pill the next morning, and we've been safe ever since. The odds of getting pregnant were like .001%. I don't even get a regular period. With my birth control, I get a period, like, three times a year. How was my uterus able to produce life? It doesn't make any sense.

Angry at this entire situation, I swing the door open and stomp out, slamming it behind me. It's not until my bare feet hit Trey's driveway that I realize I've left without shoes on. How far am I going to get without a vehicle or shoes?

I wipe the wetness from my cheeks as I hurry down the sidewalk. Apparently, I've decided that trudging around barefoot without a destination is better than being in there with my heated boyfriend who thinks I cheated on him.

I'm already past his neighbor's house when the front door reopens.

"Arella!" Footsteps come running after me. It's not long before he's caught up. His breaths are heavy.

I expect him to yell at me. To smack me for disobeying him, or to call me names because I "wasn't listening." Instead, he takes one look at the tears rolling down my cheeks, then crushes me against his firm chest.

I attempt to push him off, but it only makes him squeeze me tighter. I'm too weak to shove him away, because I want this too. Nathan never chased after me. Some nights, I'd walk around for hours before finally coming back to find him *still* drinking, *still* angry, and *still* aggressive. All I ever wanted was for him to be sorry and for me to matter to him. I never did.

I matter to Trey though. I can tell by the way he's holding me as if I'm the only thing that's *ever* mattered to him. I sob into his shirt as he buries his face in my hair.

"Arella," he says, all choked up. "Please don't leave me. We can figure this out, okay? Just don't leave me."

38

TREY

If I wasn't perplexed by this woman before, I am now. She's a good liar. If I didn't know any better, I'd believe her. But I do know better, and at the end of the day, it's her word against biology. Believing her is like believing she can get pregnant from watching porn. It's just impossible.

After I convince her not to leave, I carry her back into the house. The second I return her feet to the carpet, she runs and locks herself in the bedroom—*our* bedroom—the one we've been making love in almost every night for weeks. Something I thought we were doing with only each other.

To give her some time alone, I pace the kitchen where my panic first started. My mind hasn't stopped feeling chaotic since I saw those brochures fall out of her purse. I can't wrap my head around the idea that she let another man put his grubby little raccoon hands all over her. The knots in my chest tighten just thinking about it.

When did she even find the time? When she's not with me, she's either at work or with Javina. I guess, now that I think about it, I don't have any proof that she's at work or with Javina when she says she is. She could have been sneaking off to see another guy this whole time.

Maybe this is why she refuses to move to Paris with me—why she didn't even consider it. She didn't want to leave *him* behind. What's he got that's so special? What am I missing that made her turn to someone else to fill that void? Maybe I should have—

No. I can't do this. I can't spiral down a hole of self-pitying thoughts right now. Not while I've got a woman in my bedroom who's crying her eyes out. No matter what she did, I still care deeply about her, and I'll do whatever it takes to make this right.

Lightly, I knock on our bedroom door. Again, *our.*

Nothing happens.

I knock again.

"It's unlocked," says a sniffling voice.

I enter to find red eyes, pink cheeks, and a bunch of crumpled-up tissues on the night-stand. I want to scoop her into my arms and tell her that everything's gonna be okay. I don't, because nothing's okay. Not while there's another man's baby growing inside her.

Silently, I bunch up all the tissues and toss them into the trash. She clutches her violet blanket against her front as if she needs a barrier between us. As if she's using it to protect herself from me.

I sigh deeply. I didn't mean to upset her. I'm just hurt. I want to know why I wasn't enough for her. I'd do anything for her, including drop my band and move to Europe to protect her. I'd spend every last dime I have on making her dream bakery become a reality. I'd even trade my life to save hers if it came down to it. *How is that not enough?*

I point to the empty side of our bed. "Can I sit?"

She nods, and I settle in.

"I'm sorry for yelling at you," I say gently.

"I'm sorry for yelling too."

"I've been thinking it over, and if you say you didn't sleep with someone—"

"I didn't." She says it so resolutely, I almost believe her. I *want* to believe her. I just can't when there's evidence inside her that points otherwise.

"Then there's only one explanation. You're not pregnant."

"I've had really sore breasts for a week now, and three days ago, I woke up slightly nauseous. That's why I went to take a test at the doctors. It came back positive, as did the home tests I took."

"Maybe the tests are wrong. Let's take another." How accurate can those tests really be? There's gotta be a chance they're wrong, right?

"Okay." She agrees so quickly, it makes me think the odds are not in my favor.

I jump to my feet. "Great. Let's go."

"Now? It's past three in the morning." She gives me a look like I'm insane. Maybe I am. Actually, I know I am. I'm in love with an Ordinary. It doesn't get any crazier than that.

What if, by some miracle, she *is* carrying my child? What if she really is a Zordi and just pretends to be an Ordinary for a reason I can't comprehend? It's possible to pretend to not see far. It's possible to fake shivering. It's possible to force your body to fall asleep every night.

But then, if she was a Zordi, why wouldn't she have said something by now? If she was a Zordi and didn't know it, why wouldn't she mention that she feels a tingle in her chest whenever she's around me?

Also, how does she fake the sweat that beads over her forehead whenever we're under the hot sun? How did she fake passing out from getting roofied by Ordinary drugs? If she was a Zordi, Dex would have had to drug her with z-drugs. If she was a Zordi, she'd have powers, and she'd heal faster than she does.

The more I think about it, the more my anxiety grows. There's no way in hell that baby is mine, and I don't care that it's three in the morning—I need to know the truth, and I need to know it now.

I head toward the door. "I can't wait any longer, babe. Let's go."

Arella shakes her head and gestures at her red face and messy hair. "Trey, look at me. I'm not in a state to leave the house. How about we do this first thing in the morning?"

I don't give two fucks what she looks like right now. On her side of the bed, I collapse to my knees with my arms in her lap. "Arella, please. For once, can you just do what I ask? This is not like when I asked you to stay at the restaurant. Or like when I asked you to take me to meet your grandparents. Or to move to Paris with me. Or to accept the new car. You've been fighting me on practically everything since the day we met. Can you, please, just give me this *one* thing?"

I slap a hand over my chest. "Try to see this from my side, okay? I'm an infertile man whose girlfriend just told him she's pregnant. I want to believe that you didn't sleep with another man, but can't you understand that this whole situation is tearing me apart?"

Forty-five minutes later, we step inside a twenty-four-hour superstore that smells of stale chips and sour milk. With Arella in hand, I head straight to the aisle with condoms and pregnancy tests.

"Why are we getting four?" Arella asks when I pull multiple brands of tests off the shelf.

"We need to be sure."

She scowls at the boxes tucked under my arms. The look on her face tells me I shouldn't grab another.

I guess four's enough. "Don't worry, babe. I'm paying."

"That's okay. I can get it." She reaches for the boxes.

I lean back. "I got it."

She shifts her scowl from the boxes onto me. "You *never* let me pay. Not when we go out to eat, not on our dates, and you just bought me a brand-new car. Let *me* buy something for once."

"No."

She doesn't give up because lately, she's been making it a point to be as difficult as possible. "Why do *you* always get to pay for everything?"

"Because I'm the man." The moment I say that, I want to face-palm myself.

She scoffs and jerks her head back. "Are you saying I can't pay because I'm a *woman*?"

"No." I let out an exasperated breath. "I'm paying because these things are a smaller percentage of my bank account than yours. You work hard for your money, and all I did was lose my parents to a fucking explosion. Thousands of dollars I don't deserve appear under my name every month, so I'm paying. Besides, this was *my* idea. I was the one who dragged you out here in the middle of the night."

For a moment, her glare falters into sympathy. It looks like she's about to give in, until she crosses her arms over her chest. "Nathan always had more money than I did, and he never let me pay for anything. At first, I thought it was because he wanted to be nice. Eventually, I realized he just wanted to control me."

Ouch. I can't believe she's comparing me to that ugly scumbag right now. I cup her face with my free hand and lean in to her. "That's not what I'm doing, and you know it."

"Then when I say I want to pay for something, don't stop me."

This woman is one of the most easygoing people I know. She's also the most difficult. I've learned by now that once her mind is made up, there's no changing it. So reluctantly, I hand her the boxes.

She clutches all four against her chest. "Thank you for understanding that I need to do this."

I do understand. Things are falling out of control, and she wants to feel in control of *something*. Not only that, she doesn't want to repeat her situation with Nathan. I applaud her for standing firm the way she just did. *My strong, independent woman.*

I lower my voice. "If you want to pay, that's fine, but please, don't compare me to your ex ever again. I don't buy you things to control you. I buy you things because I want to take care of you. Because I—" *Because I love you.* The words almost leave my lips. They don't, because 4 a.m. in the middle of the family-planning aisle of a grocery store is not the right time or place. "Because you're special to me."

"I'm sorry. I didn't mean to compare you to him. I was just trying to explain why I wanted to pay."

With a palm on the small of her back, I pull her in. She steps into me and allows me to kiss her forehead, but it's not enough, so I cup the back of her neck and collapse my mouth over hers. We embrace in a hard kiss that soothes the ache in me.

The second we part, the ache floats right back in like a cold black fog. Our moment of truth is coming, and my heart knows it.

"The car is this way," Arella says after we check out.

"But the bathroom is this way." I point toward the big RESTROOMS sign hanging from the ceiling.

"What? We're doing this *now*?"

"What part of 'I can't wait any longer' wasn't clear?"

"Can't we do this at your house?"

Ouch. It stings that she didn't call it *our* house. "Arella, please . . ." I hold out the shopping bag.

With a huff, she snatches the bag. I'm about to follow her into the family bathroom when her palm against my sternum stops me.

"What do you think you're doing?"

I give her a *duh* look. "Trying to see if you're pregnant?"

"Nuh-uh. You need to wait out here. I don't want you to stand around and watch me pee on a stick."

"What's the big deal? It's not like I've never seen you naked."

"It's weird."

Things will move along faster if I stop arguing with her, so I step back with my hands up. "Fine. Just take all four, and let me in as soon as you're done."

The bag crinkles in her grasp as she vanishes behind a locked door.

After an eternity, Arella peeks her head out and motions for me to enter.

Breathe, I remind myself. I've been forgetting to do that.

"So?" I say as an electric current of nerves shoots up my core. "What's the verdict?"

"I just took them."

"Okay?" I wave my hand in a *keep going* motion.

"Do you not know how these things work?"

"Not really. Don't you just pee on it?"

"You have to wait two minutes for the results."

"Oh."

It's the longest two minutes of my life. My heavy footsteps echo as I pace the tile back and forth. Arella remains at the sink, watching the four sticks intently. I can barely contain myself.

"Are they done now?" I ask like an impatient child.

"Yeah."

I rush to the sink. *What the hell?* It's just a bunch of lines. "What do they say?"

"They're all positive."

"What's that mean? You're positively pregnant or you're positively *not* pregnant?"

She chuckles, making me feel stupid. "Positively pregnant."

39

TREY

I'm pathetic.

We've confirmed that she's pregnant, and the first thing I do when we arrive home is climb into bed and ask her to cuddle with me. She does and falls back asleep within minutes. I don't blame her. She has to work in the morning, and because of me, she'll be running on barely five hours of sleep.

I've got her back crushed to my front, and I'm pathetically gripping onto her like I never want to let her go. Because I don't. Because I'm so fucking pathetic!

I shouldn't want her. I should be telling her this is over. But I don't. I'm too weak. I still need her like I need air to breathe. All I can think about is how I can convince her to leave the other guy and be with me—only me. And to love me—only me.

I'll give her anything she wants. *Anything.* Does she want me to change? Name it. I'll do it. Does she want me to give her more attention? Less? I'll do it. Does she want me to find her a fluffy unicorn that shits glitter? What color, baby? I'll fucking do it.

The longer I hold her, the more I fall apart inside. My thoughts keep diving deeper and deeper into a black hole of *I deserve this pain* and *I'm not worth anyone's love.* That second thought is the one that keeps repeating in my head like an annoying beeping sound I can't get rid of. Why did I think for even a second that Arella could love me back? What's there to love about me anyway? I can't do anything without fucking it up.

My chest won't stop burning like I've swallowed hot coals. My throat's dry like the goddamn Sahara. It's hard to breathe because my lungs feel constricted. Every breath I suck in is laced with her scent. Someone else got this close to her. Close enough to smell her and touch her. Close enough to put his load inside her.

Someone else.
Someone else.
Someone else.

In the morning, we barely speak to each other. As Arella leaves for work in a rush, she tells me that she'll come right back when she's done so we can talk. That gives me a small sense of hope. Maybe that means she's willing to work things out.

That hope quickly drains out of me as I watch her taillights disappear, and I'm left alone. It's not long before my mind spirals again. How could this happen? What did I do wrong? What can I do moving forward to be a better man for her? To be the man she wants to spend the rest of her life with.

If she could just be honest with me, I'd forgive her. I'll even raise her child like it's mine if it means she'll stay with me.

Are there some logistics I'd have to figure out to make that happen? *Of course.*

Am I risking going to z-prison for life? *Yep.*

Am I willing to do it anyway? *Abso-fucking-lutely.*

I'm twenty minutes into murdering a punching bag when the doorbell chimes. I almost miss it with how loud my music is. *Who the hell is here?* No one ever shows up unannounced.

Except for one.

"I thought you were dead." Jess makes my zense prickle. Behind her, droplets of water sprinkle from the gray clouds above at a steady pace. I didn't realize it was raining.

"Nice of you to use the doorbell this time." I don't invite her in, and apparently, she doesn't need the invitation. She struts right past me and dumps herself onto my couch, throwing her legs up onto the cushions.

Reluctantly, I shut the door. It mutes the sound of water falling that seems to get heavier every time I blink.

Jess looks me up and down, and it's only then that I realize I'm still shirtless from my workout. I hate the way she stares at me like I'm property that belongs to her. I don't.

"Did something happen to your phone?" Jess is wearing the world's tightest pink shirt and a pair of denim shorts that cover more of her hips than her ass.

"No." I don't move from the door.

"Then why haven't you been answering my calls or texts?"

Because I don't want to or care to. "I've been busy."

"With what?"

"Stuff."

She blows out a breath, making her lips smack together. "All right, Mister-Fucking-Details. I see how it is."

"What do you want?"

"Well, damn. Aren't you a ray of fucking sunshine? Excuse me for checking up on a friend I haven't heard from. I texted you at least four times last week and, like, three times the week before that. I honestly thought you were dead."

"I'm not."

"Good." She kicks off her heels, then gets to her feet. "Got anything good to eat?"

Sighing, I follow her to the kitchen. "Take whatever you want, then leave. I've got shit to do."

"Do it later." She steals an apple from my fridge and takes a bite, leaning her elbows on the counter. "Come on, Grant. Don't you miss me? You haven't seen me in months, and now you're kicking me—" She gasps and shoots up. "You're seeing someone!"

Seeing Arella isn't the right term for it. *Madly in love with her* is more like it.

A pang of jealousy slaps me in the face as Jess takes another bite of my apple. "Tell me about her."

"Look, now isn't a good time."

"Sure it is! I'm here. You're here. We both got nowhere to be." Smirking, she heads to my bedroom. I follow and watch through unamused eyes as she jumps onto my sheets and shoves her face into the pillows. "Ya know, I'm not a Sniffer, but I can smell her. She sleeps here, doesn't she?"

I don't answer. Jess bounces off my mattress.

"She has clothes here!" she shouts from inside my closet. "Wow. You must really like this one."

"It's complicated." I lean against the doorframe, debating on whether or not it's appropriate to throw her over my shoulder and dump her back out in the rain.

Jess returns from the closet and settles on the edge of my bed. "How so?"

"It just is."

"Is it 'cause she's an Ordinary?" Jess takes my silence as a yes. "Trust me. Relationships with them Ordis never work. Been there, done that plenty. They're only good for one thing: sex without the consequence of children. I'm actually seeing this new guy. He's an Eavesdropper, like me. Things are working out so far. Maybe you should try dating Zordis again."

The idea of that is like hearing tires screeching into my ear. I don't want to date other Zordis. I only want one person. I just wish I was the only one she wanted too.

Jess stands from my bed to meet me in the doorway. She slides her hands up my bare chest. "Do you need me to remind you what being with your own kind is like?"

She intensifies her erotic emotions, knowing it'll make me want her. It's always worked before, but it's not going to work now. I'm done with this woman. I'm done with her using me. And I'm especially done with her making me feel like the only time I'm worthy of her presence is when she needs a fuck and some cash.

Arella's never made me feel like an ATM. If anything, she makes me feel like I'm worth more *without* the money. Plus, she's never tried to use my mind power to manipulate me into giving her what she wants.

So I grab Jess by her wrists as I expand my Empath power out. I need to sense anyone but her, because if I don't control my emotions, she will end up controlling me.

Her jaw drops as her confused shock rushes through my head. I wish I could say that I give a shit, but I don't.

I'm more concerned about my situation with Arella. Thinking about it again makes me want to crawl into a dark hole and never come out.

The last time I felt this terrible was when I lost Elliott. The time before that? When I lost my parents. Maybe this is my fate—to lose anybody who means anything to me. I've lost Arella to another man. Next, I'll lose Liz and—

"Seriously?"

I whip my head toward the voice coming from down the hall. Arella's standing there with her jaw dropped and tears forming in her eyes. Before I can say anything, she runs away.

40

TREY

Barefoot, I dash out in the rain after Arella and catch her by her arm, just as she yanks her car door open.

Water pelts my bare back. "That wasn't what it looked like, I swear."

She's got wet hair, flushed cheeks, and tears streaming down her face. At least, I think those are tears. They could be raindrops. "You're shirtless, and she had her hands all over you. What am I supposed to think?"

Without waiting for me to answer, she shoves me away and climbs into her car.

I grab the door and hold it open. "Please, don't go." I sound desperate—because I am. "Just let me explain."

She wipes the wetness off her cheeks with the back of her hand as she chokes on a breath. "There's no need. I know what I saw."

"Look, I know what it looks like, but I swear to you—"

"Who is she?" Arella wipes more tears from her face.

I hang my head low. "Her name is Jess."

"Your ex-girlfriend?"

I nod, and her face contorts.

"So we get into one big fight, and the first thing you do is booty-call your ex-girlfriend?"

"No. She just showed up today." It's the truth, but it sounds like a goddamn lie coming from my lips.

"What did she want? Sex?"

"Yeah."

"And you agreed?"

"No. I was about to tell her to—hold on." I put a hand up, palm forward. "Don't sit there and pretend like you're not guilty of doing worse. There's proof living inside you." At least I stopped Jess before it got that far. I can't say the same for Arella.

"This is *your* baby!" she yells so loudly, all of California probably heard her.

"I'm infertile!" I shout back, just as loud.

She throws her hands up in surrender. "Nope. That's it. If you really think I have it in me to be unfaithful to you, then I'm done. This isn't worth it."

And there it is. The truth. I'm not worth it to her. Like how I wasn't worth it to my parents to quit their mission. Like how I'm not worth anything to my uncle. Like how I'm not worth Jess's time outside of a bedroom. It's nice to know that I'm not worth it to Arella *after* I've already fallen in love with her.

Hiccuping through a sob, Arella shoves me back a step.

I manage to catch her door before she can shut it. Then I grab her arm. "Stop trying to leave! We're not done!"

She jumps. She actually jumps. Worse, her hands shoot up to protect her face. "Don't hit me."

I step back. *Hit her?* No! I would never. Why would she think—*Dammit.* I shouldn't have grabbed her like that.

My shoulders drop. "Baby, no. I'm so sorry. I would *never* hurt you like that. Ever."

Her dagger eyes slice at me. "What you've done is worse. Bruises heal, Trey. The pain I feel from seeing you with another woman will stick with me forever."

My gaze sinks to the raindrops pooling in my driveway. I wish for something to come erase this. *Anything.*

I wait.

Nothing happens.

Water continues to attack me.

"I'll prove that I didn't cheat on you," she says through a sniffle. "As soon as this baby is born, I'll get a DNA test."

"Fine, and when that test comes back with the truth, don't bother telling me, because I already know." I'm being an ass, and I don't give a fuck. I'm hurt, and I want to drown myself in this rain. Why can't she just be honest with me? I'll forgive her in a heartbeat. I'll be a father to her baby. I just want her honesty.

She shoots me a foul glare. "And when that test comes back confirming that you're the father, be prepared to pay child support."

"Child support?" *What?*

That's what this is about, isn't it? That's why she's trying so hard to convince me she's carrying my baby. She's trying to milk me like I'm a cash cow. *Wow . . .* She played me good. Not once did I think this was her game. *Well, too bad.* Someone else has already tried pulling this stunt on me. It didn't work then, and it won't work now.

I let out a scoff. "You'd be stupid to think you're getting a dime from me."

She gapes at me with a pain in her eyes that makes me want to hold her and make everything right again. But how can I? Nothing's right. Nothing makes sense.

Arella turns and reaches into her purse. When she twists back around, she's got something in her hand.

"The only stupid thing I did was fall in love with you." She slams a piece of paper against my wet chest.

I peel it off to find our happy faces in a small photograph. This. This is all I've ever wanted. To be happy. To share my life with someone who understands me and makes me feel whole. I thought that person was Arella. I thought—*Wait. What did she just say?*

Two words leave her mouth that will scar me forever. "Goodbye, Trey."

PART TWO
CAPTURED IMMUNE

PLAYLIST

Bonus Tracks:
"U Got It Bad" Usher
"SOS" James Arthur
"The Other Side Of The Door (Taylor's Version)" Taylor Swift
"Die For You" The Weeknd
"God Damn You're Beautiful" Chester See

41

TREY

"*G*oodbye, Trey."

She knew that word would crush me. She knew, and she used it anyway. *Goodbye* is the word my mother taught me to use only when I'd never see someone again.

"*Goodbye* means forever. *Bye* is just for now," my mother said to me countless times when I was a kid.

Exactly nineteen years ago, on a rainy night in September, she said goodbye to me. I never saw her again.

Arella purposely used that word to hurt me, and it worked. I'm so wrecked by it, I haven't found the strength to move yet. My bare feet are standing where her car stood in my driveway a minute ago. Where we both stood a minute ago, shouting at each other, saying things we didn't mean. *At least,* I *didn't mean them.*

Rain pelts my bare back like little bullets shooting from the sky. The hems of my workout shorts drip water down my legs. I'm not even wearing shoes, because I didn't have time to put any on before chasing after Arella.

I tried getting her to stay. I wanted to explain and make things right, but she refused to listen.

So now I'm here . . .

Alone . . .

With a wallet-size photo of Arella and me gazing deeply into each other's eyes.

It's slowly curling in my hand. She shoved it at me right before taking off. I want the happiness we had when we took this photo. The happiness I have whenever I'm with her. Whenever we're cuddling until the very last second we have to get out of bed. Whenever we're exchanging looks from across the room that say *I admire everything about you* without actually saying it.

I've got half a mind to mount my Harley and chase after her right now—after the only person who's ever made me feel whole. I'll come clean. I'll tell her everything. I'll confess that the flat tire that brought us together wasn't an accident and tell her what Zordinaries are. I'll show her my powers and explain how I know for a fact that the baby growing inside her isn't mine.

Am I risking going to z-prison? *Yes.*

Do I care? If it'll get me my girl back, *no.*

Even knowing she's pregnant by another man, I still want to be with her. I love her too much to not forgive her. I'll raise that baby like it's mine, if that's what it takes for her to forgive me too. *Will she?*

She was pretty upset after finding me shirtless with another woman. But she was off sleeping with another guy for who knows how long, so what's the difference? I guess the difference is that she *saw* me. I suppose if I saw her half-naked with someone else, she'd be harder to forgive. But I'd forgive her—after bashing the other guy's face in.

No one touches my girl.

No one.

Except, she's not my girl anymore. *Was she ever?*

"What happened?" Jess asks when I step back into my house. She's draped over my couch with a slight grin on her face.

I wasn't in the mood for her when she showed up unannounced, and I'm definitely not in the mood for her now, so my tone comes out rough. "Cut the shit. I know you heard everything." *Or did she?*

With her enhanced hearing, Jess can hear something as small as dust fall. Arella's immunity probably blocks Jess's power like it blocks mine.

"Okay, fine." She perks up. "Was that the Ordinary you've been fucking around with?"

I hate the way she says that, as if my relationship with Arella was only "fucking around." Arella means a hell of a lot more to me than that.

"How well could you hear our conversation?" My soaked workout shorts cool against my skin as I drag my feet behind the couch. I'm dripping water all over my clean carpet, and I don't care.

Jess twists to face me. "As well as any other person can hear. I didn't need my gift to catch what you guys were saying. You were screaming at each other so loud, I'm sure the moon people heard y'all."

Dammit. I didn't mean to shout at Arella. I just couldn't control myself when she kept lying to my face, demanding that I pay child support for another man's child.

Okay, technically, she wasn't demanding anything. What she actually said was that she'll be taking a DNA test to prove that I am the father and that I should be *prepared* to pay child support. Because I'm an asshole and was pissed off to shit, I told her she'd be stupid to think she's getting a dime from me, when in reality, I'd give that woman anything she wants.

Money? *Done.*

My house? *Take it.*

My car? *Here ya go.*

Just be with me.

With a sigh, I scold myself. I shouldn't have let her go. I especially shouldn't have grabbed her the forceful way I had. Add those to my long list of mistakes.

Jess continues with a sparkling grin. "Sooo, she's pregnant?"

"Yep." Admitting it out loud to another person makes it more real.

"Who's the father?"

Isn't that the million-dollar question? I wish I knew. At the same time, I don't think I want to know. I'll obsess over it, and I'll want to know everything about him so I can figure out why she chose him over me. "I dunno, but she tried to tell me it's mine."

Low laughter bellows from Jess's gut. "Wow! I'm so glad I was here to witness this. An Ordi trying to convince a Zordi she's carrying his child? Holy shit! This is better than TV."

Seriously? I glare at her. "Get out."

"What?"

With the fingers not holding my precious photo, I point at the front door. It swings wide open, coming to a firm stop just before hitting the wall. "Get the fuck out."

"Hell no! I need to know all the deets! Like, what's her motive? Is she trying to get your money?"

"Out! Now!" I give her two seconds. When she still doesn't move, I lose it. With a flick of my wrist, the couch shoots toward the door with her still on it.

"Whoa! All right, all right. I'm leaving. No need to be such an ass."

She's right. I am an ass, and she's a bitch, so I don't give a flying fuck what she thinks of me. I just lost the most important person in my life, and she's laughing about it like I'm on some stupid reality TV show. I'm done being her entertainment, and I'm done being her last-minute rebound. *Just get out!*

Once she stands, I point at the couch and fly it back to where it belongs. The second Jess has crossed the threshold, I wave a hand at the door. It slams shut behind her, and the bolt lock clicks. I hope I never have to see her face again. Ever.

I push the sopping strands of dark hair away from my face as I storm into my music room.

Minutes later, my pen flies messily across notebook paper as lyrics tumble from my mind. It's not long before I've got two new verses and a chorus written. I grab my guitar to play some chords along to the melody.

When I was eight, I learned that playing and writing music helped settle the tornado of misery swirling in my head all the time. That, and lighting stuff on fire. And throat-punching people.

As a teenager, I found out that getting drunk helps too.

As an adult, I discovered that z-drugs work the best. The higher I get, the less agony I feel. I wish I had some right now, because writing this song isn't helping.

"Fuck!" I smash my guitar against the floor. The wood breaks with a loud *crack!* as the instrument snaps in half.

For the first time since I got the call about Elliott passing away, I burst into tears. Thinking about losing my Deaf mentee kid only makes me sob harder. He meant so much to me, and I only had him for a short amount of time. Sadly, I had Arella for less.

My shoulders are shaking, and I'm wheezing. I don't even understand why I'm crying. Maybe it's because of the way things ended with her. Maybe it's because it happened on the anniversary of the worst day of my life. Either way, my relationship with her was doomed from the start. Whether it was now, like this, or later when the Superiors hauled me off to z-prison for having close relations with an Ordinary, eventually, our relationship would have ended, and I knew that.

So why the hell do I feel this broken? Why, for weeks, did I try to convince myself that we could make it work? Zordinaries and Ordinaries aren't meant to be together. We *can't* be together. Knowing that didn't stop me from falling in love with her, especially when everything with her feels more natural than blinking.

MY BODY LURCHES UPRIGHT AS I WAKE. THE SKY OUTSIDE MY WINDOW IS BLACK. I DON'T REMEMBER falling asleep, especially not on the floor. My eyes are sore, and my neck aches from the way I was lying. Next to me is my shattered guitar in a helpless heap of broken pieces. At least my shorts are dry now . . . mostly.

I flop onto my back and stare at the motionless ceiling fan. I'm not sure how long I stay like that. Maybe it's five minutes. Maybe it's five hours. It doesn't matter.

Eventually, my stomach rumbles. The sky is still black, so it's not time for breakfast. It's been a while since I ate, so I should probably eat *something*.

Inside the fridge, I find salad for two, chicken for two, and pie for two. Disgusted, I slam the fridge shut. Suddenly, I'm not hungry anymore.

The bedroom is worse. My sheets smell like her: sweet lavender and springtime. Groaning, I rip the linens off the bed and hurl them at the wall. The gentle way they slump to the floor pisses me off, so I rip my lamp from the outlet and chuck it across the room. It hits the wall, and the lightbulb shatters to pieces.

What else can I throw?

A book? *Sure.* It lands with the pages open.

Bluetooth speaker? *Definitely.* It leaves a dent in the wall.

Cologne bottle? *Hell yeah.* I thought for sure it would crack, but it merely falls to the carpet, unharmed. *Lame.*

This throwing stuff thing isn't working. *What can I light on fire?*

I glance around for something to burn and find Arella's dress on the floor. I pick it up and crush it against my nose. As I inhale, every memory I have of holding her in my arms comes rushing back to destroy me.

After I suck up my sorrows, I grab all the sheets and take them, with Arella's dress, to the laundry room. Just before tossing all the linens into the washing machine, I smash her dress against my face again. *Mmm.* It smells so good. Like a mix of happiness and the only sense of peace I've ever had.

I can't do this.

Huffing, I stomp out of the laundry room, leaving her dress on the floor.

With an achy chest, I crawl onto my bare mattress and lie facedown with my arms out wide. I could put another set of sheets on, but why? That sounds like a lot of effort right now.

My bed feels bigger without her on it. Emptier too. I can still picture her here with her back flush against my front. I'd trace my fingertips up and down her arm while kissing her neck. We'd talk about nothing and everything at the same time. I never cared what we talked about as long as I could hear her voice.

"The only stupid thing I did was fall in love with you." Those were some of her last words to me. They keep repeating in my head.

Love. What does that word mean, anyway? Liz once told me that love is a beautiful and fulfilling experience. So far, my experience with love has only been full of pain and regret.

I should have listened to Liz when she told me to stop messing around with Ordinaries. Liz was afraid I'd hurt Arella. Little did we know Arella would be the one to hurt me.

Whatever happened to that "Ari's perfect for you" thing? Those were Liz's words. She said that since I can't sense Arella's emotions, anything I feel for Arella is real and not a reflection of her feelings for me. If Arella is perfect for me, then why do I feel like I've just lost a war?

I want nothing more than to see my girl right now. More so, I want to see her happy. The image of her that keeps replaying in my mind is the way I last saw her: weepy and angry. I don't want that to be what I picture whenever I think of her. *Hold on. Where's our picture?*

I fly off the mattress and scour my bedroom. It's not here.

I sprint to the living room. I search between the couch cushions, then the kitchen. Nothing.

Where did I—Oh! My music room! I rush in there and find the photo waiting for me next to my notebook, where I wrote that sad guitar ballad about her. It's a song that will never see the studio. The lyrics are too raw. I'd never be able to sing it without choking up.

Thankfully, the rain didn't ruin the photo. It's a little curled at the corners, but it still showcases a happy couple gazing lovingly at each other.

The more I stare at the picture, the more I want to rip it up. I can't bring myself to do it though. I'm weak. Too weak to leave her when I should have. Too weak to throw her dress into the wash. Too weak to destroy the only picture I have of us.

Ripping up this picture will be like admitting it's over.

It's not over.

It *can't* be over.

Back in my bedroom, I search for my wallet. I find it lying open on the carpet. All my cash is gone—all two thousand dollars. *Of course.* Why wouldn't Jess use the time I was outside with Arella to dig through what's not hers? Unfortunately, missing cash is the least of my problems right now.

I'm carefully tucking my precious photo between the fabric of my bifold when I catch a glimpse of some writing on the back. I flip the picture over. The loopy handwriting makes my breath hitch.

I love you, Trey. You are right.
We do belong together.
—Arella

I read it again.

And again.

And again.

The sunrise appears out of nowhere. I haven't slept, I haven't eaten, and I don't feel like doing either. I also haven't let go of this picture since I saw Arella's note.

The absence of her is driving me insane. I need to do the one thing that will completely block her from my mind. Unfortunately, I promised myself—more importantly, Liz—that I would never drink that much or get that high again. Although, back then, I didn't know I'd feel so devastated.

Maybe I can black out for one day. I just won't tell Liz.

No, no, no. I scold myself for even considering it. Nothing good can come from that. Except I could feel better, even if it's just for one night. *That'll be worth it, right?* Probably not. The second I wake up sober, this chest ache will come right back. It always does.

What I truly want is a permanent healing solution, and she's probably in the arms of that other guy right now. The mere thought of it scratches at my throat, leaving it coarse and dry.

Instead, I imagine her alone in her bed, sulking like I am. I let out a groan toward the ceiling. Neither image makes me feel good.

Should I call her? Has she tried to call me? Where's my phone? After rubbing my sore eyes, I force myself to go phone hunting.

I don't find it in my bedroom. Or the living room. Or the kitchen. When I still can't find it, I search my music room twice. Nothing.

Huffing, I trudge upstairs to my workout room. Finally, I find the damn thing sitting next to my Bluetooth speaker. Now that I think about it, this was the last place I used my phone before Jess showed up during my workout yesterday.

Damn. Was that only yesterday?

My phone has five percent battery left. I've got two missed calls. Neither is from Arella. Three texts. None of those are from Arella either. They're all from Liz, dated yesterday.

> You coming to perform tonight or what?

> T?

> Shit. I'm sorry. I didn't realize it's September 5th. Don't worry about coming if you don't feel up for it.

The anniversary of seeing my parents get blown up is not the reason why I skipped out on my band's show last night, but I'll take it.

My phone vibrates in my hand. Liz's name and picture appear on the screen. I let the call go to voicemail, because I'm not in the mood to talk to Liz right now—or anybody. Well, except for one. If Arella called, I wouldn't hesitate to pick up.

A second later, my phone buzzes. It's a text from Liz.

> Are you planning to come tonight?

If I'm not in the mood to talk to people, I'm definitely not in the mood to perform. Especially not on a Saturday, when the Soul House is always packed. But if I skip again, my band manager will have my head. Monique lives for any chance to yell at me. I don't have the energy to deal with her wrath, so I suck it up, grab my leather jacket, strap on my helmet, and head toward downtown Los Angeles.

Riding my motorcycle is lonely without Arella. I can still feel her behind me and her fingers drawing figure eights over my abs. It's not until I've arrived at my destination that I realize I should have stayed home.

Arella usually comes to work with me. Whenever she doesn't, everyone asks about her. Typically, I can tell people she'll be coming when she gets off work. This time, I can't. What will I say instead? I sure as hell am not explaining what actually happened.

I find a parking spot in the back lot, then force myself to dismount my bike. I'd much rather go home, but I drag my feet to the backstage door anyway. On the keypad, I type in the access code.

Beep! The little light turns green, and I step inside.

Marcus is behind his drum set, spinning a drumstick around his fingers when he glances up at me. "Hey, man! Where you—" His face drops. "Damn. Who died?"

I must look like a train wreck. Definitely feel like one. I rub my stubbly cheeks. Maybe if I had trimmed my beard, I wouldn't look so defeated.

"Is Ari comin'?" Kevin, our bass guitarist, asks through a mouthful of chips.

"Marcus! Kev!" Emmy, our pianist, rushes out of the women's bathroom with Liz right behind her.

Liz flashes Marcus and Kevin a stern look, then pretends to zip her lips shut. The room goes silent.

The girls know. I don't know how they know, but they know. I can tell by their distraught emotions whipping me in the face like a chilly gust of wind. Plus, they're staring at me with a sorrowful look in their eyes.

I hate that look. It's the pity look. It's the same look people used to give me when I was known as the little boy whose parents died in a "house fire." *I shouldn't have come.*

Liz whispers something to Emmy, who nods, turns to the boys, and gestures toward the door. Without a word, the guys obey, and they rush outside with Emmy.

When the door clicks shut, Liz approaches me with gentle steps. The closer she gets, the deeper her sadness bleeds into my head. It mixes with the pain that's been throbbing inside me since yesterday. *I really shouldn't have come.*

"T," she says, all tender and shit.

I hate it. I hate this. I don't want to be treated like I'm wounded. I mean, I am, but I don't want to be treated like it.

"How do you know?" I ask dryly.

"Well, you weren't answering your phone, so I called Ari. She said you broke up with her."

Is that the story she's telling people? Hearing the words *broke up* doesn't help me accept it. I won't accept it. I'm still holding out for the moment someone pops out and tells me this was all just a cruel joke. *The cruelest fucking joke ever.*

I drag a rough hand through my already messy hair. "What else did she say?"

"Not much."

I swallow the hard lump in my throat. "How is she?"

Liz studies me with furrowed brows. "Uh, I'm not sure."

Is she as miserable as I am?

"How are *you*?"

I shrug halfheartedly. "Fine."

"You don't look fine. You look heartbroken."

Is that what I'm feeling? Heartbroken? I guess I wouldn't know. It's never happened to me before. No wonder people say it sucks.

Liz keeps talking to me like I'm a lost puppy. "I thought you were in love with her?"

"I am."

"Then I'm confused as to why you dumped her, but let's talk about this later, okay? We've gotta get ready for our show."

The idea of performing sounds as bad as explaining to Liz what happened. "I don't wanna talk about it."

"I didn't ask if you wanted to. We're gonna talk tonight whether you like it or not."

"Liz . . ." I sigh through her name.

She lifts a gloved hand to my face. "No. Don't argue with me. You won't win."

She's right. With her, I never win.

I guess if there's one person in this world I can talk to about Arella, it's Liz. Liz befriended me even when I was a drunk z-drug addict headed nowhere in life. Liz, of all people, will understand.

I WAS WRONG. LIZ DOESN'T UNDERSTAND, AND I DON'T THINK SHE CARES TO.

"What do you mean, you didn't break up with her?" Liz has left her satin gloves lying on the backstage coffee table and has forced me to sit on the couch with her.

The rest of the band and crew left a while ago. I delayed this conversation by taking a long bathroom break. I'd still be in there if Liz hadn't waltzed into the men's room to call me out on my bullshit. Leave it to her to know that I was simply hiding in a stall to avoid this.

"I didn't break up with her. Technically, *she* left me." I can still hear Arella's tires squealing from driving away so fast.

"Why would Ari do such a thing?"

"Because," I groan, "it wasn't working."

"Do you want it to?"

I rub my hands over my face and groan again—louder this time. "Why are you doing this?"

"Because I care about you."

It's ridiculous that Liz cares about me at all. I'm a fuckup. She should start investing her precious energy into someone who actually matters.

I slouch back against the couch. "You've never had to have a therapy session with me about any other girl before. Why do you have to start now?"

"Because Ari's different, and you know it. With her, you're more vibrant and happy. You two have something special most people can't find in a lifetime. It doesn't even make sense, because she's an Ordinary and it's totally illegal and against all biology for you to love her, but I've never seen two people more meant for each other than you and her. I know you believe that too. So why are you acting like you're just gonna let her go?"

Liz is right. Arella *is* meant for me. She's my soul mate—something I didn't even believe in until I felt the *glimmer*. I used to think getting a sickening sense whenever your soul mate was in danger was just some stupid thing Zordinaries made up to put claim on each other—until last month. I was on my way to Arella's apartment when a sudden wave of nausea hit me like bricks to the stomach. My throat went dry and I couldn't stop coughing. Then I found Arella being attacked by spiders.

The week after, when her car was hit by a truck, my body knew something was wrong. I was nowhere near her when it happened, yet sudden nausea hit me again. I got so dizzy, I threw up. Given that Arella's an Ordinary, my sicknesses at those exact times could have been a coincidence, but that's one hell of a coincidence.

"Tell me what you want, T," Liz says. "What would make you happy?"

"I dunno." Happiness seems like a foreign idea right now.

"Do you want her back?"

"I dunno."

"Yes, you do. You either want her or you don't. Which is it?" Liz isn't stupid. We both know the answer. She's just trying to get me to say it out loud.

"Of course I want her back," I grumble.

"Then go get her. Whatever you guys fought about, talk through it."

"It's not that easy."

Liz scoffs. "You're a smart man. Figure it out."

"I can't."

"Why not?"

"I just can't," I snap.

Like always, Liz isn't having my attitude. She snaps right back at me. "Why not?"

I give in. "Because she slept with another man."

"No, she didn't."

I scowl at the conviction in her tone. "How are you so sure?"

"Because Ari would never do that."

That's what I thought too—until she showed me those two lines on a pee stick. "Well, she did."

"How do you know? Did she tell you?"

"No. I know because—" I choke up. "She's . . . She's pregnant."

Liz gasps, covering her mouth with her hand. "No. Maybe the test was wrong." She's going through the denial phase. That was me for the first fifteen minutes after I saw those goddamn pregnancy brochures.

I was cleaning up my house when I accidentally dropped Arella's purse and all her stuff spilled out. As I bent to pick it up, the words *Having a Healthy Pregnancy* caught my attention. I almost fell over.

"She took four store-bought tests and a test at the doctor's office. They all came out positive." I lift a finger. "Which, by the way, does not mean she's positively *not pregnant*."

Liz screws her face up. "Hold on. You thought *positive* on a pregnancy test meant positively *not* pregnant?"

"Well, I fuckin' hoped."

"You know, for a smart man, you're kind of an idiot."

I toss my hands into the air, letting them fall to my thighs. "Thanks for the pep talk, Liz. Really made me feel *loads* better. Same time tomorrow?"

Her hands go up in surrender. "Okay, okay, I'm sorry. I'm just . . . trying to process all this. If Ari is pregnant, that means she really did sleep with someone else."

"That's what I've been trying to fucking tell you."

Liz slumps back, huffing out a breath. "Damn. That changes everything."

SUNDAY NIGHT USED TO BE *OUR* NIGHT. IT'S THE EVENING I USUALLY HAVE OFF, AND I'D SPEND those hours just being with Arella. Most of the time, we'd just talk until she fell asleep. Sometimes we'd watch movies or play card games or take walks around my neighborhood.

Sundays are special to me. We had our first date on a Sunday. I took her to my favorite pasta place in Long Beach, where I made her laugh so hard, she wheezed and slapped her knee over and over.

A couple of Sundays later, she taught me how to bake snickerdoodle cookies in my kitchen. That night ended with us throwing flour at each other and sharing our first kiss.

Then there was that one Sunday when we went stargazing at her *thinking spot*, a secluded oak tree at the top of a woodsy hill. There, she explained to me what love is.

"When you love someone, you put their happiness before your own."

Later that night, I told her what really happened to my parents, and she comforted me with a simple touch of her hand to my face.

On a Sunday after that, we made love for the first time, right under that tree. It was the most magical and sensual experience I've ever had.

As I flop onto my still-bare mattress, I mope over the idea that this could be the first of many Sundays I spend alone.

On Monday, everything reminds me of her. Little things like waking up to her side of the bed empty, or walking into the kitchen, where she's not in my T-shirt, pouring herself a glass of apple juice. Or stepping into my shower without a naked beauty smiling back at me.

My shower water ran cold five minutes ago. My body's natural equilibrium is working hard to warm me because I don't care to get out. There's nothing waiting for me beyond these tile walls—the ones that I'm pounding my head against because I'm trying to get her out of my mind.

When I finally gather enough willpower to step out, the mirror is foggy. In the middle of the glass, I swipe a towel in a circle to reveal my face. *Ew.* Bloodshot pupils. Dark eyebags. Facial hair that hasn't been trimmed in who knows how long. I look like a homeless bum.

With a towel around my waist, I drag my feet into my walk-in closet. All her clothes are still hanging up on her side. I debate shoving it all into a box and driving it back to her. It'd be an excuse to see her, but returning her things means she won't be coming back. I'm not ready to admit that yet.

On Tuesday, I don't do anything productive all day. Unless lugging my feet around my empty house and finding things to throw fireballs at counts as productive.

Around noon on Wednesday, Liz FaceTimes me. I almost don't answer, but if I don't, she'll show up here, and that would be worse.

"Hey," I mumble when her face appears on my screen. I take a seat at my kitchen counter.

"Don't even think about skipping tonight. If you don't show up to rehearsal by four, I'll drive over there and throw water balls at you until you beg me to stop."

"Can't I get one pass?" I prop my phone up against my salt shaker. It's too much effort to hold my phone up.

"Hell no. I've given you passes for two days." That's true. I skipped our recording session yesterday and our writing session the day before that. "It's not good for you to be alone, T. I know how you get."

"What's that supposed to mean?"

"Have you been staying sober?"

"Unfortunately," I say with a scoff.

"Good. Now get yourself together and show up tonight."

Let's see . . . Get pounded with water by Liz or leave my house and be forced to talk to other humans? I think I'll take the water balls.

"Come on, T. Please?"

I sigh heavily. "Fine."

"Fabulous. I'll see you later then. And for the love of all things holy, please, trim your beard."

I rub my palm against my long chin hairs. "Is it that bad?"

"You look like the Wish version of Henry Cavill."

On Thursday, only because hunger is clawing a hole through my stomach, I force myself to make some lunch. For the first time in months, I'm cooking for one—that is, if sticking a frozen pizza into the oven counts as cooking.

On Friday, I arrive home from the Soul House mentally exhausted. The fans got a half-hearted performance from me tonight. During the meet and greet, I fake-smiled for all the photos until it was finally over. All of it felt trivial. What's the point when I don't have her?

I can't take it anymore. I need the pain to stop, and I need it to stop now.

I don't register that my feet have moved until I'm already in the kitchen with the cabinet open. From it, I drag down a half bottle of bourbon, some tequila, and a tiny bit of vodka. I don't think about it as I unscrew the vodka cap and chug it all in one breath. It burns on its way down my throat.

The tequila is next. It takes three breaths to finish.

The bourbon takes four.

This isn't enough to get me buzzed, and I need to black out. Years of being a drunk have built up my alcohol tolerance. Couple that with my body filtering it out way faster than the average Ordinary can, and I'm gonna need at least three more bottles—full ones.

My nights used to be filled with popping questionable pills and trying any z-drug I could get my hands on. Hollow sex with women in skimpy outfits. Meaningless fights with big guys in bars. Talking shit to bouncers at clubs, just to get them to drive a hard one into my face. I used to do anything so I could feel something other than the emptiness in my chest.

Two years ago, I cleaned up. Liz made me realize that a pathetic trainwreck isn't what I want to be. Tonight, I don't give a shit what I am.

Through heavy rainfall, I drive to the nearest liquor store, getting there ten minutes before closing. Something makes me go apeshit in the aisles. I toss practically every hard liquor in sight into my basket.

When I arrive back home, I don't waste a second. In my silent living room, on the vacant couch, I rip the seal off a bottle and chug.

The last time I drank with the intent of passing out was after I got the call telling me the cancer had finally taken Elliott. I would have given anything to cure that precious little boy. Right now, I'd give anything to have Arella back.

She would hate me if she saw me drinking like this. The smell of alcohol triggers bad memories of her ex in her head. Because of that, I never drank around her. *And now, she's gone.*

Only once two bottles lie empty beside me do I start to feel something. The blackout is coming, but it's not coming fast enough, so I reach for another bottle. *Bottoms up.*

42

ARELLA

It's been seven days. Seven slow, tormenting days.

I can't eat. I can't sleep. I can't think.

I didn't realize how much time I spent with Trey, until now, when I'm not.

He's ruined me. And he'll continue to ruin me. From now on, every doctor's appointment I'll attend alone, every kick I'll feel from the baby, every time someone comments on my rounded belly, he's all I'll be thinking about.

I've always wanted to be a mom. I've dreamt of this moment since I was a kid, except I imagined this with a ring on my finger and the father-to-be at my side.

I'm terrified to do this alone. What will I tell my grandparents? How will I explain to my future son or daughter why they don't have a father? How does anyone explain to a child that their father thought he was infertile and—

Knock-knock-knock.

I jolt out of bed. *Is it him?* I rush to the door in my pajamas.

"Wipe that disappointment off your face." Javina's wearing a light jacket with the hood up to block the rain from all her black curls. She holds up a carton of ice cream. "Wanna have some rocky road while we plot his murder?"

I roll my eyes, mostly because when she called earlier, I told her not to come. Still, I motion for her to step inside. "We're not going to kill him."

"Of course *we* aren't gonna kill him," she says as she slips her shoes off. "We don't stand a chance against him and those huge arm muscles. We're gonna hire a hit man." Her tone is so serious, I'm no longer sure she's joking.

On the floor of my living room with the ice cream between us, I tell Javina about the blonde chick I saw Trey with. I choke up as I hash out the details of our fight, leaving out any parts that suggest I'm with child. I'm not ready to tell Javina yet. She'll freak out, and I need to be in a place where I'm not also freaking out before I tell her.

"Toward the end, we were fighting quite a bit," I say as I dig my spoon into the now half-gone ice cream.

"About what?"

"Mostly about him keeping secrets from me. For example, he was always up at three in the morning, talking on the phone. I don't think he sleeps."

"Wait." Javina draws her thick eyebrows together. "You don't think he sleeps, like, ever?"

"Ever."

"That's impossible."

"I'll tell you what's impossible. One time, we were at a restaurant, and somehow, he knew there was a teenage boy getting beat up in an alley *blocks* away."

Javina takes a moment to process that before saying, "What?"

"Exactly. Then, there was this whole thing where he kept asking—no, *begging*—me to move to Paris with him. Whenever I asked him why, he kept saying he'd tell me once we got there, otherwise, I'd leave him."

"Again, what?"

"Oh, and let's not forget that on the night he and my ex got into a fist fight, Trey left with gashes in his knuckles. When I saw him three days later, his hand looked brand new. I got so curious that two weeks ago, I asked if he's an alien."

Javina freezes with her spoon halfway to her lips. "And?"

"He claims he's not. Apparently, he's not a superhero or from the future either. Those were my other guesses."

Javina gasps. "What if he's a wizard?"

"Like from Harry Potter?"

"Nah. More like the ones from that show *Charmed*. They have magical powers and shit, and they hide it from society, but they don't need to use any wands."

I go in for another spoonful of ice cream. "I don't think he's a wizard."

"Don't completely rule it out, girl. That's what the wizards want us to do. They live among us and don't want us to know it."

"Do you really believe that?"

"I believe that alternate universes exist, so why not wizards?" She gasps with a hand to her mouth. "What if he's from an alternate universe?"

Alternate universe? *Hmm . . .* Is that the explanation for all of Trey's oddities? Maybe in his universe, never sleeping is normal. I'll have to look into that later.

"I'm still pissed that you waited this long to tell me." Javina waves her spoon in the air. "I warned him not to hurt you. I told him if he did, I'd rip his balls off with my bare hands."

I don't doubt that Javina would try to if given the chance.

She leans back against the front of my couch. "So, do ya think Trey was havin' another woman over *every* time you were at work?"

Pfft. "I didn't . . . until now."

Shaking her head, she says, "I knew pretty boy was trouble."

"What? You were the one who said, 'If you don't marry him, I will.' "

"I still would! We'd have the grandest, most expensive wedding ever. Then, once I was the sole beneficiary of his will, I'd make sure he *accidentally* fell into a mysterious cavern within three years. Can't do it too soon, or it'll be obvious it was me."

Okay, maybe Javina and I watch too many true crime shows.

"Anyway, enough about that asshat." She licks her spoon clean, then tosses it onto my coffee table. "Tell me what's up with you not being on the schedule at the daycare. All your shifts have other people's names on them."

I knew this topic was coming. I've been avoiding it. "Um, I got let go."

Javina lifts an eyebrow like, *No, seriously. What really happened?*

I return her look with a deadpan face.

Finally, she gasps. "What? Why?"

"Remember last month when I was attacked by spiders?"

"How could I forget? After hearing you describe it, I'm *still* having nightmares. You're lucky I'm even sitting inside this arachnid magnet you call an apartment."

Whenever I see a black spot on the wall, I get a flashback of being attacked by thousands of spiders, and it suddenly gets hard to breathe. Thankfully, I haven't found any creepy-crawlies yet, but that moment was so traumatizing that sometimes, everything around here looks like a spider.

I place the lid back over our ice cream. "Since I was gone for a whole week, our director said I needed to provide a doctor's note. Company policy. Trey had one, but he lost it, so he wrote me a new one instead. Our director checked up on it, and apparently, the doctor never said I couldn't go to work."

"Why didn't you tell me? I could have done something."

"I didn't tell you because I didn't want you to start a fight with our director in front of everyone."

Javina scoffs. "That's exactly what I'ma do on Monday."

"No, Javie. Please, don't. She was nice about it. She said she didn't want to fire me but had to because of policies."

"Fuck the policies. You're one of the best we've got."

"It's okay," I say, half meaning it. "I can find another job."

"Have you started lookin' yet?"

"Not yet. I've got some money stashed away, so I'll be fine." *For now.* Soon, I'll need to have enough income to support myself and an expensive newborn.

Javina and I continue talking about life, movies, and her girlfriend until she can't stop yawning. Eventually, the clock hits 1:00 a.m., and Javina leaves.

As I crawl back into bed, the heartache resurfaces like a tsunami. A minute ago, I was laughing at my best friend's jokes. Now I feel like I could burst into tears with the simple thought of him.

Under the covers, I listen to the steady pour of raindrops on my window while I scroll through our old texts. What did I ever say to make him think I'd be capable of sleeping with another man behind his back? The only thing I gain from rereading our messages is a reminder of how in love with him I still am.

The second I finish reading our texts, my YouTube app is up, and I'm typing *Flames in the Night* into the search bar. The first video that pops up is their original song "Fired Up!" I tap it, then shove my earbuds in and turn the volume up as loud as it will go. A familiar drum solo rattles my brain, followed by Trey's guitar riffs. This is the song they use as their upbeat opener for all their shows, so I've heard it plenty. It brings back good memories.

I finish that video, then scroll until I come across their cover of a Justin Timberlake song. I was there for this shoot, like I was for many others. This one stands out to me because in the middle of filming, Trey dropped to his knees in front of me and kissed me like his heart would collapse if he didn't. I'll never forget the intense way he looked at me when he came barreling through that bedroom door and seized my face without a single word.

I can't get through the whole video because it's a bunch of footage of Trey cuddling with some blonde actress playing his love interest. So I skip to the next video.

It's about to play when *Tap! Tap! Tap!*

That can't be the rain. I rip my earbuds out.

"Arella?" someone yells from outside.

The blinds are shut. I know who it is though. No one else ever calls me by my full name.

"Arella, please. I need to see you."

Need? I hop off the bed and yank the blinds up. There he is, sopping-wet hair and all. I unlock the window and crank it open.

"What are you doing here?" I hate that there's a screen between us. My racing heart wants to be near him, and this stupid mesh thing is in the way.

Rain pours over him as he slurs, "I knocked on your door, like, a ba-jillion times. Why didn't you come?"

"I didn't hear it. I was listening to—" I can't admit that I was hopelessly listening to him sing me to sleep. "Music."

"Will you let me in?"

I nod slowly, even though I want him in here so bad, I'm willing to break through this screen. Instead, I rush to the door.

I open it to find Trey more drenched than expected. His black T-shirt clings to his skin, outlining his defined pecs. Raindrops slide down his leather jacket until they hit the concrete. His jeans look like he just crawled out of the ocean.

When we lock eyes, a rush of emotions hits me like heavy sand dumped over my head. It submerges all my other emotions under its weight, replacing them with sadness, anxiety, and heartache. I mean, my heart was already aching, but now it's throbbing.

I don't get a chance to say anything before Trey steps inside and crushes me against him. His arms squeeze me so tight, I lose all the air in my lungs. With a little sigh, he buries his face into my neck. At first, I stiffen, but it's not long before my body softens into him.

The sadness weighing me down is quickly replaced by a warm sense of belonging and hope. A trickle of peace runs from my shoulders to my toes. It's an odd sensation, like an electric current rushing through me, except I think it's coming from him.

We stand in my doorway while the rain drowns my front step behind him. No words. No movement. Just arms wrapped around each other's bodies. I think we both needed this. I, for sure, needed this.

The scent of him is familiar—mostly. Manly cologne, his shampoo, and . . . *alcohol?* Has he been drinking?

"I missss you," he slurs.

I suppose that's my answer.

When I don't respond, he asks, "Do you miss me?"

I've missed you since the moment I drove away. I waited seven days for you to show up, and every minute you didn't felt like years in a dark abyss. What took you so long? Why didn't you come after me? And why are you drunk?

I pull back. "Trey, why are you here?"

He wraps his arms around me tighter, crushing me against his chest again. "I wasn't done yet."

Tears threaten to burst from my eyes. Being held by him makes me feel whole again, so I don't fight it. I'd stay in his embrace forever if I could, but I can't. So I give him another minute before saying into his shirt, "You're soaking wet."

"Sssorry." He lets me go, and I gesture for him to step all the way inside.

After he does, I shut the door, muting the rainfall, then turn to him.

He's gorgeous—a towering muscular frame that was my safe haven for three months. Light stubble decorates his strong jawline. I used to run my fingertips through that stubble whenever we made out. I used to grip that firm neck whenever he'd scoop me up and carry me into his bedroom. Everything about him is familiar, except for the heavy anguish ingrained between his eyebrows. Selfishly, I'm glad to know I'm not the only one who's miserable.

He places a tender finger under my chin and lifts my head until my eyes meet his. "Were you crying, babe? Your eyes are all puffy."

I draw back from his touch. It's doing things to me. And if he calls me *babe* again, I might let him do *anything* he wants to me. "Why didn't you take your car instead of the bike?"

"I didn't take either."

"Then how did you get here?"

"I walked."

"You walked?" That's at least a two- or three-hour walk.

"Yeah. I'm fucked up. I know better than to drive like this." He runs his fingers through his dark-chocolate hair and shakes the water out. Little droplets sprinkle onto my arms, but I don't care. I'm just relieved he's here, and that the first person he thought to go to while in this drunken state is me.

Does that mean he wants to fix things? Do *I* want that? I think about it for all of two seconds before I almost laugh at myself. Who am I kidding? Of course I want that.

"Why didn't you call an Uber?" I ask.

He scoffs a little. "I did. The dude drove me most of the way before kicking me outta his car."

"Why?"

"He asked me questions like where I was goin' and who I was tryna see. He said somethin' about how taking a drunk man to a woman's apartment meant trouble. So he forced me to get out and drove off."

Mentally, I applaud the Uber driver. Taking a drunk man to a woman's place *can* mean bad news. After surviving an abusive three-year relationship with a drunk, I know just how terrible those situations can get. However, with drunk Trey, I feel completely safe. I have full confidence that he would never hurt me. At least not physically. Emotionally, I'm stupidly wrecked.

"How much did you have to drink?" I ask.

His shoulders slump like I've caught him in a lie. Another invisible bag of heavy sand and sadness dumps over me—from him. "Please, don't be mad."

"How much, Trey?"

He glowers at the carpet. "Maybe, like, two bottles."

"Of?"

"Vodka. Tequila. Bourbon."

I squint at him. "You just named three things."

"All righty then. So I had *three* bottles."

My jaw drops. "You had three bottles of hard liquor? Like, all of it?"

"Probably. I don't really remember . . ."

"How are you still standing?" There's no way he had that much. That would kill him.

"I have a high tolerance."

No one's tolerance is that high.

After kicking off his shoes, he heads to my couch and falls onto it with a plop.

I cringe a little. "Trey, you're wet."

He shoots back up, stumbles over, and leans against me as I steady him. Tingles shoot down my legs from the warm hand he places on the small of my back. I've missed his touch.

"I'm sorry," he slurs. "It's just that I've been walking forever. I really need to sit."

"How about you take off all your wet clothes first? I'll wash them for you."

He complies, first with his jacket, then his shirt. As soon as I see his abs, I realize this is a mistake. I can't see him shirtless. It's my kryptonite.

From his pockets, he drags out his wallet and phone, then drops them onto my coffee table with two light thuds. Then he yanks his jeans and socks off. I grab all his damp clothes and head to the front door to hang his jacket up to dry. When I turn around, he's already got his boxers down.

I shut my eyes and throw my hands up. "Stop!"

"Huh?" A wave of shock rushes through my head.

"Put your boxers back on."

"But you told me to take off all my wet clothes."

"The boxers can stay." I wait a moment before I reopen my eyes.

Trey stands magnificently before me, wearing only a pair of plaid boxers. He gestures toward my couch. "Can I sit now?"

"Sure." With his clothes in hand, I head down the hall.

The world is cruel. Countless times, I've pictured him at my door with flowers, telling me he's come to his senses. He'd say things like "I realized you never would have cheated on me" and "I'm ready to be a father." We'd have the most amazing makeup sex and everything would be okay. Instead, the world drops him off here drunk, looking like a model for men's underwear. What am I supposed to do with this?

In the hallway, I open the pair of closet doors where my washer and dryer hide. I throw Trey's clothes into the washer with some detergent, then start the machine.

Footsteps thump against my carpet as a cloud of gloominess approaches me. I pretend not to notice him as he wraps his arms around me from behind and breathes a shiver down my neck. I have to grip the washing machine just to keep my knees from buckling.

"You're so beautiful," he says with liquor breath.

Instead of melting into him the way I always have, I remain strong and keep still. I need to know what his intentions are before I allow myself to give in to him. The moment I do is the moment I give him permission to break me again.

After a few deep breaths, I gather enough willpower to pry myself out of his grasp, and then I stride into the bathroom. Trey and his cloud of gloominess follow me there.

I open the cabinet above the sink. "How do you feel?"

"Sad." His gaze drops to the floor as he lingers in the doorway. "All the time."

"I meant, how does your head feel?"

"Oh. Um, it's all right. I'll probably be hungover in the morning though."

I shake out two pills from a bottle of ibuprofen and hold them out.

He pushes my hand away. "That's not gonna do anything for me."

I roll my eyes. He sounds like Javina whenever she's had too much to drink. She thinks water doesn't help either, but it totally does. "Just take them."

"I'm serious, babe. Ordinary human pills don't work on me."

Ordinary human pills? What pills *do* work on him then? Superhuman pills? Maybe in the alternate universe he's from, having superpowers is normal. Is that why I can feel his emotions right now? *Oh my god.* Am I carrying a superhuman baby inside me that can sense feelings?

Pushing down the panic in my chest, I stash the pill bottle back into my cabinet. I've still got the two tablets in my palm, though, just in case he wants to take them later.

With gentle hands, Trey pushes the hair from my face and cups my cheeks. My heart thrashes as he presses his lips to my forehead and gives me a light kiss. "I need you, baby."

Oh, how four little words can stir up so much eagerness inside me. The irrational part of me is screaming, *Yes, please!* The rational part of me wants to smack him for trying to claim to be infertile. Maybe in his alternate universe, he is infertile. But in this universe, he's definitely able to make babies.

"Trey, can you please explain why you're here?"

Sighing, he lets me go and steps back. As if he didn't hear my question, he asks, "Can I dry my hair a little? It keeps dripping down my face."

"Sure."

He drags my bath towel off the bar, then freezes. An invisible fist punches me in the gut. "What the fuck happened there?"

It takes me a second to register what his eyes are glued to. It's a gaping hole in the wall below the towel bar—evidence of my ex's lingering presence.

"Nathan," I say, and it's all the explanation he needs.

Trey's face turns sour. "When?"

"A year ago, maybe?"

"I swear, if he ever touches you again, I'll kill him."

I'd think he's just spitting out words, but the conviction in his tone and the anger radiating off him makes me think he's serious.

Trey rubs the towel all over his hair, then hangs it back up. It's not the way I usually do it. I typically spread the towel out to make sure it conceals the hole. Trey's version is messy and hugs the right side too much. I'll fix it later.

"Would you like to sit down now?" I ask.

Trey nods with his hair sticking up in all directions. I open my mouth, about to offer him a comb, then I don't. He looks cute like this.

He gestures for me to walk out first. I do and sense his cloud of despair follow me to the living room.

I set the pills on the coffee table. "I'll leave these here for you to take later."

His gloominess trails me to the kitchen, where I snatch a clean glass from the cabinet and fill it with some filtered water from the fridge.

I offer him the glass. "Drink up."

Without hesitation, he accepts it and finishes it in three gulps. I can't imagine what little time it took him to down that tequila.

"Thanks." He pushes the empty glass toward me.

I fill it again. "Want some more?"

"Maybe later." He stares at me with his captivating blue-gray eyes. If he keeps looking at me so intensely like that, I might fall under his spell again. *Not that I've fallen out of it.*

For the fourth time tonight, I ask, "Why are you here, Trey?"

"I couldn't stop thinking about you."

My heart does a pathetic little happy dance. My head scowls at my heart for being so easily fooled.

Without a word, Trey takes my hand and leads me to the couch. When he sits, he gestures for me to sit as well. I don't, and he doesn't force me either. Instead, he takes my hands into his and kisses the tops of my knuckles. Whatever wizardry spell he's casting on me, it's working.

I plant myself onto the couch next to him. "You can sleep here tonight if you want."

"I don't wanna sleep." He keeps my hands in his so tightly, it leaves no room for me to pull away, which is probably his intent.

"What do you want to do, then?"

"I wanna kiss you."

My lips tingle, as does everything between my legs, betraying me. Thankfully, my brain takes over before my body can. "No kissing. You have to sleep off all that alcohol."

He pouts a little, and it's adorable. "Can we kiss in the morning?"

Finally, I draw my hands back and scowl at him. "Did you forget that we broke up?"

"Not for a second."

I feel a little piece of his soul fall apart somewhere in that dark cloud above his head, and it makes me feel bad for him.

This man has been through a lot. Seeing his parents get murdered. Surviving his abusive uncle. Losing the only child who's ever meant anything to him. They're all reasons as to why he's so guarded, has deep trust issues, and refuses to let people in. And don't even get me started with his lack of self-worth.

I get it. It took me a long time to start healing from my abusive ex, and I'm *still* healing, so if there's anything I can do to help ease Trey's pain right now, I'm going to do it.

I hop to my feet. "Come. I'll let you sleep in my bed."

His eyes light up. "With you?"

Yes, please! "No."

The light in his eyes goes dim. "I'll stay here on the couch then."

"It's okay. You can sleep on the bed, and I can—"

"Arella, what kind of man would I be if I took over a woman's bed and forced her to sleep on these old cushions? The answer is no. I'll sleep right here."

With Trey, I've learned to pick my battles. We're both as stubborn as the other, and I can tell this is a fight I'm not going to win.

I leave him for a moment, then return with the one extra pillow and blanket I own. It's what Javina always uses whenever she stays over. When I hand them to Trey, he takes it, clutching my hand in the process.

"Cuddle with me."

I almost burst into tears. All I've wanted for the last seven days is for him to want me. Here he is, acting like he wants me more than he wants his next breath, and I can't bring myself to let him in. He hurt me—deeply. If we pretend like nothing happened and go back to the way things were, he'll hurt me again. I can't allow that.

Besides, there is no going back to the way things were. I've got his baby growing inside me now. No matter what happens from here, things will never again be the way they were.

"Please?" he begs. "It's been really hard for me to fall asleep without you."

I know how that feels all too well, so I give in.

We lie on the couch with my face pressed against his bare chest. *Oh, the scent of him . . .* He wraps the blanket around us, tucking it under my waist the way he always does. My body relaxes into him as a rush of calmness settles over me. This time, it's not just his feelings. They're mine too.

Trey leans back a little to look at me. "You wanna know something I've noticed?"

"What?"

"You're still wearing the angel wings." He grazes a thumb across the necklace he gave me. The golden wings feature a way-bigger-than-I-can-afford diamond heart in the middle. The tiny engraving on the back reads: *Paris? T.G.*

Maybe that's where the portal to his alternate universe is and he was trying to take me there with him. It would make sense since he said if I knew the reason behind why we had to go to Paris, I wouldn't go—and he's right. I have no desire to leave this universe for an alternate one. Not even for him.

"I guess I forgot to take it off," I lie. I've refused to take off this necklace because doing so feels like disconnecting from him, and I'm not ready for that yet.

He caresses my cheek with his fingertips. "I like that you're still wearing it."

I grab his hand and hold it against my chest. "Why don't you try going to sleep?"

"Do you ever think about me?" he asks as if I didn't say anything.

I clear my throat to give myself time to decide if I should lie or not. "Sometimes." *All the time.*

"I think about you constantly. You're like a never-ending song that keeps replaying in my mind. I can't stop writing lyrics about you either. Every single song I write sounds like a miserable ballad."

Boy, do I want to hear one of those! "Go to sleep, Trey."

He doesn't obey. "I've been thinking a lot about what happened. I want you to know that if the situation was different, I'd ask you to marry me. We'd raise this baby together to be the best little boy or girl the world has ever known. I'd ask you to give me more babies. We'd have a whole bunch of 'em. I'd grow old with you and support you in any dreams you want to make come true."

Tears prick the surface of my eyes. I want that. All of it. *How can I have it?*

Trey's tone goes husky. "The problem is that I can't. Can you understand how much it hurts to know that you're pregnant when I biologically cannot have babies with you? Mental images of you fooling around with another man are tearing me apart from the inside out. I constantly feel like I'm suffocating because my chest aches too much for my lungs to work."

That does it for me. I gasp for air as a cry ripples through me. I can't imagine how much it burns to think you're infertile, then find out your girlfriend is pregnant. If I were him and believed what he believes, I wouldn't be here. To him, it's obvious that I slept with another man.

When I said he should be prepared to pay child support, it probably sounded like I was after his money. I only said that because I was angry. I didn't actually mean it. If I were him, I'd hate me. No wonder he's so broken.

What breaks me, though, is that not once has he stopped to think that maybe, just maybe, this baby is his. How can he be so sure he's infertile? Did a doctor say so? Did he get a vasectomy? Was he born that way? Does he think people from his alternate universe can't have children with the people in this universe?

Suddenly, any hope I had of us getting back together vanishes. If I were him with all the baggage from his past and the knowledge he has, I wouldn't want anything to do with me.

Trey places a tender kiss against my temple. "Oh, angel, please don't cry."

I can't help it. I've been crying for a week, and feeling his pain mix with mine is only making it worse.

He kisses my temple again. "Remember when we were at your thinking spot under that big oak tree? You told me that when you love someone, you put their happiness before your own. I want you to be happy, baby. It'll kill me, but if you wanna go be with him, go be with him. If that's what makes you happy."

Wait . . . Did he just admit he loves me? He's shown me he loves me, but he's never verbalized it.

I don't have much time to process it, because he keeps going.

"I just want to know what I did wrong, first. What did I do to make you feel like you needed him instead of me? Did I not give you enough? Should I have paid more attention to you? Should I have made you feel more beautiful or bought you more things?"

I've never felt like I needed anything more from Trey than his presence. He's given me everything I've ever wanted and more. He gave me a man who listened to me. A man who truly cared about my hopes and dreams. Someone I felt safe with and protected by. Most of all, he gave me someone who made me feel loved in bed—not used and abused. Trey has made me feel the most loved I've ever felt, without ever saying the words *I love you.* How could he think he didn't give me enough?

"I think I need closure," he says, choking up. "I need a reason to let you go, because obviously, knowing that your heart is with someone else isn't enough. Tell me you're better off without me. Tell me you're happier when you're with him. Tell me you don't want me anymore. Maybe then I'll be able to move on. I just can't take this pain anymore. I need it to be over."

And there it is—the real reason he's here. Closure. He needs me to give him a reason to let me go. If that's what he came for, I'll give it to him. Maybe then we can both move on. Unfortunately, it'll be separately, but at least we can move on.

Maybe in the future, if we're ever able to mend this rift, we can do a paternity test and things will work themselves out from there. But for now, I just want his heart to stop aching.

43

TREY

The scent of freshly brewed coffee floats through the air. I pry my eyes open to find myself under a blanket I don't recognize. It's fleece, and it smells weird. This isn't my blanket. *Whose the fuck is it then?*

I lurch upward. Something in my neck pinches. It's a kink, probably from sleeping on my couch. *Hold on.* This isn't my couch. It's Arella's couch. *What the hell?*

I shoot up onto my feet. The room spins.

Dizzy.

Wobbly.

I shouldn't have gotten up so fast. I plop back down. Screwing my eyes shut, I rub my temples as a lame attempt to get the hammering in my brain to stop. It doesn't.

When I open my eyes again, I'm still in Arella's apartment. How did I get here? And why am I wearing only boxers?

On Arella's coffee table are a glass of water, my wallet, my phone, and two small pills. *Are the pills meant for me?* They look like Ordinary pills. Well, of course they're Ordinary pills. Arella wouldn't have Zordinary ones. Zordi bodies process Ordinary medicines too quickly for them to work on us.

I down the glass of water within seconds. It refreshes my dry throat—sort of. I could probably have another glass or two. Maybe it'll get rid of the spinning.

"Morning."

I jerk my head toward the voice. It's Arella, sitting at her small dining table, eyeing me with a hesitant look. *Damn, she's gorgeous.* Her wavy chestnut hair is tied into a braid falling over one shoulder. Her dark purple dress drops to the middle of her thighs. It shows off her slender legs. I have the urge to trail my fingertips up her thighs and lick every part of—*She's still wearing it.* The necklace with the golden angel wings. She's still wearing it.

"How do you feel?" she asks in her usual honeyed tone.

"Shitty." My voice comes out raspy. *Definitely need more water.* "What happened last night?"

"What do you remember?"

The last thing I remember is being a tragic wreck on my couch, guzzling as much forget-her-juice as possible. Judging by the way I woke up half naked in Arella's apartment, I'd say the juice didn't work.

I must take too long to respond, because she says, "You came over late last night. You were a little drunk."

I'm too nauseous to have only been *a little* drunk. Usually when I drink that much, I pass out for hours. I've never driven myself somewhere. I must not have drunk enough to completely shut down my body. Either that or drunk me had a very determined one-track mind.

"Did I talk a lot last night?" I ask, unsure if I want the answer.

"A little."

"What did I say?"

She lifts a shoulder. "Nothing, really."

I can't tell if she's lying or not. With her, I never know. It's one of the many reasons why this woman is still a mystery to me.

"Do you want some coffee?" she asks.

"I thought you don't like coffee?"

"I don't. I bought some a while ago in case you ever wanted some."

That was thoughtful of her. How long ago did she get this coffee for me? Why did she even care to get it? Was it before or after she slept with that other guy?

I sigh heavily and push down the pain. I guess it doesn't matter *when* she got it. What matters is that she made it for me, and it smells delicious. "Yeah, I'll have some, please."

She disappears into her kitchen. After some rustling around, she comes to me and sets a steaming mug on her coffee table.

She's so beautiful. I wish I could have her again. Just one more day. Actually, no. Every day —for the rest of my life. Any less won't be enough.

"Where are my clothes?" *Wait . . . did we have sex last night?* I'll be pissed if we did and I don't remember it.

"In the dryer. They were wet, so I washed them for you. They should be done soon. Your shoes and jacket are by the door. Hopefully, they're dry now."

I lift the coffee to my face and take a whiff. I'm glad she knows I like my coffee black without having to ask. Like how I know she likes her salads with the dressing on the side. Her pasta with white sauces, never red. Her strawberries cut into halves, never quarters, because, apparently, they taste different.

She also likes the toilet paper going over, never under. To her, I do it wrong. Apparently, reloading the toilet paper whatever way it happens to be facing is weird. What else is weird, at least to her, is the way I cover my pancakes with whipped cream until I can't see the pancakes anymore. I don't think that's *that* weird. What's actually weird is that she pours her milk in before the cereal. Like seriously? Who does that?

"How did my clothes get wet?" I want to drink the coffee, but the side of the mug tells me it's way too hot right now, so I set it back onto the table.

"You really don't remember anything, do you?" She takes a seat on the other side of the couch.

"Not a thing." I groan, mostly because she's never sat so far from me before. The space is maddening.

"You walked here. In the rain."

I raise an eyebrow at her that says, *Come on. Really?* When her deadpan expression doesn't falter, I let out a low chuckle. "I must have been insane."

"I think you just needed someone to talk to."

I hope I didn't say anything stupid. My past drunk experiences tell me I probably did. According to Liz, the saying "A drunk man's words are a sober man's thoughts" rings true for me.

Liz and I are so close that a lot of people think we have romantic feelings for each other. Whenever Liz wants to shut them up, she tells them the story of the time I got so drunk, I booty-called her at two in the morning. Except, it wasn't a booty call at all.

According to her, I begged her to come over because I had something important to tell her that could only be said in person. When she arrived, I spent the next hour lamenting over how much I loved her, as a friend of course, and how if she ever disowned me, I'd jump off a cliff. Not once did I make a move. Liz says that if drunk me wasn't interested in her sexually, then sober me isn't either.

I sure as hell am interested in Arella that way, though, which is why I'm glad I didn't force myself on her last night. *At least, I hope I didn't.*

I don't want to be away from her, but my bladder is killing me. "Can I use your bathroom?"

"Of course."

After a long piss, I wash my hands and examine myself in the mirror. I look like hell. Messy hair, pale face, and saggy eye bags. *No wonder she left me. Who'd want this?*

I do a quick sniff test to check my breath. *Gross.* It smells like rancid food that's been in a Tupperware for two weeks too long.

I crack the door open. "Arella?"

She answers from the living room. "Yeah?"

"Is my toothbrush still here?"

"Top left drawer."

I pull it open to find a bunch of those free toothbrushes from the dentist, still in the package. Next to those is the one I used the one time I stayed over. I scrub my mouth out with it. Once I'm done, I do another sniff test. *Much better.* It no longer smells like alcohol. The last thing I want is to trigger bad memories for her. *Damn it.* I probably did last night. I'll have to ask her if I did, so I can apologize for it.

I place the toothbrush next to hers, then twist around to dry my hands off. The towel rack is empty. Instead of a towel, what greets me is a giant hole in the wall. *Did I do that?* I can't tell how fresh it is.

I feel around the floor for any debris. Nothing. Maybe she cleaned it up. Maybe that's why there's no towel. Maybe she used the towel to wipe up the mess I made.

I pat my hands off on my boxers, then ball up my punching fist. My heart races as I insert it into the hole. It fits. *Fuck.*

I'm prone to violence when I'm drunk, but *never* have I directed it at a woman. If I tried to have sex with Arella last night and she denied me, would I have hit her? If I did, I'll never forgive myself.

I crack the door open again. "Arella?"

"Yeah?"

"Can you come here?"

Her soft footsteps shuffle across the carpet until she appears in the doorway.

"Did I hurt you last night?" I stare into her eyes, trying to figure out her emotions. I can't allow her to lie to me about this one. Like always, I sense nothing, and her blank expression gives me no answers.

"No," she answers easily.

I scan her face for any bruises, then her arms. *Clear. Clear.* I'm tempted to rip that dress off her body so I can check the rest of her. "Are you sure?"

"Yeah, I'm sure."

"Then where the hell did that come from?" I point a firm finger at the gaping hole.

She hesitates, and it scares me. Maybe she's too afraid to admit I hurt her, like it'll spare my feelings or some shit. *Hell no.* Fuck my feelings. If I hurt her, I need to know so I can make sure it never happens again.

I cup her face and tilt her head up to stare her dead in the eyes. "Babe, if I hurt you, you can tell me. I'll make it right."

"You didn't hurt me, Trey. That was from Nathan a long time ago."

I think she's telling the truth. If so, how have I never seen this hole before? I guess, now that I think about it, I haven't been in her bathroom much. The first time was when I shoved her ex into the bathtub. I was too focused on making sure he knew who was in charge to even look at the walls. The time after that was when I stayed over. She must have kept this hole concealed with a towel.

I let out a breath, then release her from my grasp. "You've gotta tell me if he ever tries to touch you again, okay? It doesn't matter what time, or day, or place I'm at. Call me and I'll come running. Understand?"

She nods with a look in her eyes I don't recognize. All that time spent studying this woman, and here I am, still trying to figure her out.

Together, we make our way back to her living room, where I dump myself over her couch. My brain rattles inside my skull. I should have sat down slower.

"The dryer has about ten minutes left." Arella sits, still keeping space between us. "Are you hungry? I could make you some breakfast?"

"Why are you being so nice to me? After the way I spoke to you last week, I don't deserve your kindness. I can't even believe you allowed me in last night."

"I wasn't going to leave you out in the rain."

I scoff. "You should have."

She fidgets with the end of her braid, looking anywhere but at me. I can't feel it, but I know she's sad. She's usually pretty smiley around me, and now she's not.

Make her feel better. How? *Apologize.* For what? *For being a worthless piece of shit. For doing whatever it was that made her turn to someone else.*

"Arella . . ." I say softly. "I'm sorry for being such an ass to you."

She nods, pursing her lips. "Yeah, you were an ass."

A tiny smile spreads across my lips. I've never heard her say that word before.

"I'm also sorry for, ya know . . . what you saw." I run a hand through my hair, pulling at it. "I shouldn't have allowed her to—I just wasn't thinking straight because . . . you told me that you're pr—" *Breathe.* "It's impossible for . . ." *Deep breath.* "I felt so . . ." *Crushed.* My hands shake. I fold them together as if it'll stop the shaking. "Sorry. I'm not good at this."

"I get your point."

The room goes quiet. She focuses her attention on the floor while I focus all my attention on her. Little wisps of hair fall from her braid, framing cheeks that I want so badly to kiss. Just last week, I was picking her up, tossing her over my shoulder, and carrying her to my bedroom to kiss every inch of her. Now she's carrying a tiny human inside her that she'll be kissing within nine months. It's crazy how fast things can change—and not in my favor. There's a *very* short list of the things I wouldn't do to make that baby mine.

"Have you told him?" I try to keep my tone impassive as if thinking of her with someone else isn't killing me at all.

She looks up at me. "Huh?"

I glance at her stomach, then back up at her face. "The father. Have you told him?"

Her answer comes too quickly. "Yeah."

I expected her to say something about how *I* am the father. She didn't deny the infidelity this time. Is this it? Is she done denying it? Am I finally going to hear the truth from her lips?

"How did he take it?"

She shrugs nonchalantly. "He wasn't too happy about it."

My voice cracks as I find the courage to ask, "Who is he?"

She doesn't miss a beat. "Some guy I reconnected with from college."

Seriously? She threw away our passionate, sappy romance-movie-worthy relationship for *some guy?* I thought hearing her admit it would make me feel better. It doesn't. The wound has only gotten deeper.

"What's his—never mind. I don't wanna know his name." I'll probably end up in z-prison for crimes even the Enforcers would throw up reading about. "When did it start?"

"A while ago."

"When?" I snap.

She lets out a long sigh. "It—it was before I started living with you."

I guess that makes sense, but . . . "How did you ever find the time to see him once you moved in? We were always together."

"Sometimes I got off work early and didn't tell you."

That makes my throat tighten. How many times did she leave work early to bang him, then came home to me, acting all innocent?

The clock on her wall reads nine thirty. She's usually at work by now.

"Are you off today?" I ask, desperate to change the subject.

"My nanny family is on vacation right now, and I don't work at the daycare anymore."

"Why not?"

She stares at her lap as she picks at her fingernails. "They, um, let me go."

"What for?" Arella works hard, and she's great with kids. I can't imagine why they'd fire her.

"Overstaffed," she says coolly. "I was just one of the many people they chose to cut."

Overstaffed? I thought they were *under*staffed. At least, that's what I gathered from the many conversations I overheard between her and Javina. Either way, if Arella's down a job, that means she needs money.

Wait . . . Is that why she came home early that day? Was that the day they fired her? No wonder she told me to pay child support. She's gonna need it. But what about the father of her child? Shouldn't he be—*Oh no.*

My heart sinks into my stomach. "Is he staying with you . . . and the—um, baby?"

She keeps picking at her fingernails like there's something stuck under there when I know there isn't. Patiently, I wait for an answer. It never comes.

"Arella?"

She still doesn't look at me.

I lean in closer to her. "Arella, please, tell me he's planning to take care of you."

A single teardrop rolls down her cheek as she sucks in a deep breath. She wipes it away with the back of her hand. "No, he's not."

"That son of a bitch." Nothing could ever get me to leave my child. Not money. Not a death threat. Nothing. Growing up without parents is something I'd never wish on anyone.

I was the kid who got stuck hearing about all the presents the other kids woke up to on Christmas mornings. All I ever woke up to was another day of wishing my parents weren't dead. Other kids had things like family dinners and birthday parties. I had an abusive uncle who banished me to my room just for breathing the wrong way. Other kids spent their childhoods riding bikes and playing video games. I spent mine doing odd jobs so I could make enough money to buy myself new clothes. A hard life is not what I want for this child.

I have to do something. "Go get me your bank account and routing number."

Arella's face crumples. "Why?"

"I'll send you some money." Ten grand should be enough, right? How about fifty? I know nothing about how much it costs to raise a child. A hundred grand? A million?

Last week, in the heat of the moment, I told Arella she wouldn't be getting a dime from me to support another man's child. Now here I am, about to transfer her a million dollars. I guess her scheme worked. Pretend not to want my money, with hopes that I'll hand it over myself. *Genius.* I don't even care. I'll sleep better knowing she's got enough to take care of herself and this baby.

"I don't want your money," she says.

"What?" I expected her to jump up to retrieve those bank numbers for me. "Arella, you're down a job, expecting an infant, and that good-for-nothing girlfriend thief has run away. What the hell are you gonna do?"

"I'll figure it out. I always have."

"Just go get me those numbers." I wave a shooing hand at her, then I grab my phone off the coffee table. I've already got my online bank account username typed in when she crosses her arms over her chest.

"I said I don't want your money."

I swear this woman makes it a point to be difficult. My tone comes out rough. "If you're not gonna accept it for yourself or the baby, then do it for me. I promise you, there are no strings att—"

"I said no."

I groan and chuck my phone back onto the table. "You don't make any sense. Why would you screw around, get pregnant, try to convince me it's mine, then refuse to accept any money? What are you trying to gain?"

"Nothing."

I'm losing my mind. "Is this some kind of sick game to you? Playing with my heart?"

She dips her eyebrows at me like she's offended. "No."

"Do you just enjoy torturing me?"

"Of course not."

I throw my hands into the air. "Then what? Why won't you take my money?"

"Because!" she yells. "I don't want it!"

The room goes silent.

I feel like shit, and it's not from the hangover. I shouldn't have raised my voice at her. I want to apologize, but what ends up coming out is a broken "What was I missing?"

"Huh?"

"You know . . ." I choke up a little. "What does *he* have that I don't?"

She lets out an exasperated groan. "I don't want to talk about this anymore."

My tone goes soft and desperate. "Please, Arella. Just tell me." *And don't try to spare my feelings. I'm already a fucking mess.*

"I don't know, Trey."

"Yes, you do. There was obviously *something* that made you choose him over me. What was it?"

"I don't know. I guess he just . . . he just made me happy."

An invisible dagger stabs me right in the chest. I swallow, but it does nothing to ease the ache. My gaze falls to my feet. "I . . . I . . . I thought *I* made you happy."

At least, she *seemed* happy. She laughed a lot. I made it a point to get her to smile as much as I could. What could I have done more?

I should stop asking her questions, because every answer she gives only breaks me more. The smart thing to do would be to leave. I got what I wanted: to hear the truth from her. I should be done here. So why don't I want to go?

I've never been known to do the smart thing, so I ask another question. "Do you love him?"

She gets to her feet. "I'm done with this."

I steal her hand, pulling her back down. She comes willingly, and I lift her chin to look her in the eyes. "Arella, please. Tell me. Do you love him?"

"No."

It might be foolish of me, but I believe her. The sincerity in her eyes tells me it's the truth, and I'm relieved. On the back of our photo, she wrote that she loves *me*, not him. As pathetic as it is, I want that to be true.

A loud, mechanic buzzing sound comes from her hallway, startling me.

"That's the dryer." She releases herself from my grasp. I'm left feeling hollow as she disappears from my sight.

She returns with my clothes in hand. They're warm as I dress myself. *I guess this is my cue to leave.*

I shove my phone and wallet into my pockets. "Where are my keys?"

"You walked here, remember?"

"Oh, that's right." I press a hand against the side of the coffee mug I forgot I had. It's cooled down enough for me to drink, so I down it all in one breath.

"Would you like a ride home?" she asks as I rinse the mug out in her kitchen sink.

"No, thanks." I don't deserve anything she's got to offer.

"Can I call you an Uber?" she asks as I slip into my shoes. They're still kinda damp. I shove my feet in anyway.

"I can walk."

"That's a long walk, Trey."

"I'll be fine. Thanks again for the coffee." I open the door, then turn to get one last look at her. She's hugging herself in a way that makes me want to hold her. She only ever hugs herself like that when something's wrong. I don't wanna leave. I also don't have any reason to stay, so I suck it up and step out.

The bright-ass sun scorches my pupils, making my head spin. I only get four steps away from Arella's door before realizing I'm too fucking hungover to be doing this. What makes me think I can walk home when I can barely see straight? Add the heavy burning in my chest, and I'm in no condition to be walking anywhere.

I drag my phone out to call an Uber, then stop. I wanted a reason to keep seeing her, didn't I?

Knock-knock.

She answers the door immediately, as if she was just on the other side, waiting for me to come back. She gazes up at me with wide eyes, looking so adorable, I could pick her up, crash my lips against hers, and never let her go.

Resisting the urge to do all that, I scratch the back of my head. "So, um, on second thought, I'd appreciate a lift."

Without a word, she nods and grabs her purse.

I slouch into her passenger seat as I glare out the window. The blazing sun is still burning my eyes. Arella doesn't turn the radio on as she backs her car out of its parking spot.

I bought her this car three weeks ago. At that time, I would have bought her anything she wanted. Apparently, I'm still willing to do that. If she calls me up tomorrow, next month, or even years from now asking for money, I'll hand it over in a heartbeat, no questions asked.

If for some reason I'm broke, I'll get a fucking job just to be able to send her something. One way or another, I will make sure Arella's baby is taken care of. If she won't accept my money now, she'll be accepting a mountain of diapers on her doorstep in nine months.

The silence between us has never been louder. Typically, when we're in the car, we're holding hands or I've got my palm over her thigh. Right now, we might as well be on separate ends of the earth.

At our first stoplight, Arella breaks the silence. "How would you like me to give you monthly payments for this car?"

"Don't worry 'bout it."

"I told you, Trey, I won't be accepting this car if you don't accept payments for it."

"And I told you it's a gift. No matter what the circumstances are, that hasn't changed."

The traffic light turns green, then she eases onto the gas. "Since I'm assuming you won't be cashing any checks with my name on it, I'll just drop off some cash for you once a month in an envelope."

I shut my eyes and rub my forehead. "I swear, it's like you do everything in your power to be difficult."

"I wouldn't have to be difficult if you didn't make everything so complicated."

I jerk my head back and point at my chest. "Me? *I* make everything complicated?"

"Yes. I never asked you to buy me a car. I mean, who gifts their girlfriend a brand-new car after only knowing them for two months?"

"I didn't buy you this damn car to complicate anything. I bought it to fix a problem. You needed a vehicle, so I got you one."

"Which I want to pay you back for."

I huff. "Arella, if I find any cash on my doorstep, I will take every cent of it plus triple to buy you a crib made of gold and baby clothes imported from a fucking palace. Do you understand?" I expect her to give in. I want her to. Of course, she doesn't.

"Fine. In that case, I'll be leaving this car in your driveway next week with the keys in it after I buy myself a new one."

I shake my head, biting my lip. "You're so goddamn difficult."

She simply stares out the windshield. "So are you."

"We can fight about this all you want, but I'm telling you, if this car is left in my driveway, I'm driving it straight back to your place. We can play that game for as long as it takes for you to get it through your head that this vehicle is yours and I don't want anything for it."

The car goes quiet until Arella chuckles to herself.

Obviously, I've missed the joke. "What's so funny?"

"Whenever we argue, it's always over paying for things. We fought for days when you first bought me this car. We even bickered in the middle of a grocery store at four in the morning over who was buying all those pregnancy tests. Now here we are, *still* fighting because I want to feel independent and you refuse to allow it."

That stings. How many times do I have to explain to her that I don't buy her things to take away her independence? "Arella, I have enough liquid cash to buy you private jets, superyachts, and a mansion the size of a castle. Buying you a car doesn't make even the slightest dent in my bank account. Don't you want to save your hard-earned money for more important things?" *Like, you know . . . a baby?*

"Well, I—" She stops because a vibration comes from my pocket.

I dig my phone out. It's Victor. *Shit.* When I spoke to him three days ago, I promised I'd have more answers to explain Arella's immunity within the week. I haven't told him that she left me, because he's not going to accept that as a valid excuse not to have answers. *What the hell am I gonna do?*

"Is that your uncle?"

I shove the device back into my jeans. "Yep."

"You're not going to answer it?"

"Nope."

"Is it because he's calling during regular-people time?"

That makes the corners of my lips tick up. I like how quippy she can be. I also like that even after we've been arguing, she can still make me smile. "Contrary to what you believe, my uncle and I *can* have conversations during regular-people hours."

"News to me."

Not long ago, Arella questioned me about my late-night phone calls with my uncle. That was also the night she asked me about my tinted windows, how I don't sleep as often as she does, and how my body can heal so fast.

Many Zordi homes have tinted windows so we can use our powers freely without our neighbors spotting it. Zordis only need to sleep every other evening, and our bodies can heal wounds three times faster than the average Ordinary. Couple that with the healing products my parents invented, and we can fix broken limbs within hours.

Arella noticed all of these abnormal-to-Ordinaries things about me. I didn't want to lie, so I never gave her an explanation. I can see why the Superiors forbid us from having close relationships with Ordinaries, because after a while, it gets hard to hide even the littlest things. Like our enhanced eyesight and our natural ability to regulate our body temperature.

The second Arella turns her car into my driveway, my heart races. Our time together is almost over. I don't want it to end yet. "Do you wanna come in and grab your st—"

"No."

I didn't get to finish my sentence, but okay. "Stay here then. I'll get it all for you."

She shakes her head and puts the car into park. "I don't want it. Any of it."

"What about your clothes? Your blanket? Your purple teddy bear?"

"You bought all those things for me."

"Not *all* of it." I unbuckle my seat belt. It makes a *zip* sound as it retracts upward.

"Maybe some clothes are mine, but you bought me that blanket and the bear."

"I bought them *for you*, so they belong to you."

"No," she says sternly. "They belong to you."

I don't think this woman understands how gifts work. News flash: Once it's been gifted, it no longer belongs to the gifter. "I want you to have them."

"Fine, then I want you to have this." She grabs her purse, drags her car key out, and tosses it onto my lap.

I scowl at it before chucking the damn thing behind me. It lands with a light thud against the backseat. "This car is yours, and that's final."

"Fine, then take this." She reaches behind her neck, and before I can stop her, the angel wings are detached from her body. She holds the diamond out to me on a straight arm.

I glance at her, then at the necklace, then back at her. My words come out like a shattered reflection of my heart. "Are you trying to hurt me?"

"Are you trying to hurt *me*?"

"No. I just want you to have your things back." That's not true. Really, I'm looking for any reason to prolong our time together, and apparently, arguing with her is what I went with.

"I want you to have your things back too." She shakes the jewelry. The tiny engraving on the back catches my eye. *Paris? T.G.* I envisioned the rest of my life with her in Paris. Right now, that life feels so far away.

I clench my jaw to keep from punching something, then I snatch the necklace from her. Without a word, I lean in to hook it back where it belongs.

She doesn't move as my fingertips graze her soft skin. Being this close to her is dangerous. I'm about to put my lips all over her neck. Her sweet lavender scent is making me lose control over my thoughts and even my hands. The diamond slips from my grasp and lands on her lap. She remains still as my trembling fingers pluck it back up and I try again.

Not once does she fight me as I take my sweet time getting the clasp to work—surprising, considering she's spent this entire morning doing the opposite of everything I want. Maybe she wants to keep the necklace as much as I want her to keep it. *A man can hope.*

Once the jewelry is back around her neck, I take her hands into mine and gaze deeply into her eyes as a silent plea for her not to rip it off.

When she doesn't, I lower my voice to almost a whisper. "I'll keep your stuff, Arella. Just please, keep the necklace."

44

TREY

I'm fucked. Completely fucked.

Victor has called two more times since Arella dropped me off this morning. I didn't pick up. I can't. Not without something good to tell him.

When he assigned me this mission, one of the first things he said was "Don't fuck this up."

I was determined not to. Back then, my mission seemed simple.

Step one: Get close to this twenty-two-year-old woman to find out the source of her immunity.

Step two: Replicate it, and use it to destroy the people who killed my parents.

Step three: Live out the rest of my life knowing my parents would be proud of me for finishing the research they started before they died.

Thing is, I haven't even completed step one. The moment I found out that whatever tests Victor performed on the last two Immunes killed them, my mission was over. I switched my focus from trying to discover the source of Arella's immunity to protecting it. Maybe Victor's willing to risk innocent lives for a greater cause, but I'm not. Especially not Arella's.

Suddenly, it hits me: I've been making a huge mistake.

I've been so down in the dumps over our breakup that I've forgotten the bigger picture: No matter what Arella has done, she still needs my protection. She still needs me to keep Victor away from her. *What the hell am I doing here? I need to get that woman on a plane and fly her as far away from here as possible.*

I launch off the toilet I've been sitting on for the last forty-some minutes, give myself a shake, then pull my pants up. After washing my hands, I check the time on my phone. *Wow, it's late . . .* 12:53 a.m. *What the fuck did I do all day?* Nothing, that's what. I spent all day sulking over the bullshit I call my life when I should have been working out a plan to get Arella to safety.

Since we're not on the best terms right now, I don't know how I can convince her to run away with me. Maybe that should be the first step of my new plan: Make things right with her. I'll buy her the biggest bouquet of flowers I can find and show up on her doorstep with it first thing in the morning. I'll apologize for everything that happened. I'll confess that I'm in love with her and that I have been for a while. She'll forgive me, right? She has to.

Once I've won her back, I'll convince her to go to Paris with me. If she refuses, I'll try convincing her to help me find my parents' safe house. On a password-protected voice recording hidden in my childhood teddy bear, my parents left me instructions on how to find an underground hideout. The only problem is that I've listened to the recording about a hundred times now, and I still can't figure out where the safe house is.

Maybe this safe house thing isn't the greatest idea. Plus, I don't have time to sit around trying to convince Arella of anything. That woman is too stubborn for her own good.

How about I simply ask her to go on vacation with me? I'll take her somewhere tropical, where she can enjoy a nice view from our resort window. I just won't tell her that we won't be coming back. *Damn.* I'm pretty sure that's called kidnapping. Maybe she won't see it that way if she's sipping mocktails on a beach with her feet in the sand.

All right. That's the plan.

Step one: Win my girl back.

Step two: Take her on vacation.

Step three: Drinks on a beach.

Easy peasy, lemon squeezy.

I'd like to think I can wait until the sun rises to start my new plan, but I'm too impatient for that, so I stand at the kitchen counter with my phone on speaker.

My heart pounds with each ring Arella doesn't pick up. I know it's late, but I had to give it a shot. Maybe she's still up. Maybe she—

"Hello?"

My breath hitches at the sound of her voice. "Arella?"

"Yeah?" She doesn't sound like she's been sleeping. Not that I would have felt bad for waking her up anyway.

"Um, it's me."

"I know. There's a really cool feature on phones nowadays where a person's name pops up whenever they call."

"I wasn't sure if you'd pick up since it's so late." *And because of the way we ended things this morning.*

"You've got a bad habit of making calls outside of regular-people hours, don't you?"

"That's only with my uncle." *And Liz.*

"Is everything okay?" She sounds genuinely concerned. I hate when people give a fuck about me, because I don't deserve anyone's concern. But when it comes to Arella, I want her to give all the fucks in the world.

"Not really." *Nothing's okay when I'm apart from you.*

"What's wrong?"

The words fly out of my mouth before my brain can register that I'm even saying them. "I miss you."

It takes her a few heartbeats to respond. When she does, it sounds tearful. "I miss you too."

I can't hide my shock. "You do?"

"I do."

Those two words give me so much hope. "I want you back, Arella."

A long pause, then she clears her throat. "Are you drunk again?"

"Nope. I'm completely sober."

"You really want me back? Even after I told you that I slept with a guy from college?"

Ouch. I could have gone forever and a day without ever hearing her admit that out loud again. I choke up a little. "Are you done with him?"

She only hesitates for a second. "Yeah."

"Like, completely? You don't plan to ever see him again? Or talk to him?"

"No."

"Ever?"

"Ever."

Maybe it's stupid of me, but I believe her. "Do you think you can forgive me for being a dick to you?"

"I already have." The way she doesn't miss a beat gives me confidence that she means it. "Do you think you'll ever forgive me?"

I don't miss a beat either. "I already have."

I've only been on this call with her for a minute, and hope is already filling me to the brim. Things are going so well. At this rate, we'll be sipping drinks on a beach by tomorrow night.

"Can I come see you in the morning?" I ask, but what I really want to ask is *Can I come over right now?*

There's a long pause before she says, "Trey, I think we have some important things to talk about before we start thinking about getting back together."

She doesn't need to say what for me to know what *things* she's referring to. Little does she know, I was ready to be a father to her baby since the night I found out she was pregnant. We just had a little hump to get over, and now that we are over it, I'm thrilled for this next step.

I want to have a family. More so, I want to have a family with Arella. I picture myself holding a child. I imagine the tiny human calling me *daddy*. If it's a girl, I'll vow to protect her with my life. If it's a boy, can I teach him to be a better man than me? That probably wouldn't be too hard. I've set the bar pretty low.

I sigh and slump my elbows onto the counter. "Do you think I'd make a good father?"

"Why wouldn't you?"

"Because I don't know anything about it. I've never even held a baby. How am I supposed to know how to take care of one?"

"Nobody really knows what they're doing until they do it. Babies are a learning process." The way she says all that gives me faith that I can do this. If it's something I can learn, I'm ready for the challenge.

"Don't they have classes or some shit I can take about parenting?"

The sound of Arella's giggle feels like a warm sunny day after a week of freezing rain. "*You* would take a parenting class?"

"Not alone, but I'd do it with you."

"Trey, I want you to really, *really* think about what you'd be getting yourself into. Having a baby means you can't do whatever you want whenever you want. Life changes when you have a mini human to take care of. It's a lifetime commitment. Are you sure you're ready for that?"

I don't have to think about it. "Yes, baby. I'm ready. I can't guarantee I'll win Best Dad of the Year, but you can bet your ass I'll fight for it."

I'll also fight to keep our relationship off the zovernment's radar. I don't know how yet, but I'll figure it out. All I know, without a doubt, is that I am meant to be with this woman. And nothing is going to stop me.

My phone vibrates. I don't have to look to know who's calling.

"I've gotta go, babe. Is it cool for me to come over in the morning? We can talk about this some more. Maybe look for some parenting classes coming up in the area? I could take you to some bookstores, and we could find some reading material?"

"That sounds wonderful."

I can almost hear the smile spreading across her lips and lifting her cheeks. I feel a thousand pounds lighter already. "Text me the second you wake up, 'kay? I'll come over right away."

After she agrees, I tell her good night, then switch calls just in time.

"Where the fuck have you been, kid?" Victor says through a mouthful of something crunchy. "This is the tenth time I've called today."

It's actually the fourth time, but whatever. "I forgot my phone at home and was out all day." My lie sounds pretty convincing.

"I need you to come to base."

Fuck that. I don't wanna be anywhere near Shadow Ridge right now. "What for?"

"I'm putting you on a new anti-Royals assignment. We need three agents on it, and one of the men I originally assigned to this didn't pass his onboarding tests. You're next on the list."

"What about my current mission?" *The one I've been ignoring for weeks.*

"This new mission is entry-level shit. You can handle both. Besides, you haven't been making any advancements on your current mission. Might as well make yourself useful. The briefing starts in thirty minutes."

The way he says all that means I don't have a choice. He's not *asking* me if I want to accept this new assignment so much as he's *telling* me. "Thirty minutes? I live three hours away."

"Maybe if you had answered your fucking phone, I could have given you more notice. I'll send a Teleporter. Text me your coordinates." *Click.*

Growing up, I begged my uncle to make me a ZIRDA agent. It was my dream to work for the anti-Royals department so I could help bring down the violent organized crime group who blew up my parents.

When I was nine, Victor put me through training where I learned how to throw a proper punch and to control my powers better. He kept saying that once I turned eighteen, he'd assign me my first mission. When that birthday finally came, he told me to get lost.

A few months ago, Victor called me out of the blue to assign me Arella's mission. He said, "It's top secret, typically for level-five agents, but if you think you won't fuck it up, I'll give it to you."

I was ecstatic to be handed such an honor and to be told I could skip the onboarding process. Now I'm being spoon-fed another mission, and I'd rather gouge my eyes out with chopsticks. Can Victor seriously not find any other agent to work this one? I've got more important things to do—like get Arella away from him.

My phone buzzes with a text from Victor.

We'll be meeting in room 409. Your coordinates?

With a sigh, I Google what my coordinates are and text it to him.

Within seconds, a loud *pop!* bursts into my ears like someone's cracked a whip right next to me. I wince and cover both ears.

A slender guy who looks barely nineteen appears in my kitchen. The zense in my chest tingles, telling me what I already know.

"Sorry, bro," he says. "I've gotten used to the sound. Barely hear it no more. You must be Big V's nephew."

"Yep."

"You got everything you need on you?"

"Give me a sec to get some shoes on." I head to the garage door where my shoes are, then return to the kitchen to find the dude staring at my living room.

"Where's your TV?"

"Don't have one."

"The fuck do you do all day then?"

I let out an exasperated sigh. "Are you here to judge me for my lack of screen entertainment, or are you here to take me to the Ridge?"

"Right." He holds out his skinny arm to me. "You ever been teleported before?"

"A few times."

"Super. Whatever you do, don't let go."

Reluctantly, I grab onto his arm. Without any warning whatsoever, that loud *pop!* startles me again. It's more painful this time. I'm about to cover my ears until I remember that I can't let go.

My vision blurs, and my ears ring. The sound stops when my feet hit a hard surface.

Icy-cold liquid drenches me from above. The Teleporter tugs me away from the waterfall.

"Sorry, bro. Missed the mark by a few steps."

I spit water out of my mouth, then rub away the wetness on my face. The familiar dark cavern hidden behind the waterfall greets me with a sneering *Why are you back?* I'm wondering the same damn thing. Of all the places I want to be right now, this isn't it. Especially not while wearing cold, drenched clothes. Still, I follow the Teleporter into the black of the cavern.

"You wouldn't happen to be a Pyro, would you?" he asks. "My phone's dead, so I can't use the flashlight."

If he typically uses his phone for light, that means he's either a Hydro, an Aero, or a Terra, who produces rock balls instead of lightning balls. I answer his question by making some flames appear in my palm and throwing them ahead of us.

"Thanks." The guy gestures a hand forward. "After you."

We continue down the cavern with my fireball illuminating the way. The Teleporter doesn't try to make conversation with me, and I'm glad for it. The only sounds are our echoing footsteps and the waterfall fading behind us.

After several minutes, we reach the secret entrance to Shadow Ridge. The door looks like any regular part of the rock wall. I stick my index finger into a little hole and press it against a flat scanning device inside.

Beep! Beep! Beep! A ten-foot section of the wall pushes itself inward, then slides to the left, allowing us inside.

My chest tingles as two security guards approach me, one from either side. One of them is the menacing-looking guy I saw the last time I was here. He's got a scar down his left eyebrow and a scowl that would scare away all children. The other guy, I don't recognize.

Together, they search my body for whatever it is they're told to look for. When they don't find it, they do the same with the Teleporter.

"Clear. You may proceed."

The Teleporter offers the guards a friendly *thanks* before following me to the set of four elevators. We take one of the machines down from floor six to four.

Once the elevator doors slide apart, I step off.

"Do ya know where to go from here?" the Teleporter asks, keeping the elevator open with his arm.

"I got it."

"Super. You were my last pickup for the day, so if ya see Big V, tell him I'll see him later."

"Hold on. How the hell am I gonna get back home?"

The guy shrugs. "All I know is that my shift technically ended at midnight. I just happened to still be around when you needed a lift, so I told Victor I'd do it. If you're still here in the afternoon, I can take ya back then. That's when my next shift starts."

The afternoon? I cannot be here for that long. I have baby-preparation plans with Arella in the morning.

The elevator doors close as I trudge down the hall. With each step I take, my wet shoes squeak over the tile floors and my toes squish against my drenched socks. I fucking hate the feeling of wet socks on my feet.

Following the numbered signs, I make a left, then a right. I arrive at room 409, a small meeting room, to find a young woman in the corner, setting up a zoffee cart. From the back, she doesn't look any older than eighteen. Petite frame. Pale skin. Long brunette hair tied up in a sleek ponytail.

A rectangular table with about ten rolling chairs around it separates me from her. An iPad and some manila folders lie on top of the table. A whiteboard is attached to the back wall, featuring the date Expo-markered in red.

The girl hums to herself as she plugs a coffee machine into the wall.

I knock on the door lightly as an attempt not to scare her. Total fail.

She jumps and flips around, slapping a hand against her chest. "Jesus. You scared me."

I offer her a tiny smile. "Sorry."

"Are you here for the mission briefing?" She's got a soft, mousey voice. It's not irritating to me like most people who talk like that. Hers is more soothing than anything. Like she's teaching a meditation class or trying to relax a baby.

"I am." I step into the room and take a seat in one of the rolling chairs.

"I was told the meeting doesn't start until one thirty." She checks her watch. "It's just past one. You're really early. Would you like some zoffee?"

I haven't had zoffee in forever. It's got enough caffeine in it for Zordis. The Ordinary kind does nothing for us, but it tastes good.

"Black, please."

Steam rises from the mug as she pours a healthy amount of zoffee for me. As she sets the mug down in front of me, my zense activates.

"I've never seen you before," she says with a bright smile that feels more friendly than flirty. I appreciate her for it. "You must be new or a field agent."

"Field agent." I hold my hand out for a shake. "Trey."

"Katie." She accepts my palm with her little hand. As we shake, her eyes go wide and blank. I know that look. It's the same look Liz used to get whenever she touched my hand and my most painful memory invaded her mind.

A rush of anxiety radiates off Katie as she draws her hand back. As if practiced, she erases any evidence from her face that she just used her powers on me and is nervous about it. I'm not in pain, so I'm gonna assume she's got an ability like Liz's that allows her to see into my head. I wonder what she just saw. I'm tempted to ask, but I'm not in the mood to discuss whatever glimpse into my life she just got. None of it is good.

Instead, I feign ignorance. "What's your role here?"

"I'd like to say I'm a field agent too, but for now, I'm just Victor's assistant."

"What do you do for him?"

"Whatever he wants. I run errands around base, deliver messages, do paperwork here and there." Katie sits in a seat two away from mine and gestures toward my steaming mug. "And I make zoffee. Ya know, the important stuff."

I lift my mug to take a sip. It burns my tongue a little. "Zoffee is important. It takes a skilled person to brew it well."

"Victor says I'm the best at it. He assigned me my first on-base mission today—not because I make good zoffee. I've been asking for a mission for months. I'm super excited about it."

I know she is by her excitement rushing through my head. "What is it?"

She narrows her eyes at me. "You're a field agent. You should know the rules. We don't go into details about missions amongst each other."

"Right. I was just testing you."

"Surrre you were." Katie gestures toward my damp clothing, with her eyebrows pressed together. "So did ya swim here?"

"The Teleporter ported me here right under the waterfall."

She giggles. "Sorry, I don't mean to laugh. That's just kinda funny. You don't seem to mind that you're wet though."

"It's whatever." I do mind, but what can I do about it? It's not like I possess a gift that can make my clothes instantly dry.

Victor appears in the doorway, wearing a dark brown suit. "Katie, the folders, please."

Katie jumps to her feet and grabs the manila folders from the end of the table. She hands them to Victor with a mousey "Here you go, sir."

"Thank you." Victor makes his way around the table to the head seat. Two of his bodyguards station themselves on opposite sides of the room. A third one stands outside the door. "Katie, can you text me updates on your mission as you go today?"

"Yes, sir." She takes her iPad from the table and hugs it against her chest.

"Thanks. Nothing else for now. Feel free to take a break before your assignment arrives. Shouldn't be too long."

I'll never understand how Victor can talk to people so nicely when he always addresses me with revulsion. When I was a young child, Uncle V was my best friend. He'd take me out for pie at two in the morning. We'd ride around the neighborhood on roller skates. We'd have sleepovers at his house and spend hours building blanket forts together.

After Aunt Jodi left him for her soul mate, leaving behind only an apology note, he transformed into the angry man he is today. Now he acts as if looking at me is detrimental to his health. The day he lost her was the day I lost my Uncle V.

Sometimes, I still hold out for the day he returns to that loving uncle I made all those good memories with. Deep under all that bitterness somewhere, way, *way* deep, I'm confident there's that same man who used to treat me like his own son. I'd be lying if I said that when I accepted Arella's mission, I didn't hope my success would bring that man back.

The room is silent after Katie leaves. Neither Victor nor his bodyguards acknowledge my existence, so I take a sip of my zoffee and pretend they don't exist either.

A few awkward minutes later, two field agents join us. They take the chairs across the table from me. One is a stocky short man. The other is a tall blonde woman with tattoos running up and down each arm. Victor chitchats with them for a while with a smile on his face that's never directed at me.

It's just before one thirty when Victor says, "All right. Let's get started."

Good. The faster we start, the faster I can get outta here. I want to be at Arella's apartment as soon as she wakes up.

"The Royals have been getting their hands on powerful weapons," Victor says. "By that, I don't mean guns or tanks. They're collecting Tickers. Anyone know what that is?"

When the other agents shake their heads, I raise my hand. Quickly, I realize it's a mistake.

"What is this? A fucking middle school? Put your goddamn hand down and answer the question."

Resisting the urge to snap back at my uncle, I lower my arm. "It's a Pyro with an illness called smother. Unlike Dormants where their powers just aren't active, Zordis with smother still have active flames. The flames are simply *smothered* as if their skin's a containment system. They can't produce fire outside of their bodies, but inside, those flames and energy build until they eventually explode like a bomb."

Victor nods, the most approval I've gotten from him in years. "The range of a Ticker's explosion is anywhere between five feet to five miles. It incinerates everything in its path."

"Sounds like a bad day for anyone nearby," tattoo lady says.

"Correct, and word on the street is that the Royals have found a way to control when those explosions happen. They've been kidnapping Tickers and using them to attack Ordinary government officials. Did you hear about that bombing in Lisbon six months ago? Authorities never found any traces of explosives. Can you guess why?"

"So," I say, dreading my next words, "the Royals are using unwilling suicide bombers?"

"Exactly." Victor slides a manila folder down the table to each person.

In mine is a blurry picture of an Asian woman standing outside a grocery store. The photo is paperclipped to a single sheet of paper with the name *Kim Nguyen* on it. Under that are the words *somewhere in Nevada*. There's no home address, no other names, not even a clue as to where or when the picture was taken. *What the fuck?*

When I received Arella's manila folder, it was loaded with hours' worth of reading material. I wouldn't be so pissed about this folder if the other agents didn't clearly have multiple photos to work with, paperclipped to stacks and stacks of information.

Victor continues, "Ever since word got out that the Royals are kidnapping Tickers, the Tickers have gone into hiding. Unfortunately, that makes it harder for us to track them down and protect them. Each of you has been assigned a different Ticker. Your job is to find them before the Royals do and bring them here for safety."

"What if they don't want to come?" I ask.

"Then you force them."

My face twists into hard lines. "So you want us to kidnap them?"

Victor shoots me a lethal glare. "Would you rather the Royals do so first? Better us than them, right?"

I mean, he has a point, but I still don't like the idea of taking someone by force. It's always bothered me that ZIRDA is willing to end ten lives to save ten thousand. When I was a kid, I thought I'd understand it when I grew up. Here I am at twenty-six, and I still don't understand it.

For the next two hours, the four of us brainstorm tactics we can use to find these Tickers and bring them to base. I'm not sure how Victor thinks I can find someone when all I've got is a blurry photo and a common name for a Vietnamese woman. The other agents have things like places of employment and names of relatives. I'm pretty sure Victor assigned the hardest Ticker to me with hopes that I'll fail.

Wait . . . What if that's why he assigned Arella's mission to me? What if he knew that finding an explanation to her immunity was a wild goose chase from the start? If so, what's his game? Why would he want me to get close to Arella if discovering the source of her immunity is impossible?

The meeting finally ends around seven in the morning. Six hours. Six whole fucking hours of pretending to be interested in a mission I have no intention of even starting. By tonight, I'll be on a beach, sipping out of pineapples with my girl.

After tossing the manila folder into the trash, I fold up the photo of Kim Nguyen with her single sheet of useless information and stick it into my back pocket. Then I rush out of the meeting room without saying a word to anyone.

Somehow, I need to find a way back home. First things first though; I gotta find a bathroom. We weren't given a single break throughout that entire meeting, and I consumed four cups of zoffee.

I find a bathroom down the hall and stumble into it. My head spins as I unzip my semi-dry jeans. When I finish peeing, I'm woozy as hell. I have to slap my palm against a wall just to steady myself on my way to the sinks. Nausea rises up my stomach as I wash my hands. I'm about to dry them off when vomit races up my throat.

I half run, half stagger past the urinals and back into the first stall. My knees hit the floor just as I throw myself over the toilet bowl and cough. Nothing comes out. I cough again, gagging as my body convulses like it wants to puke, but it doesn't. I wish *something* would come up, because at least then, I'd feel a little better.

For who knows how long, I gag into the toilet bowl, trying to cough up my intestines. After a while, my chest hurts from heaving and my throat's dry as fuck. *I need water, stat!* The cafeteria is two floors down. I could get water from there if my body would stop shaking.

I feel like I've been on a plane for an hour while the pilot does flips in the air. *What the hell is going on?* Was it something I ate? I haven't eaten much lately because of my lack of appetite. For dinner, I had a granola bar. Beyond that, all I've had is zoffee. Was there something in that? The other agents and Victor had zoffee from the same brew I did. Are any of them sick? Whatever this is, it's almost as bad as—I gasp. *The glimmer!* It's Arella. Something's wrong.

I push myself off the floor and stumble out of the bathroom like I would stumble out of a bar at three in the morning. When I reach the elevators, I stab the *up* button almost fifteen times, even though it lit up the first time I pressed it. A *ding!* sounds, then the doors slide open.

In my haste to rush into the machine, I run into Katie on her way out. Her face smacks right into my chest.

"Ow!" She rubs her forehead with her hand not hugging her iPad.

"Sorry." I grab her shoulders to steady her—or am I steadying myself? Either way, neither of us falls.

She offers me a warm smile as she steps back into the elevator with me. "You're just the person I came to find."

"What for?"

In her sweet little voice, she says, "I'm here to take you to the second floor. Victor needs you."

Fuck no. "Whatever it is, tell him he's gonna have to wait. I've gotta go." I'm putting my foot down this time. He didn't give me a choice earlier, and I didn't fight him on it. I'll fight him now because this time, Arella's in trouble.

"Where do you gotta go in such a rush?"

"Home. Something came up." I'm about to press the 6 button when Katie grabs my arm.

"I'm sorry. Unfortunately, I can't allow you to leave." Even though she says it in her mousey little voice, it triggers a pang of fear inside me.

"What're you gonna do to stop me?"

"Um, let's just say you don't wanna find out." Whatever gift she has that makes her confident she can overpower me must be good.

Without hesitation, she presses the 2 button, and the doors close. Then she offers me another of her sweet smiles. They're beginning to irk me.

Katie eyes me as the elevator takes us downward. "Are you okay? You're lookin' a bit red."

"I'm fine," I say as my arms go numb, my head throbs, and my legs feel like they're about to give out, and—

Ding!

I follow Katie out toward the community room, even though I want to run straight back into the elevator. Behind the glass walls, a group of four agents are on their laptops, working together. Opposite them is the cafeteria. The rest of this floor is a bunch of sleeping accommodations. Some bedrooms are better than others. The higher-level agents have rooms that are more like luxury apartments complete with their own kitchens and walk-in closets.

When I lived here, my bedroom was basically a square space where the twin-size bed took up half the floor. It included a little closet and a teeny bathroom, where the toilet always broke down. I'm pretty sure Victor assigned me that room because it's the shittiest and farthest away from everyone else.

As we pass the cafeteria, I spot a woman in her late thirties, who I've never seen before. She's reading a book floating in front of her face while she cuts into a plate of pancakes. A group of men in their forties or fifties sit at a table two away from the woman. I don't recognize any of the men either.

As soon as Katie takes two rights then a left, I know exactly where she's going. I'll bet the burn marks are still on the door from all the times I accidentally set my bedroom on fire. Whenever I got too upset, which was quite often, I'd lose control of my powers. My stuff would fly around the ceiling and bang against the walls. If my emotions were really bad, everything would catch on fire. After the fifth time that happened, Victor assigned a Hydro to live in the room across from mine. That lady's job was to extinguish my fires before they spread too far.

I follow Katie down the last hallway. At the end of it are all three of Victor's guards standing outside the closed door of my old bedroom. I was right. The burn marks are still there.

"Why are we here?" I ask.

Instead of answering my question, Katie types a four-digit code into the keypad. I doubt it's the same code from when I lived here. After releasing the chain lock that was never there before, she opens the door and steps aside for me to head in first.

My heart drops at the sight of the woman sitting on my old bed. She's wearing a white T-shirt she doesn't own. I know because it's four sizes too big. The shorts she's wearing aren't hers either. I know because they're orange, and Arella never wears orange.

I glare at my uncle across the room. "What the fuck is this?"

45

ARELLA

E*arlier*

I wake up feeling groggy with a slight headache. I'm about to get up to grab some medicine when the handcuffs stop me. *What?*

I jerk upright. I'm on a twin-size bed with yellowed sheets. The walls around me are charred from the floor to the ceiling. The clock on the wall is warped like it's been melted at one point. Parts of the carpet are blackened too. *Where am I? And has someone been burned alive here?*

"Good morning." A young woman stationed on a folding chair in the corner smiles sweetly at me. She looks about eighteen or nineteen. If she's the reason I woke up in a strange place wearing handcuffs, that wholesome look on her face is very deceiving.

"Where am I? Who are you?"

"I'm sure you have a lot of questions," she says calmly as if she wasn't watching me sleep a minute ago. "I'll answer as many questions as I can. My name's Katie."

"Where am I?"

"You're in Shadow Ridge."

Why does she say that as if it's the same as saying "Welcome to New York" or "This is Miami"? I've never heard of a town called Shadow Ridge. "Where is that?"

She places the iPad onto the floor under her chair. "Sorry. I'm not allowed to share that information."

"Not allowed by who?"

"My boss. Oh, that reminds me. He asked me to text him when you woke up." From the inner pocket of her blazer, she pulls out a phone with a pastel pink case. After she types out a quick message, she slips it back into the same pocket.

"Who's your boss?" My breaths are short, and my chest feels tight. I'd like to think this is a dream, but it feels too real.

"You'll meet him soon."

Call it a gut instinct, but something tells me I don't want to meet her boss. "How did I get here?"

"Two of our agents escorted you in. They sedated you in your sleep with a harmless injection. You're waking up around the hour you're supposed to, so that's good."

The tranquil way this girl says all that does nothing to silence the danger alarm blaring in my head. Also, how can she tell me so casually that I've been "sedated"? Is knocking people out and dragging them out of their home against their will a normal occurrence around here?

The baby growing inside me tells me Katie is anxious. It's not the same anxiousness I feel. Mine is laced with a pounding fear while Katie's is more like what I feel when I'm running a few minutes late for work.

I wish I knew how this baby is sensing other people's emotions. It happened last night with Trey and now Katie. I'd like to say it's a pregnancy thing, but I'm pretty sure it has more to do with Trey being from an alternate universe. I'd be a little more freaked out by it if I hadn't woken up in a bed that doesn't belong to me.

"Why was I kidnapped?"

"Whoa, hold on there," Katie says with a hand out, palm forward. "Let's not use such harsh words. We prefer to say that we're borrowing you."

Borrowing? She can't be serious. "Borrowing usually means you have intentions to give it back."

"Then yes, to your definition, you've been borrowed."

I suppose that means they're not planning to kill me. That's good, right? "When do you people plan to return me?"

"That, I'm unsure of. It probably depends on how long it takes to figure you out. Anyway, I think that's enough questions for now. My boss will be here soon, and I've gotta get you cleaned up. Your pajamas are dirty."

I glance down, and she's right. There's literal dirt, all brown and crusty, across the bottoms of my pajama pants. I was not wearing these when I went to bed last night, which means someone dug through my drawers and dressed me before stealing me from my apartment. *How did I get so dirty?*

"I've picked out a new outfit for you. It's on the counter next to a pair of flats." Katie points toward the bathroom. The door sits ajar, giving me a view of the toilet. From the pocket of her dress pants, Katie produces a small metal key. "I'm going to uncuff you, but only if you promise not to hurt me. It's my first day working an on-base mission, and I'd prefer it if everything goes smoothly."

She's slightly smaller than me, so I think I can take her, but I don't know what or who lies beyond these bedroom walls. Also, I think her innocent face is just to fool people. I bet she knows karate or something.

"What if I don't want to change my clothes?"

Katie shrugs. "You're welcome to stay in your dirty pajamas, but I think you'll be more comfortable not. If you really want your current outfit back, I'm happy to launder it for you first."

It boggles my mind how she's speaking to me so friendly. This isn't how I imagine most kidnappers talk to the people they've kidnapped. "I'll change my clothes."

"Great, and you promise not to hurt me if I release you?"

Only if you promise not to hurt me. "Sure."

Katie uncuffs me from the bars of the bed frame. "I'll give you a few minutes to get cleaned up. Feel free to shower too. I'm not sure when you'll get a chance to next."

That doesn't sound promising.

From the bathroom, I sense Katie's anxiety growing. I can't see her, but I know she's pacing the bedroom. Somehow, this baby knows every emotion running through Katie. From how weak or strong it's coming to me, I know her distance from me too. Since she's the only person I can sense right now, I'm going to assume there's no one else nearby. Either that, or this baby can only sense one person at a time.

I'm in the middle of showering the mysterious dirt off my feet when Katie knocks on the bathroom door, which does not have a lock. I checked.

"You almost done?"

"Almost." I turn the shower off and step out to examine myself in the mirror. There's no evidence that I've been hurt in any way. I suppose that's a positive.

I come out wearing black flats, a white T-shirt that dwarfs me, and a pair of ugly orange shorts. I return to the bed where Katie, if that's her real name, cuffs me back to the bed frame. I go willingly because I don't know what else to do.

From watching true crime shows with Javina, I've learned that the victims who comply with their kidnappers' demands are the ones with the highest percentage of making it out alive. So far, it doesn't seem like Katie wants to harm me. I'm sure her boss does though.

Whatever happens, I have to get through this alive—for the baby. The first chance I see of a possible escape, I'm taking it.

"You've got really long hair." Katie stands in front of me, stroking my hair. I lean backward, but she cups the back of my neck and forces me toward her. In one swift movement, she unhooks my necklace and tucks it into her bra.

"Hey, what are you—"

"I'm just tying your hair up for you," she says, giving me a firm *shut up* look.

I don't know why, but I do. With the hair tie around her wrist, she pulls all of my long waves into a ponytail. As she finishes, she gently tugs on my hair, forcing my head back. My attention lands on a small security camera bolted to the ceiling behind her. Is she trying to tell me we're being watched? *Maybe she's here against her will too.*

"There!" Katie says, stepping back to admire her work. "Now you won't have to worry about getting that long mane of yours tangled up during your stay."

"My stay? What is this? A hotel?"

"It's no five-star resort, but it's not a crappy side-of-the-road Motel 6 either."

"Then what is it?"

She doesn't answer. Instead, she plants herself back onto the folding chair and returns her iPad to her lap. For a few minutes, she does stuff on the tablet in silence. I don't say anything because I'm too busy scanning the room for possible exits.

No windows. No vents big enough for a person to climb through. There are two doors: the one to the bathroom, which I've already inspected for exits, and the other that Katie is so obviously guarding.

"There's no way out," she says, not looking up from the iPad. "You might as well stop searching. Despite what it looks like from inside this little bedroom, you're not in a house. You're in an underground facility surrounded by about two hundred trained agents. Beyond that is a forest that stretches as far as your eyes can see."

That's all great information to note to the police once I get out of here. *If* I ever get out of here. If what Katie's saying is true, I don't think I'll see my home again until they want me to.

A steady vibration comes from Katie's pocket. She pulls out her phone to read the screen. *Wait.* That's not her phone. It's mine!

"Your *Grammy* is calling. Is she expecting you or something?"

Last night, I called my grandma with the intention of telling her about the baby, but she was already asleep. Instead, I left her a voicemail saying I had something important to talk to her about. It must be morning now—not that I could peek out a window to be sure.

My phone stops vibrating. Seconds later, it buzzes with a text.

"What did she say?" I ask as Katie reads my phone screen.

"She said, 'Hi, sweetie. Sorry, I was sleeping last night. You said you had something important to tell me? I'll call again in a bit.' " Katie returns my device to her pocket. "Are you pretty close to your grandma?"

"Yeah."

"So she'll find it weird if you don't call her back?"

"Definitely."

With a long sigh, Katie drags out her pink phone again. She types something on it, then waits for a reply. It comes a few seconds later. "My boss says you need to call your grandma back and talk to her as if you weren't here."

"You mean, as if I'm not being held captive?"

"Exactly."

"And if I refuse?"

She folds her hands together in her lap. "I think my boss would prefer it if you called."

"Look, I don't know who your boss is, but I'm assuming he's the reason I was kidnapped, so I'm not going to do anything he wants me to. If he's saying he wants me to call my grandma and tell her that nothing's wrong, I'd rather jump into a pit of flesh-eating snakes."

Katie blinks at me before returning her thumbs to her phone. After a moment, she straightens her back. "He's almost here."

Less than thirty seconds later, the door opens and in walks a tall man wearing a brown suit. The big gray mustache above his lips barely hides the scowl on his face and the emotions to match.

Three other men accompany him. Two step into the room and stand on opposite corners. The third guy stations himself outside the door as Katie shuts it.

I can sense them. Every single one of them. Katie, Mustache Man, his two bodyguards, and the one out in the hall. Turns out this baby *can* sense more than one person at a time. They just have to be close enough.

"You need to call your grandma back now." As Mustache Man speaks, the long horizontal scar on the front of his neck moves up and down. Either he had surgery or someone tried to slit his throat. My bets are on the latter.

Something about his face makes me squint at him. He looks familiar. Like an actor I've seen in a movie. I can't place him though.

I don't respond to Mustache Man with words—only glares. He glares back with his piercing eyes. I want to know his name and everything about him so that when I leave here, I'll have everything the police need to put him behind bars.

"Are you going to call your grandma back or not?"

Again, I remain silent. I'm not going to comply with his demands that easily. *So much for everything I've learned from those true crime shows.*

"Katie!" he shouts so loudly, she jumps. "Proceed with Plan B. He's in the bathroom on the fourth floor. I'll work on trying to convince her by the time you return with him."

"Yes, sir." With her iPad in hand, Katie retreats out of the room.

I almost shout at her to not leave me alone with this scary man, but she's already gone. Strangely, without her, I feel more vulnerable.

Mustache Man approaches me. The closer he gets, the more his irritation twists into curiosity. He wants something from me. I can see it in the way his eyes are staring straight into my soul. What does he want?

"Leave us," he says. Almost instantly, his two guards exit the room. They don't go far though. I still feel their presence right outside the closed door.

Now that it's just me and Mustache Man, he closes the distance between us in two strides. As he does, his blue eyes turn black like he's being possessed by a demon. I crawl backward on the bed, screaming at the top of my lungs.

"Get away from me!"

"Hold still," he says and reaches for my neck.

I swat him away with my free arm. "Don't touch me."

"I said hold still." He grabs me by the neck and forces me to meet eyes with him. His eye color has returned to blue, but it's not long before a cloud of black takes over his pupils again. It's like something out of a horror movie.

"Let me go!" My words come out stifled from how solid his grip is around my throat. I claw at his fingers.

Surprisingly, he releases me and takes a step back. I cough and gasp for air as he runs a hand through the top of his salt-and-pepper hair.

His frustration radiates toward me from where he stands. "I don't even know why I'm trying. Of course it won't work."

Whatever he was trying to do to me, I'm glad it didn't work. Above all else, I'm glad he wasn't trying to sexually assault me—although I have a feeling that whatever he was trying to do is much worse.

Something about him isn't right, and it's not just because his eyes can turn completely black. There's something oddly familiar about him.

Minutes later, when someone bursts through the door shouting, "What the fuck is this?" it hits me.

This man looks like an older version of Trey Grant.

46

ARELLA

For a second, I'm relieved to see someone I know. However, when Trey doesn't immediately punch Mustache Man and carry me out of here . . .

"The girl's grandmother is expecting her to call," Mustache Man says. "I've asked her to call the old lady back and act normal, but she's refusing. Think you can persuade her?"

Trey's body goes stiff. Anger radiates off him so strongly, I can't sense Mustache Man anymore, or Katie, who has returned herself to the folding chair in the corner.

Trey barely moves as he glares at his older look-alike. "What the hell is she doing here?"

Mustache Man speaks calmly yet firmly. "I figured that since you're gonna be busy working your new mission, we could go ahead and accelerate your first one."

I've got to be dreaming. There's no way that Trey, *my* Trey, is a part of this.

Trey doesn't stop glaring at Mustache Man. "Why wasn't I consulted first?"

Mustache Man narrows his eyes at Trey. "What makes you think I need to consult *you* before making any decisions? Now, do you think you can convince her to call her grandma or not? If the answer's no, get the hell out and go be useless somewhere else."

Finally, Trey turns his attention to me. His chest rises and falls like he's not getting enough air. I hold back tears as we lock eyes and I silently plead with him to stop whatever's happening.

He must not hear my plea, because he clears his throat and says, "I'll convince her to call."

I burst into tears, covering my mouth with my free hand. *This can't be happening.* My breaths are sharp as Katie hands my phone to Trey, and he accepts it.

Mustache Man heads toward the door. "Katie, send me a full report when it's done, then return her phone to me. I'll be in my office."

"Yes, sir." Katie stands to open the door for him.

Mustache Man points to the bulkiest of his three bodyguards. "I want round-the-clock security on this Ordinary. You're first."

"Yes, sir," the man replies.

Even with the door shut, my baby senses Mustache Man and his two guards as they head down the hall. After several footsteps, I don't sense them anymore. I'll assume that's because they're out of my baby's range, not because they disappeared off the face of the planet.

Now I'm left alone in a silent bedroom with Katie and this master of deception I used to call my boyfriend.

Suddenly, everything starts to come together: Trey's late-night phone calls, his irregular sleeping habits, the mysterious air about him. He's been living a double life this whole time. He's a criminal. I think I prefer him being from an alternate universe over this.

"Could you give us a few minutes?" Trey asks, slipping my phone into his back pocket.

Katie nods. "Sure thing."

Trey waits until the door clicks shut behind her before he eyes the charred walls. At first, I think he's looking for an escape route like I did, but once his eyes land on the camera behind him, he turns back to me.

For a moment, he just stares. It's nothing I'm not used to. He's always had a habit of staring at me, except this time, it's not in admiration. He's looking for something. I'm not sure what.

I jolt back a little when he drops to his knees at my feet. Silent tears roll down my cheeks as he continues to scan my body up and down.

"Did anyone hurt you?" His question comes out in barely a whisper.

I can't respond, because if I do, I'll burst into tears again.

"Arella . . ." My name comes out like a plea. "Did anyone hurt you?"

There's no evidence of it on his face, but the baby senses relief from him when I shake my head. I want to tell him that, technically, no one's hurt me. Not as much as it hurts to see him here and to know that he's involved in this.

"How did you get here?" His voice is still a whisper.

My words come out through choked tears. "I woke up here."

He grits his teeth together. "So they fucking kidnapped you?"

It's nice to hear someone call it what it is. I want to say, *Of course they kidnapped me. Do you think I willingly drove here myself?* What I actually say is "Who's *they*?"

He ignores my question. "Why are you handcuffed to the bed?"

I glower at him and wipe my damp face off with the bottom of the gigantic T-shirt I'm wearing. "You're asking me like *I* should know? When I woke up, I was already cuffed to this stupid bed, and that Katie girl was sitting on that chair, watching me sleep. Do you think I have any clue what's going on? I don't even know where I am."

"You're in Three Rivers."

"Your hometown?"

A nod.

"Why am I here?"

My question is met with silence. Trey springs back onto his feet and groans while running a hand through his hair the same way Mustache Man did. They've got to be related. Mustache Man is probably his dad. Trey's story about how his parents were killed was just a cover-up for his parents being criminals or to gain my sympathy. I can't believe I trusted anything he ever said to me.

In a regular tone, Trey asks, "Can you call your grandma back?"

"No."

"Arella, you have to."

"Says who? Mustache Man? The guy who a minute ago was choking me by the neck and—"

"He did what?" Trey's entire body goes rigid.

I shoot dagger eyes at him. "Don't be so surprised. If he's willing to sedate and kidnap me, he's probably willing to do much worse."

"You were sedated?" To himself, he says, "That explains why I didn't feel it right away." *Feel what?*

Trey's hands clench into fists as he sucks in a deep breath. When he lets it out, his fists relax. "Did he do anything else to you?"

How can I explain that Mustache Man probably tried to melt me with his black eyeballs without sounding like I'm crazy? Does Trey know he can do that?

"Who is he?" My tears are starting to let up because I'm more angry than shocked now. I want to know what's going on, how Trey is involved, and most of all, I want to go home.

"His name is Victor. He's the CEO of ZIRDA California, which is a secret organization that, um . . ." Trey's gaze falls to a burn spot on the carpet. "It's complicated."

A secret organization? That, along with some words Katie said earlier, like *mission* and *underground facility surrounded by about two hundred trained agents*, makes me feel like I've been sucked into some messed-up spy movie.

"Better question," I say. "How do *you* know Victor?"

"He's, um . . . my uncle."

I knew they were related. Maybe that means Trey wasn't lying about his parents getting blown up. Victor is probably the abusive uncle who took him in after the explosion. "Did you help your uncle kidnap me?"

"No. Fuck no. If it wasn't obvious, Arella, I'm just as shocked to see you here as you are to see me."

"He's your uncle!" I shout. "You really want me to believe you had nothing to do with this?"

"I didn't!" he shouts back.

I must be dumb, because I actually believe him. Mostly because my baby senses how angry he is about this. Correction: *our* baby. Oh my god, I'm pregnant with a baby who belongs to a man with a PhD in lying. *How is this my life?*

Trey paces the room, pulling at his hair before finally turning to me. "Could you please call your grandma?"

Does he really think saying *please* will change my mind? "I said no."

"Look, I know you're probably scared right now, but trust me, everything's gonna be okay." The way he says all that makes me think he's trying to convince himself, not me.

"Why should I trust *you*? You're one of them!"

How could I not have known? This should have been the first question I asked him on our first date: *Hey, is your uncle a crazy dude running a secret organization in an underground facility crawling with secret agents?* My second question should have been *Are you one of those secret agents?* The next guy I meet, I'll make sure I know the professions of *all* his uncles before even considering having dinner with him.

I glare at Trey with the most venomous look I can muster. "You've been one of them this whole time, haven't you?"

His silence is all the answer I need to lose any hope I had left in him.

47

ARELLA

I'm firm in my refusal to call my grandma. Eventually, Trey and Katie give up asking. Trey simply hands my phone back to Katie, and then she tells him to leave. At first, he hesitates, but eventually, he shuffles toward the door.

On his way out, I catch a glimpse of the big guy guarding my exit. He looks like the white version of Dwayne "The Rock" Johnson. I don't know how I'm going to escape with that man around. I can't take him on. He's triple my size.

When the door shuts, Katie flashes me a gentle smile. "Are you allergic to anything?"

My response is automatic. "Liars and people who don't use their blinker."

She giggles, covering her mouth with a hand. "I'm glad you can still make jokes, given how scared you must be, but I was asking if you have any food allergies."

She's wrong. I'm not scared. I'm terrified. I'm making jokes because it's keeping me centered. Otherwise, I might be hyperventilating in the fetal position right now.

"No allergies," I say.

"Excellent. I'll be right back."

She leaves and returns a few minutes later with a food tray in hand. On it is a bowl of cereal, some milk in a glass, an apple, and a granola bar.

She sets it onto my lap. "Eat up."

"No."

She frowns at the food. "Do you not care for Cheerios?"

"I don't care to eat any offerings from criminals."

This girl has the *audacity* to look offended. "I haven't committed any crimes. You don't have to eat if you don't want to, but for your information, lunch doesn't start in the cafeteria for another three hours. Judging by what's on your schedule today, I think you're gonna want all the energy you can get."

I don't like the sound of that. "What's going to happen to me?"

Katie doesn't answer with her mouth, but the pity in her eyes tells me all I need to know.

I glance at the food, then back up at her. I'm about to ask if it's poisoned but figure if it is, at least I won't have to endure whatever it is they've got planned for me, so I pick up the apple and take a bite.

My breakfast is long gone by the time Katie's iPad chimes. She leaps off her chair and plucks that precious metal key out of her pocket. "It's time."

"For what?" I have a good feeling that whatever she's got to say next won't be good.

"To take you downstairs. Before I uncuff you, I wanna tell you that your stay here will be more comfortable if you don't try to run. The last person tried and was put into a straitjacket. Those things are uncomfortably heavy. I don't think you want that."

The last person? That means I'm not the first. If that's the case, what happened to the others? Do I even want to know?

Katie continues, "I was the one who suggested not restraining you at all. I told Victor it would help you be more agreeable. He wasn't fond of that idea, so we compromised with restraining only one of your arms instead. I know you don't have any reason to trust me, but I sure hope you won't purposely ruin my chances of proving to my boss that I can have good ideas. So, do you think you can be agreeable?"

"I'll be agreeable if you give me back my necklace."

For the second time, Katie shoots me a firm *shut up* look. It quickly disappears and fades into a warm smile. "Glad you're promising to behave. Now let's get you downstairs."

This girl is either a psychopath or she's up to something. Maybe she's both. She'd better not think I'm going to simply brush off that she stole my necklace. It doesn't matter that the man who gifted it to me is a . . . well, I'm not sure what he is. A spy? A secret agent from another universe? Whatever he is, I still want my necklace back.

Katie leads me down the hallways, passing a plethora of numbered rooms like in an apartment complex. The big guy who was guarding my door follows closely behind me. After a few turns, we pass what looks like a community area across from a cafeteria. A few people are scattered around the tables, typing on laptops.

In the elevator, I make a mental note that there are six floors. I also note that they're keeping me captive on the second one. Katie presses the 1 button, and then the doors slide together.

Katie cuddles her iPad close to her chest as the machine takes us down. I'll bet there are lots of important things on that device. Like incriminating notes, names of all the secret agents here, and a way for me to send for help. I've got to get that iPad from her.

Ding! The elevator opens to a new floor.

I follow Katie down the wide hallways while the big guy tramps behind me in his heavy boots. I log as many details of this place into my brain as possible. White walls, gray doors, cream tiled floors. Behind a glass wall is a group of six rowdy men. Two are wrestling each other on padded mats while the other four cheer them on.

In a fitness room, two men and three women are running on treadmills or lifting weights. I don't get a long enough glance to memorize any of their faces. I'm not even sure how any of this information is going to help me later, but I continue to memorize things anyway.

We pass a few more rooms, but they don't have windows for me to see through. The signs on the outside say things like *Fireball Throwing Practice*, *Terra Training*, and *Artificial Sunlight*. I don't know what any of that means.

Through a set of double doors, we enter a giant auditorium with a square boxing ring in the center. Empty rows of seats stretch from the boxing ring all the way up to the back walls. In the ring are a group of people having a conversation. One of them is Mustache Man, otherwise known as Victor, Trey's uncle and the man who organized my kidnapping. The baby senses excitement from him instead of the frustration that was simmering in his gut earlier. Whatever he's excited about can't be good for me.

Katie stops at the bottom of the stairs leading into the boxing ring. She gestures for me to step up.

I don't.

"Get in," Victor orders.

Three. Besides Victor, there's three of them in the boxing ring, and they're all ready to do whatever it is they do to their captives in there. *No thank you. Hard pass for me.*

Victor snaps his fingers. "Craig, assist the girl, will you?"

I yelp when the big guard scoops me off my feet. Then he stomps up the stairs in his boots and drops me into the center of the boxing ring.

I don't move a muscle as Victor throws a leg over the ropes to stand on the other side of the ring. Then he draws a circle in the air with his finger. "Surround her. One of you at each corner."

As if they're robots—maybe they are—all three people plus Craig migrate to separate corners of the box. I stare at each one, memorizing anything about them that can help the police identify them later.

Craig, if that's his real name, is a forty-something white male with neck tattoos that seem to run all the way down to his fingertips.

Guy two is another white male, maybe late thirties, with muscles practically bursting out of his shirt. Short brown hair. No visible tattoos.

The other two are women. The first one is Asian—maybe Korean. She's the shortest of them all. She also looks the youngest, maybe nineteen or twenty. She has a pixie haircut with blue highlights, plus floral tattoos running down her upper arm, and she's chewing on a piece of gum.

Female two looks in her mid-twenties. Slender figure, long curly red hair, and lots of freckles.

Okay, now all I have to do is remember all that . . .

"Let's try one at a time first," Victor says from the sidelines. His deep voice echoes throughout the emptiness of the auditorium. "Derek, you first."

The muscular guy steps forward and snaps his fingers in my direction. I glance around, looking for something coming at me, or something to fall onto me from the ceiling. When nothing does, he snaps again.

"Maybe I need to touch her." Derek comes to my side. I think about running, but his stern gaze makes me stay in place. Besides, there's nowhere for me to go.

I flinch when he grabs my arm and holds it. His grip gets tighter as I try to jerk away from him.

"Let go." I yank my arm back until he releases me.

"What the . . . ?" He gapes at me. "Pixie, come here for a sec."

The Asian woman pops up from her squat. In mid-stand, Derek snaps his fingers, and she stills like she's been paused in a movie. She doesn't blink. She doesn't chew on her gum. I'm not even sure if she's breathing. My mouth pops open as my eyes go wide.

"So my powers *do* work." Derek snaps his fingers again.

Pixie finishes her stand like the movie's been unpaused. She must know what happened, because she narrows her eyes at Derek. With two fingers, she points at her eyes, then at him. "I'm watchin' you, jackass."

Victor waves a hand at the big guard. "Let's keep this movin'. You're next, Craig."

As Derek returns to his corner, Craig points a firm tattooed finger at me. His strides are long as he closes the distance between us. The closer he gets, the more I back away.

"Don't come any closer." My voice betrays me. It comes out weaker than I wanted it to.

Craig backs me into the ropes, pinning me there. I punch his chest, but it's as effective as punching a statue. He doesn't even flinch. He continues pointing a finger at me, even pressing it against my forehead—hard.

"How are you doing that?" His shock flashes through my mind.

Doing what?

"Sorry, Derek." Craig unpins me, then points a finger at the muscular guy. With the sound of a balloon releasing air, Derek shrinks to the size of a small dog. I scream, but I'm the only one who does. None of the other people look slightly surprised—not even Katie, who's typing away on her iPad from the front row of the auditorium seats. Is seeing people shrink like that normal around here?

In a tiny, high-pitched voice, Derek shouts, "Hey! Unshrink me!"

Pixie draws her arm back like she's about to pitch a baseball. In the palm of her hand, a ball of water appears. She tosses it at mini Derek, and it lands right over his little head, drenching him.

"That's fucking rude!" Derek shouts in his high-pitched voice. "Craig, unshrink me, you bastard!"

Craig points his finger at Derek. With the sound of air being blown into a balloon, Derek returns to his normal size. He leans against the ropes for support. "Damn. That shit hurts," he says as he wrings out the bottom of his drenched shirt.

"The shrinking or the water ball?" the Asian woman asks.

"The shrinking, bitch. Yours, I barely felt."

I don't even see the water ball grow in her hand before it's launched across the room. Derek ducks, and the water splashes all over the floor.

"Missed me, bitch," Derek says, grinning.

A third water ball appears in the woman's hand. She raises it into the air as it doubles in size. "Call me a bitch one more time."

"Enough!" Victor shouts. "Pixie, since you're so eager to use your powers, why don't you go next?"

"Gladly." Pixie's water ball evaporates in a cloud of steam in her hand, then she marches toward me and stops barely a half step from my face. I log more of her features into my brain: nose ring, sharp eyebrows, plump lips. How am I going to remember all this?

Her minty breath wafts over my nose as she puckers her lips into an O shape. She blows air at me. I wait for something to happen, maybe for my face to melt or my eyeballs to pop out. Nothing happens.

Pixie steps back as her genuine confusion races through my head. "No fucking way." She takes the gum out of her mouth and blows air at me again.

Then she blows a third time.

Finally, she twists on a heel, puckers her lips, and blows air in Derek's direction.

He slaps his hands over his ears. "Ow! Stop!"

Pixie does and returns her gum to her mouth. She smirks at me as if we're good friends. "I just love fuckin' with him."

"Ruby," Victor says, "how 'bout you try?"

The redhead doesn't move from her spot. Instead, she simply raises her open palm out to me and hisses through her teeth. When nothing happens, she advances toward me. Her black booties click with each step she takes until she's right in my face.

"Is it workin'?" Derek asks.

"Do you hear her screaming in pain?" Ruby says.

Screaming in pain? What is she trying to do to me?

"If you touch her, will it work?" Victor asks.

Ruby places her hand on my arm and hisses again. When nothing happens, she releases me. Then she directs her hisses at Derek. He drops to his knees and screams like he's being attacked by giant cobras. When Ruby puts her arm down, the screaming stops.

"What the fuck?" Derek is still on his knees, clutching his stomach. "Going through an incinerator would be less painful than that."

Ruby shrugs, smirking a little. "I had to make sure my powers still worked."

Who are these people? Better question: *What* are they? They seem to have abilities of some kind and are testing them out on me. For some reason I don't know and am deeply grateful for, their powers don't work on me. *Why?*

Maybe Javina was right about Trey being from an alternate universe. Except, it wasn't him who was sucked into my universe; I've been sucked into his. It's the only explanation I have for everything I'm witnessing.

"Gather 'round her," Victor orders. "Let's try all four of you at the same time."

Derek, Craig, Pixie, and Ruby trap me against the ropes as they fix their gazes on me. I don't pause. My body doesn't shrink. I don't hear anything that makes me want to cover my ears. I don't collapse to my knees with pain either.

"Pixie, give her a splash," Victor says. "Everyone focus!"

Pixie raises both arms as a giant water ball forms in her hands. I raise my arms to try to block her, but she wins. Icy-cold liquid drenches me.

I spit out the water and wipe at my face.

"Well, she ain't immune to elemental powers," Pixie says.

There's that word again. *Powers.* How did these people get their powers? If they are *people* at all.

"Do it again," Victor orders.

The second water ball is even colder.

I shiver as the four of them continue trying to accomplish whatever it is they want to accomplish. The longer nothing happens, the more the cloud of irritation above Victor grows.

"How are you doing that?" Victor asks.

I wish they would stop asking me that as if I know the answer. My jaw quivers as I push the wet hair from my face.

"All right, let's be done," Victor says. "Pixie, help the girl out."

The other three step back as Pixie waves her hands in circles. In slow steam clouds rising to the ceiling, all the water soaking my body disappears. My shirt that was soaking wet a second ago feels like it just came out of the dryer. *What kind of magic is this?*

"Katie!" Victor shouts, and it makes her pop out of her seat. I think she's been typing notes on her iPad this whole time. "Take the girl back to her room. Give her the questionnaire."

In her mousey little voice, Katie says, "Yes, sir."

Together, Katie and Craig escort me back to the elevators. I think about running, but now that I've discovered they're wizards, I don't stand a chance.

Back on the second floor, we take a few turns down the hallways before we reach my corner jail cell disguised as a bedroom. On the doorframe is a chain lock that disheartens me. I didn't think I had any chance of escaping before. Now it seems impossible.

Katie types a few numbers into a keypad on the door. When it beeps, she gestures for me to step inside. I do, because what else can I do?

While Craig stations himself outside my door, Katie clicks it shut. The sound of the chain lock sliding into place makes me choke up.

"Take a seat," Katie says, pointing at the bed. She plops onto her folding chair and offers me a smile. "I'll leave you uncuffed if you promise not to attack me."

I stay standing where I am. "Why do you have to cuff me at all? I don't have magic powers to fight you with. There's no way I can get out of here. Although, if I did attack you, it doesn't seem like your powers work on me, so maybe I *could* win in a fight."

"First off, the cuffs aren't really to keep you from attacking me or to keep you from leaving. It's more to keep someone from taking you. We've been having a problem with double agents lately, so you can never have too much security on your assets."

She's calling me an asset like I'm something they own. *Am I their slave now?*

Katie continues, "Secondly, it's not magic, and please, don't say that word out loud around here. Most Zordis get really offended when our gifts are referred to as *magic*. Third, some of our powers *do* work on you. It's only the internal ones that seem to have no effect. And lastly, I don't need my powers to subdue you. I grew up learning karate."

I totally called that. "Zordis? That's what you call yourselves?"

"We don't just *call* ourselves that. It's what we are. The technical term is *Zordinary*, but we shorten it to Zordi."

"And you're what? Aliens? Mutants? Lab experiments gone wrong?"

Katie lets out a little laugh. "You have quite the imagination, don't you? We're humans, just like you, except we have gifts. Now how about you sit down? It's my turn to ask the questions."

Sighing, I do as I'm told and plant my butt onto the mattress.

Katie taps around on her iPad, then says, "I've got a pretty long list of questions. All you've gotta do is answer them honestly. Think you can do that?"

The questions start off normal enough: Where did you grow up? Do you have any siblings? What did you study in college?

Once the questions are about my family, it gets weird: Did your mom or dad have a sexually transmitted disease at the time of your conception? Was your mother on any drugs or prescriptions while she was pregnant with you? Have you or your parents ever been bitten by an exotic spider?

I don't understand how these questions are relevant. How would I know if my parents had an STD at the time of my conception or if my mother was on drugs? That's not a typical dinner conversation. Even if it was, I never got the chance to ask.

"I told you already," I say exasperated. The warped clock on the wall reads eleven thirty. It's been almost two hours since we began this stupid interrogation. "My parents died in a car accident when I was three. I don't even remember them."

"Do you think there's a chance your parents were Immunes too? Like, maybe it runs in the family?"

"No! No! No!" Normally, I don't like to shout. Right now, I want to shout so loudly, the sky can hear me. I haven't seen the sky yet today, so I'm questioning if it still exists. "I don't know the answers to your dumb questions! I didn't even know I was immune to anything until today!"

Katie's expressionless as I chuck a pillow at her. She doesn't even flinch as it hits her shoulder and flops onto the floor. I let out a scream toward the ceiling, then burst into tears.

It's quiet for a moment while I cry into my hands, letting out all the emotions I've been bottling in since I woke up. I feel Katie's gaze on me as she waits for me to stop sobbing.

When I don't, she slaps her thighs and stands from her chair. "Welp, I think it's time for lunch. I'll be back in a bit. We can finish the questionnaire after you eat."

There's more? How can there be more?

Five minutes later, Katie returns with two food trays. My sobbing has subsided and turned into occasional hiccups. I'm regretting every decision I've ever made that landed me here, and all I want is to crawl into my nice comfy bed at home and never come out.

"Do you prefer turkey or ham? I made one of each. I'll have whatever you don't want."

"Turkey," I say somberly.

She hands me one of the trays. "I made it myself. If you want, I'll take the first bite, so you know it's not poisoned."

"Don't bother. If it is poisoned, at least it'll end this misery."

Katie puckers her bottom lip out into a little pout. "Oh, come on. Am I really *that* bad to hang out with? I think you'd prefer me over the last guy. He was kinda mean. He also had a gut that hung over his belt and a beard so long, you could braid it. Honestly, he looked like an ogre. And that's saying something, because Zordis are naturally pretty fit. We have higher metabolisms than Ordis, so that guy had to really let himself go to get all that flub."

That explains how Trey has such perfectly toned abs. All this time, I thought he just put a lot of effort into his exercise. Turns out, he's got a mutant body that makes it easy for him to look fit.

"Can I sit with you?" Katie eyes the other side of the twin bed. "This chair is aching my bum."

"Sure."

We rest our food trays between us, then take a bite into our sandwiches. If someone snapped a photo of this moment, it'd look like Katie and I are best buddies, having a friendly bedroom picnic. In reality, I met this girl this morning and I know nothing about her, except that she works for a man who organizes federal crimes. Oh, and that she's a thief. *Is my necklace still in her bra?*

"You asked me a million questions earlier," I say. "Can I ask you some now?"

"You can ask, but I can't promise I'll give you the answer, even if I know it."

"I'll take all the answers you can give me. First, I want to know what your *mission* is."

Katie swallows her food, then says, "Victor assigned me to be your overseer. I'm in charge of making sure you're fed, dressed, and arrive on time to your appointments. Honestly, I think *overseer* is just code for *glorified babysiter*. This wouldn't have been my first pick from the pool of on-base assignments, but it's a stepping-stone."

"What would have been your first pick?" I open my bag of chips.

"My dream is to be a field agent, doing stuff out in the world where I can make a big difference. That's not to say the people who work on base aren't making a difference. Of course the janitors, the cooks, the maids, and even me, as Victor's assistant, are important. We're the oil for the gears to function properly—the gears being the field agents.

"But this type of work doesn't light my soul on fire, ya know? It's hard to feel like I'm making an impact when I'm confined down here all day and night. I guess if I had to pick something on base, I'd like to be in project management. I could help write up mission plans for the field agents and make sure they're getting done."

By the way Katie talks about this place, it sounds like a well-functioning establishment—not a place that houses kidnapping criminals.

I finish the bite I'm eating, then say, "So, this is just a job to you? Like, you're getting paid for this?"

"Yes, technically this is a job. Just like anyone else, I get paychecks, and I have days off where I'll go see my family and stuff. But to me, working for ZIRDA is much more than that. I want to build a career here. When I'm old and retired, I want people to say my name and think, *Wow. She saved a lot of lives.*"

How can Katie talk about saving lives when I feel like mine is at risk? "What does ZIRDA stand for?"

"Zordinary Innovations Research and Development Agency. We began as an organization who designs and improves inventions that progress the lives of Zordis. For example, our agents are the ones who created the z-net, which is an Internet that only Zordis can access. It was also our agents who invented z-ink, which is the ink our kind uses to print books that only our eyes can see. Over the decades, ZIRDA has become more than just inventors. Now we also work to fight off the Royals, who are the biggest organized Zordi crime group in history."

I take a sip of water and ask the question that's been on my mind since this morning. "What's Trey's role here?"

"Field agent."

That's not the answer I was looking for, so I try again. "What's his mission?"

"I'm not sure exactly. Agents aren't allowed to speak in detail about our missions with each other, but it's only right to assume that his mission is to get you to give Victor what he wants."

A little piece of my heart breaks as I flashback to meeting Trey on the side of a busy highway. It's hitting me now that maybe my flat tire wasn't an accident. I choke back some tears and say, "I'm going to assume that Trey's mission is to figure out how I'm immune to your people's powers, but what happens after that?"

"I'd assume that ZIRDA will try to replicate your immunity so we can use it to take down the Royals."

"What makes them so bad?"

"Everything. While most Zordis believe that living in peace with Ordinaries is optimal, the Royals believe that because Zordis have powers, we're the superior humans. They think Zordis should be the ones running the show, and they hate that we are the ones who have to hide our true selves. Some Royals even go to the extreme and believe that all Ordinaries should be eradicated. They've gone as far as mass genocides and biochemical weapons that cause worldwide viruses killing off only Ordinaries. The Black Plague, the Spanish flu, SARS—all started by the Royals."

I have no idea if she's feeding me lies or not, but for now, I'll assume she's telling the truth. What reason does she have to lie about where the Black Plague came from? "And Ordinaries are . . . ?"

"People like you."

"Is that like muggles in Harry Potter? Non-magic folk?"

Katie scolds me. "Again, it's not magic. It's called gifts or powers."

"How did you get them?"

"We're born with 'em," she says, like it's common knowledge. "It's passed down by genetics. Which reminds me, would you mind if I held your hand for a moment? I'm curious to see if my powers will work."

I respond by holding my arm out to her with full confidence that she won't hurt me.

After setting her half-eaten sandwich down and wiping her fingers off on a napkin, she takes my hand and closes her eyes. A few seconds later, she lets me go and picks up her sandwich.

"Did it work?" I ask.

"No. I can't control when my body power works, anyway, but it's safe to assume that no matter how hard I try, it won't work."

I don't have a clue as to what *body power* means, and I don't care to ask. My brain is too overloaded with all this information. Secret agents with magic powers fighting the bad guys who apparently caused the Black Plague? And they want to use *me* and my strange immunity to their magic to defeat them?

I never signed up for this.

48

TREY

"**S**on, *your mama and I wanted to make sure that you'd be safe and taken care of. That's why everything we have is now yours, including a safe house by our secret rock.*" My father's words replay from the button-size device I found in my old teddy bear. I don't know why I'm listening to this. I've played the recording so many times now that I have it memorized.

My mother's voice comes next. "*When you get to the rock, take a hundred steps away from Cheesy. There, you'll find the safe house. You're the only one who can get into it. Remember that Trackers can't sense you once you're inside and underground.*"

No matter how many times I play this recording and scour the woods, I can't find the safe house. Before, I searched for it out of curiosity. I wanted to see what my parents left behind for me. Now it's the only way I can keep Arella safe. I *need* to find it.

The sun beats down on me as I comb the same wooded area in Julian, California, as I have multiple times before. *Inside and underground.* I understand the underground part—hence all the holes surrounding me that I dug and refilled. It's the *inside* part I'm having trouble with. *Inside what?* All that's around me are trees, trees, and more trees.

As I continue searching, I play the recording again. The one line that keeps sticking out to me is "*Aunt Debbie is the only person you should trust, and the only person you should take with you.*"

Why is my mother's sister on the trustworthy list but my father's brother is not? Did my parents know something about Victor that I don't? If they didn't trust him, does that mean I shouldn't either? Not that I do anyway.

Even while I was actively working my mission, any time I discovered anything about Arella that seemed out of place, I never told Victor about it: her parents dying on the same night as mine. How that news article stated that three-year-old Arella—I mean *Hannah Calder* —died too. How whenever I made her orgasm, I was able to break through her immunity walls. Something in the back of my mind kept me from telling Victor any of that, and I'm glad for it.

For weeks, Victor was adamant that I bring Arella to him for a bunch of bullshit tests. I had a feeling that if I didn't do it, he would send someone who would. I never thought he'd go as

269

far as kidnapping her. *Is he fucking serious?* That's not how ZIRDA ever handles things with Ordinaries. Usually, ZIRDA is more discreet and causes no harm. I thought he'd simply send another guy to get Arella to fall for and start the process over. Now that I know he's willing to kidnap innocent Ordinaries, I'm starting to question all of his decisions.

Victor has been the CEO of one of the largest ZIRDA bases in the United States for the last nineteen years. During that time, I've witnessed him shut down Royals operations before they even began. I've seen him personally train the new agents and help them draw up missions to keep Ordinaries safe. Throughout the years, he's accomplished a lot of good. That's why I usually give him passes for treating me like dirt.

Without ZIRDA working to develop and distribute the necessary life-saving vaccines to save Ordinaries from all those bioweapons the Royals have unleashed, there might not be many Ordinaries left. Without ZIRDA, the Royals would have a higher kill count. Without ZIRDA, the Royals probably would have won by now.

I fully support ZIRDA's purpose. I even commend Victor for running ZIRDA California for all these years. It's not a job for the weak. But being the CEO of a ZIRDA base doesn't mean he can do no wrong. And with Arella, he's wrong. Sedating her? Kidnapping her? Handcuffing her to a bed? Is this what he did with the last two Immunes instead of asking them to be part of a secret medical study the way ZIRDA usually does? Are his crazy methods the reason why the other two Immunes are dead?

On my way out of the Ridge earlier, it hit me why Victor didn't give me a choice to come to the base: He needed me preoccupied while he sent some agents out to kidnap my girl. I'll bet anything that Kim Nguyen isn't even a real person. I'll bet he simply stole that picture off the Internet and purposely prolonged that briefing meeting to keep me busy.

My parents would have never stood for this. Maybe this is why they stopped trusting Victor. Maybe the three of them disagreed on how ZIRDA should handle missions, and this is what drove them apart. Whatever happened, I need to stop dwelling on the past. Instead, I need to focus on getting Arella out of Shadow Ridge.

The base is completely guarded and crawling with other agents. If I had to guess, I'd say there are at least a hundred people there. Maybe two hundred. I won't make it three feet into the hallway with Arella in tow without someone stopping me. Whether it's Katie or that guard Victor has stationed outside, or the security guards, *someone* will stop me.

I slump onto the dirty ground with a huff. This plan is impossible, especially because I'm doing it alone. I could recruit help, but who? The only other Zordis I've had contact with recently are Liz and Jess.

Liz doesn't even know that I'm a ZIRDA agent. Even if she did, I refuse to bring her into this. I'm not willing to risk her life, and I think that's what it'll come down to in order to get Arella outta there—risking lives.

I'd be willing to risk Jess's life, but there's no way in hell she'd help me. Especially not after the way I kicked her out of my house. Besides, the thought of having to see her again is more unappealing than seeing a dog get run over.

So, it's up to me and only me. Whatever I'm planning to do, I have to do it quick. I have no idea how many days the previous Immunes lasted in the Ridge before their innocent lives were stolen. Arella's already been in there for half a day. The sooner I can get her out, the better.

I play the recording again.

"When you get to the rock, take a hundred steps away from Cheesy."

Back on my feet, I return to the rock my parents used to bring me to all the time. We used to camp here and lie down on blankets, stargazing. I know now that it was their way of helping me remember this place.

Cheesy is the name I gave a tree off in the distance. It's covered in holes. When I was a kid, I thought the holes were from birds and other animals. Now I'm pretty sure my parents put those holes there on purpose to give me a sense of direction. Telling a young child to take a hundred steps north or south isn't as effective as "take a hundred steps away from Cheesy."

For the gazillionth time, I start at the big rock, then turn my back to the holey tree and walk forward while I count my steps. *One, two, three . . .*

One hundred steps later, I'm back in the general area I've been scouring every time I try looking for this damn safe house. There's nothing here. No house. No sign that there ever was one. No bunker entry. Not even a trapdoor.

I hike around for a while, trying to see if there's anything I missed. Eventually, I give up. I'm pretty certain there's no safe house here.

With a heavy heart, I climb back onto my Harley and begin the long ride back to Shadow Ridge. Ideally, I'd have a safe place to take Arella to once I get her outta there, but she can't wait until after I find my parents' invisible safe house. For now, I just need to rescue her. I'll figure the rest out later.

Shit plan, I know, but what else can I do?

49

TREY

At the entrance to Shadow Ridge, I stick my finger into the fingerprint scanner hole. *Beep! Beep! Beep!* The large door slides open. Two security guards are waiting for me on the other side.

I expect them to ask me why I'm here without being summoned, but they don't. *Odd.* Typically, field agents aren't allowed to enter the Ridge unless they have an appointment. I'm not gonna question it though. If they're slacking on their duties, I won't complain.

Carlos, the guard I used to pull pranks on as a kid, greets me with a grunt. "You again?"

I'm not in the mood to give him shit, so I keep my mouth shut.

"What?" he says. "No smart-ass comment? No rude remarks about my gray hair or my big-ass nose? Are you goin' soft now?"

"Just pat me down so I can get going."

"Sheesh. Someone's got their balls caught in a zipper."

As Carlos frisks me, I scan the security room. Multiple screens of all sizes show footage of people walking down hallways and gathered in the community room. The more screens I see, the more I think my already impossible rescue mission seems more impossible. They've got their eyes on everything, and there are people everywhere.

The other security guard stares me down from his rolling chair with a look on his face like he wants to strangle me. He's the guy with the eyebrow scar, who I wouldn't have even considered pulling pranks on as a kid. It's not normal for Zordis to have scars. With our ability to heal quickly and the healing products my parents invented, a Zordi has to *want* a scar to have one, or the injury had to have been pretty severe.

"Clear," Carlos says and steps back.

Without a word, I head toward the elevators.

I press the *down* button as my heart sprints like I'm running from a bear. I thought once I got in here, I'd know what to do. Not only was I wrong, but I'm starting to think this is a suicide mission.

The base has been having an issue with double agents lately. People might assume I'm one of them, which, technically, I am. No, I'm not working for the Royals, but I'm working for myself. If an agent sees me trying to walk outta here with Arella, they won't know that, and they won't hesitate to kill me. I doubt Victor would stop them either. I definitely should have thought this through more.

Ding!

One of the four elevators arrives and invites me in. I wait for two women to step out before jumping inside and pressing the 2 button. I don't know if I have permission to see Arella, but I'm going to. I need to make sure she's okay and assess the situation before I formulate the rest of my get-her-the-fuck-out plan.

When the elevator doors reopen, my breath hitches. It's her. She's still in that giant white T-shirt and those tattered orange shorts. We lock eyes, and it takes everything in me to not throw her over my shoulder and run. I'll throw fireballs at anyone who tries to stop me if that's what it takes. The only reason I don't do exactly that is because Katie and Victor's hulk-size security guard are standing right next to her.

"Oh, hey!" Katie says in a cheery tone. "That was quick."

"What was?"

The three of them join me in the elevator as Katie says, "I left you a voicemail, like, thirty seconds ago. Victor wants to see you immediately."

I had shut off my phone on the way here. I didn't want it to make any noise while I was in the middle of sneaking Arella out. "What's he want?"

"We're about to find out." With her hand not holding the iPad, Katie presses the 1 button.

"You mean you don't know?"

"He didn't tell me. I was just told to bring the Immune down to the battle box again."

I narrow my eyes at Katie because, surely, I didn't hear her right. "Again? As in . . . she's already been there?"

I scan Arella for any signs of cuts or bruises. She looks normal enough—if I ignore her puffy red eyes and that bleak expression.

"Not to worry," Katie says. "Unlike what the battle box is normally used for, that's not what happened this morning."

My memories of being in the battle box consist of fists and lightning balls hurling at my face. The battle box is where agents train in hand-to-hand combat and test their powers on each other. Arella belongs nowhere near that thing.

"Then what *did* happen this morning?" I try not to sound as enraged as I feel but fail.

"Victor asked three of our most powerful field agents to come in to test their powers on her. They tried a few methods to see if it would work."

"What kinds of methods?" I'm still failing at keeping my voice in the chill zone.

"The kinds that didn't work. Maybe that's why Victor wants you here. You've spent the most time with her. Maybe he thinks you can provide some insight on how we can crack her secret."

I've already cracked Arella's secret. *Well, sort of.* I know that I can break through her immunity walls by making her orgasm, but that's it. If anyone asks for more answers beyond that, I don't have them. I don't know how or why it's then and only then that I can sense her, and I don't care to know. The only thing I care about is keeping her safe.

Ding!

Arella doesn't look at me as the four of us step off the elevator. She still doesn't spare me a glance as we make our way down the wide halls. I'm aware that I deserve her cold shoulder, but it still stings. I wish there was a way for me to silently tell her that I'm working on getting her out. *Just hang in there, baby.*

As I follow Katie, I count how many agents we pass. Twelve. Some in the fitness center. Some heading into the pool room. One janitor mopping the floors. One security guard patrolling.

I can't see an exit route from here. Especially not when we're on the first floor, and the only exit to the surface is on floor six. At least, that's the only exit I know of. As a kid, I heard rumors of secret passageways in and out of Shadow Ridge, but I never found them. I'm sure Victor knows them all, but I doubt he'll share that precious information with me.

Katie leads us through a set of double doors and into an auditorium. In the battle box is Victor with two young women. One has long red curls and is wearing black leather pants. The other has short blueish-black hair and is chewing on some gum. Both women have eager energy shooting at me. *What the hell are they so eager about?*

"Look at that!" Victor says. "He's here already. I guess we can go straight into the second part of tonight's plan. Join us in the box, kid."

Something tells me I don't want to. Something also tells me I don't have a choice.

"Ordinary, are you gonna come up willingly this time, or will I have to ask Craig to assist again?"

Craig must be the name of Victor's security guard, because he's about to lift Arella when she throws a hand up.

"Don't touch me. I'll do it myself."

I trail her up the stairs and through the ropes, resisting the urge to ask if she's okay. Meanwhile, Katie and Craig take seats on the sidelines.

"What's going on?" Sparks flicker between my fingertips—a reflex I've developed from being in the battle box so often before. Also, I'm not liking the smug way those two women are looking at me.

Victor ignores my question as he nods at the Asian woman. "Go ahead, Pixie."

The woman puckers her lips. Before I can produce a single flame, an agonizing high-pitched sound shoots into my ears. I slam my palms against the sides of my head. It does nothing to block the pain. It hurts like hell. There are no other words to describe it. Just hell.

I drop to my knees. "Stop! Stop!"

It doesn't stop. If anything, it gets louder and stings more. In the corner of my eye, I see Pixie glance at Victor. He nods, then she stops blowing. The pain subsides, leaving a ringing in my ears.

"Goddammit!" I shout. At least, I *think* I shouted. I can barely hear myself. "What the fuck was that?"

Victor acts like he didn't hear me. He turns to Arella. "Use your immunity to shield him from Pixie's gift."

Arella draws her eyebrows together. "I . . . I don't know how to do that."

"Try."

Out of nowhere, tiny invisible pitchforks attack my ears again. This time, it's louder and more excruciating. I wouldn't be surprised if my eardrums were bleeding. No matter how hard I press my palms to my ears, the agony stays the same.

Arella yells something. I can't hear what though. Her mouth looks like she's screaming "Stop! Stop!" The terrorized expression on her face makes me want to hold her and tell her I'll protect her, but I can't get off my knees long enough to get to her.

When Pixie closes her mouth, the sound stops. More importantly, so does the piercing pain. I fall onto my hands, gasping for air as the ringing returns.

"Fuckin' warn a guy!" My shouting sounds muffled.

Arella rushes to my side, dropping to her knees, with her hands cupping my face. Her touch feels like drinking an ice-cold bottle of Healing Water—therapeutic and refreshing.

Her lips move, but I can't make out the words. *Is she asking me something?* She yells at Victor, but I can't hear that either. They shout at each other for a moment before the ringing fades and my hearing slowly returns.

"We'll stop once you do what you're told," Victor says.

"I told you already! I don't know how!" Arella turns back to me with tears pooling in her eyes. "Trey, please tell me you're okay."

I offer her a weak grunt as I get to my feet. Arella holds me steady as I use her shoulder to keep me upright.

I scowl at the pathetic excuse for the only relative I have left. "Whatever you're trying to get her to do, it won't work."

"It will," Victor says. "She just needs the right motivation."

"No!" I slash my hand through the air. "You're treating her immunity as if it's a gift like ours. Like it's something she can use and control. For all we know, it's not possible for her to control it at all, let alone project it."

"It *is* possible. We got the last Immune to project his immunity onto someone else, which means she can too. She just needs to focus."

What? Victor never mentioned he got that far in this research. Why didn't he tell me? What else hasn't he told me?

"Ruby! Your turn!"

The redhead takes one look at me and hisses through her teeth. I collapse to my hands and knees again. The feeling of a hundred—no, a *thousand*—snakes biting into my skin takes over my entire body. I scream out as my muscles clench and burn. My arms give out, and I fall face first onto the floor.

"Stop!" Arella launches herself at Ruby. Pixie holds Arella back as Ruby keeps her eyes trained in my direction.

My body convulses like I'm being tasered from all sides. I lied earlier. Pixie's eardrum-stabbing power isn't hell. This is. Pure, unfiltered hell.

"Project your immunity onto him!" Victor orders.

"I can't! Just stop! Please!"

Victor slices a hand through the air. Finally, Ruby drops her arm. The agony on my skin fades. My body is left with a lingering burn.

I turn onto my back, panting as my vision goes blurry. I can't feel my thighs or anything below them. I would have taken Pixie's ear pain over whatever the hell that bullshit was.

"Let me go!" Arella shouts. A second later, she kneels at my side.

I can't see her because I can't get my eyes to reopen. I only feel her warm palm press against my stubbly cheek.

"Trey!" She says my name through a broken sob. "I'm so sorry. I don't know how to make them stop."

"I told you already," Victor says from across the battle box, "you just need to focus. Imagine yourself protecting him with metal shields or maybe some armor. If you don't save him, he will die. Ruby, hit him again."

I brace myself for the pain. It doesn't come.

"You sure, Big V?" Ruby says. "I went pretty hard on him. He might need a break."

"He can handle it."

No, I can't! I don't get a chance to say that out loud because the stinging ache in my limbs returns. I lose all control over my convulsing body. Someone could be throwing knives into an open wound in the middle of my chest and it would feel like butterfly kisses compared to this.

My limbs tremble against the floor.

Nausea.

Throbbing.

Vomit rises in the back of my throat.

Arella drapes her body over mine as if it'll shield me from the stinging pain. It doesn't. Not even a little bit.

"Stop!" She sobs into my chest. "Stop hurting him!"

"Project your immunity onto him!" Victor shouts.

"I can't! Stop! Please!"

"Ruby, go harder!"

Seriously? There's a setting above this one? The torture increases. It's like snake venom, and bee stings, and being mauled by a jaguar, and—

Arella pulls me into her lap, clutching me against her front. She rocks back and forth as my body trembles in her arms. Tears pour down her cheeks as she screams, "Stop hurting him! Stop hurting him! Stop hurting him!"

Somehow, I find the strength to get some words out. "Arella, please, make it stop."

She takes my face into her hands and gives me a squeeze. "I don't know how."

"Please," I beg because she's my only hope. "Make it stop."

My vision's blurry again. I can't feel my legs. *Are they still attached to my body?*

Arella breathes deeply as she mutters inaudible words to herself and rocks me in her grasp. If this is my end, I won't be too mad about it. I'm in the arms of the woman I love. What could be better?

Suddenly, the burning stops. My body goes limp. I don't gasp for air this time. My lungs are too tired for that. Instead, my breaths come out short and ragged. Arella's tears roll down her face and onto my cheeks. I want to wipe her tears away, but I can't feel my arms.

"I never told you to stop!" Victor shouts.

"I didn't," Ruby says through hisses. "I'm still going."

Victor gasps at the same time Pixie does.

"She did it," Pixie says. "She actually did it."

50

TREY

"You monsters!" Arella keeps me tight against her body, and I'm grateful for it. "How could you do this to him? He's barely breathing."

"The kid knows it's for the greater good." Victor stomps toward her and stops only to yank her up by her arm.

I tumble out of her grasp and onto the battle box's floor, too weak to catch myself. I still can't feel my limbs.

"Ruby! Do your thing."

I cry out as the invisible snakes sink their teeth into my skin again.

"Stop!" Arella collapses next to me. She cups my face and shuts her eyes. It takes a moment before the agony disappears and my body stops shaking.

"Are you stinging him?" Victor asks.

"Yes," Ruby hisses.

"Outstanding! That's twice in a row."

I can't open my eyes enough to see it, but I know Victor's grinning. I'll bet this is one of the happiest days of his life. He gets to see me suffer while he performs tests on an Immune. Win-win for him.

"Pixie, how 'bout you give it a shot?" Victor says.

"No!" Arella cups my face tighter. She presses her forehead against mine, whispering something I can't make out. I wait for the ear pain to come. It never does.

"She's blocking it," Pixie says.

I pry my eyes open just enough to see my girl with tears streaming down her cheeks. With a quivering hand, I wipe one away.

I've always been amazed by this woman. At first because she was immune. Then because of her inner strength. Then because of how she got me to fall in love with her so effortlessly. Now she's projecting her immunity onto me. She's absolutely incredible.

For the second time, Victor pulls Arella up by her arm, snatching her away from me.

Arella punches him in the chest. "Let me go!"

Panting, I twist onto my side, then hoist myself onto my elbows. It takes a few breaths before I'm able to push myself onto my knees.

"Quit manhandling her!" My voice comes out coarse, like I've smoked a pack a day for fifty years.

Victor ignores me as he shoves Arella toward the Asian woman.

The flames between my fingers flicker.

"Hold hands with Pixie," Victor orders.

Pixie grabs Arella's hand and keeps her there.

"Ruby, do your thing on Pixie."

Screaming, Pixie falls to her knees. The stings mirror onto my body for a second before I draw back my Empath power to avoid it.

"Stop!" Pixie shouts.

Ruby drops her hand immediately.

Pixie lets go of Arella's hand and pants. "Jesus fucking Christ! Couldn't you have gone easy on me?"

Ruby grits her teeth together apologetically. "Sorry, Pix. That was on my lowest power."

Victor points at Ruby. "Go hold the Ordinary's hand."

With a few clicks of her heels, Ruby does what she's told. Once her hand is joined with Arella's, Pixie is ordered to blow at her. Ruby shrieks toward the ceiling, clutching one of her ears, until the pain stops.

"Sorry, Roobs," Pixie mimics. "That was on my lowest power."

Victor crosses his arms over his chest. "Ordinary, do whatever you did on Trey on the girls."

Arella shakes her head. "I don't even know what I'm doing."

"Go hold Trey's hand again."

Arella doesn't waste any time obeying that request. She stands at my side and grips my arm like it's a lifeline. I think about running and dragging her with me, but I doubt I can make it out of here without one of us getting hurt. For once, I'm glad I can't sense her emotions. The expression on her face is enough for me to know that she's scared to death. *I'm scared too, baby.*

"Both of you," Victor says. "Hit him with all you've got."

A piercing sound stabs my ears as my body burns like it's on fire. Arella squeezes my hand harder, closing her eyes. I fall to my knees, counting at least ten seconds of pure agony before it finally stops. Arella kneels at my side, gripping onto my hand so tight, it hurts. I plant my other hand against the floor to keep myself from collapsing over. My breaths come out in heavy pants.

"Let go of him," Victor says.

"No!" Arella squeezes my hand harder.

Victor wrenches her up by her hair. Hearing her scream hurts me more than what those women have been doing to me. I don't think about it as I shoot up onto my feet, grip Arella by her waist, and yank her behind me. Flames appear in my palm, and I chuck them at the back of my uncle's head. My fireball misses and falls to the floor before disappearing into a cloud of smoke. Stupid, because I rarely miss. My trembling fingers are throwing me off.

Victor twists on his heel and shoots me a death glare. "Did you just throw a fireball at me?"

"I told you to quit manhandling her!"

The auditorium goes silent. The look in Victor's eyes screams murder. The anger radiating off him says he'll do it. I wouldn't put it past him.

Surprisingly, Victor relaxes his shoulders and turns to the women. "Thanks for your time, ladies. You're dismissed."

Without a word, Pixie and Ruby exit through the double doors. The second they're gone, Victor comes at me with a fist up. I push Arella out of the way and duck. She stumbles to the side as I back the other way. As I hoped, Victor follows me, hurling another fist at my face. This time, it lands. My head snaps to the side as pain explodes up my jaw.

"How dare you attack me!" He aims a kick at my chest. I manage to get out of the way, only to get sucked into a tornado. Spinning, it carries me toward the ceiling. Victor circles his wrist in the air as his tornado whips me from side to side, round and round. "I should have gotten rid of you after the police dropped you off on my goddamn doorstep! If I wasn't the only living relative you had left, I would have unloaded your dumb ass with someone else. You've been nothing but a fucking nuisance, you worthless piece of shit!"

I kick, and swim, and jump. I even try using my telekinesis. Nothing works to get me out of his spiraling tornado. I'm trapped, and I'm dizzy.

"I should kill you right now for throwing that fireball at me. Teach you a fucking lesson!"

The air is sucked from my lungs as the tornado disappears. From the ceiling, I fall straight back into the battle box and land on my front. My head bounces back from the impact as agony flares up my cheek. Wheezing, I force myself onto my knees only to find Victor pointing a finger at Arella.

"Quit that shit!" he says.

My girl shoots a dirty look at him. "You've spent all day trying to get me to do this, and *now* you want me to stop?"

The auditorium goes silent again.

From the stands, a deep voice says, "She's got a point, boss."

Victor directs a glare at Craig. "Nobody asked you."

I get to my feet and march across the battle box to stand in front of Arella protectively. "This is over. You have no right to treat her like this. No right to be yelling out orders to her or manhandling her like she's a fucking ragdoll. She's an Ordinary. A person that we, as ZIRDA agents, have sworn to protect."

"Well, aren't you Mr. Righteous tonight?" Victor scoffs and even has the nerve to chuckle. "You don't get it, kid. Within the last day, this Ordinary has gone from being unable to tap into her immunity to activating it while making skin-to-skin contact with you. Then, just now, she projected it onto you while you were near the ceiling. That's way more progress than the last Immune.

"Don't you see? She's it! She's the key we've been looking for. The ultimate win against the Royals. Once we can get her to fully control and project her immunity, she can help us wipe them out of existence. And once we can replicate her immunity to make the rest of us immune too, this could be the end for the Royals. It all begins here—with her."

Having the right intention doesn't justify purposely hurting innocent people. Clearly, Victor has no boundaries when it comes to completing his life's mission of eliminating all the Royals. I'm certain that he'll kill off as many Immunes as it takes to finish the job. Yes, the Royals tried to kill him and they succeeded in killing his younger brother—my father. We both lost people we loved at the hands of the Royals, but at some point, we need to say enough is enough.

When Victor first assigned me to Arella, he said the goal was simply to find out the source of her immunity. No one was supposed to get hurt or kidnapped. Somewhere between here and there, he has justified doing whatever it takes to get what he wants. We can find another way to bring down the Royals. A way that aligns with ZIRDA's values of protecting Ordinaries.

I wish I could say all that to Victor, but it won't change his mind. He's so blinded by his need for vengeance that he's drifted too far off the path of what's right. He thinks it's okay to kill one to save a thousand, but if that one is Arella, he'll have to get through me first.

"Craig, get your ass up here and make yourself useful," Victor says.

In an instant, Craig is in the battle box with us. I keep Arella close behind me.

"Craig has the ability to shrink anything down to the size of a grain of rice," Victor says to Arella. "Unless you want Trey to be squashed under my shoe, you'll project your immunity onto him."

Without a single warning, Craig points at me, and I'm falling. Except, I'm not. The room has gotten bigger. Every passing second makes everything sound louder and echoey.

My already aching body doubles over as I clutch my stomach. Vomit sprays out of my mouth onto the floor, and then I cough as another wave of vomit rises inside me. Arella's shriek vibrates through the air as a giant shoe appears above me.

Someone shakes my arm. My eyes pop open.

Katie leans back into a chair and stares at me with a honeyed smile. *How is this girl always so happy?* If I wasn't an Empath, I'd think it's fake, but the energy I sense from her is light and content.

"Good morning," she says and holds out a bottle of Healing Water to me. She glances at the iPad in her lap. "Actually, no. Good afternoon! How ya feelin'?"

I sit up and glance around. Sterile white cabinets. A sink in the corner. A beeping sound coming from a machine. An IV is taped to my arm, connected to a bag of fluids. I'm on a hospital bed with crisp white sheets. I've been here before. Many times. This is the infirmary on the third floor of Shadow Ridge.

I accept the Healing Water and unscrew the cap. It's hard to move. My arms are sore, and my fingers have lost some dexterity. Still, I put my lips against the opening of the bottle and chug. It's the berry-flavored kind—my least favorite. I didn't even check the label before consuming it. Still, I drink it all in one breath.

"Wow," Katie says. "That's one hell of a party trick."

I press a button on the side of the bed. The top half of the mattress folds upward until it's in a comfortable position for me to lean against. My hazy head has a pounding migraine, and I swear I can still hear Pixie's ringing in my ears.

"Where is she?" My voice comes out scratchy.

"In her room."

The fuck she is. If Arella was in "her room," she'd be in her apartment. "Why aren't you there with her?"

"Victor told me to check on you. He wanted me to make sure you were okay."

I scoff, and it hurts my throat to do so. "He hasn't cared about my well-being since I was a kid. Why start now?"

Last night, Victor almost killed me. I'll bet if no one was around, he would have. When I was trapped in his tornado, I sensed his rage and need to bang me against the ceiling until every bone in my body was in pieces.

"Victor has to care about you somewhat," Katie says. "He's asked me to check on you at least five times a day since that night in the battle box."

That night in the battle box? Instantly, the haze clears from my head. "Say again?"

"I said that Victor's gotta care about—"

"No, no. Not that. What was the last part?"

"Um, that he's asked me to check on you multiple times since that night in the battle box?"

My body stills. "And how many nights ago was that?"

"Three."

"Three?" *She's gotta be kidding me.*

"Being shrunk does a lot of trauma to a person's body. Not to mention you were shrunk and reshrunk almost ten times in a matter of five minutes."

I don't remember that. I must have passed out by that point. I point to the IV sticking out of my arm. "What the hell is this for?"

"Fluids and pain medication, according to the nurse. She said you'd need at least another two days to fully heal, but Victor insisted on getting you back into the battle box today."

I let out a *fuck that* chuckle. "What makes him think I'm gonna willingly allow people to torment me like that?"

"I don't think you have a choice. Victor won't stop this research just because it causes you a little pain."

"A little? I was knocked out cold for three days! I'd rather be a lion's chew toy than ever get volun-told to participate in that bullshit again."

"While you've been out, other people have been volunteering. Victor's tried countless methods to get the Immune to project onto someone other than you. So far, every test has been unsuccessful." Katie straightens her back and smiles. "Now do you think you can get up? We don't want to keep Victor waiting."

51

ARELLA

Two days ago, I woke up to Katie strolling into my prison room, carrying a food tray.

"Wakey wakey!" she said in her overly cheery voice. I wasn't sure if she did that because she's naturally cheerful or if she thinks it would make me less anxious about being held captive against my will. "I wasn't sure what you'd want, so I grabbed one of everything." She placed the tray onto the nightstand. It was covered with an assortment of baked breakfast goods and a glass of milk. Then she drew out a metal key from her pocket to uncuff my ankle from the bedframe.

Before going to sleep the night before, I had convinced Katie to cuff my ankle instead of my wrist. It was hard to sleep with my arm like that.

"Last night was a big night for you," Katie said. "You made the first step to controlling your immunity. Victor's so thrilled, he added four new meetings to your calendar to try it again."

I hated how she said all that like I was an employee here. I sat up and rubbed the crust from my eyes. "Where's Trey?"

Katie scooted her folding chair closer to the bed. Her energy, all anxious and apprehensive, wafted toward me. "He's still in the infirmary."

"Is he okay?"

"He's not dead, if that's what you're wondering." Between Katie's uneasy emotions shooting at me and the troubled look on her face, I assumed Trey wasn't doing too hot.

When Craig the Hulk shrunk him over and over, Trey threw up four times and coughed up blood. No matter how much I begged, Victor refused to let me hold him. That heartless man kept pinning me down and screaming at me to project my immunity onto Trey from across the battle box. Projecting onto Trey while he was in the tornado had felt like a one-off chance. I didn't know how I had done it or how to do it again.

I cried hysterically while Victor kept shouting, "Focus! Focus!" into my ear. Because, you know, shouting at people like that is helpful. When Trey, the size of a cat, slumped onto the floor and didn't look like he was breathing, I lost it.

I screamed at the ceiling, and somehow, I did something to make Trey return to his normal size. After that, no matter how hard Craig tried, he couldn't shrink Trey again.

Then and only then did Victor call for someone to drag poor, unconscious Trey to the infirmary. In the meantime, Katie and Craig escorted me back to my prison room. With my ankle cuffed to the bed, I cried myself to sleep, wondering if I'd ever see Trey again.

Hearing that Trey was still alive gave me a tiny bit of relief—assuming Katie was telling the truth.

When I finished eating breakfast, Katie directed me to the shower and handed me a new set of clothes. I could already tell this outfit would fit me better.

"It's from my own closet," Katie said. "We're about the same size, so I figured why not? Your current outfit was plucked from the lost and found. If you want your pajamas instead, they're clean now."

"I appreciate you sharing your clothes with me."

Twenty minutes later, I stepped out of the bathroom, wearing a plain black V-neck and some gray leggings.

For the rest of the day, they kept me in the "battle box"—a fancy name for their torture station disguised as a boxing ring. I held hands with countless *volunteers*, as Victor called them, while Pixie and Ruby tormented each person with their powers. I tried everything I could to protect them but failed.

Around nightfall—not that I knew for sure, because I hadn't seen a single window in this place—Katie dropped me off in a small lab room with a lady wearing a white lab coat.

Throughout the night, White Coat Lady performed a series of tests on me—Everything from checking my reflexes to drawing blood samples to taking my handprint. She examined every part of my mouth, eyes, ears, and vagina. I had never been so violated in my life, and that was saying a lot after spending three years with a man who used to force himself on me. What was she looking for?

White Coat Lady spent another eternity asking me health-related questions, some of which Katie had already asked me. Some of my answers made her ask follow-up questions. Other times, she just nodded and moved on.

Once the interrogation was over, the White Coat Lady secured me to a medical bed. The leather straps were so tight against my wrists and ankles, they pinched my skin.

"Shield yourself from the shock," she said as a sizzling lightning ball appeared in her palms. "No!"

The lady dropped the orb onto me. A surge of electricity rippled through my veins. I screamed out, and my body convulsed, tugging against the restraints.

"Picture something around your body." Another sizzling ball appeared in her hand. "Armor, a box, a glass tank, anything that will protect you."

The glowing ball landed on my chest again. I yelled toward the ceiling as brutal torture tore through my limbs.

She did it again.

And again.

And again.

Every time, I was unable to protect myself, no matter how badly I wanted to. From the content emotions I sensed from her, she didn't feel bad for hurting me.

I heaved for air when the electrocution finally stopped. *Is it over?* Something pinched the side of my neck, then White Coat Lady placed a syringe onto a metal tray.

My words came out between short breaths. "What did you just do to me?"

"It's a z-drug called perrizophine," the lady said, like she drugged people all the time without their consent. She probably did. "This small dose will deactivate your immunity for a few hours. At least, we're going to see if it does."

I didn't know if it deactivated my immunity, but it had definitely deactivated my baby's ability to sense people. All of a sudden, I couldn't sense White Coat Lady's emotions anymore.

The door opened, then Victor sauntered in. The sight of him disgusted me. "Any progress?"

"Not much," White Coat Lady said.

"Did you hit her with the perrizo yet?"

"Just did."

"Great. Lemme take a look at her."

White Coat Lady stepped back to give Victor some space. With both hands, he held my head still. As he stared into my eyes, I balled up some saliva in my mouth. The second a black cloud smoked up in his pupils, I spat at him.

Victor bounced back with a groan. "You nasty little bitch."

I'd been called worse by my ex, so I didn't care what he called me.

White Coat Lady held out a towel to Victor. "Sir."

Victor wiped his face off, then tossed the towel behind him. "Got any duct tape?"

From a drawer, the lady pulled out a roll of silver tape and ripped off a piece. Victor took it from her. I squirmed as he tried to seal it over my mouth. Since I could only move so much, he won our battle. I panted through my nose as he ripped a second piece of tape off the roll.

"For good measure," Victor said as he stuck it over my mouth.

Within seconds, that black cloud took over the whites of his eyes again. What was he trying to do? Burn a hole through my face? Read my mind? Or maybe—I internally gasped. Was it mind control? That was how all these people worked for him so willingly, wasn't it? He was trying to turn me into one of his minions. Maybe it worked on the other people, but it wouldn't work on me. Well, they weren't *people*, exactly. They had to be aliens. Aliens who could take the form of humans.

If not that, maybe they were X-men. Katie claimed they were simply humans who were born with powers. Were X-men born with powers? I couldn't remember. I'd only seen one X-men movie, and it was a long time ago.

With a huff, Victor stepped back, and his pupils returned to normal. "It's no use. Not even the perrizo is lowering her immunity walls. I suppose since the z-drug didn't work, we can rule out that she's part Zordi and that immunity is her gift."

White Coat Lady crinkled her face. "How could she be part Zordi? It's impossible for us to reproduce with Ordis."

Ahh. That explained why Trey said he was infertile. It wasn't that he couldn't make babies. He just couldn't make babies with regular humans. It all made sense. Except, not. If it was "impossible" for these aliens to reproduce with humans, then how did I get pregnant?

Victor scoffed loudly. "It's also impossible for someone to be immune to our powers, yet here she is. I'm not saying I had bets on her being part Zordi. That was just one of the many theories I came up with to explain this freak of nature."

Me? A freak of nature? Of all people to be calling someone a freak of nature, why was it the man who could turn his eyeballs completely black?

The two of them continued talking, but I couldn't make out their words anymore. Suddenly, my eyelids felt heavy . . .

YESTERDAY, I WOKE UP FROM A NIGHTMARE, DRIPPING WITH SWEAT. I GASPED FOR AIR AS I SPRUNG upright.

Katie's chair was empty. The only light was coming from the crack under the door. It was too dark to read the wall clock. It must have been early if Katie wasn't around yet.

I had to use the bathroom, but I couldn't get in there with my ankle handcuffed to the bed. As far as I knew, Katie was the only person with a key, and I had no way to contact her.

After a while of tossing and turning, I concluded that I couldn't fall back asleep while my bladder was that full. The thought of wetting the bed was too embarrassing for me to consider. Maybe I could ask that guard to get Katie for me.

Wait . . . Where's the guard? Normally, I could sense his presence out there, even if he was only feeling content. I didn't sense anyone outside the door. I sat up again to see if I could spot his shadow through the bottom crack. No shadow.

Why would Victor leave me unguarded? Maybe something happened and everyone left. That terrified me. They wouldn't ditch me here all alone, restrained to a bed, would they? Why was the idea of that worse than the idea of them taking me back to the battle box?

A while later, the door crept open, then Katie tiptoed in. She used the flashlight on her phone to see her way to her chair. Quietly, she sat and did something on her iPad as the sound of that dreaded chain lock slid into place.

So there is *someone out there.* Why couldn't I sense them? Why couldn't I sense Katie either? That drug the White Coat Lady injected into me had to have worn off by now.

Oh no. I glanced at my belly and gave it a rub. *Please be okay.*

Katie glanced up from her iPad and found me staring at her. She jolted back and slapped a hand over her chest. "Ah! You scared me."

"Sorry." I half meant it.

"I didn't realize you were awake." She stood to flip the light on.

I squinted from the brightness.

Katie returned to her chair, scooting it closer to me before settling back onto it. "How did you sleep?"

"I had a bad dream."

"What was your dream about?"

Victor holding me back while those two women torture Trey until he takes his last breath. What else? "Um, I'll just say that you people aren't only scary in real life."

"I'm sorry." She offered me a sympathetic look. I couldn't tell if she meant it or not. Her emotions weren't coming to me. "What's that like?"

"Being surrounded by scary people?"

"No, dreaming."

I tilted my head to the side. "You've never had a dream?"

"Zordis don't dream. For some reason, we can't. There's no study that explains why, but there are theories. The one I believe the most is that because we only need to sleep every two days, our brain completely shuts down during that time. Therefore, no dreams."

"Weird." But not as weird as how they could go two days without sleeping. That explained why Trey was up all night so often.

"Sooo," Katie said, "what's it like?"

"Um, I guess it's like living real life, but it's in your head and crazy things can happen."

She nodded slowly with her mouth partly open, like she was trying really hard to understand the concept of a dream. "Fascinating. I've heard that sometimes it feels like a hallucination or like you're watching a movie."

"I guess so."

"I'd like to experience a dream one day. It sounds fun."

A long silence sat between us. It felt partly awkward and partly calming. Most of my time here had been chaotic. That was the most normal conversation I'd had since being kidnapped.

Katie cleared her throat. "He's still in the infirmary, in case you're wondering."

I was wondering, so I was glad she told me without me having to ask. "Is he okay?"

"The nurse said his vitals look better than yesterday. He still hasn't woken up though."

"Like at all?"

"At all."

The poor guy. Trey must have been in really bad shape if he couldn't wake up. *Wait . . .* I narrowed my eyes at Katie. "How do I know he's still alive? What if you people have already killed him, and you're lying to me about it?"

"I guess you'll just have to trust me. If you don't, you can trust that Victor won't get rid of the only person you've successfully projected your immunity onto. Anyway"—Katie slapped her thighs with her palms—"are ya hungry? Should I go get you some breakfast?"

"Actually, could you let me into the bathroom first? I've had to go for a while."

"Sure thing." She released my ankle, and I practically ran to the toilet.

After I did my business, I checked the water. Only yellow, no red. I leaned down to inspect it a little closer, just in case I missed a speck. Still no red. I was sure of it though. I'd been sure since the moment Katie walked into this room and I couldn't sense her. Maybe I wasn't bleeding now, but I would eventually.

I braced myself against the sink as the reality of what had happened sunk in. I was sad. Why was I so sad? It was an unplanned pregnancy with a man who turned out to be a mutant with superpowers. Two nights ago, I saw fire come out of his hand. His *hand.* Who knew what else he could do?

His baby had the power to sense other people's emotions. If a Zordi fetus could do that from inside the womb, what else could it do? Would it have thrown fireballs inside me? Would I have had the power to make fire come out of my hands too? How insane! I should have been relieved that the baby was gone, but I wasn't.

Before I was kidnapped, Trey and I talked over the phone about raising this child together. Stupidly, I believed with all my heart that it was something he wanted. Especially since he still wanted me after I lied about sleeping with "some guy from college." I figured that once we had patched things up, I could confess that I'd lied and prove he was the father, then everything would be okay.

I didn't realize how much I wanted to be a mother—until the opportunity was stolen from me. I collapsed to the tile floor and cried into my hands. It wasn't a silent cry either. It was one of those ugly cries with my mouth fully open as I wailed.

The bathroom door jerked open and hit me. Katie popped her head in. "You okay?"

I shook my head, unable to answer with words.

She gestured for me to move over. I did, scooting closer to the toilet so she could get in. Once she was through the door, she clicked it shut.

Katie sat on the floor with me and rubbed a tender hand over my shoulder. "What's wrong?"

I didn't have it in me to explain. The only thing I had the strength for was to cry. Katie didn't force me to speak. She simply circled her arms around me and hugged me tight. I let her because something about her made me feel at ease. Plus, I was willing to take any form of comfort.

We stayed like that until my sobbing subsided. I wasn't sure how long it was.

Through hiccups, I asked, "What happens to you people when you die?"

She pressed her eyebrows together. "What do you mean?"

"Like what happens to your bodies?"

"Um, we just . . . die. Obviously, we lose our powers, and everything about our bodies become like Ordinaries. Well, except for Shifters. If they die in another form, whether it's an animal, an object, or another person, they'll stay that way."

Shifters? Apparently, that wasn't just a thing in books and movies. "Does anything special happen when a Zordi dies *before* they're born?"

At first, Katie's face scrunched together, then her eyes went wide and she whispered, "Are you pregnant?"

"Was." That single word almost made me burst into tears again.

Still hushed, she said, "Are you saying you were pregnant with . . . a Zordi?"

I nodded.

That mousey voice of hers disappeared as she continued whispering, "That can't be. Our biological makeups are too different for fertilization to happen. The Ordinary egg isn't strong enough to hold the nature of a Zordi sperm."

I stared at the bathroom floor. "Maybe whatever makes me immune to your powers also makes me immune to all that."

Katie thought for a moment, then shook her head. "Nope. It's impossible. Your immunity has nothing to do with your reproductive organs. For you to have conceived a child with a Zordi, you'd have to be a Zordi with Zordi eggs in your ovaries. It's impossible for you to be one of us because you don't have any gifts. And if immunity was your gift, it would have been turned off by the perrizophine. Last night, your body was affected by only the sedative part of the perrizo, and you took to it faster than the average Zordi, which further confirms that you're an Ordi. Also, our zense doesn't activate around you."

"Zense? What's that?"

"It's a little tingle we get in our chests whenever we're within an arm's length of each other."

"Interesting." By the look on Katie's face, I could tell she was about to ask, so I beat her to it. "No, my chest doesn't tingle around you guys."

"Immune *and* a Mind Reader. You really are something special." She leaned in to me again, lowering her voice. "How are you so sure you were pregnant with a Zordi baby?"

"I've only slept with one man recently. And for the last few days, up until last night, I was sensing everyone's emotions."

Katie gasped, then lowered her voice so much, I could barely hear her. "Your baby was an Empath. You must have been at least seven or eight weeks along. That's when our mind powers begin developing in the womb."

That timing was right. "Mind powers?"

"All Zordis are born with three gifts. Our mind power is the most powerful because it begins developing the earliest. Our body and elemental powers are determined before birth, but those don't develop until we're about a year old. Then, it's not until puberty when our powers become fully developed."

It was nice to know that my baby couldn't have thrown fireballs or made tornados inside my uterus.

Katie went back to whispering. "Does he know?"

I match her tone. "Does who know what?"

"The father. Trey." She points at my stomach with her eyes. "Does he know?"

"Yeah, I told him."

"He didn't think the baby was his, did he?"

I shook my head as a single tear rolled down my cheek. "No, he didn't."

"I wouldn't have believed you either. Even now, knowing that your baby was sensing emotions in the womb, it's *still* hard to believe." Katie leaned in to my ear, then said softly yet firmly, "Victor cannot find out about this."

I whisper back. "Why?"

"Think about it. He's already doing whatever he can to find out the source of your immunity and to get you to control it. Imagine what he'd do if he knew you could carry a Zordi child."

I pictured myself restrained to a bed as a bunch of Zordi men violated me while Victor sat on the sidelines, taking notes. It would go on for months to years before I was pregnant again. Assuming it was possible for me to carry a half-human, half-wizard baby to term, Victor would have his hands on the world's first half-and-half baby. I didn't even want to think about what he'd do with that child.

Katie stood and offered me her hand. "Come on. We've gotta get outta here before they find it suspicious that I'm in the bathroom with you for this long."

Sighing, I took her hand and allowed her to help me off the floor.

52

ARELLA

I t's been three days since I've seen Trey alive. I trust that Katie's telling me the truth, but I won't fully believe her until I actually see him. She's been giving me updates on his condition after she checks on him every few hours. So far, he still hasn't woken up. Knowing he's been out cold for this long worries me.

"Welcome back," Victor says as I step into the boxing ring. I do it willingly because I don't want Craig touching me again.

I can't sense Victor or Craig's energy. I can't sense Pixie, Ruby, or Derek either. Suddenly, I feel the most alone since being kidnapped. Before, I had the presence of my unborn baby. Now I have no one. I don't even have Katie. After she fed me breakfast, she left, and I haven't seen her since. It was Craig who brought me lunch and escorted me down here.

While I hug myself in the corner, Victor speaks to his four minions in a low voice. I can't make out anything he's saying. Judging by the head nods coming from the others, it looks like Victor's giving them instructions.

Behind me, the double doors open with a squeak. Katie strolls in with Trey at her side. He looks rough: messy hair, dark beard lining his jaw, and grayish skin. His gaze never leaves me as he climbs up the stairs and into the battle box. Meanwhile, Katie finds a seat in the front row of the auditorium.

"Now that everyone's here," Victor says, "let's start. Ordinary, go hold Trey's hand."

I don't need to move because in an instant, Trey is at my side. A troubled storm brews in his eyes as he intertwines his fingers with mine. I hate how normal it feels to hold his hand and to feel the warmth his touch sends up my arm. He's the very reason I'm here, and I shouldn't be comforted by him. Still, I'm relieved to see him alive. No matter what he's done or how we got here, he doesn't deserve to be tortured.

Victor takes a few steps back until he's leaning against the ropes. "Today's objective is to see how versatile the Ordinary's immunity can be. Once we get an idea of that, we'll take more time in the upcoming days to explore each of her skills to strengthen them."

Days? That's how long they plan to torture Trey in front of me? One second is already too long.

"Ordinary, your first goal is to see if you can project your immunity onto Trey without us hurting him first. Think you can do that?"

"She has a name," Trey growls.

Victor points a stern finger at him. I squeeze Trey's hand to protect him from whatever powers Victor is about to use on him. Nothing happens. Instead, Victor shouts, "Don't speak unless you're spoken to."

Trey squeezes my hand back as if to say he'll protect me; however, *he's* the one who needs protection. "Stop referring to her as *Ordinary*. She has a name."

"I will call her whatever the fuck I please. Now, are you gonna shut your goddamn mouth, or do you wanna keep being a nuisance?"

Trey grits his teeth together. "I never signed up to be your test puppet."

"You signed up for this when you accepted this mission."

"No. I signed up to find out the source of her immunity. This"—Trey gestures around the room—"is not what I—"

"Shut your fuckin' mouth!" Victor crosses his arms over his chest. "If you delay this session one more time, I'm releasing you from this mission. Actually, I'll be releasing you from all of ZIRDA. Speak another word without my permission. I dare you. Craig can escort you straight out to the waterfall, and you'll never be allowed back for any reason. Is that what you want?"

Trey clenches his jaw together as he sucks in a breath and slowly lets it out. I can't sense the anger radiating off him, but I can definitely see it. Keeping his job must be important to him, because he doesn't say another word.

"Anyway," Victor says, "Ordinary, project your immunity onto him. When you're ready, Pixie will blow his ears. Again, your goal is to prevent him from feeling any pain before it comes. Got it?"

I glance up at Trey, who looks back at me with a *you can do it* confidence in his eyes. It makes me believe I can.

"Take a moment to prepare yourself," Victor says. "Let Pixie know when you're ready."

I close my eyes and replay the things they did to Trey three nights ago. I hear him screaming. I see his body shaking against the floor. I picture him throwing up blood. Then I open my eyes, squeeze Trey's hand, and give Pixie a nod.

She closes the distance between us until she's three steps away. Then she puckers her lips and blows.

"Fuck!" Trey tries to cover his ears as I squeeze his hand with all my might. Barely a second later, he puts his arms down and breathes normally again.

"Did she do it?" Victor asks.

"I'm blowing," Pixie says. "He seems to be okay."

"Good." Victor claps as if we're part of a show. He should get a refund for his ticket because I never auditioned for this play, and I don't want to keep performing in it. "Immune, let's try that again. This time, *really* focus."

I squeeze Trey's hand with both of mine. Pixie blows again. The same thing happens. Trey screams in agony as he uses his free hand to cover an ear. *Does that even do anything?*

"Try again," Victor says.

And this goes on for the next half hour. No matter how much I beg, Victor keeps ordering Pixie to hurt Trey, who's on his knees, gasping for air. I kneel in front of him and cup his face. His cheeks are red, and the whites of his eyes are too.

"I'm so sorry," I plead in a low voice, hoping he'll forgive me. "I want to shield you from the pain, but I don't know how."

"Don't apologize," he whispers as he wipes the tears from my face with his thumb. "None of this is your fault."

My body hiccups from all the sobbing I've been doing. Trey knits his brows together and presses his lips into a hard line. He looks like he's a second away from putting me over his shoulder and making a run for it. A part of me hopes that's why he's still here and is just waiting for the right time. I'm not the only one who needs escaping anymore.

"Stand up," Victor orders. "Let's raise the stakes a little. Ruby, how 'bout you try?"

Oh no. Not her. Whatever power Ruby has seems to feel like death crawling through the bloodstream.

Trey helps me to my feet, and I seize his hand. He closes his eyes, bracing himself for the pain. I shut my eyes too, just as Ruby raises her arm and hisses. *Don't hurt him. Don't hurt him.* I wait for Trey to scream, but he doesn't.

"She's blocking it," Ruby says.

I don't dare open my eyes because I can't lose concentration. I don't know if she's still stinging him or not.

"Pixie, you give it a shot."

A moment later, Pixie says, "She's blocking mine too."

"Excellent!" Victor says, clapping. "What progress! Let's move on. Immune, your next goal is to protect Trey from an ice ball. Derek?"

On cue, Derek stands from his squat and draws an arm back. A sparkling ice sphere flies through the air, straight at Trey's head.

"Fuck that." Trey ducks and drags me down with him. The ice ball lands behind us and shatters against the floor. I don't get a chance to take another breath before a second ice ball soars through the air and hits Trey right in the stomach. He coughs and falls to his knees as another ice ball whizzes through the air. It hits him again, right in the face. That's going to leave a mark.

"Stop!" I shout. "I don't know how to shield him from stuff like that."

"And three days ago, you didn't know how to shield him at all," Victor says. "So try harder!"

Derek readies another ice ball and launches it at Trey. I rush in front of Trey and brace myself for the impact. It never comes. Instead, I'm tackled to the floor as the ice ball flies past me and shatters into pieces.

"What are you doing?" Trey shouts as he does a push-up over me.

"What do you think I was doing?" I yell back as I shove him off me. "I was trying to save you!"

"By using yourself as a barrier? Are you fucking crazy?"

"Obviously, my immunity isn't working. What else do you expect me to do?"

We get to our feet as the auditorium goes quiet and I ignore the pain in my tailbone.

Trey shakes his head at me as he says in a low voice, "Don't ever do that again. Ever."

Victor taps his chin. "Maybe testing with elementals is rushing things a little. Let's go back to internal powers, shall we? Immune, your next goal is to project onto Trey without touching him and to do it before Ruby has a chance to bite him with her powers. Let her know when you're ready."

A part of me wants to tell Victor he can go shove a stick up his ass. The other part of me is realistic and knows I don't have a choice. So I close my eyes and concentrate. The auditorium remains quiet for almost a minute. No one dares to interrupt my process. Finally, I keep my eyes shut as I raise up a thumb.

No one says anything for a moment.

Victor is the first to break the silence. "Are you attacking him?"

"I am," Ruby says through hisses. "She's blocking it."

"Excellent! What an improvement!"

I reopen my eyes, then Trey falls to his knees, shrieking. *Oh no!* I rush to cup his face. At an instant, he stops screaming.

In the corner of my eye, I see Ruby lower her hand. "She must have stopped projecting while I was still biting him."

"Interesting," Victor says. "Let's try this. Immune, come to me."

I don't. Not that I can anyway, because Trey rushes off the floor and stands in front of me.

"No," Trey says.

"What?" Victor snarls.

"I said no! Arella doesn't want to be a part of this. She never did. We're done."

"We'll be done when I say so." Victor strides over and takes me by the hand, tearing me away from the only person here who cares about my well-being. "Pixie, Ruby, Craig, you three hit Trey with your mind powers at the same time. Derek, I'll hold her down while you throw ice balls at her."

"What?" Trey shouts. "Hell no! You've gotta be crazy if—"

"Go!"

Trey drops to the floor as he covers his ears and screams. Slowly, his body shrinks until he's the size of a cat.

"Stop!" I rush toward him, but Victor yanks me back by my hair. An ice ball zooms at me and hits my arm. I cry out as the pain shoots up my shoulder.

"Project your immunity onto him," Victor orders.

Another ice ball soars toward my face. I duck while Trey's high-pitched wails echo throughout the auditorium. Victor sidesteps to dodge the ball, and it shatters against the floor.

"Stop!" I shout, but another ice ball is already whizzing through the air. It hits my stomach. I clutch my front as I fall to my knees and burst into a sob. "I can't save him! Not while I'm being attacked!"

"That's the point. You need to learn how to project your immunity, even when you're distracted and under pressure. Derek will stop hurting you once Trey stops screaming."

I punch at Victor's hands that are still gripping my hair. "Let me go!"

A spiky ice ball rockets straight at me. I duck to the side. The spikes glisten under the light as it flies past my arm so close, it tears the sleeve of my shirt. Victor releases my hair to dodge the ball.

Free now, I race to save Trey. I'm halfway across the boxing ring when my feet are lifted off the ground in a tornado. The air leaves my lungs as I spin in circles. Then I collapse to the ground, back at Victor's feet.

He jerks me up by my arm and pins my back against the ropes. "That worthless piece of shit is going to die if you don't help him."

Trey's screams echo from across the boxing ring.

"Project your immunity onto him. Focus. Picture yourself projecting a shield around him. What color is it? What shape is it? What is it made out of? Center your mind around those concepts." Victor steps aside and gives Derek a nod.

Derek doesn't waste a second producing another spiky ice ball in his hand and chucking it at me.

"I'm imagining the shield," I say through tears as I dodge the sharp sphere. "It's not working."

"Try something else. Bubble wrap. A brick wall. Couch cushions. A house. Pick something. Imagine every little detail of it and focus!"

I close my eyes and center all my energy in Trey's direction. I imagine the bubble wrap. He keeps screaming. I imagine the brick wall. Then the couch cushions. Then the house. He's still screaming as Victor continues shouting at me. I don't know why he thinks that's helpful. It's making me lose all my concentration.

With deep breaths, I tune Victor out. Then I imagine a wave of ocean water rushing toward Trey, drowning him with my immunity. While he's under that water, no one can touch him. No one can hurt him. The water circles around him, while still giving him pockets of air to breathe in. He's safe under my water. He's protected. They can't hurt him.

Finally, the screaming stops. I open my eyes. The sound of a balloon being blown into resonates through the auditorium as Trey's body expands back to normal size. Craig is still pointing at him, Ruby is still hissing, and Pixie is still puckering her lips, but the screaming has stopped.

Victor grins and claps. "Good job."

I rush across the floor and drop to my knees. Trey's body is limp as I cradle him against my chest. He pants heavily as tears stream down both our faces.

"How could you do this to him?" I shout at all of them because I don't blame only Victor. He may be their leader, but the rest of them are all choosing to do this too. And for what? A stupid paycheck? Is torturing people really worth a few dollars?

Suddenly, Trey lurches upward. He raises an arm into the air with his fingers outstretched. A small garbage bin whizzes through the air from across the room. He catches it in midair and heaves into it. I stand and step back as the smell of vomit fills my nostrils.

Any other time, I'd be reeling over just witnessing Trey move an object by merely summoning it with his hand, but it's the least weird thing I've seen all week.

"Anyone got a theory as to how this Ordi is immune to our powers?" Derek asks.

"She's probably an alien," Pixie says.

Funny, I've been thinking the same thing about them.

"She's gotta have a gene defect," Ruby says.

Trey's coughs echo throughout the auditorium as he vomits into the garbage bin some more.

"We've done thorough DNA testing on her," Victor says. "We've also cross-referenced her results with the other Immunes. There's no DNA pattern to link them. Not a single one."

"What's your theory, Big V?" Derek asks.

"Oh, I dunno. I have a few. Everything from radioactive spiders to sorcery. No matter what we do, we can't figure it out."

They're all having this conversation as if the man they just tortured isn't puking his guts up right in front of them. Doesn't anyone care about Trey?

"I've gotta give him some credit," Ruby says, staring at Trey with an *ick* face. "Most people throw up within the first minute."

"Ladies," Victor says, "why don't you two take Trey up to the infirmary? Derek, you are dismissed."

I feel helpless as Pixie and Ruby slump Trey's arms over their shoulders and drag him out of the box. I'm about to follow them when Victor seizes my arm. He holds me tight and waits until the women have left with Trey before he speaks.

"What did you picture in your head?"

I yank my arm back and shoot him a nasty look. "Don't touch me."

Victor slaps me across the face, and my head snaps to the side. I've had worse, so I simply cup a palm against my burning cheek and continue glaring at him like he's more disgusting than a maggot in my sandwich.

"Answer my question. What did you picture?"

"I'm not telling."

I expect him to smack me again. I even brace myself for it. Instead, Victor narrows his eyes at me before turning to his security guard.

"Hey, Craig. Don't you think Katie will look just as cute when she's the size of a button?"

From the stands, Katie's eyes go wide. The second Craig takes one giant step toward her, I blurt, "A brick wall."

Victor raises a hand, making Craig stop in his tracks. "Come again?"

"I imagined a brick wall."

"What color?"

"Red and brown."

"How tall?"

"I don't know? Pretty tall? It surrounded him in a circle. Kind of like he was at the bottom of a well." I can't believe how convincing I sound.

Victor takes a moment to process what I told him, then says, "Interesting."

53

TREY

"How long was I out for?" I ask Katie when I wake up in the infirmary again. She's on a chair at my bedside, typing something on her iPad.

In her sweet little voice, she says, "It's been about seven hours."

I drop my head back onto the pillow and let out a breath of relief. I swear, if she would have said I'd been out for another three days, I would have waltzed up to my uncle with the biggest fireball I can make and hold it against his face until his skin melted off.

I rub my face with my palms. "What time is it?"

"You just missed dinner. It's almost nine."

Dinner? That sounds good. The emptiness in my stomach is beginning to get excruciatingly painful. I can't remember the last time I ate.

"Want some Healing Water?" Katie holds out a bottle of heaven to me.

This time, I read the label first. Lemon-lime, my favorite. When I finish drinking it, I toss the empty bottle into the air and point at it as it flies across the room and lands in the trash.

I'm surprised my powers are working. Last night after I climbed into this medical bed, I pointed at the blanket to pull it up, and it barely hovered. Poor thing fell limply to the floor. No matter how many times I pointed at it, it wouldn't rise.

Technically, I don't need a blanket, since my body will regulate my internal temperature during my sleep, but I like having a blanket for the comfort it provides. I was too weak to bend over to pick it up, so I figured I'd ask the nurse to do it whenever she came in to check my vitals. I fell asleep before she arrived. It was either her or Katie who must have picked up the blanket and draped it over me.

Katie crosses one leg over the other, then places her hands over the iPad in her lap. "So, you're a Kinetic?"

"Yeah." I press a button on the bed. With a mechanical buzzing sound, the mattress folds upward.

"You like it?"

A little *eh* grunt comes out as I exhale. "I like it more than my mind power."

"Do you wanna share what that is?"

Usually, Zordis don't openly discuss what their mind powers are. Many powers are seen as intrusive or dangerous, so it's cultural to keep that information private. Mine is a power that falls into the intrusive category. I'm not a person who'll tell people what my mind power is unprompted, but when asked, I don't mind sharing. "I'm an Empath."

A rush of adrenaline races through Katie. She's good at hiding her emotions. If I wasn't an Empath, I wouldn't have a clue that her anxiety just spiked, because she shows no signs of it on her face. If knowing I can read emotions makes her nervous, that means she's hiding something. Now I want to know: What's she hiding?

"I'm a PMT," Katie says as she works to regulate her nerves. I'm pretty impressed. Within seconds, she's back to feeling content.

I rack my brain, trying to figure out what PMT means.

"Premonitioner," she says.

"So, you're a Seer?"

"Not exactly. Seers can control what they see and get their visions on demand. PMTs can't control either. We see whatever decides to come to us, and our visions come randomly. Mine only come when I touch someone's hands, and it doesn't happen every time I touch someone. My visions can last up to ten seconds, but typically, it's just a two-second flash, and it's always from that person's point of view. Because I rarely have context, I rarely understand them."

"You had a vision the first time we met, didn't you? When we shook hands."

She nods slightly.

"What did you see?"

A tiny smirk creeps over her lips. "I saw you punch me."

"What?"

"Yeah. Right here in the face." She points at her left cheek.

"Well, shit. I'm sorry." I've never hit a woman before. I'm not sure why I'd start now or why Katie. The girl looks as fragile as a carton of eggs. If I punch her, she'll be down for the count. "Do your visions always come true?"

"Not always. If they're bad, I'll do things to prevent them. Like once, I went to lunch with a friend and I got a vision of her falling off a boat to her death. She hasn't been on a boat since."

"Do you know why I hit you?"

She shakes her head. "That's the thing, my visions only show me *what* happens, never *why*."

"I can relate. My powers only tell me *what* people feel, never *why*."

"Speaking of which, how are you feeling? Better enough to get back into the battle box tonight?"

I let out a deep *you've gotta be fucking kidding* laugh. "Hell no."

"Victor won't like that answer, so I'll just tell him you need a few more minutes to rest before we head down there." Katie picks up her iPad and begins typing, except the device is backward. The screen faces me. I'm about to say something until my name catches my eye.

Trey, read carefully. Camera behind me. On the way to the elevators, we'll pass a supply closet on the right. It's unlocked. Put your hand over my mouth and drag me into it. I'll explain there. Ask me for more Healing Water when you're done reading this and you're ready to go.

My heart rate kicks up. I do everything I can not to show it on my face. What does she need to explain to me in private? Is this a trap? Should I do it anyway?

Only one way to find out. "Could I get some more Healing Water?"

Katie shines one of her many smiles my way. "Of course."

After she discreetly flips her iPad back over and clicks a few buttons, probably deleting all evidence of that note, she heads to the mini fridge in the corner. When she comes back, she has another bottle of Healing Water in her hands. This time, it's the plain water flavor.

I drink it in its entirety with a good feeling that I'm gonna need all the healing I can get.

"Welp," Katie says with a slap of her thighs, "we should get going. Don't wanna keep Victor waiting."

I let out a bitter grunt as I slide my aching body off the bed. Katie plucks my leather jacket off a hook by the door and hands it to me. I slip into it, then follow her out of the infirmary.

The hallway is silent as I trail behind her. We pass a security guard patrolling the area. He barely looks up from his phone as we cross paths. Every echo of our footsteps makes my heart pound harder. The anxious energy simmering in Katie's gut makes me anxious too. I read the signs outside each door as we pass them.

My heart skips a beat when I spot a door coming up marked SUPPLY CLOSET. I expand my powers to check if anyone's around. The closest emotions I sense are from four people in a room around the corner. I don't waste a second. I snatch Katie into my arms with a hand over her mouth. She pretends to struggle as I drag her into the closet with me.

Once inside, I let her go and she turns the lock. A tiny fireball appears in my palm, illuminating the many mops and spray bottles around us.

"We don't have much time," Katie says in a low voice. My flames dance across her sweet and innocent facial features, but gone is her mousey voice and that ever-present smile. Replacing it is a firm tone coupled with a frown that means business. "There aren't cameras in here, but there are out there. If someone up in security saw you nab me, we have about one minute before they're here, so listen carefully."

"Wait." I put my hand up, then magnify my mind power toward the security room. In that general area, I sense energy from two people. Neither seem alarmed. "We're good."

"How are you so sure?"

"Do you really want me to explain, or are you gonna tell me why you told me to kidnap you into a supply closet?"

"Right. Okay, Victor is planning to get rid of you the second the Immune projects her immunity onto someone besides you. He's pretty confident she can do it. I overheard him giving orders to Craig to shrink you, then play off your death like it was an accident during testing. You need to get outta here. Tonight. And take the Immune with you."

Why doesn't it surprise me that my uncle has plans to off me?

"There's a tech lab down the hall." Katie points in that direction. "Go past the elevators, take the first left, then two doors down is room 317. In the far back right cabinet are perrizo guns—the sedative kind, not the normal kind that Enforcers use to subdue people's powers in z-prison. I've preloaded two guns for you. Each one carries thirty shots. Aim well. One shot will subdue your target's powers and make them drowsy. Two doses should knock 'em out within seconds. Do not—I repeat—do *not* kill anyone on your way out. Half of these agents are *real* ZIRDA agents."

My face screws together. "What do you mean, half?"

"I don't know if I have time to explain. Are you sure we're good? Check again."

I do, even though I know we're okay. "My empathy power has been stretched throughout this entire floor and up to the security room this whole time. I'll let you know if anyone's coming."

"Excellent. I'll try to make this quick. Basically, this ZIRDA base has been compromised."

"Compromised? By who?" As soon as those words leave my mouth, I know the answer.

"The Royals, duh. More specifically, Victor. Over the years, he's been slowly getting rid of the real ZIRDA agents and replacing them with Royals. He's done it so discreetly that it took this long for anyone to notice."

Victor? A Royal? It doesn't make any sense. How could he work for the same people who murdered his younger brother? Plus, they tried to kill him too. Katie's gotta be lying.

I eye her through slits. "How do you know this?"

"ZIRDA Toronto was the first to recognize that there was something fishy going on here. Every time they collaborated with ZIRDA California to defuse one of the Royals' schemes, somehow, the Royals were always two steps ahead.

"A few months ago, Toronto sent two agents here to do some snooping on the pretense that those agents needed more-intense training. They were never heard from again. I was sent here from ZIRDA Minnesota to find out what happened to them and try to uncover what's going on here. Victor thinks I was sent here because I want to be a field agent and my CEO thought I needed more experience at a larger base first. Thanks to my submissive-girl act, Victor took me in as his assistant.

"Through some snooping, I found out Craig shrunk and crushed those two Toronto agents under Victor's orders. But that's not all I've uncovered. There's heavy shit going on here. Everything from human trafficking to suicide bombing, and they're creating another bioweapon."

Suicide bombing? It hits me. Those Tickers—the ones Victor sent those two agents out to find—Victor doesn't want to protect the Tickers. He's the goddamn Royal who's been kidnapping them to use as unwilling suicide bombers. *Fuuuck. I think I'm gonna be sick.*

Katie continues, "I send weekly notes to my CEO about my progress here. Victor thinks I do that because she's monitoring my experience to determine when I'm ready for field work. Really, I'm just encoding secret messages to her about what I find here. Since Victor reads and approves all my notes to her before I send them out, I can only give her so much info. She's building a case against him and trying to get some other ZIRDA bases involved to take him down."

I let out a scoff. "You've been here for how long now? Why is Victor still in charge? What the fuck is taking so long?"

"These things take time, okay? We've gathered the evidence, and my CEO has been in contact with some of the other bases, but a proper takedown can't happen overnight. If it makes you feel any better, after this last Immune arrived, I asked for reinforcements. I'm determined to keep her alive."

A little hope sparks in my chest. "That's great. When are your people coming?"

"Um, I dunno. It could be days. Could be weeks. That's if they're sending anyone at all. They'll only come if they think it's safe to."

"What if your life was in danger? Shouldn't they make saving you a priority?"

"I knew the risks when I took this field assignment. My CEO told me up front that she'd rather let me die than risk more lives. I told her I wouldn't want it any other way."

Kill ten to save ten thousand. Seems like the other ZIRDA bases believe in that mentality too. Except, this base isn't ZIRDA anymore. At least, fifty percent of it isn't.

Wait . . . "How do you know that half of this base is still ZIRDA and the other half isn't?"

Katie shrugs nonchalantly. "I don't know—not for sure, at least. In my time here, I've only *theorized* that it's fifty-fifty. I've only been able to confirm that seventeen people here are good."

I whisper yell. "Seventeen? That's it?"

"Well, you can't expect me to run around asking people what side they're on. I have to be discreet about it. Including you, that's eighteen."

"How are you so sure I'm not a Royal?"

Katie gives me a *come on* look. "Victor wouldn't try to kill you if you were. Also, I did my research. Back in May, Victor assigned a field mission to some guy in the LA area who had no prior record of being a ZIRDA agent. I thought for sure you were another Royal that Victor recruited to test out his *infatuation theory.*

"When I researched you, I discovered that your parents died under mysterious circumstances. All of ZIRDA knows that's code for 'The Royals did it.' That was my first sign you weren't one of them. Once I met you, I was one hundred percent sure. The agents before you personally brought in their Immunes for testing. Your Immune was taken in by other agents, and you seemed genuinely livid to find her here."

Because I fucking was.

Katie's words are making my knees weak. I'm not sure if I should believe her or demand proof. We don't have time for that though. Also, something she said is rubbing me the wrong way.

"What do you mean by 'Victor's infatuation theory'?"

"You really haven't figured it out yet?" Katie pauses to look at me. I make my fireball bigger just so she can see my *I don't have a clue* look. She rolls her eyes at me like I'm an idiot. I feel like one. "Many, many years ago, ZIRDA discovered that some rare Ordinaries are immune to our gifts. As a research and development agency, naturally, they brought in these Immunes to analyze. The Immunes were told they were part of a top-secret medical study led by the government, and they were even paid for their services. Ya know, normal ZIRDA stuff."

This is information I've known. I let Katie continue anyway.

"Eventually, the Royals found out about the Immunes too. They began kidnapping the Immunes from ZIRDA to try to weaponize them. I've estimated that at least five have died from Victor's brutal tests over the last nineteen years. With the last three Immunes he found, yours included, he's been trying out his *love* or *infatuation* theory. He thinks with the right stakes on the line, he can get an Immune to project their immunity onto someone else.

"Since kidnapping Immunes and torturing their families in front of them would give away his cover, he came up with this plan to plant a Royal into the Immunes' lives. The Royal would get the Immune to fall in love with them. Then Victor would arrange their kidnappings to make the Immune think they were both in danger.

"Once here, he'd have some agents torture the Royals the way he did with you. The rest of ZIRDA wouldn't think it's suspicious because it's one of our agents getting hurt. Because you know, it's okay to torture our own people if it's for the greater good." Katie rolls her eyes and huffs.

"Anyway, Victor's plan failed. The two previous Immunes he tried the love theory on never developed strong enough feelings. The last Immune got close, but once he found out the woman he loved never loved him back, he could no longer project his immunity onto her.

"So, Victor needed someone to play the lover part who didn't know his end game. He needed someone who could take on this mission and develop the feelings back to make the infatuation stronger."

I blow out a breath as the weight of the world comes crashing onto my shoulders. "And that's where I come in."

"Yep. You were the perfect guy for Victor to use. Single, good-looking, around the same age as the Immune, and you even live in the same area. Over the last few weeks, he's been running tests on you to see if you've developed the infatuation he wanted you to. I process most of the mission notes that Victor receives from our field agents. One of the notes came from an agent Victor has stationed at a hospital in LA named David Jordan."

That's the zoctor I spoke to after Arella was in the car accident Victor caused. Is that doctor actually a ZIRDA agent or is he a Royal?

Katie continues, "David Jordan's note included some MRI results and a paragraph about your reaction to finding out that she'd been hurt. Once Victor knew that you were 'visibly distraught,' he was ready to move on to the next phase of his plan: getting you here with her. That's when Victor assigned me my first on-base mission. He said that she'd arrive within the week, but she never did.

"For the next month, Victor had plans to send agents out to nab her three times. Each time, you must have said something to make him put it off, which only excited him more. It further confirmed that you had real feelings for her. I think he allowed you to put it off because he wanted you to continue falling for her, with hopes that a deeper connection would yield better results. Something must have happened between you and the Immune last week, because all of a sudden, Victor wrote up mission plans to get you here immediately."

I know exactly what happened. Victor must have found out that Arella and I broke up, and decided he needed to get us here before our feelings faded. But how did he know? Did he have someone watching us?

"I hate to say it," Katie says, "but Victor's infatuation theory worked. He's had the most success getting your Immune to project onto—"

I slap a hand over Katie's mouth, then I squeeze my fireball out. She doesn't protest. A few seconds later, the two people I sensed coming down the hall stroll past our supply closet.

"You wanna join me in the Artificial Sunlight room tonight?" a woman asks.

"Ya know," a man says, "I've worked here for almost ten years, and I've never been in that room. What's it like?"

"Seriously, Mark? It's like a beach vacation in there. And if you've got the room to yourself, it's like you're on your own private island where the sun is always shining."

The rest of their conversation trails off as they turn the corner toward the elevators. I take my hand off Katie's mouth, and she breathes again. My fireball returns to my hand with a burst of heat and light.

I speak first. "How can I get Arella outta here safely?"

"You must have had some type of plan already cooking in your head. What was it?"

I scratch the back of my neck. "Um, I was just gonna sneak her out of her room."

"How were you going to unlock her handcuffs?"

"Easy. I'm a Kinetic. I can wave at almost any lock to open it."

"Okay. How were you going to get past the Hulk?"

"Um, I dunno. Maybe I'd tell him that Victor sent me to take her down to the battle box alone."

Katie narrows her eyes at me and cocks her head to the side. "What if I was in the room?"

I shrug my shoulders with another *I dunno* look. "Maybe I would have told you the same thing?"

"But I'm assigned as her overseer. I'd know if Victor wanted her there or not. What kind of dumb plan is that?"

"Listen, I never said it was any good."

"It's shit, is what it is."

I think I prefer the mousey version of Katie. This one is mean. "All right," I huff, even though she's right, "you come up with something better."

"I already have. That's why those perrizo guns are preloaded for you. Again, room 317. Far back right cabinet. Once you get those guns, aim at whoever you see. Once everyone's gifts are subdued, you'll have a better chance of getting outta here with the Immune—alive.

"Now, before you go, remember that vision I had when we first met? I lied about what I saw." Katie reaches down her shirt and pulls out a shiny object from her bra.

I move my fireball closer to it, then gasp. It's Arella's angel-wings necklace. But why does Katie have it?

"In my real vision, you were outside an apartment building, asking a woman where her angel-wings necklace was. You said something about it being proof. Later, when I saw the Immune for the first time, I realized she was the woman from my vision. And there she was, wearing an angel-wings necklace. I thought maybe she didn't have it in the future because Victor stole it. I took it off her to give to you. Hopefully, I just prevented my vision from happening."

"Thank you, Katie. You have no idea how much this necklace means to me." I accept the jewelry. As our hands touch, Katie's breath hitches and her eyes go blank. Seconds later, she blinks and returns to the present.

I place the necklace into my front jeans pocket for safekeeping until I can hook it back where it belongs. "Did you just get another vision?"

"Yes. I—I think I just saw your death."

My lungs stop working. "What?"

"And I think it's soon."

Shit. "Describe your vision to me. What did you see?"

Katie shuts her eyes and thinks. "Um, you were running from some men. Probably Royals. Three of 'em. They catch up. One is a Slasher. He stabs you. Left side of your stomach. You collapse to the ground as the other two drag the Immune into a van. You get stabbed again, and that's it. Everything goes black. My visions never black out like that unless . . . well, you know."

I gulp as the trauma of seeing my parents' mutilated faces whips through my mind. Is the Slasher who attacked them the same one who's going to kill me?

"On the bright side," Katie says, "this vision means you manage to get the Immune outta here alive."

Her words give me no reassurance. "Where am I when this happens?"

"I'm not sure. I saw shops. One had cats in it. Lots of 'em. Toy cats. Golden with one arm waving."

Golden toy cats waving? What the fuck? What kind of shop sells those? "What time of day was it?"

"Maybe late afternoon? The sun was out for sure. God, they're going to kill you in broad daylight. The bastards."

Hell no, they're not. "I'll make sure to avoid any shops with waving cats while the sun is up from now on."

"Good." From the inner pocket of her jacket, Katie pulls out an ID card with her name and face on it. "Take this. You'll need it to access room 317."

I shove the card into my back pocket. "Thanks."

"Oh, and you'll need the code for her door. It's 5634."

Goddammit. How am I supposed to remember all this? I repeat the numbers in my head a few times. "Okay. Got it."

"All right. You ready for the most important part?"

"There's more?"

She tilts her head back to look me square in the eyes. "You need to punch me."

"What?"

She points at her cheek. "Right here in the face. And do it hard."

"No way."

"Trey, you have to. I can't blow my cover. Why do you think I told you to drag me in here? When they review the camera feed, it needs to look like you attacked me, interrogated me in this closet, then stole my ID card."

"There has to be another way."

"There isn't. And if you wanna continue dinking around in this closet forever, we can, but we've already spent a lot of precious time in here."

"Goddammit," I groan because she's right.

"Look, Trey, my parents were killed by the Royals too. I was ten, and I've wanted to be a field agent ever since. I've been training since I was eleven, so I've gone through much worse than one punch." She braces herself against the shelves, then closes her eyes. "Don't hold back, okay?"

I can't believe I'm about to do this. Sighing, I form a fist, draw back, then release.

Katie's head snaps back as she moans. "Jesus, fuck. You couldn't have held back just a little?"

"But you said—"

"Kidding, kidding. Kind of." She rubs her cheek with her palm as she slumps onto the floor. "Now go."

54

TREY

The sign reads 317 Weapons Technology Lab.

On the black device near the door handle, I wave Katie's ID card. It beeps, and a little light flashes green. I let myself in and shut the door behind me.

The room is dark. Instead of turning the lights on, I toss a fireball into the air. My flames hover beside me as I pin my back against the door. My hands shake as my breaths turn ragged.

Can I really pull this off? Me against a hundred? Maybe two hundred? *Fuck.* The idea of that many people coming at me at once is gruesome. I won't stand a chance. I can't do this. This is crazy. *Why the hell am I doing this?*

An image of Arella pops into my head. She's probably handcuffed to my old bed right now, scared out of her mind. She's probably more freaked out than I am. Trapped in a place with people she doesn't know? That's frightening. I can't imagine what went through her head when she saw everyone using their powers.

I have to do this. I have to save her. And if I die in the process, at least I died trying.

I expand my empathy outward. The closest emotions are from several rooms down the hall. It's two people, and they're . . . well, they're having a good time, that's for damn sure. I don't think I'll have to worry about them getting in my way.

Up in the security room, everything seems normal. Two people. Both are content. They've got too many screens to keep an eye on for them to have noticed me casually strolling into this room. The rest of the base seems clear too. No one feels alarmed or is running toward me. For the moment, I'm good, so I rush to the back cabinets.

Hold on . . . Did Katie say left or right? *Shit!*

I think she said right. I pull the door of the top cabinet. It clicks against the lock. I wave a hand at the keyhole and try again.

The cabinet opens. Inside are a bunch of small throwing knives lined up in four neat rows. Knowing ZIRDA, they're probably much more than simple throwing knives. They could be laced with something. Either way, they aren't perrizo guns.

Just in case, I take two knives and shove them blade-down into my back pockets. They're fucking huge, though, so they stick out like Excalibur in the stone. With these things in my jeans, I won't be able to walk around casually anymore.

I drag the leg of my jeans up. I'm about to stick one knife into my sock when I stop. Whatever this knife is laced with probably shouldn't touch my skin. How can I—*oh, I know!* I kick my shoes off and take one sock off. Then I drag the sock over my other foot. I put one knife back where I found it, then stick the second knife between the two socks until it's secure. When I shove my feet back into my shoes, it feels weird. One foot is bare while the other is double-socked. It'll have to do though.

With a thunk, I shut the top cabinet, then unlock and open the bottom one. Three rows of handguns stare back at me. *Which ones are the preloaded ones?* I bring my fireball closer to them. On the bottom row, two of the weapons are facing the opposite way of the others. I pick one up. It feels heavy. I pick up one of the firearms from the top row. It's definitely got less weight to it. *Thank you, Katie!* She definitely made this idiot-proof.

I shove the preloaded guns into the front of my jeans, then hide them behind my unzipped jacket. It's been years since I've shot a gun, but with the help of my telekinesis, I'll be able to make every shot count. I'll have to, because what I have is enough shots to knock out thirty agents, which isn't even close to what I need.

I leave room 317, acting as nonchalant as possible. Then I freeze. Down the hall, that security guard who was on his phone earlier steps out of a dark room with a short blonde girl. They both have guilty, satisfied smiles on their faces that drop the moment they see me.

Without a word, I make my way toward the elevators as if to say *I didn't see nothing.* I sense them stay where they are while I press the *down* button. My heart thrashes against my ribs because if those two weren't busy worrying about getting caught in their own dirty affairs, they might question why a field agent was in the weapons room.

Ding! The elevator arrives, and I rush into it.

When my ride lets me off at the living quarters, I step out with a dry lump in my throat.

In the community room, half the tables are occupied by agents playing poker. It must be tournament night, which explains why it's so empty on the third floor. As a kid, I used to stand outside those glass windows and watch them play, knowing exactly who was bluffing and who wasn't. *Couldn't poker night be any other night but this one?* Why couldn't they all be in their rooms, where they can't see me?

A few of the agents glance up as I pass by. I keep my face impassive, even though my heart is pounding like I've been running laps around a football field. One guy stares a little longer than he should. *Is he an Empath too? Can he sense me freaking out?* Eventually, his head drops back to his cards and he goes back to playing the game.

The closer I get to my old bedroom, the shorter my breaths get. What am I gonna say to that hulk-like Shrinker who's always guarding Arella's door? The same story I was gonna sell him before? But Katie said my idea was dumb. I should come up with something else, and I'd better do it fast because I've got less than thirty seconds.

I turn the corner. *Fuuuck.* Craig eyes me as I saunter down the hall. I hope I look casual enough. The man's energy swings at me, all alert and defensive. I brace myself for the burn that rips through my body whenever he shrinks me, just in case he decides to.

When I reach him in my normal size, I offer him a tiny smile. Not too big, where he'll think I'm up to something, and not too small, where it looks super fake.

"What are you doing here?" Craig says like it's peasant-minded of me to even think I belong in his breathing space.

"I'm here to take the Immune to Victor."

"What for?"

I begin to think of a lie until the truth hits me. If Victor had actually told me to bring Arella to him, he wouldn't have told me why. He would have simply said, "Just do it," so I shrug nonchalantly. "Dunno. He didn't tell me. Just ordered me to come pick her up."

Craig steps aside to allow me access to the keypad.

Suddenly, my brain freezes up. *What was the code again?*

A heartbeat passes. Then another. And another.

"You ain't got the code?" Craig's wariness spikes inside me.

"Nah, I got it." I type in some numbers as I silently pray to the keypad code gods. *Please be correct.*

When the light blinks green, it takes everything in me not to let out a sigh of relief.

I open the door and step into the dark room. I'm about to close the door when a hand slams against it.

Craig peeks his head in. "Where's Victor's assistant? Wasn't she at the infirmary with you?"

The lie comes out easily. "She was. She's already with Victor. She said something about getting there before me so she could have him approve some notes."

"I see." The door shuts.

This time, I do let out a sigh of relief.

"Arella?" I flip the light on.

She sits up and squints with a hand cupping her forehead. "Trey?"

The sound of my name coming from her lips is like hearing my old favorite song for the first time in years. It's familiar. It's soothing. It's everything I've been living for.

I wave a hand over the handcuff around her ankle. It falls to the floor with a clank.

She rubs her ankle. "What's going on?"

"Just follow me and stay close, okay?"

Like the stubborn person she always is, she crosses her arms over her chest. "Tell me where you're taking me first."

It hurts that she doesn't immediately shoot off the bed and into my arms. She doesn't trust me anymore. I understand why, but it still stings. It takes me a second to recover internally. When I do, I whisper, "I'm busting you outta here."

Her eyes go wide as she springs off the bed and slips her feet into a pair of flats. *That's more like it.*

I open the door to find Craig standing there with his phone held up. "You son of a bitch. Almost had me there. I just heard from Victor. He's not even on base."

I'm about to reach into my jeans for a perrizo gun when a searing burn takes over my body. The room grows bigger and bigger with each sharp breath I suck in. I clutch my stomach. Vomit is coming.

Arella's screams echo above me as a giant Craig squats over me. His enormous hand is about to grab me as I snatch one of the guns from my jeans. I'm not sure what damage a tiny perrizo gun will do to him, but it's all I've got.

Suddenly, the burning stops. I fly into the air as the room returns to normal.

"What the hell?" Craig stumbles backward, hitting his back against the wall. Shock, then anger, courses through my head as he glares at me, then at Arella.

It hits me what she just did. I can't believe she did it so fast.

"You bitch." Craig balls his hand, draws back, aims at her, and—

Ssspt! My shot misses. It hits the wall behind him. Craig freezes and glances back at the little needle sticking out of a burnt area in the wall. He shoots me a venomous look as a lightning ball grows in his hand.

"You bastard!" He launches his sizzling ball at me.

I duck. The ball hisses as it zips past me and scorches the wall.

Another glowing orb soars toward my chest. As I step aside to dodge it, another one flies straight at my face. I wince as it stops barely a fingertip from my nose, then falls to the floor and disappears. Another lightning ball flies through the air. This time, it stops a fist away from my face and also drops to the floor.

"What the fuck?" Craig shouts, then points at Arella. "It's you again, isn't it? You're blocking my powers from—"

Ssspt!

"Ow!" The needle hits his shoulder. He plucks it off, then flicks it to the carpet.

I still have the gun up, aimed at him. The look on his face tells me I'm in for it. He opens his palm. This time, no sparks appear. Shock consumes him as he closes, then opens his hand again. No sizzling. No glowing light. Nothing.

Before he can make another move, I pull the trigger. *Ssspt!* The shot hits him right in the chest. This time, he doesn't pluck it off. Instead, he wavers, then falls face-forward with a heavy thud.

I'm about to let out a sigh of relief when a siren blares. *Brehh! Brehh! Brehh!* "Intruder alert! Intruder alert!"

In the hallway, red lights flash from the ceiling. Next comes a man's deep voice over the speakers. "Floor two. Royal spy. White male. Leather jacket. Blue jeans. Pyro. Kinetic. Empath. Kill on sight. I repeat, kill on sight."

Fucking great.

I expect Arella to look as terrified as I feel. Instead, she glances up at me with a firm confidence in her eyes. She grabs my hand and slips her fingers between mine.

With the most conviction I've ever heard her speak with, she says, "I'll make sure they can't hurt you, Trey. Just get me out of here."

55

TREY

B rehh! Brehh! Brehh!

The siren is maddening. At least the words *intruder alert* have stopped repeating. The red lights are still flashing though.

I sense a mass of people racing toward us. There's so many, I can't count them all. They're running from the community room and jumping down the stairs with a *ready to kill* energy that erases all the assurance Arella just instilled in me.

I grip her hand tighter in mine. "Don't let go, 'kay?"

She nods, then we step over Craig's unmoving body and sprint out of the room. The red lights are brighter out here, making it hard for me to see. Halfway down the hall, I stop and turn around, jerking Arella with me.

"What are you doing?" she shouts over the siren.

I tug her with me back toward the bedroom. Then I point a finger at the one shot of perrizo sticking out of the wall. It flies toward me and stops a breath away from my nose. The tiny cylinder is still full of green liquid. *Perfect!* I pluck it from the air and shove it into my pocket. I'm gonna need every dose I can get.

Hand in hand, we run again. I pull one of the perrizo guns out of my jeans and throw it into the air. It hovers in front of us while I pull out the other gun and hold it up. We're about to turn the corner when I get an idea. Arella's body slams into mine as I stop.

"Ow!" She rubs her forehead.

"Sorry." Never letting go of her hand, I kneel and slide a gun down the hall. The weapon skates across the floor past a few closed bedroom doors before coming to a halt. I snatch the weapon hovering in the air and slide it down the hallway too. Then I pin my back against the wall and close my eyes.

The crowd of people darting toward us is turning the corner.

Now they're halfway down the hall. Suddenly, the lead person stops.

"Where'd these guns come from?" a woman asks.

I peek one eye around the corner and lift my hand. The guns swoop into the air. As I pull an imaginary trigger with my finger, the guns go *Ssspt! Ssspt! Ssspt!*

One by one, the agents' lightning balls fizzle out and the flames in their hands turn into smoke. The agents grip their necks and shout profanities.

"It's a perrizo gun!"

"Who's controlling it?"

A man punches the air behind the gun. "Not a Vanisher."

A woman toward the back points at me. "There! It's him! The spy!"

Fuck. I keep pulling the imaginary trigger. The lead woman goes down first. Then the guy behind her. Then the guy behind him. One after another, they fall with thuds, until everyone's lying on the floor.

I feel bad. It's likely that half these people are the good guys. I don't have time to dwell on it, though, because more people ready to kill me are on their way.

I tug on Arella's arm. "Come on!"

We rush over the sea of limp bodies, trying our hardest not to step on anyone. There's between twelve to fifteen of them, which means I don't have many perrizo shots left.

"Are they dead?" Arella asks.

"No, just sedated." It amazes me how she can be so concerned about these people after what's happened to her.

I wave a hand at the floating guns. They fly ahead of us as I scan the walls for any shots that missed. *One, two, three.* I point at each spot of green sticking out of the wall. They flutter down the hall, after the guns. I pluck the dose out of my pocket and toss it into the air. With a *zip!* it goes flying too.

Arella and I freeze mid-step when a man dashes around the corner. He aims a rock ball at us and releases. I aim one of my floating doses of perrizo at him.

Ssspt!

Halfway to me, the rock ball explodes, and the debris falls to the floor. The man plucks the tiny green cylinder off his arm.

Ssspt! He collapses to his knees.

One of the bedroom doors opens. A young woman in pajamas comes stumbling out. The red lights flash across her sleepy features. "What's with all the noise?"

You shoulda stayed in bed, lady. I point at two floating doses, then point at her. *Ssspt! Ssspt!* She collapses too.

From around the corner, a fireball rockets toward my face. The floating guns clank against the floor as I grab Arella and drag her down with me, covering her with my body. The fireball whizzes over my head. Heat singes the top of my hair, and I pat my head to put out the sparks.

Another burst of red-hot flames shoot at us. I open my palm. A fireball appears in it, and I toss it at the one threatening to burn us. The flames collide in the air with a blistering explosion. Arella screams as I cover her with my body again. The sparks land all over my jacket, and some on the back of my neck.

"Ow." I rub the speckles of pain away, then hoist Arella onto her feet. "You okay?"

Instead of answering me, she screams and tackles me to the floor. I wrap my arms around her as we fall onto my back, and she lands on my chest. Pain erupts up my spine as a glint of green flies through the air where I was just standing.

"Another!" Arella shouts.

I spot it coming at us and close my fist. The needle pauses in midair, then darts back toward the woman who shot at me—with my own damn gun. She tries to avoid it, but I swerve the needle to follow her. The needle lands in her collarbone. She groans as she plucks it off and flicks it to the floor.

Arella pushes herself off me. We get back onto our feet just as the woman with both my guns in her hands points them at me and fires. I close my fists again, forcing the needles to stop and drop to the ground. Then I wave my hand at the guns and they soar out of the woman's grasp, then twist to face her.

Ssspt! She falls onto her side.

Heavy footsteps thunder around the corner. A group of agents appears with their hands armed with element balls. Flames, lightning, rocks, and spiky ice fly through the air. I wiggle my fingers at both guns.

Ssspt! Ssspt! Ssspt! The element balls tumble to the floor in midair.

A female agent stares at her empty hands. "It's perrizo! Avoid the shots!"

Yelling, the agents charge at us. There's too many of them. I can't shoot fast enough. Arella and I retreat backward as we dodge fireballs. The flames land around us, then smoke out on the floor.

Ssspt! Ssspt! Two men in the front tumble to the floor, tripping the others. I keep my focus on my floating guns and continue pulling the triggers. One by one, the agents fall down, except one guy who ducks and aims a fireball at my guns. It hits one gun, which explodes with a deafening *BOOM!*

Pieces of metal firework through the air. I throw my hands up just in time. Barely a finger from my cheeks, the shrapnel stops. As I drop my hands, the pieces tumble to the floor. Arella gapes at me, wide-eyed.

I pull her behind me as I spot a perrizo dose on the floor. It's still green. As I wave my hand at it, it flies into the air and straight into the neck of the guy who blew up my gun. He grunts as he plucks it out. I aim my remaining gun at him.

Ssspt! He face-plants against the floor.

A middle-age woman appears from around the corner and points at me. I let out a wail as my skin burns with searing heat. The woman keeps her fingers aimed at me as I fall to my knees.

"No!" Arella slaps her palms against my face, holding them there.

Within seconds, the pain stops. *Thank fuck.*

Brehh! Brehh! Brehh! The siren seems to have gotten louder. I push back onto my feet and take Arella's hand in mine.

A flash of green whizzes toward me. I sidestep it just in time. Skin Burning Lady has my last gun in her hands. She pulls the trigger again. I clench my fist. The needle stops in the air, turns, then flies right back at her. She dodges it and shoots at me again. Twice. I halt both needles in the air and spin them around.

Ssspt! Ssspt! They hit her at the same time. She plummets, landing over the guy at her feet. I point a finger at my gun. It flies out of her grasp, toward the ceiling, and hovers there.

I scan the walls and spot several perrizo shots sticking out, still green. I point at them, then they zip down the hall at the five agents sprinting at us. Four of the doses hit, making the two biggest guys collapse to the floor. The other three agents open their hands. I wave a hand, making the last of my floating perrizo shots rocket toward them. Their shock consumes me when their element balls disappear in their grasps. With deep frowns, they charge at us.

I point a hand at my gun hovering near the ceiling. The weapon clicks, but nothing shoots out. *Fuck.* The gun drops to the floor as I drag Arella behind me, then arm my hands with fireballs. I launch them into the air. The first one hits the female agent right in the head. She wails at the top of her lungs as the smell of burnt hair stings my nose.

The two men behind her dodge my other fireballs, so I throw more. And I keep throwing them until both men are on fire. I'm about to tell Arella we'll run past them when a woman appears from around the corner and gasps. She raises her arms into the air. A giant water ball bubbles over the three agents' heads. Then another and another. More keep coming until the agents are drenched and their clothes aren't flaming anymore. Wet and angrier than before, they put their fists up and sprint toward me.

"Arella, get back!"

She races down the hall behind me as one of the drenched men smashes his fist against my face. Miserable pain explodes through my cheek. The man aims his fist again. This time, I duck and hurl a punch right back. I make contact with his nose with a loud *crunch!*

"Fuck!" He clutches his face as he collapses to the floor.

Someone jerks me back by the collar of my jacket. A large fist slams right into my temple. My vision goes blurry as the man slugs me in the gut. I bend over, clutching myself as I cough.

"Grab the girl!" the man shouts.

The woman with pieces of hair sticking out of her almost-bald head darts toward Arella. Screaming, Arella runs back the way we came. I throw a fireball at the woman, but it misses and hits the wall, then smokes out.

The man's fist thumps against the side of my head again. Two more men rush out from down the hall and join him. I block a punch. They land a kick. I throw a fireball at one. He ducks it. From down the hall, another woman appears and aims a lightning ball at me. It lands on my chest, and my body convulses.

The men punch me again.

And again.

And again.

A second lightning ball hits my arm, sending burning waves of hell through my bones. Another kick in the face. Another punch in the stomach.

One of them drags me up by the front of my shirt. Somehow, I find the strength to put my hands on his head. Flames come rushing out of my palms. The man stumbles back, grasping his face.

Another lightning ball whirls at me. I duck just in time. More fire lights up my palms, and I launch it into the air. One after another, flames blast out of my hands until I can hear every single agent screaming. I keep chucking fireballs as I run backward toward Arella.

Brehh! Brehh! Brehh!

When I turn the corner, I find my girl on the other end of the hallway, being dragged across the floor.

"Let me go!" Arella shouts as she punches at the almost-bald lady.

The lady keeps her grip on Arella's hair, then stops at a door and stabs the keypad with her finger. She gets the door open just as a fireball lights up my palm. I'm about to throw it when I stop. What if I miss and hit Arella? I can't risk it. Instead, I wave a hand at the door. It shuts in the lady's face.

"What the—"

"Let her go!" I yell.

The lady shoves Arella down, then sprints toward me. Big mistake. I have a clear shot now, and I take it. My fireball spins through the air until it lands on her, but she doesn't catch on fire. My fireball simply rolls off her wet clothes and falls to the floor.

"You traitor!" The lady heaves a fist at my face. I duck and trip her with my leg. She falls, and I climb on top of her, straddling her hips. My fists collide with her face, one after another. Once her head falls limply to the side, I stop.

Shooting back up, I rush to Arella. She's already back on her feet and meets me halfway.

"Did she hurt you?" I ask, scanning her body for any blood.

Arella clutches her cheek. "She punched me a few times, but I'll be okay."

I'll take a better look at her later. For now, I grip her hand, and we run back down the hall. As we go, I scan the walls for any last doses of that precious green liquid. I find none.

After we get past the sea of unconscious bodies on the floor, we turn the corner.

"Give me a fucking break," I mutter as three men from the other end dash toward us.

The biggest guy points his fingers at the floor, making it vibrate beneath my shoes. I lose my balance and fall backward into the hard wall. Arella is torn from me as she falls onto her knees. Over the trembling floor, I crawl toward her.

"Are you o—" I don't get to finish my sentence because I catch a glimpse of red-hot flames flying toward us.

Arella shrieks as she throws her hands up over her head. I crouch over her and brace myself for the fiery impact, but it never comes. The fireball stops just before hitting my cheek. It tumbles to the floor, then smokes out.

A second fireball whirls through the air. Arella screams again with her hands up. This time, the flames stop an arm's length away.

My mouth falls open. "How are you doing that?"

Her arms tremble. "I have no idea."

I help her onto her feet. "Well, keep doing it, 'cause it's working!"

Brehh! Brehh! Brehh!

I grab Arella's hand as we dash toward the three men coming at us. With my free hand, I throw fireballs at them. One after another, after another. The men do the same at me, but none of their fireballs reach me. Each one hits the invisible wall that's always two steps ahead of me. Their balls roll to the floor and disappear in puffs of smoke. I've never been more impressed by Arella. She's doing the impossible.

Feeling safe behind Arella's immunity shield, I pull the leg of my jeans up and grab the knife from my sock. I aim it at the biggest dude, then throw. It's about to hit the guy's chest when he throws his arms up and the knife stops in midair. The man twists his wrists, then the knife comes rocketing back toward us.

I raise a hand to stop it, but it doesn't stop. And it's aimed straight at Arella. Just as the metal slices through her invisible wall, I jerk her toward me, but it's too late.

Her scream pierces my ears as the knife slashes the side of her arm. The blade somersaults onto the floor with a few clanks, leaving a trail of blood in its path.

All the air leaves my lungs as Arella rips her hand out of mine to cover the fresh wound on her upper arm. She falls to her knees, screwing her face together in misery.

I've barely got a second to catch my breath before the knife zips off the floor, straight at me. I clench my fist. The knife stops just in time. With a twist of my wrist, it flies back the other way.

"Fuck!" The big guy stumbles backward, clutching the weapon sticking out of his chest until he collapses onto the floor and goes limp.

I point at the knife again. It shoots out of his body and straight at the next guy. He swerves away, but I twist the knife around, and it hits him in the back. With a wail, he falls onto his front. The wailing stops as his head droops to the side.

"Mark!" The last guy stares at his friend in devastation before shooting me a killer glare. "You piece-of-shit Royal spy!" His fireballs whiz toward me, one after another.

"No!" Arella shouts as she raises a bloody hand into the air.

The flaming balls stop so close to my cheeks, their heat prickles my skin before they roll onto the floor and vanish.

"How the hell are you doing that?" the guy shouts.

The blaring siren suddenly stops, then everything goes quiet. A second later, the red lights stop flashing too. Why did they—two women with high energy sprint from around the corner. One has short black-and-blue hair. The other has long red curls.

"Oh, come on," I say through a groan. "Anyone but them." I brace myself for the stabbing in my ears and the bites on my skin, but they never come. I glance behind me. "You're doing great!"

Arella, still kneeling and clutching her bloody arm, shakes her head. "I'm not doing anything."

"Ah!" The guy with fireballs in his palms falls to the floor. His hands are smoky as he clutches his ears. He screams as his body jerks and shudders. It's only seconds before he bends over and vomits. I almost feel bad for him because I know the feeling all too well.

Pixie stops blowing, then hooks her thumb at him. "I think he's one of us."

"How do you know?" Ruby asks.

"Look at him. You really think the Royals are gonna recruit someone as scrawny as this dude?"

"I'm not the Royal!" the guy shouts and shakes a finger at me. "He is!"

Two fireballs appear in my palms.

"Nah," Ruby says. "Trey's one of the good guys."

My jaw drops. *Whhhaaat?*

"Sorry it took us so long," Ruby says. "We got a little held up on the way down here."

Pixie saunters past me and peers down the hall. A sharp whistle leaves her lips. "Damn. Homeboy was busy. You gotta see this, Roobs."

Ruby dashes past me to glance down the hall. "Holy moo maker! Are they all dead?"

"No," I say as my fireballs disappear into smoke between my fingers. "They're all sedated, I think."

"How did you do that?"

"Perrizo guns."

The women glance at each other, then back at me.

"You got any more?"

I shake my head. "I used every shot."

"Dammit," Pixie says, snapping her fingers. "We might need—"

"Trey?"

The little hairs on the back of my neck stand up as Arella's frail voice calls my name. I hurry to her as she tips backward, and I catch her just before her head hits the floor.

"Arella?" I can't breathe. "What's wrong?"

Through half-closed eyes, she says, "I—I feel weak, and sleepy, and . . ."

Ruby steps up behind me in her clacky black boots. "What happened to her arm?"

"She was hurt by that knife." Because my hands are busy holding Arella up, I nod my head toward the two guys lying limply on the floor. I swallow hard. That could have been Arella.

Pixie marches toward the guy with the knife sticking out of his back. She pulls it out and holds it up as blood drips from it. "I can't tell for sure, but I think it's laced with perrizo. There's a bunch of these in the Weapons Tech lab on level three." After wiping the knife off on the guy's shirt, she sticks it into her back pocket.

"Got anything to tie her arm with?" Ruby asks me.

I shrug my jacket off, then drag my shirt over my head. Ruby helps me tie it around Arella's limp arm, then I slip my jacket back on and zip it up.

"Okay," Ruby says, "let's get her outta here."

56

TREY

Armed with my two new bodyguards, I cradle Arella and carry her down the hall. She's struggling to keep her eyes open.

The smell of ripe vomit attacks my nostrils as we approach the cafeteria. When we turn the corner, countless bodies are draped over the floors. There's puke everywhere.

"They're not dead," Ruby says. "At least not *all* of them."

"Don't feel too bad," Pixie says. "Most of the dead ones are Royals. We think."

"You think?" I say.

"Well, there ain't no way to be sure, is there? We took guesses. Educated guesses. Sometimes you can tell just by lookin' at 'em. Like that scrawny dude back there—totally not a Royal.

"Victor knew the other ZIRDA bases have been investigating him, so lately, he's been bringing in *real* ZIRDA agents as a lame attempt to get people off his case. But he only keeps the weak and pathetic ones on base—like that Katie girl. The powerful ones, like us, he sends out on useless missions as field agents to keep us away from here."

I adjust Arella in my arms as I continue following the women. "How did you guys know Victor's a Royal?"

"We were transferred here from ZIRDA New York," Ruby says. "We work closely with ZIRDA Toronto. They were the first to smell something fishy here."

"Speaking of which," Pixie says, "Victor disappeared tonight. When we heard the siren and your name over the intercom, we figured you was tryna save the Immune and got caught. The first thing we did was rush to find Victor. One of his guards told us he was off base."

"Where is he?" I ask.

"We dunno," Ruby says. "We didn't get a chance to find out before his guards attacked us. They must have figured we were using the alert as our chance to kill Victor—which, I suppose they weren't wrong."

Pixie rubs the side of her head. "That one guard punched me so hard, I swear I saw stars like they do in the cartoons."

"What happened after you guys got away from Victor's guards?" I ask.

"We rushed down to help you, duh! On the way, we ran into a bunch of agents rushing down from all the other levels. Since we didn't know which side people were on and we had already blown our cover, we screamed out, 'Victor's a Royal!' Anyone who didn't look surprised and tried to shut us up, we aimed to kill."

My arms are getting achy from carrying Arella like this. She's still slumped against me as we pass more bodies lying on the floor.

"This guy is dead. I made sure of it." Pixie gestures toward a buff guy lying facedown in a pool of his own blood. I think his name was Derek. "I knew he was a Royal from the moment I met him. When I looked him up later, I found out he's the guy who arranged that school shooting at a Zordi elementary school in Texas last year. Many agents' kids went to that school. Not a single child came out alive."

God, I fucking hate the Royals.

When we finally arrive at the elevators, Ruby presses the *up* button as Arella's head droops backward. My heart collapses into my stomach. I can't tell if she's breathing. *Oh, baby, please be breathing!*

Pixie must read my mind, because she places two fingers against Arella's neck. "She's alive. Just knocked out."

I let out a breath of relief.

Ding!

As we step into the elevator, I expand my empathy up and out. "There's a group of people in the security room. I can't fight them off with my arms full."

"It's the other ZIRDA agents," Ruby says as the elevator closes then rises. "After the battle down here, we told the ones who were still alive to guard the entrance. Don't let anyone in or out, and detain Victor on sight—those were their orders."

The elevator reopens, and we're greeted by three men armed with lightning balls. They close their hands the moment they see Pixie and Ruby.

"Is this the guy?" one of them asks.

"Yeah," Pixie says, "and we've gotta help him protect this Ordinary at all costs."

At an instant, the men surround me like they're the Secret Service and I'm the president—or, more specifically, Arella is.

The women lead me into the security room, where a group of bloodied-up men and women are gathered around the monitors. Sadly, there's no more than twenty of them. *Is this really all who's left?*

Lifelessly leaning against the corner is that security guard with the eyebrow scar. He's bleeding out from a deep wound in his chest.

Pixie hooks a thumb toward the guy. "Did y'all make sure he was a Royal before ya offed him?"

"He was definitely a Royal," a familiar voice says from behind me. "He was one of the men who kidnapped the Ordinary and brought her here."

I spin around to face Katie. She's got a bright red mark on her cheek where I punched her. I still feel bad about that.

"What if the dude only kidnapped the Ordinary under Victor's orders?" Pixie asks. "Victor could have fed him some bullshit to get him to do it."

Katie arches a brow at her. "If anyone from ZIRDA gave you orders to drug and kidnap an innocent Ordinary to bring here, would you have done it?"

"Hmm. Point made. Now what about this guy?" Pixie points at the other security guard duct-taped to a chair. It's Carlos—with some duct tape around his mouth too.

"We weren't sure about him," Katie says. "That's why we detained him instead."

The gray-haired man shakes his head and mumbles something under the tape. His emotions tell me he's scared shitless. Is he scared because we suspect he's a Royal and might kill him, or is he scared because he *is* a Royal and we'll kill him? Hard to tell.

"Listen up, guys!" Pixie shouts. "We've gotta help Trey get this Ordinary outta here. Ruby and I will leave with him to help keep her safe. We could use at least two more while the rest of you stay here and guard the base. Who's got the best gifts to come with us?"

A slender Black man in the back raises his hand. "I have enhanced speed."

Pixie flashes him a thumbs-up. "Thanks, Dash. Anyone else?"

"I want to come," Katie says. "I have the power to—"

Errr! Errr! Errr! A high-pitched alarm goes off.

"Incoming!" a blonde woman shouts with her attention on the monitors. "Looks like ten. Maybe fifteen. They're being ported in next to the waterfall."

The group shouts over each other at the same time.

"They're running through the cavern!"

"What do we do?"

"What if they're on our side?"

"They're not! Victor's with them!"

I catch a glimpse of Victor on a screen, barking orders to people. I hug Arella tighter against me. Is that why Victor left the base? He went to recruit more of his fellow Royal buddies? *Fucking traitor.*

"Secure the entrance!" someone shouts.

The blonde searches around, then slams her hand against a red button labeled EMERGENCY LOCKDOWN.

Ruby turns to Pixie. "How are we gonna get this Ordinary out now?"

Pixie's voice booms over everyone else's. "Does anyone know another way outta here?"

"There are secret passageways," I say, "but I don't know where they are."

Ruby scoffs. "Well, that's helpful."

From his chair, Carlos mumbles and wiggles his body.

Pixie rips the tape off his mouth so fast, it looks painful. "Here's your chance to prove you're one of us, old man. Do you know another way out?"

"There's a tunnel," Carlos says, "in the Artificial Sunlight room."

"Where in that room?"

"Untie me, and I'll show you."

Pixie glances up at Ruby. "Think we can trust him?"

Ruby shrugs. "Do we have a choice?"

"Tell 'em, Trey," Carlos says. "You've known me since you were a kid. I let you play all those damn tricks on me over the years, and I never once ratted you out to Victor. You know I'm good!"

The women turn their attention to me, waiting for an answer. I wish I could say for certain that we can trust Carlos, but I can't. How can I know what side anyone's on, when my own uncle has been on the dark side this whole time?

"I don't know if I can vouch for him," I say and sense Carlos's stomach drop.

"Whatever you're gonna do," the blonde says, "do it fast! They're trying to blast through this door with their powers!"

Pixie slides the knife out of her back pocket and uses it to cut apart the duct tape restraining Carlos to the chair. "Try anything funny and I'll blow those little ears off your head. Got it?"

Carlos nods, then hops to his feet. "Follow me!"

With Arella still in my arms, I trail Carlos to the elevators with Pixie, Ruby, Katie, and the Speeder at my side. Together, we climb into the machine as Ruby stabs the *close doors* button repeatedly until the doors shut.

Katie turns to Carlos. "How do you know about this tunnel?"

"I used to patrol before I got assigned to entrance duty. When you patrol for almost twenty years, you tend to know things."

"What if he's leading us straight into a trap?" the Speeder asks.

Pixie pats his shoulder. "Good thing you're here, Dash. Once we get to the tunnel, you can run through it first to make sure it's good before we all go."

The Speeder nods. "Sounds like a plan."

"If it counts for anything," Carlos says, "I was with ZIRDA for many years before Victor took over."

I wish that counted for something, but if the Royals can turn Victor, they can probably turn anyone.

Ding!

"Let me go first," Pixie says.

Without anyone having to say it, they all shift to stand in front of me as the elevator opens. Ruby even prepares her hands with fireballs. I appreciate the effort, but I already know we're good. I don't sense anyone on the other side.

Pixie steps out and peeks around the corners before calling out, "Clear!" Only then do the rest of the group step off the elevator and Ruby's hands smoke out.

Carlos leads us to the Artificial Sunlight room, where he holds the door open for everyone else. I step inside with Pixie and Ruby protecting my front while Katie and the Speeder guard my back. I stare at Arella's chest to make sure it's still rising and falling. Slowly and slightly, it is.

Carlos shuts the door behind him. "Follow me."

A fake sky stretches above us with an artificial sun so bright, it stings my eyes. I wait a second for my vision to adjust and return to normal. Blazing heat attacks my skin. On cue, my body's natural equilibrium kicks in.

Since Victor made up a rule that this room was for agents only, I've never been in here. Seeing it for the first time makes me feel like I've been transported onto a deserted island. A sandy beach covers the floor as far as I can see. Glistening blue water sweeps over the shoreline in calm waves. Some blue tables are stationed around the beach with padded lounge chairs under giant white umbrellas. If someone showed me a picture of this room, I wouldn't think it was indoors.

Carlos points toward the rocky, tree-covered cliffs in the distance. "The tunnel is just on the other side of that."

As we hike across the beach, Pixie presses her fingers against Arella's neck again. "She's good."

"Thanks for checking."

"Aren't your arms tired, bro? She's, like, all deadweight."

I let out an exhausted grunt. "My arms are so numb that I can't feel them anymore."

"How about one of us carry her for a bit?"

I'm about to accept her offer until I realize it means I'd have to let Arella go. It's not that I don't trust them to keep her safe. Pixie, Ruby, and Katie have more than proven that they're willing to take risks to help save Arella. Carlos and this Dash guy are still in yellow status, but for now, I'm choosing to allow them near my girl. Either way, none of these people will protect Arella to the extent that I will. If it comes down to it, I'll take a fireball for her. I'm not sure if any of them would do the same. For that reason, she's staying as close to me as possible, even if it makes my arms fall off.

"Never mind," Pixie says. "That was a stupid question."

"I'm sorry," I say. "It's not that I don't trust you. It's—"

She puts a hand up. "Say no more. If it was my baby sister, I wouldn't give her to someone else to carry even if my arms were broken."

I'm glad she understands.

A sudden burst of panic rushes through my head as double the emotions invade my mind. It's all coming from the sixth floor above us. "Fuck."

Everyone turns to me. "What?"

"I think the Royals just got through the main entrance."

"Shit," Ruby says. "Maybe we should have secured the door to this room in case they—"

Dash disappears with a *whoosh!* and a gust of air that blows Ruby's curls into her face. The ground rumbles for a moment, then a few seconds later, Dash returns with another *whoosh!* "We're good now."

"What did you do?" I ask.

He smirks and nods his head toward the door. "Take a peek."

We all turn.

Katie gasps with a hand to her mouth. "I can't even see the door anymore."

I can't see the beach behind us either. A forest of dark green trees now stands between us and the door.

"I'll keep working my Earth powers," Dash says. "Just keep going."

As we close the distance between us and the other side of the cliff, Dash remains a few steps behind. The ground rumbles with each tree that pops out of the sand. From the branches, he grows thick thorny vines, making it almost impossible to see through his forest.

When we finally make it to the other side of the cliff, Carlos stops to examine a large crack running up the rocky wall.

"There's a hidden keypad here somewhere." Carlos sticks his hand between the crack and feels up and down. We all wait a moment before he sighs. "I—I can't find it. Maybe I'm looking in the wrong crack."

Pixie whips the knife out of her back pocket and points it at the old man's face. "Or maybe you're just purposely wasting our goddamn time. Is there even a tunnel here?"

Carlos throws his arms up in surrender. "I swear there is!"

"Point to where the entrance is," Katie says. "I'll get it open."

With Pixie still pointing her knife at him, Carlos gestures toward a part of the cliff that looks the same as all the other parts of the cliff. "It's around there."

"How big is it?" Katie asks.

"I dunno. Maybe big enough for a small car to fit through?"

"Okay. Everyone, stand back."

I take about three steps backward. So does everyone else.

Katie shakes her head at us. "Um, no. You're gonna want to have a lot more space than that, I promise you."

Without a word, everyone takes another ten big steps back until our feet almost touch the waterline. It must be far enough because Katie twists around to aim her stare at the cliff.

Suddenly, a square part of the cliff glows red, then *BOOM!* Debris fireworks through the air. Rocks the size of watermelons land in the sand with hard thuds. A cloud of dirt and sand makes me cough. In the corner of my eye, I see Carlos lift his hand and circle it above his head. A gust of wind blows the debris away. Once the air clears, it reveals a dark tunnel and a grinning Katie.

Carlos lowers his arm, then the wind stops. "Told ya there's a tunnel."

Pixie shoves her knife back into her pocket, then pats Carlos on the shoulder. "You did good, old man."

"Where does this tunnel let out?" Ruby asks.

"The forest, I assume," Carlos says. "I haven't actually walked through it. I just knew it was here."

"Dash?"

"On it." With a *whoosh!* the Speeder disappears.

This time, he's gone for almost ten seconds. The whole time, I expand my powers upward to sense how things are going upstairs. From what I can tell, a lot of people have died. The number of people I can sense has almost halved. Thankfully, I don't sense anyone on their way down here—yet.

Whoosh! "The tunnel is about a half mile long. It lets out into the forest. I even surveyed the area up top. It's clear."

Ruby lights up her palms with fireballs, then throws them into the tunnel to light the way. "All righty, peeps. Let's get this Ordinary outta here."

I'm so overwhelmed with gratitude, I'm speechless. This is the ZIRDA I know: a team who works together to do good things, to save Ordinaries, and to keep the Royals from causing harm. This is what I thought I was working for this whole time. This is what I've wanted to be a part of my entire life.

57

TREY

Ruby leads the group with her fireballs flickering against the tunnel walls. I've got Pixie on my left and Katie on my right. Carlos and Dash are at my heels. I think I trust the men now—not enough to ask one of them to carry Arella, but I trust them enough to let them walk behind me without wondering if they'll try something. Even if they do, the women will stop them. I'm sure of it.

"Is Pixie your real name?" I ask as our footsteps echo with each step. The silence was killing me.

"Nah. I go by Pixie here because my real name is Anna Jung. It's kinda lame and plain for how badass I am, huh?"

"That's not as lame as *my* real name," Ruby says. "My family's been calling me Ruby since I was born, and I've been going by it ever since. Barely anyone even knows what my real name is."

"*I* don't even know what your real name is," Pixie says. "And we're besties."

"Tell us," Carlos says, grinning.

Ruby shakes her head with a chuckle. "Hell no."

"Helga?" Pixie asks.

"Ew!"

"Olga?"

"No."

"Gertrude," I say because that name just sounds funny.

"Definitely not."

"Bertha?"

"Okay, stop." Ruby rolls her eyes. "It's Agatha, after my great-grandmother."

Pixie spits out a laugh. "Agatha? No fucking way."

A baseball-size fireball appears in Ruby's palm, and she holds it close to Pixie's face. "If you ever call me that, I'll burn you alive."

Pixie throws her arms up in surrender, still laughing. "Noted."

"What's your real name?" Carlos asks Dash.

"Henry," Dash says simply. "But everyone's called me Dash since I was toddler."

"And you, Katie?"

"My name is actually Katie," she says. "Not short for Katherine either. It's just Katie."

"I take back what I said about you, girl," Pixie says, keeping a steady pace at my side. "I called you weak earlier, but apparently, you're not. That timid voice and submissive personality fooled me good."

Katie lets out an adorable chuckle. "Where's my Oscar?"

"That's one hell of a mind power too," I say, ignoring the burning ache in my arms. I don't know how much longer I can carry Arella like this. "Now I know why you were so confident you could overpower me when I tried to leave."

"I only said that to scare you. I can't blow *people* up—just things."

"I see. I guess if you could blow people up, you probably wouldn't exist."

Even before Zordinaries went into hiding, the zovernment controlled what powers remained in our genetic existence. Whenever a gift is classified as too dangerous or deadly, the zovernment puts it on the Extinction List. Then anyone with that power is sterilized to prevent others from being born with that gift.

There used to be people who could control minds, swap minds, and some even had a death touch. Now that those people haven't reproduced for almost thirty generations, those powers don't exist anymore.

"Deadly people slip through the cracks all the time," Ruby says. "Especially if they're a child of a Superior. My sister is living proof of that."

"What do you mean?" I ask.

Ruby twists around and walks backward as she raises a brow at me. "Think about it. Once our powers come in around the age of one, our parents are required to register our gifts with the zovernment, right?"

"Right?" I say like a question because I don't know where she's going with this.

"My sister's body power is one that skipped a few generations in our line, so there isn't a record of this gift being in our genetics. She can make your blood literally boil until it kills you from the inside out. Do you really think my parents were going to register her as a blood-boiling killer? That's instant extermination, my dude."

"What? I thought the zovernment just sterilizes those babies."

"Mm-hmm." Ruby turns around to face the front. "That's what the zovernment says they do because that's what they want you to *think*. In reality, they just take those babies away and pop them into an incinerator."

Katie slaps a hand over her heart. "Oh god."

"Sorry for the visual, but that's exactly what happens. It's easier, faster, and it's the most effective way of preventing that baby from ever being a danger to people in the future."

Kill one to save the others. Seems like the zovernment has adopted that ideal too. Am I the only one who doesn't think that's okay? Isn't there another way?

Ruby continues, "Now, let's say you work for the zovernment and you know that's where those babies end up. No zovernment official in their right mind would ever register their own child with a gift on the Extinction List, knowing it's a death sentence for their baby, so people lie. They cover it up. They go into hiding. Whatever it takes to save their kid. According to the zovernment, my sister can look at any animal to hear its thoughts—you know, something completely harmless and not life-threatening at all, and most importantly, hard to prove."

"Honestly," Dash says from behind me, "if it was my kid, I'd do the same."

"Me too," Carlos says.

Me three. I'd kill a hundred people before I let anyone take my child away from me. I guess that doesn't make me any better than the zovernment.

I glance at the woman in my arms with my shirt still tied around her knife wound. The man who threw that knife at her is now lying either sedated or lifeless in a pool of his own blood, and I have no regrets. I'd do it again if it meant saving her, and I feel the same for the unborn child growing inside her belly. This baby isn't mine, but it's Arella's. That means it's a part of her, which means I'll stop at nothing to make sure it's safe too.

"Does anyone know of a good place I can take Arella once we get outta here?" I ask.

"Our ZIRDA base in New York might take you in," Ruby says. "And I promise, our CEO is *not* an undercover Royal."

"I dunno," Pixie says. "The boss would need some convincing. You know how she is about bringing in outsiders."

"But Trey's not an outsider. He's a fellow ZIRDA agent."

"Who is related to Victor. She won't trust him. She might think it's a trick Victor came up with to get him into our base."

Being associated with that monster by blood disgusts me. What would my dad say if he knew his older brother ended up joining the group of criminals who ended his life? Suddenly, it hits me: What if Victor's the one behind the murder of my parents? His neck was slashed on the same night that my parents were blown to bits. What if that was just a cover-up to make it seem like he wasn't involved?

The story Victor told me was that the Royals showed up at his house, demanding he take them to Shadow Ridge, and when he refused, they slashed his neck and left him for dead. If the Royals had really wanted him dead, wouldn't they have slashed him enough to make sure he couldn't survive?

"I can take you to ZIRDA Minnesota," Katie says. "My CEO will take care of you two in a heartbeat."

That sounds amazing. "How are we gonna get there?"

"Any way we can. Walk. Steal a car. Ride a bus. Stow away on a plane. Whatever it takes."

The idea of having an entire ZIRDA base, a *real* one, protecting Arella makes my heart swell. With them, no Royal will be able to get within twenty steps of my girl.

Eventually, we arrive at a long set of narrow wooden stairs leading upward.

"This is the end of the tunnel," Dash says. "It's just up these stairs, then we come out of a tree. Let me go first again to make sure it's all clear." With a *whoosh!* and a slight gust of air, Dash disappears. At the top of the stairs, some moonlight shines through a small door. The rest of us climb the stairs in silence.

When Dash doesn't come back right away, I stop and project my empath power upward. Like how Trackers can't trace people who are underground, my empath powers can't sense anyone above ground while I'm under it, so I get nothing.

Pixie pauses a few stairs ahead of me. "You okay?"

"Something's not right." My heart rate kicks up a notch. "It's been at least ten seconds, and Dash isn't back yet."

"Roobs?"

"On it." In an instant, Ruby runs up the stairs.

The rest of us stay where we are while she heads to the surface. Just as she exits the top, she screams. Then come the wails of a bunch of men.

"Help!" Ruby shouts. "I can't fight them all myself!"

Without wasting a second, Pixie, Katie, and Carlos race up the stairs.

"Stay here!" Pixie shouts to me.

Stay here? And do what? Wait for them to either win or die before I can get Arella to safety? *No fucking way.* If they're being attacked up there, they're gonna need all the help they can get.

I scurry back down the steps and gently lay my unconscious Arella over the tunnel floor. My arms gain a tiny sense of relief from letting her go.

"I'll be right back, baby. I promise." Then I sprint up the stairs two at a time, shaking the ache out of my arms.

The second I step out of the hollowed tree, madness swarms my head. Shock, anger, and fear shoot at me from all around. Lightning balls whizz through the air. The forest catches on fire with each fireball that misses its human target. A rock ball the size of a basketball flies straight at my face. I duck just in time, and it hits the base of the tree behind me.

Everyone is screaming and shouting. It's too dark, and there's too much commotion for me to make out who is who. All I know is that there are more of them than there are of us.

A large man wails as he drops to his knees and covers his ears. Behind Pixie, another large man charges at her with his arm transformed into the shape of a machete.

"Pixie! Behind you!" I run to help her until I trip over something soft on the ground and fall on my face. When I turn to look back, I gasp.

At my feet, Dash's lifeless body stares back at me. He's bleeding out of a deep gash in his neck. They must have killed him the second he got up here. I guess that proves he really was on ZIRDA's side.

"I'm sorry," I whisper to him as I hoist myself onto my feet. Just as I do, a loud *pop!* pinches my eardrums. A slender man appears in front of me. It's the Teleporter who brought me here.

He hurls a fist straight into my nose. I stumble backward as pain explodes up my face and something wet trickles into my mouth. Blood. Salty and metallic. I wipe at it with my hand, then launch my bloody fist back at him. He disappears with another *pop!* as I stumble forward, and my fist catches nothing but air.

Pop! The man kicks me from behind. I face-plant into the ground, then turn and aim a fireball at him.

Pop! My fireball hits a tree, setting it ablaze.

Pop! The Teleporter appears on top of me. He straddles me and punches my face. Then he does it again. And again. And again. He grabs my neck and chokes me as a punishing jolt of lightning races down my legs. I scream out in pain, clawing at his fingers digging into my throat.

This isn't my end. It can't be. Arella needs me.

I draw my arms back as some flames flicker between my fingertips, but I can't gather enough strength to produce a fireball.

Suddenly, the lightning stops and the man groans in agony. His body convulses as he falls onto his side. I kick him away from me.

"Stop! Stop!" he shouts.

A hissing sound comes from behind me.

"St—" The guy vomits in his own mouth, then coughs as he chokes on it. Seconds later, his body goes still.

Ruby offers me a hand and helps me off the ground. "Grab the Ordinary and get outta here!"

"What about you guys?"

"We'll hold them back! Just go!"

I don't need to be told twice. I climb back into the hollowed tree and race down the steps. Arella is exactly where I left her, unmoved and unharmed. I heave her limp body into my still-aching arms, then sprint back up the stairs.

When I step out, the women and Carlos are guarding the entrance. Ruby has two men shaking on the ground, wailing like dying cats. Pixie has another three people on their knees, with their hands clasped against their ears. A few guys are swirling around in Carlos's giant tornado. Katie is throwing ice balls at two women as a tree behind them glows red.

BOOM! The tree explodes. The women attacking Katie go flying through the air. When they land on the hard ground, the emotions of one of them leaves my head.

"Run!" Katie shouts. "We'll cover you!"

Since I don't know where in the forest I am, I don't know which way to go. But anywhere is better than here, so I pick a direction and sprint.

I'm barely five steps away when Katie screams from behind me. "No! Carlos!"

Instinctively, I turn just as Carlos's emotions disappear from my head. A giant tree root sticks out from the ground, piercing him right in the chest. Three people scream as Carlos's tornado vanishes and they fall to the ground. It only takes them a second to get onto their feet. One of them punches Katie in the stomach as the other two run toward me.

I drop Arella's feet to the ground to free a hand, then chuck fireballs at the men. Clumsily, I hug Arella's upper body against mine, dragging her with me as I stumble backward and dodge the fireballs flying toward us.

"Arella!" I shout as I shake her. "Wake up! I need you!"

Her immunity would be so fucking helpful right now. Fighting people off is a hell of a lot harder without her invisible wall of protection.

The men are gaining on me. Another fireball rockets through the air and grazes my arm. The heat sears my skin before the fireball lands in the grass behind me, setting it on fire. The ground rumbles beneath my feet as two tree roots pop out of the ground. Their sharp ends fly straight toward my chest. I fall backward and land on my back just as the roots swipe the air where I was just standing. I lose my grip on Arella, who rolls away from me and lands on her side.

The Terra attacking me points his fingers at the ground again. The dirt rumbles beneath me until another tree root shoots out of the ground and circles my legs.

"No!" I shout as the roots drag me away from Arella.

In the corner of my eye, I see the Terra lift his hands into the air. His roots whip me upward, then slam me back onto the ground. Searing pain tears through my ribs. I clutch my side as I'm lifted into the air again, then my face crashes against the hard ground. More agony fires throughout my ribs. I cry out as the tree roots fling me toward the sky a third time. I'm bracing myself for the impact when suddenly, the roots stop. I dangle above a tree as the man below me cries out in pain.

"You little bitch!" Ruby says through hisses.

The tree roots around my legs glow red. They're warm against my jeans until they slowly break apart and release me. I fall to the ground, landing face first—on my ribs again. The agony burns like hell.

"Sorry," Katie says. "I didn't know how else to get you down."

I push onto my knees and clutch my side. I taste blood again, and it's so hard to breathe.

"Get up, Trey!" Katie shouts as she tosses ice balls at someone behind me.

What the hell does she think I'm trying to do, have a tea party? "Give me a fucking second, will ya?"

"We don't have seconds. You need to get her away from here."

I'm barely back onto my feet when Pixie shouts, "No!" Then she puckers her lips and blows toward the large man hoisting Arella over his shoulder.

Katie and I race toward the man as he drops Arella onto the ground and clutches his ears. My girl limply rolls onto the ground.

With a grunt, Katie hurls her fist into the man's face. Then she draws back and does it again. The petite woman sure hits hard. The man's pain mirrors onto my own face, but it's nothing compared to the agony in my torso.

"Go, Trey!" Katie shouts. "Get her outta here and hide!"

Aching, I pick up Arella off the ground and cradle her against my burning chest. Then I run.

58

ARELLA

A rustling sound makes my eyes flutter open. I'm lying on my right side with my head against a hard floor—a dirty floor. It's covered in mud, dry leaves, and who knows what else.

It's dark. Some slivers of moonlight shine through the cracks of . . . tires? I'm lying under a large table pushed against a corner with tires stacked around it. *Where am I? How did I get here?*

Wherever I am, it smells like rotten wood and stale dung that's been rained on. *Gross.* At least I'm out of that evil lair now. *Well, I think I am.* Why else would there be moonlight?

Someone's lying behind me with their arm limp beneath my neck. Their other arm rests over my ribs. It's Trey. I don't need to turn around to see his face for confirmation. I know it's him by the sound of his steady breaths and the familiar way his muscular body feels against mine.

My left arm is throbbing. There's something wrapped around it. I reach up to feel it. It's a shirt. *When did a shirt get tied around my arm?* The last thing I remember is that knife slashing me. Everything beyond that is a blur.

I have to get out of here. I have to get away from Trey and anyone else with magical powers. They're trouble. Every last one of them. Once I get away, the first thing I'm doing is contacting the police. They'll keep me safe for sure. After that, I'm going to find a baked potato and some bacon. I'm so hungry, I could probably eat the whole pig right now.

With the gentlest of fingers, I pick up Trey's arm draped over me and slowly rest it over the nasty floor. His breathing remains steady. Dry leaves crunch and crackle beneath me as I move to sit upright. I go slow, careful not to wake him up. *So far, so good.*

Once I'm upright, I take a closer look at the tires barricaded around me. They're stacked in rows, three high. I only need to move one row to give me enough room to get out. *Maybe if I go slow enough . . .*

More leaves crunch beneath me as I maneuver into a kneeling position. Trey moans softly as his head slumps against the floor. I hold my breath and wait for him to move again. When he doesn't, I exhale.

At the row of tires farthest from Trey's ears, I give the bottom tire a gentle push. It doesn't budge. I push again, harder this time. With a light dragging sound, the tires shift forward a tiny bit. I stop and eye Trey. Thankfully, his eyes are still shut.

I'm about to push the tires again when a rustling sound makes me freeze. I think it's coming from the other side of the wall. It might be a small animal outside or the wind blowing leaves around. When the rustling stops, I resume my escape.

The tires make another small noise against the floor as I push them again. Trey doesn't move. I give them another shove. This time, I feel resistance. Something on the other side is blocking the tires from moving any farther. *Dang it!*

I peer out the small opening I've made. It looks like I'm in a barn. Straight ahead is a rusty car—or what's left of it. Next to that are a couple of old tractors with missing wheels. More rubber tires lie in a pile near the wall. A line of old, broken shovels leans up against some shelves. Everything is covered in dirt.

Trey lets out another tiny moan, making me stop and stare at him. A beam of moonlight shines through my small opening, hitting him just right. I let out a little gasp. Trails of dried blood drip from his temples, all the way down his neck. The bruises on his cheeks are a bright shade of red and purple. A cut on the side of his lip is crusted over in blood. *How did he get so banged up?* It must have happened after I passed out.

Even with all the gore covering his face, he looks peaceful. I don't think I've ever seen him asleep before. Correction, I've *never* seen him asleep before. I almost feel bad for leaving him like this. Not bad enough to stick around though. I want nothing to do with him and his supernatural friends. Not unless one of them has the power to turn back time to before I was kidnapped.

Since the opening isn't big enough for me to crawl through, I'll have to move the row of tires next to it. It takes me a few pushes, but eventually, my opening becomes big enough. I'm about to crawl out when another rustling sound stops me. I yelp as a huge rat scurries across my legs, making me jerk backward, straight into Trey.

"Ah!" His arms flail around as the rat climbs up the tires and weasels its way out the other side.

All the tires fly across the barn as Trey shoots out from under the table and onto his feet. Two fireballs magically burst into his hands, one in each palm. They're so big and bright, they illuminate everything around us.

"Stay down!" He takes a firm stance in front of me as his head swivels from side to side. "Where are they?"

"Who?"

"The bad guys!"

"Not here."

He turns to me, still holding the flames. "Then why did you scream?"

"It was a rat."

Finally, his fire goes out, drowning the barn in darkness again. He slaps a palm against his forehead. "Fuck."

He dashes across the barn toward the pile of tires and seizes one off the top. It must have belonged to a tractor because I've never seen a car with a tire that big before.

"What are you doing?" I ask as he rolls the tire to me and flops it at my feet. "You know we'll need the rest of the vehicle for this to be of any use, right?"

A little smile tugs at the corners of his lips. "Only you can make me laugh when we're being hunted by people who won't hesitate to drive tree roots through my heart."

The mental image of that makes my throat tighten.

Trey points at the large tire. "Do you think you can work your magic on me?"

Funny that he calls *me* magic when *he's* the one who can make flames come out of his hands. "Why?"

"Because all they need is my DNA to give to a Tracker, and they'll know my exact location by sensing the use of my powers. If they were tracking us when I used my powers just now, it probably won't take 'em more than a few minutes to know we're here. Then all they need is a Teleporter, and they'll be here within seconds. I need you to make me immune so I can fly us outta here before they arrive."

And *this* is why I need to get away from him. *He's* the one they're tracking. Not me. Still, my current choices are to get out of here faster *with* Trey or slower *without* him, so I offer him a firm nod. "I can do it."

"Great." He sits in the hole of the tire, then spreads his legs apart and pats the space between them.

I accept the invitation by leaning my back against his front. He hisses through his teeth, and I stiffen up. "Are you okay?"

He groans and winces. "I'm fine."

My heart pounds uncontrollably as he wraps his arm around my waist like a seat belt. Internally, I scowl at my heart for betraying me. My body can't react this way around him anymore. *Not allowed.*

My stomach betrays me with butterflies when Trey slips his fingers between mine. Everything in my body tells me I'm safe—except for my head, which is shouting, *He's dangerous! Get away from him!*

I flashback to the night I questioned Trey about his abnormalities. After he refused to tell me his secret—one I didn't realize could be this insane—I asked, "Are you dangerous?"

Without hesitation, he said, "No. Not to you."

"Who are you dangerous to?"

"Anyone who tries to hurt you."

I think he knew at that time. He knew people were going to kidnap me, and he did nothing to prevent it. Maybe he's not dangerous to me directly, but he's dangerous by association. The second I'm able to, I'm getting away from him. Far, far away.

"You ready?" Trey's breath on the back of my neck sends warm tingles down my spine.

Stop! I mentally shout at myself. Screw my body for loving the feel of him on me. Actually, screw the world for putting me in this situation. Why give me a man I feel safe with, only to make being with him the most life-threatening situation I've ever encountered? It doesn't make any sense.

"Arella?"

I pull myself out of my swirling thoughts and imagine my waves of water crashing around him. I visualize the water soaking him from head to toe, drenching him with my immunity. "Okay, I'm ready. Just don't let go of my hand."

By now, I'm pretty confident in my ability to project my immunity onto Trey without having to touch him. The hand holding is simply for assurance. At least that's what I'm telling myself.

"I'll start slow, then I'm gonna go fast, 'kay?" Trey lifts his free hand, then the tire carries us into the air and we soar through the giant hole in the barn's ceiling.

It blows my mind how he's doing this. Seeing him move a trash bin from one side of the room to another is one thing, but this? The fireballs, the skilled fighting, the being a member of a secret underground spy ring thing. What else don't I know about him?

We zoom over a quiet house, then above some woods and a small lake.

More woods.

Another house.

More woods.

Then it's just woods for a while.

"Arella, I think you're cutting off the circulation in my leg."

I release the death grip I didn't realize I had on his calf. "Sorry."

"It's okay. I won't let you fall, babe. Just relax."

Relax? He wants me to relax? I haven't been able to relax for what feels like weeks. Now he's telling me to relax while I'm jetting across the sky on a smelly tire to get away from my abductors? *Yeah, right.*

"Don't call me *babe*," I say with a little bite to it.

His hands droop a little. Then he clears his throat and says somberly, "Sorry."

How can so much pain come out in one little word? If I could still sense other people's emotions, I'm sure I would have felt his heart shatter in his chest. Suddenly, I feel bad. Not bad enough to take it back though. This man has no right to be calling me *babe* anymore.

He clears his throat again. "Are you ready to go faster?"

"Sure." My head jerks backward into his shoulder as we speed through the air like we're on a roller coaster. "Can I turn around to face you? The wind is making it hard for me to breathe."

"Of course. Do you wanna land first?"

"I think I can flip around up here." Slowly, I rotate, sticking one leg into the air over his head, then dropping it at his side. The entire time, he holds me tight around my waist and never lets me go. I wish he didn't make me feel so safe, yet so terrified at the same time. It's not that I'm terrified of him; it's the people who are after me *because of him.*

I lock my ankles together behind him while my hands find the back of his neck for support. He winces and lets out a pained grunt.

I release my grip a little. "Am I hurting you?"

He forces a tiny smile. "I'm just a little sore."

He's totally lying, but that's nothing new. Either way, I'll try to stay still so I don't hurt him anymore.

Now that we're out of the darkness of the barn, I'm able to get a better look at his bloody face. It's worse than I thought. I think he's bleeding from the side of his head. But that's just a guess, because there's so much blood covering him, it's hard to know where it's all coming from.

I feel the need to take a wet rag to his face and an urge to kiss the pain in his eyes away. It's the same pain I saw in him the first time he saw me handcuffed to that bed—and all the other times he looked at me while I was in the evil lair.

I believe him when he says he had nothing to do with physically abducting me. If he did, he wouldn't have been so genuinely shocked to see me there. I know he cares about me, too. Why else would he have attacked his uncle for manhandling me? Why else would he have risked his life to save me? Even though he's part of the reason why I needed saving in the first place, I won't discredit that he's the one who got me out of there.

"Thank you, Trey," I say in a sweet whisper. "That was brave of you."

Trey's face crinkles as more anguish swims across his face. He bites down on his bloody lip and shakes his head. I wait for him to say something, but he just keeps staring at me with that broken look in his eyes.

It takes a while for him to whisper back, "That wasn't bravery."

"What was it then?"

"I dunno, but I don't feel brave." He lets out a ragged breath like he's about to cry. It makes me tear up too. I want to cry whenever I think about how they tortured him until he went unconscious for three days. And then they tortured him *again*. No matter what he's done, he didn't deserve that.

"Arella, I'm so sorry." He chokes on his words. "None of this was supposed to happen."

I glance over the edge of our flying tire, unable to look him in the eyes. If I do, I might burst into a sob.

The forest is dark and quiet. The treetops seem to wave goodbye at us as we pass them. I feel Trey's gaze on me as I swallow the dry lump in my throat.

His apology feels sincere. I wish I could tell him that it's okay. I wish I could tell him that what happened to me wasn't his fault. But it's not okay, and some of this *is* his fault, and I'm ready to know how much.

59

ARELLA

I stare over the edge of the tire as the wind blows against my back. "If I ask you some questions, will you answer them honestly?"

"Yes," Trey says with a firm nod.

"What planet are you from?"

He scrunches his eyebrows together. "Earth. I'm not an alien."

Pfft. "You could have fooled me."

"Do you see antennas coming out of my head?"

I run my fingers through the top of his hair to check and my hand gets caught in the dried blood matting up his dark strands. "They could be coming out of your butt or something. I've seen a lot of wild stuff recently. Nothing can surprise me now."

"You've seen me naked. Many times. Don't you think you would have noticed if I had antennas sticking out of my ass?"

You'd think so, but then again, I didn't know he could make fire come out of his bare hands. How am I supposed to trust my ability to notice things—ever? "If you're not an alien, then what are you?"

"Human . . ." He scowls hard and has the audacity to look offended.

"You said you'd be honest, remember?"

"I *am* human, Arella, just like you. Except I was born with powers—and I guess I have a few bodily differences."

I pull my long hair to one side and hold it there to keep it from flying into Trey's face. He hasn't complained about it, but I can't imagine he likes being continually whacked by my waves. "I didn't know there could be humans born with powers."

"That's because you're not supposed to know. The entire world used to know about Zordis. Our kinds used to live cohesively. Eventually, we were forced to go into hiding because Ordinaries began mass-murdering us."

"How did that happen when you guys can overpower us with your superpowers?"

"First off, superpowers is a term only used when referring to superheroes, like the ones in comics and movies. Our gifts are simply passed down by genetics. Think of it like getting your nose from your dad or your hair from your mom. There's nothing super about that."

I wonder who in Trey's line of genetics had the power to sense emotions like my baby did.

Trey continues, "Secondly, there are more of you than there are of us. Back in the early 1300s, Ordinaries created a poison and distributed it through alcohol. While it did nothing to an Ordinary, it was deadly to Zordis. Two million people dropped dead over the span of a year, and no one knew how it was happening.

"Once the drug was discovered, the zovernment decided we couldn't live in harmony with Ordinaries anymore, so a bunch of Scrubbers came together to wipe the memories of all Ordinaries and erased any evidence of our existence."

A secret society of people with powers that the entire world used to know about, who then erased everyone's memories because they were being murdered by poisoned alcohol? This is getting crazier by the minute. "And the zovernment is?"

"The Zordi government. Also called the Superiors. Casually, we call them the Supes. It's made up of Keepers and Enforcers. Keepers are the head honchos who make the rules. Enforcers are like the police."

"And Scrubbers—are those like people who go around with that thing from *Men in Black*, zapping people's memories away?"

Trey lets out a light chuckle. "No, they don't need a zapping thing, just their powers. One of my Zordi schoolteachers said that eighty-nine of the most powerful Scrubbers in the world came together to erase and alter all Ordinaries' memories at once. Sorta like how you project your immunity onto me, they did the same onto everyone in the world."

I tilt my head to the side. "Zordi school?"

"Yeah. From the age of one, when our body and elemental powers come in, to eighteen, in addition to Ordinary school, all Zordis go to Zordi school at night. We learn things like our people's history, our biology, and the way our powers and bodies work. It's like Ordinary school, except without math since that's universal."

"Hmm. It sounds like there's way more to this Zordi thing than simply having"—I almost call them *superpowers* again—"gifts."

"There is. We have our own culture, lifestyles, holidays, and festivals. There are a few islands around the world that are only inhabited by Zordis for those who refuse to acknowledge that Ordinaries exist. Everyone there gets to use their powers freely."

"Liz is a Zordi, isn't she?"

At first, he hesitates, then nods and says, "Yes, she is, but how could you tell?"

"Because she looks like one. You all have this impossible beauty about you. Everyone's so healthy-looking, with perfect skin and straight teeth. Katie said you guys have higher metabolisms too. Liz has the same beauty you and Katie do. Also, I can't imagine you could be as close to her as you are and be able to keep this big of a secret from her."

He purses his lips and nods. "You're right. I wouldn't. It's actually against Zordi laws to have close personal relationships with Ordinaries. My relationship with Liz would probably cross that line."

"Where is the line?"

"Dating, for sure. Kissing and sex are definitely off the table. Basically, we just need to keep as much of a distance as it takes to prevent Ordinaries from noticing that we're different."

Trey broke all those rules with me. We dated, we kissed, and we had lots of sex. I noticed he was different the first time we went out for dinner. I should have questioned it more back then. I should have demanded that he tell me how he knew that teenage boy was getting beat up in an alley from all the way at the restaurant. Instead, I ignored it because I was charmed by his beauty, his humor, and the way he made me feel so protected.

"What happens if the zovernment ever finds out that an Ordinary knows about Zordis?"

Trey swallows hard. "It means a scrub for the Ordinary and z-prison for the Zordi who caused the exposure. Depending on intent, it could mean death."

This is a lot for me to process. It's as if I've recently discovered that math exists and I'm trying to understand all of its elements from simple addition to calculus in one day. It feels impossible, yet I'm curious and I want to know it all. I suppose that's a little counterproductive when I'm also trying to forget that any of this ever happened.

However, it's not the existence of Zordis I want to forget. I mean, not all Zordis are bad. I wouldn't say Trey's a bad person, and neither is Liz. I never got the feeling that Katie was bad either. It's not having powers that makes them bad. It's how they use them, and that's the part I want to forget.

I want to forget that Victor had Trey spinning in a tornado while he threatened to kill him. I want to forget hearing Trey's screams while they caused him so much pain, he could barely breathe. I want to forget that Derek threw spiky ice balls at me while Trey fought for his life only a few steps away. Just like those spiders in my apartment, I've got a good feeling these moments will haunt me in my sleep.

With a light finger, Trey tucks some of my stray hairs behind an ear. That entire side of my body tingles, betraying me again. "I know you probably have more questions, but I have some I wanna ask you."

My voice comes out breathy. "Okay . . ."

"First, you're still making me immune, right?"

"Mm-hmm."

"Great. Second question: What do you think about when you're doing it?"

"Water," I say easily. "A wave surrounding you, protecting you with an impenetrable liquid shield."

"Wow." He chuckles under his breath. "That's ironic."

"How so?"

"Water is my weakness. It's ironic that you, my only other weakness, would imagine it drenching me as protection."

"*I'm* your weakness?"

His expression falters like he's baffled over how I didn't already know that. "Of course. I'd do anything for you."

No one's ever said those words to me before—and with such conviction. A light fluttery tingle fills my belly. I push it away because I can't let his charm put me under his spell again.

"Where are we?" I ask as an attempt to change the subject. All I've seen for the last however long we've been airborne is trees. Not a single house or road in sight.

"We're currently flying over the Sequoia National Forest."

"Where are we going?"

Trey lifts a hand, making our tire fly higher into the air. "We're gonna do this until the sun rises. Then we'll have to find a different mode of transportation."

"You mean, like, the *Ordinary* kind?"

"Yeah, that."

My stomach twists into knots as the question I've been wanting to ask him for days slithers into my head. I swallow hard as I gather the courage to make the words leave my mouth. "Was it all a lie?"

Trey's gaze locks with mine as his lips part. Something in his eyes dies a little as he sucks in a pained breath. "Arella, I—"

"Was my flat tire an accident?"

The way his face drops makes me wish I wouldn't have asked. For a while there, through that brokenness in his eyes and the sorrow in his voice, I wanted to give him the benefit of the doubt. I wanted to pretend like he merely got caught up in this mess too, like he wasn't part of a grander scheme from the start. Like it was only *after* we started dating that his uncle saw an opportunity and took it.

Trey hangs his head low. "No, it wasn't an accident."

My heart shatters to pieces. How could I be with a man for three whole months and not realize he was pretending the entire time? I'm impressed. His acting skills are top-notch. He should win an award for those amazing performances he put on. Everything from prancing around the grass with that invisible woman to making me think he was in love with me too. He even had Javina fooled, and barely anything gets past that woman.

How long did he know of me before pursuing me to find out the source of my immunity? How did he even know I was immune in the first place? Was he stalking me? If so, for how long? And why did he have to pop my tire? Was he trying to make me feel helpless so he could swoop in and play the hero? I almost laugh. It worked, so I guess it wasn't that terrible of a plan.

God, I feel so stupid! I allowed him to spin a web of lies right in front of me, and I walked straight into it—willingly. He made me believe he actually wanted me. I should have known that a man as rich and as gorgeous as him wouldn't pursue me of his own accord. Of course he had an ulterior motive.

Oh, god . . . and I slept with him! Worse, I was going to have his baby. I saw the rest of my life with this guy. I wanted him there when I opened my first bakery. I wanted to be with him as he toured the world with his band. I can't believe I thought all those things could happen when, this whole time, he was just using me.

My nose stings as I hold back tears. I want to slap him and curl into him at the same time. I hate that he's the one who hurt me but is also the only person I want to hold me until the pain goes away. *Was any of it real?*

Trey scowls at me. "Stop that."

"Stop what?"

"You look like you're questioning everything I've ever done or said to you. Arella, I need you to know that it may have started off as a way to get information from you, but that's not how it ended. I realized halfway through that I'd fallen in—"

"Tell me," I say, cutting him off because I don't want to hear him finish the rest of that lie. I fold my arms over my chest. My hand hits the T-shirt tied around my left arm, and it irritates my wound, but I don't care. The pain that shoots up my shoulder and down my arm is nothing compared to the agony throbbing in my chest. "Tell me everything, and don't leave anything out."

"Okay," he says so calmly, it only pisses me off more. "Where would you like me to start?"

"From the beginning! Where else?"

"Well, there's the beginning from when I met you and the beginning from when my parents died."

I squint at him. "What do your parents have to do with you manipulating your way into my life?"

"Okay, okay. It sounds like I'm gonna need to start from when my parents died."

After a deep breath, he tells me all about the night he witnessed his parents' murder. Everything from when the Royals burst through the front door and attacked him, to seeing his mother get beat up by a man twice her size, to when his dad threw him on the couch and kinetically tossed him out the window just before the house exploded into a mushroom of fire.

"I didn't have any other relatives, so I was forced to live with Victor. After he became the CEO of ZIRDA California, he moved to Shadow Ridge, so that's where I grew up. You already know that Victor was abusive to me. He liked to beat me up and call me things like *worthless kid* and *piece of shit*. He hid the fact that my parents left me money until the day I turned eighteen, when he finally told me about my inheritance, then told me to get lost.

"After I left, I didn't hear from Victor until he called me in early May, out of the blue. He said there was an Ordinary in the LA area who was immune to Zordi powers and if we could find out the source of her immunity, we could work to replicate it and have the upper hand against the Royals. He explained that he needed someone to get her to tell them everything about herself and the best way to do that was to pretend to date her. I've wanted the Royals gone since I was seven, so I didn't hesitate to say yes."

I think back to all those times Trey asked me about my grandparents and my parents. Yes, I found his questions odd, but not odd enough to come to the conclusion that he was on a secret mission to learn everything about me to relay back to his devil of an uncle.

Trey drags a hand through his matted hair as he sighs. "Tonight, I found out from Katie that Victor's actually a Royal. His real plan was to get us to fall for each other so he could torture me in front of you until you learned to control your immunity.

"Once you did, his plan was to get rid of me, then who knows what he wanted to do from there. If I had to guess, he probably would have kept you locked up in the Ridge for as long as it took to find a way to replicate your immunity. If not that, he'd probably torture you into projecting onto his Royal buddies while they carried out their missions of destruction."

The idea of spending my entire life locked up in that underground hideout scares me. What scares me more is knowing that my grandparents and Javina would have spent the rest of their lives wondering what happened to me. I doubt *kidnapped by her ex-boyfriend's uncle* would have been at the top of their list.

Trey continues, "Since I thought Victor was operating under ZIRDA, I never thought he'd go as far as kidnapping you. I was under the impression that this was just about getting information. No one was supposed to get hurt, Arella, especially not you.

"ZIRDA is an organization of good people who do good things. They started as a research and development agency that ended up also being the people who fought to protect Ordinaries from the Royals. Because, ya know, the fucking zovernment wasn't doing anything about the Royals' bioweapons, nor were they stopping the Royals from going around murdering innocent people for no goddamn reason.

"After Victor told me he planted those spiders and caused your car accident, I should have known he wasn't with ZIRDA. A *real* ZIRDA leader would never purposely risk an Ordinary's life. It doesn't make any sense why he'd work for the very people who murdered his little brother, so the possibility that he switched sides never even occurred to me. Even now, knowing what I know, it *still* doesn't make any sense. What reason does he have to work for the Royals? What did they say to him to get him to turn?"

I gather all my loose hairs to one shoulder again. "You've said that Victor used to be like a second father to you, then, like flipping a switch, he treated you like trash. What if he's under someone's mind control? Is that a thing in the Zordi world?"

Trey gives me an *I dunno* shrug. "It's a gift that's on the Extinction List, but I just found out today that some people still slip through the cracks, so who knows? Victor being under mind control makes a hell of a lot more sense than him willingly joining the criminals who believe that Zordi humans deserve more than Ordi humans just because we were born with powers."

He lets out a long sigh. "Fuck, Arella. If I had known about Victor earlier, I woulda kidnapped you myself—in a heartbeat. I wouldn't have wasted all that time trying to convince you to move to Paris. Within minutes, I woulda had you duct-taped to a seat on a private jet on the way to Europe."

I was wrong when I thought Trey had done nothing to prevent my abduction. Turns out, he had tried, although his plan was stupid. *Move to Paris? Seriously?* Couldn't he have come up with something better? Something with a higher chance of my cooperation? I don't know what that would be, but anything would have been better than *let's move to another country forever.*

I shake my head at him, but mostly, I shake my head at myself. I fell in love with a man from a world of people with powers who live in secret among those without powers. And the only reason we met was because his manipulative uncle sent him on a mission to find out if I had a gene defect or if I had ever been bitten by a radioactive spider. Nothing Trey and I had was real.

Now here we are on a floating tire after I was kidnapped and he was brutally tortured and we almost died trying to get away. And for what? Even after dodging all those fireballs, we *still* don't know what makes me immune. What did anyone gain from all that?

"Arella." Trey says my name like a plea. "Please tell me what's going through your head because that look on your face is scaring me."

"What look?" I snap.

"Um, you look sorta mad."

"Because I *am*. Wouldn't you be if the one and only man you decided to let into your heart after being in an abusive relationship turned out to be a fake? What was your plan after you got the information you wanted? Were you just going to break up with me and move on like the moments we shared never happened? Like it didn't mean anything?"

He lets out a pained breath. "At first, yes. But once I fell in—"

"You pretended to like me and got me to fall for you knowing what my history was like with Nathan. You knew that I felt like I'd never find someone who could treat me right, yet you kept going on with your deceitful mission anyway."

He softens his tone as if it'll calm me. "The goal was to casually date you for a few weeks. Things between us weren't supposed to go as far as they did. Real feelings were never supposed to get in the way."

"How do you think I would have felt when you suddenly ended things between us once you finally got the information you wanted?"

He gestures toward the forest below us. "Should I land so we can talk this through?"

"No," I shout with my hands in fists. "I want answers, and I want them now."

He lets out a long sigh. "My plan wasn't to break up with you. It was to get you to break up with me."

I force back the tears threatening to stream from my eyes. "Right, like that makes it any better? Either way, you would have conned me into falling for you, only to disappear from my life. Do you really think I wouldn't have been hurt by that? How am I ever supposed to trust another man ever again?"

"You're right, Arella. You're one hundred percent right. That's one of the reasons why I couldn't leave you. The idea of hurting you hurt me."

I throw my arms up and let them flop back into my lap. "Well, look at us now, Trey. I'm hurt—emotionally and physically. If you wanted to keep me from getting hurt, you failed. Just like how you failed your mission to find out what makes me immune. I hope it was worth it, because I swear to you, the second this nightmare is over, I never want to see your face again."

Trey's breath hitches. He stares at me with his mouth slightly open like he can't believe what he just heard. I mean what I said though. The second this is over, I never want to see him again. I don't even want to think about him. I want to move on with my life as if he never existed and none of this ever happened.

With a hard swallow, Trey breaks his gaze from mine and stares down at the trees with a somber look on his face.

Neither of us says anything for a while. I said all I wanted to say, so I just keep my eyes on the forest as I try not to cry.

Occasionally, I steal a glance at Trey. Every time I do, I wish I hadn't, because with each glance, the light in his eyes is dimmer. They're glossed over with a pain in him I've never seen before. Seeing it makes the large crack running through the middle of my heart break deeper.

After a long time, Trey clears his throat and looks up at me. "Arella?"

My heart skips a beat at the sound of my name on his lips, but I'm still mad, so I huff out a breath. "What?"

His Adam's apple moves up and down as he swallows hard. His voice comes out low and husky like it's taking all his energy just to speak. "At your thinking spot, you told me that when you love someone, you put their happiness before your own. If you're saying that once this is over, you never want to see me again . . ." He lets out a ragged sigh, looking anywhere but at me. "Then okay. If that's what makes you happy, then when this is over, I'll force myself to walk away."

Hearing him say it out loud makes it more real, and suddenly, it terrifies me. Never see Trey again? *Is that really what I want?* I think about it for a moment, only to come to the conclusion that I don't know. What I do know is that being with him is dangerous and it's detrimental to my life. That should be reason enough to never want to see him again.

"But before I do that," Trey says, still avoiding my eyes, "I want you to know that I never pretended to like you. I've always liked you. From the moment I saw you, I was completely and utterly captivated by you. Then, the more time I spent with you, the more I fell in love with you."

I try to convince myself he's feeding me a spoonful of lies, but he sounds so genuine.

"You hooked me in with your kindness and your sense of humor. I fell in love with your laugh and the way you made me feel whole. I fell in love with the way you were fixing me without ever making me feel like I was broken. You made me feel like I had a purpose, and you still do. My purpose is to keep you safe and to make you happy.

"So, once you're safe, I'll do whatever it takes to make you happy. And if that means I never get to see you again, then . . ." He shakes his head at himself, biting his bottom lip. After letting out what sounds like a painful breath, he finally looks up at me, and the light in his eyes completely disappears. "I'll do it, Arella. I'll walk away."

I'm not sure who he's trying to convince that he *can* do such a thing—me or himself?

60

TREY

There's a gaping hole in my chest where my heart used to be. My lungs feel tight, and I can't really feel my arms anymore. I've always known that emotional hurt can also make a person physically hurt. I found that out when I was seven.

The pain I feel now is different from the pain I felt when I lost my parents. It's not that one pain aches more than the other; it's just a different type of ache. It's been nineteen years since my parents died, and I still feel the gut-wrenching agony in my chest from that. How many years will it take before I stop feeling the agony of losing Arella?

It took me a while to come to the conclusion that walking away is what's best for her. It'll kill me to do it, but I'm going to do it. I love this woman with my entire soul, and if never seeing my face again is what she wants, then okay. I just hope I'll be able to function after walking away, because the mere thought of having to do it makes me want to leap over the edge of this tire.

Eventually, the trees below us aren't as dense and we fly over a house. A light-blue Subaru sits in the gravel driveway, parked behind a rusty white pickup truck.

With a soft thud, I land the tire next to the driver's side of the Subaru. Up the long driveway stands a house with a ton of windows. Inside, it's dark. The five emotions I sense coming from the house are all muted, which means they're sleeping.

Arella wastes no time hopping off my lap as if she can't get away from me fast enough. The last twenty-ish minutes up in the air felt like hours. Neither of us spoke, and she barely even looked at me. I wish I could say it's just her pregnancy hormones making her give me the cold shoulder, but I'm pretty sure Arella would be acting this way, pregnant or not. I know I deserve it, but it still hurts.

"What are we doing here?" she asks in a low voice.

I reply in an equally low voice, "We're getting the *ordinary kind* of transportation."

Her mouth pops open. "You mean we're going to steal a car?"

"What did you think I meant when I said we were gonna get a different mode of transportation?"

"I thought you meant we were going to take a bus or something."

I throw my arms up and spin around. "Do you see any bus stations 'round here?"

She glares daggers at me. Maybe I should tone my attitude down a bit. Yes, I'm emotionally damaged and my ribs are screaming at me with every breath I take, but that doesn't mean I should take it out on her.

"Relax." I almost call her *babe,* then stop myself. "We're just gonna *borrow* a car."

"Like how your uncle *borrowed* me?"

Ouch. She might as well have shanked me with a serrated knife straight through my chest. It probably would have hurt less.

I'm ashamed to call Victor my uncle. Before, I excused his cruelty toward me because I thought he was doing good things for the world. Now that I know he's just a piece-of-shit double agent, I have no excuses for him. I want nothing to do with him, and I'd appreciate it if Arella would stop calling him my uncle. That man is not family to me, and he hasn't been for a long fucking time.

Arella crosses her arms over her front. "We're not stealing a car."

I wave a *don't worry about it* hand through the air. "I'll pay 'em back later."

"How?"

"When this is all over, I'll come back and leave them cash on their front step for whatever this car is worth, plus triple." I pause and wait for her to give in. When she doesn't, I sigh exasperatedly.

We don't have any other options, and she knows it. She's just so mad at me that she's being difficult on purpose. Unfortunately, we're running out of darkness and I can't keep talking nicey-nice to her anymore, so my tone comes out firm. "Look, Arella. The sun's about to come up, so we can't fly on this tire for much longer. We need a car so we can go find a Healer who can fix your arm. The closest Healer isn't for at least another few hours—by car. I'd suggest we walk, but that'll take us days, and I can't wait that long because I'm pretty sure I've got a broken rib, and this shit fucking hurts." I point to my right side, where my throbbing pain is coming from.

Ignoring the misery, I continue my rant. "I'm exhausted from using my powers, both from flying us over a whole-ass forest and from fighting off all those dickheads trying to kill me. Now, can we *please* steal this car so we can get the hell outta here before the family that lives inside that house wakes up and calls the police?"

Arella softens her defensive stance and gapes at me. "You have a broken rib?"

"I think so. Maybe a few."

Her jaw drops. "A few? Trey, why didn't you tell me?"

"It's not important."

"Not important? Not even when I was using you as a chair earlier? You winced every time I moved even a little bit, and you didn't think it was important to tell me you have broken ribs?"

I shrug, and it feels like fire in my ribs to do so. "I'm fine."

"You're *not* fine. We need to get you to a hospital."

It's my turn to gape at her. "Are you serious? We're not going to a fucking hospital. That's like putting a beacon on our heads to tell the Royals exactly where we are. We're gonna go find a Healer who can fix me up faster than any hospital can. Now, as much as I enjoy standing around arguing with you, we've gotta get going." I hook a thumb toward the Subaru. "You gonna let me steal this car or not?"

She ponders it for a moment, then says, "Fine, but we're not stealing *this* car."

"You got somethin' against Subarus?"

"No. I have something against stealing from a family with small children." She points through the back window.

My eyes follow her finger to two car seats strapped into the back. "What's your point?"

"It's expensive to have babies. This family is off-limits."

Our lives are in danger, and of course Arella still cares more about some children she's never met than she does herself. She's been pregnant for, what, a few weeks? And she's already thinking like a mother. I wish I could say I'm bothered by this, but it only adds to the many reasons why I love this woman.

Reluctantly, I grunt and return my ass to the tire. My side burns the entire time I bend and adjust to sit comfortably—well, as comfortably as I can get.

I spread my legs, then gesture for her to join me.

Arella hesitates. "How should I sit so I won't hurt you?"

"The way you were before, facing me. Much better than when you leaned your back against me."

Once she's back on top of me, I offer her my hand to put hers in. She understands why without me having to say it. After she tells me she's ready, I fly us over the treetops again.

Two empty roads over, we approach another house.

I'm about to land when Arella says, "We can't steal from these people either."

"Why not?"

"They only have one car. What if someone needs to go to work in the morning?"

The third house we find has four vehicles parked along the gravel driveway. The one at the end is a rusty tan Nissan Altima. I almost drop my jaw when Arella doesn't pick a fight with me about swiping it.

With her hand in mine, I wiggle my fingers at the locks. They pop up with a click, then we climb in.

The car smells like toe jam and expired yogurt. The backseat is covered in fast-food wrappers that have been collecting there for who knows how long. Dripping down the steering wheel is a questionable crusty white spot. I can't imagine what it looks like under a microscope. I'm so fucking grossed out, I'd rather be back on that tire, but the sun's peeking up. We can't risk being seen anymore.

Behind the wheel, I take Arella's hand again, then point at the empty keyhole. The engine sputters to life, then I ease us away from the house.

"How did you do that?" Arella asks from the passenger seat. She keeps her hand in mine, even though I don't need her immunity anymore. Now that the car is started, I won't need my powers for a while. Still, I won't draw my hand back, nor will I say anything about it. I'll only have Arella for as long as she needs me to keep her safe. I don't know how much longer that'll be, so for now, I'm going to selfishly take as much of her as I can get.

The headlights on this car suck ass. They're so dim, I can barely see what's ahead of me. "How did I do what?"

"Unlock the car and start it without the key?"

"Do you know how locks work?"

She cocks her head to the side. "Sort of."

"You know how keys have those ridges that go up and down? All it does when you stick those ridges into a lock is push the mechanisms up a specific way to unlock it. I simply use my Telekinesis to do the same."

"But how do you know how far to push up those mechanisms?"

"I just feel it, I guess. Like it just clicks in my brain when I've got all the right ones up. Kinda like pushing a button and stopping once you feel resistance."

She nods with her lips pursed. "Interesting."

With one hand on the wheel, I make a right turn. Then I glance at the dashboard and groan. "We're gonna have to stop for gas soon."

"How soon?"

"We've got a quarter tank-ish. There's no way in hell we'll make it to Las Vegas on that."

She twists at the hip to face me. "Why are we going to Vegas?"

"To find a Healer." Has she already forgotten that I told her that's what we're trying to do?

"And the closest one is in Vegas?"

"No, the closest one is in LA, but we can't go to that one. The Royals know I'm injured. I'd be surprised if they weren't waiting for us outside the Healer's shop in LA right now." And outside my house, Arella's apartment, our friends' houses, the Soul House, and any other place we're connected to.

"Wait. If they're expecting you to go to a Healer, then why are we going to one? Shouldn't we do the opposite of what they think we'll do?"

She's right, but I don't know any other options for us. "Can your immunity fix broken bones?"

"No."

"Then we're going to Vegas and hoping for our lives that Victor doesn't already have people waiting for us there too." I don't know what I'll do if Victor ever gets his hands on Arella again. Actually, I do know. It's violent and inhumane. I'll make sure he can never touch another innocent woman ever again, and I won't even feel guilty about it.

"How can a Healer heal me if I'm immune to their powers?"

I slow the car and stop at a stop sign. After checking both ways, I ease back on the gas and keep heading straight. "They can't, but they'll have Healing Goo that'll work on you."

"Okay. What happens after we visit the Healer?"

"We'll go into hiding."

"Where?"

I wait until we pass a dark blue pickup truck driving on the other side of the road before I answer. "Ideally, I'd take you to the safe house my parents left for me, but I can't find it. So, we're going with Plan B."

"Which is?"

I run a hand through my hair until my fingers get caught in some dried blood. "Um, I haven't figured that part out yet."

Her jaw drops. "What?"

"Hey," I say defensively, "my only plan was to get you away from Victor. I haven't been able to strategize beyond that."

"So you expect me to just blindly go along with this nonexistent plan of yours? I thought you had more than this."

"I do. My plan exists. It just exists . . . in the future."

She laughs—a really condescending laugh. "The *future*? That's wonderful. That's just wonderful."

"All right, Miss Sarcastic-and-judgy, I'm open to ideas if you've got 'em. Do you know of a place we can stay where they can't find us? Preferably underground."

"Why underground?"

"Trackers can't sense people while they're underground. I mean, I could go without using my powers forever, but there are Trackers out there who can sense people without waiting for them to use a gift. They're rare, but they exist. It's better to be safe than sorry. Plus, in general, if we're underground, it'll be harder for them to find us."

Our car reaches another intersection. I turn left, hoping it'll take us toward Nevada. If Arella asks if I know where I'm going, I'll lie because there's no way in hell I'm admitting to her that I'm driving off of *gut feelings*.

I'd use my GPS if I still had a phone. Earlier, after I hover-logged through the forest with Arella slumped over my shoulder, I climbed onto my motorcycle that was hiding behind some trees, then placed Arella over my lap, straddling my front and rode off. I kept her secure against me with one arm while I controlled my bike with the other. We rode away from Shadow Ridge until my damn motorcycle ran out of gas. That's when I stashed my bike out of sight and continued on foot.

At one point, I stopped to give my arms a break from carrying Arella. When I pulled my phone out of my pocket, it came out in two pieces. I don't know why I was surprised, because if my ribs got smashed, it's likely my phone did too, so I ditched the broken device on the side of the road and kept carrying Arella until I found a place for us to hide.

A smelly barn wouldn't have been my first choice, but at that point, I would have settled for any type of shelter. I was exhausted, everything ached, and I needed to sleep so my body could heal. Unfortunately, the little nap I had did nothing for me. I still feel like I've been hit by a train—multiple times.

Now that I think about it, even if I had my phone, I probably wouldn't turn it on anyway. What if Victor was tracking me on it?

"Is your parents' safe house underground?" Arella asks.

"Yes, but like I said, I don't know where it is. I know the general location, but that's it."

"How do you know the general location?"

"My parents left me a message—sorry, a *riddle*, in my childhood teddy bear telling me about it."

Her eyes go wide as she gasps. "That's the bear that kept asking you for a password!"

"Correct."

She perks up in her seat. "What's the password and riddle? Maybe I can help."

I don't want to, but I have to let go of her hand to be able to dig into my pocket. Otherwise, I'd have to drive with my knees, and my body is way too fucking sore for that.

After shifting Arella's diamond necklace to the side, I find the button-shaped device. I haven't pressed it since I was whacked against the ground, so I hope it still works.

I press the button.

Nothing happens. No robotic voice saying, "Password?" Not even a sign that it's *trying* to work.

I press the device again.

Still nothing.

I flip the device over and find a small crack down the center. *Great.* With a sigh, I toss it into the sea of trash behind me. "Good thing I've got it all memorized. The password to unlock the message was a song my mother wrote for me to encourage me to keep moving forward in life."

"Can you sing it?" Arella asks.

So I do. "When you're lost without me, you'll always have Andy. When you feel you don't belong, hug this bear and sing this song. Look to the sky when you feel down. Know that things will turn around. Work twice as hard to the finish line. Now it's your time to shine."

"That's some password," Arella says.

"Yeah, I know." After a deep breath, I recite the recorded message from my parents, word for word, and try not to choke up at the end. Speaking the message to someone is like admitting out loud that my parents knew whatever mission they were working on could kill them, and they still chose their job over me. I hate having to verbalize that my parents abandoned me on purpose.

"Are you sure that's it?" Arella asks when I finish. "Did they leave you a map or something? A follow-up message in a second bear?"

"Maybe they did and it got blown up when the house exploded. I dunno. Either way, that's all I've got."

Arella bends forward and opens the glove compartment. She's pretty brave to poke through it with her bare hands. I wouldn't be touching anything inside this biohazard of a car if I didn't have to.

"What're you looking for?"

"Something to write on. Aha!" She holds up a crumpled receipt like she's won a prize. "Now I just need . . . aha!" She holds up a pen with the most adorable *I did it* face. "Sing that song and tell me that message again. I'm gonna write both down."

"Why?"

"Because maybe once it's transcribed, we'll be able to see a secret message."

I raise a skeptical eyebrow. "You think my parents left me a cypher?"

"They could have."

"They died when I was seven. I wasn't smart enough to decode a cypher at that age. My theory is that they gave my Aunt Debbie information that was supposed to help me decode this but that information died with her."

"Come on, Trey," she says, slumping her shoulders. "At least let me *try*."

"Fine." Slowly, I tell her the lyrics to my mother's song. Arella scribbles each word down until it fills the entire backside of the receipt. When she's done, she sits back to admire her work.

"This is wonderful! Now tell me the message."

I say every single word exactly as my parents said it, until Arella's got a backside of another receipt covered in her loopy handwriting.

As we continue down our route, Arella reads the words to herself over and over. I remain quiet while she thinks, admiring her determination to solve this puzzle. If I thought my parents had left me a cypher, I would have done this already. I won't tell Arella she's wasting her time though. The more she's thinking about this, the less she's thinking about how mad she is at me.

I'm going to make this up to her. I don't know when, and I don't know how, but someday, someway, I'm going to make up for my mistakes.

61

TREY

This starving car has been begging for me to feed it with gas for the last fifteen minutes. Every minute or so, it yells at me with an annoying *Ding! Ding!* and a flashing gas-tank icon.

If we run out of fuel, I'll have to use my powers to hover this car down the road as if I was driving it, because the goddamn sun is up. I'm not confident I can do that. Arella and I on a rubber tire is one thing, but a whole-ass car? And for how long?

I'm so exhausted, I could close my eyes and fall asleep within seconds. I'm so hungry, my body is withering away. My head's pounding, and I can barely breathe without my ribs throbbing. Using my powers will only weaken me more, and if I get so weak to the point that my powers shit out again, then what? I can't imagine Arella will let me steal another—

I gasp when I see it. It's like a light at the end of the longest and darkest tunnel, right there on the corner of an intersection, next to a Subway. A sandwich sounds amazing right now. I doubt it's open at—I check the clock on the dashboard—seven in the morning.

Arella peers up from the two receipts she's written on. "Oh, goodie! A gas station. It's about time."

She has no idea.

"You gettin' anywhere with that?" I pull the car up to the closest gas pump and shift the gear into park. I sense one person inside the general store. A maroon Hyundai Elantra is parked at the side of the building. It must belong to the employee inside.

Carefully, Arella folds the receipts in half, then half again, and slides them into the side pocket of her leggings. "I think I have to be at your secret rock for any of this to make sense. I have some theories though."

"Like what?"

"What if when your mom asked you to take one hundred steps, she was thinking they were kid-size steps?"

"Tried that. I took kid steps and adult steps." I unbuckle my seat belt and feel something sticky on my fingertips. *This car is so fucking nasty.*

"Could the song be a clue? Like the part that says, *work twice as hard to the finish line.* Maybe that means you need to take two hundred steps, not one hundred."

Now that's an idea! If that works, this woman is a genius. "I've never thought of that. How 'bout we take a trip there after we see the Healer?"

"Sounds good."

"Great. Now could you help me shut this car off?"

She places her palm into mine, takes a deep breath, then nods. "I'm ready."

I point at the ignition, and the engine stops rumbling. Arella's about to open her door when I stop her with a hand over her thigh. "What are you doing?"

She gives me a *what do you think I'm doing?* look. "Going to the bathroom?"

"Can you wait 'til I'm done pumping?"

"Why?"

"Because I need you at an arm's length at all times."

"I'll be fine." She rolls her eyes, and I can't understand why. Does she not realize how much danger we're in? Or how much it'll kill me if something happens to her again? She reaches for the door handle a second time.

I grab her arm. "Arella, please. Don't make this harder for me than it already is. How can I protect you in there if I'm all the way out here?"

"I wouldn't need your protection if you hadn't put my life in danger in the first place."

Ouch. I never meant for her to get hurt. Once I realized she could be, I did what I could, short of kidnapping her myself, to try to get her out of Victor's reach. And that was back when I thought he had good intentions. If I had known he was a double agent, I one hundred percent would have tied her up and flown her to a deserted island—save her first, answer questions later.

"Arella . . ." My voice cracks at the end of her name. "I am so s—"

She throws a hand up to silence me. "Whatever. I don't want to fight about this. Just go pump the gas. I'll hold it in."

I stare at her as I debate whether or not to continue what I was gonna say. What good will an apology do anyway? No words can ever erase what's happened to her.

My chest feels like it's weighed down by a grand piano as I exit the vehicle. I barely read the machine's screen as I press buttons. I can't remove the way she just glared at me out of my head. As I stick the nozzle into the car, I clench my jaw to hold back from breaking down.

While the gas pumps, I glower into the distance with my back facing the car. I can't let her see the bullshit falling from my eyes. I blink it away as I force my body to suck in a deep breath. Slowly, I let it out. Then I suck in another. I should do it again, but it's hurting my ribs, so I quit.

When I'm done with the gas, Arella doesn't speak to me as we head toward the general store. She barely even looks my way when I hold the door open for her. I know I deserve the silent treatment. That doesn't make it hurt any less.

A bell above the door rings as the door shuts behind me. Bright lights shine above the many aisles of candies, snacks, and trucker hats. No one is at the counter. One person's blah energy wafts toward me from behind a door marked OFFICE. EMPLOYEES ONLY.

I'm like a puppy with separation anxiety as Arella and I head into separate bathrooms. It's the first time she'll be out of my sight since I got her away from Shadow Ridge. I'm hesitant to leave her, but if the Royals suddenly appear here, I'll know it the second I sense more than one person.

After I do my business, I scrub my bloody hands off with soap and water at the sink. In the mirror, a gory version of myself stares back. Dark untrimmed beard. Bruised cheeks. Gashes in my lips. Lines of crusty red drip down my face. I look like a victim in a horror film.

I stick my head under the faucet to wash off my face and hair. It hurts like hell to bend into the sink like this. Still, I do it until the water runs clear. When I glance back up at the mirror, the blood is all gone—mostly.

I hiss through my teeth as I unzip my leather jacket. Spots of black and blue cover my torso. The area where my ribs are on fire has the worst discoloration. With a light finger, I press on it. Big mistake. It stings so much, it sends the pain all the way down to my calves. *We've gotta get to that Healer—stat.*

Carefully, I zip my jacket back up, then exit the bathroom. Since I took so long, I thought Arella would already be out here waiting for me, but she's not. A quick glance around the general store shows no signs of her either.

I knock on the women's bathroom door. "Arella?"

No answer.

I knock again, harder this time. "Arella?"

I curse that I can't sense her. I turn the knob, expecting it to be locked, but it opens. The bathroom is empty. My stomach plummets.

I sprint across the aisles. "Arella!"

She's nowhere in sight. *Did she return to the car?*

I bolt out of the store. At the car, I peer through the windows. She's not here. *Where the fuck is she? Did they find us? But how?* I would have sensed them arrive. Arella would have screamed, and I definitely would have heard that.

A spike of anxiety comes from inside the store. I still only sense one person. Why are they suddenly—it hits me. *She's asking for help.*

I rush back toward the store with so much adrenaline that I almost forget about the agony in my torso. The bell above the door rings as I sprint inside. Exactly like before, no one's at the counter. Not missing a beat, I jump over the counter and burst through the office door.

At least, that's what I was *trying* to do.

Instead, my body slams into the locked door, and it ignites a fire throughout my rib cage. I brace myself against the wall and groan as I press a hand against my side. It takes me a few seconds to recover. Once I do, I wave a hand at the doorknob and stumble in.

A thick man wearing glasses sits in a rolling chair behind a messy desk, with a cell phone pressed to his ear. He takes one glance at me, then his fear whips me in the face.

"Could you explain that again, sir?" a woman says from the phone.

I march up to the pudgy guy with the DENNIS name tag pinned to his polo shirt. I snatch the device from his hands and glare at the screen. The numbers 9-1-1 flash back at me. I press the big red End Call button, then chuck the phone onto his desk. "What did you tell them?"

Dennis puts his hands up in surrender. "I—I told them that some people appeared out of nowhere and kidnapped a young woman out of the store."

"What?"

"I—I saw it happen on the security cameras." He points to a computer monitor showing a bunch of empty aisles.

"What do you mean, some people appeared out of nowhere?"

"Like they j—just appeared. Like out of thin air. Then they disappeared."

I pull at the ends of my hair. *You've gotta be fucking kidding me.* I just went through hell getting her away from them, and they stole her back within mere seconds with a goddamn Teleporter?

How did they even track us here? Arella assured me she was making me immune the whole time and—*Wait* . . . How did the Teleporter pop Arella out of here when she's immune? There's no way. Also, why did this man's anxiety only spike now and not while I was in the bathroom when he would have seen it on the cameras? He's lying, and I bet I know who told him to.

I grit my teeth together as I grab Dennis by his polo and yank him toward me. "Where is she?"

"I—I told you! They took her!"

"No, they didn't." I shake him. "Where. Is. She?"

The man shrinks into himself. "Please! Don't hurt me! She just told me to call the police and to tell you that some guys appeared like magic and took her. I just did what I was told. She looked like she was bleeding. I thought I was helping her!"

"No! *I'm* the one trying to help her! Do you realize what you just did by calling the police? Now *they* know exactly where she is. They're probably on their way right now."

Some rustling comes from the other side of a door marked SUPPLIES. I drop Dennis back into his chair and run to the supply closet as the door swings open.

Arella slams into my chest on her way out. My ribs light on fire again. I take a moment to gasp for air, then I lay it on her.

"What the hell are you doing?" I grab her by her shoulders and shake her. I'm not trying to stay calm anymore. I can't. I've never been so angry with her. "Why did you tell him to call the police?"

She shoves me off her. "Because I want someone I can trust to come get me."

Ouch. She'd rather trust a bunch of strangers in uniforms than me. Add that to the growing list of things she's said that will tear me apart at night. "Arella, the Royals have people planted all over the system. We can't trust anyone! Now come on. We've gotta go before they get here." Seizing her unwounded arm, I tug her toward the exit.

She jerks her arm back and stands her ground. "No. I'm not going anywhere with you."

I press the heels of my palms against my temples. "Please, please, tell me you're joking right now."

"I'm not. Staying around you is dangerous. *You're* the one they're tracking. Not me. Wouldn't it make the most sense for me to get as far away from the thing they're tracking as possible?"

I toss my arms up and let them flop to my thighs. "Fine. Let's say we do that. Where are you gonna go? It's not like you can run back to your apartment, or Javina, or your grandparents. They'll find you there. And once they do, who's going to protect you?"

"They won't find me. I'll hide."

I scoff. "Where?"

"I can't tell you! What if they capture you and torture you for that information?"

I screw my eyes shut and pinch the bridge of my nose. She's being difficult on purpose, and the only thing it's accomplishing is wasting time. "You're not telling me where because you don't know of a place to go."

"Okay, maybe that's true. If it is, it's not much different from your nonexistent plan, except my plan is better because mine doesn't involve sticking around the thing they're tracking!"

I hate that she's mostly right. The only thing she's got wrong is that, while I might be dangerous by association, I'm also the only person in this world who's willing to die to keep her alive. She's safer with me than she is without.

I debate throwing her over my shoulder, chucking her into the car, and driving away. Save her first, answer questions later. She can be mad at me all she wants. At least then she'll be safe. The Royals could be here any—

Pop!

From right outside the gas station, three people's emotions enter my head.

62

ARELLA

Trey may be trying to protect me, but I wouldn't need his protection if I hid somewhere by myself, then got help from someone the Royals weren't tracking.

I thought once Trey realized I was missing, he'd drive away to look for me, and then once the police got here, I could be safe with them. Not once did I think the cops were Royals too. Is the entire government system infested with bad guys?

Pop!

Trey's eyes go wide. He grabs my hand and drags me back toward the supply closet I was just hiding in.

"Arella, I swear to fucking god if they get their hands on you again, I will lose any sanity I have left. So please just do what I say, get to the back of this closet, and don't come out for any reason. Got it?" Without waiting for a response, Trey shoves me into the closet and shuts the door.

I'm drowned in darkness. The only light coming in is from the tiny crack under the door.

From the other side, Trey whispers, "Get under that desk and hide, or they'll kill you too."

Earlier, I got a glimpse of the inside of this tiny supply closet. It's full of boxes, mops, and a vacuum. None of it looked organized, and there's no way I can get to the back without making noise. Besides, I can't see anything. So I stay exactly where I am.

It's silent for a few seconds, then that bell above the door rings.

"You check the bathrooms," a woman says off in the distance. "Bruce and I will go this way."

"Yes, ma'am," a man says.

Seconds later, the office door handle clicks.

"Locked," a deep voice says. I picture the voice belonging to a seven-foot man with huge arm muscles and a thick chest.

The woman scoffs. "Seriously, Bruce? You're a Porter. Since when has a locked door ever stopped you?"

"Right." *Pop!*

What comes next sounds like utter chaos: people shouting, things toppling over, and a shriek that would leave a man's mouth only if he was kicked in the balls or stabbed in the chest.

"What the fuck?" Dennis shouts. "Fire just came out of—"

"Get down!" Trey yells.

Someone screams at the top of their lungs. It's not Trey's screams. It didn't sound like deep-voiced Bruce or the woman either, so it must have been Dennis.

"Find the girl!" Bruce says. "I've got him!"

A loud yelp grabs a hold of my heart like someone is reaching into my chest and sinking their sharp nails into it. I'd know that sound anywhere because it's the same sound I heard for days as they tortured him in front of me.

I'm about to leap out of the supply closet to save him when a thought hits me: Whatever I can do out there is the same thing I can do from right here. Closing my eyes, I picture Trey in my head and imagine shoving him into an ocean. Waves of water surround him like a liquid shield. Within seconds, his screaming stops, then a man grunts with pain.

"What the hell?" Bruce shouts.

I keep imagining my waves surrounding Trey as someone kicks against the locked office door. It must be the other guy trying to get in. He kicks again. Then again. And again, until the door crashes against the floor.

"You help Bruce!" the woman says. "I'll find the girl."

Instinctively, I grab the closet's door handle and pull it back. I feel for a lock, but there isn't one. From the other side, the woman attempts to turn the handle. My heart races as I put all my weight into keeping the door shut. The woman tries turning the knob again and yanks. This time, the door opens a crack, and I catch a glimpse of her before I yank on the doorknob and brace my feet against the doorframe to secure my precious barrier.

"Get away from there!" Dennis yells.

Bang! Bang! Bang!

I jolt with each loud gunshot that echoes through the air. Just outside the closet, someone's body thumps against the floor, blocking all light coming through the door's bottom crack.

"Lisa!" a man shouts. "You worthless Ordinary! You fucking killed her!"

"Get away from me!" Dennis shouts.

"Ow! You'll pay for that."

"I said, get away!"

Bang! The door rattles as someone's body thumps against it.

"And I said you'd pay for that," a man says from right outside my door.

Dennis cries out in a half squeal, half yelp. He gurgles, then his screaming stops. His thick body thumping onto the floor makes me gasp.

With a grunt, the man picks up the woman's body and moves her away from the closet. I pull on the door handle with everything I've got, but it's not enough. The man twists the handle, and the door is yanked open.

Trey lets out a gut-wrenching wail. If he's wailing, that means he's alive, but that also means I've lost concentration.

A bald man grabs me by the front of my shirt. "I've got her, Bruce!"

I punch and kick at my captor as I picture waves of water surrounding Trey again. A second later, his wailing stops.

"How are you doing that?" Bruce asks, and it's the first time someone's asked that question and I've been happy about it.

"Hurry up and kill him!" my captor says as he blocks my punches.

"What the fuck do you think I'm trying to do?" Bruce chucks an ice ball at Trey's head.

Trey dodges the spikes, then runs the other way as he tosses a fireball at Bruce. The flames miss, hitting a stack of cardboard boxes instead. The boxes catch on fire with flames crackling toward the ceiling.

A flash of flying dark gray metal catches my eye. I yelp as my captor releases my shirt just as a large filing cabinet hits him. The metal bangs against his head with a bone-crushing *clank!* I'll never be able to unhear.

The man falls to the floor with the heavy metal cabinet landing on top of him. I expect him to get right back up, but he doesn't even stir.

"You bastard!" Bruce shouts as he punches Trey in the face. Trey stumbles backward, clutching his cheek. Bruce, who's almost twice the size of Trey, kicks him in the stomach. Trey falls backward with a grunt, then Bruce climbs on top of him.

"Arella, run!"

Bruce wraps his hands around Trey's neck. Trey claws at the man's hands as I glance around for something I can hit the guy with, something heavy, like a fire extinguisher, or a large—I gasp. A handgun! It's lying on the floor inches from Dennis's limp body.

I dive toward the weapon as if someone else was going for it too. It's heavier than I thought it would be. I've never held a gun before. *Are they always this heavy?* My hands shake as I hold it up and aim it at the man straddling Trey. *Oh no.* What if I miss? What if I hit Trey? How do I do this? Do I just pull the trigger?

Suddenly, an ear-piercing alarm blares from the ceiling. Seconds later, the sprinklers activate and rain onto everything.

Trey wails as Bruce beats his large fists into Trey's ribs. I keep imagining my ocean waves surrounding Trey as I aim my weapon. I can't get a good shot though. Bruce keeps moving, and my hands keep shaking. I command my feet to get closer, but they don't listen. They're frozen where they are.

"Run!" Trey shouts as he grabs the man's face. A burst of red flames appears in his hands. Bruce screams over the blaring alarm and falls backward, clutching his head.

Now that he's away from Trey, I aim the gun and pull the trigger. *Bang!*

I miss. I pull it again. *Bang!*

And again. *Bang! Bang!*

The man's body jolts twice, then he stops moving altogether.

My ears ring as the gun slips from my shaky grasp. Water drips down my forehead and into my eyes.

Trey's propped up on his elbows, gaping at the dead man, then loses his strength and slumps onto his back.

I rush over to him. "Trey!"

His breaths are sharp as I take his face into my hands. The side of his head is bloody again. So are his nose and his lips and, well, everything.

"Arella . . ." My name comes out in a scratchy broken tone. I barely hear it over the high-pitched beeping of the fire alarm. He points. "My leg."

I slap a hand over my chest and gasp. Something has sliced through his jeans and cut into his left thigh so deep, I could stick my fingertip into it. His blood has already soaked through his jeans, all the way to his calves.

Trey pushes himself back onto his elbows to get a better look. "It's pretty deep, huh? Those fucking ice balls. I tell ya, they can be sharp as hell."

I take another glance at his thigh, and it makes me queasy. It's one thing to see this stuff on TV; it's another to see it in real life.

After I suck in a deep breath of courage, I get to my feet and dash to the supply closet. It takes me a bit of rummaging to find a first aid kit on the top shelf.

When I return to Trey's side, he's lying on his back with his eyes closed, breathing heavily. I set the first aid kit down next to me, then work on getting his belt unbuckled.

Trey grabs my hands. His voice comes out coarse and weak like it's taking all his strength just to speak. "Arella, listen to me. They could be sending more people. You need to go."

"Okay. Let's stop the bleeding first." I reach for the button on his jeans.

He grabs my hands again. "No, Arella. The wound is too deep. I'm . . ." He lets out a painful exhale. "I'll only slow you down. I'll probably bleed out anyway. Just forget about me and get outta here."

Tears well into the corners of my eyes. I shouldn't have asked Dennis to call the police. All I wanted was for this nightmare to be over. I never meant for anyone to get hurt. Now Dennis is lying lifeless on the floor from whatever Baldy did to him as revenge for the woman who is now bleeding out from the holes Dennis put into her. Baldy is still unmoving under that heavy filing cabinet and barely a step from where I'm kneeling is the large man I shot. All of that didn't happen just for me to leave Trey behind to bleed to death. No way.

"You'll be okay," I choke out. "We just have to stop the bleeding until we can get you to a Healer." I get the button of his jeans undone, then I slide the zipper down.

Trey grabs my hands a third time. "Arella, this is not the time to be difficult. More of them could be here any second. A fire department is probably on their way too. Go look through that employee's pockets for his car keys. Then—"

"No!" I shout as tears fall from my eyes. "You're going to be okay. Just let me wrap you up."

"We don't have time for that. Just leave me. You were right earlier. *I'm* the one they're tracking, not you. So you need to get into that guy's car and—"

"No!" I shout over the constant beeping. My body trembles with a sob as I grab his hand and pin it against the floor. "I'm *not* leaving you! No matter what you say, I'm not! So you can either keep fighting with me and waste time, or you can just let me stop the bleeding!"

He stares at me with his mouth slightly open and his eyes dazed. Once he realizes this is a fight he won't win, he gives me a curt nod. Then he flops onto his back and sucks in a sharp breath. "Be quick."

I'm still crying as I cut the jeans off his body with scissors from the first aid kit. Once they're off, I toss the denim aside. His entire leg is dripping with blood. Some of the red has soaked his boxers too. Ignoring the queasy feeling in my belly, I pour an entire bottle of hydrogen peroxide over his wound.

"Fuck!" Trey chomps on his bottom lip as he groans through his teeth.

"I'm sorry," I say as I clean off as much red from his leg as I can with antiseptic wipes. Honestly, I don't even know if this is what I should be doing. I'm a professional with Band-Aids over the knee on children, but this?

A few minutes later, I have Trey's thigh wrapped in gauze and medical tape as tight as I can get it. Hopefully, the pressure will keep the bleeding at bay for now. Once I've got him on his feet and leaned against the wall for support, I go dig through Dennis's pockets. In the first pocket I shove my hand into, I find a set of keys.

When I turn back around, Trey has hobbled over to his jeans and is emptying the pockets, shoving all his stuff into his jacket pockets. Then he tosses the bloody jeans aside and throws a fireball at them. "Okay, let's go."

63

ARELLA

We're parked at the side of a Walmart. The sun blazes high in the sky, making Dennis's car hot. We're almost out of gas, so I don't want to waste it on air conditioning. I'd roll the windows down, but I can't risk someone looking in and seeing that I've got a bloody man sleeping in the front seat.

A while later, I'm halfway through eating a banana when Trey finally stirs and blinks his eyes open.

"Morning," I say.

He sits up, adjusting the seat with him as he squints out the bright window. "Where are we?"

"Walmart." I swallow down the rest of my banana, then toss the peel into a plastic bag with my sandwich and granola bar wrappers already in it.

"Where exactly is this Walmart?"

"Barstow, California—according to the signs I passed on the way in." When we left the burning gas station, my only goal was to get as far away from it as possible, so I drove without knowing where I was going. As far as I can tell, I took us in the general direction of Las Vegas . . . *I hope.*

"Barstow," Trey repeats. "I think that's still another two or three hours from Vegas."

I tear a banana off the bunch and hold it out to him. "Want one?"

He accepts the fruit from me, then peels it open and takes a small bite.

"Does your body naturally heal faster than an Ordinary's?" I ask.

"Yep. Zordis heal during sleep, just like Ordinaries, but much faster."

"I see that. The bruises on your face are almost gone. I can tell where they were, but it looks like what my bruises look like after a week. Is your special healing thing powerful enough to fix broken ribs or a deep thigh wound?"

He groans as he takes another bite of the banana. "I fucking wish."

"Are you hungry for anything else?" I reach back to grab the other three grocery bags from the backseat. I dig through one as I say, "I've got a sandwich, granola bars, chips, apples, and water. If there's anything else you'd like, I can run back in to grab it."

"I'll take a water, please."

I pull out a bottle and hand it over.

Trey chugs it all in one breath, then scarfs down the rest of his banana. He tosses the peel into the same bag I tossed mine in.

I pluck an apple from the food bag. "Here."

He shakes his head. "I should take it slow. I haven't eaten much for days."

I drop the apple back into the bag. "Oh, right."

Now that I think about it, that makes sense. Ever since I was kidnapped, he's been in the infirmary for most of that time. Any time he wasn't in there, he was getting used as a test dummy for people's powers.

I dig through the second bag and drag out a pair of black sweatpants. "I figured this would be more comfortable for you than jeans. I also got you a new shirt, socks, boxers, and some clothes for me too. We can change after I redress your wound."

From the third bag, I pull out some first aid supplies. While in the store, I almost bought some ibuprofen until I remembered it wouldn't do anything for him. Do Zordis have special pain medications they can take? If so, where can we get some?

"Thanks, Arella. All of this is great."

"Thank yourself," I say, gesturing toward his wallet sitting in the cup holder. "You paid for it."

"With cash?"

"Of course. I've seen movies."

When I made it to this Walmart, Trey was still out cold, so I dug through his jacket pockets for his wallet. That's when I caught a glimpse of his bare chest and realized the shirt tied around my arm is probably his. Up until that point, I hadn't thought about where this shirt had come from.

Knowing this man literally took the clothing off his back to give to me makes me feel even worse for trying to ditch him. At the time, getting away from him seemed like a good idea. Now, knowing the Royals have people everywhere, I'm positive the safest place I can be is with Trey.

"Fuck." Trey hisses through his teeth as I clean around his wound with baby wipes. His thigh isn't bleeding as much as it was before, but it still looks gnarly.

After I rewrap his wound with clean gauze and fresh medical tape, I use more baby wipes to clean off his bloody face. The whole time, he lies still and stares at me with an admiration in his eyes that gets my stomach to flutter with love-sick butterflies. This time, I don't try to fight the feeling. For me, there's no resisting this guy.

I unzip his jacket to reveal a red and purple discoloration over his right rib cage. I can't imagine how painful it is. The rest of his torso doesn't look any better. He groans while I help him get into his new shirt—a plain black one, of course. After that, I help get the rest of him into fresh clothes.

"Do you want to put your jacket back on?" I ask, holding it up.

He pants heavily as he slumps back into his seat. "Not right now. That requires more moving."

I set his jacket onto the backseat, then get dressed in my own pair of black sweats and shirt.

"Matching outfits," Trey says. "I likey."

"I don't think I've ever worn all black before. I feel like a ninja."

"You sure shoot like one." He places a gentle hand over my knee. "Thank you for saving me."

I can't look at him as I say, "I wish we could have saved Dennis."

Trey keeps his hand over my knee. "That man was so brave. When that lady ran toward the closet, he didn't hesitate to shoot her. He helped save you."

"And I'll never be able to repay him for it."

"I'll never be able to repay *you* for saving me."

I offer him a warm smile. "I suppose we're even now."

He scoffs. "Not even close. You only needed saving *because* of me."

"Technically, I put you in danger too. I was the one who told Dennis to call the police."

His gaze falls to his lap. "I'll admit that even though it makes me sad, I understand why you did that. You also didn't know the Royals have connections with the police."

"And you didn't know your uncle is a psychotic evil maniac with henchmen."

He scoffs again, shaking his head. "Don't remind me."

I place my hand over his on my knee. "Like I said, we're even now."

"It doesn't feel that way, but I'll take it." He turns his hand over to intertwine his fingers with mine. A warm tingle spreads up my arm, all the way to my shoulders.

It's always felt natural for us to hold hands. Like the way it's always felt natural for us to kiss and make love. If Ordinaries aren't meant to be with people like him, then why does being with him feel so right to me?

"Arella?"

It's official: No matter what happens, I'll always love the sound of my name on his lips. I flick my eyes up to meet his. "Yeah?"

He gives my hand a little squeeze. "Thanks again for not leaving me behind."

I roll my eyes at him. "I can't even believe you asked me to do that."

"I didn't ask. I was telling, but I shoulda known you'd be difficult."

Pfft. "If I wasn't difficult, you'd be bleeding out right now."

"Actually, someone would have found me by now. And if it was the Royals, I'd be dead."

I shake my head at him. "I can't believe you were so ready to accept that fate."

"Well, I thought I was gonna die like, fifteen different times recently, so yeah, I was ready."

"I'm glad you're alive. Now let's get you to a Healer."

Given how we left the gas station in a chaotic, gory, fiery mess, Trey and I conclude it's best if we aren't anywhere near Dennis's car. The Royals or the cops are probably looking for it, so we ditch the car at the Walmart and head a few blocks down to a Greyhound station. Over my shoulders is a newly bought backpack filled with food, water, first aid supplies, and Trey's jacket.

The sound of buses releasing air surrounds us as Trey and I step up to the Greyhound station. Correction: I step up. Trey is limping.

I'm glad I cleaned his face, because even without all the blood covering it, people are staring at us. More specifically, the *women* are staring at Trey.

I almost forgot what it's like to be out in public with the YouTube-famous, gorgeous musician Trey Grant. In LA, we couldn't walk into a single restaurant without someone approaching him for a picture. Thankfully, no one stops us as we make our way past all the people waiting on benches for their buses.

"How can I help y'all?" a lady says from behind the ticket counter. The name tag on her shirt reads LATOYA.

Trey flashes her a sweet smile. "Could I get ten tickets, please?"

The lady barely looks up at him from her computer. "Where to, sir?"

"I'll take one-way tickets for the next buses to Los Angeles, San Diego, Las Vegas, New York, and Houston. Two each."

Finally, the lady looks up at him. From behind her glasses, she knits her eyebrows together. "Is you sayin' you want one bus that will take you to all dem places?"

"No. I'd like tickets for five different buses to all of those places. Two each."

The lady skeptically eyes Trey, then me, then him again.

Trey doesn't miss a beat. From his wallet, he holds out two hundred-dollar bills. "Please?"

Latoya doesn't hesitate to seize the cash and stuff it down her bra. Sighing, she turns back to her computer. Then her long sparkly nails clack against the keyboard. "Don't ask questions, Latoya. Don't ask questions. Just mind ya damn business," she mutters to herself.

A few minutes later, Latoya tells us our total. Trey pays all twelve hundred of it in cash, which only makes her shake her head at us more.

As she hands us five sets of tickets, she says, "Whatever y'all is up to, I ain't want nothin' to do with it. If anyone asks, I was just doin' my damn job."

"And if anyone asks," Trey says, "we were never here."

She flashes him a thumbs-up. "Deal. Now get outta here before y'all get my ass fired."

We exit the ticket booth as Trey slips the tickets into his sweatpants pocket. Then he smiles down at me. "You still hungry?"

I hike our backpack higher up my shoulders. "Starving."

"Me too. Our bus won't leave for another twenty minutes. Let's get something to eat."

The building next to the ticket office is a mini food court. Square tables are scattered around the center area and blissful-looking food stands are lined up around the exterior. The options range from burgers to pizza to Chinese and more. At the end sits a little shop filled with candies, bottled drinks, and souvenirs.

It doesn't take us long to decide on something. We're so hungry, everything sounds good. Together, we join the short line for Panda Express. Not long later, we have two Styrofoam containers of Chinese takeout in hand. We pick the closest table and sit on opposite ends to devour our meal.

"Mmm," I moan as I have my first bite. "This is the most amazing Chinese food in the world."

Trey stuffs his face as he nods. "Heaven is what this is."

I'm halfway done with my lo mein when I ask, "Did you buy all those tickets to throw them off our trail, or are we going somewhere other than Vegas?"

"Still Vegas."

"How did you know which cities to buy tickets for?"

Trey scoops up a spoonful of his fried rice. "I picked cities that have Chinatowns, because every Chinatown has a Healer. Hopefully, if they're tracking us, and I'll bet they are, they'll have a good time trying to figure out which Chinatown we—"

Something behind me catches Trey's attention. His eyes go wide as he drops his plastic fork. Under his breath, he mutters, "Fuck."

I freeze and resist the urge to glance behind me. "Are they here?"

"No," he whispers. "Look."

My chair squeaks against the floor as I spin around. I follow Trey's gaze to a small TV hanging from the wall. I gasp as a female news anchor stares into the camera, saying words I can't hear, while a picture of me is shown beside her head.

The closed captions read, " . . .twenty-two-year-old, Arella 'Ari' Rance, who was reported missing by a friend yesterday. The friend says Rance hasn't answered her phone for a few days, which is unlike the missing woman. When the friend stopped by Rance's apartment, the place had been broken into and Rance was nowhere to be found."

The captions continue as a photo of Trey replaces mine. "Police say their number-one suspect is Rance's most recent ex-boyfriend, Trey Grant. Grant has not been seen or heard from since around the same time Rance went missing. Grant has a violent criminal record, including two counts of disorderly conduct and one misdemeanor."

The news anchor continues as Trey's photo slides off screen. "This morning, we had the opportunity to interview one of Grant's ex-girlfriends. This is what she had to say."

My already racing heart thumps faster as the screen changes to video footage of a blonde woman being interviewed outside a red house. I recognize her right away.

Someone holds a microphone up to Jess's moving lips as the captions read, "Trey and I have been on and off for the past few years. Whenever he gets too angry, he pops me in the face, and I leave. Weeks later, he'll beg for me to come back with promises that he'll change. But you know men like him; they never do."

The screen returns to the news anchor with another picture of Trey. "We've asked close friends of Grant for comments. None have agreed. If you have any information that can help the police locate twenty-two–year-old Ari Rance, please call this tip line."

I turn back to Trey, who drops his head into his hands. I reach over the table to rub his shoulder. "It's okay. When this is all over, I'll clear your name."

"I hate her," he says under his breath. "I fucking hate her. I've never laid a goddamn hand on her like that, and she's gonna go tell a news station that I abused her for years? Is she fucking serious?"

I draw my hand back and rest it over the table. "Are you really more mad about that than the world thinking you've kidnapped me?"

"Kind of." He huffs out a frustrated breath. "I have it in me to kidnap you, but I would *never* abuse a woman like that."

"Okay, *I* understand what you mean when you say you've got it in you to kidnap me. I know you'd do it if it meant protecting me, but please, if anyone else asks, especially the police, don't say that out loud."

Trey offers me a tender smile as he puts his hand over mine on the table and squeezes it. "Thank you for understanding me. That is *exactly* what I mean. Now let's finish eating. Once we're done, we're going shopping."

64

ARELLA

"You look good in a hat," I say as we claim the farthest seat in the back of the bus. We're some of the first people to board. I slide in next to the window, then set our backpack at my feet.

Trey settles down next to me. "You do too."

I wince when he accidentally rubs against the shirt tied around my arm.

"Oops. I'm sorry, babe—I mean, Arella."

I almost forgot I had told him to stop calling me *babe*. I'm fine with him calling me that. I only told him not to because I was angry.

I press against my arm to ease the ache. "It's okay. It doesn't hurt much unless it's bumped. I'm more worried about your ribs and thigh than my arm."

"Funny. I'm more worried about your arm." Trey stands and gestures for me to stand as well. "Let's switch spots so I don't bump your arm anymore."

After we switch, Trey glowers out the window from behind a pair of black sunglasses—another purchase from the souvenir shop. I've got a matching pair covering my eyes. I think he's trying to see if anyone out there is a Royal. Can he know that someone's a Royal just by looking at them?

Katie said Zordis feel a special tingle in their chests whenever they get close to each other. Does Trey's tingle work from a farther distance?

Katie also explained that every Zordi has three powers. Trey's elemental power is Fire, and his body power is telekinesis. I don't know what his mind power is, nor will I ask right now because I don't want him to lose concentration on whatever he's doing. Whatever his mind power is, it was able to tell him that a teenage boy was getting roughed up in an alleyway, and it's able to tell him if someone's a Royal just by looking at them.

The bus is about half full when the bus driver finally shuts the door, and we roll away from the Greyhound station. Only then does the tension in Trey's shoulders relax.

Since the closest people to us are three seats away with headphones on, I turn to Trey and ask in a low voice, "Are there a lot of your kind in the world?"

"Lots. Most live in Europe and Asia."

"And is everyone either a ZIRDA agent or a Royal?"

"No. Most are just regular people. Think of ZIRDA like a secret organization that does research, develops products, and also works to stop the Royals. Then think of the Royals as violent gang members."

I tilt my head to the side. "Why is it up to a research facility to stop violent criminals? Didn't you say you guys have a special government?"

"The zovernment is useless when it comes to getting rid of the Royals. A part of me thinks the Royals pay them off. It wasn't until after the Royals caused the Black Plague that ZIRDA started their anti-Royals department, and only because at the time, the zovernment was too busy still trying to clean up the mess from the mass genocide and worldwide scrub job. Considering that was over six hundred years ago and the Royals are still around, I think it'll take more than the zovernment and ZIRDA to get rid of them."

I take a moment to process all that before asking, "Why don't the zovernment and ZIRDA work together to fight off the Royals?"

"Because that's not how things work. That's like saying, why don't the cops team up with regular civilians to stop crime? To the zovernment, ZIRDA is just a bunch of researchers who *think* they're vigilantes. To ZIRDA, the zovernment is nothing more than some elites in uniforms who only care about keeping Ordinaries from finding out about us."

"Interesting." There is still so much I want to learn about Trey's world, but my eyelids are getting heavy. I fall asleep within minutes.

When I wake up to our bus pulling into the Greyhound station in Vegas, Trey is wide awake.

"Why didn't you take a nap?" I ask as I lift my head off his shoulder.

"How can I protect you if I'm sleeping?"

My heart does a little backflip in my chest. It's endearing how much he cares about me and isn't afraid to show it.

"Besides," Trey says, "I was enjoying watching you sleep. Whenever you stayed over and it wasn't my night to sleep, I used to spend those hours just holding you and trying to sync my breaths with yours."

With anyone else, that statement would be creepy. With Trey, it's wholesome. He told me once that he used to hate cuddling until he cuddled with me. I'm happy to know he likes cuddling with me enough to do it for hours upon hours without getting bored.

I tilt my head back so he can see my smirk. "When this is over, I'll be sure to tell the media that watching women sleep is one of your favorite hobbies."

Trey lets out a light laugh. "They'll love that."

We're the last to leave the bus. When our feet are back on the ground, Trey spends a moment scanning the crowd.

"I think we're good." He takes my hand, then leads me toward a row of taxis waiting for passengers.

We pick a taxi toward the front of the line and climb into the backseat.

"Gold Coast Hotel and Casino, please," Trey says.

Fifteen minutes later, the driver drops us off outside a large white building with wide arches in the front. Some gold letters at the top of the building read CASINO.

I wait until the taxi is gone before saying, "I thought we were going to Chinatown."

"We are."

I glance around us because I must be missing something, but even after a second look, I confirm that there's nothing here that remotely resembles a Chinatown. No Chinese characters on buildings. No pagodas. No dragons with open mouths scaring off the evil.

"In case anyone asked him, I didn't want the driver dropping us off *inside* Chinatown," Trey says as he begins half walking, half limping down the sidewalk. "We're only a few blocks away."

"How many is a few?" One block already sounds like too much. This backpack is heavy, my body is sore, and these flats I'm wearing are almost paper thin. I might as well be barefoot.

"Would you like me to carry you?"

"Are you serious? You have broken ribs, and you can barely walk on your own."

He shrugs nonchalantly. "I carried you with my broken ribs before. And I did it for miles."

"What? When?"

"How do you think I got us to that barn after my motorcycle ran out of gas?"

My mouth drops. "You had me on a motorcycle while I was passed out?"

"Yep."

"Where is it now?"

He shrugs again. "On the side of a road somewhere."

"But you love that thing."

"Not as much as I love you."

My heart skips a beat as I gaze up at him. His eyes meet mine with a look that says, *I mean those words with every fiber of my soul.*

Earlier, when we were on the flying tire and he confessed his love to me, I didn't know how to feel. At the time, I was trying to process the idea that we didn't meet by accident and that he spent weeks fake-dating me solely to gather information for his uncle. Hearing him say the L-word again now, I *still* don't know how to feel.

I keep putting one foot in front of the other. "Didn't you say that besides your memory box, your motorcycle is your most sentimental possession?"

Trey told me once that I'm the first woman he's ever taken on a motorcycle ride. He said his motorcycle is special to him because it's what he rode while he traveled the states, searching for his *place in the world.* He said he had never wanted to share that experience with anyone else until he met me.

"You remember me saying that?" Trey says.

"Of course. You don't open up a lot. Whenever you do, I take notes."

He keeps his attention on the sidewalk. "I've opened up more with you than I have with anyone else."

"That's not true. Don't you tell Liz everything?"

"Nah. She has to force it out of me. And trust me, I make her work for it."

Liz has told me on more than one occasion that Trey is like a puzzle box: *"No matter how hard you twist and turn him, he won't open. However, if you're patient and keep working on him, you'll be rewarded with bits and pieces, but it's still never the full picture."*

At the time, I wasn't sure if I agreed with Liz's description of Trey. I thought after he had shared with me that his parents hadn't actually died in a house fire that I had unlocked everything I needed to know. Turns out, Liz was right.

I play with the straps of our backpack as I ask, "Have you ever told Liz that you love her?"

Trey's answer comes easily. "No. Not soberly, anyway. She claims I said it once when I was wasted, but I don't remember it, which means it doesn't count."

"It probably counts for her. I actually think it counts more because it was unfiltered."

"I don't love Liz the way I love you, if that's what you're wondering."

"I'm not. I've seen how you two are together. The kind of relationship you guys have is pretty exceptional, but not romantic."

He lets out a little scoff. "You should say that to the media. Maybe they'll stop making up stories about me leading her on."

"Okay, to review, the list goes: Trey Grant did not kidnap me, he does not abuse women, he likes to watch women sleep, and he does not want to bang Liz Hart."

A bright smile lights up his face, and it's the brightest one I've seen on him in what feels like weeks. "Yes. In that order."

I miss these moments between us when we're just talking, all light and playful. I miss the way things were when simply being with him was enough. I miss feeling like as long as I had Trey by my side, everything else would fall into place. Can we ever be like that again?

I don't know how that can happen, considering that law forbidding Zordis from being with Ordinaries. If the zovernment is afraid that I'll find out about their world, that ship has sailed. Maybe now I can be an exception. Is that a thing? Can they make exceptions?

I can't be the first Ordinary who has found out about Zordis. Trey mentioned that they erase the memories of those people, but since they can't do that with me, what would happen instead? I'm not sure if I want to find out.

I know we've made it to Chinatown when some reddish-orange pagoda roofs with curved edges appear in the distance. The signs say things like THAI FOOD, PHO, and SUSHI. Still no dragon statues warding off bad people, but there is a golden statue of an Asian man riding a horse.

Trey leads me past a bunch of shops. Most of them look slow and empty. The parking lot is pretty vacant too.

We're walking past more shops when Trey stops and his body goes rigid. I follow his gaze to a storefront window, where a bunch of miniature golden cat statues are waving at us with one arm. Trey stares at them like they're about to spring alive and attack him.

Suddenly, he grabs my hand. Then he flips around and scans the parking lot.

I give him a moment before asking, "Is everything okay?"

"Uh, yeah." With a tug on my arm, we continue walking. Not even for a second does Trey release his firm grip on me. I don't mind. It's giving me a sense of comfort and safety.

His mind power must be some type of danger alarm. That's how he knew that teenage boy was getting hurt. That's how he can know if a Royal is close. If his danger alarm went off just now, why aren't we trying to hide?

My feet are achy by the time we stop outside a store with a turned-off neon sign that says GINSENG. The inside is dark and messy. Cardboard boxes are scattered all over the floor.

A handwritten note on a blank sheet of paper is taped to the inside of the door.

Closed for remodeling. Reopen Oct 1.

"You've gotta be fucking kidding me," Trey grumbles.

"Is there another Healer nearby?"

Trey responds to my question by banging on the glass door. "Hello?"

I seize his arm. "Stop! Didn't you read the sign? They're closed."

He ignores me and slams his other palm against the glass. "We need help! Please!"

"Trey!" I try shoving him from the store, but it's like trying to move a house. He barely budges. "Stop it. No one's here."

"Yes, there is. Two people are inside this shop, and they heard me. They're just refusing to come out."

"How do you know? Can you see through walls?"

He knocks again. "Please! It's urgent!" He bangs some more until his fist stops in midair. "Thank fuck. Someone's coming."

A short Asian man in his early sixties glares at Trey and me as he unlocks the door. He opens it a crack just so he can yell at us in his thick Chinese accent. "Can you read duh sign? Open October one! Right now, not October one!"

"We need your help," Trey says.

"Come back October one." The man is about to shut the door when Trey sticks his arm through the opening.

"Please, I'm begging you. She's hurt. All she needs is a little Healing Goo."

I'm not the one who needs the most healing; Trey is.

The gray-haired man wiggles a finger in the air. "You know duh law. No healing foh her."

"She already knows about us."

The Asian man scolds Trey like a father would a son for swearing when he shouldn't have. "You should be in z-prison then. Now go away before I report you to duh Enforcers."

"Please! She's sliced badly." Trey points at the bloodstained T-shirt wrapped around my arm.

The Asian man is still unfazed. "Maybe next time you don't play with sharp tings."

"She was kidnapped by the Royals. They're the ones who hurt her. Please? I'll pay whatever you want."

"Royals?" The Asian man's eyes go wide as he shoves, or attempts to shove, Trey from the door. "No, no, no! Go away! Do not bring dem here. I don't want trouble."

Trey opens his mouth, probably about to beg again, when a woman yelling from inside the store stops him. She's yelling in Chinese, and she doesn't sound happy. The Asian man responds in the same language in an equally yelly tone. The woman shouts back, then appears from around a shadowy corner. She looks a few years younger than the man—probably his wife.

With a hand to her chest, she gasps. Slowly, she approaches the door. The whole time, she stares at Trey with her mouth wide open. It's not the same astonishment he usually gets from the young women who recognize him off social media. This lady's shock feels different. Maybe she recognizes him from the news. If that's the case, why is she not running to call the police? Instead, she's . . . tearing up? *Huh?*

"Are you . . ." She takes a step closer. "Are you Trey Grant?"

Trey grips my arm. He looks like he's about to run away and drag me with. "Who wants to know?"

"Wow. You are not a kid anymore, but it's definitely you. You look so much like your father." The lady turns to her husband, scolding him. "Trey Grant shows up at our door, and you want to kick him away? How ungrateful!"

The Asian man throws his arms up. "How was I supposed to know who he is? He is not wearing a name tag."

"Please excuse my husband's cluelessness." With a beaming smile, the lady shoves her husband aside and waves for us to enter their shop. "Come in, come in. Let me get a better look at you."

I glance at Trey, who looks back at me with a weary look. Still, he grips my hand tightly, and we enter the store.

While the Asian man locks the door behind us, the lady gapes up at Trey. He's almost two heads taller than her.

"Wow. You're so big, and tall, and very handsome. Look at your arms." She takes the liberty of squeezing his muscular bicep. "I can't believe it's really you. And who's your friend? She's so beautiful. Very long hair and—" The lady with no boundaries is about to touch my waves when Trey extends a protective arm in front of me and pulls me behind him.

"Don't touch her. Tell me who you are. How do you know me?"

The lady is unbothered by Trey's *ready to attack* stance. She slaps a hand against her forehead. "Oh, right! I apologize. I'm being rude. Of course you don't remember. My name is Li-Fong. Most people call me Li. You used to call me Auntie Li-Li. This is my husband, Tao. Your parents were our best friends. Come, come. I'll show you."

Trey gives me a look like, *should we follow this lady?* I respond with a shrug. Curiosity must take him over, because he grabs my hand again. Then we follow the eager woman through her dimly lit store that smells of herbs, spices, and dry earth.

"Watch your step," Li says. "We're remodeling. There's stuff everywhere."

She's not exaggerating. The shelves are covered with giant glass jars filled with dehydrated things. I can't even begin to guess what they are. Boxes are stacked on top of each other so high, I'd need a ladder to reach the top. I can barely see any of the wood flooring through this chaos.

Li takes us down a long flight of stairs, flipping lights on along the way. The steps creak under our feet. When we reach the bottom, she flips more lights on. The basement is one big room that's dim, cool, and has equally as much stuff everywhere.

One half of the basement is a little kitchen featuring cluttered countertops and a dining table for two. Opposite of that is a small living room with a loveseat and some end tables covered with old books.

The other side of the basement looks like a giant office, with an array of desks, chairs, and storage shelves along the walls. Every surface is littered with big books, glass jars, and tattered boxes.

On a desk in the corner is a bunch of papers with Chinese characters written on them. From the bottom drawer, Li drags out a photo album and flips some pages until she finds what she's looking for. She removes one of the 4x6 prints from the book and hands it to Trey. He accepts it with the hand that's not holding mine.

"This picture was taken when you were only a year old," Li says.

Trey gapes at the photo with his mouth slightly open. I steal a glance too. The picture features five people standing outside this shop with a banner above them that says GRAND OPENING!

Younger versions of Li and Tao are standing next to Trey's mom, who's holding baby Trey over her hip. On the other side of Trey's mom is a younger version of Victor. In the picture, he's smiling so brightly, I barely recognize him. I've only ever seen Victor scowling. It's weird to see him look so happy.

"Your parents came to visit on opening week to help us kick off this shop," Li says. "For many years, they visited almost every month. They always brought you to play with our kids, who are slightly older than you. I doubt you remember them either."

"I don't," Trey says with his attention still glued to the photo.

"My husband is the original Healer who provided the teardrops for your parents to research and develop the formula for healing products. Our cut of the royalties allows us to live a pretty good life."

"Uh . . ." Trey points to the picture. "This is definitely me, and that's definitely my mom, but that's not my dad. That's my uncle, Victor. My dad and Victor were born only fourteen months apart, and they looked a lot alike, so a lot of people got them confused."

Li stares at Trey for a lingering second before she turns to Tao, who's leaned against a table behind us. She says something to him in Chinese. Tao responds in Chinese with a half shrug. Li says something while gesturing at Trey, and Tao responds in more Chinese. They do this back and forth for a moment before Li's attention returns to Trey.

"All right," Li says. "We decided you should know the truth."

Trey's shoulders go taut. "What truth?"

"Victor is not your uncle. He's your father."

65

TREY

I'm not breathing. I—I don't think I know how to anymore.

"Maybe you should sit down." Li snaps her fingers. "Tao, hurry. Bring him a chair. One for the girl too."

The world seems to blur as Tao appears behind me with two clanky folding chairs. I don't register anything he says as he puts a hand on my shoulder, gently shoving me into a chair. My ribs ache as I sit.

Tao says more stuff to me. I know because his mouth is moving, but his words aren't making it to my brain.

The knot in my chest tightens as my fingers tremble. My breaths are short. My mouth feels dry. I feel like I'm going to fall over. *Breathe*, I command myself. I shut my eyes and try to take in a breath, but my lungs don't obey. If I can't get myself under control, this entire place will go up in flames.

A warm pair of hands cups my face, jump-starting my lungs. Finally, I can breathe again. I know whose hands these are because they're the same hands that have always centered me before.

I open my eyes to find Arella's brown ones staring back at me. She's kneeling in front of me with concern etched into her furrowed eyebrows. Behind her, Li and Tao are whispering to each other in Chinese.

"I'm sorry," I choke out, staring at my shoes. I can't look anyone in the eyes.

Arella doesn't take her hands off me. "You're okay, honey. Just breathe."

I suck in a deep breath through my nose, then let it out through my mouth. She just called me *honey*. She hasn't called me that in too long. Hearing it offers me a tiny sense of peace.

"Tao asked you if you'd like some water," Arella says.

I keep my focus on her, hoping she'll continue to calm me. "Water sounds great."

Tao's legs leave my sight. On the other side of the basement, a fridge door opens, then closes. Then Tao returns with two bottles of water. He hands one to Arella, then one to me. I place mine in my lap while I continue trying to pull myself together.

Li grabs another folding chair from the other side of the room and sets it in front of me to sit on. Tao does the same, then Arella climbs into her own chair until the four of us make a square. As if reading my mind, Arella scoots closer to me, placing her hand over my thigh. It's exactly what I need.

Li folds her hands together in her lap. "I can tell you as much or as little as you'd like, Trey. Just tell me when you're ready."

"I'm ready," I lie.

"How much do you want to know?"

"Everything," I say breathlessly. "I want to know everything."

"All right. Um, how about I start from the beginning? Your mom, Suzie, and I met during our first year at California State University in Fresno. We became instant best friends and did everything together. That's the year she met Andy too. They began dating right away. He proposed the next year and they got married the next."

Li leaves our talking square and returns with the photo album she had earlier. She pulls out a 4x6 print and hands it to me. In the photo, my mom is wearing a lacey white dress. Two ladies stand on each side of her. One is Aunt Debbie. The other is a younger version of Li. They're wearing matching burgundy dresses and holding bouquets of flowers.

"I was a bridesmaid. Suzie's sister was the maid of honor. Small wedding. Close friends and family only. Victor flew in from New York just to attend. Over the years that Suzie and Andy were together, she and Victor didn't have many interactions. Victor was super focused on finishing his engineering degree, and he spent a lot of time with his fiancée, Jodi, in New York. After he finished his degree, Victor and Jodi moved to Three Rivers, where Victor started working at ZIRDA. Shortly after, they were married as well.

"Suzie and Andy had already been ZIRDA agents for about a year. They were researching how to transfer the healing ability from a Healer's tears into a usable product. It was Andy who theorized that it *could* happen and the both of them who put in the years of research to *make* it happen.

"In the end, it was Suzie who made the groundbreaking discovery of which chemical component of a Healer's teardrop gave it its healing abilities. She named it *Chemical T*, after Tao."

I've never heard the history behind Chemical T's name before. As a kid, I thought my mother named it after me. Now I'm realizing it couldn't have been named after me. She discovered the chemical before I was born.

Li continues, "Once Suzie and Andy knew which chemical component had the healing ability, they needed a way to extract it from the teardrops. That's where Victor comes in. He was the engineer who designed the machine that could remove Chemical T. Smart man, that one. He designed, built, and modified hundreds of machines before it worked.

"Anyway, through long nights working in the lab together, Suzie and Victor fell in love. You should have seen them, Trey. Your parents were made for each other. From the way they looked at each other to the way they could communicate without saying a single word. There's no doubt in my heart they were soul mates."

I know the feeling. That's exactly how I feel about Arella. There's not a single doubt in my heart that she's meant for me.

Li continues again, "The night Suzie found out she was pregnant was the night I found out about the affair. Tao and I had already moved here to Vegas, so Suzie and I didn't get to see each other much. We were still best friends though. We spoke on the phone every day. I thought we didn't keep secrets from each other until she called to tell me she was pregnant with her husband's brother's baby.

"That weekend, she and Victor drove out here so we could talk. That's when Tao and I got the whole story. They told us that the affair had been going on for a while and that no matter how many times they tried to end it, it felt like torture to be away from each other. They cried over how much they already loved their unborn baby. Getting pregnant only reinforced their love for each other and confirmed how badly they wanted to be together. I told them they should be together, until they explained why they wouldn't divorce their partners. It was a wholesome reason, really. Very selfless. Those two always had the good of Zordi people in mind."

"What was the reason?" I ask, desperate to know. "Why couldn't they be together?"

"At the time, Andy was in the midst of creating a liquid solution that could preserve Chemical T. You see, the chemical doesn't survive outside of a Healer's body for more than five minutes. That's why it took so long for Suzie and Andy to discover the chemical in the first place. Can you imagine putting something under the microscope to study for over a year, not realizing that the chemical component you're looking for had died off within five minutes of it leaving its source? The time they wasted . . ." Li shakes her head with a sigh.

"Because Andy was in the middle of creating the preservation solution and was near completion, your parents decided they couldn't tell him they were in love. They were concerned that if Suzie left Andy, he would quit working on the project and they would never see it finished, so your parents made the tough and heartbreaking decision to raise you as if Andy was your father.

"In the end, it took Andy another year to finish the preservation solution. Then it took them all another three years of research to create healing products in the forms of a beverage, an ointment, and a mist.

"For all those years, Tao and I watched how much it killed Victor to have to say he was your uncle. The only times he ever got to freely be your dad was when they came here to visit us. Here, Victor didn't have to hide how much his spirit brightened every time you sat in his lap. He could barely take his eyes off you as you ran around and played with our kids. The way he looked at you was the same way he looked at your mother—with pure love and happiness."

I think I'm in shock. I can't move. I can't do anything but blink. Everyone's staring at me, waiting for me to react. I don't know how to, mostly because I don't believe it.

Does this lady really expect me to believe that the cruel and abusive man I grew up with is my father? The man who allowed adults to beat on me until I bled—when I was a kid? The man who refuses to call me by name and opts for demeaning terms? The man who used me in his Royal-based schemes, who just days ago almost murdered me? That man? My *father*? No way in hell.

"How did my mother know for sure that Victor was my father?" I ask. "If she was having sex with both of them, it could have been either of them."

"I asked the same thing," Li says. "Turns out, when Suzie found out she was pregnant, she and Andy hadn't been intimate for months. Once the decision was made to raise you as Andy's son, Suzie went home and seduced him that night. Two weeks later, she made a show of being shocked by a positive test. When you were born, she told everyone you were early. Since Andy and Victor look so much alike, no one questioned it when you grew up looking like Victor, because you looked like Andy too. Tao and I were the only ones who knew the truth."

"No!" I burst out of my chair. It falls behind me with a *clank!* The unopened bottle of water in my lap tumbles to the floor and rolls away. My ribs burn from the sudden movement. "You're lying! Victor can't be my father."

Tao, who has barely spoken a word this whole time, calmly says, "Ask yourself, Trey, what reason do we have to lie?"

I think about that for a moment, then sigh. He's right. They have nothing to gain from lying to me.

"Here," Li says as she hands me the entire photo album. She points to one of the pictures on the page. It features a toddler me sitting in Victor's lap. He's hugging me tight as he kisses my cheek with a light in his face I've never seen in him before.

I flip the page to find more pictures of me with my mom and Victor. Most of the photos look like they were taken somewhere in this shop. Some are of me learning to walk while Victor holds my hands. There are a few photos where he's got me sitting on his shoulders with my little fingers gripping his dark hair.

In one picture, my mom stands with me on her hip, feeding me a blue popsicle. The colorful evidence is all over my face. In the background, Victor stares lovingly at my mother the same way I always stare at Arella.

I flip the page again, and my heart drops. These images were shot so early that my mom is still pregnant. Victor has his hand splayed across her rounded belly as he kisses her temple. In another photo, they kiss each other's lips as he hugs her from behind and cradles her belly like it's his entire world.

The more pages I flip, the more I get a glimpse into a past that seems impossible. My mom and Victor look genuinely and hopelessly in love with each other.

"We assumed you already knew," Li says. "After Suzie and Andy were killed, didn't you go live with Victor? Why didn't he tell you the truth? By that time, Jodi was long gone, and without Andy around, he had no reason to keep it a secret anymore. We figured he would have told you right away."

"I thought you guys were *best friends*?" I sneer. "Wouldn't he have told you if he had told me?"

"Actually, as soon as Jodi left him, Victor broke things off with your mother. She was devastated. None of us could understand it. One day, he was completely in love with her. The next, he didn't want anything to do with her. It was like if he couldn't have Jodi *and* Suzie, he didn't want either of them at all. Around that time, he also stopped speaking to us. No matter how many times we've reached out over the years, we never heard back. Years of friendship right down the drain."

Now *that's* the coldhearted Victor I know. Selfishly, it makes me feel slightly better that I wasn't the only one he pushed away. But why my mother? If he was as in love with her as these pictures depict, what changed?

The room goes silent as I gather my thoughts. I feel sick, and disoriented, and confused, and *fuck* . . . my ribs are killing me.

As if reading my mind, Tao stands and points toward a padded medical chair in the corner. "You came here for some healing, right? Let's do duh lady first."

"Actually," I say, snapping out of my bewildered state, "you won't be able to heal her. She's immune to Zordi powers. You can use healing products on her though."

Tao glances at Li with a look that says, *What's duh boy talking about?*

Li responds with a *hell if I know* shrug.

I don't blame them. It's as strange for me to say that someone's immune to Zordi powers as it is for them to hear it.

"What do you mean, she is *immune*?" Tao asks.

"See for yourself."

Tao gestures toward my T-shirt wrapped around Arella's arm. "Can I heal foh you?"

Arella nods. Tao kneels by her chair, then carefully peels the bloody fabric off her skin. She winces a little.

"Just sit still." Tao closes his eyes, then hovers his hand over Arella's knife wound. A moment later, when nothing happens, his mouth pops open. "How?"

I'll never get tired of seeing the shock on people's faces when Arella amazes them with her —what can only be described as—magic. "Told ya."

"Let me try," Li says, perking up. "Tell me a lie."

"Um, I hate bacon," Arella says, and it makes me smile. This woman loves bacon. Whenever she eats it, she moans like I'm eating her out.

"Hmm," Li says. "My inner alarm didn't go off. I can't see through your body either." Li aims her gaze at me. "I can see through Trey's body though." She turns back to Arella. "Tell me another lie."

Arella thinks for a moment. Then her eyes flick up to me. "I'm not in love with Trey."

It takes my shattered heart a second to realize she means the opposite. I haven't forgotten that each time I've confessed my love to her, she's never said it back. I didn't tell her I love her with hopes that she'd return the words, but I'd be lying if I said I wasn't *hoping* she'd say it back. In a way, she just admitted that she loves me. It's not the same as actually hearing her say *I love you*, but it's close enough.

"Hmm," Li says. "Try another one. Something obvious, like one plus one is five."

"Um," Arella says, "the grass outside is blue."

Li gasps with a hand to her chest. "Wow. She really is immune."

While Li grabs the healing products for Arella, Tao asks me to climb into the medical chair. I don't hesitate to obey. With a few cranks of a lever, the back of the chair reclines, and suddenly, I'm staring into a blinding chicken lamp clamped above me.

"The ceiling lights down here are kinda dim, huh?" I say.

Tao scoffs as he examines my face. "Landlord said to install good lights down here, it be over three thousand dollah and I am responsible for pay. I said no thank you, went to duh store, and got three lamps for less den thirty bucks. Do same job, but cheaper."

"Didn't Li say you guys get royalties from healing products?"

"Yes. One percent."

I do the quick math in my head. "That's still six figures a year."

Tao wiggles a finger at me. *Tsk. Tsk.* "Having money does not mean you should spend it on three-thousand-dollah lights when thirty-dollah ones do duh same job."

I feel that. I collect fifteen percent on my parents' inventions and still buy plain shirts online that come in a three pack for twenty bucks.

Tao lifts my shirt up, then gasps. "Aiyah! What duh hell happened?"

"Royals," I say, and it's all the explanation he needs.

Closing his eyes, Tao hovers his open palms above my torso. "Three broken ribs and a lot of bruising. How long ago did dis happen?"

"Twelve hours, maybe?"

He slaps the side of my head. "Why you not come sooner?"

"Ow!" I rub the spot he hit. "We got here as fast as we could."

"Not fast enough. Now be quiet so I can work."

Tao's warm palms press against my aching ribs. The light pressure he applies makes me wince until, gradually, the pain fades away. Several seconds later, the pain is completely gone.

Next, Tao places his hands on either side of my face. Soon after, my cheek isn't throbbing anymore and my headache has vanished. The soreness at the back of my head disappears too.

When he drags my sweatpants down and tears the gauze off my thigh, he makes some more *tsk-tsk* sounds. He places his hands over my thigh, and I hiss when he applies some pressure. This time, it takes at least a minute before the pain disappears. Once it does, I take a look at my thigh. Minus the remaining blood on my skin, it looks normal again. Not even a scar to show for it.

Tao leaves me for a second, then comes back with clean hands and a wet towel. After he wipes off the blood from my leg, he does one more pass on my body. Everywhere he hovers his hands, the aches diminish until they're gone.

"Done."

I sit up and press a finger against my ribs. No tenderness. No agony. I don't even flinch. Why didn't we start with this instead of Li's crazy story?

Arella is in the middle of getting her arm wrapped with gauze when I kneel at her side.

"Wow." Her eyes go wide. "You look brand new."

"I feel it too."

Tao taps my shoulder and hands me a bottle of Healing Water. "Foh her face bruises."

"I'm almost done," Li says as she finishes taping the gauze around Arella's arm. "Although, I'm confused as to how the Healing Goo will work if she's immune to our powers."

I unscrew the cap off the lemon-lime Healing Water and hand it to Arella. She accepts it with her free hand and chugs.

"For some reason," I say, "Arella's not immune to healing products. I've used them on her before, and she takes to it. I think it has to do with the power coming at her from *outside* her body. She can get burned by a fireball, but if someone's got the power to incinerate her from the inside out, she'd be immune to that."

"Interesting," Li says, then taps Arella's shoulder. "All done, beautiful girl."

"Thank you." Arella finishes the Healing Water, then tilts her head back to look at me with crumpled eyebrows. "When did you ever use healing products on me?"

"How do you think you recovered from that car accident so quickly? That Sprite I kept giving you wasn't Sprite."

She stares at the empty bottle in her hands. "Huh. I never would have—"

Thud! Thud! Thud! Someone pounds against the front door upstairs. Instinctively, I seize Arella's hand. She jolts out of her chair and squeezes mine back. By the concentration in her eyes, I'm certain she's projecting her immunity onto me.

"Seriously?" Tao groans. "Can people not read my sign? We are closed until October one. Right now, not October one. I'll go tell dem to go away."

"Wait," I whisper. "It could be the Royals. They might have tracked us here."

"I'll check." Li narrows her eyes at the ceiling in the direction of the front door. "Three large men, and they don't look like they're here for herbal medicines."

Thud! Thud! It's louder this time.

"Shit," I mutter.

"Should we fake like we aren't here?" Tao asks.

"No," Li says. "These guys look like they'll let themselves in if we don't first."

Tao closes the photo album. "Quick! I'll hide the pictures. You hide the kids."

It takes me a second to realize that *the kids* is referring to me and Arella.

Li clutches Arella's other arm. "Follow me."

Practically leaping over the many boxes on the floor, Li takes us to the farthest back corner under the stairs. It's dimmer back here. A bunch of glass jars are stacked on bookshelves. In the corner against the wall stands a freezer chest that Li shoves aside to reveal a dusty floor. She steps onto one of the wood planks, and up pops a square section of the floor. It's just wide enough for a person to crawl through.

"Get in," Li says.

Using the questionable wood ladder, Arella climbs down first. I follow shortly after. The second my head clears the flooring, Li shuts the trapdoor and we're surrounded by black. There isn't a single crack of light with how sealed it is. The floor rumbles above us as Li returns the freezer chest back to its spot.

"Can you make me immune?" I ask.

Arella grabs my hand. "Done."

I imagine a tiny flame on the tip of my finger, and it appears. My little fire illuminates the space that's just tall enough for me to reach up and barely touch the trapdoor. It's not wide enough for me to lie down though—not that I'd want to. It's dustier than hell, with cobwebs hanging along all four walls.

I move my little flame to see Arella. Her face is crumpled with concern.

"Don't worry, baby," I whisper. "I won't let anyone hurt you." She hasn't given me permission to call her pet names again, but I won't correct myself this time.

Without warning, she slams her front against mine and circles her arms around my back. Then she buries her face in my chest. I'm so shocked that I can't move. A heavy weight lifts off my shoulders as her warmth envelops me.

Eventually, I regain my composure and wrap my arm around her too, squeezing her so tight, she exhales a little breath. The relief that eases through me almost makes me tear up. It's been eating at me that Arella no longer trusted me or felt safe around me. This is proof that she knows I'll do anything to protect her. If any of those men lay a finger on her, I won't hesitate to kill 'em.

Things are quiet for a minute before some heavy pairs of footsteps come stomping down the stairs.

"Then you won't mind if we look around," a deep voice sneers.

"Excuse me," Li says sternly, "we are closed."

"Dat is what I told dem," Tao says. "Dey not listening."

"We aren't here to shop, ma'am. We're looking for fugitives. Have you seen either of these two?"

"No. I have been in my shop all day since seven this morning. I have seen no one except my husband because everybody else actually reads the sign that says we're closed. We're in the middle of remodeling."

"I can tell," a second guy scoffs. "It's a fucking shit show in here."

The first guy speaks again. "This will only take a minute."

"You can't just barge into someone's business and trample around like you own the place!" Li shouts. "Get out of here before I call the Enforcers."

"We *are* the Enforcers," a third voice says.

"Are not." The confidence in Li's tone is unmatched.

"Yes, we are. See?"

Li chuckles. "Fake badge. Also, I'm a Detector. The alarm in my head is going off right now. So you have three seconds to get out before I call the *real* Enforcers."

A pair of footsteps tramp on the floor above us. I put out my flame as if the man can see it. Blackness engulfs us as Arella curls into me, gripping my shirt. I clench her tighter, just in case the man has the power to reach through the floor and snatch her from me. Zordi powers don't normally work between surface level and underground, but I'm not taking any chances.

"Three," Li counts like an annoyed mother.

"We're almost done, old lady. Chill the fuck out."

"Two."

The man above us isn't moving. What is he looking at? Can he see us through the floor?

"I think you liars are forgetting what the consequences are for impersonating an Enforcer," Li says. "What is it? Five to ten years? I hear they drug you up good with perrizo in z-prison. Do you need me to finish counting to one?"

The man above us sighs. "Come on, boys. They ain't here. Let's go."

I don't let out a breath until I hear their footsteps trudge up the stairs and out the door. A moment later, a gentle pair of feet shuffles back down. I imagine it's Tao after relocking the door.

Arella and I remain silent, still hunched into each other as we wait to be released. Our freedom doesn't come right away. Instead, Li and Tao speak to each other in Chinese for a while. I'm fluent in English, conversational in French and Spanish, and I know enough American Sign Language to get by. Whatever Chinese language they're speaking has now made it to the top of my list of languages to learn. I'm going to assume they have a reason for not immediately releasing us, and although I only met them within the last hour, I trust them.

Arella tilts her head up and brushes her lips against the base of my neck. A bright beam of light shines inside me, filling the dark hollow hole where my heart used to be. It's not just that she's breathing on me and almost kissing me that's got me reeling; it's that she's doing it so tenderly, willingly, and unprompted.

Mere hours ago, we were on a flying tire, where she told me she never wanted to see me again. She meant it so much that she even tried to lose me at a gas station. Now she's letting me hold her like I'm the only person she wants holding her forever.

My little fireball reappears on my fingertip again, and I move it near her face. She gazes up at me with her big brown eyes, the fear in them from earlier dissolved. Replacing it is that lustful trusting look I've wanted to see for days. It's the look she used to give me before all this shit happened.

I free my hand that was glued to the small of her back, to push some of her hair behind an ear. She closes her eyes and melts into my touch the way I always melt into hers. Before I even realize I'm doing it, I lean down to plant a heavy kiss against her forehead. When she doesn't pull away, that light in my chest shines brighter. Then she sighs and squeezes her arms around me tighter, making me choke up a little.

If I never have to leave this dusty, dirty, cobweb-infested underground hideaway, I'll be happy. It's like a sanctuary down here when I've got my girl back in my arms.

66

TREY

"I apologize that it took so long," Li says through the opening of the trapdoor. "They lingered outside our shop for a while. I kept watching them through the walls, reading their lips. From what I could catch, they're convinced you're in the area. They've gone scouring to find you but have made plans to return later. They think you're waiting until nightfall to come here for healing. You should go before they come back."

I help Arella climb up the wooden ladder first, then I do the same. Li shuts the trapdoor, then Tao shoves the freezer chest back over it.

"Is it still light outside?" I ask, taking a breath of clean, not-musty air.

Li glares up at the ceiling, then nods. "Yes. The sun is starting to set though."

"Could we stay here until it's dark?"

"What if they return and you're still here?"

"We'll take that chance."

Arella places an affectionate hand over my forearm. I'm living for any moment when she willingly touches me.

"Are you sure?" she asks me. "If they've gone out to look for us, that means they aren't around here. This might be our chance."

I scratch the back of my head. "Um, so, I'm not trying to be dramatic or anything, but if we leave now, I'm gonna die."

The three of them scrutinize me with their eyebrows dipped.

I should probably explain. "Yesterday, well, I think it was yesterday—all my days are blending together. Anyway, it doesn't matter what day it was. The point is that Katie, a Premonitioner, told me that she saw my death. It was right outside that shop selling all those waving cats. The Royals stab me and kidnap Arella in the daylight. So, if we could stay here until dark, that'd be great."

With a firm nod, Li claps her hands together. "Who wants some duck?"

A half hour later, Arella and I are sitting at a small dining table with some bowls of rice, roast duck, and a side of brothy soup. Our gracious hosts took their meals to eat upstairs. They said that if the Royals come back, they'll stomp on the floor three times as a signal for us to hide. In the meantime, they'll work on putting their store back together since it'll help make it look like they're not hiding people in their basement.

I finish my meal within ten minutes. Arella cleans out her bowls shortly after I do. As I wash up our dishes, she dries them and puts them back into the cabinets.

The next time I see Katie, I'll have to thank her profusely. Not only did she help save Arella's life, she saved mine too. Without her knowledge, we definitely would have left earlier. Then the Royals would have found us outside and Katie's premonition would have come true.

To continue waiting out the sunlight, Arella and I head to the love seat to rest. So far, we haven't heard any stomping, and I hope we never do.

For a while, Arella cuddles with me in silence. She's sitting between my legs with her back flush against my front and her head resting against my chest. Tenderly, I play with her hands, grateful to be this close to her again.

Things are quiet as I enjoy the feel of her body against mine, especially since my ribs no longer ache. Earlier, when she fell asleep on my shoulder on the bus, it hurt like hell to stay in that position, but I didn't care. I would have rather ached as her pillow than been more comfortable away from her.

I've never been one to enjoy silence. It's hard for me to be alone with my thoughts. Whenever I am, my mind spirals into reminding me what a worthless human I am, walking around without a reason to live. I felt that way until Arella came into my life. With her, I not only enjoy silence but prefer it. She calms my mind in ways I can't explain. With her, I have a purpose. She's my reason to live.

Arella breaks the silence. "Why didn't you tell me earlier?"

"Tell you what?"

"That Katie had a premonition about your death. You freaked out when you saw those waving cats, and you said nothing."

"I didn't wanna scare you."

She tilts her head back to look at me. "Trey, how am I supposed to protect you when you keep information like that from me?"

"*I'm* the one who's supposed to protect *you*."

Her mouth draws into a hard frown. "Why can't we protect each other?"

"I don't want you to worry about me."

She turns around to straddle my lap, and I'm not mad about it. I even pull her in closer, keeping my hands around her hips. Gently, she caresses the back of my head with her nails, sending tingles down my spine. "Will you make me a promise?"

My gut instinct is to say yes because I want to give this woman anything she wants, but I can't lie to her. There are certain things I won't promise her, and they mostly involve anything that goes against her safety. "Depends what it is."

"Will you promise me that from now on, we'll be a team? You protect me, and I'll protect you."

Something is tugging at my lips, because I can't stop them from smiling. "Is it really that important to you to protect me?"

She creases her face together like I'm an idiot. "Victor got me to project my immunity onto you by trying to murder you in front of me. What does that tell you?"

Good point. "I'll make you that promise on one condition."

"What?"

"You have to promise me that we'll be a team—forever. I protect you, and you protect me —forever. Deal?"

She beams and nods. "Deal."

"Oh, and also, promise me that if someone's throwing an element ball at me, you won't jump in front of it."

"Deal."

"And promise me that you'll never try to abandon me at a gas station ever again."

She nods again. "Deal."

"Great. Now can I also go back to calling you *babe*?"

Her lips curve into a warm smile. "I'd like that."

I don't realize my hand is clutching her face, guiding her toward me, until my mouth is already consuming hers. My kisses start off tender—light pressure, short breaths, and gentle touches—until suddenly, I'm not gentle anymore. I pant as I claw at her body to come closer to mine, because even when she's straddling me, she's not close enough.

"Trey . . ." She moans as I lay her over the couch cushions and climb on top of her. I put a leg on either side of her hips, then attack her neck with my lips. Her soft hands reach under my shirt, clawing at my abs.

I melt into her touch, groaning against her collarbone. "Arella."

I kiss up her neck as she arches her head back. I've missed this so much. The taste of her sweetness. The smell of her intoxicating scent. The way she lets out breathless whimpers as I keep sucking on her skin.

Naturally, I grind my hard cock against her inner thigh. She digs her fingernails into my back, making me let out an uncontrollable grunt. The things this woman does to me. The power she has over me with just one touch. I'm hers. For as long as she wants me, for whatever she wants me for, I'm hers. All hers.

My lips travel upward until I find her mouth again. Panting hard, we return to what can only be described as an animalistic make-out session. We scratch at each other's clothes. She breathlessly moans my name over and over. I thrust my hips against her, attempting to find any sort of release from the torment we've been going through.

I know this chaos isn't over, but for now, right here, I have Arella. She's alive, she's safe, and she's allowing me back into her heart. This is all that matters. This is what I risked my life to get back. This is my reason to keep risking it all.

I love this woman with every part of my soul. To be without her is to be without sunlight and air and food and water and whatever else I need to survive. I'm never going to allow someone to take her away from me ever again. I'll spend the rest of my life fighting to be with her if that's what it takes.

"Arella?" I whisper against her lips.

"Mmm?"

"I love you."

She doesn't hesitate. "I love you too."

I might pass out from how happy I am to hear those words from her. A rush of flutters fills me to the brim. I've never felt so full like this. So completely and utterly full.

I lean down to plant one long, hard kiss against her lips, then pull back again. "Do you think you can ever forgive me?"

"For what?"

"You know, blowing your tire so I had an excuse to meet you. Trying to use you to make my dead parents proud. Spending three days passed out in an infirmary while you were trapped in a place with people you didn't know. Putting your life in danger. Should I go on?"

"Trey, most of that wasn't your fault. Actually, none of it was. Now that I know the whole story, I would have done the same thing if I were you. Fake-date someone to find out information that could result in taking down the people who killed my parents? And to stop those people from killing more people? When that's all it was supposed to be, I would have taken that mission in a heartbeat. You never meant for me or anyone to get hurt. The only thing you did wrong was trust the wrong people. I forgive you for what happened, but I think the more important question is, do you forgive yourself?"

I don't have to think about my answer. "No, but maybe someday."

Arella grabs my face and pulls my mouth to hers. She kisses me so long and hard, it takes my breath away.

I pant for air as I do a push-up over her. "I really don't want this to stop, but I think we should get going."

Twenty-some minutes later, I've got our heavy backpack over my shoulders. Tao filled it with a fuck-ton of Healing Water, Healing Goo, and Healing Spray. I hope we won't need it, but it'll be good to have.

"Come back to visit anytime, okay?" Li says as she leads us to the back door of their shop. "Don't wait twenty years this time."

I chuckle lightly. "I won't. Thank you again for everything. Seriously. You guys saved our lives."

Li stops at the door, then turns to give me a smile and pinch my cheeks. Her eyes glisten a little. "I'm so proud of you, Trey Grant. You've grown up to be such a strong and handsome good boy."

My insides flutter as Arella and I exit their shop. Li will never know how much her words mean to me. That's the first time someone other than Liz has ever told me they're proud of me. Hearing it from Li is like hearing it from my mother.

Tao's black SUV is exactly where he said it would be: two spots away from the dumpster. With his key, I unlock it with a *beep*. Arella and I climb in, I toss our backpack onto the backseat, then we're off.

"I can't believe they just *gave* us their car." Arella shifts to get comfy in the passenger seat. "I mean, it's a freaking Lincoln."

"I bet they'll have enough money on their next royalty check to buy another." I glance into the rearview mirror. So far, so good. "Also, I'll come back some other time and thank them tenfold."

"Are we going to go search for your parents' safe house now?"

"Yep." I check the rearview mirrors again. There's a car behind us. An elderly lady is driving with an elderly man in the passenger side. Probably not Royals. Also, their emotions are pretty content.

"How do we know that Victor doesn't know about your parents' safe house? Now that we've discovered he and your mom were a thing, what if she told him about it?"

"I thought about that earlier, and I think we're okay. My parents' message said that the only person I should trust is Aunt Debbie. That tells me Victor wasn't on the *trustworthy list* for a while. Probably since the day Aunt Jodi left him and he broke things off with my mom.

"Now that I think about it, it was around that time when my parents started bringing me out to Julian, California. I remember because Victor had just started treating me like a plague-ridden toad. Whenever my parents brought me out there to stargaze, I'd wish on all the stars that my Uncle V would find another wife. I wanted him to be happy so he'd be nice to me again."

All the emotions I had as a kid during those days come rushing back to me. Victor used to be my favorite person in the world. He was the one I'd beg my parents to let me call, so I could ask him to come play with me. He was the one I'd look forward to seeing every weekend. He was the one who taught me how to swim and to roller-skate.

We were so close that we had a secret word. Whenever either of us said *crystal*, it meant that whatever just happened stayed between us. It started one Christmas morning when Victor and I snuck downstairs to the decorated tree and opened one of my presents early.

In the midst of shooting Uncle V with my new Nerf guns, I bumped into the Christmas tree and one of my mom's precious crystal angel ornaments fell. The wings broke off, and there was no fixing it. My mom never found out where her angel ornament went, because Victor and I made a pact to never tell anyone. From then on, whenever we had to keep something a secret, we'd say *crystal*.

That was the last Christmas I ever spent with Victor. Suddenly, he stopped coming by to take me out for late-night ice cream and walks around the neighborhood. My loud nights filled with Victor and me wrestling on the carpet while I avoided Aunt Jodi's glares became quiet nights with just my parents, asking them when Uncle V would come back to visit.

"Let me see if I've got this right." Arella ticks off her points on each finger. "Victor was in love with your mom but was married to Jodi. After Jodi left him for another man, Victor's so heartbroken that he dumps your mom. Then he starts treating his own son like trash?"

I purse my lips and nod. "Sounds about right."

"That doesn't make any sense. With Jodi gone, wouldn't he have felt more free to be with your mom? What if your dad—or the person you thought was your dad—found out about the affair and threatened to hurt Victor if he kept seeing your mom?"

"That's possible, I guess. Either way, I'm not gonna try to make it make sense. The only person who can tell us why he did what he did is Victor, and to say we're not on the best *let's sit down and hash out the past* terms is putting it lightly."

Arella and I talk for a bit longer before she eventually falls asleep.

When we finally arrive in Julian, California, it's well past three in the morning. The sky is black, the roads are quiet, and the emotions coming to my head are mostly muted.

Arella's eyes flutter open as I tap her awake.

"We're here," I say as I gesture toward the Y-shaped tree my parents always parked their car at. I shut the Lincoln off, then grab the backpack.

After locking the car, I take Arella's hand and lead her through the woods.

"If we don't find it," I say as my fireball floats in front of us, "we could go to my cabin in Colorado. It's not underground, but it can be a good transition place while we figure out our next steps."

While the cabin property is under my name, I don't think Victor knows I have it. I bought that cabin well after I moved out. Then again, he could easily look up properties I own and send his men there. *Maybe my cabin isn't a good idea.*

"We *are* going to find this safe house," Arella says with a hell of a lot more confidence than I have. She's gripping my hand pretty tight to ensure that her immunity works on me.

I'm not anywhere closer to understanding her magic more than I was on day one. From what she told me in the car before she fell asleep, she doesn't even have to think that hard about projecting it anymore. She said it's been coming pretty easily to her. This woman is truly extraordinary.

I step over a fallen tree, then help Arella over it too. "What makes you so sure we'll find it?"

"Because we're not leaving until we do."

I've told myself that countless times. Every time, I've always left with dirt all over my jeans and no safe house. If Arella's that confident, though, I'll try to be too.

A while later, we arrive at the big rock.

"*This* is your secret rock?" Arella knocks on it with her knuckles. "It looks like any other big ol' rock on the ground."

"Because it is. I think my parents put this here to help my seven-year-old brain remember where Cheesy is." I point toward the holey tree a few steps over.

Together, Arella and I take one hundred steps away from Cheesy. The whole time she counts, I expand my Empath power out to cover the woods. No one is nearby, which means we're safe. I've never been so grateful for this gift until now.

"Ninety-nine," Arella says. "One hundred."

We reach the same area I've always come to. There's nothing here but nature.

"Can I assume all these former holes in the ground are yours?" Arella gestures toward all the patches of dirt around us.

"What can I say? I was determined. Now as you can see, there's nothing here. No safe house. No bunker. No trapdoor. No sign. No nothin'."

"Let me look around for a bit. Keep holding my hand and move your fireball with me so I can see, please."

"Yes, ma'am." I salute her like she's my drill sergeant.

For a while, I follow Arella wherever she goes as she scours the woods. When she finds nothing, as I've been telling her, she says, "We took a hundred adult steps. Where do you usually end up when you take a hundred kid steps?"

"About twenty paces back." Hand in hand, I lead her there as my fireball follows us.

"Next to this tree?" She places a hand against the bark of a skinny box elder.

"Yep, and I've looked everywhere around this tree. There's nothing here. My parents' message said *inside and underground*. You see all these dirt patches? I've dug almost fifteen feet down starting from the base of this tree and all around it. I've even drilled into the trunk to see if there's anything inside it. It's a regular tree."

Arella steps around the trunk, running her hand along the rough bark. I move my flames to follow her gaze.

She tilts her head back and squints her eyes. "Have you ever looked for anything up in the branches?"

"No. The safe house is *underground*, remember?"

"And your mom's song says to 'look to the sky when you feel down.' Haven't you ever done an escape room?"

"A what?"

"An escape room," she says as if saying it again means I'll suddenly know exactly what she means. "Seriously? Javina and I love them. It's a fun place where someone locks you and your friends in a room, and you have to solve puzzles in under an hour to get out. I think your mom is hinting for you to look up. Can you move your fireball that way so I can see better?"

I do as I'm told, even though there's no way in hell my mom would have given me a hard puzzle to solve. I was a kid when she died. Still, I float my fireball up the trunk and stop once the flames get too close to the leaves. "Any higher and I'll light this thing up."

"That's close enough. Walk around the tree with me."

Again, I do as I'm told, even though—I gasp. Right there, way up in the bark of one of the thick branches, is a carving.

"What?" Arella asks.

"There's something carved into the bark."

"Where?"

I point up. "Right there."

She squints. "I don't see anything."

"Babe, it's right—" I slap a palm against my forehead. "Oh, did you know that Zordi eyes are different from Ordi eyes?"

"How so?"

"Zordis can see things farther out than Ordinaries can. It's like our eyes have the zoom and focus function of a camera. Maybe I can see it but you can't."

"Well, what's the carving of?"

I bring my fireball down. "212E."

"What's that mean?"

"No fucking clue. You're the escape-room genius here. You tell me."

From her pocket, Arella pulls out the two receipts she wrote on the back of. "Look to the sky when you feel down. Know that things will turn around. Work twice as hard to the finish line. Now it's your time to shine." She taps the receipts against her thigh as she thinks to herself. "Turn around. Twice as hard to the finish line."

"Are you thinkin' we need to turn around?"

She nods. "Toward the east. Four hundred and twenty-four steps."

"Why four hund—Oh! Twice the steps! Wow. Maybe my mom's song *was* a hint. This whole time, I just thought it was her way of telling me to keep my head up because things will turn around as long as I work hard."

"I'm sure she meant the song that way too. Now which way is east, because I have no idea."

Finally! Something I can contribute! I point to our right. "It's that way."

Four hundred and twenty-four steps feels like a lot as an adult. I can't imagine how I would have felt as a kid. When my parents said I should bring Aunt Debbie with me, I think it was more of a request than a suggestion: one, because I needed someone to drive me here, and, two, because they must have told Aunt Debbie that my mom's song included instructions.

"Four twenty-two, four twenty-three, four twenty-four." Arella stops taking her kid-size steps and glances at the huge tree standing in front of us. Its long branches loom above our heads like an umbrella. The trunk is so large, it would probably take at least three of my arms to wrap around it. Any other time, any other place, I'd see this tree and think nothing of it. Tonight, I've got a feeling this is it.

"What now?" I ask.

Arella paces around the tree, towing me with her. "I'm not seeing anything. Can you use your special eyeballs to check up top?"

My special eyeballs? I let out a light laugh, then do as I'm told. We walk around the tree twice, but I find nothing.

"Hmm." Arella squats to examine the base of the tree.

I move my flames closer to help her see. "Anything?"

"Not yet."

Suddenly, something shiny catches my eye. *Now it's your time to shine.* The last line of my mother's song. I wave at my fireball, and it floats back up to my eye level. The flames illuminate a shiny reflective device inside a little hole in the tree. It's the same size as the hole in the rocky entrance to Shadow Ridge. I'm about to stick my index finger into the slot when Arella grabs my arm.

"What are you doing?" She gapes at me like I'm crazy. "You see a mysterious hole and you're just going to stick your finger into it? What if you get your finger chopped off?"

"Relax. I think it's a fingerprint scanner."

"How do you know?"

"It looks like the same kind we use to open the door to the Ridge." I stick my finger straight into the hole.

Nothing happens. No beeping. No ten-foot door sliding open. No guards greeting me with scowls on the other side. I glance around to see if there's something off in the distance I might be missing. I don't see a trapdoor that's popped up from the ground, or an opening of any sort.

"What's supposed to happen?" Arella asks.

"I'm not sure. Maybe I'll try a different finger." I stick my middle finger into the hole. Nothing happens. I try my ring finger. My thumb. My pinky. Same thing. I hope this isn't the part I needed Aunt Debbie for, because her fingers are long gone.

"Try your index finger again," Arella says. "Harder this time."

After I blow some dirt out of the hole and wipe my finger clean on my sweatpants, I stick my index finger back in. Something clicks inside the tree, then a large part of the bark pops forward. I pull the bark back to reveal a hollowed-out tree trunk.

"It worked." Arella's jaw drops. "This is so cool. Like a real-life escape room, except we're trying to get in, not out."

It's nice that she finds this amusing. I guide my fireball up the hollow. It's a tight space, barely big enough for my broad shoulders. Downward is a flight of stairs. I flick my wrist, and my flames travel all the way down until they hit a metal hatch door.

"Me first," I say as I step into the hollow. Our backpack hanging on my shoulders hits the walls of the tiny space. "Stay close, okay? And don't let go of my hand."

"Trey, we haven't stopped holding hands this entire time. I'm not planning on going anywhere."

And I hope she never does.

67

ARELLA

One-handed, Trey turns the hatch door's wheel. It squeals as it twists to the open position. Together, we lift the heavy door. Trey waves his hand, making his fireball float down the hatch, revealing a set of stairs and a living room. I can't see much else beyond that.

"I'll go first to make sure it's safe," Trey says. Finally, we release each other's hands. "Don't come down until I say so, 'kay?"

After I nod, he heads down and disappears into the darkness. The wooden stairs creak under his feet.

A minute later, he pops his head up the hatch and holds a hand out to me. "Watch your step, babe."

Once my feet touch the carpet, Trey points at the hatch door. It shuts with a light thump, drowning us in pitch black. A new fireball brightens the room. He tosses it into the air, then searches the wall until he finds a light switch. The ceiling lights flicker on with a light buzzing sound.

I spin to examine our surroundings. "How is there electricity down here?"

"No clue." Trey slashes a hand in the air, then his fireball disappears.

Against the wall sits a small couch with a recliner next to it. They are covered with protective plastic sheets. In the middle of the room stands a coffee table with a layer of dust on it so thick, I can't see the surface. Everything looks like it hasn't been touched in years. Probably as many years as Trey's parents have been gone.

Trey drops our backpack onto the dirty carpet at his feet. "Let's look around."

I follow him toward the small kitchen, where a thick layer of dust and dirt covers everything from the countertops to the appliances. He peels the fridge open. The inside looks like a science experiment gone wrong. It smells like it too. Whatever was in there before is now unrecognizable lumps of black goo.

Trey slams the fridge shut. "Let's never open that again."

"Agreed."

We head down a hall, where he flips on another light. Trey opens a door on the right to reveal a small bathroom with a sink, a toilet, and a one-person shower.

"How is there plumbing down here?" I ask.

"Babe, did you forget that *you're* the one who found this place? I'm seeing it for the first time, just like you are. I don't understand how anything works down here."

I point at my chest. "*I* didn't find this. *We* found it together."

"I couldn't have done it without you solving my mom's riddle."

"And I couldn't have gotten here without you telling me which way is east."

He smirks handsomely. "Glad I could contribute."

Across the hall is another door that creaks as he opens it. A bedroom greets us with two queen beds covered with protective plastic. A large dresser stands against the opposite wall. Trey pulls open the drawers. They're full of clothes for an adult man and an adult woman. The bottom drawers are full of clothes for a seven-year-old boy.

"It's good to know they weren't *trying* to abandon me," Trey says. "That doesn't change the fact that they set up this entire safe house because they knew there was a chance they *could* die but continued on with their mission anyway."

"You also knew there was a chance you could die when you came back to the Ridge to save me, yet you did it anyway."

Trey shakes his head as he slams the drawers shut. "That's different."

"How so?"

"I don't have a child waiting for me at home."

That's a good point. I can't imagine what it's like to be Trey, to have lost his parents at a young age in a traumatic way, only to discover that they chose their jobs over him. I don't know the full story, so that statement might be oversimplifying his parents' decision, but the bottom line is that they chose to risk their lives, knowing they could be abandoning their son in the end. What could have possibly been more important than him?

I leave Trey's side to go explore the nightstands. In one of the drawers are some passports and ID cards. I recognize Trey's mom in one of the passports, but the name next to her face isn't Suzie Grant; it's Linda Johnson. Trey's dad—I mean, the man he thought was his dad—is pictured in the other passport. The name next to his face is Michael Johnson. There are two other passports as well. One is for Aunt Debbie, and the other is for seven-year-old Trey. They have fake names next to their faces too.

"Looks like your parents were prepared to leave the country," I say.

Trey comes up behind me and glances over my shoulder. "Daniel Johnson? What? Do I look like a fucking Daniel to you?"

I place the passports back where I found them, then head toward the closet. I slide the doors open to reveal an air mattress, extra pillows, linens, towels, and cleaning supplies.

Trey doesn't waste a second to grab the towels. "Let's clean this bedroom up so we can sleep in it."

I roll out the vacuum. "Good idea."

Together, we work to remove the layer of dirt and grime from . . . well, everywhere. I vacuum the carpet three times over, but it still feels grimy on my feet. Meanwhile, Trey wipes off every surface in the bedroom and cleans the bathroom.

"At least we can sleep now," Trey says a while later from the bedroom doorway.

I'm gathering all the dirty towels into a pile on the floor. "How long do you think we should stay here?"

"Until we figure out what to do next. We'll have to resurface for some food in the morning. I found cans of soup and beans in the kitchen cabinets, but I refuse to let you consume anything in here. It's all probably so toxic, one bite will kill your baby."

My body stills. I didn't realize Trey still thinks I'm pregnant. I suppose he has no reason to think otherwise. I haven't had much free time to think about the loss of our baby, let alone explain it to him. We've been a little too preoccupied with running for our lives for the baby topic to even come up.

"Are you hungry?" Trey asks.

"I can wait until the morning."

"Okay. I'm gonna use the bathroom. When I come back, I have something to tell you."

I have something to tell you too . . .

With a sigh, I stand back to take a look at our cleaning job. The bedroom looks and smells less musty than before. The protective cover that was over one of the beds is now lying in a heap on the floor.

I don't waste a second getting under the covers. As I lay my head against the weird-smelling pillow, my eyes get heavy. My exhausted body is ready for a long, uninterrupted night of rest. The last places I slept were handcuffed to a lumpy bed, the dirty floor of a barn, a rocky bus, and the front seat of a Lincoln. I'm excited to sleep in an actual bed tonight—without the handcuffs.

Trey reenters the bedroom with damp hands, patting them off on his shirt. "I dirtied up all the towels while cleaning. Didn't think about saving one for our hands." With a plop, his sweatpants fall to his ankles, then he drags his shirt over his head.

My eyes don't leave his abs and muscular shoulders as he joins me under the covers. I'm used to seeing him in only his boxers. This is how he normally sleeps. So why are my insides tingling this much?

Trey props himself up on an elbow and tenderly tucks some of my hair behind an ear. "You look cozy."

I lean into his touch, hoping he'll continue to do it. "I'm exhausted, and this bed is comfy."

"Would you rather we talk in the morning?"

"No." I sit up and prop my pillow against the wall behind me. "I'm curious about what you have to tell me."

He sighs deeply, and it makes my body tense. The blankets ruffle as he sits up. "There's no easy way to say this, so I'm just gonna say it. Do you remember when you told me about your parents? About how they were driving home on a rainy night in September of '95 and drove right over a cliff?"

Of all the things I thought Trey had to tell me, I didn't think it would relate to my parents. I side-eye him. "Yeah?"

"Well . . ." He scratches the back of his neck. "I researched them. Aries and Bella Rance, right?"

"Right."

He bites his lip and stares at his hands for a moment before looking back up at me. "The reason I thought to research them in the first place is because my parents also died on a rainy night in September of '95."

I blink as I process that information. "Are you saying they died the exact same month?"

"No, babe. I'm saying they died the exact same *night*."

"What?"

"Yeah, that was my reaction too. At first, I couldn't find anything on an Aries Rance or a Bella Rance online. After some digging, I ended up Googling for deaths over a cliff in September of 1995. Turns out, there was only one couple that happened to, and it happened on the same night my parents were killed. And here's the other part: It happened in Three Rivers, near the same mountain range Shadow Ridge is hidden under."

I gasp with a hand over my mouth. "Do you think there's a connection?"

"I don't know exactly what, but there's gotta be one. Back then, ZIRDA was already doing research on Immunes. My parents were some of the researchers. The subjects were told it was part of a top-secret medical study put on by the government. My theory is that *you* were one of my parents' research subjects."

"I suppose that's plausible." I hope the tests being performed at that time were more humane than the ones Victor was doing.

"It would explain why your family was around Shadow Ridge that night. Now, are you ready for the next part?"

The next part? My heart's still thrashing over finding out that my parents died on the same night as Trey's parents. Do I really want to hear more? "I'm going to assume by the hesitation in your tone that this next part is crazier."

"It is. I think the Royals who killed my parents are the same ones who killed yours. Somehow, the Royals found out about ZIRDA studying some rare Ordinaries and they wanted to take the Immunes for themselves. On that rainy night, they shoved your parents down a cliff to make it look like a car accident so they could kidnap you. My theory is that my parents saved you from them."

I gasp as it all clicks together. "That's why they showed up at your house that night. They were looking for me."

"Most likely. My parents must have handed you off to another ZIRDA agent to take you to your grandparents before they rushed home. That's why I think your grandparents know something. Why else would they have moved you around every year?"

"You think they moved me around to hide me from the Royals?"

"One hundred percent."

I ponder that for a moment, then say, "Why keep me in California though? If there were people coming after me in this state, why keep me here?"

"Unfortunately, the Royals don't only reside in California. They've got people everywhere, all around the world. Unless your grandparents were going to hide you in a hole your entire life, no matter where they took you, the Royals would have found you."

"Wow. This is a lot to process."

"I know, and I'm sorry to throw this all on you at once, but are you ready for the last part?"

My eyes bulge. "There's more?"

"Last thing, I promise. The articles I read about your parents' car going off a cliff weren't about an Aries and Bella Rance. The couple's names were Stanley and Robyn Calder. And . . ." Trey clears his throat. "Their three-year-old daughter, Hannah Calder, supposedly died with them."

Three-year-old daughter? Hannah? Died? If what Trey is saying is true, then there's a lot more to that night in September of '95 than I thought. This whole time, I thought my parents' death was just a tragic car accident. Do my grandparents know what really happened? Was my name Hannah at one point?

For the next hour, Trey and I talk through theories of what could have happened that rainy night. The only thing that comes out of our conversation is that we have more questions than answers.

Trey yawns, and it's the first time I've ever seen him do it. "Are you ready to sleep now, babe?" he asks.

"Actually"—my heart rate kicks up—"I have something to tell you too."

He fixes his attention onto me. "What's up?"

I haven't had a chance to plan out my words. Like Trey said earlier, there's no easy way to say it, so I come out with it. "I lied to you."

His expression remains impassive. "About what?"

"There was never some guy from college."

He presses his eyebrows together and tilts his head to the side. "Huh?"

"I never cheated on you. There was never a guy from college. I only told you that because you told me you needed a reason to let me go, so I gave it to you."

"What? When did I say that?"

"When you were drunk."

He pauses to think, then stares at my belly. "But—"

I put a hand up before he can say anything about us not being able to conceive. "You said your powers are passed down by genetics, right?"

"Yeah?"

"Maybe you don't know because it might go back a few generations, but was there ever someone in your family who could sense other people's emotions?"

"Yes?" His eyes narrow. "Why?"

"Well, um, because, the baby—um, since the baby could do it, so could I. I sensed your heartache that night you were drunk. That was the first time. Then I could sense all those people in the Ridge too."

He inhales a sharp breath. "What?"

"At first it was only the people who were within a few feet of me. Later, the baby could sense people farther out. It could tell exactly where someone was by sensing what direction the emotions were coming from and how strong they were."

"You . . . you're preg—oh my god! And it's . . . it's mine!" Trey shoots off the bed and rakes his hands through his hair. It's not in frustration, the way he typically does it. He looks more confused than anything. "But—but how is that possible? To have a half-Zordi, half-Ordi child? That's not—wait. Who cares how it's possible? My baby's an Empath, just like me. Holy shit! I'm gonna be a dad!"

My eyes go wide. "Oh, Trey. Hold on."

He doesn't hear me. He climbs back into bed, rips the blanket off my legs, then presses his ear to my stomach.

"Trey, I—"

His shuddering body stops me. He grips onto my legs, then lets out a cry.

I place my palms over his back as his shoulders tremble. "Are you okay?"

It takes a few heartbeats before he arches his head back, and I can finally see the tears rushing down his face. "Arella, I'm more than okay! I'm gonna be a dad! I've always wanted a family. I haven't had one in so long. I'm gonna work so hard, baby. I promise you. I'm gonna work so hard to be the best dad this little baby could ever have."

I burst into tears. *This* was the reaction I wanted when I was scared to tell him I was pregnant. *This* is what every woman dreams of seeing from her man the second she gets that positive pregnancy test.

Trey swipes his thumb under my wet eyes. "I'm gonna teach them how to play guitar and piano. You can teach them how to bake and how to be a good person. We'll do things like go to amusement parks. I've never been to one. That's something good dads do with their kids, right? I'll take them to baseball games and out for movies. Disney World. The zoo. Oh, god. I've always wanted to go to a zoo."

"Trey . . ." I say through tears as I try to find the right words.

"Look, I know I don't know anything about babies, but I'm gonna learn. I'll take classes. I'll read books, and do lots of Googling. I'll take really good care of this baby. I'll take really good care of you too, Arella. I promise."

"Trey, stop."

"I can't. I'm so fucking happy right now. Fuck, I'm even crying. I don't think I've ever cried from happiness before. Look at me. I'm such a goddamn sap, and I don't even care. I'm gonna be a dad! I'm gonna be—"

"Trey!" I finally find the strength to shout through my tears. "Listen to me!"

Ultimately, he settles, taking my hands into his. "What, baby?"

"Oh, honey. You just made it harder for me to tell you."

"Tell me what?"

I've never seen anyone so wholesomely happy about being a dad before. I squeeze his hands to give him reassurance that everything will be okay. "Honey, the baby is gone."

68

ARELLA

I expect him to burst out with a loud *What?* but he doesn't. Instead, he stares at me with a deadpan look like he doesn't understand the language I'm speaking.

"I'm sorry, Trey. Maybe I should have started with that." I didn't because I needed him to know that I had never cheated on him. I needed him to know the baby was his. I didn't expect him to react so strongly about being a father.

"W-what do you mean, *gone?*"

"As in, I'm not pregnant anymore." I'm surprised by how well I'm keeping myself together. I wasn't sure if I could say it out loud without crying. However, after seeing how happy Trey was just now, I think he's going to lose it, and at least one of us has to stay strong.

He squeezes my hands tighter in his. "No! That's . . . no! But—you . . . H-how? How do you know?"

"Because the morning after I was electrocuted, I couldn't sense other people's emotions anymore."

"Electrocuted?"

"Yes. While you were in the infirmary, Victor sent me to a lab. There, a lady did a bunch of tests on me. One of them was dropping lightning balls on me to try to get me to shield myself from them. I couldn't do it, and I'm pretty sure that's what caused the baby to—"

I'm right. He does lose it. He flies off the bed and heaves a hand through his hair. Now *that* is in the manner I'm used to seeing. "No! This can't be. I—Goddammit! Victor! That fucking . . . There's not even a word horrible enough to describe what I feel about him right now."

Trey paces the room. "He's probably the goddamn Royal who organized the murder of my parents. He kidnapped my girl, then he killed my baby. How can one man cause so much damage? Why? What did I ever do to him?"

The blanket Trey ripped off me hovers into the air. I grab it as the dresser drawers open and all their contents float out. Shirts, pants, and boxers drift around the room. "Trey."

He's not even looking my way. "And he's supposedly my biological father? You've gotta be fucking kidding me! If he really was my father, why would he kill my mother? A woman he supposedly loved?"

"Trey," I say louder as I grab a pillow from the air, trying to keep it against the bed.

He continues pacing the other side of the room. "I can't allow him to keep tormenting me. Everything that man does is toxic. He's going to keep hurting people if I don't stop him. He'll keep coming after my girl too. You'll always be in danger for as long as he's alive. I can't let that happen."

The pillow I'm holding down bursts into flames. My scream makes Trey spin around as I toss it onto the floor.

"Oh, shit!" He waves a shaky hand at the flaming pillow. The flames don't stop. "Fuck."

"Trey, make it stop."

"I—I'm trying." His chest rises and falls as he gasps for air. He has that desolate look in his eyes again—the same look he got after Li told him that Victor is his real father.

Suddenly, I know exactly what I need to do. I jump off the bed. The second I take his face into my palms, everything in the air falls to the carpet. The flames consuming the pillow disappear into plumes of smoke. It takes a minute for Trey's breathing to slow. The entire time, my hands never leave his face.

After several deep breaths, he finally makes eye contact with me. That desolate look is gone, replaced by sorrow. He wraps his muscular arms tight around my waist. "I'm sorry, babe. Are you hurt?"

"I'm okay. Are you?"

He nods slightly, and I don't need Li's lie-detecting power to know he's lying.

I drop my hands, then turn to find what's left of that pillow in a burnt heap on the floor. The carpet beneath it is scorched too. It hits me that the bedroom I was locked inside of at the Ridge was probably Trey's at one point.

"Good thing we have extra pillows," I say.

"Good thing we're underground."

"Good thing the fire didn't spread."

With a tender finger, he tucks some of my hair behind an ear. "Good thing I've got you. Did you know you have a special power where every time you touch me, it calms me?"

"I've noticed."

Trey leans down to kiss my forehead. "Thank you for being everything I never knew I needed."

My heart swoons. He's everything I never knew I needed too.

I leave him to grab a new pillow from the closet and toss it onto the bed. "This has happened before, hasn't it?"

His gaze falls to the carpet. "Yeah, lots. It started after my parents died, then it stopped sometime after I turned sixteen. It hasn't happened since until today. I don't know what it is or how to prevent it."

"When does it usually happen?" I ask, even though I know the answer.

"Whenever I get too emotional, or anxious, or depressed."

"I think they're panic attacks."

"Hmm" is all he says. Then he spends a moment staring at the carpet.

Eventually, we get back under the covers. Trey pats his shoulder, then gestures for me to scoot closer. I don't hesitate to nestle into the crook of his arm. As he wraps his limbs around me, his hand bumps my gauze. It doesn't hurt.

"It's been long enough," he says. "Can I take this off for you?"

"Sure." I expect him to peel it off. Instead, he points at my arm. The gauze flies away and lands on the floor. My skin under it looks brand new.

Trey inspects my arm, then nods his approval. I let out a sigh as I nuzzle deeper into him and rest a hand over his pec. He points at the light switch, and it flips with a click. The room goes dark. A night-light plugged in on the other side of the room illuminates everything just enough for me to not feel like I'm stuck in a box with no exit.

For a while, neither of us says anything. All that fills my ears are the sounds of our soft breaths. I shut my eyes and relish the warmth of being in Trey's arms again.

I'm about to drift off to sleep when he says, "Babe?"

I don't open my eyes. "Mmm?"

"I think you're right."

"About what?"

His chest rumbles against my face as he says, "The panic attacks. I think that's what they are too."

"I'm no doctor, but I'm, like, ninety-nine percent sure that's what it is. You exhibit all the signs of it. Short breaths. Shaky hands. A blank look in your eyes. You said it started after your parents were killed, which means it probably stems from that trauma."

"How do I stop it?"

"There's no way to *stop* it, really. I think it's something you just learn to live through and manage until they go away on their own. In the meantime, you could go see a therapist and see if that helps."

"I'd have to see a zerapist, but yeah, I'll think about doing that."

"Ahh," I say when it clicks. "Because you can't talk about your world with Ordinaries."

"Exactly. And because we have different bodily functions, we have to see people like zoctors and zutritionists."

"But if your car breaks down, can you see a regular mechanic?"

"Yes. There are no such things as zechanics because there aren't special cars just for Zordis."

Now that I think about it, that all makes sense.

Trey shifts under the blanket until he's on top of me. He opens his palm, and a little fireball appears in it. He tosses it into the air, and it hovers above us as he caresses my cheek. I'm grateful that he brought out the flames. I wouldn't be able to see the intense look in his eyes otherwise.

"I love being able to openly talk to you about my world, baby. I love you so much—with all my heart. I want to marry you and have babies with you and grow old with you. I want it all with you. Say you want it with me too."

I don't hesitate. "I do."

He grips the back of my neck as he drops his mouth over mine. His lips are as eager as his tongue. My hands caress down his bare back as he peppers tender kisses over my neck. I arch my head back and moan as he sucks my skin into his mouth.

In a low voice against my collarbone, he says, "We're meant to be together, Arella. I know it within the depths of my soul. You're it for me, and I'll spend the rest of my life convincing you that I'm it for you too."

"I don't need to be convinced, Trey. I already know you're the one for me."

He shifts onto his side and props himself up on an elbow. His other hand caresses me behind my ear in little circles. Shadows from his fireball dance across his features as he says, "When this is all over, I'm gonna get you a ring. It'll be so big, the fucking astronauts will be able to see it from space."

"That sounds great, honey, but what about—"

"No. Don't say it. I know there are logistics, but I don't care. No zovernment is going to keep me away from you. We can't get married legally, but I'd love to at least see a ring on your finger. We'll know what it means, and that's what matters to me. If you want to have a small ceremony with some friends and your family, we can do that too, just without the paperwork. We can do it wherever you want. I'll buy everyone plane tickets to Paris if that's your dream wed—oh!" Trey pops up and slides off the bed. "That reminds me. I have something for you."

He flips the light on, using his hand this time, then his hovering fireball smokes out. He digs through our backpack to pull out his leather jacket. From the inner pocket, he drags out something shiny.

"My necklace! How did you—"

"Katie gave it to me. She said she had a vision that made her think Victor might have stolen it, so she took it before he could."

That Katie, saving the day again. "We owe that girl."

Trey scoffs. "No kidding."

Once I've got all my long waves pulled up, Trey rejoins me in bed and hooks the jewelry around my neck. The entire time, he stares me in the eyes like he wants to devour me. Maybe he does. I wouldn't mind.

I let my hair back down, then run my fingers along the diamond. "Have I ever told you how much I love this thing? It's stupid because it's just a necklace, but it means so much to me because it came from you."

"*You* mean so much to me."

Roughly, I grab the back of his neck and pull him on top of me. He comes willingly and goes straight for my lips. His kisses are hard and desperate. Mine are just the same. The way we move so in sync only solidifies how perfect we are for each other.

I drag my shirt over my head, then shove my pants down. Once my bra is off, Trey doesn't waste a second wrapping his tongue around my nipple. I arch my head back and moan toward the ceiling as I cup the back of his head and wrench him closer.

"Oh, baby," he says against my breast. "You taste so good."

He keeps licking me as he rolls my other nipple between his thumb and fingers. I claw my way down his back until I reach his boxers and pull them down just enough to give me access to his dick. He groans into my chest as I stroke his thick shaft up and down.

"Don't be gentle with me," I say breathlessly.

As if that's what he's been waiting to hear all day, he shoves his boxers down all the way, then pulls my legs up. I rest them against his shoulders.

He slides his tip against my damp opening and moans. "Fuck. You're so wet."

"You did that to me." I gasp as he plunges into me, no warning or anything. My fingernails dig into his arms as I let out a yelp. I know I asked him not to be gentle, but I didn't expect him to shove it in *that* hard.

He plants a hand on either side of my head. "Fuck, baby. You're so tight."

I half moan, half scream as he draws back and shoves it into me again.

He stills. "Are you okay, babe?"

"Yeah," I lie through a pant. "Give me more."

He draws back and thrusts again. This time, the pain is partly pleasure. With each of his thrusts, he kisses my neck and grunts into it. His deep, guttural sounds turn me into a puddle.

I grip his shoulders as I eventually stretch to his size. After a while, the pain transforms into satisfying bliss. With each pump, his chest slides up and down mine as if he needs to be as close to me as possible. His deep groans mix with my breathless whimpers and the sounds of our bodies smacking together. I wanted it rough, but I'll accept these slow and steady thrusts for now.

"I love you, Arella," he whispers into my ear. "I love you so fucking much."

"I love you too, Trey," I say as my head bangs against the pillow over and over.

His breaths send warm air down my shoulder. "I promise I'll always love you—no matter what. And I'll always fight for you. And protect you. And treat you right. And make love to you with my whole heart like I am right now."

"Yes, Trey," I moan. "I want that. All of it. But harder."

"Harder?" He pushes himself up. "You want it harder?"

"Yes, Trey. Fuck me."

His mouth parts, then he licks his bottom lip. "Beg for it."

"Please!" I scream. "Fuck me!"

"Again."

"Please! Give it to me as hard as you can."

"Good girl." He slaps a hand on either side of my hips and keeps me against him as he gets to his knees. Then he slams his cock into me over and over. With each thrust, he yanks my hips into him so our bodies meet as hard as they can. I scream his name to the ceiling and clench my hands into the sheets.

"Fuuuck . . ." he says between grunts. "You're taking it so good, baby."

I can't respond. Not when he's pounding into me so hard like this. It's taking all my energy just to keep up with him. The mattress creaks beneath us again and again. I screw my eyes shut as the pleasure consumes all my senses. Just when I think it can't get any better, his thumb finds my clit.

"I need you to come for me," he says through moans. "I need to feel your emotions rush through my head."

I have no idea what he means by that, and now is not the time to ask, because I can't think about anything except the feel of his thumb rubbing me to my climax. Like he has before, he goes in little circles, using the perfect amount of pressure. I head straight for the edge.

"Oh, god," I breathe out. "That feels amazing."

"Tell me how you want it, baby."

"Just like that. Don't stop."

He doesn't. He doesn't go any harder or faster either. He just keeps his rhythm as he continues pumping his cock back and forth inside me and rubbing my clit. I keep my eyes closed and take in every ounce of pleasure he's giving me until I reach the edge and jump over it.

I scream out as the pleasure ripples through me. I pulse around his shaft as tingles shoot down my legs in waves. He continues rubbing me until my breathing slows into long pants and my body relaxes.

When I open my eyes, I find him staring at me through dazed blue-grays. Without wasting another second, he pulls my legs up higher and relentlessly drives into me. I grip onto his firm arms to hold myself as still as possible for him. His pumps feel even better after my orgasm. I'm so sensitive, I can feel every vein of his cock against my inner walls.

"Fuck, babe," he says through deep grunts, "I'm gonna come."

"Come inside me."

"Oh, god." He thrusts into me harder. "Beg for it, baby."

"Come inside me, Trey. Please!"

"Beg some more."

"Please! Come for me!"

"Fuuuck . . ." He thrusts a few more times before he stills, then fills me with his load. He pulsates over and over, grunting as he drains his final drops inside me. His hands lock my hips against his as if he needs to make sure I can't get away.

Don't worry, honey. I don't plan to.

After one last pump, he collapses over my chest. Together, we pant until our breaths slow.

I'm sweaty, but he's not, which is nothing new. I'll assume that has something to do with the way his body functions differently from mine.

"That was amazing," he says against my breast. "Whenever you orgasm, your emotions rush through my head."

"How?"

"I have no idea. Your immunity walls just come down—only for a few seconds though."

Interesting. "I better never fake it, then."

He chuckles a little. "I'll know it if you do."

I grab his face and guide him up to kiss me. Then I whisper against his lips, "Do you want to do that again?"

He pulls out, making me gasp. "Hell yeah."

69

ARELLA

I jolt awake, gasping for air. Everything is dark except for the little night-light in the corner. It takes me a second to remember where I am. I've been waking up in a lot of strange places lately.

Trey places a gentle hand over my waist and gives me a tender squeeze. "You're okay, babe. I'm right here."

I relax my shoulders and flop my head back over the pillow. "I had another nightmare."

"About what?"

"Lightning balls and spiky spheres of ice."

He leans in closer to caress my face. "I'm sorry, angel. I hope these nightmares don't stick around like the spider ones have."

"Me too." I let out a little sigh. "What time is it?"

"Earlier, the clock on the microwave said it was just past noon, but I have no clue if that's accurate or not."

"How long have you been awake?"

"Not long. Maybe a half hour."

I sit up and rub my eyes. "Could you turn the light on?"

Trey sits up too, and points at the light switch. It clicks, then the room brightens to life.

I squint and blink a few times before my eyes adjust to find my man in a gray polo and a pair of light wash jeans. He doesn't normally wear polos or light wash jeans. It was probably the closest thing to what he prefers to wear that he could find in here. "Telekinesis is a really cool power to have. I wish I had that."

"You have a power that's waaay cooler than mine."

"My immunity isn't a *power*, and it's not as useful as being able to move things with your mind."

"First off, your immunity *is* a power. It's not a Zordi power, but it's still a power—a powerful one at that. Second, telekinesis is my *body* power. So, it's mostly my hands doing the work. My mind plays a huge part, but without my hands, it couldn't happen."

I take a moment to let that information settle in. "There's still a lot for me to learn about the Zordi world, isn't there?"

"You know, my plan once I got you to Paris was to tell you everything about my world. I didn't wanna tell you in advance because I didn't want you to freak out and leave me before I could get you somewhere safe. You seem to be taking all this pretty well. Maybe I should have just told you. We might have avoided all this."

"No, you did the right thing by not telling me. If you had, I definitely would have left you. When I first saw people using their powers, I was terrified."

"I'm so sorry." He takes my hands into his and gives me a light peck on the knuckles. "What's the first power you saw?"

"Whatever power Victor has that makes his eyes go black."

Trey thinks, then his face scrunches together. "He doesn't have a power that makes his eyes go black."

"Yes, he does."

"Victor is an Aero, an Animal Empath, and he has enhanced taste. None of those can make his eyes go black."

"I know what I saw, Trey. He held me down, stared at my face, then this creepy black cloud took over the whites of his eyes. I saw it multiple times."

"Hmm." His eyes gloss over in deep thought.

"While you think about that, I'm gonna go brush my teeth." I slide off the bed and head toward the bathroom.

After I've got fresh breath, I join Trey back in the bedroom. He stands in front of the night-stand with the drawer open, holding his fake passport, staring at it with a far-off look in his eyes.

I rub a palm over his shoulder. "What're you thinking about?"

He continues staring at the name *Daniel Johnson* before he sighs and sets the passport down. Then he shuts the drawer, takes my hands into his, and leads me to sit on the edge of the bed with him.

"Babe," he says through a long sigh, "I'm gonna say something to you, and it's gonna sound crazy."

"Is it crazier than telling me that our parents were killed on the same night, and that the media said I died with them, and that my name was probably Hannah Calder at one point?"

"This is equally as crazy."

I'm not sure if I can handle any more bad news, but . . . "Okay, let's hear it."

"I'm gonna go back."

I freeze as I try to comprehend what he means. "Go back?"

"I thought about it all last night and some more when I woke up this morning. Katie told me that Victor's been running tests on Immunes for the last nineteen years. Do you wanna take a wild guess as to what happened to the others?"

"I don't have to guess. I already know."

"I have to stop him. Otherwise, he'll continue killing more innocent people. So, I have to go back."

I swallow thickly. "What are you going to do?"

He stares at me without blinking. "You already know, so please don't make me say it out loud. The idea of having to do it is already making me nauseous."

I'm not going to make him say it, because he's right: I do know. I'd like to think I'm the type of person who'll talk him out of this, but seeing how the Royals at the gas station didn't hesitate to kill an innocent man, I have no compassion for them.

"Judge me if you want, but I've made my decision."

I give his hands a loving squeeze. "I'm not judging you, honey. Actually, I think this is very heroic of you."

He scoffs lightly. "I'm not doing this to be a hero. Honestly, the root of this decision is pretty selfish. We can't hole up down here for the rest of our lives. You deserve better than that, and as long as Victor is alive, you won't be safe. So, selfishly, I'm doing this for me. For you. For us. For our future family together. I won't be able to sleep knowing someone is searching for us with the intent to hurt you. And if we have kids, then what? Our babies could never live a normal life if we're always on the run. I don't want that."

I had these same thoughts yesterday when we were in Tao's Lincoln. While Trey drove, I asked myself, *When can we stop running?* After some deep thought, the answer was clear: As long as Victor is breathing, I won't be safe. I'll always have to run. The only way to stop running is to stop Victor.

I give Trey a firm nod as I make my decision too. "Okay. Let's go."

He gapes at me. "What?"

"I said, let's go."

He lets out a humorless chuckle. "No, no, no. *You're* not going. *I* am."

"I'm coming with you."

He jumps to his feet and slashes a hand through the air. "Hell no! Not in a million years. It could be dangerous."

"And that's exactly why I need to go. You won't stand a chance against Victor and his Royal minions without my immunity protecting you."

"No. Fuck no." He shakes his head with a look in his eyes that says he won't back down. "Abso-fucking-lutely not."

I'm not going to back down either. "I said I'm coming."

"Arella, this is not the time to be difficult."

"You promised we'd be a team, remember? You protect me, and I'll protect you."

"This *is* me protecting you. You need to stay here until I come back."

I get to my feet as I cross my arms over my chest. "And what if you don't come back?"

"Then at least you'll be alive."

"But that means you aren't, which means I'm still in danger. If I go with you, at least we'll have a *chance* at winning."

He points a hand toward the ceiling. "We don't know what the situation looks like up there. When we left, the Royals had just gotten through the cavern entrance and people were dying. Then once we got through the tunnel, we were attacked by a swarm of Royals. Pixie, Ruby, and Katie held them back to give me a chance to get you to safety. They risked their lives to save you. The last thing I'm gonna do is bring you straight back to the place we fought to get you out of. Also, I have no idea which side won. If it was Victor's side, that probably means the Ridge is crawling with hundreds of Royals by now."

I put a hand over my hip. "All the more reason why I *need* to come. If it's you against hundreds, we might as well say our goodbyes now because you're definitely not coming back."

Trey's body stiffens. I know *goodbye* is a trigger word for him. I didn't mean to use it against him like that. Still, if given the choice, I wouldn't take it back. I'm right, and he knows it. If he leaves without me, it'll be the last time we ever see each other.

"Arella," he says, choking up, "I can't lose you again."

"I can't lose you either."

Roughly, he yanks me to him and smashes me against his chest. We stand there for a while, just holding each other. He doesn't say anything. He doesn't move either. This reminds me of the night he held me for the first time. It was right after he fought Nathan in my apartment, and it was the first time I had felt safe in a man's arms in years.

I tilt my head back to look at him. "Last night, you promised you'd always fight for me, right?"

"Yeah."

"How about we fight together?"

He captures my face between his hands, then plants his mouth over mine. His kiss is full of agony. As he slips his tongue between my lips, it feels like he's using me to heal himself, like he needs my kiss to quell his anxieties and kill off his demons all at once. I'll gladly be his emotional Healing Goo if it means he'll always kiss me like this.

He's about to pull away when I grab him by the collar of his polo and drag him back toward me. We embrace again until we're panting and my lips are numb.

Trey presses his forehead against mine. "All right, babe. Let's go find something to eat while we make a plan."

70

TREY

The waterfall concealing Shadow Ridge's cavern pours into a small lake. Crickets chirp throughout the darkness as Arella and I crouch behind a bush overlooking the shimmery water. I can't believe I allowed her to come. Earlier, when we stopped at a drive-thru, she went inside to use the bathroom, and I almost put that Lincoln into drive and left her there. It's not like she could have found her way to the Ridge without me. The only reason I didn't take off is because she's right. Without her immunity protecting me, I'd be waltzing straight into a death trap.

"You need me to go over the plan again?" I ask in a low voice.

"Nope. I've got it all up here." She taps her temple three times.

"Do you remember what the most important part is?"

"Yes. If you die, I need to get out of there as fast as possible."

"Right. Don't try to save me. Don't try to stop the bleeding. Just go."

She gives me a curt nod, but that defiant look in her eyes tells me she only agreed to my terms to shut me up. She's already proven that she won't leave me behind if there's even a *chance* I'll make it, and that's the part that worries me the most. If I'm about to die, I need her to forget about me and save herself.

"All right. Stay close and—" Suddenly, a bunch of people's emotions cloud my head, all coming from inside the cavern.

Arella stills, but she doesn't say anything. She just watches me with wide eyes, wondering why I've frozen up.

More emotions invade my head as ten—no, fifteen—no, twenty-some people come marching out the Ridge's entrance.

"I sense people coming out," I whisper. "They're walking through the cave now, toward the waterfall."

"How many?" she whispers back.

"Maybe close to thirty."

"Do you think they saw us on the camera feeds and are coming out to kill us?"

"I'm not sure, but they're not in a rush, nor do their emotions feel urgent." Which is why I'm so confused.

We remain where we are as I continue sensing the large group approaching the waterfall.

"Get your fucking hands off me!" a man shouts.

I'd know that voice anywhere. It's Victor, and he sounds lethal.

"Keep it moving, asshole," a woman yells back. She steps out from behind the waterfall first, making my heart drop. She's not just any woman. She's an Enforcer, a fully uniformed zovernment official, with her blonde hair tied into a tight bun at the top of her head.

From her holster, the Enforcer whips out a gun. "I said to keep it moving! Otherwise, I'll shoot you with another dose of perrizo to knock you out. Then I'll drag your ass across the ground instead. Is that what you want?"

I grip Arella's arm and hold her tight as if the Enforcer is threatening her, not Victor.

In silence, Victor steps out from behind the waterfall. He's handcuffed and attached to a long chain. On that chain are the rest of the people I sense, marching out of the cave behind him, cuffed at the wrists and fixed to the long chain. I recognize a few of the people as the left-over ZIRDA agents from before. The others, I don't recognize at all. I can only assume that means they're on Victor's side.

Three men step out from behind the waterfall, wearing the same light-blue uniform as the Enforcer woman. How many Enforcers are here? And how did they find this ZIRDA base? ZIRDA hides from the zovernment just as much as they hide from everyone else. Did someone call the Enforcers here as an attempt to get Victor arrested? If that's the case, why are the Enforcers arresting *everybody*?

"Stop at that tree and don't move," the female Enforcer yells at Victor, then marches past all the chained people and shouts down the cavern. "Did you get everyone?"

A deep male voice from behind the waterfall answers her. "We're gonna go back to do one more sweep."

"Great." The female Enforcer points at the three men in uniforms. "You guys keep an eye on these delinquents. I'm gonna go help with the sweep." As she heads back into the cave, the last people on the long chain step out.

I recognize Ruby and Katie right away. Neither woman looks too banged up. *Thank fuck.* But where is Pixie?

Just as a *whoosh* of air blows Arella's hair into my face, someone's emotions pop up behind me. Then something sharp pricks my neck, making everybody's emotions disappear from my head.

Arella yelps as she slaps a hand over her neck. "Ow."

Suddenly, my wrists are heavy. A pair of thick cuffs has appeared around them. Arella's wrists are cuffed too. They're so heavy, they make her fall over into the grass.

Another *whoosh*, then a slender Hispanic man in a light-blue uniform stops running in front of me. He presses a finger against the wired device in his ears. "I found two more hiding in the woods. They were on their way back in when they saw us coming out." The man pauses for a moment, then says, "Yes, ma'am. I'll add them to the chain."

"Wait, no," I say. "We're not with them."

"Yeah, sure. I've *never* heard that one before." In a mocking, high-pitched voice, he says, "No! I'm not a Royal. I haven't committed any crimes or killed any Ordinaries."

"We haven't."

"Yeah, yeah. Good try. Now, get up, and don't try to run. You won't get far."

Even if this man wasn't a Speeder, I wouldn't try to run. I've been trying to make a fireball appear in my hands while he talked, and I haven't seen a single spark.

Katie gapes at me and Arella as we step out of the tree line with the Enforcer behind us. "Trey?"

"What the hell are you two doing back here?" Ruby says.

"Where's Pixie?" I ask because that's the more important question.

Ruby shakes her head and furrows her eyebrows together. In a choked voice, she says, "At least she went down doing what she loved most—kicking a Royal's ass."

A little piece of my heart breaks for that strong woman I barely knew. She spent more time torturing the hell outta my ears than anything, but in the end, she helped save me and Arella. She's a fucking hero in my book.

The Speeder attaches Arella to the chain first, then he does the same to me.

"You okay, babe?" I ask.

She offers me a slight nod. "You?"

I nod back. Physically, yes, I'm okay. Emotionally, I'm fucking terrified. *How the hell are we gonna get outta this one?*

The Speeder presses a finger to the device in his ears. "Y'all almost done in there?" A pause. "Cool. I'll do another sweep of the perimeter."

With a *whoosh*, the man is gone.

I eye the other three Enforcers guarding the people in cuffs. Each Enforcer looks like he could easily toss a tank over a building.

I turn to Katie and ask in a whisper, "What happened after I left?"

"We kept those Royals away from you for as long as we could. But after they killed Pixie and knocked Ruby unconscious, I surrendered. By that point, it was six against one, and all I could do was hope that you'd gotten far enough away. After that, Victor ordered his people to lock up all the agents in the cells. In case you can't tell, there aren't many of us left."

I cock my head to the side. "The cells?"

"You know, like, jail cells?" She flashes me a *duh* look. "That's where Victor has contained us for the last day or so."

"I didn't know there were jail cells here." Which is stupid, because I lived here for almost eleven years. Victor probably keeps the cells hidden in one of the many areas he forbade me from wandering around.

Katie continues, "We think he was keeping us alive for a possible ransom from ZIRDA or to torture us for information. We were in the middle of plotting an escape when the Ridge got raided by the Enforcers. They think this is a Royals hideout. We tried telling them that we're ZIRDA agents, until the Royals started doing the same. Since the Enforcers can't tell who is on what side, they're taking us all to z-prison. They said once we prove our innocence, we'll be released."

"That's right," the biggest Enforcer says from where he stands. "We'll be interrogating you all thoroughly, so you bestah get yo stories straight."

"Settle down, Cameron," the Enforcer closest to Victor says.

"Don't you tell me to settle down," Cameron says. "A Royal killed my son. I live for moments like this."

From inside the cavern, a woman babbles words so fast, I can't make them out.

"Please, you have to believe me," the woman says. "You—"

"I told you, lady," a man says, cutting her off, "you can prove your innocence to the Keepers."

"But you have to listen to me," the lady says. "I'm not a criminal."

When she steps out from behind the waterfall, I can't believe my eyes. "Aunt Jodi?"

Her skin looks unhealthily pale, and she's skinnier and more frail-looking than I remember, but it's definitely her. I'd recognize her anywhere, because that's the face of the woman who used to glare at me just for walking past her.

Jodi continues rambling as an Enforcer secures her handcuffs to the end of the chain behind me. "No, please! You have to listen to me. That man over there is not who he says he is."

I can't believe it's really her. I haven't seen her since I was six.

"I've been imprisoned here for twenty years!" she shouts as the Enforcer ignores her and huffs his way back into the cave. "I'm not a criminal!"

Is that true? Has Victor really kept his wife locked up here this whole time? Victor told my parents that Jodi packed up all her stuff and left, leaving behind only a note about finding her soul mate. I guess since that story came from Victor's lips, none of it is to be trusted.

"Aunt Jodi?" I say, cutting into whatever she's yelling to the Enforcers.

She flicks her attention to me, then her entire face drops. At first, she doesn't say anything; she just stares. The way she's looking at me isn't the way she used to look at me when I was a kid. There's no disgust, no loathing, not even an ounce of hatred in her eyes. Instead, she's looking at me like she's trying to figure out if I'm real.

"Trey?" My name leaves her mouth in a soft whisper.

"Yep," I say with a nod.

"Oh, god." She chokes up as tears stream down her pale cheeks. "Trey. You—you're so grown up."

"Well," I say dryly, "it's been, like, twenty fucking years."

She places her hands on my forearm, and it takes everything in me not to throw her off. "Trey, listen to me. You have to believe me, because these damn Enforcers won't."

"Shut up, Jodi!" Victor shouts from the front of the chain. "Shut your goddamn mouth."

Jodi ignores him. "Listen, I'm not Jodi. She's a fucking liar, and so are her goddamn parents. They lied about her mind power because it's on the Extinction List. Jodi doesn't have a photographic memory, like they made everyone believe. She's a Mind Swapper. Twenty years ago, she stole my body. I haven't seen a single ray of sunshine until just now. Please, you have to believe me."

I suck in a long breath as I muster up the courage to ask the question I think I already know the answer to. "If you're not Jodi, then who are you?"

"I'm Victor."

71

TREY

"Shut your mouth, Jodi, or I'll fucking kill you," Victor shouts. The chains rattle as he points a stern finger at me. "I'll kill him too."

Jodi shakes my forearm to grab my attention back. "Remember that one time we made a blanket fort? We ate spray cheese out of the can, and you told me you had a crush on a girl at your Zordi school. Oh, what was her name? God, I can't remember. Maybe that's not the best way to prove—"

"Don't listen to her," Victor says. "She's a goddamn liar."

Jodi ignores him again. "One time, I took you to the zoo. It was just you and me. When we got to the open aviary, you grabbed one of the small birds walking around and stuck it down your shirt. You wanted to take it home. No matter what I said to you, you refused to let the bird go. Eventually, the zookeepers got the bird out of your grasp, and they kicked us out. Do you remember that?"

I shake my head. "I don't remember ever going to a zoo."

"That's because she's a liar!" Victor says. "She's making this all up to try to save her skin."

All thirty-ish people hooked to this long chain between me and Victor gawk at us with wide eyes and silent mouths. The three Enforcers guarding us are silent too. Like me, they're probably unsure what to believe.

Jodi takes her hands off me and runs them through her greasy, matted hair. The chains clink against her thick handcuffs as she thinks. "Oh! I know! One Christmas morning, I came over early and we snuck down to the tree. We opened up those Nerf guns I got you. While we played, you bumped into the tree and—"

"Stop!" I shout so loudly, it makes Arella jolt back a step. I lock my attention onto Victor. "What happened next?"

"Huh?" he says.

"If you're really Victor, then you'll know what happened after I bumped into the Christmas tree."

He scoffs condescendingly. "Of course I know what happened. You tipped it over."

I turn my attention back to Jodi, whom I'm now pretty sure isn't Jodi. "What happened next?"

"You broke your mama's crystal angel ornament."

"And?"

"The wings broke off. We spent the rest of that morning trying to glue it back together but ended up breaking the head off too, so we dumped the thing in the neighbor's trash bin and made a pact to never tell anyone. That's how we came up with our secret word."

"Which is?"

Jodi doesn't hesitate. "Crystal."

I choke up as the realization sinks in. This whole time, it wasn't my sweet Uncle V who abused me and called me names. It was Jodi in Victor's body. Now that I think about it, it makes sense. It was always Jodi who treated me like shit, not Victor. This whole time, I thought he started treating me like that because he was sad about losing his wife. Turns out, he did it because his wife stole his goddamn body. *What the fuck?*

"So?" Cameron says, breaking the silence. "Who got it right?"

"Yeah," another Enforcer says from behind me, "we wanna know."

"Jodi is correct," I say, then shake my head. "I mean Victor. More specifically, Victor in Jodi's body."

Cameron chuckles to himself, shaking his head. "Damn. The Keepers gon' have a heyday with this one. A Mind Swapper? I thought them fuckers was extinct by now."

This explains why Arella saw Victor's eyes go black. It was Jodi trying to swap minds with Arella. I can't imagine what would happen if it had worked. For someone as toxic as Jodi to have immunity? I don't want to know all the things she'd do with that ability.

My dad places his female hands over my forearm again. "Jodi told me your mama's dead. Is that true?"

The pain in his eyes makes me think about lying, but I can't do that to him. "Jodi blew her up. She blew up both my parents."

"I didn't blow up anyone," Jodi sneers from Victor's body. It's disgusting that her mind has been living in my dad's head for this long and no one knew it. "They blew themselves up. My men's orders were only to detain Suzie and Andy. I had plans to torture them in front of Victor. Whatever happened that night, they killed themselves and took my men with them. I had nothing to do with it."

It's official: Jodi is a fucking nutcase. Abusing me is one thing, but keeping her husband locked up for twenty years, with plans to torture people in front of him for her pure enjoyment? Nutcase.

"Why didn't you kill me when you could?" I shout at Jodi. "I was seven. It would have been easy to get rid of me. Why keep me around for so long?"

If she tells me she kept me around just to torture me too, I won't be surprised.

Jodi chuckles deep from Victor's throat. "I had just killed Debbie and made it look like an overdose. That same night, your parents blew themselves up. How was I supposed to kill you too without raising suspicion? One death is an accident. Two is tragic. Three is a pattern. With the cops and social workers up my ass, it was either keep you alive or get investigated."

"What?" my dad shouts. "You told me Debbie took Trey in! You fucking lied!"

"Of course I did! I couldn't tell you that he was living on the floor right above you."

"What?" my dad turns to me. "Trey, you—you lived here?"

"Yep," I say. "From the day after the explosion, I lived here until the day I turned eighteen, when she kicked me out."

My dad gapes at me, then at Jodi. "You heartless bitch!" He runs at her with his fists up. He doesn't get very far though. The chains connecting him to me and thirty-some other people stop him. "You stole my body, locked me up for twenty years, and the whole time, you kept my son away from me right above my head!"

The Enforcers on the sidelines aim a perrizo gun at my dad, but they don't shoot him.

"You're a psycho!" my dad says. "A deranged lunatic!"

"And you were screwing around with your sister-in-law behind my back!" Jodi shouts. "Then you had a fucking baby with her and tried to hide it from me. I knew the second you laid eyes on Trey that he was yours. Nobody looks at a little boy like that unless they know it's their son."

Everything makes sense now. That's why Jodi always treated me like I was diseased. The whole time, she knew about Victor's affair. She knew I was his son.

Jodi glares at me. "Why don't you look surprised?"

I shrug nonchalantly. "Because I already knew."

"That Victor is your real father?"

"Yep."

My dad drops his jaw—well, technically, he drops Jodi's jaw. "How long have you known?"

"Since yesterday. Li and Tao told me."

"I knew it!" Jodi sneers. "Those chinks must have been hiding you underground somewhere."

My opinion of Jodi was already low based on my memories of her. It dipped even lower after I found out she's a Royal who stole my real father's body. Now she's racist too? What's next? Is she a pedophile? A Nazi? An animal abuser? I wouldn't be surprised by any of those.

In the corner of my eye, I see Cameron press a finger against his earpiece. "Nah, he ain't back yet." A pause, then he turns to one of the other Enforcers. "How long do ya think Eduardo's been gone for?"

The man shrugs. "A few minutes?"

"Hmm. He doesn't usually take that long to run the perimeter. Apparently, he's not responding to—"

BOOM!

The tree behind Cameron explodes, rocketing chunks of wood through the air. Cameron falls over and doesn't get back up. Screams echo around me as I instinctively leap in front of Arella and cover her with my body.

"We're under attack!" an Enforcer shouts.

A mass of people burst out from the tree line. Lightning balls sizzle through the air. A flaming fireball hits an Enforcer in the back and sets him on fire.

"Send backup now!" the Enforcer behind me shouts.

The chain line explodes with a deafening *BOOM!*, releasing everyone from it. With my cuffs still on, I grab Arella's arm and yank her toward me.

Then I shout at Katie over the screaming. "Please tell me these people are from your ZIRDA base!"

"No!" Katie yells over another loud *BOOM!* "They're Royals! Look!"

My attention whips to where she's pointing. A woman with short brown hair opens her palms toward Jodi's cuffs. With a smaller *boom!*, the cuffs fall off Jodi's wrists. With each small explosion, the heavy metal falls off all the Royals' wrists.

"Grab the Immune!" Jodi shouts, pointing at Arella.

My heart sinks as a bunch of large men charge toward my girl. Ruby and Katie step in front of her with their cuffed fists up. I know exactly which side people are on by the way they either help protect Arella or try to fight their way past the human wall surrounding me and her.

I keep Arella close to me as a fireball flies straight toward Katie's face. She screams with her arms up to block it. The fireball stops barely an arm away from her, then rolls to the ground and smokes out.

Katie's eyes bulge as another fireball rockets toward her face. The flames hit the same invisible wall, fall to the grass, then smoke out.

I gawk at Arella, who's got her eyes trained on the other element balls launching toward the people surrounding her. Each ball stops in the air, then disappears.

"What the hell?" a Royal shouts.

"It's you, isn't it?" Ruby says to Arella.

"I don't know how long I can do this," Arella says as she stops an ice ball from crashing over Katie's head. It falls to the ground and shatters into pieces.

"Keep that up!" Ruby says, then she runs toward the guy running at her with a knife in his hands. She ducks his weapon, then turns and kicks him in the back. Using her heavy metal cuffs, she bangs him on the head, and he drops to the ground.

As the Royals close in on us, the people surrounding Arella use their cuffs to keep the Royals away from her. People shout and cry out as they fight each other. From the corner of my eye, I see two men in cuffs charge at me, each one holding a knife in his hands. Katie tackles one to the ground while I kick the other in his gut. Then I bash my cuffs against his face. It only takes one hit for him to drop his knife, but it takes another hit for him to slump to the ground.

"Get off me, asshole!" Katie struggles with the man straddling her. He's trying to dig his knife into her neck. I rush up beside him and bang my cuffs against the side of his face. He yelps, then falls onto his shoulder. Katie picks up the knife he dropped and drives it straight into his stomach. He cries out again.

A woman charges at me with a water ball in her palm. It hits me in the face, drenching me with an icy-cold liquid. Agony explodes up my jaw as she punches me, then kicks me in the stomach.

"Get away from my son!" My dad tackles the woman into the grass. Then they roll around, punching at each other. The woman straddles my dad's frail body and drenches his face with a steady stream of water.

I'm about to help him when Arella screams out from behind me. I twist around on my heel, then gasp. A thick man has Arella by her neck in one hand and a knife in his other. As I run to save her, the man draws the knife back and aims it at her stomach.

"No!" Katie shoves Arella out of the way. Then she screams as the man drives the knife straight into her side. She cries out as the man pulls the knife back and aims for her throat.

I grab the man by the back of his shirt and yank him away from her. He stumbles, falling onto his ass. Then I heave my cuffs into his face.

Then again.

And again.

Once he limply thuds onto the ground, I stop.

"Trey!" Arella is hunched over Katie, putting pressure over the knife wound in Katie's stomach. "Help me! We have to save her!"

I kneel at Katie's side. The glint of bloody metal sticking out of her neck makes my lungs stop working. Her body shakes as she gurgles, then she goes limp and her head droops over.

Of all the people to die, I never wanted any of them to be Katie.

"Come on, Trey!" Arella cries. "Help me!"

I choke up as I grab Arella by her arm. "Babe, she's gone."

"No! She can't be!"

I drag Arella off the grass to meet my eyes. Her bloody hands tremble against my shirt. "We can't save her, Arella. She's gone."

"No!" Tears stream down her face as her knees buckle. "Katie!"

"I'm so s—" The wind gets knocked out of me as someone tackles me into the dirt. Jodi in Victor's body climbs on top of me and jabs something sharp into my side. I gasp for air as pain ripples through my stomach and down my leg. I feel every agonizing inch of the dagger as Jodi slides it out of my body.

She raises the weapon into the air again and spits into my face. "You worthless piece of shit! I never should have—" She flies off me as someone yanks her away.

"That's my son!" My dad climbs on top of Jodi and bashes his cuffs against her face. Then he grabs Jodi's dagger and drives it into her chest.

"Trey!" Arella drops to her knees at my side, putting pressure over my wound. "Oh, god!"

I groan in pain as Jodi kicks my dad's skinny body off her. Then she straddles my dad and stabs him in the stomach with the same dagger she just pulled out of her chest.

"No!" I scream as Jodi stabs him again, then again, and again.

My dad screams until his female body goes limp. Then he's not screaming anymore.

"Nooo!" I jerk upright, then everything stills. I try to stand up, but I can't. I can't even blink. All the screaming around me stops, and the air goes silent like we're in a library.

Jodi freezes on top of my dad. Her knife hand is drawn back, but she's not making a single move. A fireball flying above me is frozen in midair. The flames don't dance. The wind doesn't blow the trees. The crickets don't chirp.

Arella's mouth falls open at the hush surrounding us.

"Holy shit!" a man shouts from barely ten steps away. "That one just moved."

"That's impossible," a woman says. "I just froze everything except us within a quarter-mile radius."

"I swear, I saw that girl move."

"Which one?"

Arella stills, but her hands tremble against my wound. I reach out to protect her, but my arms don't budge. My heart races as two pairs of footsteps stomp their way toward us.

A male Enforcer I haven't seen before steps into my view and points a firm finger at Arella. "It was this woman right here."

The female Enforcer at his side produces a water ball in her hand, then drops it over Arella's head.

Arella gasps for air as the chilly liquid drenches her and drips onto my chest. I can feel the bitter cold, but my body doesn't react to it.

"What?" The female Enforcer grabs Arella by her arm and drags her onto her feet.

"Let me go!" Arella screams, making my heart thrash against my tight lungs.

"How are you doing that?" the female Enforcer asks, then gasps. "Oh my god! She's an Ordinary."

The male Enforcer presses a finger against the device in his ears. "Yes, we just arrived. Everything is under control now. Everyone's been immobilized. We're ready for the other

Porters." A pause. "Sounds good. And boss, you're not gonna believe this, but there's an Ordinary here, and she's moving." Another pause. "I mean exactly what I said. I'm standing right next to her, and my zense isn't activating. Not only that, but she can move, even after the immobilization." Another pause. This time, it's longer. "Aye. We'll take her in for a scrub."

"No!" Arella tries hitting the female Enforcer with her cuffs, but it's no use.

The female Enforcer shoves Arella to her knees, then points a gun at her neck. I try to protect her, but my limbs won't budge.

"Stay down," she says, then turns to her partner. "What if the scrub doesn't work on her like my immobilization isn't?"

The male Enforcer shrugs. "I guess we'll find out."

PART THREE
SCRUBBED MIND

PLAYLIST

72

TREY

I bang a fist against the wood table. "Where is she?"

The Keeper sitting across from me sighs. With the long sleeve of his navy-blue uniform, he rubs the fingerprints off the golden nameplate pinned to his upper chest. It reads ORTIZ. "Mr. Grant, if you don't want to cooperate with me, I'm happy to ask the Enforcers to put you back behind bars until you do. Now answer my question."

I burst out of my metal chair. It falls behind me with a *clank!* against the hard floor of this stuffy interrogation room. This bullshit little space is barely bigger than a bathroom stall. Plus, it's musty, it's windowless, and, most of all, it's Arella-less.

"I've been cooperating with you for the last three days!" I shout at the useless example of a Superior in front of me. "Now I'm done cooperating, because every time I ask you where she is, you refuse to answer. If you don't tell me now, I'll tear this whole place apart until I find her!" *And that's a fucking promise.*

Ortiz leans back in his chair and chuckles. "This prison is packed with Enforcers whose powers aren't subdued by perrizo—while yours are. How do you plan to tear this place apart without your gifts?"

Each injection of perrizophine forced onto every inmate is supposed to last twelve hours. To ensure there's never a chance an inmate's perrizo has worn off before their next injection, doses are handed out like candy every eight hours.

I never realized how much I relied on my Empath power until now. I have to pay attention to people's facial expressions and body language to guess how they're feeling. Even then, it's just a guess. When I get outta here, I'm never talking shit about my mind power ever again. And I say *when* because it's a matter of when, not if.

Three days ago, I woke up in a large holding cell, surrounded by the remaining ZIRDA (Zordinary Innovations Research and Development Agency) agents and double that number of Royals, the chaotic assholes who think all Zordis are better than Ordinaries, just because we were born with powers—something outside of our control. The Enforcers stated that if we could prove we hadn't broken any laws, they'd let us go.

One by one, they took us into an interrogation room. Depending on our answers to their questions, a Detector on the other side of the wall either confirmed that our words are true or that we've lied.

On day one, every Royal was taken out of the holding cell, interrogated, then relocated to separate cells to await their trials that will determine how long they'll be incarcerated for. Depending on the severity of their crimes, they could be trapped in prison for the rest of their lives. I hope that's the case for all of them.

As for the ZIRDA agents, they were also interrogated on day one, then released within twenty minutes of their interrogations starting. I'm not that great at math, but I'm good enough to know that three days is a hell of a lot longer than twenty minutes.

The first ZIRDA agent to be freed was Ruby. She was also the only person left I knew by name. Everyone else I knew by name had been killed: Dash the Speeder, who helped me get Arella out of Shadow Ridge by making sure the hidden tunnel was safe. Carlos the security guard, who helped fend off the Royals while I got Arella to safety. Pixie the Ear Blower, who was barely twenty years old and one of the bravest people I've ever known.

The youngest to die was Katie. She's the one I owe the most. She preloaded some perrizo guns for me, which was crucial in our escape. Katie is also the one who pushed Arella out of the way when a Royal tried to stab her with a knife. Sadly, Katie ended up on the other end of that knife.

I barely had time to process Katie's death before Aunt Jodi, in Victor's body, stabbed me in the side. Then Victor, in Jodi's body, tackled her to the ground. They tried to kill each other until the Enforcers showed up seconds later, but it was too late. Victor—who I thought for all my life was my uncle but was really my dad—had already stopped breathing.

Jodi had suffered some injuries too—a few blows to the head and a dagger to the chest. She didn't make it long enough to see the prison's Healer. I did, though, and now I don't even have a scar to memorialize that battle.

I'd like to say I've had a moment to mourn the loss of my dad, but I've been too busy trying to figure out what the zovernment has done with my girl and wondering why they're still keeping me here when they've already deemed me innocent.

They're not holding me for being a Royal, nor are they holding me for committing crimes as a ZIRDA agent. Surprisingly, they aren't holding me for exposure to an Ordinary either. After their many questions, all of which I answered with the truth, they determined that since I used my powers to protect Arella and only did it *after* she'd already found out about the existence of Zordinaries, they're dropping the charges.

So if I'm not being convicted for anything, why am I still here? More importantly, why am I talking to a Keeper? Keepers are high-level zovernment officials who make the laws. Enforcers are the ones who enforce those laws. The people who were arrested with me were all interrogated by Enforcers, which makes sense because this is mid-level Enforcer work. So why is there a *Keeper* sitting in front of me?

Ortiz points at my knocked-over chair. "Pick that up, sit your ass down, and answer my question."

Glaring at the man, I scoop up my chair and set it upright with a *clank!* Then I plant myself back onto the metal and cross my arms with a huff.

"What else do you know about her immunity?" Ortiz asks for the third time. Since he's so insistent about getting my answer to this question, I'm gonna assume *this* is why they're still keeping me around. Arella must be an anomaly to the zovernment too.

"I've already told you everything I know."

Like it did the last two times I said that, a device on the wall glows red with the word LIE.

Whoever that Detector is who keeps pressing that LIE button on the other side of that wall needs to stop.

This Keeper already knows I was sent on a mission to find out the source of Arella's immunity. He also knows I never found it. I told him that she was able to project her immunity onto me multiple times. I even told him the way she did it was by imagining waves of water drenching me. I've told him everything I know—except one thing.

What I haven't told him is that I was able to break through Arella's immunity walls by making her orgasm. I don't want the zovernment knowing that, for two reasons: First, I don't want them to take advantage of that knowledge and scrub her memories. Second, they've already let me off the hook for fake-dating an Ordinary. I doubt they'll be as relenting if they find out I had sex with her too.

Sadly, getting locked up for that is the least of my worries. My biggest concern is that they'll find out Arella and I were able to conceive, even though it's biologically impossible for us to do so. I still have no idea how that happened, and it doesn't matter. What matters now is that the Keepers don't find out about it. Who knows what they'll do with that information. If it's anything close to dissecting Arella to study her reproductive organs, fuck that. This is why I need to know where she is, because if they've already locked her up for research, then I need to bust her out.

"You can't tell lies in here." Ortiz folds his hands together over the table. "So how about you stop wasting—"

Knock-knock.

The door unlocks, then opens to reveal a slender Asian woman in a fancy-ass burgundy suit. Her heels clack against the floor as she lets herself into the room. "Thank you for your time, Mr. Ortiz. You may dismiss yourself."

Ortiz lets out a scoff and wrinkles his face together. "Excuse me? I'm in the middle of an interrogation. Who are you?"

In a sweet tone, the twenty-something woman says, "I'm Mia Wang, Executive Keeper."

"Executive Keeper?" Ortiz chuckles under his breath. "Yeah, right. Those people never come out from behind their desks."

"I assure you, Mr. Ortiz, when needed, we do *come out from behind our desks*. I am here to speak to Mr. Grant. Therefore, you are no longer needed." Mia gestures a shooing hand out the door again.

Ortiz remains in his seat. "You can't be serious. Where is your badge?"

Without hesitation, Mia pulls back the left collar of her silky shirt and suit jacket. Right over her heart is the *official crest of the Keepers* branded into her skin. It's something I've only ever seen in books. Only the highest level Executive Keepers get that symbol branded onto their skin. They're the Executive Keepers who are allowed more information than the other executives and the lower level Keepers—like this toe-jam sniffer who's just dropped his jaw.

It doesn't take more than a second for Ortiz to hop onto his feet and scurry out the door. With an apologetic smile, he closes and locks my precious exit behind him.

Mia makes her way to Ortiz's newly vacated chair and sits. With a smile, she says, "How are you today, Mr. Grant?"

I'm not fooled by her gentle voice or the way she just asked that question like she actually cares about my answer. "Been better."

"I hear you've been pretty concerned about the Ordinary the Enforcers found you with."

Concerned is not the right word for it. Obsessively tormented over her well-being is more accurate. "Where is she?"

Like Ortiz, Mia doesn't answer me. "I only have one question, Mr. Grant. Once you answer it, you'll be free to go."

My heart thrashes like it's trying to escape from my chest. Whatever this lady wants to ask me can't be good. "What do you mean by *free to go*?"

"As in, you're welcome to leave." She says that too casually. Like, *waaay* too casually.

"After I proved my innocence, you Supes have kept me drugged up here for three days while interrogating me for hours on end. All of a sudden, an Executive Keeper with the official crest shows up and tells me I just have to answer one question, then I'll be *free to go*?"

"Yes, sir."

I can't think of what information this woman wants from me that would grant me my freedom. "What's your question?"

"My question is: When Miss Rance was kidnapped, did you feel the glimmer?"

My eyes go wide because that is the farthest thing from what I expected her to ask me.

Since falling in love with Arella, I've felt the glimmer three times. The first time was when she was attacked by spiders. The second time was when she was in a bad car accident. The third time was after she realized she was kidnapped. Each time, nausea took over my body, my limbs went numb, and my chest felt tight like someone had a vise grip on it.

"Your honesty is important, Mr. Grant." Mia stares me down with an impassive look.

Without my Empath power, I can't even begin to figure out what this woman is up to. A Zordi can only feel the glimmer when their *soul mate* is in danger. We're taught in Zordi school that our kind is meant to be with *only* our kind. So why did this Keeper even think to ask if I felt the glimmer with an *Ordinary*?

Does the zovernment already know it's possible for us to be soul mates with Ordinaries? Does that mean they also know it's possible for our kinds to reproduce together? Based on what this Keeper is asking me, yes.

Why does it not surprise me to find out that the zovernment spreads false information? I guess after finding out that Aunt Jodi stole Victor's body for over twenty years and that my uncle is actually my biological father, nothing can shock me now.

I must be taking too long to answer, because Mia says, "I'm just looking for a simple yes or no, Mr. Grant. Did you feel the glimmer when Miss Rance was kidnapped?"

Should I lie? If I do, that stupid device on the wall will glow red again. Why does knowing if Arella is my soul mate or not matter anyway? And why is it so important that they had to send an Executive Keeper to ask me about it? In America, the Executive Keepers are based in New York City. Did this lady come to California all the way from New York just to ask me *one* question?

I repeat her words in my head. *When Miss Rance was kidnapped, did you feel the glimmer?* Suddenly, it hits me: The keyword here is *when*.

"No," I say, because technically, I didn't. Arella was sedated in her sleep before she was taken, so she didn't know she was in danger until *after* she woke up. The glimmer doesn't activate if the person in danger doesn't know they're in danger.

Mia glances at the wall, where a light glows green with the word TRUTH. She narrows her eyes at me as she thinks for a moment. She's smarter than I thought, because within a few heartbeats, she clears her throat and asks, "Did you ever feel the glimmer *after* she was kidnapped? Maybe once she woke up from the sedatives the Royals injected her with?"

I go silent again. How do they know Arella was drugged? Did they interrogate her too?

My hesitation makes Mia stare at me. "Again, Mr. Grant, your honesty is important."

I lean back into my chair and side-eye her. "Important for what?"

"That's classified information."

"Classified?" I scoff. "Like how you Keepers are keeping millions of Zordis away from their possible Ordi soul mates?"

A slight smile turns up the corners of Mia's lips. "So you admit you felt the glimmer?"

I lean over the table and lower my voice. "How can you live with yourself? We have the right to be with our soul mates, even if they're Ordis."

Mia leans toward me as she, too, lowers her voice. "That's a small price to pay to keep our kind safe, don't you think? Can you imagine what would happen if we openly told the general public that it's possible for Ordinaries to be our soul mates? Our kind would expose themselves left and right in retaliation. Then once the Ordinaries find out about us, they'll want to get rid of us again.

"Our kind cannot survive another mass genocide. Plus, it'll be harder for our Scrubbers to do another worldwide scrub. People have more technology now than they did back then. The Ordinaries will come after us with more than just poison. Knowing where Miss Rance is will be the least of your worries."

I hate to admit it, but this Keeper is right. Ordinaries are not ready to know about the Zordi world again. They're too fearful of anything they don't understand. There would be more than just murders and genocides. The world would erupt into chaos.

Mia presses her back against her chair. "Final question, Mr. Grant, then I will see you out the door."

"You said I only had to answer one question, then I was free to go. I've answered it. Now let me go."

She ignores me. "Did you know she was pregnant with your child?"

I try to keep my face impassive because I don't want to give her an answer. Unfortunately, my silence and lack of shock are all the answer she needs.

Mia's chair squeals as she pushes it back and stands up. "Thank you for your time today, Mr. Grant. I'll walk you outside."

I stay where I am. "That's it?"

"Yes, sir. That's it." Her heels *clack-clack-clack* as she heads toward the door.

What is going on? This Keeper just found out that I broke the second most enforced Zordi law—to never engage in sexual activities with an Ordinary—and now she's just gonna let me go? Wait . . . why the hell am I questioning this? If she's freeing me, why am I still sitting here?

Fifteen minutes later, I'm out of my z-prison jumpsuit and wearing the clothes I was arrested in: some light-wash jeans and a gray polo with a slit in the side from where Aunt Jodi stabbed me. All the bloodstains have been washed out, which I'm not mad about. Some of that blood was Katie's, and I don't need to walk around with a display of sacrifice all over me.

When I step out of the bathroom in my laundered outfit, Mia says, "Follow me."

At the prison's main entrance, a gray-haired man in a light-blue Enforcer uniform waits for us with my leather jacket neatly folded in his palms. On top of my jacket is my wallet.

"Thank you," I say as I shove my wallet into my back pocket, then slip into my jacket. With it on, I feel closer to normal, although I won't feel completely normal until I'm holding Arella again. That's why the moment the Enforcer disappears behind a door marked MAIN OFFICE, I turn to Mia.

"Where is she?"

As if she can't hear me, Mia opens one of the double doors, then holds it wide for me. Sunlight shines onto my shoes, the first glimpse of the outside I've had since being arrested. I'm about to take a step out when I stop. What if this is a trick? Having sex with an Ordinary is a huge offense. To the zovernment, *for a ZIRDA mission* is not a valid excuse for breaking the law. Why are they just letting me go?

"Are you hesitating because you'd rather stay behind bars?" Mia asks.

Fuck that. I step out into the bright September sun and squint. It only takes a second for my Zordi eyes to adjust, then I can see clearly. I'm no expert, but based on where the sun is, I'd say it's three o'clockish.

Mia joins me outside, then clicks the door shut behind her. "What time was your last dose of perrizophine?"

"Around ten this morning."

"Great. That dose should wear off around ten tonight. When it does, drink lots of Healing Water. It'll help counteract some of the side effects from coming off a long period of being under perrizo. Since your time here was short, I expect your side effects to be minor compared to the people who leave z-prison after decades of being locked up. If the side effects become unbearable, try eating some bananas. For some reason, they help."

Healing Water. Bananas. Got it. Now back to the important stuff. Since the way I asked my question before didn't yield results, I reword it. "Do you know where Arella is?"

Mia ignores my question again. "Do you know where *you* are?"

"The z-prison in Corcoran."

"Correct. On the outside of these brick walls is a van waiting to take you home. We don't normally give inmates rides. Given your situation, I pulled some strings to arrange it for you."

My situation? What does that mean? Is she talking about how I didn't know I was going to be released today, or that I don't have any family to come pick me up? Either way, I appreciate the ride.

Mia continues, "The driver has specific instructions to take you home and nowhere else, so don't even try."

"In other words, don't ask him to take me to wherever you're keeping Arella?"

Mia lets out a big sigh. "Mr. Grant, we aren't keeping Miss Rance anywhere. She's safe at home, where she has been since this morning."

Since this morning? That means they've kept her for the last three days too. Is that why they're finally letting me go? They finished their studies on her, and now they don't need to keep me locked up anymore? That's some bullshit.

I try not to sound angry. "Why did you guys keep her for that long?"

Mia blinks up at me with an expression I can't read. For a second, I think she's about to answer my question, until she turns back toward the doors and opens one. "If you know what's good for you, Mr. Grant, you'll stay away from her."

My anger comes out this time. "Why did you guys keep her for that long?"

"Don't forget about the bananas, okay? They really do help." Without another word, she disappears behind the door, and it clicks shut.

I think about rushing back in and demanding that she tell me what they did with Arella for three whole days, but I doubt that will help anything. Plus, now that I know where my girl is, I feel a pull to head straight there.

Three and a half torturous hours later, the van driver drops me off outside my home. No matter what I said to him, he refused to take me to Arella's apartment.

I race to open my garage. The loud door lifts to reveal only my car. *Shit.* I'd forgotten I ditched my motorcycle on the side of a road after I got Arella out of Shadow Ridge. My bike would have been faster, but my car will do.

Since running inside to find my keys will waste precious time, I plant myself behind the steering wheel and wave a hand at the ignition. Nothing happens, so I do it again. Then I facepalm myself. *I'm such an idiot.* If my empathy power isn't working, then my telekinesis isn't either.

I sprint through my house to find my keys. Once I do, I'm back in my car with the engine started.

THE OUTSIDE OF ARELLA'S APARTMENT LOOKS THE SAME AS IT ALWAYS DOES. THE CAR I BOUGHT FOR her is parked in her usual spot. I pull my Lexus right up next to it, then half run, half stumble toward her door.

Knock-knock-knock.

My hands shake against my leg as I wait for the door to open. I'm itching to hold her. I need my world to feel right again.

When the barrier keeping her from me finally opens, my heart fills with relief. There she is, and she looks unharmed. Her long chestnut hair cascades down her shoulders in soft waves. The hem of her white sundress falls just above her knees. Her eyes are warm and gentle—the way they always are. She looks like an angel. Partly because she's so beautiful, partly because I can't believe she's finally standing in front of me.

"Arella." Her name comes out breathily as I scoop her into my arms and crush her against my chest. "I've been so worried about you. Are you okay? Please tell me you're okay."

She doesn't return my hug or melt into my body the way she normally does. Instead, she goes stiff. Then she pushes herself out of my grasp and takes a step back. "Um, yeah? I'm okay."

I keep examining her arms and legs, looking for any signs of cuts or bruises. "Did they hurt you?"

She cocks her head to the side and creases her eyebrows together. "Um, no?"

I slap a palm over my heart. "Oh, thank fuck. I'm so glad you're—"

A movement on Arella's couch catches my attention. Someone I've never seen before stands up and stares at me with narrowed eyes and a crumpled forehead. White male in his early twenties, light brown hair, looks like he keeps up with his workouts, and he's got a french fry sticking out of his mouth. Two fast food bags sit on Arella's coffee table along with two fountain drinks.

I hook my thumb toward the guy. "Who the fuck is he?"

Arella blinks at me. "Better question: Who are *you*?"

73

ARI

I wake up from the anesthesia surrounded by a handful of nurses and doctors.

"The procedure went perfectly," one of them says from behind a light-blue medical face mask. "I'm gonna help you get off this bed and into this wheelchair. Then I'll bring you right back to your boyfriend."

Things are still fuzzy as I'm wheeled back to the same pre-op room I was in earlier. There, the nurse helps me back into the bed.

"How did it go?" Caleb asks the nurse. He's stationed on a chair in the corner when he stands to come hold my hand. I offer him a warm smile as our fingers intertwine.

We didn't plan to get pregnant, but when I told him the news, he was thrilled. We were in the midst of talking through possible names when we got the terrible news that we'd lost our baby.

Since I was already over nine weeks along and the baby wasn't coming out naturally, I opted for a D and C. Caleb has been supportive and loving throughout this entire experience. He promised he'd treat me to some burgers for dinner since I've had a huge craving for fries lately.

"Everything went splendidly," the nurse says with a bright smile. "Zero issues."

Caleb gives my hand a light squeeze. "That's awesome. Thank you so much for taking good care of her."

The nurse turns back to me. "Remember, you'll be sore and have some light bleeding down there for about two weeks. After that, your body will return to normal. Do you have any questions before we start the process of discharging you?"

"Nope," I say as the fuzziness begins to leave my head.

"Great. You rest up then. I'll come back in a bit when the anesthesia has fully worn off. After that, we'll get you up and walking, then you'll be ready to head home."

The nurse is right, I am a little sore down there.

I feel slightly more at ease by the time Caleb and I are back home. Together, we sit on the couch to enjoy our dinner. Typically, we eat at the kitchen table, but I want to sit somewhere more comfy while I devour my fries.

"It's been a while since we've had In-N-Out," Caleb says as he unwraps his burger.

"The last time was back when we first met." I shove some fries into my mouth, then let out a satisfied *mmm*. "We had In-N-Out on our third date."

He counts on his fingers. "That was only three months ago. I suppose that's not *that* long ago, but it sure feels like it."

I feel the same about my relationship with this beautiful man. We haven't been together for that long, but it sure feels that way. In only three short months, Caleb and I have gone from being strangers on the side of a highway, to going on a few dates after he helped me fix my flat tire, to falling madly in love, to finding out we were going to be parents, to losing our baby. I can't imagine going through all of that with anyone else.

Knock-knock-knock.

Caleb eyes me with his mouth full. "Are we expecting anyone?"

"It's probably Javina," I say as I wipe my fingers off on some napkins. "She texted me before my surgery, saying she'd stop by after she gets off work."

When I open the door, it's not Javina. Instead, a man with dark chocolate hair and a stubbly beard stares back at me. He lets out a tiny breath of relief as our eyes lock. Relief from what? I don't know. I'm about to tell him that we aren't interested in whatever he's selling when he says my name.

"Arella." It comes out breathless. In a flash, he wraps his arms around me and clutches me against his firm chest.

I freeze. How does this man know my name? And it's my full name too. Everyone calls me Ari. Barely anyone even knows that Arella is my full name.

"I've been so worried about you." The snug way he wraps his muscular arms around me sends a warmth down my spine. His hold feels desperate, possessive, and protective—three things I don't expect to feel when being hugged by a man I've never seen before. "Are you okay? Please tell me you're okay."

It takes me a second to regain myself. When I do, I push the man away and step back. "Um, yeah? I'm okay."

His gaze skims my body up and down. "Did they hurt you?"

Did *who* hurt me? The doctors who performed my surgery? How does this man know that I just had surgery? "Um, no?"

He slaps a hand over his chest and lets out a breath. "Oh, thank fuck. I'm so glad you're—"

Behind me, Caleb must move, because the man's eyes dart away from me. Then his entire face crinkles together. With a thumb pointed at Caleb, he says, "Who the fuck is he?"

This guy sure has a potty mouth. "Better question: Who are *you*?"

The strange man drops his jaw. It takes him a second to say, "W-w-what?"

I don't think I stuttered, but I repeat myself anyway. "I said, who are you?"

His eyebrows press together so hard, it makes his forehead wrinkle. "What do you mean?"

I feel like *who are you?* is a pretty straightforward question. What does he mean by what do I mean?

"Arella, it's me, Trey."

"I'm sorry. You must have the wrong apartment." Even as I say that, I know it's not true. This guy is staring at me like he can't comprehend why I would ask who he is, and he just held me like he's been desperate to for days. Plus, he knows my full name. This man is exactly where he thinks he should be.

Caleb steps up behind me and places an arm around my shoulders, protectively pulling me back. "Who are you?"

He has barely gotten the words out when this Trey guy leaps into our apartment and shoves Caleb away so hard, he's launched backward several steps. Even more protectively than Caleb just did, Trey pulls me behind him and stands in front of me like a shield.

"Don't you dare touch her."

Caleb throws his arms up in surrender. "Hey, now. No need to get violent, okay? We'll give you whatever you want. Just don't hurt my girlfriend."

"Your *girlfriend*?"

I step away from the crazy man. "Who are you?"

The man whips his attention back to me. "Baby, it's me, Trey. Trey Grant." He points at his chest. "*I'm* your boyfriend, not him."

I keep my voice calm so I don't aggravate this man any further. "I'm sorry, but I've never seen you before in my life."

"What?" At first, he stares at me with his mouth slack. Then I see it in his eyes the moment something clicks for him. He gasps with his entire body jerking backward. "You've been scrubbed."

Scrubbed? Am I supposed to know what that means? I flick my eyes up to Caleb. The look on his face tells me he doesn't know what *scrubbed* means either.

Trey closes the distance between us in two large steps. With rough hands, he grabs my face. "Baby, look at me. We can beat this, okay? Whatever they did to you, you can fight it. Look into my eyes. Try to remember me."

My body stills. I don't want to move, because I'm afraid of what's going to happen if I do. I don't know what this man's intentions are, nor do I know what he's capable of. He's built like he could fight off truckloads of soldiers. "Um, could you, please, take your hands off me? You're scaring me."

Trey gazes into my eyes as if he's trying to figure out if I'm serious. When he realizes I am, his shoulders droop and his arms fall to his sides. "Arella, please. Try to remember me. If there's anyone who can do it, it's you."

Caleb still has his hands up in surrender. "Look, buddy. I think you should leave."

Trey ignores Caleb and keeps his attention trained on me with a desperate look on his face. "Arella, come on. You can fight this. We met on the side of a highway, remember? You had a flat tire, and I helped you put a new one on."

How does this guy know how Caleb and I met? And why is he claiming that's how I met *him*? Now he's *really* scaring me.

He keeps talking. "We started dating after that and—"

Caleb cuts him off by rushing to my side and pulling me behind him. "Ari, go call the cops. This guy is a psycho."

"I'm not a psycho!" Trey shouts. "I'm telling the truth!"

Caleb scoffs. "You're the literal definition of a psycho. Unstable and aggressive."

What is Caleb doing? When someone is being crazy, the last thing you should do is call them crazy. It only makes them more crazy.

"Arella, will you just look at me? You know me. Deep in there somewhere, you know me."

I eye the man up and down, trying to entertain the idea that I *might* know him. Tall, light skin, dark hair, broad shoulders, a leather jacket. The more I stare at him, the more I'm certain I've never seen him before. He's got a gorgeous face that was carved by gods. I'd remember a face like that.

"I'm sorry," I say. "I don't know who you are."

⌇⌇⌇

"WHAT HAPPENED AFTER THAT?" JAVINA ASKS. SHE SHOWED UP BARELY TEN MINUTES AFTER THAT Trey guy left. We're sitting in the living room with Caleb as I finish telling her the whole story.

"Caleb told him to leave before we called the cops," I say. "Without another word, the guy got right back into his car and left."

Javina shakes her head, huffing. "Why do the weirdest and worst things always happen to you, Ari? As if your abusive ex isn't enough, last month, you got into a bad car accident. Then this week, you lost your baby. Did you piss off the karma gods or something?"

After my car accident, I was sent to the hospital by ambulance. I came out with some whiplash, stitches, and bruises. My parents were killed in a car accident. I'd pick wearing a neck brace for two weeks over death any day.

While I was away from work, Caleb took good care of me. He brought me food, cleaned for me, and treated me like a queen. I don't know how I could have gotten through it without him.

"That man was a psycho," Caleb says from the floor. Javina and I are taking up my small couch, so there's no room for him up here. He always says he prefers to sit on the floor, but I know he's just being gracious. He never sits on the floor when it's just us. "He kept grabbing you. I was afraid he was going to hurt you."

I wasn't. Trey's tight grasp on me felt too protective for me to think he had intentions to hurt me. Yes, the man scared me, but mostly because he claimed to have met me the same way I had met Caleb.

"What did you say his name was?" Javina asks.

"Trey Grant," Caleb says.

Javina thinks, then gasps. "Oh my god! I know him!"

I blanch. "You do?"

"Yes! I mean, not personally, but I know *of* him." From the coffee table, Javina grabs her phone. A few seconds later, she shows me a Google image page. "Is this him?"

The blue-gray eyes that stared at me earlier look back at me from Javina's screen. "That's him."

Caleb pushes off the floor and leans closer to Javina. "Lemme see."

Javina shows him her screen.

Caleb points a finger at her phone. "Yeah, that's the guy. Who is he?"

"He's a musician," Javina says. "He's in a band called Flames in the Night. They play at a bar in downtown LA every weekend. Rachel and I were there a few months ago for the first time. I've been watching all their music videos on YouTube ever since."

"Okay . . ." Caleb pretzels his legs back together. "That doesn't explain why he showed up here, claiming that *my* girlfriend is *his* girlfriend."

"Yeah, that's weird." Javina shrugs. "At least now you know who he is."

Later that night, after Javina heads home, Caleb leaves for his night shift as a security guard at the Los Angeles County Museum of Art. The alone time gives me freedom to do my own Googling.

Trey Grant's Wikipedia page is the first link that pops up when I type his name in. I read the entire thing word for word. What I gather from the limited information is that Trey seems to be a normal guy who loves music. He's been with his band for four years, and they released a few cover albums together before releasing an original album. They're known for being a diverse group of talented individuals who went viral on YouTube with their music. He even has a foundation that supports children with deceased parents, in honor of his parents passing away when he was young. There's nothing on his Wiki page that suggests he's an escapee from a mental hospital.

Naturally, my research gravitates toward the next best thing: social media. Because of my ex, I deleted all my social media accounts when we broke up, so I have to create new ones to be able to continue my research. Once I do, under a made-up name, I scroll through Trey Grant's platforms.

At first glance, it doesn't look like he manages his own accounts. He must pay someone to run his pages for him, because the content is full of candid pictures of him playing guitar, sitting behind a piano, or singing to a large crowd. As for his other band members, their content is a little more personal, with pictures of the things they're eating and videos of them doing silly dances.

I head to YouTube next. It only takes me one video to become captivated by Trey's sultry singing voice. It sounds familiar, but at the same time, so new. Still, I don't find anything that suggests he's a weirdo.

Judging from the video comments, Trey's fans think he and the half-Hispanic woman in his band are dating—or, at the very least, friends with benefits. It also sounds like he has a reputation for being a bit of a bad boy.

That triggers me to take my research back to Google, where I type, *Trey Grant criminal record.*

My heart thumps wildly as I pull up his past charges: two counts of disorderly conduct and one charge for fleeing the police. Obviously, this man has a history of being violent and doing things he shouldn't. Knowing that, I'm surprised he left as willingly as he did. However, that probably means he's bound to reappear soon.

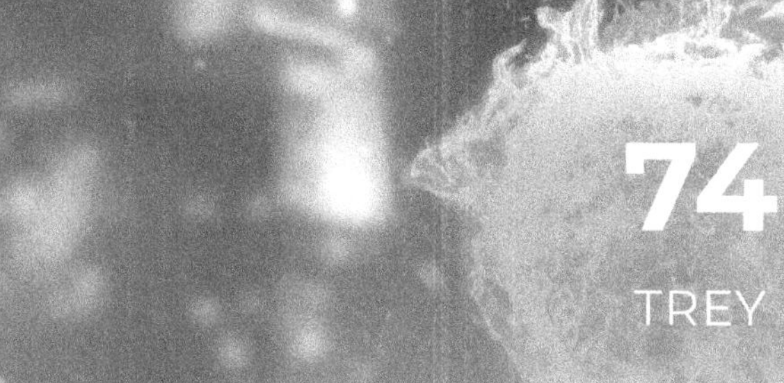

74

TREY

"She's been scrubbed!" I meant for that to come out a little less panicky.

"What?" Liz stands on the other side of her open front door, giving me a furrowed look. "Who's been scrubbed?"

"Arella. They took her, then they interrogated me in z-prison for three days before finally letting me go. I just went to her apartment, looked straight into her eyes, and she didn't recognize me. They fucking scrubbed her!"

Liz puts her gloved hands up, palms forward. "Wait, wait. Let's start from the beginning. Who's Arella?"

I gasp. "No! Not you too!"

Liz side-eyes me like she's trying to figure out if I need to get checked into an asylum. It's the same look Arella gave me earlier. "Why don't you come in and sit down, T?"

I get only two steps into Liz's house before my legs buckle and I fall to my knees. *This can't be happening.* I can't breathe. My throat feels like I'm swallowing sand. *Is everybody scrubbed?*

Liz grips my arm and helps me to my feet. "Come on, T. Let's get you on the couch, then I'll get you some water. Once you're calm, you can tell me everything."

It takes me a while to become calm enough to speak again. I start off by telling Liz about my ZIRDA mission and how, over time, I fell deeply in love with Arella. Then I tell her about the baby, Arella's kidnapping, and how I found out that the person I thought was my uncle was actually my biological father, who was actually Aunt Jodi the whole time.

Liz ogles me like I'm telling her a horror story. "Oh my god. That's a lot to process."

"Oh, I'm not even done yet."

"There's more?"

"Yep. I found out today that the zovernment already knows that our soul mates can be Ordinaries. They also know that we *can* reproduce together. They only tell us we can't so our worlds don't mix again. They don't want to have to deal with another mass genocide, so basically, they've conditioned us to think Ordinaries aren't an option."

"Wait." Liz shakes her head like she can't believe what I just said. I don't blame her. A part of me is still trying to believe it too. "Does that mean there are a bunch of half-Ordi, half-Zordi people walking around?"

"Um, that, I don't know. I didn't even think to ask because I was so fixated on getting to Arella. Oh, by the way, when I got there, she was with some dude who claimed to be her boyfriend."

"Damn." Liz blows out a long breath. "In my memory, you called me up and said you needed a break from band stuff. You told me you were going to hop onto your bike and travel around for a week or two. Then you asked if I could tell Monique so you didn't have to hear her yell at you about it."

At least when the Scrubbers altered Liz's memory, they gave her a fake one that's reasonably believable. If that had actually happened, my band manager definitely would have yelled at me for taking two weeks off without notice.

I clear my throat as I prepare to say something stupid. "I have to go back."

"Back where?"

"To the prison."

"What?"

I knew it was stupid. "I don't mean behind bars. I mean that I need to go back so I can beg them to unscrub her."

"Is that even possible?"

"Fuck if I know, but I'm gonna find out."

THE SKY IS DISMALLY DARK BY THE TIME I PULL MY VEHICLE UP TO THE Z-PRISON'S GUARD BOOTH. The barrier arms are down, blocking my car from going any farther.

I told Liz not to come with me, but she insisted. She gawks out the window at the empty road stretching ahead of us, then at the gigantic building at the end of it. "I've never seen a z-prison before. It looks kinda eerie."

I roll my window down at the same time an Enforcer in his light blues peeks his head out the booth window.

"Sorry," he says from under a gray mustache. "Visiting hours are over."

The zense in my chest tingles from his nearness. "I'm not here to see an inmate. I'm here to see Mia Wang." *That is, if she's still here.* She could be back in New York by now.

"I dunno who that is, but either way, y'all can't be here right now."

"She's an Executive Keeper. I was just here earlier today and spoke with her. I need to talk to her again."

"This is a z-prison, sir, not a zovernment office. If you're trying to talk to a Keeper, go bother them instead."

"Find me someone who can get me in contact with Mia." *Oops.* I didn't mean for my words to come out so demandingly. I'm just still on edge from hearing Arella ask me, *Who are you?*

"Excuse me?" The Enforcer screws his face together as a tiny wave of anger floats into my head. The perrizo is slowly wearing off, but it's not fully out of my system yet. If it was, I'm sure I'd be sensing heavier emotions from this man. "You have no right to be making demands around here. If you're trying to see a Keeper, an Executive Keeper at that, you've come to the wrong pl—"

Ring. Ring.

The Enforcer slides his window shut, then picks up the booth phone and holds it to his ear. There's a long pause as he listens to whatever is being said on the other line. He nods a few times, says words I can't make out, nods again, then hangs up the phone.

The window slides back open. "Miss Wang will meet you out here in ten minutes. Stay in your vehicle until she arrives."

"Thank you." I roll my window up, then turn to Liz. "She must have known I was coming. This oughta be good."

The ten minutes I'm forced to wait feels like ten hours. Eventually, a black Cadillac Escalade with blinding headlights rolls down the road and stops on the other side of the barrier arms. The front passenger door pops open, then Mia Wang slides out. She's still wearing her burgundy suit and matching high heels. Whoever is driving the vehicle remains in the car with the engine running.

Mia approaches my window as I roll it down. She bends at the hip to meet my eyes. I'm about to ask her how she knew I was coming when she says, "I'm a Seer. Besides, even if I wasn't, I had a feeling you'd be back."

"Is that why you're still here?"

"You were my main reason for coming to California, but I had other things to take care of here. Things I'm not doing right now because I'm standing outside, talking to you. You've got some nerve, Mr. Grant. We've had to make quite a few exceptions for you. Dropping charges for exposure to an Ordinary. Dropping charges for having sexual relations with an Ordinary. Getting you that ride home. And now this. Do you realize you can't just show up to a z-prison and demand to speak to a Keeper? Given your situation, I'm allowing you one free pass, so make it count."

I step out of my car and shut the door behind me. I expect Mia to be a little intimidated because I'm a full head taller than her, but the woman doesn't look fazed at all. I guess she didn't get that official crest branded onto her chest for nothing.

I cross my arms. "What did you do to her?"

Mia sighs as she tucks some of her long black hair behind an ear. "Didn't I tell you to stay away from her?"

"Did you really think I was gonna listen?"

Mia sighs again, heavier this time. "How about we go for a walk?"

I bend to peek my head into the car. "You cool to stay here for a bit?"

Liz nods. "I'll be fine."

Mia gestures down the road leading away from the prison. She doesn't say anything as we fall into steady steps side by side. Maybe she's waiting for me to speak first, so I ask my question again.

"What did you do to her?"

"You already know what happens to Ordinaries who get exposed to our world. Why are you surprised the same thing happened to her?"

Because I didn't think it was possible to scrub her. Erasing and altering memories is a mind power that would affect Arella internally. She's immune to that. "How did you do it?"

"With a Scrubber, of course."

"Yes, but how?"

Mia chuckles under her breath. "Mr. Grant, if you know how to pleasure a woman right, then you should already know that it's possible to bypass her immunity walls." She throws up a hand, palm forward. "Before you get too worked up about that, no, we did not sexually violate her."

I let out a breath because that's exactly what I was about to accuse the zovernment of doing. "What did you do instead?"

Mia's heels clack against the road as she pulls all her long hair to one shoulder. "Do you know what happens to the human brain during climax?"

"I dunno. Dopamine, I'm guessing."

"Correct. That, along with a bunch of other hormones, are released. Most importantly, the brain shuts down the control center that has to do with fear. Getting a person to orgasm is not the *only* way to shut down that control center. As you've already figured out, when those fear controls are put into overdrive, she gains the ability to control and project her immunity. So it's simple: Shut down the fear and her invisible shield comes down."

That makes a ton of sense now that I think about it, except . . . "How did you shut down her fear?"

"Our zoctors did it with the right mix of drugs and hormone injections." Mia puts another hand up. "Don't worry. She was under anesthesia, and she doesn't remember a thing."

Since the zovernment knows so much about how to scrub an Immune, I'm going to assume Arella wasn't their first. I wouldn't be surprised if the zovernment was or is hosting research sessions on Immunes in a secret facility somewhere.

"What about when Arella woke up?" I ask. "Wouldn't she have questioned why she was put to sleep by a bunch of people she didn't know?"

"The Ordinary had a Zordi fetus inside her that stopped developing. She would have had to undergo a surgery for the removal anyway, so we took the liberty of doing both procedures at the same time."

I swallow hard as I'm flashed back to the short moment when I thought I was going to be a dad. I hadn't felt that kind of happiness in . . . well, ever. I've always wanted a family, and the idea of having my own had brought me more joy than I realized it would. Then Arella told me our baby was gone.

I'll never forgive Jodi for all the things she's taken from me. First, my parents, even though she claims she didn't cause the explosion. Then she kidnapped Arella, killed my unborn child, and murdered my dad in front of me. Selfishly, I wish Jodi hadn't died. She's now free of the demons that turned her into the monster she was, instead of suffering with them like I am.

I keep my feet moving as I ask, "Am I right to assume that this isn't the first time an Ordinary has gotten pregnant with our kind?"

Without hesitation, Mia nods. "Yes. While it *can* happen, it doesn't happen very often, and very rarely does the baby grow to term. Even when Ordinaries reproduce with other Ordinaries, one in every four pregnancies ends in a loss. When it comes to Ordis reproducing with Zordis, losses happen ninety-nine percent of the time."

"So what you're saying is that the chances were pretty high that we would have lost our baby anyway?"

Another nod. "Most likely."

I'm not sure if that information is comforting or depressing. If the zovernment knows that only one in every hundred pregnancies between our kinds grows to term, that means it has happened enough times for them to have gathered that statistic, which means Mia probably knows the answer to my next question. "When those babies are born, are they half Zordi?"

Mia side-eyes me with a slight smile creeping onto her lips. "Are you asking because you're wondering if Miss Rance is part Zordi?"

"The idea has crossed my mind."

"Like I said, it's rare for a Zordi and Ordi baby to grow to term, but when they do, they're born as one or the other—never both. Miss Rance is full Ordinary, which means it is in your best interest to stay away from her."

I open my mouth, about to ask the question that's burning in my mind, when Mia throws her hand up, palm forward. "No, Mr. Grant, we cannot unscrub her." The way this woman knows what I'm about to ask before I ask it is a little unsettling. "Do you realize that your situation was one of the biggest scrub jobs the zovernment has had to do in decades? This wasn't like erasing the memories of all the people at an Ordinary school when a Zordi child got too emotional and lost control of their powers. This wasn't a situation where someone simply used their powers in public, thinking no one was around. Your situation was much more than that.

"Your face was plastered all over the news as a kidnapper. Even people who lived out in the middle-of-nowhere Montana heard about the man who disappeared and took his ex-girl-friend with him. People were looking into your criminal history and your past, and your fans went wild on social media. If we didn't erase all evidence of this incident from the Internet and alter everyone's memories, you would have come home to news reporters on your front lawn, waiting to get a statement. The FBI would have gotten involved, which comes with the risk of exposure, so we did what we had to do.

"Most importantly, we did this big scrub to protect the Immune. We couldn't allow her face to remain plastered all over the news. If there's attention on her, it's only a matter of time before the Royals discover her again and try to use her for her immunity."

I guess that's a positive. If the world doesn't remember Arella, that means the Royals don't either. That means she's safe.

"Do you know what makes her immune?" I ask as I turn around to head back toward my car.

Mia follows me. "I don't."

I give her a narrowed look.

"You don't have to believe me. That doesn't change the fact that the zovernment doesn't have an explanation for her immunity."

From the tiny waves of calmness I'm sensing from Mia, I think she's telling the truth. Now it's time to ask the other question that's been burning on my mind. "Why didn't I get scrubbed?"

"Because if you forget everything that happened, how will you ever learn to never make those mistakes again? Need I remind you, Mr. Grant, you had an illegal relationship that resulted in high-level exposure and nationally televised news."

I throw my arms up, letting them flop to my sides. "So what am I supposed to do now? Just move on with my life as if I never met her?"

"That would be the wisest decision, yes."

"But she's my soul mate," I say as if it'll change anything.

"That's a small price to pay to avoid all the chaos that comes with worldwide exposure. Think of this sacrifice as your duty to our people."

That's some bullshit. I feel no sense of duty to the Zordinary community. The only thing I feel is a need to be with Arella, but she's with that other guy, which reminds me . . . "Who's that guy who claims to be her boyfriend?"

Mia sighs heavily. "For the record, I was against replacing you in her memories with another man, but the Scrubber insisted it was necessary. Apparently, the memories you created with her became such deep core memories that they were quite hard to fully erase. Therefore, the Scrubber altered them to reflect someone else."

A light flickers on in my chest. If Arella's memories run that deep, maybe there's a chance I can get her to remember me.

"May I ask you a question now?" Mia asks.

"Sure," I say through a sigh.

"Did Miss Rance ever feel the glimmer?"

"Is it possible for her to?" I thought the glimmer was something that's unique to only Zordi bodies.

"It is possible. Despite what you're taught, a soul-mate connection is not something that's limited to only Zordis. Ordinaries with Ordinary soul mates *can* sense when their partners are in danger. Their symptoms just aren't as severe, and they usually ignore them. However, if an Ordinary makes a soul-mate connection with a Zordi, they will experience the glimmer like any other Zordi does. And before you ask, no, we have no idea why that is. We can only assume that because one of the soul mates on that connection is a Zordi, the glimmer affects the Ordinary the same."

"So what you're saying is that the glimmer exists between both our kinds, but we Zordis just have a stronger connection to it?"

"Yes," Mia says with a firm nod. "Actually, that's a great way to put it. I'm going to use that at my next meeting with the other execs."

"To answer your original question, no, I don't know if she ever felt glimmer-like symptoms. If she did, she never mentioned it."

The glimmer exists to warn us that our soul mates are in danger when we're not around them. It's not as strong when we are already with our soul mate when something bad happens since we already have that knowledge. Whenever something bad happened to me, I was already with Arella, so if she did feel anything, she was too busy fighting off ice balls to pay attention to it.

"You realize that this is cruel, right?" My words come out partly angry and partly choked. "You're aware that Arella is my soul mate, yet you guys scrubbed her, and now you're telling me to just forget about her."

"What's done is done, Mr. Grant."

Well, fuck me then.

When I return to my car, Liz perks up, ready to hear everything. "So? How'd it go?"

I put my car into reverse and back away from the guard booth. The whole time, Mia watches me from outside the Escalade, as if making sure I'm actually leaving.

It's not until I'm at least a mile away from the prison that I say, "Basically, the Keeper said I'm shit out of luck and that I need to move on as if none of it ever happened."

"What? But Arella is your soul mate."

"That doesn't matter to them. They only care about keeping Ordinaries from knowing about our world."

While I drive us back to LA, I go into some details about my conversation with Mia. The whole time, Liz is quiet while she takes it all in.

Once I'm done, she says, "I think we both know you're not gonna stay away from her."

I chuckle humorlessly. "You know me too well."

"So what are you *actually* gonna do?"
My answer comes easily. "I'm gonna get her to remember me."

75

TREY

Despite how much I want to show back up at Arella's apartment, Liz convinces me to sleep on it.

Around noon, I wake up on Liz's couch, feeling like shit. My mind is hazy, and my body aches from head to toe.

I stumble into the bathroom like I'm hungover, even though I haven't been drinking. After a quick piss, I stare at myself in the mirror. The skin around my eyes is dark purple. I look like I either lost a bar fight or have some weird skin condition.

Liz's footsteps thump down her stairs as I make my way back to her uncomfortable couch. I didn't want to sleep here last night, but I also didn't trust myself to stay away from Arella.

"Holy balls!" Liz clasps an ungloved hand against her chest. "What happened to your face?"

"I think it's a side effect from coming off perrizophine."

"You look like the Joker."

"Thanks, Liz." I huff. "You're just the person everyone needs when they're going through one of the worst times of their lives."

"Sorry, T. I'll, um, be right back." Her footsteps thump back up the stairs. A minute later, she's returned to the living room with her makeup bag in hand. "I did a quick search on the z-net. It sounds like Healing Water and bananas can help."

So I've heard. "You got any?"

"Yep." Liz disappears into her kitchen, then comes back with a cold bottle of Healing Water and two bananas. "Sorry, they're a little overripe."

"I'm not picky." I take the bananas and peel one open. Then I inhale half of it in one bite and wash it down with some Healing Water. "I'm gonna try to talk to her today—without that other guy there."

Liz unrolls her makeup bag over the coffee table. "Does he live with her?"

"Fuck if I know." I swallow down the rest of the banana, then peel open the second one.

"Whatever you do, T, just don't scare her again. Try to see it from her point of view. To her, you're just a crazy guy who showed up on her doorstep yesterday, claiming to be her boyfriend."

I slump my shoulders, feeling the weight of the world on them. "But to me, she's my everything."

"Yes," Liz says tenderly, "but she doesn't know that. How would you react if some chick you've never seen before showed up on your doorstep, claiming to be your girlfriend?"

I take a small bite of my second banana and actually chew it this time. "I'd probably think she's some deranged fan with an unhinged obsession."

"Exactly."

I didn't mean to freak out Arella. How was I supposed to know her memory had been wiped? If I had known, I might have handled things a little differently. "Okay, I'll try to be calm."

WHEN MY CAR PULLS UP TO ARELLA'S APARTMENT COMPLEX, I'M NOT CALM. I'M NOT EVEN CLOSE to it. My hands are jittery, my throat is scratchy, and, worst of all, the skin around my eyes is still purple. No matter how much makeup Liz put on me, the purple was still visible. I ended up just washing off the makeup.

Thanks to the Healing Water and bananas, the body aches and that hazy feeling in my head have diminished. Before coming here, I stopped at home for a quick shower and a change of clothes. I hoped the purpleness would disappear during that time. It didn't, and I still look like shit, but I don't care because I need to see my girl.

Based on the way hundreds of emotions are shooting at me all at once, I'm gonna say my powers are back to normal. I draw in my range to a five-foot circle around me, turning the intense emotions screaming in the back of my mind into a low hum. Then I aim my gift at Arella's apartment.

No emotions come to me. That could mean one of two things: either she's not home or she is home and that other guy isn't. Only one way to find out.

Knock-knock.

A shuffle of feet comes toward the door, then stops. The barrier never opens. She must have seen me through the peephole and is now pretending she's not home. I didn't prepare for this. All I planned out was what I was gonna say once she opened the door. The thought never crossed my mind that she'd be too scared of me to open the door at all.

I knock again. In the gentle tone I would use if I was speaking to a wounded puppy, I say, "Arella, I'm not gonna hurt you. I just want to explain."

A short pause sits between us, then her firm voice comes from the other side. "If you don't leave, I'm calling the cops."

I suck in a deep breath as I try to calm my shaky hands. "Can I just talk to you? I promise I won't touch you."

There's another pause—longer this time. Then the bolt lock clicks. The door opens, but it doesn't open all the way. A chain lock stops it, giving me only a three-inch view of the woman who completes me.

I crumple my eyebrows at the metal line blocking me from her. "Since when have you had a chain lock?"

"Since last night when my boyfriend installed one to keep crazy men from barging in again."

Hearing her call someone else her boyfriend hurts more than hearing her call me crazy. "I'm sorry about that. I didn't mean to scare you."

"Say what you came to say, then leave."

It stings that she's trying to get rid of me so quickly. I'm beginning to think getting her to remember me is gonna be harder than I thought. If she's not willing to listen to me, how can I explain anything? "Arella, I—"

"My name is Ari."

Ouch. I've always called her Arella, and she's always loved it. "Yes, that's what other people call you, but I don't."

"Why?"

"Because Arella is a unique name that suits you better than Ari."

She shoots me a dirty look. "Are you sure it's not just because you saw that it's my legal name and you didn't know I went by anything else while you were stalking me?"

"Is that what you think I've been doing?"

"How else would you have known how I met Caleb?"

"Who's Caleb?"

"My boyfriend."

Could you please *stop calling him that?* "I don't know how you met Caleb."

"Yesterday, you claimed that you and I met on the side of a highway. That's how I met Caleb."

"What? No, no, no." That must have been one of her core memories the Scrubber inserted Caleb into. What other core moments were altered? "Look, Arella, I—"

"It's Ari."

I refuse to call her that. *Ari* is not who she is to me. "Look, I know this is gonna sound insane, but you've had your memories erased. You know me. You just don't remember it. I met you on the side of a highway, then we fell deeply in love. I'm confident we had the kind of love that can't be erased."

"How can someone get their memories erased?"

When I ran through this conversation in my head, I knew she'd ask me that, so I prepared an answer. "You were in a bad car accident. You hit your head and got amnesia. Now you've forgotten me and you think that other guy is your boyfriend, but he's not."

"If that's the case, then why weren't you at the hospital after my car accident?"

I didn't prepare for her to ask me that. "Um, I couldn't be there."

"Why not?"

"Well, um, because I was in prison." That's probably not the best answer, but it's partly true, and I've got nothing else.

"Prison? For what? Stalking women?" Her words drive an invisible dagger straight into my chest.

"Of course not."

"Then what were you arrested for?"

"Um . . ." I think hard, trying to come up with a version of the truth. "I was doing things I shouldn't have done in public."

"Why isn't that on your criminal record?"

"Because they dropped the char—Wait, you looked up my record?"

She lets out a little *pfft*. "A strange man shows up at my door claiming to know me. Of course I'm going to look him up."

"I *do* know you, and I can prove it. Ask me anything."

"I'm not going to play this game." She's about to shut the door on me when I stop it with my foot.

"Arella, please, just hear me out."

"It's Ari," she says sternly. "And that's the last time I'm going to remind you."

Fuck. I need to stop calling her Arella. It's not benefiting me. I throw my hands up, palms forward. "Just ask me anything about you. I'll know the answer."

"The only thing that's going to prove is how good of a stalker you are."

"Then ask me questions even a stalker wouldn't know. I'll get them right."

Her shoulders rise and fall as she sucks in a breath and thinks. After a moment, she says, "What's the only food I'm allergic to?"

"Huh?"

"I said, what is the only food I'm allergic to?"

Well, fuck. I'm only one question in, and I'm already failing. "Ar—I mean . . . I'm sorry. I—I don't know the answer to that."

"I thought you said you *know* me?"

"I do. I just . . ." I shove a hand through my hair. "Of all the meals we've had together, you've never mentioned being allergic to anything. I guess I just assumed you didn't have any allergies."

"Okay, answer this one then: Where's my birthmark?"

"Your birthmark?"

"Yeah, you know, a mark on someone's skin they've had since birth. If you know me so well, where's mine?"

I rake my fingers through my hair again as I think back to all the times I had the privilege of seeing Arella naked. I can't recall seeing any marks on her skin. "I—I didn't realize you had one."

"I thought you said we were in *love*. If we were, you must have seen me naked and saw my birthmark. It's in a pretty obvious place."

This is not going the way I hoped it would. "It's probably not *that* obvious, because I've kissed every single inch of your body, and I swear to you, I've never seen a birthmark."

That quiets her. I wish I knew what she was thinking. The blank look on her face tells me nothing. "One more chance. If you get this wrong, then you either leave or I'm calling the cops."

"Deal."

"What was the name of my childhood dog?"

Dog? She's never mentioned having a dog. I've never seen a picture of her with a dog either. I slump my shoulders. "I . . . I don't know. With how often you moved, I didn't even realize you had a dog."

She blinks up at me from behind her long black lashes. The look in her eyes kills me. There's no recognition in there anywhere. "We had a deal, sir. You leave or I'm calling the cops. Maybe your old prison cell is still vacant and they'll give it back to you."

With that, she slams the door in my face.

76

ARI

I'm in the middle of telling Javina about my interaction with Trey earlier today. Caleb is at the museum, so it's just me and her, hanging out in my kitchen.

"Where was Caleb when Trey showed up?" Javina asks as she cracks open a can of root beer and takes a sip.

"At the gym."

"I see. So what questions did you ask Mr. Obsessed-with-you?"

I lean back against the counter and fold my arms together. "I asked him what food I'm allergic to, where my birthmark is, and what the name of my childhood dog was."

"Childhood dog? I didn't know you had a dog."

"I never did. I don't have a birthmark either, and I'm not allergic to any foods."

"Ahh . . ." Javina says when it clicks. "Trick questions on the spot. I like it. What were Trey's answers?"

"He got them all right. He said of all the meals we've had together, I never mentioned being allergic to anything. He said he's kissed every inch of my body and he's never seen a birthmark. Then he said with how often I moved, he didn't realize I ever had a dog."

"So he *does* know you."

Pfft. "Lucky guesses."

Javina shakes her head, then takes another sip of her soda. "I dunno 'bout that, babes. If someone were to ask me those questions, I woulda taken shot-in-the-dark guesses. Your allergies? Peanuts. It's the number-one food allergy people have. Your birthmark? It's on your back. It's a big area, and tons of people have birthmarks there. Your childhood dog's name? Bub. No matter what people name their dog, everyone calls their dog Bub."

Knock-knock.

Javina and I freeze.

"Who's here?" I ask, even though I've got a good feeling who it is.

"Stay here." Javina sets her root beer onto the counter, then heads to the door. She steals a peek through the peephole, then whispers, "It's him."

I stay where I am and whisper back, "Don't open it."

My best friend sucks at listening. "Don't worry. I've got this." With the chain lock in place, Javina slides the door open until it clicks against the metal.

"Javina," Trey says. I can't see him, but I recognize his voice. Hearing it just kicked my heart rate up.

Javina tilts her head to the side. "You know who I am?"

"Yeah, you're Arella's best friend. Your favorite color is pink. You enjoy spa days, massages, and you like to call me *pretty boy.*"

Javina glances back at me with a *what the hell?* look. I flash her the same look back. How does this guy know what Javina's favorite color is or that she enjoys spa days? She hasn't had one in almost a year. Is that how long he's been stalking me?

Javina turns back to the man outside my door. "What else do you know about me, pretty boy?"

"Uh, you're dating Rachel. You drive that red Toyota Corolla parked right there. Um . . ." He pauses to think. "I know that Arella keeps root beer in her fridge just for you, even though she hates root beer."

Javina glances back at me again with her eyes bulging out of their sockets. Without making a sound, she mouths, *What the fuck?*

"Look, I know this must be weird for you since you don't remember me. I'm sure Arella has told you all about me by now. I know you're protective of her, but I promise, I'm not here to hurt her. I just want to show her something."

"Show her what?"

"It's a picture of her and I. It's proof."

Javina holds her palm out. "Hand it over, pretty boy."

"Could you ask her to come to the door?"

Javina flashes me a silent *what do you think?* look. My head tells me I should call the cops, but my heart tells me I'm not in danger around this man. If he wanted to hurt me, he would have already.

Trey's breath hitches as Javina steps aside and I step into his view. Earlier, he looked like he was recovering from two black eyes. Now the purple is gone. His skin looks perfect. Not a single out-of-place wrinkle or any signs that he's ever had a blemish.

His eyes are an ocean blue of somberness and fear. Why is *he* the one who's scared? He's the stranger who keeps showing up at *my* door, knowing things he shouldn't, and spewing out made-up stories of me losing my memory.

"Here." Trey hands me a wallet-size photo of him and I staring lovingly into each other's eyes. In the photo, I'm wearing a dress that's currently hanging in my closet. Around my neck is a necklace I've never seen before. It's a pair of golden angel wings around a huge sparkly heart-shaped diamond. "Four days ago, you were wearing the angel-wings necklace in this picture. It's a necklace I bought for you, and it's got an engraving on the back with my initials on it. Besides this photo, it's the only other thing that exists that's proof I'm telling the truth. Please tell me you have the necklace somewhere."

"I don't," I say as I hand the photo back to him. He doesn't take it. "Great job with the photoshop, though. That woman looks just like me."

"Because it *is* you. You just don't remember taking the picture."

"Right, because I lost my memory after a *bad car accident.* If that was true, how do you explain that Javina doesn't remember you either?"

His arm muscles flex as he scratches the back of his head. I try my best not to stare.

"Okay," he says, "I might have lied about the car accident thing. That's not actually how you lost your memories."

"Then how did it happen?"

"Um, I can't say. But if you could *try* to remember me, maybe you'll remember how that happened too."

I throw the photo at him. It falls flimsily to his feet. "Take your photoshopped picture and leave."

I'm about to shut the door on him when he shouts, "Wait! I can prove this wasn't photoshopped. You wrote a note on the back." He picks up the picture and hands it to me again.

Out of curiosity, I accept it. My lungs constrict as I read the note written in pen:

I love you, Trey. You are right.
We do belong together.
—Arella

It's in my loopy handwriting with my signature.

I was freaked out before. Now I'm terrified. How does he know what my handwriting looks like? How many times did he practice writing in my handwriting before he perfected it on the back of this photo?

Over my shoulder, Javina stares at the note. "I dunno, babes, that looks pretty legit to me. It's either real or a hella-good forgery."

"It's not a forgery," Trey says. "I swear."

"You've already admitted to lying about the car accident," I say. "How can I trust that you aren't lying about this too?"

"I only lied about the car accident because I can't tell you the truth about how you lost your memories. If I do, they'll put me back behind bars."

"Who's *they*?"

"The, uh, the government."

I press my eyebrows together. "What?"

"Yeah, I know it sounds weird, but again, if you can try to remember me, maybe—"

He gasps as I rip his photoshopped picture in half, then half again.

I toss the pieces at him. "Go away, and stop coming back. The next time you do, I won't hesitate to call the cops. This is your last warning."

"Nooo!" He falls to his knees, grasping at the photo pieces on the ground. "No. No. No." His breaths become shaky as he gapes up at me with the ripped-up picture in his palms. Disbelief mixes with the tears glistening over the surface of his eyes. "Why did you do that? This is the only thing I have of us."

"There is no *us*! I don't know who you are! Now leave!" I slam the door shut and twist the bolt lock.

My silent apartment feels too silent. I thought telling him off would feel good, but it doesn't. Instead, I feel . . . I'm not sure what the right word for it is. It's like I'm a sailor not at sea who knows I'm supposed to be in the water, but I don't know why. Meanwhile, something keeps pulling me back to shore.

Javina beams at me. "Damn, girl. That was spunky."

After letting out a long breath, I sneak a glance through the peephole. Trey is exactly where I left him: on his knees, with the photo pieces in his palms. Except now, he's got tears rolling down his cheeks. He looks like he's barely breathing as he stares at the ripped photo.

My heart breaks for him. I must have really hurt him. Then again, he's a stalker. A lunatic. A deranged man. Whatever I want to call him, they all point to the same thing: This guy is off his rocker.

"Is he still there?" Javina whispers.

"Yeah," I whisper back.

"What's he doing?"

"I don't know. He's just . . . staring at the ripped picture." I feel the need to apologize, but for what? I don't owe him anything.

Eventually, Trey stands and wipes his damp face off on his shirt. Then he stares at the ground with a desolate look in his eyes. His chest rises and falls with each breath he struggles to suck in. I've never seen someone so sad. He's either a really good actor or he actually believes the crazy story he's been feeding me and is truly hurt by what I just did.

With a blank look in his eyes, he turns on his heel and walks away.

At the living room window, I pull the blinds back a tiny bit to see him slowly dragging his feet toward his car like they're weighed down by a ball and chain. He's still got that bleak expression on his face as he opens the driver's door and sits behind the wheel.

Then he just sits.

And sits.

And sits.

The whole time, he stares at his steering wheel and barely blinks. He's in his car for so long that Javina gets tired of peeking out the window with me and heads to the couch with her root beer in hand. As for me, I'm not planning to leave this window until he's gone.

"Seeing a man that pretty look so sad hurts me," Javina says. "I'm about to go out there and offer him a blow job just to wipe that godforsaken frown off his face."

I'm still holding the blinds open just enough for my right eyeball to see outside. "He could just be putting on a show."

"A show for who?"

"For me—to make me feel bad for him so I'll believe his crazy story."

Javina sucks in a breath through her teeth, shaking her head. "I dunno, babes. Your handwriting on the back of that picture looked hella real to me."

"But how? I don't recall writing a note on the back of a picture I never took."

Javina gasps so loudly, I drop the blinds. "Oh my god. What if he's from an alternate universe?"

"A what?"

"You know, a world like ours, but not. Maybe whatever he was imprisoned for was so bad that his universe banished him to our universe. And in his world, you were his girlfriend, but he doesn't realize he's been banished, so he thinks you're his girlfriend, when really, his real girlfriend is back in his universe."

"Javie . . ." I say with a *come on* face, "that sounds even crazier than the lies he's trying to feed me."

"Hey, if it's possible for D. B. Cooper to jump out of a flying plane with a bag full of cash and never be seen again, then alternate universes are possible too." She gasps again. "What if that's why no one ever found D. B. Cooper or his parachute? What if he parachuted through a portal into another universe?"

I roll my eyes at her. "Maybe it's time we lay off the true crime shows for a while."

In the parking lot, an engine starts. I peek through the blinds again and catch a glimpse of Trey driving away. "He finally left."

Javina finishes the rest of her root beer, then stares at the empty can in her hands. "Don't you find it a little odd that he knows you don't like root beer and that you keep it in your fridge just for me?"

I join her on the couch. "That's what stalkers do; they watch you until they know every little detail about you."

"Yeah, but that's a pretty *specific* thing to know, and something you can't find out just by sitting outside someone's house. Also, I'm not gonna lie; calling him *pretty boy* feels right."

"What are you trying to say?"

She shrugs a shoulder. "I dunno. I'm just thinking out loud. Anyway, I should dip out. Will you be cool on your own?"

"Yeah, I've got a chain lock now."

Javina disappears into my kitchen to toss her can into the recycling, then heads to the front door to slip her shoes on. "Call me if pretty boy comes back, 'kay?"

"Okay." Now that I'm hearing her call him that again, I suppose it does sound right.

Javina opens my apartment door, then gasps.

I shoot up from the couch. "What?"

"He left the pieces of the photo on the ground." Javina picks them up and holds them out to me. "Here. Put these under a microscope."

"Why?" I open my palm for her to drop the pieces into.

"To look for alternate universe dust, duh. If this picture came from his world, there's probably evidence of it on there somewhere."

I roll my eyes as I chuckle softly. "Okay. I'll get right on that."

Once Javina is gone, I return to the couch to examine the photo. I don't have a microscope, but I do have packaging tape. On the coffee table, I arrange the photo pieces to reflect their original form. Then I stick a large piece of transparent tape over the picture. After cutting off the excess tape, I sit back to investigate the mended photo.

Javina is right, the handwriting does look legit. The photo looks real too. I stare closer at the necklace I'm wearing in the picture. I don't recognize it. Trey claims I was wearing this necklace four days ago. If that's true, where is it now?

77

ARI

I haven't seen Trey in over three weeks. At least not in real life. In my dreams, he's the star of the show.

It's been happening a few times a week. One of my dreams was of us at a restaurant together. Trey and I had just finished our pastas when he asked me to dance with him. After I refused, he frolicked around the dance area by himself with an invisible woman in his arms. The whole time, I laughed until my belly hurt.

Another one of the dreams I had was of us baking snickerdoodle cookies together. Trey and I were in a kitchen I didn't recognize, when suddenly, we were throwing flour at each other. It ended with us making out until I was breathless.

My dream last night was a terrifying one. I was getting dressed in my bedroom when I saw a spider. Usually, one spider doesn't freak me out; I'll simply grab a shoe and stomp on it. But this spider was huge—so big, I could see the little hairs on its legs.

Suddenly, it wasn't just one spider anymore. There were tons of them. Hundreds, maybe thousands, came crawling out from every crevice of my bedroom. I screamed and jumped onto the bed, but they followed me there. Then they were crawling on me like they were trying to eat me alive. I kept wailing and screaming until I was lifted off my feet and rushed out of my apartment. The person who saved me was Trey.

Why am I suddenly having dreams about this man? And why so frequently? I haven't told anyone about my dreams. Not Caleb, and especially not Javina. I already know what my best friend will say. It'll be something along the lines of Trey being from an alternate universe and how his presence here is causing my dreams to be snapshots of things that happened in his universe.

Javina hasn't given up on the alternate-universe theory. She even came up with a name for the alternate version of me: Alterella. "You know," she said, "because he calls you Arella. Maybe in his universe, you go by your full name."

Javina's theory could be right. It would explain why Alterella signed her name as Arella instead of Ari.

I'm storing Trey's taped-up picture in a book that Caleb would never open. He doesn't know I have this photo, and I don't want him to know. He might trash it. I don't know why I'm so keen on keeping it or why I think to look at it as often as I do, but I can't bring myself to get rid of it.

Keys jingle outside my apartment door. I peek my head out from the kitchen just as Caleb steps inside and kicks his shoes off.

"Hey, muffin," he says as he shuts the door and secures the chain lock. I had left it off knowing he'd be home soon. He still has beads of sweat running down his forehead from his workout at the gym.

"Lunch will be ready in ten," I say.

"Sounds awesome. I'm going to take a quick shower, then I'll be right out."

After his shower, Caleb emerges from our bedroom wearing a pastel pink button-up. It's one of my favorite shirts on him because he always looks so happy in it.

"Smells good," he says. "What did you make?"

I set two bowls across from each other on our cozy kitchen table. "Quinoa salad."

Caleb plants himself into his chair, practically drooling. "Thanks. This looks awesome."

"How was your workout?" I ask as I sit and take my first forkful.

"Good. Rakesh and I worked on our upper body today. He's a beast. I could barely keep up with him."

Caleb has been best friends with Rakesh since they roomed together in college. They go to the gym together almost every day, even on Saturdays, like today. When they're not at the gym, they love to explore bookstores and go hiking together. If Caleb is not with me or at work, there's a pretty good chance he's with Rakesh.

"Did Rakesh ever hear back about that personal trainer position?" I ask.

"Yeah. He didn't get the job, but he applied at a different gym, and he already got an interview."

"Wonderful. I hope he—" My entire body locks up as my eyes land on a spider on the wall. It's big, it's black, and it's got hairy legs.

Suddenly, I feel it again, all those spiders crawling up my body. I feel their legs on my skin. They're attacking me! They're trying to eat me! They're . . .

The room tilts as I fall off my chair. When my body hits the floor, the room goes black.

78

TREY

The second the nausea hits me, I'm on my new motorcycle in a flash. As I race toward Arella's apartment, I pray to the glimmer gods that this one isn't life-threatening. I can't lose her this way, not when she doesn't know who I am.

Cars honk at me from all directions as I weave between them on my bike. This one revs up to speed faster than my old one, and I'm living for it.

My arms feel numb as Arella's apartment complex comes into view. Her car is sitting in the lot. *Thank fuck.* I had no idea where she was, and this was my best guess. If she wasn't here, I would have torn this city apart looking for her.

When I park, I yank my helmet off and chuck it in the grass. Then I shake my numb arms out as I sprint to her apartment door.

I pound on it. "Arella?"

"Just put the knife down," a man says calmly.

Arella shouts from the inside. "Get away from me, or I'll stab you!"

I pound on the door again. "Arella?" I'm about to wave a hand at the lock to open it when the door bursts open.

Arella stands on the other side with a kitchen knife in hand. The moment she locks her eyes with mine, I see it—recognition. "Trey!"

My name. *She just said my name.* I didn't realize how much I was yearning to hear it come from her lips.

The knife falls from her hand, then she throws herself at me. She wraps her arms around my torso as she buries her face into my chest. Instinctively, one of my arms latches around her back as my other hand fists her soft hair.

Tears pool in the corners of my eyes. For the last three weeks, I've spiraled down hours of dark thoughts, wondering if I'd ever get my girl back. Now she's back. I don't know how, but she's back, and I'm never letting her go.

"Oh, Trey," she says into my shirt. "Thank God you're here."

My blackened world fades back to color. That constant knot in my chest loosens. My lungs feel less constricted. I'm sucking in air, and it no longer feels like a battle.

"Arella," I say into the top of her hair. "What happened, baby?"

She leans back and points at a wide-eyed Caleb standing in her living room. "I don't know. I woke up in my bed, then all of a sudden, this strange man walked into my room. He keeps saying I'm his girlfriend."

I glance at Caleb as if he knows what the fuck is going on. The look on his face confirms he's just as confused as I am. With one hand firmly around Arella's waist, I use my other hand to grab her face and force her attention back to me.

She looks straight into my eyes, and I see it again—recognition. It makes me so happy, a tear actually rolls down my cheek.

"Tell me, baby. What's the last thing you remember?"

"Like, before I woke up?"

I nod.

"Um, I—I don't know."

"Think, babe. Think real hard for me. Do you remember being at the Ridge?"

She doesn't hesitate. "Yeah."

"Do you remember us getting arrested?"

A nod.

"Do you remember when a bunch of Royals popped out of the woods and attacked us?"

"Yes. Then you got stabbed, and I was putting pressure on your wound when, all of a sudden, everything froze."

That was the last time I saw her before I was knocked out and woke up in z-prison. "Do you remember anything after that?"

She thinks for a moment. "Not really. The next thing I remember is waking up and this guy walking into my room."

I hold her tight against me. "It's all right, baby. I'm here now."

I get to hold her for all of two seconds before Caleb shouts, "What the fuck is going on?"

I wish I had an answer for him, because I want to know too. How did Arella suddenly get all her memories back? Well, *most* of them. She doesn't have any recollection of what happened after the Enforcers showed up.

"Ari, why are you letting this man touch you? He's a psycho."

Arella leans back and furrows her eyebrows together. "Who are you?"

"I told you already. I'm your boyfriend."

"No, you're not. *He* is." She gestures toward me, making my heart leap out of my chest. I didn't realize how satisfying it would be to hear Arella tell someone that *I'm* her boyfriend and not him. That title doesn't even fully encapsulate all the deep feelings I have for her, but I'll take it over being called her stalker.

"Wow." Caleb chuckles humorlessly. "You must have hit your head really hard."

I've been staring at Arella this whole time, but that statement makes me flick my eyes up to Caleb. "She hit her head?"

"Yes. We were just sitting down for lunch when she saw a spider on the wall. Then she fell off her chair and hit her head on the floor. I picked her up, laid her in bed, and was just getting her a glass of water when she woke up and screamed at me to get out of our apartment."

"*My* apartment," Arella says with a scowl.

"*Our* apartment," Caleb says.

"What is happening right now?" Arella gapes up at me as if I've got the answer. "Who is this guy and why is he—" She lets out a painful scream. It retightens that knot in my chest.

Her entire face crumples as she clasps her palms against her temples. She screams again, then her knees buckle.

I catch her as she slumps to the ground. "What's wrong?"

"My head. It hurts."

"Where?"

"All over. Something is pinching my brain and my temples."

In one swift motion, I scoop her into my arms and cradle her against me as I march toward her bedroom. Confused energy seeps into my mind from behind me. Caleb follows me and watches my every move as I lay Arella on her bed and cover her with blankets.

I have no idea why her head hurts. I'm going to assume it has something to do with how she suddenly remembers me, but how do I stop the pain?

"Ah!" She clasps her hands to her temples again. "Oh, God. My head."

I turn to Caleb. "Tylenol. Ibuprofen. Do you have either of those?"

With a nod, the dude disappears, then he returns with two pills in his palm.

I accept the white tablets from him and offer them to Arella. "Here, babe. Take these."

There's a glass of water on her nightstand that I hand to her as well. She takes the pills with a large gulp of liquid, then sets the glass back onto her nightstand.

"Maybe I should sleep it off," she says.

"Sure. Maybe that'll help."

She lays her head onto her pillow, then places a gentle hand over my forearm. "Will you cuddle me?"

I never enjoyed cuddling until I met Arella. Once I cuddled with her, it was practically all we ever did together. Hearing her ask me to cuddle her is like hearing a perfect chord on the grandest piano of all grand pianos.

Without hesitation, I kick my shoes off, then shrug off my jacket and let it drop to the carpet. Then I climb onto her mattress and slip under the covers with her. Arella scoots closer to me, then lays her head over my shoulder and rests a hand over my abs. I squeeze my arms around her as happy tears fall from my eyes.

I ignore Caleb's glare as I pull the blanket over Arella some more and tuck it under her back. Then I breathe in her intoxicating scent of lavender and springtime, allowing it to relax me. I haven't felt this at ease since . . . I can't remember. Since before Arella was kidnapped, that's for damn sure.

My girl tilts her head back to look at me. "Trey?"

I'll never get sick of hearing her say my name. "Yes, baby?"

"Don't leave me, okay? Stay here until I wake up."

It would take an act of God to make me leave her.

79

TREY

There's evidence of *him* everywhere. He's got clothes in the closet. Jackets hanging up behind the door. Colognes on the nightstand. A pair of his worn socks lying on the floor. I haven't gotten a closer look at the rest of Arella's apartment yet, but I can only imagine there's more of him around.

The Keepers sure went through a lot of effort to plant Caleb into Arella's life: altering her memories, moving him in, giving them a shitload of fake memories together. It was a good effort, but in the end, I was right. I had known my girl could fight it. I had known she could overcome the scrub. Her immunity probably played a huge part in that, but I'm going to give most of the credit to her inner strength—one of the first things about her I fell in love with.

Now that she's come back to me, I'm gonna make sure she stays. Fuck the Keepers, and fuck their stupid laws. If this isn't proof that they can't keep my soul mate away from me, I dunno what is.

Whenever Arella wakes up, we'll figure out a plan together. We'll run away to somewhere the zovernment can't find us. We'll start a family, and we'll grow old together. Whatever Arella wants, she'll get. All I want, all I need, is to be with her. As long as I've got that, I'll—

"She knows you," Caleb says, cutting into my thoughts. He's stationed on a chair in the corner, where he has been since Arella fell asleep. Like a fucking creep, he's been watching me hold her for the last twenty minutes. No matter what I said, he refused to leave. "How does she know you?"

"Could you speak quieter?" I say in a low whisper. "I don't want you to wake her."

The pastel-shirt-wearing motherfucker has the nerve to cross his arms over his chest and shoot daggers at me with his eyes. "Answer my question, asshole. How does she know you?"

"Speak quieter, asshole, or I'll throat-punch you so hard, you'll never be able to speak again."

In a lower tone this time, he says slowly, "How . . . does . . . she . . . know you?"

"We met on the side of a highway."

"That's how she and I met." The dude narrows his gaze at me. "How is it possible that we both met her the same unique way?"

Maybe because you only met her after the goddamn Keepers placed you here. I don't bother coming up with an answer for him because I don't care enough. The only thing I care about is the woman in my arms.

After a long silence, Caleb speaks again. "The only reason I haven't torn you away from my girl is because she specifically asked you to stay. If she hadn't, I would have called the cops by now."

"Call her *your girl* again and I'll set you on fire." The guy probably thinks that's an empty threat, but my palms are already sparking up.

He scoffs. "You're kinda possessive of her for a man she didn't remember an hour ago."

"She remembers me now, so you can go fuck off." *Preferably over a cliff.* The tallest damn cliff he can find.

"How did she forget you?"

I let out a frustrated sigh. "Don't you have something better to do? Like, I dunno, fall into a pool of sharks?"

"Actually, sharks aren't as violent as people think. More people are killed by cows every year than sharks."

"That's great. Since you're such a know-it-all, why don't you go on *Jeopardy!*? I'm sure they'd love to feature you and your pastel-as-fuck pink shirt."

He shrugs with a grin I want to slap off his ugly face. "I'm just sayin', dude. If you're going to wish death upon me, you should wish for cows over sharks."

"Seriously, could you just fuck off?" *And take all your shit in Arella's apartment with you.*

It takes him a moment to finally stand. "Fine. I'm going to go finish the lunch that my *girl-friend* cooked for me, but the second she wakes up, I'm comin' right back."

As he exits the room, I imagine chucking a big-ass fireball at the back of his head. If I wouldn't get imprisoned for exposure, I probably would.

Finally, for the first time since we were in my parents' safe house, I'm holding my girl—alone. I relish how the sounds of her steady breaths calm me and the way she looks so innocently beautiful when she's asleep. She's an angel who was made specially for me, and she fits in my arms like we're two perfect pieces of a puzzle. Little does Caleb know, our puzzle doesn't have room for a third piece.

Barely five minutes pass before Arella stirs. I remain still in case she's just fidgeting a little, but she moves some more, then her eyes flutter open. When she tilts her head back to look at me, my heart sinks to my stomach.

The recognition is gone.

A high-pitched scream fills the room as Arella launches herself off the bed. "Get away from me!"

My world stops turning.

Caleb dashes through the open door, then my gut wrenches as my girl dives straight into his arms.

She points a shaky finger at me. "Caleb! He—the crazy guy—he's in our bed."

Our bed. That one little word jabs me in the gut. My breath hitches as Caleb protectively snakes his arm around my entire reason for existing.

"Calm down, muffin. Everything's okay."

Muffin? What the fuck?

"It's not okay!" Arella shouts. "The crazy guy is *in our bed*!"

I'd be fine going the rest of my life without ever hearing her say "our bed" in reference to

Caleb ever again. Slowly, I slide off the mattress with my hands up in surrender. My movements only make Arella curl into this other guy more.

All the color that lit up my world a minute ago quickly fades. That pitch-black fog of depressive darkness floats back into me, clouding my vision.

Caleb cups her face the way I did earlier, forcing her attention to him. "What's the last thing you remember?"

"We were having lunch," Arella says. "Then I saw a big spider."

"What else?"

Her eyes cast down as she thinks. "Um, I think I passed out."

"You did, but you're okay now." Caleb pulls her closer to him. My body stiffens as she softens into his chest. "I've got you, muffin."

Seeing her in his arms like that is like watching a horror movie: It's terrifying, but I can't look away.

Caleb shoots me a glare. "Get out." He keeps his arms wrapped tightly around my girl as she turns her head to look at me. Still no recognition.

Swallowing hard, I keep my hands up in surrender as my eyes lock with hers. In the calmest voice I can manage, I say, "You just remembered me."

Her eyebrows dip. "What?"

"Just now, before you fell asleep, you remembered me."

"What are you talking about?"

I flick my gaze up to Caleb. "Tell her."

The dude blinks at me in silence, and it's all I need to know he's not gonna back me up. Why would he? To him, I'm the guy who's trying to steal his girl.

"Come on, man," I plead, "tell her the truth."

"Get out," he says.

He's a lost cause, but Arella isn't. That recognition earlier is proof that every moment we've ever shared together is still inside her somewhere. Maybe those memories are buried deep—way, way deep—but she can access them. There's hope. I can get through to her. I just have to figure out how.

"Arella, twenty minutes ago, you—"

"My name is Ari!" she shouts so loudly, I drop my hands and jerk back a step. I trip over my shoes and catch myself on her nightstand. "If you ever call me Arella again, I'm going to file a restraining order against you. Actually, I'm going to do that regardless. I told you to stop stalking me."

"I'm not stalking you. I'm telling the truth. Just now, you remem—"

"No! I don't want to hear you feed me a bunch of lies. Just leave, and stay away from me!"

My breaths come out shallow as all the hope I just had fades away. The disgusted look she's giving me is confirmation that no matter what I say, no matter what I do, she's not coming back to me.

She doesn't remember me.

End of story.

She doesn't remember the nights we spent cuddled in my bed, talking about her dream bakery until two in the morning. She doesn't remember taking me to her *thinking spot* under that giant oak tree—the place where we made love for the first time. She doesn't remember the battles we fought together to stay alive. She doesn't remember any of it.

Without her memories, this woman standing in front of me isn't Arella. Suddenly, it hits me that she's been right this whole time: Her name *is* Ari, because Arella is gone. Arella died the moment that Scrubber altered her memories to remove me. Unless she can remember us falling in love and all the hell we went through together, this woman in front of me is just a woman who *looks* like the woman I love.

The realization hits me like a baseball bat to the face. First my parents, then my Deaf mentee kid Elliott, my unborn baby, my dad, and now her. This is my fate, to lose anyone who has ever meant anything to me. What did I do to deserve this curse? I would never wish this torture upon anyone. Not even Aunt Jodi, who I hate with every piece of my broken soul. Who's next? Liz? The rest of my bandmates? My dog? I don't even have a dog, but if I did, I'm sure it wouldn't be safe either.

Tears collect on the surface of my eyes. I need to get outta here before they drip down.

I stare blankly at my shoes as I shove my feet into them. My breaths come out sharp as I pluck my leather jacket off the floor and slip my arms through it. I feel Ari's and Caleb's gazes on me as I force my feet to shuffle around the bed.

As I pass them, I keep my eyes glued to the carpet. I can't look at them. I shouldn't, anyway. I don't know them, and they don't know me. To them, I'm just a stranger in their home. I don't belong here.

I slam their apartment door shut behind me as I drag my feet outside. I'm about to reach my bike when I realize my helmet is missing. I twist on my heel and find it in the grass, exactly where I chucked it. My vision blurs with wetness as I bend to pick it up.

As soon as I pull the helmet over my head and my face is covered, I burst into a silent sob. It's the kind that consumes my entire body and shakes my shoulders. Tears roll down my cheeks in steady streams as I spend all my energy forcing my feet toward my bike. It's hard to move when the air feels like black sludge entering my lungs.

A door opens behind me. "Trey!"

Fuck. It's her voice. For a second, I think about turning around and scooping her up. I'd rip my helmet off and kiss her until she's breathless. She'd say my name again and look up at me with that precious recognition in her eyes.

But it's not her. It wasn't her when I showed up here after leaving z-prison, and it wasn't her I gave my photo to either. My Arella is gone, and no matter how much this woman sounds, looks, or even acts like Arella, she *isn't* my Arella.

That's why when she calls my name again, I don't stop. Actually, my slouchy walk toward my motorcycle turns into a dead run. I have no desire to talk to a woman who reminds me of someone I lost. Someone I have zero chances of ever getting back.

"Trey," she calls again as I straddle my bike.

The key is still in the ignition. I turn it, and the engine awakens with a soft rumble. I'm about to back out of my parking spot when she runs up next to me and places a hand over my forearm.

"Trey, wait!" Her touch doesn't feel like Arella's. It feels more like pain and heartache. "Can I talk to you for a second?"

I can't answer her with words, because if I do, they'll come out through a choked sob. Silent tears are still rolling down my cheeks, wetting the inside of my helmet. I'd wipe them away, but that would require removing my helmet. I can't let this woman see me cry. She wouldn't understand, and from what I know about her, she doesn't care to, so I simply pluck her hand off my forearm, give it back to her, then roll my motorcycle back.

Like Arella, this woman is difficult as fuck. She runs behind my bike and throws her hands up. "Trey, please! Wait!"

With a sigh, I twist the key. The engine dies like the way I am on the inside with each passing moment I'm in this woman's presence.

She returns to my side. "I just want to talk to you."

I circle my hand in the air as if to say, *So talk then.*

"Can you take off your helmet?"

Holding back my sobs, I shake my head.

"Please? It feels weird to talk to someone when I can't see their face."

If this woman is anything like Arella, she won't give up until she gets what she wants. The faster I do what she asks, the faster I can get outta here.

Looking anywhere but at her, I reluctantly drag my helmet off and set it on my lap. A light breeze blows against my damp skin as I stare at the bike key I want to twist so badly.

Ari lets out a little gasp. "Oh, Trey . . ."

I bet she didn't expect to see me like this. I probably have red cheeks and even redder eyes. I drag the bottom of my shirt up to wipe off my wet face.

In the corner of my eye, I see her attention drop to my bare stomach. She stares at my abs while I dry my cheeks. Her fingers used to trail little figure eights over my abs whenever she rode on the back of my bike. She doesn't remember that, but I do. I'll remember it for the rest of my miserable existence.

"Oh, Trey . . ." she says again. I wish she'd stop saying my name. It's in Arella's voice, and I used to love hearing her say my name. Hearing it was like hearing my favorite song pop on the radio. Hearing it now is like hearing skips on a record player. It's still Arella's voice, but something is off about it. "I didn't mean to hurt you."

I bet if I could sense her emotions, they'd be somewhere between shock and pity. I don't want her pity. The only thing I ever wanted from her was for her to hear me out. For her to *try* to remember me. But she didn't want to hear me out. She didn't even want to try.

Arella never pitied me. Even when I told her about witnessing my parents' murder, the only way Arella ever looked at me was with understanding. I don't think I'll ever find that again.

Since this woman isn't getting to the point, I muster up the courage to force out some words. They come out more broken than I intend them to. "Just, uh, s-say what you came out to say so I can l-leave."

"Um . . ." In the corner of my eye, I see her rub the ends of her long hair between her fingers. Arella would do that whenever she was anxious. I'll miss seeing that. "Caleb confirmed that what you said is true. He said that I remembered you."

I'm surprised Caleb told her the truth. I didn't think he would.

"How did that happen?" she asks.

I keep my eyes glued to anything but her. "Don't you think that if I knew, I'd do anything and everything in my power to make it happen again?" *Permanently this time.*

She goes silent as my question sinks in. "Um, Caleb also mentioned that I said something about you getting stabbed. He said I remembered putting pressure on your wound. Is that true?"

Slowly, I nod, unsure where she's going with this.

"Where did you get stabbed?"

"In my side."

"Can I see it?"

Ah. That's where she's going with this. She wants physical proof that I was stabbed because simply hearing it from her stupid boyfriend isn't enough. Suddenly, I wish I hadn't been fixed up by the z-prison Healer, because then I'd have something to show her. Unfortunately, if I wasn't healed, I probably wouldn't be here.

Either way, having proof changes nothing. I know that now. Even if she saw the remnants of a stab wound, she still wouldn't remember me. She would still have another man waiting for her in their apartment. She would still have no recollection of us falling in love. Therefore, this conversation is pointless.

"I don't have a scar from it." I tap my fingers against my helmet, itching to put it back on.

She cocks her head at me. "How is that possible?"

"The same way it's possible for you to not remember a single thing about me."

"So, like, magic?"

It's offensive as fuck to call anything from the Zordinary world *magic*. Our gifts are passed down through genetics. There's nothing magical about that.

"Is there anything else you wanted to talk to me about?" I ask, a little clipped. I know I shouldn't be mad at her. It's not her fault I've been erased from her head, but all my energy is being used to keep my shoulders from shuddering. I only have so much energy left to say things nicely.

"I guess not."

"So can I go now?"

Her face drops, and I'm not sure why. What did she expect from this exchange? For me to have all the answers? I don't, and I'm more upset about it than she is.

She swallows thickly. "Yeah, you can go."

I waste no time dragging my helmet back over my head, then turning my bike key. The engine rumbles again. Ari steps back, giving me enough space to back out. Once I do, I ride away from her, leaving behind my entire heart in her hands.

It may not belong to her, but it belongs to her soul. Arella is still in there somewhere, and I want what belongs to her to stay with her.

80

ARI

"So?" Caleb says when I shut the door behind me. "Did you see a scar?"

I'm speechless. I'm not sure what I wanted from that encounter with Trey, but I didn't expect to come out of it feeling so confused and empty. I suppose I wanted answers, but all I've got is more questions.

I slump into my chair at the kitchen table. My quinoa is still waiting for me to eat it. I don't feel like eating though. "No, I didn't see a scar."

"So he was lying then."

The evidence—or lack thereof—sure points that way. However, I'm not convinced that's the whole story.

"Hopefully, that's the last we'll ever see of him," Caleb says. "I'll help you file that restraining order on Monday."

"Okay," I say impassively. I can't think straight. My mind is reeling.

Caleb told me that after I woke up from fainting, I freaked out and didn't know who he was. Apparently, I kept yelling at him to get out of our apartment. When he refused, apparently, I ran into the kitchen and threatened him with a knife. Why would I do that? More importantly, why don't I *remember* doing that?

According to Caleb, Trey showed up shortly after, pounding on our door, and when I heard Trey's voice, I ran straight to him.

"You remembered him," Caleb told me. "You said something about how he got stabbed and you were putting pressure on his wound. Then you got these painful pinches in your head. He brought you to our bed, then you asked him to cuddle with you. I'm not gonna lie, babe. It was pretty fucking strange to see you talk to that man like you knew him."

Why don't I remember *any* of that? The last thing I remember is seeing that spider; then I woke up in my bed with Trey in it.

I stand with my bowl in hand. From a lower cabinet, I pick out a Tupperware container and spoon my lunch into it.

"You didn't eat much," Caleb says.

"I'll try eating more later." I snap the lid onto the container, then place it into the fridge, knowing I probably won't eat it later. As I close the door, the room spins around me and a wave of nausea hits me in the gut. A pair of strong arms catches me as I stumble backward.

"Muffin?"

"I'm okay," I lie. "Just got dizzy all of a sudden."

"You want to sit down?"

"Sure." The nausea whips around my stomach as Caleb leads me to the couch. We're only halfway into the living room when I feel like— "I'm gonna throw up."

In a flash, Caleb lets go of me and rushes into the kitchen. A trash bin appears in front of me just as I start hurling. My chest heaves as I cough up the little that's in my stomach.

Caleb holds back my long hair as I puke some more. Once the vomit has subsided, he helps me over to the couch. "Do you feel any better?" he asks.

"No," I say as I lay my head back. "My arms feel numb, and I feel like I might throw up again."

"That's it. I'm taking you to the ER."

The nausea has simmered down a bit now that we're at the ER. The numbness in my arms is lighter too. The twisting knot in my chest hasn't disappeared though.

A small medical bed sits in the middle of my sterile room. A white paper sheet is draped over the top of the bed, and the air smells of lemony disinfectant.

"Take a seat, Miss Rance," says the nurse, who points two fingers toward the bed.

I do as I'm told while Javina plops into a chair. Since there's only one chair, Caleb leans his back against the wall, crossing his arms over his chest.

On our way to the hospital, I called Javina to ask if she could meet us here. Depending on how long this takes, Caleb will have to leave for work, and he didn't want me at the ER alone.

The nurse checks my temperature, then takes my blood pressure. After he tells me that everything looks normal, he says, "We only have one doctor in tonight. She's currently with another patient but should be around to speak with you shortly."

"No worries," I say. "I can wait."

"Thanks. I'm gonna go check in the next patient. Just holler at any of the nurses out here if you need anything."

The second the nurse slides the glass door shut behind him, Javina perks up. "Okay, tell me what happened!"

Together, Caleb and I tell her a shortened version of what happened with Trey. Caleb even tells her about all the stuff that happened while I was under some kind of memory spell. "The way he stared at her while she slept creeped me the fuck out."

"I have a theory," Javina says. "I think Trey was banished here from an alternate universe and doesn't know it. With his presence in our world, I think Ari's memories are merging with the memories of the Ari from *his* universe. Maybe that's how she suddenly remembered him but she actually doesn't, because technically, those things didn't happen to her; they happened to Alterella."

Caleb arches his brow. "Alterella?"

"I know, I know. I'm a clever woman," Javina says with a flip of her black curls. "Anyway, what if traveling through alternate universe portals heals all wounds? Maybe that's how he doesn't have a scar from being stabbed."

The room goes silent as Caleb glances between me and Javina a few times. Then he hooks a thumb her way. "Is it just me, or is Javina making some sense?"

"What?" I blanch. "She's making no sense at all. There's no such thing as alternate universes."

Caleb shrugs a shoulder. "I didn't think so either—until you screamed at me to get out of our apartment, then laid in our bed with another man who you claimed was your boyfriend."

I can't believe Caleb is actually considering Javina's theory. Usually, he's so pragmatic.

"Shit, Trey can be *my* boyfriend if he wants," Javina says, fanning herself with a hand. "I'd willingly throw myself into a volcano if it means that hunk of delicious meat would belong to me."

I roll my eyes at her.

"I'll do some research on alternate universes tonight while I've got downtime on my shift," Caleb says. "Which reminds me, I've gotta get going. I still have to run home and get my uniform on before I head to work. Will you be okay with Javina?"

"Of course, love." We give each other a quick kiss.

Barely a minute after Caleb leaves, an Asian woman in scrubs strolls into my room with a friendly smile. "Hello, I'm Doctor Park. Could you confirm your full name and birthdate for me?" After I do, she washes her hands at the sink, then turns to me. "All right. Tell me why you're in today."

"I'm not really sure what's wrong with me. One second, I was putting food away. The next, I got really dizzy and—"

"Doctor Park!" a guy shouts from outside my room. "Emergency! Ambulance patient! Arriving now!"

"Please excuse me." The doctor rushes out of my room. She doesn't even bother sliding the door shut behind her.

Javina, as curious as ever, pops out of her chair and shuffles toward the sliding glass.

"Status?" the doctor says from a distance.

"Twenty-something white male," a man says. "Motorcycle accident. Witnesses say he rode straight into an oncoming truck at full speed. Thankfully, he was wearing a helmet. Broken arm. Unstable vitals. He's breathing, but he's coming in and out of consciousness."

"Which room do we have open for him?"

Their voices trail off as they head down the hall.

Javina slides the door shut, then heads back to her chair. "Sounds like a doozy. I hope the poor guy is okay."

Twenty-something white male on a motorcycle? It can't be. It'd be too much of a coincidence. Then again, it wouldn't be the hardest thing for me to believe lately.

"You okay, babes? You're lookin' kinda pale."

My lungs feel tight as I force myself to breathe. "Javie . . . um, Trey is a twenty-something white male who left my apartment earlier on a motorcycle."

She gasps. "You don't think . . . I mean, there's tons of people in this city. He can't be the *only* guy who fits that description, right?"

The air goes still around us. We must come to the same conclusion at the same time, because just as I'm about to hop down from my bed, Javina jolts off her chair. Without a word, she goes to do the exact thing I was about to do: slide the glass door back open.

"Out of the way!" a woman shouts from down the hall.

Chaos erupts outside my room. Javina and I peek our heads out the door as a bunch of EMTs rush into the hospital with a man on a stretcher. They wheel him down the hall so fast, I don't catch a glimpse of him. I know it's Trey though. My gut is telling me so.

For the next hour, Javina talks my ear off about alternate universes. She even scours the Internet for articles about how other universes could work, and she reads them to me. The more she tells me about the possible trillions of galaxies and beings out there, the more I believe her.

"He could be from the future," Javina says. "Maybe in the future, they have things that can wipe memories and that's what his government did with you as his punishment for breaking the future's laws about falling in love with people from the past."

"I think I prefer your alternate-universe theory," I say. "It's a little more believable."

Eventually, Doctor Park returns, slightly out of breath. "I apologize for the wait. Whenever we get someone in by ambulance, those patients always come first."

"What's the guy's name?" Javina asks, because she has no boundaries.

"I'm sorry," the doctor says, "I can't share that. Patient privacy."

"Is he going to be okay?" I ask, because, like Javina, I'm too curious for my own good.

"I'm sorry, I can't tell you that either. Let's talk about you instead. Tell me why you're in today."

Since my weird symptoms from earlier are no longer present and all my vitals are normal, the doctor determines that I simply need some water and rest.

"If the dizziness comes back, please don't hesitate to return," she tells me.

"Thank you," I say as I hop off the bed.

"You're good to go." The doctor sucks in a long breath through her teeth. "Now I'm off to see my next patient. I hope they're as nice as you two were about the wait."

Javina and I must be on the same page again, because we wait for the doctor to leave before we glance at each other in silent agreement of what we're about to do. She takes my hand as we exit the room, then she practically drags me down the hall—the same hall the man on the stretcher was wheeled down earlier.

"I'm so curious to know if it's him," she says.

"Me too." Even though I already know it's him, but I can't tell her that. I'll sound crazy if I tell her that my heart feels a strange pull to head this way.

We casually pass each room, where either the curtains are drawn shut or the people inside are not Trey. At the end of the long hallway, two people step out of a room. One is my nurse from earlier. The other is a woman I recognize as Liz Hart, Trey's best friend. His bandmate that all his fans say he dates on and off. She looks as beautiful as she does in their YouTube videos, maybe even more.

Javina stops dragging me down the hall and stops mid-step to turn to me. In a whisper, she says, "That's Liz Hart. She's in his band."

I haven't told Javina about all the research I've done on Trey, so I act like this is new information. "Should we ask her if he's okay?" I say instead.

Javina gives me an *I dunno* look.

"He's going to get admitted soon," the nurse says in a low voice as he slides Trey's room door shut. "He'll have to stay for at least a night. Depending on how he is tomorrow, he could be discharged, but that will be at his doctor's discretion."

"Am I able to stay the night with him?" Liz asks.

"Of course. Is there anything I can get for you in the meantime?"

"I'm good. Thank you."

The nurse heads toward Javina and me as Liz turns back toward Trey's room. She's just sliding the door open when I blurt out, "Liz?"

Her head whips up, and we lock eyes. For a split second, I regret what I just did, but it's already done, so, with Javina in hand, I head down the hall. This time, it's me who's dragging her.

"Hi?" Liz says warily as she slides the door closed.

"Um, hi," I say as we reach her. "I'm sorry to bother you. I just recognized you from down the hall."

"Oh, you're a fan. Um, now isn't really the best time."

"Actually, I'm not a fan."

That makes her tilt her head to the side and narrow her eyes at me. I suppose it sounds weird to say that I recognized her, yet I'm not a fan of her band.

Thank God for Javina. "She's not, but I am. I went to one of your shows a few months ago, and I've been watching all your music videos ever since. My favorite? The video for 'Fired Up!' The flames in it looked so real!"

Liz relaxes a bit. "That's because they *were* real."

Javina's mouth dramatically pops open. "Shut up. That wasn't just special effects?"

"Nope. One-hundred-percent real flames. Trey built that set all by himself, then set it on fire, just for our video shoot."

"That's so cool! Anyway, I'm Javina." My friend throws her hand out for a shake.

Liz accepts it with her satin-gloved hand. She wears cute gloves in all of her band's music videos. I didn't realize it was something she did in real life too. "Nice to meet you."

I offer her my hand. "Ari."

At first, she takes my hand and shakes it. Then she freezes. "Wait. Did you just say Ari?"

"Yeah."

She narrows her gaze on me again. "Is that short for anything?"

"Arella."

Her eyes go wide; then she blinks at me. Trey must have told her about me. I wonder what he said.

Finally, Liz and I let go, and I take a step back. An awkward silence fills the air as neither of us knows what to say next.

Again, thank God for Javina. "Is Trey okay? We saw him getting rushed in."

Liz sighs deeply. "Yeah, he's okay. He wasn't when I got the call from the hospital. They weren't sure if he was going to make it, but he's stable now."

"What happened?" I ask, desperate to know.

"They said Trey was on his bike when he crashed into a truck. Both parties were going over the speed limit. No one died, but Trey got banged up pretty bad. Actually, he's the only one who got hurt. What I don't know is how he lost control of his bike. I mean, to go straight into oncoming traffic?"

Judging from the timing, Trey's accident happened shortly after he left my apartment. At the time, he was upset, crying, and barely breathing right. Is that why he lost control of his motorcycle? Did he almost die because of me? Because I said things that hurt him?

I swallow thickly. "Is it all right if I see him?"

"He's asleep right now. He's under sedation."

"I don't need to talk to him. I just want to see that he's okay." *That he's alive.*

Liz thinks, then says, "Um, yeah, sure."

Javina takes a step back. "I don't need to see the man. You go, Ari. I'll be in the waiting room."

Liz reopens the glass door, then gestures for me to step inside. Trey's room is bigger than mine was, and filled with more machines. That same lemony disinfectant smell lingers in the air. Some cords dangle from Trey's upper body, and there's an IV sticking out of his arm—the arm that's not in a cast.

I don't know what comes over me. All of a sudden, I'm tearing up and my chest feels numb. It doesn't feel like the numbness that dominated my arms earlier. This numbness feels more emotional than physical. It doesn't make any sense though. I'm not emotionally attached to this man. Why does seeing him hurt and helpless affect me this much?

Liz gestures toward a chair. "You wanna sit?"

I don't take my eyes off Trey. "No, thanks. I won't be staying long." I feel the urge to apologize to him. Earlier, I yelled at this man to get out of my apartment. I even threatened him with a restraining order. Now he's all drugged up in an emergency room, with a broken arm, and I feel responsible.

"Sooo . . ." Liz says as she settles into the chair she just offered me. "You don't have to answer this if you don't want to, but, um, why are you at the ER?"

"I got really nauseous earlier and threw up. I wasn't sure what was wrong, so my boyfriend brought me here to get checked out."

"Nauseous?" Liz repeats with a lift of her brows. "And you threw up?"

"Yeah."

"Did it happen all of a sudden?"

"Yeah."

"Did your body go numb? Like, your arms especially?"

My body freezes. "Yeah . . . ? How did you know that?"

She blinks at me, then flicks her attention to Trey, then back up to me. "Lucky guess."

I want to ask her to clarify how she came to that highly accurate lucky guess, but I'm not sure how to word that question without sounding accusatory.

"Could I ask you something, Ari?"

I nod. "Sure."

"Do you believe in soul mates?"

What an odd question to ask someone you just met. I take a moment to think about it. *Soul mates.* What is the definition of a soul mate? Someone you're meant to be with? "I suppose I haven't put much thought into the concept."

Liz uses her gloved fingers to drag her reddish-brown curls behind an ear. "Well, I believe in soul mates. I believe that there's someone for each person in this world. Someone who sets our soul on fire when we're together and makes us feel like we're empty when we're apart.

"While I hope that everyone in this world is blessed enough to find their soul mate, I also believe that some may never find theirs at all. In addition, I believe that sometimes, even after we find ours, things can happen that tear us apart."

I crinkle my eyebrows together. "Why are you telling me this?"

She shrugs like there's no hidden meaning to what she's saying. "I was just wondering if you believe that even when soul mates are torn apart, somehow, in some way, they're still connected to each other, whether that's mentally, emotionally, or even *physically*."

Is Liz trying to tell me that Trey is my soul mate? I stare at the sleeping man. The man who has been the star of my dreams for the past three weeks. The man who's got me tearing up at the sight of him in a cast, even though I don't know him. The man who got into a motorcycle accident today after leaving my apartment, and around the same time, I suddenly got dizzy. Are our minds and bodies connected to each other's in some way? Some alternate-universe or futuristic way?

I shrug nonchalantly, ignoring the chill running down my spine. "Like I said, I haven't put much thought into the soul mate thing."

A soft knock sounds on the door, then the glass slides to the side.

The nurse flashes Liz a warm smile. "We're ready to take him upstairs."

Liz stands from her chair. "It was great to meet you, Ari. You really are gorgeous."

Why is she saying that as if Trey has talked her ear off about how *gorgeous* he thinks I am? My heart warms with the idea that he spoke about me to Liz in that way.

I steal one last look at him. He looks peaceful, even with all the cords and medical stuff surrounding him.

With a heavy heart, I force my feet out the door. The second I leave his side, my body yearns to go back.

81

TREY

My eyes flutter open. An IV is taped to my arm. It's hooked up to a bag of fluids hanging above me. I glance around and conclude that I'm in a hospital room. It sure smells like it.

My mind feels groggy. My body feels like I fell off a building. Maybe I did, because my right arm is in a cast. I want to sit up, but when I try to lift my head, it feels weighed down by sand.

Liz is sitting in a chair by the window, reading a book while munching on some pretzels.

"How long have I been here?" I ask.

My question makes Liz set her book and pretzels onto a rollable table, then pop out of her chair. Her shoes click against the floor as she drags her chair closer to my bed.

Once she's settled back down, she offers me a warm smile. "Hey, T-Bear. You've only been here for a night."

"Did I get a zoctor?"

"A doctor, but your hospitalization wasn't Zordi-related, so anyone could have treated you. After they discharge you, we can take a trip to Chinatown so you can see a Healer."

"That sounds good." With a few bottles of Healing Water, my arm will be fixed within days. With a Healer, it'll take five minutes, tops.

"How ya feelin'?"

Physically or emotionally? My answer is the same either way, so I say, "Shitty."

"As expected. You were hit by a truck, after all."

"A truck?"

"You don't remember that?"

The last thing I remember is the woman who looks like Arella rushing out to me from her apartment. She asked me about my missing stab wound. The next things I remember are bright lights and people shouting. That's about it.

"Liz." My voice comes out scratchy. "She remembered me."

"Huh?"

"It was only for a few minutes, but she remembered me." I go into the whole story. The entire time, Liz listens without a single interruption. Once I finish, I say, "I wish I knew what caused her mind to flip to remembering me, then back to forgetting me."

"Do you think that happens with everyone who gets scrubbed, or just her because she's immune?"

"If I had to guess, I'ma say it's just her."

A heavy cloud of anxiety floats toward me from Liz. She chews on her bottom lip as she picks at her fingernails.

I eye her, wishing I was a Mind Reader instead of an Empath. "What?"

"Oh, nothing." She waves a nonchalant ungloved hand through the air. "We can talk later. For now, let's just focus on getting you to full health."

"No. I want to talk now."

She hesitates. "Are you sure you're ready to have a serious conversation?"

"Yes," I lie.

With a long sigh, she leans in closer to me. "T, you've barely been eating, and you're always staring off into the distance with this blank look in your eyes. Getting you to come to band rehearsal is a battle, and whenever you perform, it's so robotic. At least you show up willingly to our writing sessions, but everything you write is so dark and depressing."

That's a very long-winded way of saying, *T, you've been miserable.* "How 'bout you stop sugarcoating what you're trying to say and just give it to me straight?"

"Okay, fine. When I got the call about you being at the ER and they told me what happened, I couldn't help thinking maybe . . . I dunno. Look, I don't want to accuse you of anything, but I don't want to assume either. Because you've been feeling so wrecked, I wasn't sure if—" She sucks in a deep breath and blows it out. I'd make this easier for her, but I'm not sure what she's trying to get at. "T, they told me you rode your bike straight into oncoming traffic."

Ah, I see now. "You want to know if I did that on purpose?"

"Yes. That's exactly what I want to know."

"I didn't," I say without hesitation.

Liz clasps a hand over her heart. "Oh, good. I was so worried that was the case. What made you lose control of your bike, then?"

My answer comes easily. Saying it out loud is harder. "I—" I clear my throat. "I, um, was having a panic attack."

"What?"

"You know, they're these moments when my heart races and I feel like I can't breathe, or move, or think, or anything. And whenever it gets really bad, my powers go haywire."

"I know what panic attacks are. I just didn't realize you got them, but I guess that makes sense. You've been through a lot of trauma."

With the arm that isn't in a cast, I drag the blanket draped over me a little higher up my chest. "I used to get them a lot when I was a kid. I thought I grew out of it, but I guess not."

"Did something happen to trigger this one?"

I swallow like there's something stuck in my throat. Knowing what triggered the panic attack is one thing; admitting it to someone is another.

Liz waits patiently while I gather my words.

"After she reverted to forgetting me, I came to the conclusion that my Arella is gone. Without her memories of me, that woman is nothing more than a woman who looks like her. Coming to that realization hit me hard."

I choke up, holding back a wave of tears. "Even now, there's still a part of me that wants to pursue my original plan of getting her to remember me. Obviously, she's still in there some-where, but I don't know how to draw her out. I'm not even sure if it's possible to do so permanently, and everything I'm doing is only scaring away the woman who goes by Ari."

Liz goes quiet as she takes that all in. After what feels like a long time, she says, "So if you're not going to pursue her anymore, what are you going to do instead?"

A thunderstorm of pain crashes through me like it probably did when I ran into that truck. The only difference is that I'll remember this agony. I lose my voice as I whisper, "I have to let her go."

Liz offers me a sympathetic smile. "I'm glad you came to that decision without me having to tell you."

I eye her through slits. "How long have you known that was my only option?"

"I figured it out while I was sitting in your car outside the z-prison, waiting for you to be done talking to that Keeper."

"Why didn't you tell me sooner?"

"Because you suck at listening to me. You would have fought me on it, and you would have done what you did anyway."

She's right—as always.

"I dunno how I'm gonna do it, Liz. I've spent the last three weeks trying to stay away from her while I figure out a new plan to get her back. The entire time, I've been dying inside. She's all I think about. She's all I care about. She's all I want. How am I supposed to go on like this?"

82

TREY

I raise my fist to knock on Ari's door. I'm about to make contact when I stop, and my hand drops to my side. I shouldn't be here. I don't even know why I'm here. What am I trying to get out of bothering her again?

It's been two weeks since I got out of the hospital. It took me that long to realize that staying in LA wasn't right for me. Mostly, it's not right for Arella. The only thing I'm doing by being here is causing her pain and distress, and I don't want that. I want what's best for her. I want her to be safe and happy. Since she *is*—just not with me—I decided it's best to leave.

I made this decision yesterday. Since this would affect my bandmates the most, I told them first. They took it hard. Liz took it the hardest. She cried for over an hour, and I felt like an asshole for being the cause of her tears, but I have to do this. Liz was understanding about that, which only made me feel like more of an asshole.

Now I've got a brand-new not-totaled motorcycle sitting in the parking lot of Arella's apartment complex—*Ari's* apartment complex. Next to my bike is a backpack full of clothes and toiletries.

I have a few stops to make on my way off to wherever the fuck I'm going. I didn't plan for one of those stops to be here though. Somehow, on my way out of California, I ended up here. Now I'm standing outside her door like a fucking weirdo, refusing to knock while also refusing to leave.

I should just get this over with. Maybe she's not home. I glance back at the parking lot, where her car is sitting. That doesn't mean anything though. She could be somewhere with Javina or her—uh, boyfriend. I don't sense any emotions coming from her apartment, but that doesn't mean anything either.

I raise my fist to her door again, then stop. What if she yells at me? I'm not sure if I can take another bad interaction with her. Nor can I take hearing her call me *the crazy guy* in Arella's voice.

Again, why am I here? This woman has nothing to offer me that could make things better. To her, I'm a stranger, and it'd do me some good to remember that.

Still, a big part of me just wants to see her one last time. She still *looks* like Arella, even if she isn't. Seeing her again could be worth the heartache I'll feel from hearing her tell me to get lost.

I lift my fist back up to her door, then stop again. Once she opens this—*if* she opens this—what will I say? More importantly, what will she say back? Will she look at me like I'm a lunatic, the way she has been? Arella never looked at me like that. She always looked at me like she felt safe with me. This woman doesn't feel safe with me. Not one bit. I don't blame her either. When I see things from her point of view, I know her actions are justified. So are the actions of her—uh, boyfriend.

Still, if I leave LA without seeing her one last time, I'll obsess over it. I'll regret not knocking. I'll regret not trying to leave things with her on a good note. I'll be tormented over what could have happened if I had knocked. *If I had been brave . . .*

I bring my fist back up to her door, then pause. What if she calls the cops on me? She's threatened to enough. After waking up in her bed with me in it, I don't doubt she would hesitate to make that call this time. Do I really want to deal with the aftermath of that? What's worse—living with regret or living behind bars?

I drop my hand back to my side. I shouldn't be here. If she's in there and saw me pulling up on my bike, she's probably already called the cops. They could be here any minute. I should go before they arrive.

With a heavy heart, I stare at the door I used to shove her back up against. I used to pin her arms above her head and kiss her until our lips felt raw. I wish I would have appreciated those moments more while they were happening. Since my photograph of us is gone, those memories are all I have left. A part of me wishes I had never shown Ari that picture. Maybe then I'd still have it.

I'm not sure why the Keepers allowed me to keep that photo. It was in my wallet when I got arrested, and it was still in there when I got out of z-prison. They went through my entire house to get rid of anything that belonged to her, so I'm sure they went through my wallet too. Why would they let me keep a photo? To torture me? To rub it in? To make sure I'd always remember my greatest loss?

Last night, I spoke to Liz about the possibility of finding a black market Scrubber. It's illegal for them to scrub people outside the zovernment's permission, but I'm sure I could find one I could talk into erasing my memories. Everyone's got a price, and I'm willing to pay it. It'd make things easier. I could move on without this pain.

When I shared this idea with Liz, her response was "If neither of you remember the love you created together, then it'll be like it never happened. Is that what you want? Is that what Arella would want?"

I already knew I could never go through with getting scrubbed, for that exact reason. If everything Arella and I went through together only exists in my mind and I get rid of it, then it'll be like none of it ever mattered. I don't want that. I just needed Liz to validate that living with this physically debilitating hole in my chest is better than forgetting about the happiest moments of my life.

I place a palm against Arella's door and whisper to it as if she can hear me from the deep depths of where she's being suppressed. "I'm sorry, angel. This isn't me giving up on you, but I have to let you go. I know I promised to always fight for you, but I don't have any fight left in me. I think I'm doing the right thing. I just hope you see it that way too."

With that, I turn on my heel and force my feet to walk away.

83

ARI

The sound of a motorcycle pulling up outside makes me race from my kitchen to the living room window. The engine stops as I peel the blinds back to find Trey Grant yanking his helmet off. He hangs it on a handlebar by its strap, then rests his backpack on the ground against his bike.

His bleak expression matches the gray clouds as he dismounts his motorcycle and makes his way to my door. His arm is out of the cast, and I can't figure out why. It's only been two weeks since he was in the hospital. There's no way his broken arm healed that fast. An injury like that takes a month to heal at best.

I tiptoe to the door and ready myself to open it. If Caleb was here, he'd already be calling the cops. I probably should, but I don't want to. Maybe it's naive of me, but I don't get the feeling that Trey is here to hurt me.

I glance through my peephole to find him raising his fist to the door. Then he stops. He's got that desolate look in his eyes again. I have an overwhelming urge to do something to get rid of it. His arm drops back to his side as he chews on his bottom lip.

Why isn't he knocking? Why is he just standing there, staring at the ground?

A few moments pass before he raises his hand to the door again. After he knocks, I'll wait a few seconds before opening the door so it doesn't seem like I was standing on the other side, watching him.

But the knock doesn't come. His hand drops back down again.

He's thinking heavily about something. I wish I knew what. Judging from the pained look in his eyes, it's nothing good. Whatever he's thinking about, he keeps thinking for several heartbeats before lifting his fist again. It looks like he's about to knock, but he doesn't.

Instead, he chews on his bottom lip some more while he contemplates whatever he's contemplating. Maybe he's trying to figure out how he's going to say whatever he wants to say. He must figure it out, because for the third time, he lifts his fist to the door. And for the third time, he drops it back down.

Why is he hesitating so much? I've wanted to talk to him since I saw him in that arm cast. About what? I don't know. I just have this yearning inside me to hear his voice. I've been hearing it in my dreams. Last week, I dreamt of hearing him sing in the shower. In my dream, I didn't hesitate to strip naked. As I entered the shower, his breath hitched and his eyes glazed over. The next thing I knew, he crashed his lips against mine and pounded into me against the tile wall while I moaned his name and begged for more.

That's not the only sexy dream I've had about him. Last night, I dreamt that we were at my thinking spot and he was giving me a guitar lesson—at least, he was *trying* to give me a guitar lesson. It's nice to know that even in my dreams, I still suck at playing an instrument. Eventually, the guitar got thrown into the grass and he pinned me to the ground. We panted with desire as we tore each other's clothes off. Soon, that desire turned into a need. When he slipped his thick erection inside me, I gasped from his size. He filled and stretched me so much, it was painful at first. Once the pain went away, I couldn't get enough of him.

I woke up with that vivid dream so fresh in my mind that I slipped my hand under my panties and rubbed myself until I came. I didn't even feel guilty about the orgasm coming from the thought of another man doing me, because I hadn't had an orgasm like that in months.

I still haven't told anyone about my Trey dreams. They continue to play out in my head a few times a week, giving me snapshots of a life I never had. What if my mind is merging with the mind of Alterella's and I'm seeing moments she and Trey shared together? I cringe at myself for even considering that as a possibility, because it would mean accepting that my best friend's outlandish theory has any merit.

For the fourth time, Trey's fist rises to my door, but he pauses again. I almost open the door to put us both out of this misery. He came all the way here to see me at the risk of going back behind bars. Obviously, whatever he's got to say is worth the risk, so why is he hesitating? Maybe he doesn't want me to actually file that restraining order I've been putting off.

Once again, Trey lifts his hand to the door, except this time, it's not a fist. It's his palm. He keeps it there as he whispers something to himself. I can't hear what, but he looks tearful as he says it. Whatever he says, it's brief; then he turns and walks away.

I don't know what comes over me as I undo the chain lock and whip the door open.

"Trey?"

He's three steps away when he twists back around with his arms up in surrender. "I was just leaving. No need to call the cops."

"I wasn't going to."

"Oh." He drops his arms. "Thanks for not doing so already. I'm sorry. I didn't mean to bother you." With a hard swallow, he heads back toward his motorcycle.

I can't let him go like this. I want to know what he came for. Without thinking, I blurt out, "I heard you're moving."

He turns on his heel with his brows knitted together. "How'd you hear that?"

"Javina told me. She read about it on your band's social media page this morning."

With a deep sigh, he shakes his head. "I specifically told my manager not to post anything for at least a month. I knew she wasn't gonna listen."

"Are you going to fire her?"

"I can't. She's too good at what she does, and there's no one else in this world who would ever put up with my shit."

That makes me chuckle. "Are you a hard man to handle?"

"According to Monique, I'm the worst. Now that I'm moving—and I only told her yesterday—I think she's gonna let me keep that well-deserved title."

The screenshot of the social media post Javina sent me didn't specify how long Trey will be moving away for. It also didn't say if he'd be working on new music with his band while he's gone. All it stated was that Trey would be moving for an undetermined amount of time and everyone will continue on without him until further notice.

I echo the most asked question from his fans in the comments section. "Are you quitting the band?"

"No," he says somberly. "Just taking a long break."

"Where are you moving to?"

A shrug. "I dunno."

"When are you moving?"

"Right now." He gestures toward his bike and backpack.

"That's all you're bringing?"

Another shrug. "I don't need much."

"So let me get this straight: You're moving *right now*, but you don't know where you're going?"

"Yep."

"It doesn't sound like you've thought this through."

"Welcome to every big decision I've ever made." He shoves his hands into his jeans pockets. "Anyway, this moving-without-a-plan thing isn't new to me. When I got kicked out at eighteen, I packed up what I had, bought a car, and went wherever life took me. The only difference now is that I've got a bike instead of a car."

I wonder who he lived with after his parents died and why that person would kick him out. I think about asking, but that seems like too personal of a question when we barely know each other. At least, *I* barely know *him*.

Instead, I ask, "Why are you moving?"

He stares at his shoes, then out at the parking lot, then up at the gloomy sky, then back at his shoes. "I just need a change of scenery, I guess."

I hold back the question I'm dying to ask: *Are you moving because of me?* I'd feel bad if the answer is *yes*. Los Angeles is big enough for the both of us. He doesn't have to leave.

Trey continues, "When I got kicked out, I was told to go 'find my place in the world.' I guess I'm still looking for it."

I draw up the courage to ask the question I want the answer to most. "Why did you come here?"

He looks anywhere but at me. "I'm not sure, but like I said, I'm sorry for bothering you."

"You didn't. *I* was the one who opened the door, remember?"

He offers me a tiny forced smile. It doesn't light up his face the way his smiles do in my dreams. It doesn't crinkle the corners of his eyes either. I wish I could see those smiles from my dreams in real life. I'd prefer it over this dark and wretched version of him.

Since I'm not ready for him to leave yet, I say, "Your arm sure healed fast."

Finally, he looks at me. "How did you know I broke my arm?"

"I was at the ER when you were brought in. I overheard the nurse telling the doctor about it."

His entire face drops. "Why were you at the ER?"

"I got sick, so Caleb brought me in to get checked."

"You got sick?" The pure concern lacing his voice makes my insides flutter. "With what?"

"I don't know. It came all of a sudden. I got dizzy and I threw up, but I'm fine now. It went away by the end of the night."

I can practically see the gears turning in his head as he blinks at me. "Around what time did that happen?"

The answer he's looking for isn't a time on a clock. He's wondering if I got sick around the exact moment he got hit by a truck. It's something that's been weighing on my mind over the past two weeks. I try not to think about it too much, because whenever I do, I get chills. How did my body know Trey was hurt, and why did it react in that way?

"It happened around the same time you got into your motorcycle accident." I give him a moment to see if he'll react. He doesn't. He just keeps gaping at me. To try to elicit a reaction, I add, "My arms went numb too."

He gasps, then quickly hides it behind clearing his throat. That confirms he and Liz know something I don't. I think about asking, but I don't even know what I'd be asking about.

Trey licks his lips, then drags a hand through his dark hair. Three nights ago, I dreamt that I ran my hands through his hair as he laid his head in my lap. I can't remember what we were talking about, but it made him laugh a lot. I'd like to hear that laugh in real life.

"I'm glad you're feeling better," he says.

"I'm glad you are too. You looked pretty rough that night—with your arm in a cast." I added in that last part as a subtle attempt to get him to explain his magical fast-healing arm.

He doesn't. Instead, he crinkles his eyebrows together. "You got to visit me?"

"Yeah. I recognized Liz out in the hall and asked if I could. She didn't tell you?"

He huffs out a breath. "Nope."

"She asked me a weird question that night." I'm getting tired of standing with the door open, allowing all my precious air conditioning to escape, so I step out and shut the door behind me. Then I lean my back against the door and stick my hands into my dress pockets. "She asked me if I believe in soul mates."

"What did you tell her?"

"That I haven't put much thought into the concept."

He shifts his attention to the ground. "I see."

"What about you? Do *you* believe in soul mates?"

"I didn't used to."

I arch my eyebrows. "But you do now?"

A nod.

"What changed your mind?"

He stares deep into my eyes, almost like he's trying to stare into my soul. "I met someone who didn't just change my mind—she changed everything for me. Before her, I didn't think I was capable of falling in love. Even more, I didn't think anyone could ever fall in love with me. She proved I was wrong, and being with her made me believe in soul mates."

"Liz told me she believes soul mates are connected to each other emotionally and physically. Do you believe that too?"

"Yes," he says without any hesitation.

"Do you also believe that not all soul mates end up together?"

He chuckles humorlessly under his breath. "I think you might have had the same conversation with Liz that she had with me last night. She told me that being someone's soul mate means your souls are perfectly matched for each other but it doesn't necessarily mean you'll end up together.

"She said that sometimes, soul mates are only together for a brief moment, like it's the right person but the wrong time or situation. She said that many things can tear soul mates apart, like geographical location, certain laws, death, and even unforeseen circumstances."

Do the unforeseen circumstances he's talking about have anything to do with falling through a portal into an alternate universe, tearing him away from Alterella?

I pull my long braid to one shoulder. "What do you think happens to those people who lose their soul mates? Are they just doomed to be alone forever?"

"That's the same question I asked Liz last night. She said most people never find their soul mates. Instead, they find a compatible partner, someone who makes them happy but they aren't a perfect match."

"So is that what you're going out in the world to find? A compatible partner?"

He sighs and runs a hand through his hair again. "No, I want to find my place in the world."

"What if your place in the world is the one you're about to leave?"

"If that was the case, then why do I feel like I don't belong?"

I imagine Trey as a lost soul, floating around the earth as a little orb, looking for a place to land. What if his soul never finds the place where he belongs? Will he just float around for all eternity? Finally, I say, "Well, Trey, I hope you find what you're looking for out there."

Somberly, he says, "Me too."

"Will you send me a postcard from wherever you end up?"

He gives me a slow nod. "Sure."

"Do you need me to write down my address for you?"

"Nah. I can figure it out."

"Okay." I place a hand on my doorknob but make no effort to turn it. A part of me doesn't want this to end; however, Caleb will be getting home from the gym soon, and I don't want to find out what happens if he sees Trey here. He might actually push that restraining-order thing through. I don't know why, but I just don't feel like it's necessary. It especially isn't now that Trey is moving. "I suppose this is goodbye then."

Trey's entire face falls, and the dim light in his eyes turns dimmer. His shoulders go taut, then suddenly, he doesn't look like he's breathing anymore.

What did I say wrong? "Trey?"

He doesn't answer. I'm not even sure if he heard me.

I say his name again, a little louder. "Trey?"

His gaze flicks up to me, and my breath hitches. He's looking at me, but I'm unsure if he's actually *seeing* me. There's a hollowness in his eyes that wasn't there before. I feel a need to go to him, to cup his face in my hands and tell him that everything will be okay.

I resist the urge. "Don't forget about the postcard, okay?"

He blinks slowly, as if he's trying to process my words. Once he does, he swallows, then nods. "I won't."

"I'll look forward to getting it."

A long silence sits between us. I can't bring myself to go back inside. I know I should though. On the other hand, I want to soak up every second with this man. I want to understand him and know what happened to bring him into my life. Why do I feel this strong connection to him?

Trey clears his throat. "I can't leave. Not while you're still standing out here."

"Do you need me to go inside?"

He gives me a slight nod with that hollow look still in his eyes.

"Okay." I turn the doorknob my hand has been holding for a while. "Goodbye, Trey."

He doesn't say goodbye back. All he does is stare at me longingly as I step back into my apartment and shut the door.

84

TREY

It feels weird to leave a black bag full of cash on a stranger's doorstep. It took me a while to even find the right house. It looks different in the daylight.

I put a written note inside:

To the owner of the Nissan Altima I stole,

I'm sorry for stealing your car and for any trouble that caused. I really needed it at the time, and I promised the person I was with that I would return someday to pay you back. This money should cover the cost of the vehicle, plus more.

My next stop is Chinatown in Las Vegas. I arrive at the traditional Chinese medicine shop about five minutes before closing time.

When I step through the front door, the scent of dried earth and spices fills my nostrils. The store no longer looks like a tornado ran through it. Now it features tidy shelves with containers perfectly facing forward, red paper lanterns hanging from the ceiling, and visible wood floors. Near the register sits a golden toy cat. It waves at me with one arm.

In the back of the store is an Asian man with graying black hair, stocking some shelves. "Can I hep you find someting?"

Tao doesn't recognize me, and I didn't expect him to. When I met him, Arella was with me. Anyone who interacted with Arella and me no longer has those memories.

I didn't plan out what I wanted to say, so I stutter out, "Um, is Li here?"

Tao heads down a hall, then shouts down the staircase. "Li! Another customer here to talk with you."

"Who?" a woman yells back.

"Aiyah. Just come up." Tao sighs as he reappears from the hall. "Our customers always prefer to talk to her, not me. Every time, she always ask who, like I know everybody's name."

A pair of footsteps marches down the hall, then Li steps into the light. She looks the same as last time: long black hair that falls past her shoulders, a gentle smile, and kind eyes.

Like she did before, she gasps with a hand to her chest. As she approaches me with slow steps, she keeps staring at me. I already know the words she's about to say.

"Are you Trey Grant?"

"Yep, that's me."

"Oh my god. You are so big, and tall, and very handsome. And you have strong arms." Also like before, she gives my bicep a squeeze. "Wow! I can't believe it's really you."

It's nice to know that some things don't change. Maybe if I had re-met Arella like a normal person, things might have turned out differently. Would she have fallen in love with me again? Would I have the same conversations with her that we already had before? Would I feel the déjà vu I feel now? Would she be standing here with me as I right my wrongs?

Then again, with that other guy in her life, she wouldn't need me the way she did before. Back then, she needed me to show her that a man can love her with all his heart and treat her like she's gold. I hope Caleb is treating her right. Arella deserves to be loved, even if it's not me doing it.

I hold out a black bag to Li. "This is for you."

She accepts the bag and unzips it. "Oh no! We cannot take this."

"You can, and you will. This is money I owe you for helping me out six weeks ago."

As expected, she crumples her eyebrows together. Tao does the same.

With a sigh, I ask, "Do you guys have a few minutes for me to tell you a story?"

"Of course," Li says. "Tao, you close the store. I'll take Trey downstairs."

On my way to Vegas, I considered not telling them anything at all and just leaving the money at their door. By the time I arrived, I had come to the conclusion that they deserve to know why "Victor" stopped talking to them all those years ago. Also, I have to clear my dad's name. I can't let his best friends live out the rest of their lives thinking he was cruel enough to cut things off with my mother out of the blue, then cut them off too. My dad would have wanted me to do this for him.

It takes me a while to get through the whole story because Li and Tao ask for a lot of details. When I finally finish, Tao says, "Victor was always a good man."

"You know he loved you very much, right?" Li says. "He always looked at you like you were his entire world."

"I know that now." I wish I could say that the thought of my real dad loving me outweighs the bitterness I feel toward Jodi, but it doesn't. Because of her, I was robbed of the relationship I could have had with my father.

I leave Li and Tao with a promise to visit again in the future.

Back on my bike, I head northeast.

The next morning, I arrive in Colorado. At my secluded cabin in the woods, I have full intentions of getting sleep, but no matter how many times I toss and turn, I can't manage to shut my eyes long enough. Being alone with my emotions and having nothing to do is only making me feel more lonely.

Usually, I enjoy having a break from people's emotions rushing through me all the time. But without other people's feelings distracting me, this heartache is only getting worse. Being here isn't clearing my head like it did when I lost Elliott. Instead, it's making me imagine jumping off one of the nearby cliffs. But before I can talk myself into actually doing that, I pack up and leave. I still have unfinished business, so I can't rid the world of me just yet.

The next afternoon, I arrive in a chilly Bloomington, Minnesota. It wasn't hard for me to find out where Katie's family buried her. Not at all to my surprise, Katie was a well-loved person and her funeral was a heavily attended event. Her friends and family posted about it all over social media.

At the cemetery, I dismount my bike. Then I walk around with flowers in my hand for almost forty-five minutes before I finally find her name on a gravestone.

Katie Williams
April 4, 1995–September 19, 2014

A lump forms in my throat as I bend to lay my bouquet of flowers near her name. "Everything you did for us was so brave, Katie. Thank you for saving her life."

For the next few hours, I sit with Katie and reminisce over how she helped me plan Arella's escape in a supply closet, then later jumped in front of a knife to save a woman she barely knew. Arella won't remember the courage Katie showed, but I will. If Katie was here, I'd bet anything she'd have some words of wisdom for me. I could really use some right now.

Once my ass is unbearably numb, I stand up, shake out my legs, then hop back onto my bike.

The next early evening, I make it to New York City, where Pixie's family buried her. It takes me even longer to find her gravestone because the cemetery is ginormous compared to the one in Minnesota.

Anna Jung
Daughter, sister, aunt, friend.
September 6, 1994–September 19, 2014

Both Katie and Pixie died way too young.

I give Pixie some flowers. Then I sit with her for a while, remembering how she tortured my ears, then ended up sacrificing herself so Arella and I could run away.

The sky is dim when I finally gather enough willpower to stand up. Paying my respects to Pixie was the last thing on my to-do list. Now what?

My stomach growls and claws at me to fix the emptiness. I haven't eaten much since I left LA. Not that I ate much while I was *in* LA. I guess I could get something to eat while I figure out where to go next.

Later that night, I'm slouched in a booth at a burger joint with a basket of food getting cold in front of me. I've had a couple of fries, but they can't seem to go down right. They keep sticking in my throat.

"You 'ight, sweetie pie?" asks my plump Black waitress. A wave of concern rushes through me from where she's standing.

"I'm fine," I say without looking up at her.

"You sure? You been sittin' here for almost two hours, and there ain't a single bite outta yo burger yet." She stares at me as her mood drops. "Oh, baby. I know that look. Either someone died or you just got yo heart broken. Which is it?"

This woman is perceptive as fuck. "Both."

"I'm sorry, sweetheart. Is there anything I can do for ya?"

Can you turn back time? Bring back my dad? Get me my girl back? "No, but thank you."

"Why don't you try to eat a li'l bit, baby boy? It might make ya feel better."

"I'll try."

An hour later, I've gotten all of one bite out of my burger. The other patrons have left, and the staff is mopping the floors.

My waitress stops by my table again. "You need anything else, hon?"

"Just the check."

"No way. You ain't even eat nothin'. I ain't chargin' you for that. Why don't you just go on home? Maybe tomorrow will be a better day."

I would do that . . . if I had a home to go to. Nowhere feels like home when *she's* not there.

I leave a few hundreds on my table, then grab my backpack and head out into the darkness.

The street is busy with moving cars, couples strolling side by side, some guys on bikes, and a group of teenagers taking a selfie together. An old dude stands next to a parking meter, smoking a cigarette. The cool early November air blows his cigarette smoke into my face as I drag my feet past him.

I've never been much of a smoker. My substances of choice were always alcohol, pills, and injections. I wouldn't mind some of those right now.

As I make my way down the sidewalk toward where I parked my bike, I pass stores that are closed for the evening, and restaurant owners turning their glowing OPEN signs off.

Eventually, I reach a crosswalk, but I don't bother waiting for the light to tell me when it's safe to go. If another truck hits me, maybe it'll actually take me out this time.

Liz would backhand my chest for thinking that. She would backhand me for thinking most of the self-harming thoughts I've had lately. She would also hit me for strolling straight past my motorcycle and into a bar.

An all-female band plays a sultry ballad from the stage as I hang my backpack on the back of a barstool and sit. The place is packed with men and women who are dancing, laughing, talking, whatever.

"Hey, handsome." Excitement spikes inside the pale-skinned bartender as she sets a coaster down in front of me. "What can I get you?"

"How 'bout a shot of whatever you feel like pouring?"

"Comin' right up." A few seconds later, she sets a shot glass with amber liquid in it onto my coaster. "This is—"

I don't let her finish telling me what's in my glass before I seize it. When I thunk it back onto the counter, it's empty. "Another, please."

"Sure." Without hesitation, she grabs a bottle and pours more liquid into my glass. When I thunk it back onto the counter again, she doesn't wait for me to ask; she just pours. I down my third shot, then gesture for her to give me some more.

She does, then asks in a cutesy little voice, "So where ya from?"

I drop the glass back down and wipe off my wet lips with the back of my hand. "California."

"Ooh." She leans against the counter, pressing her perky tits together. Her brunette hair falls off her shoulders to cover her cleavage. The woman is quick to grab all her locks and move them to her back. "Where in California?"

I'm not in the mood for small talk or her titties, so I point at my empty shot glass. "Another."

85

TREY

"Housekeeping," someone says from outside my hotel door.

I pry my eyes open to glance at the digital clock on the nightstand. The little red lines say it's just past noon, which means it's well past checkout time.

The ceiling looks like it's spinning. The back of my head throbs like I've been bashed with a sock full of coins. My bladder is about to burst, so I tear the blankets off me and stumble toward the bathroom.

My hotel door opens. An older woman strolls in, then gasps and covers her eyes. "Sorry! I'll come back later."

I glance at my morning wood swinging around. *Oops.*

After I'm done using the bathroom, I return to the bed, and my eyes go wide. A woman is lying on the side of the mattress I didn't wake up on. Her long brunette hair is sprawled out all over the pillow.

Fuck. What trouble did I get into last night?

I pluck my boxers off the floor and shove my legs into them. Then I find my jeans and shirt and put those on too. I make sure to be extra loud as an attempt to wake up the woman, but she doesn't even stir.

Begrudgingly, I kneel at her bedside and shake her shoulder. "Hey."

She doesn't move.

I shake her again—harder. "Hey."

Slowly, her eyes open. I think she's the bartender from last night, but I don't know for sure. I don't remember much beyond stopping at a liquor store before stumbling into the first hotel in sight. Did I ask this woman to come with me, or did she invite herself?

"Morning, handsome."

I don't bother with the pleasantries. "Did we fuck last night?" *Please say no. Please say no.*

Topless, she sits up and rubs her eyes. "We tried."

We tried? I push off my knees and onto my feet as I scan the floor for her clothes. "What does that mean? And please, explain in detail."

With a sigh, she catches the bra I toss at her. "It means you brought me here with the intention to fuck but you couldn't get it up."

What? That's never happened to me before.

"Don't worry," she says as she slips her arms through her bra straps. "I understand. You were really fucking drunk. You guzzled two liters of Karkov like you'd been trapped in the Sahara for days. And that was *after* all the shots you already had at the bar. I'm surprised you're not dead."

If only I could be so lucky. "I have a high tolerance." I pluck her shorts and panties off the floor, then toss them to her.

"You're a good kisser. If you weren't so wasted, I'm sure you would have fucked just as good."

I'm so disappointed in myself for making out with another woman barely three days after leaving LA. This isn't why I left. Thank fuck I can't remember it. The only kissing-related memories I want are the ones I have of kissing Arella. Drunk me probably thought getting laid would be a good way to get over her. Hungover me knows it wouldn't have worked. Nothing will.

"Do you need money for a taxi?" I ask as a hint that she should leave. I don't even know her name, and I don't care to.

"I'll be fine. I don't live too far from here. I work at that bar because I can walk there from my apartment. I would have walked home last night, but by the time you passed out, I was also too drunk to function."

I don't think I ever told Arella that I love how she doesn't drink. While we were together, her soberness kept me sober.

"Who's Arella?"

My attention flicks to the woman who's getting dressed like she's in a contest to see who can put panties on the slowest. "What?"

"You kept talking about her last night, saying things like 'You're not Arella' and 'You don't taste like Arella.' Is she an ex-girlfriend?"

I suck in a deep breath while also sucking in as much patience as possible. I can't be a dick to this woman. She did nothing wrong, except try to sleep with a guy who belongs to someone else.

The person I was many months ago would have definitely given her the night of her life last night. I'd probably be doing it again right now since she seems so willing, but I'm not that person anymore. I don't know who I am, but I'm not him.

I muster up the nicest tone I can. "Look, I don't wanna be an asshole, but last night shouldn't have happened. Also, it's past checkout time. I think you should go."

"Ahh." She nods in understanding. "She's your wife. Please tell me you're at least separated?"

If I was married to Arella, I wouldn't be here. I'd be at home with my wife, making sure she's happy, fed, and living any type of life she wants. I'd be asking her to make babies with me and thanking every star in the sky for each precious moment I had with her.

The bartender sighs. "Of course you're not separated. Why is it always *me* who finds the married ones?" She shakes her head at herself as she zips up her shorts. "Just my fucking luck."

I don't think I ever told Arella this either, but I like that she doesn't swear. I mean, she has, and she will occasionally, but it's not a habit of hers. I didn't appreciate that about her enough.

Finally, the woman grabs her small purse off the table by the TV, then slips into her shoes and leaves without another word.

⸎

AFTER ANOTHER WEEK IN NEW YORK, I CONCLUDE THAT THE BOOZE ISN'T DOING ENOUGH. ARELLA has never even been to New York, yet I feel her everywhere I go. The restaurants I force myself to eat at have food she would have loved to try. The stores I walk past feature flowy little dresses on the mannequins that she would've looked beautiful in. The bars I hop between play songs over the speakers that remind me of her.

I thought I could do this. I thought I could be a better man than I was, but it turns out, I can't. It's not like she remembers the man I was anyway. A man who stayed away from drugs. A man who could deal with his inner demons. Why bother trying to be him when she's not around to see it?

It's surprisingly easy to find z-drugs. All I had to do was download an app. Within two hours, I had jaderro in my hands, and the needles to inject it with.

As the liquid races up my veins, I lay my head back on a hotel pillow and wait for it to kick in. I went straight for the good stuff this time because if I remember correctly, jaderro is the shit that will knock me out for a couple of days. I've already booked this room for the next week and asked for no housekeeping. Hopefully, I can spend the next forty-eightish hours not thinking about her. And when I wake up, I'll do it again.

Usually, jaderro takes about two minutes for the effects to appear. It's only been thirty seconds, and my vision is already blurry, and my body's getting warm and tingly. My nose itches, but when I move my arm to scratch it, my arm feels heavy like my bones have pebbles in them.

The slight nausea will come next, but at least it'll be accompanied by the calm high. I wait for what feels like forever for that high to arrive. When it finally does, I'm euphoric, relaxed, and sleepy. My chest doesn't feel achy anymore, and my mind feels numb. *I could get used to this.*

⸎

TWO WEEKS LATER, I STARE AT THE EMPTINESS OF MY NEW PENTHOUSE IN MANHATTAN, WISHING IT was my house in LA with Arella in it. The only reason I signed the lease for a penthouse this morning is because it was the first available place I could find to rent in this goddamn city.

I tried nine different apartment buildings before I found this one. Every other place was either not move-in ready, the person in charge wasn't around, or they were already full with a wait list that's months long. I don't have months because Liz is coming to visit me tomorrow for Thanksgiving.

This isn't a surprise. She told me she'd be coming to visit over the holidays before I even left LA. I procrastinated on finding a place to live until the last possible day because, well . . . I'm an idiot.

475

Liz thinks I found this place two weeks ago and that I chose this city for the vibrant nightlife. In reality, I chose New York City because I happened to be here after I finished doing all the things I wanted to do. I guess one perk is that the many emotions rushing through my head drown out some of the achy ones in my chest. This is better than being at my lonely cabin, that's for damn sure.

Liz thinks I've been enjoying things like exploring Times Square and seeing Broadway shows. In reality, I've been hotel-hopping and getting wasted at the nearest bars. Any time a bartender cuts me off, I stumble into the next closest bar until those people cut me off too.

The thing about getting an Ordinary bartender is that they think ten shots is enough for me. I need the whole damn bottle to feel buzzed, another to feel drunk, and a third to feel nothing. Feeling nothing is my goal.

My other goal is to wake up alone. So far, I haven't found any more brunette surprises in my bed. All I ever find are empty bottles and a used needle.

Unfortunately, I can't do any of that shit tonight because Liz's flight arrives in the early morning. I need to be sober so I don't look like a wreck when she gets here. Plus, I have to make this place look like I've been living here for more than twenty-four hours.

So I head to the store.

The next day, Liz's face drops the second she enters my apartment. "What the hell is this?"

"It's called a penthouse," I say like a smartass, because that's not what she's talking about.

She drops her carry-on suitcase onto the floor, then backhands my arm. "Why is there nothing in here?"

"What are you talkin' about?" I rush to open my kitchen cabinets and gesture at all the dishes I bought yesterday. "See? I have stuff."

"T, you have zero furniture. My voice is echoing against your walls."

"I have furniture." I lead her to the bedroom, where a blow-up mattress is lying on the floor. "See?"

She flashes me an *are you serious?* look. "Haven't you been living here for, like, two weeks now?"

I'm about to spew out some bullshit excuses when she throws a gloved hand up. "Don't even start with me. Where do you expect me to sleep for the next four nights?"

I point at the air mattress. "We can't just share that?"

She rolls her eyes at me, then grabs my hand. "Come on. We're going shopping."

I don't move. "Liz, it's Thanksgiving day. Nothing's open."

"Haven't you ever heard of Black Friday sales? I'll bet tons of places are open today."

THE NEXT WEEK, I WOBBLE INTO MY NEWLY FURNISHED PENTHOUSE LIKE I'M ON A SWAYING SHIP. One hand clutches a paper bag, concealing the bottle I'm guzzling. My other hand steadies me against the wall as I kick off my shoes. I wave a hand at the door, and it slams shut behind me.

I take another swig as I half run, half fall into my bedroom. From under the bed, I drag out the cardboard box my silverware set came in. From it, I pull out my syringe and a little jar.

Usually, one dose will put me out for two days. Two days hasn't been long enough. Every time I wake up, I still wish I hadn't. *Let's see what a dose and a half can do.*

A minute after the liquid enters my bloodstream, my vision blurs and my body goes tingly again. I shove all my supplies back into the silverware box and re-hide it under the bed. Then I climb onto the mattress and lie back to wait for that euphoric feeling to take over.

Once my body finally relaxes and my mind numbs, I close my eyes and bask in the feeling of floating on a cloud.

What's she doing right now? Does she ever think of me? Probably not as much as I think of her. Probably not as fondly either. If she thinks of me, she probably thinks about how scared she was when she woke up and found me in her bed. If I could, I'd turn back time to the moment I saw that recognition in her eyes. I'd figure out how it happened and make sure it stayed that way.

Fuck, I'm thirsty. I should get some water.

I pry my eyes open, then slap my palm over my face. It's so bright in here. Blindingly bright. Where did all this light come from? Did I somehow get transported next to the sun?

My skin tingles, but instead of tingling inside my body, it's tingling *outside* my body. I remove my hand from my face to find an army of little cockroaches no bigger than a thumbtack crawling up my shoulder and over my chest. I swat at them, but they don't go away. It's as if my hand goes straight through them. The little bugs continue crawling over me in a single-file line as if marching to the beat of a drum. Once they reach my other shoulder, they crawl over the bed, then over someone's hand.

I sit up with a jolt. A gorgeous woman has appeared on my sheets. "Arella?"

She's lying on the pillow next to mine, smiling up at me the sweet way she used to.

I gape at her. "What are you doing here?"

She doesn't answer me. Instead, she continues to lie there as the tiny cockroaches crawl over her the way they just did on me. In a single line, they start at one of her shoulders, then march across her chest until they reach the other.

I try to swat the bugs off her, but all my hand catches is air. Why isn't she reacting to them? If she's afraid of spiders, I'd assume she's afraid of tiny roaches too. Also, why did my hand go straight through her body?

"You're not really here, are you?"

Without a word, Arella pats the empty space next to her and gestures for me to lie back down. I do, never taking my eyes off her.

In silence, she caresses the side of my head, around my ear, then down my neck. I close my eyes and melt into the feel of her touch. Even if it's not real, it *feels* real, and that's all that matters.

I wake with a jolt. I'm nauseous as I trudge into the bathroom. When I come back out, my phone tells me three days have passed. Three whole days of feeling nothing. What a treat! And that was after I got to see my girl again. Now *that* was a treat.

I remember most of it. The whole time, she just caressed me. She never said anything. She never left me either. She just lay there, drawing figure eights over my abs. I haven't been that happy since . . . I can't remember. *Wait, actually, I do remember.* It was when she looked up at me like she knew me.

I can't wait to see her again. But first, I need to get something to eat, then I have an errand to run. After all that, I plan to come right back here so I can see my girl.

Since I've got a case of the munchies, it doesn't take me long to inhale the sandwich and bag of chips I get from a little restaurant down the street.

Once my stomach is no longer growling, I head into a souvenir shop to look for a postcard. Hallucinating Arella made me realize I never did the last thing she asked of me.

"Will you send me a postcard from wherever you end up?"

I guess since I have a place in New York now, this qualifies as the place I ended up.

I must stare at the spinning rack of postcards for too long, because a young male clerk comes up behind me and asks, "You need help pickin' one out?"

My problem is when she sees this in her mailbox, I want her to think, *The man who sent me this postcard is the man I'm supposed to be with, instead of the fuckwad I'm currently with.* Sadly, none of these generic pictures of the New York City skyline or the Statue of Liberty say that.

"Sir?"

I snap out of my thoughts. "Um, I can't decide. Could I just get one of each?"

"Sure." With a smile, the clerk plucks one of each postcard off the rack.

Back in my quiet apartment, I sit at my kitchen counter with my stack of postcards and a souvenir pen. I flip through the postcards for almost twenty minutes before deciding on the one that reads, *Greetings from New York City.* It features some artwork of the city's skyline and the iconic statue. No, it doesn't say, *Please come back to me,* but it's colorful and bright, and Arella likes that shit.

I stare at the back of the card for almost an hour before I write.

> ARELLA,
> I ENDED UP IN NEW YORK CITY. IT'S BUSY HERE, AND I THINK YOU'D LIKE THE BEAU-
> TIFUL VIEW FROM MY APARTMENT. ITS BEAUTY REMINDS ME OF YOU. HOPE YOU'RE
> DOING WELL.
> —TREY

I lean back in my barstool to read it. On my third pass, I shout the F word to my bare walls. I wrote her name as Arella without even thinking about it. She's going to get this in the mail and toss it straight into the trash.

I draw a big X through my note, then grab another postcard.

> AR,
> I ENDED UP IN NEW YORK CITY. IT'S BUSY HERE, AND I THINK YOU'D LIKE THE BEAU-
> TIFUL VIEW FROM MY APARTMENT. ITS BEAUTY REMINDS ME OF YOU. HOPE YOU'RE
> DOING WELL.
> —TREY

I sit back to read it over, then draw a big X through my words again. I can't tell her that the beautiful view reminds me of her. That sounds too forward. She'll think I'm still obsessed with her. I mean, I am, but I don't want *her* to know that.

With a long sigh and another postcard, I try again.

> AR,
> I ENDED UP IN NEW YORK CITY. IT'S BUSY HERE. HOPE YOU'RE DOING WELL.
> —TREY

No, no, no. I can't sign my name! What was I thinking? What if her boyfr—no. What if

Caleb sees this before she does and trashes it once he knows it's from me? I've gotta keep my name off it. She'll know who it's from.

> Ari,
> I ENDED UP IN NEW YORK CITY. HOPE YOU'RE DOING WELL.

There. That's good, right?

I read it again, then scowl at the postcard. It's so lame. Nothing about this screams, *I love you*. Most of all, it doesn't scream, *I miss you so much, it hurts*.

86

TREY

I've figured out the perfect concoction to manifest my hallucinations of her and still remember them. I need exactly two bottles of vodka and a dose and a half of jaderro. Anything less than that and she doesn't appear. Anything more and I pass out before I can see her at all.

Whenever I do see her, she never says anything. She just lies there, caressing my face. Sometimes I talk to her. I tell her about the moments we've shared that live in my mind rent free. I tell her how much I miss cooking dinner with her in my kitchen. I tell her how much I used to love seeing her in my shirt that covered everything from her collarbone to her upper thighs. She never responds with anything but a sweet smile. Whenever I'm not talking to her, I just lie back and admire her beauty.

After I wake up from the high, I usually go get a sandwich. Then I write notes on a bunch of postcards I'll never send and fall into another high where I'm happy and get to talk to the only person who's ever truly healed me.

These postcards have turned into a therapeutic exercise. I write things on them I wish I could say to her. Then I shove them into my bedroom drawer and never look at them again.

I've just shoved my most recently written card into that drawer when I drop to my knees to dig under my bed for my supplies. This will be my last high for the week because Liz is coming to visit me for my birthday. Whenever I wake up from this one, I'll have to get my place cleaned up for her and pretend like everything is fine.

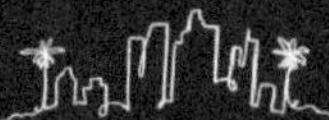

She drops her suitcase onto the floor, then stares at me with her anxiety nipping at my head.

I wait for her to explain why she's looking at me like that. When she still doesn't say anything, I urge her to. "Liz?"

"Oh, T. You're using again." She says it like a statement, not a question.

How the fuck does she know? I feign innocence. "Huh?"

"Don't play dumb with me. Did you forget that you were an addict when we first met? I know what you look like right after a high."

Well, shit. I only woke up a few hours ago. My eyes are probably still sunken, and my skin is probably a little gray.

Liz heads straight to my couch, then pats the space next to her. It's not a suggestion. It's a request. Reluctantly, I join her with my glass of water, feeling like a student in trouble with the principal.

"I'm not mad at you," she says, making it worse. "I just want to know what's going on. How long have you been using?"

I hang my head low as I place my water glass on the coffee table. "Not long."

"How long, T?" Of course, she's not gonna let me off the hook that easily.

I sigh heavily. Lying never works with Liz, so I go with the truth. "I started the week after I came to New York."

Her face screws together. "That was back in November. It's March."

"Yep."

Her jaw drops. "Were you using when I came for Thanksgiving?"

Yes. "Probably."

"Then you were using when I came for Christmas?"

Yes. "Most likely."

"T, why didn't you tell me?"

"Because I knew you'd make me stop. Why do you think I worked so hard to hide this from you?" *Obviously not hard enough.*

"Of course I'm gonna make you stop."

I shake my head. "I don't wanna stop."

"You have to."

"Why?" I say like a whiny child.

"Because it's not good for you."

A scoff. "I don't care what's good for me."

Liz rolls her eyes like that's the dumbest thing she's ever heard. Little does she know, I mean that statement with everything that's left in this dark and lonely hole in my chest.

"Which z-drug is it?"

"Jaderro." There's no use lying now. She already knows. I hate my body for giving her the clues so easily. I was able to hide it during her last two visits. Why couldn't I this time? Is it because I've been using it longer? Is it because I didn't wake up sooner? Is it because my apartment looks like a trash dump?

A sharp gasp leaves Liz's mouth. "Jaderro? T, that shit is the worst of the worst. If you inject even the tiniest bit too much, it can kill you."

I fucking hope so. Although, it hasn't killed me yet, so maybe I'm immune.

Liz scolds me. "Don't do that."

"Do what?"

"Look happy about the thought of dying."

It's not the dying part that would make me happy. It's the part where I could stop living this worthless thing I call my life. The air between us goes stale as my unspoken words stay behind my lips.

"Where is it?" she asks.

"Where's what?"

"Your supply."

I scoff-laugh. "Like I'm gonna tell you."

Before I can stop her, Liz hops onto her feet and storms into my bedroom. I catch her by her waist just as she tears the top drawer of my nightstand open—the drawer where I keep all those handwritten postcards. She doesn't know about those, and I don't want her reading them.

"Put me down!" she shouts as I throw her over my shoulder.

I march out of my bedroom, then wave a hand at the door. The wood slams behind me as I return Liz to the living room.

She smacks my back so hard, it stings. "Put me down, or I'll drench you with a waterball."

This time, I listen. I set her feet onto the carpet, then stand in front of her with my arms crossed. "I'm not letting you in there."

"You can't keep doing this, T."

"I can, and I will. It makes me happy, Liz. Don't you want me to be happy?"

"Of course, but this isn't the way." She doesn't get it. She's never done drugs, so she doesn't know what it's like. She doesn't know how good it feels.

"This *is* the way. It's the *only* way. When I'm high, I'm almost as happy as I was when I was with her." Actually, it's not even close, but it's *something*. And something is better than nothing.

"But this isn't healthy for you. You need to find happiness another way."

I cross my arms over my chest like a challenge. "Fine. How?"

"Come back to LA."

"I can't." *But I want to so fucking bad.*

"Yes, you can." Liz softens her stance. "I miss you, T. The whole band and crew misses you too. It's not the same without you. Our band needs all five of us to function properly. It's not good for you to be alone out here. You need something to do and to surround yourself with people who care about you."

I miss my friends too, but not enough to make me move back. "Nope. Sorry. Can't."

"Like ever?"

"Maybe if she moved out of the state."

"What if she never moves?"

"Then I guess I'm never going back." If I do, it'll be too easy for me to end up sitting in my car outside her apartment, waiting for her to come out, just so I can catch a glimpse of her. Then I'll truly become the stalker she thinks I am.

Liz pouts a little. "When you told us you were leaving, you said it was only for a while. Not forever."

"But here in New York, whenever I get the urge to see her, I'll have a whole plane ride to realize it's a bad idea. Here, I can see her when I'm high and she never looks at me like she doesn't know who I am."

"Wait. You see her? As in, you hallucinate her?"

"Yes, and it feels so real! When she touches me, it's like she's really there. I'm happy again, Liz." I put my hands together like I'm praying. "Please don't take that away from me."

87

TREY

T*wo months later*

"Happy birthday, angel. You're even more beautiful at twenty-three."

Arella responds the way she normally does: with a soft smile and her eyes glued to mine. Her long chestnut hair drapes over her shoulders in loose waves I want to claw my hands into and pull on until she's close enough for me to feel her warm breath on my lips.

I want to touch her, but whenever I do, my hand just falls to the mattress. That's why I usually stick to only looking at and talking to her.

"Sorry I haven't seen you in a while. Liz came to visit last week, and she thinks I quit jaderro last month. Thank fuck she's not a Detector. I probably shouldn't have lied, but she wouldn't get off my back about it. Deep down, I think she knows I haven't quit. How can I, when this is the only way I can see you?"

Arella's hand slides up my chest, leaving behind a trail of tingles. Then she cups my face. I close my eyes and lean into her touch, indulging in how soothing it feels.

"This is all I need to be happy, baby. Just you and me here, where nothing else matters and no one's trying to hurt you or take you away from me."

Her hand stops caressing my face. I open my eyes, and she's gone. *Not again.*

I roll onto my side and throw my feet over the bed. Then I dig out the silverware box and ready my arm for another dose. My little glass jar is almost empty. It's got about a dose left. *Might as well finish it out.* Lately, the jaderro has been wearing off too fast, so I've had to shoot up in the middle of my hallucinations. It's annoying, but you gotta do what you gotta do.

The hallucination returns the same as it always does. First the bright light, then the cockroaches, then she shows up. This time, she stays a little longer than usual. I try to talk to her, but suddenly, the nausea overwhelms me. I lean over the side of my bed just as the vomit rises up my throat. It splatters over my carpet with bright stars and rainbow colors.

I wipe my mouth off with my hand, then turn back around to stare at my girl. Suddenly, she's not the only person I'm seeing anymore. Two people in suits have appeared in my bedroom. One is a woman whose blonde hair has a strip of purple in the front. The other is a man with a goatee. Behind them are more bright lights and neon colors.

"I told you he's getting bad," the woman says. "I really think it's time to intervene."

"But our job is to keep out as much as possible," the man says.

I cock my head at them. "Are you guys real?"

The woman continues like she didn't hear me. "If he proceeds like this, he's going to kill himself. What's more valuable? Keeping out or this?"

The man thinks, then sighs. "You're right. Let's do something."

Usually, Arella can hear me, but she never talks. These people are talking, but they can't hear me. *Strange.* That extra dose is really fucking me up. First the puke, and now two people in suits?

I blink a few times as if it'll reset my vision. Suddenly, a loud *pop!* sound cracks through the air, then the woman disappears. I blink a few more times, and after another loud *pop!,* the man is gone too.

I wake to the sound of something beeping. It's coming from outside my bedroom. *What the hell could be beeping?*

"Could you go check on the patient in six twelve?" a woman asks as the beeping stops. "She pressed her call light again."

Getting my eyes to open feels like trying to pry apart a stubborn mussel shell. Once I succeed, a blurry image of a dim hospital room appears. Cords are attached to my arm.

"Hey, T," someone softly says from my left.

I slowly turn my head to find Liz sitting on a chair at my bedside, with a closed book in her lap. "Where am I?"

"A hospital," Liz says nonchalantly.

"H-how did I get here?"

"Ambulance."

I squint at her. "Did I get into another accident?" I can't see why. I haven't ridden my bike in months. Anywhere I go, I walk. That is, if I go anywhere at all. Lately, I've been getting food delivered because the thought of having to put pants on is daunting. My trash is overflowing with takeout containers and pizza boxes.

Liz chokes up as she says, "T, you almost died."

"What happened?"

"I called you multiple times for two days straight, and when I didn't get a response, I booked the first flight out to New York. I broke my way into your penthouse, which wasn't hard, by the way. You left the front door unlocked. I found you lying on the floor next to a puddle of vomit."

That's odd. I'm usually pretty good about locking my door.

Liz continues, "At first, I tried to shake you awake, but you didn't respond. I exploded into tears, thinking I'd lost you. I hated myself for waiting as long as I did to fly over. When I realized you were still breathing, I called for an ambulance. You've been here for two days while your zoctor has pumped you full of medications I can't even pronounce."

I reach out and gesture for her to give me her hand. She takes her gloves off first, then places one palm into mine. "I'm sorry, Liz. I didn't mean to put you through that."

She falls into a quiet sob, making me feel like the shittiest friend ever. I can't imagine what that was like for her. To rush into my bedroom and find me unmoving on the floor? If it had been me with her, I would have lost my fucking mind.

"I'm so sorry, Liz," I say as if my apology can erase the panic she must have felt.

"T, please be honest with me. Did you overdose with the intent to . . ." She hiccups a tearful breath. "God, I can't even say it."

"I know what you're trying to ask. It's the same thing you wanted to know the last time I was in a hospital, right?"

She nods, wiping her tears off with a few fingers.

I debate lying to save her from the pain, but she can always see through my lies. "Liz, you and her are the only beneficiaries of my will. Everything I have would have been split between you two. That's millions for each of—"

"No! I don't want millions of dollars. I want you!"

I scoot over to one side of the medical bed, then tap the empty space next to me. Without hesitation, Liz climbs up and digs her face into my chest. As I circle my arms around her and pull her close, she cries even harder.

Usually, I'd offer to kick the ass of the person who made her cry. This time, it's me, and I don't know how to handle that. Instead, I give her a soft kiss on her forehead.

"I'm sorry, Liz." I choke up as I kiss her forehead again and silently beg for her to stop crying. "I'm so sorry."

I don't think my apologies are doing anything. Her body is still shaking.

I end up turning two nurses away before her tears finally subside and I can breathe again.

"I can't lose you, Trey."

Wow. She hasn't called me *Trey* in a long-ass time. She only does it when she's being super serious.

"I don't have a family, T. You're all I've got. If I lose you, I won't have anyone."

"You could find a new best friend."

"Not one I can hold hands with. Not one I can have sleepovers with, where they'll hold me all night to keep the nightmares away."

Zordis can't dream, but Liz does. *Sort of.* Technically, they're the horrifying memories she's caught over the years, replaying in her head. It happens whenever she sleeps, and it wakes her up after only two or three hours of rest. Because she never gets enough sleep, she has to sleep every night like an Ordinary.

Back when Liz stayed over for Thanksgiving, we shared my bed. To help her fall asleep, we put on a movie. Normally, we cuddle during movies, so it didn't feel weird to cuddle in my bed while she fell asleep, and when she woke up in the morning, I was still holding her because I didn't want my movement to wake her. She slept through the night—a full seven hours—and she didn't have a single night terror.

The next night, we tried it again. I held her while she slept, and she got another full night of rest without a single replay of anyone's trauma.

When she stayed over for Christmas, we found out that if I left her while she was sleeping, the nightmares crept into her head within a few minutes of my disappearance. But one hundred percent of the time, if I stayed in bed and held her, the nightmares stayed away.

Like how Liz doesn't question how she can touch my hands without seeing my parents get blown up anymore, she doesn't question how this is possible either. There is still so much that Zordis don't understand about our powers.

I'm the only person Liz can touch hands with without seeing their traumatic past. I'm the only person who can keep her nightmares away too. Everything we have has happened over many, many years, and it all happened organically. Now that I think about it, I realize it'd be hard for her to rebuild our friendship with someone else and I'm angry with myself for almost taking that away from her.

Liz tilts her head back to look at me. She's not crying anymore, just hiccupping from the previous cries. "You've always said you'd do anything for me, right?"

I nod, knowing exactly where she's going with this. She's gonna try to convince me to go sober again.

"Remember when we first met and how I encouraged you to be sober?"

"Yep. You said there's a better version of me who exists under the drug habits and fistfights."

"Um, sure. That's not how I remember it, but if that's what you heard that got you to clean up, then sure. Either way, the point is that you quit the drugs cold turkey. If you did it once, you can do it again. The thing is that I can't just encourage you to quit. You have to *want* to quit. The only thing I can do is say things to help you want it."

"Lemme guess." I lean back a little to see more of her. "You're gonna say I need to quit so I can be here to help you keep the nightmares away?"

"Nope. Guess again."

Outside my hospital room, that beeping sound chimes again. I ignore the commotion. "You're gonna tell me there's still that better version of me beneath the drugs?"

"Closer."

I think hard. "You're gonna say this isn't the man I want to be?"

Liz smiles up at me. "Even closer."

"I'm done guessing. Just tell me."

"I was gonna say this isn't the man *she* would want you to be."

That slams me right in the gut. I wasn't expecting Liz to say that, because she normally avoids bringing Arella up. Liz doesn't mind when *I* bring her up, because that means I'm choosing to talk about her. But Liz avoids mentioning her so I don't get that "sad and depressing look in my eyes."

I swallow hard. "She doesn't know me well enough to have an opinion on who she wants me to be."

"No, T. I'm not talking about Ari. I'm talking about Arella. Ari doesn't know you, but Arella does. You've said it yourself: Your girl is still in there somewhere. If she saw you now, what would she think?"

If Arella saw the terrible things I've done in the last six months, she'd be so disappointed in me. Getting wasted in bars until they kick me out, shooting poison up my arm, barely eating or doing basic things like drinking water or combing my hair. I've lost so much weight, my cheeks are sinking in. The thing is, though, Arella's not around to see me, which is why I don't care what type of man I am.

Liz continues in her same gentle tone, "If she suddenly reverted back to remembering you and came looking for you, how would it make her feel to find you like this? Is this the man you want her running back to?"

"But she's *not* running back to me, Liz. She's not even *walking* to me."

"But what if she was?"

88

ARI

O*ne year later*

"WHERE ARE WE GOING?" I ASK FROM THE PASSENGER SEAT OF JAVINA'S CAR. THE AIR conditioning is on high to combat the intense heat from the early afternoon sun. I turn the vents to face me.

"I told you already," Javina says as she makes a left turn. "We're going to a softball game."

"Really?" When she said that earlier, I thought she was joking. Javina does that sometimes. She likes to answer questions with the wrong answer. Like yesterday, when I asked her what book she's currently reading, she said, "It's called *101 Ways to Kill Your Best Friend and Get Away with It*." I just rolled my eyes and moved on. "Why are we going to a softball game?"

"I was gonna surprise you, but I'll just tell you. I entered a contest where if I won, me and a plus-one got to be extras in a music video. And guess what? I won!"

"No way!" Now I see why she told me to dress nicely. "What exactly does being an extra mean?"

"Don't worry, babes. There's not a lot of acting involved. Our only job is to sit on the bleachers and cheer."

A while later, Javina pulls into the parking lot of a softball field. The scorching June sun beats down on my skin as I exit her red Corolla. A pair of giggly young women in skimpy skirts strolls past us toward a table featuring a sign that reads, EXTRAS. CHECK IN HERE.

"Did the email say if we'd have a chance to meet the band?" the woman with pink hair asks.

"Nope," her friend says. "But I don't care. I'm not leaving here without a picture with Trey Grant."

I whip my attention to Javina. "Excuse me?"

She grits her teeth together with a guilty smile. "Oh, um, did I forget to mention that this video shoot is for a band called Flames in the Night?"

I meet her at the trunk of her car and slap her shoulder. "No, you didn't mention that, because that's something a *good* friend would have done. Why didn't you tell me that important piece of information?"

"Because then you wouldn't have come. Duh."

Actually, I would have. I've been suppressing this deep urge inside me to see Trey again for the past year and seven months. *Not that I've been counting . . .*

I still see him a few times a week in my dreams. Some dreams have repeated so often, I've memorized them. Like the dream where Trey is lying on the floor of a gas station office with a gash in his thigh so deep, I can see the inside of his leg.

Every time I have that dream, it happens the same: Trey always says, "I'll only slow you down. I'll probably bleed out anyway. Just forget about me and get outta here." I always fight with him until he allows me to bandage his wound, and then I help him stand and we drive away from the gas station in someone else's car.

In my free time, I've been doing research on dreams and what they could mean. The best explanation I could find to explain Trey almost dying in my dreams is that I'm afraid of losing him. But how can I be afraid of losing someone I don't have?

Javina takes my hand and leans into me with a low voice. "Look, Ari, you can be mad at me all you want, but I've been in love with this band for years. You know that Rachel and I were going to their shows almost once a month until they went on tour. Now they're back, and they're filming videos again.

"They don't ask for extras often. The two times they did in the past, I didn't win an invitation. Now I finally did! I know this must be weird for you, given the whole thing where he came from an alternate universe and thought you were his girlfriend, but could you please pretend like that didn't happen for a day and just enjoy this with me?"

"I'm not mad at you, Javie."

She leans back with her brows knitted together. "You're not?"

"No. I just would have appreciated a heads-up."

"Oh. In that case . . ." She flashes me a cheesy smile. "Hey, babes. Just so you know, we're gonna go be extras in a music video that Trey Grant's band is filming."

I roll my eyes. "Gee, thanks. I'm so glad you told me that *ahead of time* so I could mentally prepare to see the man who's been starring in my dreams for a year and a half."

"You're *still* having dreams about him?"

"They haven't stopped."

I finally told Javina about my dreams a few months ago because I wanted to get her opinion on them. Her crazy theory is that my dreams aren't dreams. She thinks they're Alterella's memories. Somehow, I knew she was going to say that.

Caleb still doesn't know about my dreams, and I don't plan to tell him. I don't want him reading into them as something with a deeper meaning. Despite what Javina says, I still think they're just dreams. At least, that's what I'm telling myself.

After we get checked in, we're ushered toward a set of bleachers facing a small diamond field. Javina and I have two seats smack-dab in the middle of the stands. Within ten minutes, the bleachers are full of other extras. The crew gave us blue pom-poms to wave. The bleachers on the other side of the field are full too, except the extras there have red pom-poms.

The Black woman who checked us in earlier stands in front of our bleachers with a microphone. "Hello, everyone! I'm Monique, the band's manager. Thank you for coming."

The crowd cheers with hoots and hollers.

"I love the enthusiasm! Two things before we get started: First, there is to be no video recording or pictures taken during the filming of this video. If any of the crew catches you with your phone out, you'll be asked to leave. No exceptions.

"Second, many of you have already asked me if there will be a photo opportunity with the band. The answer is yes. After we film all the scenes we need, anyone who wants to get a photo can line up on the other side of this dugout." Monique gestures toward the red team's dugout. A bunch of people wearing red jerseys are sitting in it. None of them are Trey. "Any questions?"

When no one raises their hand, Monique says, "Great. Now I'd like you to meet Mateo, the video director." She gestures toward the short Hispanic guy leaning against the fence. A Giants baseball cap covers his curly brown hair.

Mateo steps forward and takes the microphone from Monique. "Hey, hey! I'm excited to be here, and I need you to be excited too. Your only job today is to give us high energy. The band will be acting out a few rehearsed scenes on the field with some hired actors. I need you to act like you're at a real softball game. When someone on the blue team makes it on base, you cheer! When someone on the blue team scores a run, you scream! When anyone on the red team does that, you boo 'em. Got it?"

The people on my bleachers let out a high-pitched *whoo!* in unison. Javina is one of them. I shout out a loud *yes!*

"Awesome!" Mateo says. "The last scene we're filming today is of Trey scoring the winning home run. His job today is to actually hit a ball that far. Since that could take a few tries, we'll need you to be on your toes for that. The second he hits the ball out of the park, we need you on your feet, going wild. Can ya do that?"

The extras scream out again. Javina and I join them with cheers and claps.

"That's the energy I want!" Mateo says. "We'll begin this shoot in ten minutes."

With a wave goodbye, Mateo and Monique head toward the away team's bleachers. Once there, they give the away team a similar speech. Eventually, Monique heads back toward the parking lot while Mateo steps up to home plate.

A rumble of chatter comes from the home team's dugout. Unfortunately, I can't see any of the players from where I'm at. I'm anxious to see what Trey looks like now. Does he look the same? Different? Older? I've kept away from cyberstalking him, even though I want to often. I don't because I don't feel like I have any business doing that. But now that I'm here, my curiosity is flying through the roof.

The chatter in the dugout fades as a bunch of people wearing blue jerseys runs out onto the field. The fans on both bleachers cheer for them. The players I recognize are the ones in Trey's band. The drummer and bass guitarist head toward the outfield as the band's pianist trots toward first base. Then there's Liz. She heads to home plate, wearing catcher's gear. Still no Trey though. A guy from the red team carrying a baseball bat over his shoulder joins Liz at home plate, completing the scene to look like a real softball game.

Mateo glances around, then gestures toward the empty pitcher's mound. "Where the hell is pretty boy?"

Liz says something to the director, but it's not loud enough for me to catch it.

Javina leans over to me and whispers, "Apparently, I'm not the only person who calls him *pretty boy.*"

"I'm right here," a deep sultry voice says, making my heart spark with heat.

Trey steps out of the closed-off concession stand wearing a blue jersey, dark jeans, and a baseball cap. My breath gets caught in my throat, and my hands are suddenly sweaty. I didn't expect my body to react like this at the mere sight of him.

The two giggly women at the front of the bleachers cheer for Trey as he jogs to meet with the video director at home plate.

Mateo says stuff I can't hear as he gestures toward the field. In unison, Trey, Liz, and the batter nod their understanding.

Since Trey's facing away from me, I can't get a good look at his face, but I can get a good look at his back, and it's not a sight to complain about. His body fills out his jersey in all the right places. GRANT is printed in big block letters over his thick shoulders. *Has he always been that muscular?*

"Pretty boy looks like he's been goin' to the gym," Javina says with a waggle of her eyebrows.

"Okay, people!" Mateo says into the mic as Liz kneels behind home plate and Trey jogs over to the pitcher's mound. "Let's do this! Cameras ready?"

The three guys with heavy cameras on their shoulders nod.

"Action!"

Once the batter is in position, Trey underhand throws the ball to him. The batter swings and misses. They do a few takes of this until the batter finally makes contact with the ball. It barrels toward left field as the people on the away team's bleachers make some noise.

The band's drummer races toward the ball and catches it in his glove with ease. The people in my bleachers pop up to cheer. I join them, waving my pom-poms in the air.

The next batter is a woman with her long blonde hair in a ponytail sticking out of her helmet. Trey pitches her the ball. She hits it, drops her bat, then runs until she makes it to second base. The red team cheers from the dugout as the fans on their bleachers do the same. Everyone on my side shouts out some boos.

An hour later, my throat is sore. I've never seen the filming of a music video before, so I didn't realize how much work goes into these things. They have to film things over and over again until they get the right shot.

During the scene where Liz has to slide home, they make her do it fifteen times before the director is satisfied with how the dirt looks as it kicks up behind her. I never would have thought little things like that mattered so much.

This whole time, Trey hasn't looked my way once. I don't think he knows I'm here. Javina mentioned that all the coordination to be here came from the band's manager. I doubt anyone from the actual band is part of that process.

I keep obsessing over what's going to happen when Trey does see me. Is he going to want to talk to me? If so, what will he say? What will *I* say? I'm not sure if I even want to talk to him. I mean, I do, but I don't. What if it's awkward? What if it ends badly? Or worse, what if he pretends like we don't know each other and just ignores me the whole time? I think that will hurt the most, even though it shouldn't. I shouldn't *want* to talk to him as much as I do, but I do. I shouldn't think about him as much as I do either, but I do.

"Last scene!" Mateo's voice booms over the speakers a while later. "Six-pack, you know what you gotta do?"

Trey nods from his position at home plate as he practices swinging his bat. "Hit a homer, run around the bases, get water dumped over my head."

"Exactly. Easy peasy, lemon squeezy. We'll all be home in no time."

Trey chuckles from deep in his belly. It's a laugh I've heard in my dreams but never in real life. Hearing it makes my insides flutter. "You've got more faith in me than I do, Mateo. You saw how I did during rehearsal yesterday. I couldn't hit a home run to save my life."

"Yeah, but now you've got loads of people watching. I'm hoping the pressure will whip you into shape. Aaand action!"

A guy wearing red on the pitcher's mound readies himself, then tosses the ball toward home plate. Trey swings and misses, then shakes his head at himself.

"You've got this, Willie Mays!" Mateo shouts with his hands cupped around his mouth. "Let's try that again."

A woman on the side of the field throws the pitcher a new ball. He catches it in his glove, then readies himself again as Trey raises his bat into the air. When the pitcher releases the ball, Trey swings, and it's another strike.

"Try again," Mateo says.

Trey strikes out with the next ball.

And the next.

And the next.

"Come on, Pete Rose!" Mateo says. "You can do this!"

Trey chuckles beautifully. "I'm telling ya, man, I think my bat is broken."

Mateo puts the microphone up to his lips. "Let's pump him up, guys! Trey! Trey! Trey!"

Everyone in the bleachers, even the red side, joins in on Mateo's chant.

Javina throws her fist into the air each time she shouts his name. I cup my palms around my mouth and chant too.

Trey shakes his head at the crowd as he gestures for everyone to calm down. "Thanks, but I think this might be faster if someone else hits a home run and we just edit the person to look like me in post."

"No can do, buddy-boy," Mateo says. "We need this shot to look as authentic as possible. Now channel your inner Babe Ruth and knock this shit outta the park."

The giggly woman with the pink hair cups her mouth. "If you hit this next one, my friend will let you take her out on a date."

The friend playfully slaps the woman with pink hair on her shoulder. "Caitlyn!"

Trey turns to offer the ladies a warm smile. "Thanks for the encouragement, but I—"

His eyes lock with mine, then his smile drops. The world stills as he stares at me, mouth partly open. His intense gaze from those blue-grays steals my breath away. He's blinking at me like he's not sure if I'm real.

In the corner of my eye, I see the giggly women turn around to find out what he's gaping at. A few others whip their heads around too. Then suddenly, everyone's staring at me, making me want to curl into a turtle shell.

Trey rubs his eyes with his fingers, then glances back at me. We lock gazes again, and I almost wave at him as a peace offering. Before I get the chance to, he tears his attention off me.

With a shaky voice, he calls out, "Liz?"

She runs to him from the dugout. "What's wrong, T?"

He grips her forearm and says something to her I can't make out. Whatever he says, it makes her turn to look at the bleachers. When she catches sight of me, her eyes go wide, then she turns back to Trey. She says something in a low voice. He responds by sucking in a deep breath and nodding back.

Javina nudges my arm with her elbow. "I think they're talking about you."

I'm speechless. *I think so too.*

89

TREY

Like the bestest friend a man can have, Liz rushes to me as soon as I call out for her. "What's wrong, T?" she asks.

I grip her arm to steady myself as I lean toward her ear. "I swear to you, I haven't done drugs for over a year, but I think I'm hallucinating right now."

"What?"

My lungs feel full of shrapnel as I prepare to hear her tell me I'm losing it. "I see *her*. In the bleachers."

Liz turns to glance behind me, then her eyes go wide and she lowers her voice. "You're not hallucinating. I see her too. Are you okay?"

I draw in a deep breath of relief and nod. It's good to know I'm not hallucinating. "Did you know she was gonna be here?"

"Nope. Do you want me to get Monique to ask her to leave?"

"No." *Absolutely not.* I don't know why she's here, but I've been dying to see her. Whatever force of nature brought her here today, I'm grateful for it.

"Then do you think you can hit us a home run so we can all go home sometime, oh, I dunno . . . today?"

"Yeah, I'll try to pull myself together."

"I believe in you, T." With that, Liz returns to the dugout.

I resist the urge to glance back at the bleachers—at *her*. Instead, I suck in a long breath and slowly let it out.

I do it again.

Then again.

My zerapist told me that deep breathing can be helpful when I feel like I can't control my emotions. I need it to work right now. Otherwise, Liz is right and we'll be here all day.

If I had known Arella was in the stands this whole time, I would have tried harder to hit this homer. Now I'm determined to nail the next one.

"You good?" Mateo asks.

"Yep," I lie, then raise my bat into the air.

He flashes the cameramen two thumbs up. "Action!"

The pitcher readies himself, then underhands the ball to me. I eye the ball as it hurls toward me. Then I swing.

Crack!

My bat hits the ball just right, and the ball flies through the air until it lands on the other side of the fence. As the crowd goes wild, I go for a run around the bases. At home plate, someone dumps water over my head as my fake softball team surrounds me with cheers and slaps on the back.

The cameramen rush over to film our celebration, reminding me that I'm supposed to be smiling. *I can't look at her. I can't look at her.*

Once Mateo gets all the footage he needs, he calls out, "That's a wrap!"

Monique grabs the microphone from him. "Thank you, everyone! Extras, if you'd like a picture with the band, please line up behind this dugout."

Liz hands me a white towel as the people around me disperse. "I knew you could do it."

"I had to once I knew *she* was watching." I dry off the back of my neck, then my hair.

"She and her friend are getting into the picture line. Do you think you can handle that?"

"Probably not, but I'll do my best."

I spend the next twenty-some minutes taking pictures with fans and mentally preparing myself to see her again. What I don't mentally prepare for is not seeing her at all. When Javina appears from the other side of the dugout, she struts her way onto the field—alone.

Excited energy radiates off her as she hands her phone to Monique. We all smile for the camera, Javina says a few words of praise to my bandmates, then she leaves. The entire time, I hold my tongue back from asking her where Arella is. As the next person in line steps out, I feel Liz's eyes on me.

She mouths, "You okay?"

I only stare at her because I don't know the answer to that. Why didn't Arella come out? Where did she go? Did she not want to see me? That last thought hurts the most because I wanted to see her more than anything. Even if we didn't speak to each other, it would have made me happy just to *see* her. To get a better view of what she looks like now. To hear if she still sounds the same. Maybe I could have wrapped my arm around her shoulder for the three seconds it takes for Monique to snap a photo.

The next smiles I make feel harder to fake. Once the band is done meeting with the last person in line, I glance behind the dugout for her. She's not there. A heavy stone sinks into my stomach as I force my feet into the concession stand, where I've left all my things. The rest of the band's stuff is in here too. Otherwise, it's vacant. My bandmates are still out there, chatting with some fans who have stuck around.

I focus on sucking in deep breaths as I drag my semi-dry jersey over my head and slip into a black V-neck. Then I brace my hands against the wall and try to gather myself.

Deep breath in. Slow breath out.

Deep breath in. Slow breath out.

This deep-breathing bullshit isn't working. What else has my zerapist taught me to help control my panic attacks? I can't remember them right now. What good can those methods do me if I can't fucking remember them? Maybe I should get them tattooed onto my inner left forearm, next to the other tattoo I got recently.

Suddenly, the door pops open.

"How ya doing, T?"

I push away from the wall and plaster on a face that will make Liz think I'm not breaking down. "I'm trying not to look into it too much."

"That she didn't come to meet the band?"

"Yeah," I say somberly as my gaze dips to my feet.

"How do you feel about that?"

Devastated. Destroyed. Incinerated by a hundred fireballs. "When I look at it from her point of view, I understand. What reason does she have to see me? If I had to guess, I'm gonna say Javina dragged her here without her knowing it."

"I'm sorry, T. Do you think you can keep it together for just a little longer? There are two very eager fans standing outside, waiting for you."

"What do they want?"

"They asked if they could get a picture with just you. I told them I'd ask you first. If you don't think you can handle it, I can tell them to leave."

I draw in a long breath, then let it out. "I think I can handle that."

Liz places a gentle gloved hand over my forearm. "You are welcome to break down all you want when we get home, okay? We can order pizza and do whatever you need to feel better."

I pull her in for a firm hug. "Thanks, Liz. I love you so much."

Something I've been working on with my zerapist is getting over my fear of saying *I love you.* Through many, many, *many* sessions together, my zerapist concluded that one of my biggest regrets is not telling Arella sooner that I loved her. Now I make it a point to tell Liz whenever I think of it, because someday, I may not get the chance to.

"I love you too, T-Bear." Liz stands on her toes to place a short kiss on my cheek, just as the door opens.

Kevin, our bass guitarist, freezes and stares at us, wide-eyed as the door shuts behind him. His emotions match his expression. "Uh, did I just see somethin' I shouldn't have?"

"You're good, Kev," Liz says with a nonchalant wave of her hand.

"Um, okaaay?" He looks like he's about to ask a question, then he puts his arms up in surrender. "You know what? It ain't my business."

Liz and I kiss each other in private all the time. Usually, she kisses my cheek and I kiss her hand or her forehead. It's not romantic, but if someone doesn't understand the type of relationship Liz and I have, I'm sure they think otherwise.

With all the rumors that have been spreading online about Liz and me lately, catching us in a private moment like that probably makes Kevin think those rumors are true. I don't care enough to say otherwise. I've never felt the need to explain my relationship with Liz, and I'm not about to start now.

I grab my duffel bag, then head toward the door. "I'ma go take a picture with those fans, 'kay?"

"When you're done, come back to get me," Liz says.

"Yes, Mom," I say, because she hates it when I call her that.

Liz rewards my nickname for her with an eyeroll.

As I step out of the concession stand, two women approach me with thrilled yet flustered energy.

"Trey," Pink Hair Girl says.

"Hi, ladies." I don't bother with faking a smile, because I'm gonna have to when I take the photos with them. I only have so much energy for faking it. "Liz told me you guys want a picture."

"Yes, please."

I set my bag to the side, then place an arm around Pink Hair Girl's shoulders first. Her friend snaps a photo, then they switch places and I fake smile again.

"These look great!" the brunette says as she checks the pictures.

I don't bother looking because I don't care.

"So," Pink Hair Girl says, "I told you earlier that if you hit the next ball, my friend would let you take her out on a date. You must have really wanted that date."

The brunette flashes me a hopeful smile.

I slap a hand over my chest. "Sorry, ladies. I'm seeing someone right now."

Their faces drop. "You are?"

I nod as convincingly as I can. "Yep."

"Like, is it serious?" Pink Hair Girl asks.

"Pretty serious."

"Who is it?"

"I can't say. We're, um, keeping things private."

"It's Liz, isn't it?" the brunette says. "It's gotta be Liz."

I could have guessed they'd say that. Our fans seem to think that it's impossible for two people as close as Liz and me to be single for this long and not fuck each other. To me, what's actually impossible is the idea of having meaningful intimacy with anyone but Arella. "No, it's not Liz."

"Are you sure? Because we could have sworn we just saw you two kissing when Kevin opened that door."

Of course they saw that. "Is there anything else I can do for you ladies? If not, I've gotta get going."

Disappointment slams into their guts as they shove their phones back into their pockets. "Thanks for the picture, Trey."

"You're welcome. Have a good night." I toss my duffel bag over my shoulder, then open the concession stand door. Kevin is sitting on a chair, typing on his phone. Liz is tying up her shirt in the front.

"You ready?" I ask.

"Just a sec." Liz spends a minute switching her sneakers out for some heels, then gathers all her things into her bag. " 'Kay. Ready."

Together, we head toward the half-empty parking lot. Most of the crew is gone already. Some guys are still around, cleaning and packing up the equipment. Those two women I took pictures with are climbing into their car. I just told them that Liz and I aren't dating, yet here we are, walking to her car together, about to go home together. Sometimes, I can see why people write shit about us.

Liz and I pass a few more vehicles before we come across the trunk of one with the hood up. It's a red Toyota Corolla I've seen many times before.

"It's just a blown fuse," Javina says from behind the hood. "This happens all the time."

"All the time?" Arella says in her *are you serious?* voice.

"Once I change the fuse, this baby will be just fine again."

"Does that mean we need to go get you a new fuse?"

"Nah." Javina's footsteps round the front of her car to the passenger side. "This happens so often, I've got a stash in the glove—oh, hey, guys."

"Everything okay?" Liz asks as her heels stop clicking against the pavement.

I stop behind her with my chest pounding and my mouth dry.

"We're fine," Javina says. "My car does this thing where sometimes, this one fuse will blow and it keeps the prindle in park. Until I change the fuse, there ain't no movin' it."

Arella peeks her head out from behind the hood, and we lock eyes again. I lose my breath. She's much more beautiful in real life than she is in my hallucinations. Gone is that bright light that's always shining behind her, those stupid cockroaches, the occasional rainbow stars, and those people in suits.

Arella's long chestnut waves cascade down her ribs the way they always have. She still has those same angelical features and the same eyes that mesmerize me in every way. The only thing that's different about her is that she looks slightly older.

I resist the urge to grab her, to bring her into my chest and squeeze her and tell her that I'm still deeply in love with her and—

"Dammit!" Javina says as she finishes digging through her glove box, pulling out an empty plastic container. "I'm all out of fuses. Ari, could you call us an Uber?"

Arella snaps out of our little staring contest. "Sure. Where to?"

"Wherever the closest auto parts shop is."

Liz perks up. "I could drive you."

Javina's grin looks like the one she gave me when I treated her to a spa day years ago. "You would do that?"

"Of course. It'll be faster than waiting around for an Uber."

"That'd be great! Thank you." Javina turns to her best friend. "You wanna chill here while I go real quick?"

"Um . . ." Arella locks eyes with me again as I silently plead for her to say *yes*.

Liz butts in before Arella can come to a decision. "Trey will stay back with you and keep you company, won't you, T?"

Silently, I nod, trying not to look as eager as I feel. Then I realize it's rude to assume Arella even *wants* me to keep her company, so I clear my throat and add, "If that's what *you* want."

Arella smiles as her cheeks pinken. "Sure."

It's not an enthusiastic *yes*, but I'll take it.

90

ARI

I plant myself on a bench while Trey drops his duffel bag onto the ground. Then he joins me on my right, sitting as far away as possible. I'm not sure if it's because he wants to have distance between us or if he thinks it's what I want.

To say my heart is working in overdrive is to say the least. It's pounding so hard, I can practically hear it. Neither of us says anything as we stare at the parking lot, where Liz and Javina just drove out. I have so many things I want to ask him; however, I'm not sure if I *should* ask them.

Trey sucks in a deep breath through his nose, then slowly lets it out through his mouth.

Then he does it again.

And again.

I should probably say something before he passes out. "That was an impressive home run you hit."

He flashes me a warm smile that contradicts the gloom in his eyes. "Thanks."

"I didn't know you knew how to play softball."

His attention drops to his hands in his lap. "That's because you don't really know much about me at all."

He's right, and he's wrong. I know *some* things about him. Probably not as much as Alterella knows.

"I played baseball with my—" He blows out a ragged breath. "I played baseball when I was a kid. Softball is similar enough. Don't be too impressed though. That's the first time I've ever hit a ball that far. It'll probably never happen again, so I hope the camera guys got a good shot of it."

"Grant!" a man in Trey's crew calls as he heads toward a black SUV. "That was one hell of a homer!"

Trey plasters a fake smile onto his face. I know it's fake because it looks different from the genuine ones I've been seeing in my dreams. "Thanks, man."

The SUV's headlights brighten as the crew member unlocks his car, then gets in and takes off.

I run my fingers through my hair before pulling all my loose waves to one shoulder. "I'm glad I came. I had a lot of fun."

"Can I assume that Javina dragged you here without telling you why?"

"That's exactly what happened." I chuckle and flash him a small smile, hoping he'll return it.

He doesn't.

A silent moment sits between us before I ask, "When did you move back to LA?"

"I didn't. I fly in every Thursday to do band stuff and leave on Sundays."

If he has to fly, that means he's living somewhere pretty far. "Where do you live now?"

"New York City."

That's the biggest city in the states that's as far away from me as possible. Is that why he chose it? "Living in New York sounds expensive."

"It is. Especially since I live in a penthouse I never wanted."

"That sounds fancy. I bet all the dates you bring home are impressed by that."

He shrugs a shoulder as he stares at his dirty shoes. "I wouldn't know. I've never brought home a date."

"Oh. Are you one of those guys who keeps all his dates outside the home?"

"No, I'm just a guy who doesn't go on dates."

I tilt my head to the side with an *oh, come on* smile. "With a face like yours in a big city like New York, do you really expect me to believe you have a hard time finding a date?"

He shrugs one shoulder again. "I wouldn't know. I haven't tried. The only girl who's ever been inside my apartment is Liz. And the first time she ever saw it, she was *not* impressed."

"Why? Do you have a bad view?"

"The view is fine. It was the lack of any furniture whatsoever."

"Why didn't you have any furniture?"

He plays with his hands in his lap. "I had just moved in the day before—but don't tell her that. She thinks I'd already been living there for two weeks."

I'm about to ask why he would lie about something like that, but the question I actually want to ask comes out instead. "So you and Liz finally got together, huh?"

That makes him tear his eyes from his hands and look at me with furrowed brows. "What?"

"You and Liz. I'm happy for you," I say as convincingly as I can. "Friends-to-lovers is one of the best romantic relationships you can have because you guys already know each other so well."

I picture them together and try not to feel jealous. I have no reason to feel jealous, but I do.

"Wait," Trey says. "I'm confused. What makes you think I'm with Liz?"

Now it's my turn to stare at my hands. "I, um, I was waiting for Javina outside the bathrooms when I overheard you telling those two women that you're seeing someone. I heard them say they saw you and Liz kissing."

"Did you also overhear me tell 'em I'm not seeing Liz like that?"

"Yeah, but I thought you lied because you want to keep your relationship with her private."

"I lied to those girls about seeing someone because I recently figured out if I tell people I'm taken, they'll leave me alone faster than if I tell them *no*. Liz is just my best friend. Nothing more."

I side-eye him. "Best friends who kiss?"

"Not on the lips. Now *that* would be weird." He makes a genuine *ick* face that makes me *almost* believe him.

"Javina said she saw something online about how you two live together now. Is that true?"

"Kind of. I stay at Liz's place whenever I'm in LA."

If he's in LA every Thursday and doesn't leave until Sundays, that means he lives with Liz for half the week. That's living together, if you ask me. "What happened to your house?"

"I sold it to Marcus and Emmy, our drummer and pianist. They were looking for a place together, and I was looking to get rid of mine, so I sold it to them for almost nothing, furniture and everything else included. The only things I took back were my clothes and some other personal belongings, which are now in a storage tub at Liz's house."

If his house is the one I keep seeing in my dreams, then . . . "Wow. That sounds like an amazing deal."

"It was a win for both sides. They needed a house, and I couldn't step foot into mine anymore without—" His face falls as he circles his thumbs around each other. "Anyway, I was happy to give it to them straight up, but they insisted on paying *something* for it. Kevin did the same with my car. I wanted to just give it to him, but he insisted on paying *something*."

That was nice of Trey to sell his house and car to his friends for a low price. "So if you aren't seeing anyone and you're not going on any dates, then what have you been up to for the past year and a half?"

He takes a moment to think before he says, "When I first moved to New York, I spent the first six months being a bum until Liz convinced me to get my shit together. She said I needed to do three things: come back to the band, get some hobbies, and see a therapist regularly. So I guess that's what I've been doing.

"My band finished our second original album, and we just got back from tour last month. Now we're working on filming new content for our YouTube channel. At the end of July, we'll go back to playing our regular weekend shows at the Soul House."

"It sounds like you're staying busy," I say. "How do you have any time for your hobbies?"

"I have more than enough time. I go to the gym Mondays through Wednesdays. I read while I'm on the plane. When I stay over at Liz's, we watch movies. We're currently going through all the Disney canon films in order. She thought it was weird that the only Disney movie I'd ever seen was *The Lion King*. *Mulan* was last week. *Tarzan* is tonight."

"So those are the hobbies you chose? Working out, reading, and Disney movies?"

"I guess so." He kicks a small rock, and it skips across the ground. "Do you have any suggestions for something else I could be doing?"

"What are your interests?" I ask, even though I feel like that's something I should already know about him.

"Making music," he says without hesitation. "That's about it."

"What part of the music-making process do you enjoy the most?"

"Probably the writing and producing part."

"Maybe you could write and produce for other artists?"

He stares off into the distance and slowly nods. "Yeah. Maybe I could."

I pull my leg up onto the bench and turn to face him more. "Do you like it in New York?"

"It's all right."

"What made you pick New York?"

He goes quiet as he ponders that. His eyes stay glued to the ground as he says, "I'm not sure if I picked New York. I think New York picked me."

"Does that mean you've found your *place in the world*?"

He doesn't waste a second to say, "No."

"But you've been living there for over a year."

"That doesn't mean I feel like I belong there."

A group of Trey's crew members leave the softball field and wave at him as they get into their cars and leave. Now the only car left in the lot is Javina's, with the hood still up.

Trey keeps his eyes on the little rocks at his feet like they're the most mesmerizing things in sight. Why is it so hard for him to look at me while I feel like I can't take my eyes off him? I notice everything he does and doesn't do. Like the way his hands fidget like he's itching to touch me. The way he steals glances at me whenever I'm not looking directly at him. It's like he doesn't want me to see all that sadness in his eyes. I've even noticed the way he's purposely speaking softly as if he's trying not to scare me away. Little does he know, I've been anticipating the day we'd meet again. There's a question I've been dying to ask him.

"I never got your postcard." That didn't come out as a question the way I intended it to. Still, I hope this will open up the conversation about the one thing that's been running laps through my mind since he disappeared from my life.

Trey doesn't respond. Instead, his face falls. Even from the side, I don't miss the way his eyes turn more gray than blue.

"Did you forget my address?"

"No," he says somberly.

"Did you not have a stamp?"

"No."

"Could you not find any postcards?"

He still doesn't look at me. "I bought a few for you. I even wrote a message."

He actually wrote a card for me? Why didn't I receive it? I made sure to check the mail every day before Caleb could. "Maybe it got lost in the mail."

Trey bites his lip as he shakes his head. "It didn't. I—I never sent it."

"Oh." I try not to look disappointed. "Did you forget?"

"No."

"Oh." I want to ask what happened, but I don't know how to do that without suggesting I've been waiting for his postcard since the moment he left my front stoop. Every day, I checked the mail, thinking, *Today will be the day*. It never was.

Finally, he glances over at me with an ocean of anguish on his face—his gorgeous, I-want-to-touch-it-so-badly face. "I'm sorry I never sent you a postcard."

"Why didn't you?"

"I . . ." His gaze falls back to his lap, where his hands are fidgeting again. "I dunno. I just couldn't do it."

"What stopped you?"

"Anything and everything. The idea that what I wrote wasn't good enough. The idea that Caleb would see it before you and he wouldn't give it to you. The idea that even if you did get it, you'd just read it once and throw it away. Should I go on?"

It sounds like he overthought this so much to the point where it debilitated him from doing it at all.

"What did the postcard say?" I ask, trying not to sound like I'm dying to know.

"Which one? The first one or the hundredth one?"

My jaw drops. "You wrote on a hundred postcards for me?"

"It's probably closer to two hundred now."

"And you couldn't send just *one*?"

"I didn't think it mattered to you. Honestly, I'm surprised you even remember asking me for a postcard. I figured as soon as I left that day, you haven't thought of me since."

I've thought about you every day. Those words get stuck in my throat because I shouldn't be saying things like that to him. Nor should I be asking, "Do you ever think of me?"

He scoff-laughs. "Does the sun rise?"

Yes. "How often would you say you think of me?"

He gazes at me with such a deep and intense look that my lungs forget how to function. I don't tear my attention away from him as he communicates his answer to me through his unblinking eyes and silent lips.

I tell him I received his wordless answer by nodding my acceptance of it. I'd like to tell him that I probably think about him just as often, but I don't know how.

"I'll try to send you a postcard when I get back to New York," he says.

"I'd really appreciate that."

Just then, a silver Malibu pulls into the lot next to Javina's car. Liz steps out first, then Javina. They have good timing, because the tension between Trey and me was getting hard to handle.

Silently, Trey and I meet our friends at Javina's open hood.

"Did you get a new fuse?" I ask Javina, feeling Trey's stare on my back.

"Lots," Javina says. "I got a snack too. Can you hold this?" She hands me a plastic shopping bag with some chips and a root beer in it, then works to get a fuse out of its package.

With the bag in my hands, I smile at Liz. "Thanks for giving Javina a ride."

Liz offers me a warm smile back. "No problem. There's an auto shop not too far from here, so it didn't take long. Plus, Javina bought me a snack too."

After Javina pries the old fuse out with her pliers, she sticks in a new one. Then she gets behind the wheel and starts the car.

"We're all good!" she shouts out the window. "The prindle works now." She steps out just as Trey gets her hood closed for her. "Thanks, pretty boy."

"You're welcome." He smiles, and this time, it looks genuine. It's almost like he missed hearing her call him that and it was nice to hear it again.

"Thanks, Liz," Javina says. "Next time I need an Uber, I'ma hit you up."

I hold Javina's snack bag out to her. "Here."

She tries taking it from me, but it gets snagged on my ring. I unsnag the bag's loops from the diamond as Trey sucks in a little gasp. His face falls as his eyes remained glued to my left hand.

Liz plasters a big ol' smile onto her face. "That's a pretty ring, Ari."

"Thanks." Naturally, I stick out my hand for her to see it better.

Trey's gaze follows my ring as all the color drains from his face.

"Did you pick it out?" Liz asks.

"No, Caleb did."

"When's the wedding?"

"Tomorrow." In the corner of my eye, I see Trey's shoulders slump as he sucks in a frazzled breath. His attention is still stuck on my ring.

"Congrats," Liz says. "I'll bet it's easier to find a wedding venue on a Sunday versus a Saturday."

"Oh, we didn't rent a venue. We're just having a small ceremony with close friends and family in his parents' backyard. Nothing too fancy. We picked tomorrow because it's the anniversary of the date Caleb and I met."

Liz's attention darts up to Trey, who now looks like he's going to collapse from a lack of oxygen.

"I'll be in the car," he whispers to Liz. Then he half runs, half stumbles into her passenger seat and slams the door.

"Sorry," Liz says with an apologetic smile. "He's just a little dehydrated. We've been under the hot sun all day."

We all know that's not why Trey ran away. A part of me wants to apologize to him, but for what? For getting married to Caleb? For trying to hide it from him? The entire time Trey and I sat on that bench, I kept my left hand out of his sight. I don't know why I didn't want him finding out that I'm engaged. I just didn't. Maybe it was because I wanted to avoid this awkward situation.

Javina and I say our goodbyes to Liz, then get into the Corolla. I steal a glance at Trey, who's slouched in Liz's passenger seat with his eyes closed. He's sucking in deep breaths so heavily that his chest looks pumped. I stare at him until Liz starts her car and drives away.

Javina unscrews the cap of her root beer and takes a sip. Then she places the bottle into the cup holder and opens her chips. As she crunches on one, she hands me the box of unused fuses and her pliers. "Could you put this in there for me?"

I take the stuff from her, then press the button to open her glove box and gasp. "What's all this?" At the bottom of the compartment are a bunch of fuses that look exactly like the ones in my hand.

"Oh, shit. Forgot about those."

"You had extra fuses this whole time?"

She shrugs. "Okay, sue me. I saw an opportunity, and I took it. While we were in the picture line, you said you wanted to talk to him, then you chickened out at the last second."

"Because I didn't want to talk to him in front of a bunch of people."

She flashes me a *duh* face. "Which is why I saw the opportunity and took it."

I gape at my mastermind of a friend. "Did your car even break?"

"Yes. It wasn't until they showed up and I dug through my glove compartment when the idea came to me. Without hesitation, I dumped out the fuses and presented an empty box. You can be mad at me all you want, but my plan worked. You got to talk to him without people there, didn't you?"

"Yes, but—"

"How'd it go?" She bites down on a chip.

"Fine, I suppose."

"Did you ask him why he never sent you a postcard?"

I nod as I replay Trey's long answer in my head. All his overthinking, his somber tone, that depressing darkness in his eyes.

"And?" Javina impatiently circles her wrist in the air.

"He said he never sent one because he didn't want Caleb to see it first and not give it to me." Technically, Trey said much more than that, but that's as much as I'm going to share.

Trey also said he'll send me a postcard when he gets back to New York. I plan to check my mail every day for it.

91

ARI

O*ne year later*

The summer sun sets behind me in hues of pink and orange as I drive down the gravel road toward my thinking spot.

The last time I made this trip, it was because Caleb and I got into the biggest argument we've ever had. I sat under my oak tree at the top of a grassy hill until the moon came out and I felt better enough to return home.

The time before that was the month after our wedding. I had to sort through my thoughts to figure out why I couldn't stop looking for a postcard that wasn't coming and never came.

I also wanted to figure out why, as I read my vows to Caleb, I kept imagining Trey crashing our wedding. He didn't, and the wedding went as planned. Tomorrow is my and Calebs's first anniversary. Tonight, I'm heading back to my precious thinking spot because I have more thoughts I need to sift through.

When I pull my car up to the side of the road where I usually park, there's a motorcycle already there. My heart skips a beat the way it always does whenever I see a motorcycle— especially if the person riding it is wearing a black leather jacket. It's never *him*, but my chest always thumps as if it is.

I step out of my car to examine the bike. Nothing on it screams, *I belong to Trey Grant!* but something inside me knows this is his.

More eager than I was before, I snatch my blanket from my car. Then I dash through the woods and hike up the narrow trail faster than I normally do.

When I reach the top of the hill, someone is lying under the oak tree. From the silhouette of the person, I think it's a man—a very *still* man. He's lying with his arms straight at his sides. I can't tell for sure if it's Trey, but I'm pretty certain it is. My thrashing heart says so.

As I approach him, he still doesn't move. When I get within five steps of him, I see why.

He has a pair of wireless headphones in his ears. His eyes are closed, and his steady breaths tell me he's either sleeping or very relaxed.

"Trey?"

He doesn't move.

I take two steps toward him and speak louder. "Trey?"

Still no movement.

I poke his arm. "Trey?"

He jolts upright. "Ahh!"

I step back and throw my hands up in surrender. "Sorry!"

He stares up at me with his mouth agape. Then his eyebrows press together as he slowly draws out his earbuds. "Arella?"

I haven't heard someone call me that in years. The last person who did was him. "It's Ari."

He shakes his head at himself. "Right. Sorry. I didn't mean to—" He lets out a sigh. "I just —" Another sigh. "Sorry. I wasn't thinking. That just came out."

I know what he's trying to say. He only called me *Arella* out of habit. It's how he knows me, and how he thinks of me, but he can't say that because it'll make him sound crazy.

I've had over two and a half years of thinking to come to the conclusion that this man isn't crazy. If he was, he wouldn't be living in New York just to stay away from me. He respects that I don't know him, and he purposely keeps his distance. Crazy people don't do that.

"I'm sorry I scared you. I called your name, but you didn't respond."

"Sorry. I was listening to something and zoning out." He stands as he shoves his earbuds into the inner pocket of his leather jacket. "What are you doing here?"

I fidget with the blanket hanging over my arm. "What are *you* doing here?"

"I come here every Sunday."

My brows arch. "*Every* Sunday?"

"Mm-hmm."

"What for?"

He glances around at the quiet woods, then up toward the oak tree's leaves looming over us like an umbrella. "To think."

"How long have you been doing that?"

He waggles his head from side to side. "About a year."

"A whole year? How do you know about this place?"

"I . . ." His voice trails off as he gazes straight into my eyes. Then his attention travels to my neck, down my arms, past my shorts. Then he scans my legs.

What's he looking for?

His eyes meet back up with mine. "Did he hurt you?"

"Did *who* hurt me?"

"Your hus—" He clears his throat with a fist to his mouth. "Your . . . Caleb. Did Caleb hurt you?"

"No? Why would you think—" I gasp. *He knows about Nathan.* He knows my ex is the reason I found this place. He knows that sometimes after Nathan hit me, I'd drive here to get away from him. How does Trey know that? I've never told anyone about this place. Not even Caleb.

Trey grabs his backpack that was leaning against the tree trunk and swings it over his shoulder. "I'm sorry. It was wrong of me to make assumptions. I'll leave so you can have your thinking spot to yourself."

He knows I call this my thinking spot—another thing I've never said aloud to anyone. If I didn't already have enough evidence that this man came from an alternate universe, I do now. Since he knows things I've never told anyone, the only explanation is that Alterella told him before he fell down a portal and ended up here.

Now that I think about it, it makes sense that he knows about this place. I've seen us here before in my dreams. Correction: I've seen him and *Alterella* here before in my dreams.

Trey is already five steps away when I realize what's happening.

"Wait!" I run to step in front of him. "You don't have to leave. *You* were here first."

He stops and gives me a little shrug. "It's all right. I've already been here for a few hours. I'm happy to—"

"But I want you to stay."

He knits his eyebrows together. "You do?"

"Yeah. I'd appreciate your company."

"You would?"

I let out a chuckle. "Why are you acting so surprised?"

"This isn't acting. This is genuine shock. Some of the last times we saw each other consisted of a newly installed chain lock, your dude kicking me out, and your best friend meeting my band solo because you didn't want to."

I don't regret leaving the photo line that day, because what I got instead was a thousand times better. "For the record, I did want to."

"You did?"

"Yeah. I wanted to talk to you, but I chickened out at the last second."

"You *wanted* to talk to me?"

"Yeah."

He gapes at me like he can't understand that concept. "Why?"

"I wanted to ask you about the postcard. I still haven't gotten one, by the way." And I'm totally *not* bitter about it.

His eyes cast down to the grass. "I'm sorry."

"Did you forget to send it?" I ask, but I already know the answer.

"No."

"Did you overthink it again?" I flash him a teasing smile, hoping it'll help get rid of that melancholy look in his eyes.

It doesn't. "Abso-fucking-lutely."

"Did you even write me a card?"

"Yep."

I want to ask how many he wrote. Instead, I ask, "What did you write?"

"I shouldn't say."

"Why not?" I try not to sound like this is all I've been thinking about for the past year.

"Same reason I never sent it."

"Which is?"

"You're really gonna make me state the obvious?"

"It must not be that obvious if I'm oblivious to it."

"Arel—sorry." He shakes his head at himself again. "I . . . I didn't send the postcard because by the time I got back to New York, you were already married and, I dunno. It just felt weird to send a postcard with deep thoughts on it to a married woman."

"Deep thoughts?" My smile spreads from one ear to the other. "Now I *have to* know what you wrote on that postcard."

He shakes his head at me, but there's a hint of a smile on his lips—a genuine one. I want to keep seeing it. I want to spend the rest of this night making him smile until his cheeks ache.

I gesture toward the tree. "How about we sit and talk for a bit? I bet by the end of this evening, I'll get that secretive information out of you."

With a light chuckle, Trey heads back under the tree and drops his backpack at the base of it. "We'll see about that."

92

TREY

She's a treasure to look at. A goddamn treat for my eyes. A sight I wasn't sure was real at first. I've visited this tree every Sunday for the last year, and not once has anyone ever come up here.

When I first saw her, I thought I was hallucinating again, even though I've been staying sober. By that, I mean everything: No drugs. No alcohol. Not even a drop. I don't trust myself. If I have even one drink, it'll easily turn into two, then ten, then I'll be too gone to make good decisions again. After that, it won't be long before I'm back to seeing bright lights and swatting away cockroaches that aren't there.

Is it miserable to live with this raw pain throbbing in my chest all the time? *Yep.*

Am I doing it anyway? *Yep.*

Am I happy about it? *Fuck no.*

Whenever I get the urge to drink myself into oblivion, I just remind myself of what Liz said: *"Is this the man she'd want you to be?"* Most days, that's enough for me. Other days, I need distractions. Having to fly to and from LA is the best at keeping my mind off self-medicating.

"You cut your hair," I say as Arella unfolds her blanket and drapes it over the grass. Then she sits and gestures for me to join her. I don't hesitate to obey as a tiny-little-itty-bitty light flickers on inside my chest.

"Do you like it?" she asks.

"Yeah. Shoulder-length hair is cute on you."

"Do you like it better than my really long hair?"

"I wouldn't say I like it more or less. I'm sure you'd look cute with any hairstyle." Hell, she could be bald right now and I'd still be in love with her.

"What were you listening to before I scared you?"

"A meditation app."

"You were meditating?"

"Yeah. It's something my z—" I clear my throat to hide my almost slip of the tongue. "Around this time last year, I went into my weekly session with my therapist and asked her to teach me more methods to control my thoughts. She recommended meditating."

"I never pictured you as someone who likes to meditate."

That's because I'm not the type, but after I saw that shiny diamond ring on her finger, I was willing to try *anything* to keep myself from relapsing.

I still remember bursting into my zerapist's office that Monday afternoon. I flopped onto her couch and choked out, "She got married yesterday."

"To that Caleb fella?"

"Yep. Not only that, but they picked the date they supposedly met. The date that *I* met her."

That date is coming up again tomorrow. I bet Caleb has special plans to take her somewhere nice for their anniversary. I bet he's already picked out a thoughtful gift for her, like a new apron with her dream bakery's name on it, or maybe some custom-designed baking tools. After he gives it to her, she'll thank him by getting into the sheets. The sheets of *their* bed, inside *their* apartment, in their own little world of perfection where *he* has her and I don't.

But I have her now. She's sitting in front of me, and she's *willingly* talking to me. Not only that, but she asked me to stay. This time, it's not because she reverted back to remembering me, either. She asked me to stay as *Ari*. I don't know why. I'm not gonna question it though. I don't question miracles.

"Do you feel like meditating helps?" Arella asks. Or should I say *Ari*? I'm not sure how I should refer to this woman in my head. All I know is that I'm not calling her Ari out loud. Doing so feels like admitting she was never Arella at all.

"Meditating calms my thoughts. It's why I started coming to this tree. My therapist said I needed to find a place that was secluded to meditate at. This is the only secluded place I know of within driving distance of the two places I live."

"Are you still in New York?"

I nod.

"Do you still stay with Liz while you're in LA?"

"For now, yes, but Liz's boyfriend recently moved in. Even though they turned her office into a guest room for me, I've been looking into getting an apartment for myself."

Arella arches her brows. "Liz has a boyfriend?"

"Yep. Colton."

"Do you like him?"

"Yeah. He's a good man, and he adores Liz even more than I do."

Colton is as obsessed with Liz as I am with Arella. It's been pretty validating to know that it's normal to feel that way about your soul mate. At first, I thought that was just me. Turns out, all soul mates are like this with each other.

According to the z-net, when soul mates are separated, it's one of the worst emotional pains imaginable. Also according to the z-net, the emotional pain never goes away. When I read that, I scoffed out loud and said, "That's promising."

Liz's response was to look up at her soul mate with gratefulness that he was standing right next to her and he knew who she was. Colton gave her the same look back. I hope they never get separated, and I hope they never get their minds erased either. I don't wish this torture upon anyone, especially not Liz and Colton. They're the closest people I have to family.

Even though Arella doesn't remember who I am, I'm still grateful to be under this tree with her. I don't need her to remember me to enjoy her company or to appreciate hearing her voice.

"Have you found any potential apartments yet?" she asks.

"Some." If I really wanted my own place, I would have gotten one by now. The only reason I'm hesitating is because I don't trust myself to live alone in LA yet. Living with Liz and Colton keeps me grounded. I'll know I'm ready for my own place once I can go a day without considering drowning myself in alcohol.

"Enough about me," I say, holding back a huff. "Tell me what's been going on in your life."

She perks up with a smile that sends warmth through me. "What would you like to know?"

Everything. Where do you work now? How's your baking blog going? Do you still want to start a bakery? Are you still obsessed with bacon? Do you still always order your salads with the dressing on the side? Have you had another relapse moment of remembering me?

I don't ask any of that. I can't. What I ask instead is "What did you come here to think about?"

She gives me a narrowed stare. "I'll tell you that private information if you tell me the deep thoughts you wrote on that postcard for me."

The chuckle that leaves my mouth takes little effort to get out. "You haven't forgotten about that, huh?"

"I told you I was going to get it out of you by the end of this evening."

"You can try and beg all you want, Miss Rance, but that information is staying sealed behind these lips."

The smile on her face falls. At first, I think it's because I said something to offend her, then it hits me: Her last name probably isn't Rance anymore. The look in her eyes tells me she's thinking the same thing, but she doesn't correct me.

Like the kind person she is, she changes the subject. "If you're not going to tell me what you wrote, then at least tell me if you've been on any dates lately. The last time I saw you, you were lying to women about being unavailable so they'd stop pursuing you."

Her tactic works, because my little pang of hurt fades away. "That hasn't changed. I'm still lying to women about that. I just did it last night at my band's meet and greet, and the tipsy woman *still* wrote her number on my arm—in Sharpie. I had to scrub for almost ten minutes before it finally came off so my fake girlfriend at home wouldn't see it."

Dramatically, Arella rolls her eyes. "Wow. Must be hard to have to chase women away all the time."

I lift a finger into the air. "You know what's actually hard? Keeping up with this lie that I have a girlfriend. Last month, I did an interview for a podcast highlighting up-and-coming bands. The interviewer wanted to know more about how I met my invisible girlfriend than anything regarding my band's music."

"Naturally. That's the juicy stuff that sells."

"Yep," I say with a sigh. "Apparently, nobody wants to know about the inspiration behind our original songs or what we're releasing next. They just want to know how my girlfriend feels about my relationship with Liz and if she'll ever get over her *camera shyness.*"

Arella lets out the most adorable laugh. It floods me with memories of when I used to make her laugh like that on my couch until two in the morning. "You tell people your fake girlfriend is camera shy?"

"How else am I supposed to explain our lack of pictures together?"

Arella continues laughing, and I want to keep making her do it.

"If you have enough money to buy weekly plane tickets," she says, "then you have enough to hire someone to pretend to be your girlfriend. Actually, I'm sure there's a long line of women out there who'd do it for free."

I cringe at the idea of having to talk to a real person and actually bring her places. "That sounds like more work than actually having a girlfriend. I'm not *that* committed to this lie."

"You're pretty committed to your band though. Flying back and forth every week can't be cheap."

"It's not."

"Once you get your own place in LA, do you think you'd move back here permanently?"

"No," I say without hesitation.

"Why not? What's keeping you in New York?"

It's not what's keeping me *in* New York; it's what's keeping me *out* of Los Angeles. Without me saying it, I think Arella knows that. I'm sure by now, she's guessed that the real reason I left LA wasn't to go find my place in the world. I already know where my place is; it's wherever she is. Since I can't have that, I guess I'm looking for a place where I can feel half as happy. I haven't found it yet, but I'm trying to have faith it exists.

Liz has complete faith it exists. Colton does not. Unlike Liz, Colton and I believe that trying to find a "compatible partner" after being with your soul mate is a shit idea. I'd consider finding a compatible partner if I had never found Arella at all. It's easier to settle for less when you've never had the best.

Now that I know what true happiness feels like, having anything less is like trying to use spotty dial-up that drops every two seconds after using high-speed Wi-Fi my whole life. It's just unacceptable. Can it work? Sure, but it'll take a lot of effort, waiting, and frustration to get what I want. The whole time, I'll be wishing I had high-speed Internet instead.

"Somehow," I say, "we came right back to talking about me."

"That's because you're more interesting to talk about than I am. Not everyone comes from an alternate universe."

I cock my head at her. "Huh?"

"You know, a world like this one, but not. It's Javina's explanation for how you know so much about me. At first, I thought she sounded nuts, but the idea has grown on me."

I blink at her as I attempt to grasp the concept of alternate universes. "What's Javina's explanation for how I got here?"

"You fell through a portal."

I chuckle at how nonchalantly she said that. "And what's her explanation for why there aren't two Trey Grants walking around?"

"The Trey Grant from this universe is still in prison. Basically, you just took his place."

"I see." From Arella's point of view, I guess this theory makes sense. "Do you think Javina can show me where that portal is? I'm ready to return to my own world now."

"I'm sure Alterella misses you."

"Alterella?"

She gives me a moment to put it together.

Once it clicks, I laugh. "That's clever. Who came up with that?"

"Javina, of course. I'm not that witty."

Alterella. I repeat the name in my head a few times. It rolls off the tongue nicely. "So what you're saying is that there's an alternate version of you out there somewhere?"

"Yeah, and that's the version of me who's your girlfriend. She looks, talks, and acts exactly like me, which explains why you mistook me for her. She's probably at home right now, wondering where you've been this whole time."

The idea that a version of Arella could be out there somewhere, waiting for me, doesn't sit right. I don't like the thought of making her wonder if I'll ever come back for her or wonder if the reason why I didn't is because I stopped loving her. I couldn't stop, even if I tried.

"Well," I huff, "it's been over two and a half years. I hope she's quit waiting by now."

"Don't you *want* her to wait for you?"

"Fuck no. I want her to be happy, and waiting around for someone who's not coming is not happiness. Sounds like hell to me." *I would know. I'm doing it.*

Arella squints at me like she can't understand why I'd feel that way. "You'd rather she moved on with someone else than wait around for you?"

"If that's what makes her happy, yes."

"But what about you? What about *your* happiness?"

I shrug and pretend like the dark cavity in my chest isn't throbbing at all. "My happiness doesn't matter."

"Of course it does. Everyone deserves to be happy."

It's been so long since I've felt happy, I don't even remember what it feels like. "I'd rather she be happy than me."

"Why can't you *both* be happy?"

"Because that's not how the world works. Somebody once told me that when you love someone, you put their happiness before your own. I'm more than willing to do that for her." *For you.*

"Did you hear that line from my grammy? She says that to me all the time."

"Nah, I heard it from Alterella."

She erupts with laughter. "Oh my god. I can't believe you actually used that name."

For the next two hours, we sit on her blanket and talk while the sun sets. She makes me smile so many times, I lose count. The achy heaviness in my chest feels lighter, and I don't think about getting drunk once.

Eventually, Arella glances at the time on her phone and tells me it's time for her to go. I fake a smile to hide the way my stomach sinks and my throat goes dry.

"Could I walk you to your car?" I ask, trying not to sound as hopeful as I feel. I want as much time with her as I can get.

"Sure." If she's excited about the idea, she doesn't show it. She doesn't sound repulsed either. That's good, I guess.

I help her fold up her blanket, then together, we head through the dark woods.

When we reach her car parked behind my motorcycle, she leans her back against the driver's door and looks up at me. "You wanna know something weird I've been thinking about lately?"

I want to know everything you think about. "Sure."

"Apparently, when I bought this car, I paid for it in full—in cash."

"What's weird about that?"

"I don't remember doing that. And with my income, I could never afford a vehicle this nice, nor would I ever have enough in the bank to pay for it in full."

A lump forms in my throat because it's not like I can tell her that the car came from me. She wants to believe that I came from another universe. If that belief is what made her feel comfortable enough to stick around and have a two-and-a-half-hour conversation with me, then I'm gonna roll with it. "Maybe Caleb helped pay for your car," I say, because I'd rather give him the credit than burst this bubble of make-believe we have.

"I've asked him about it. He doesn't remember doing so, nor does he have the income to."

"Maybe your grandparents lent you some money for the car." I'm grasping at straws now.

"They can't afford anything this nice either." She looks me square in the eyes. "You know who can, though? A person who has enough money to buy things like penthouses and weekly plane rides across the country."

She gives me a moment to respond, but I don't. If I admit that I bought her this car, it'll ruin the vibe we've created. Plus, she didn't like that I bought her this car when she loved me. How will she feel about it now, when she doesn't love me at all?

"I had a great time with you," I say as an attempt to change the subject.

At first, she stares at me, probably debating whether or not to force an answer out of me. Then she relents and offers up a tender smile. "This was fun. I'm glad we ran into each other."

I take a step back toward the woods. "Drive home safe."

She unlocks her car and grips the door handle. "You too. I mean, you're flying, but you know. Just get home safe."

"Thanks." This should be when I turn and walk away, but I don't. I can't. Not while she's still here and I can still look at her.

I take another step back as she opens the door and tosses her blanket onto the passenger seat. Then she glances back up at me. "Trey?"

I lock eyes with her as my ears throw a confetti party from hearing her say my name. "Yeah?"

"Thank you for the car."

My stare tells her a silent *you're welcome*, then I take another step back and wave.

Without another word, she plops behind the wheel and starts the engine. I stare at her red taillights going down the road until she turns the corner and disappears from my sight.

Back at the tree, I flop onto the grass and gaze up at the stars. I missed my flight, but I don't care. I'm so high off joy right now, I feel like I'm floating on a cloud. Missing my flight was worth it.

93

ARI

"What do you think I should wear for dinner tonight?" I ask Caleb when I step out of the bedroom.

He's lying on the couch and doesn't look up at me from his phone. "Where are you and Javina going?"

"What do you mean?"

He still doesn't look at me. "How am I supposed to give you a suggestion if I don't know what type of place you guys are going to? Like, is it fancy?"

Oh. My. God. He forgot. "Caleb."

Finally, he pries his attention away from the screen. "What?"

"I'm not going out with Javina tonight. I'm going out with *you.*"

"What? But—Oh, shit!" He jerks up and swings his legs over the front of the couch. "It's our anniversary today, isn't it?"

"Yeah, and three weeks ago, you said you'd take the night off so we could go out for a nice dinner."

"Oh, muffin. I'm so sorry. I completely forgot to take it off. I have to work tonight."

I pout a little. I was looking forward to this because Caleb and I haven't had quality time together in a while. I work days at a bakery, and he works night shifts at a museum. Normally, I get off just in time to come home to make him dinner before he runs off to work. By the time he's off, I'm in the middle of my REM cycle, dreaming about a person I shouldn't be dreaming about.

Last night, my dream was the one where Javina and I were in Trey's house, chatting on his couch, when we saw him pulling into the driveway in a brand-new white crossover—the vehicle that I now own.

Javina whistled through her teeth as we stepped outside. "Damn, pretty boy. Lexus ain't doin' it for ya no more?"

Trey flaunted a megawatt smile from the driver's seat with the door open. "I'm good with my car. This one's for Arella."

I gasped. "Honey, you didn't . . ."

He beamed proudly. "I did."

"Why would you do this? After all the reasons I told you not to?"

Javina gaped at me like I was crazy. "Ari! Ungrateful much?"

Trey hopped out of the car with his arms up in surrender. "I bought the car under your name. It's all yours. Fully paid for. No strings attached."

I pretzeled my arms together. "I'm not accepting it."

"How 'bout you get in and drive it around before you make that decision?"

I was about to protest again when Javina threw her arm up. "Shotgun!"

That's the fifth time I've had that dream. The times before were the reason I thought to ask Caleb if he remembers how I paid for an expensive new car without any financing.

I mentioned it to Trey last night, and his silence confirmed he's the answer to that mystery. It's things like this that make me question my reality. Why doesn't my life add up right? And when it does, why does it always point to Trey?

"This explains why you weren't in the kitchen, making dinner." Caleb stands from the couch and shoves his phone into his back pocket. "I was beginning to wonder if you'd have food ready in time."

"I'll go see what I can whip up for you quickly."

"Don't worry 'bout it. I'll just grab something on my way to work, but that means I've gotta leave now." He leans in to peck my cheek. "I'm sorry I forgot. How about I take you out on Thursday instead? I have that night off."

"That's movie night with Javina." I think about offering to ask Javina if we can skip our movie date, but I'm not going to ditch my best friend just because my husband forgot about our first wedding anniversary. "Plus, don't you have something with Rakesh that night?"

"Oh, that's right. We're doing this tournament thing at the gym. We can win a prize if we beat the other pairs that night."

"Yeah, you told me that three weeks ago when we made these plans to go out tonight." *Which is why he was supposed to take it off.*

"I'm sorry, muffin. I'll buy you a nice gift, okay?" He kisses my cheek again, then heads into the bedroom to put on his uniform.

I'm left alone in the living room, holding back tears. *I don't want a nice gift. I want to spend time with my husband.*

LATER THAT WEEK, AS I DRIVE BACK TO MY THINKING SPOT, TOXIC THOUGHTS CONSUME MY HEAD. The one that keeps repeating is *Trey wouldn't have forgotten about our anniversary.* I scold myself for thinking that, because it's not right to compare my husband to another man. Caleb has been stressed out with work lately. I'm sure that's why he forgot.

My heart thumps wildly as I pull off the gravel road behind a motorcycle. Trey wasn't kidding when he said he comes here every Sunday.

I step out of my car with my purse in one hand and my blanket in the other. The sun is beginning to set behind the woods, looking like a Bob Ross painting. When I make it to the top of the hill, Trey is in the same position he was last time: lying on his back under the oak tree, unmoving.

"Trey?" I say as I approach him.

He doesn't respond.

"Trey?" I say louder.

He keeps his eyes closed and his earbuds in.

I don't want to scare him again, but . . .

"Ahh!" he shouts when I poke him. He jolts upright and tears the wireless devices out of his ears. When his eyes land on me, his face lights up. "You're back."

"I am." My heart flutters from how happy he looks. I didn't expect to see him smile that big.

"Did you have some more thinking to do since you didn't get to do it last time?"

"Yeah."

"Would you like me to leave?"

I unfold my blanket and lay it down. Then I gesture for him to join me. He gladly takes that as my answer.

"Were you meditating?" I ask as we settle onto the blanket together.

He crosses his legs into a pretzel. "Mm-hmm."

"Could I do it with you?"

"You want to meditate?"

"You said it helps clear your head, right? I could use some of that."

"Uh, sure." He hands me one of his earbuds, then sticks the other one back into his ear.

I put the device in but hear nothing. "How do I do it?"

"I'll choose a short guided meditation for us. Then you just listen to what the lady on the app tells you to do."

"Do I lie down first?"

"You can stay sitting or lie down. Whichever you prefer."

"It seems like you prefer to lie, so I'll try that." I settle on my back and gaze up at all the leaves and branches above me.

Trey lies next to me, making my heart beat faster. He taps on his phone a few times, then a soft melody plays into my ear. A calming female voice tells me to release every thought from my mind and focus on one body part at a time, starting with my forehead.

By the end of the ten-minute session, my entire body feels relaxed and a little tingly. We sit up and face each other.

"What do you think?" Trey asks as he returns his earbuds to their case.

I try not to admire the way the sunlight hits the curves of his cheeks just right. "That was wonderful. I feel less stressed now."

He shoves his earbuds case into the side pocket of his backpack behind him. "What are you stressing out about?"

"Same thing I came to think about last week."

"The thing you refuse to share with me?"

The person here who refuses to share things the most is him. "I made a deal with you, remember? I'll share that information if you share the deep thoughts you wrote on that postcard."

"Oh, I have a gift for you." He grabs his backpack and unzips the big pocket.

He brought the gift with him? "How did you know I was coming?" *I* didn't even know I was coming until the moment after Caleb left for work and I climbed into my car.

"I didn't," Trey says. "I just hoped."

We lock eyes as a warmth rushes down my spine. How long has he been sitting here, waiting for me to show up without knowing if I would or not?

After we break our intense stare, he pulls out a flat paper item from his backpack and offers it to me. I gasp at the colorful artwork of the New York City skyline. In the background is a silhouette of the Statue of Liberty.

"I wrote this card for you the night after my band's video shoot at the softball field."

I flip the postcard over and read it.

WHENEVER THE SUN OR MOON IS OUT.

I knit my eyebrows together. "Am I supposed to know what this means?"

"You asked me a question that day, which I never answered. This was my answer."

"What did I ask you?"

"You asked how often I think about you."

I read the postcard again.

WHENEVER THE SUN OR MOON IS OUT.

I can practically feel the nerves radiating off him as he waits for my reaction to this very sweet and personal message. I hug it to my chest. "Thank you, Trey. This means a lot to me."

The darkness in his eyes dissipates a little. "It does?"

"Yeah. It took a lot of courage for you to give me this." And now I can *finally* stop obsessively checking my mail.

"It was my therapist who convinced me to give it to you."

"You talk to her about me?"

"Technically, I talk to her about Alterella, but you come up occasionally."

Javina would love to know that Trey actually uses the name she gave my alternate-universe self. Javina doesn't know that I found Trey under my thinking tree last Sunday. Caleb doesn't know either, and I don't plan to ever tell him. This place is still my secret spot, and now Trey feels like a part of it.

"What have you told your therapist about me?"

Trey lets out a little laugh. "I can only open up so much at a time. Giving you this postcard means I've reached my limit for the week."

"Does that mean I'll have to come back next week to get you to open up again?"

He perks up. "Yes. That's exactly what it means."

"Okay, I'll put it in my calendar. Next Sunday evening is officially *hear Trey open up* time. I'll book it for seven thirty since that's the time I got here today."

That dimness in his eyes illuminates again. "Could you make it a reoccurring event?"

"Maybe," I say with a smirk. "I'll have to see if what you give me next Sunday is juicy enough to warrant a weekly visit."

"I don't open up a lot, so anything I say will be juicy."

"I'll be the judge of that."

We smile and stare at each other for a long moment before Trey forces his attention away. "So . . ." He clears his throat. "I think it's time you held up your end of the bargain and tell me what you came here two weeks in a row to think about."

Technically, I came here the first time to think. Tonight, I came to see him. "I'm not sure if you want to know. It has to do with me and Caleb."

He hides his discomfort behind another clear of his throat. "I can handle it."

"Are you sure?"

"Hey, now." He smiles playfully and narrows his eyes at me. "Are you trying to back out of our deal?"

That makes me giggle. "No, I'm just being honest with you. If you'd really like to know, I'll tell you."

"I'd really like to know."

I pause, trying to come up with a way to say it without hurting him, although it's probably going to hurt him regardless of how I put it. "Caleb and I have been trying to have a baby."

His entire face falls, and all the light that was flickering in his eyes earlier goes black. "Oh."

"We've been trying since before we got married, and still no baby. It's been frustrating and exhausting to have to track my ovulation cycle and time things right, only to get my period again two weeks later." I'm going to assume Trey knows what I mean by "time *things* right." "I've been to the doctor to get checked out for infertility, and they said nothing is wrong. As for Caleb, he refuses to get checked out."

"Why?"

"He says he knows nothing is wrong with him because we've gotten pregnant before. It was over two and a half years ago, but we lost the baby."

Something heart-wrenching breaks in Trey's eyes, then his gaze falls to the grass. "I see."

"It's been a pretty heavy and frequent topic of argument between us." That's putting it lightly. Caleb hates whenever I bring up baby stuff, so much that I've stopped mentioning it at all.

"What does he have to lose from doing a few tests?"

"That's exactly what I said. The answer is nothing. I don't know if he's scared or just being lazy."

Trey pauses to think about that. "I don't know the guy, but if I had to guess, I'd say he's scared. Maybe he doesn't wanna be told he's the problem."

"Right, but maybe if we knew what the problem was, we could move forward with a solution. My doctor has already talked to me about fertility treatments, but I don't think that's an option for us."

"Why not?"

"Because it costs thousands of dollars we don't have."

"I'll pay for it," Trey says without any hesitation.

"What?"

"I said I'll pay for it. Whatever it costs. The treatments, exam fees, medications, whatever. I'll cover the whole thing."

I gape at him. "You would do that?"

"Yep. Just tell me how much it is, and I'll send it to you."

I can't believe how easily and nonchalantly he's offering me his money. Does he not realize how much fertility treatments cost? "I didn't tell you this as an attempt to get financial help. I only told you because you wanted to know."

"And now that I know, I want to help."

"You want to help Caleb and me have a baby?"

"No," he says firmly. "I want to help *you* have a baby. Your dude just happens to be part of that picture."

"But why would *you*, of all people, want to pay for it?" I hope without me having to say it, he knows what I mean by that.

He gives me a *duh* look. "Wouldn't having a baby make you happy?"

"Of course."

"Then that's reason enough for me."

I let out a little *hmmph*. "Thank you, Trey, but I can't accept."

"Figures."

Like we did last time, we talk and laugh together while the sun goes down. Trey makes me laugh so hard, my knee's tender from how often I've slapped it.

A few stars twinkle in the black sky as Trey walks me to my car. I've got my precious postcard in my hands, and I already know where I'm going to put it: right inside that book Caleb will never open.

"Could you do something for me?" I ask.

"Anything."

My heart skips a beat from the way he says it so eagerly. "Next week, could you leave one earbud out or turn the volume of your meditation down so I don't have to scare you again?"

"Of course. I would have done that tonight, but I'd already convinced myself you weren't coming."

I stop at my car and turn to face him. "I'll be here next week. Promise."

"I'm looking forward to it."

That should be my cue to leave, but I don't. It's already past ten thirty. I stayed a little longer this time because I was making him laugh so much, I wanted to keep hearing it. Now I probably won't make it home until midnight. Then I'll have to sleep and be up by six to get ready for a day at the bakery. That's not enough sleep for me, yet here I am with a pair of feet that won't get into my car.

"What time is your flight tonight?" I ask.

"An hour ago."

"You missed your flight?"

"Yeah, but it's okay." He shoves his hands into his jean pockets. "I'll head to the airport soon and ask them to get me on the next flight. No big deal."

"I'm sorry. I should have asked when your flight was so we could get you there on time."

"It's fine, really. I'll miss a hundred flights if it means I get to see you."

The smile that curves up my lips is automatic.

94

ARI

"Hey, you." Trey smiles at me from under the oak tree. This time, he's not lying under it. He's sitting in the grass with his back leaned against the thick trunk. He had his eyes glued on me the whole time I walked over to him from the woods.

"Are you ready to open up and tell me more of your deep thoughts tonight?"

He closes the book he was reading and lets out a laugh I've been craving to hear for a week. "Is that all you came for? A glimpse into my deep thoughts?"

"Yes, and as soon as I get it, I'm leaving." I grin at him so he knows I'm joking. Then I shake out my blanket and drape it over the grass.

Trey joins me on it. "I have something for you."

"Another postcard?"

"Nope." From his backpack, he pulls out a white envelope.

I take it from him and open it, then gasp. It's a check for a hundred grand. "Nope. Nuh-uh. No way."

"Look, I already knew you were going to decline. That's why I wrote you a check. You don't have to cash it now, but I want you to have it in case the time comes and you decide you want it."

"Trey, I'll *never* want this."

"Think of it like a donation." He says that as if handing someone a check for a hundred grand is no big deal.

"I'm not a charity."

"I'm sure they have charities for infertility out there. Think of this like I'm donating to them, but this is my way of making sure all the funds go to you."

"I appreciate the thought, but no, thank you." I hold the envelope out to him.

He doesn't take it. "Could you at least keep the check in case you change your mind?"

I tear the envelope in half, then half again. "I'll never change my mind, but thank you."

Trey glares at the papers as I toss them behind me. "You've got a bad habit of doing that."

"Doing what?"

"Ripping shit in half."

"Oh, that reminds me. I have something for you too." From my purse, I slip out the taped-up photo I tore apart over two years ago. "Here."

His breathing stops as I place the photo in his palm. He stares at it with wide eyes and trembling fingers, then flips it over to read the back. As if he just remembered that he needs to breathe, he sucks in a shaky breath and lets it out. Then he flips the photo back over and stares at the front again. When he finally looks up at me, his eyes are watery.

In a soft whisper, he says, "Thank you for giving this back to me."

"You're welcome. I'm sorry for tearing it up."

"It's fixed, and I have it back now. That's all that matters." As he blinks away the water in his eyes, he pulls his wallet out of his backpack. With gentle fingers, he slides the picture into the crevices of his bifold.

Playfully, I ask, "Was this picture in your wallet when you fell through the portal? Is that why you still had it?"

"Yep," he says with a light chuckle as he returns the wallet to his backpack.

"Why did you get Alterella an angel-wings necklace?"

"Because I called her my angel." In my dreams, he mostly calls her *Arella* or *babe.* Only occasionally have I heard *angel.*

"Did you know the name Arella means *angel*?" I say, because originally, I thought that's why he bought her an angel-wings necklace.

"I didn't know that. I guess that's fitting."

"Did you know my parents named me Arella because it's a combination of their names, Aries and Bella?"

Trey stares at me, and I can practically see the gears turning in his head. Whatever thought just crossed his mind, he ignores it and says, "I've been thinking about getting my middle name changed."

"What is it now?"

"Andrew. I wanna change it to Victor—to honor my dad because he died trying to save my life."

I have so many questions about that, but I doubt he'll be open to talking about something so serious. Instead, I ask, "Is that what the letter V in your tattoo stands for?"

Trey's attention shifts to the tattoo on his left forearm. I've been stealing glances at it over the past three weeks. He doesn't have this tattoo in any of my dreams. The first time I ever saw it was when we sat on that bench outside the softball field.

His tattoo is an acoustic guitar that stretches across the entirety of his inner left forearm. The body of the guitar is shaped with a blend of fiery red flames mixed with bright blue waves of water. Going up the neck are sprigs of purple lavender that start off as guitar strings until they spread out into more lavender sprigs, surrounding the guitar's neck. At the head of the instrument is the letter V. When I first saw the V, I thought it looked like a sideways L for Liz.

Trey runs a finger up and down his tattoo. "Yeah, the V was added in honor of my dad."

"Does the rest of your tattoo have any meaning?" *More specifically, does the lavender have to do with me?* Lavender is my favorite color and scent. I use it for everything—my pillows and blankets, my shampoo, conditioner, hand soap—and it's my go-to candle scent. It's a pretty specific thing for him to have included in his tattoo.

"The guitar represents my love for music, and it was the first instrument I learned to play. The fire and water represent my friendship with Liz. She's the water; I'm the fire. She's got a matching water and fire tattoo on her forearm. Hers is just shaped into a circle instead of a guitar."

I don't miss how he avoids mentioning the lavender at all. "You guys live together, got matching tattoos, and you *still* expect your fans to think you're not dating?"

He offers me a careless shrug. "A few trolls and bad media aren't gonna stop me from doing what I wanna do. I could be dead and people would still spread rumors about Liz and I sleeping together behind Colton's back."

"Does that ever bother Colton?"

"Nah. He sees how Liz and I are in private. We're close, but even he knows the romantic feelings aren't there and never have been. He's so comfortable with it that he doesn't even care when we cuddle."

"You cuddle with Liz?"

"Sometimes. Less now that she's got Colton."

It must be nice to have such a strong platonic relationship. "Was Alterella ever bothered by your relationship with Liz?"

He pauses to think. "Eh. I wouldn't say she was bothered. When we first met, she was curious, but once she became good friends with Liz, she never questioned it."

"How close were Alterella and Liz?"

"Pretty close. They liked to talk about boy bands and make fun of me behind my back— and sometimes to my face."

Liz seems like a really good friend and someone I'd get along with. I do love boy bands. I wonder which ones are Liz's favorites. Are they the same as mine? "In your alternate universe, did JFK get assassinated?"

Trey presses his eyebrows together. "Yeah?"

"Lincoln too?"

"Yep."

"Did your people land on the moon?"

"Yes?" He jerks his head back a little. "Why are you asking me all this?"

"I'm trying to figure out what the differences are between your world and mine."

He chuckles. "I'm amused, so please, keep going."

"Did Martin Luther King Junior say, 'I have a dream'?"

"Yep."

"Was there a Black Plague?"

"Yep."

"Did the *Titanic* sink?"

He freezes. "The Ti-what?"

"*Titanic*. You know, the ship that hit the iceberg in 1912, split in half, then went down, taking fifteen hundred people with it."

"I've never heard of such a thing."

My eyes go wide, then Trey bursts into a laugh. "I'm just fucking with you. Yes, *Titanic* sank in my universe too."

I backhand his chest. "Don't do that!"

He continues laughing as he rubs the spot I hit. I love seeing him laugh. He's doing it the same way he does in my dreams. It's light, it's beautiful, and best of all, it doesn't sound forced.

We banter for a while as the sky fades to black. Eventually, it hits me that we've been talking for so long, I forgot about getting a deep thought out of him. When I mention this out loud, he says, "All right. You can have one deep thought from me tonight. What would you like to know?"

I debate between asking him about the lavender in his tattoo and the question I asked him last week. Since I've already got a good feeling about what the lavender represents, I go with the latter. "What have you told your therapist about me?"

"Damn. I was hoping you'd forget about that."

"Not a chance."

It takes him a moment to come up with the right words. "I told her that you look like my version of Arella. She knows about what happened after I showed up at your door, thinking you were her."

I let out a *pfft*. "That's not juicy at all. I could have guessed that."

"If I give you something juicier, will you come back next week?" He gives me a hopeful stare.

I'm planning to come next week no matter what he shares with me. Still, I smirk at him. "That depends on how juicy your information is."

"Okay. Lemme think." He spends a whole minute staring at the grass in deep thought. "If I share this with you, will you promise not to judge me or get weirded out?"

I perk up. "Ooo. I like where this is going already. Yes, I promise not to judge or get weirded out."

"Okay." He sucks in a breath, then slowly blows it out. "Last week, I told my therapist that I got to see you at this tree. I told her you were planning to come back tonight and that it was the only thing getting me through the week.

"I also told her that while we were here together, I kept forgetting that the rest of the world existed. It wasn't until I walked you to your car when I finally remembered you were going home to someone else and I'd be going back to an empty apartment in New York.

"My therapist has been working with me on living in the moment instead of dwelling on the past or dreading the future. It's been a struggle for me. All my thoughts are either about wishing I'd done things differently or how anxious I am about living the next day without . . ." He sighs as the words get caught in his throat.

"Anyway, when I'm with you, it feels easy to live in the moment and just enjoy your company. Sometimes I feel *some* anxiety because my mind drifts to when you have to leave, but when I catch myself doing that, I just do what my therapist taught me. She said to take an imaginary katana to those *out*-of-the-moment thoughts and bring myself back to living *in* the moment."

My heart leaps out of my chest over and over again. That's the most endearing thing anyone has ever said to me. I don't even remember Caleb's vows from our wedding, but I'll probably remember everything Trey just said for the rest of my life.

Without saying it, he basically just told me he wants me, and it's the most wanted I've felt in months. It doesn't feel like he wants me for anything more than my presence either. Simply being around me seems to be enough for him, which is how I feel about him too. I don't want him to give me anything, or to perform for me, or to fake a smile. I just want to sit here with him, hear his voice, see him laugh, and occasionally catch a whiff of his familiar scent.

I tuck a loose wave of hair behind my ear. "If I share something with you, will you also promise not to judge?"

"With all the shit I've done, I have no right to judge anyone, so yes. I promise."

I come out with it before I can change my mind. "I haven't had sex in three months."

"What?"

"You heard me."

He knits his eyebrows together. "But . . . I thought you're trying to have a baby."

"That doesn't mean I've had any sex."

He tilts his head to the side. "Do you not know how baby-making works?"

"Caleb and I have opposite schedules, and whenever I try, he says he's not in the mood."

"Wait, wait, wait. Are you telling me that even when you initiate it, he says *no*?"

"Basically. It's gotten to the point where I don't even try anymore because I keep getting denied."

Trey gapes at me with his mouth fully open. "Is the dude an idiot?"

I shrug with my hands out to my sides. "I think it's stress. Work has been crazy for him."

"But . . . but . . . he's got *you*." Trey doesn't expand more on that, as if saying having *me* is explanation enough.

"Maybe once work settles down, he'll get back in the mood."

Eventually, Trey forces his jaw shut and huffs out a breath. "I hate to admit this, but I've got you beat. It's been over two and a half years for me."

"What?"

"You heard me."

I don't believe him. How can a single man who looks like he belongs on a billboard advertising a diet and gym routine that actually works go that long without getting laid? I don't even think I'd believe him if he told me it's been over two and a half weeks.

"But women practically throw themselves at you."

With pursed lips, he shakes his head. "None of them are what I want."

"What are you looking for?"

"Not them." He chuckles at the way I'm still gaping at him. "I dunno why you're surprised. I've already told you I haven't been on any dates."

"You don't have to go on a date to have sex. I'm sure you've had a plethora of one-night stands."

"In the past, yes, but not anymore."

"What changed?"

He locks his eyes with mine, and it's all the answer I need: Losing Alterella changed him. Or losing *me*. I'm not sure anymore. Our worlds are blending together too much for me to keep them separated.

Trey clears his throat. "Let's just say that once you've had high-speed Wi-Fi, it's hard to go back to spotty dial-up."

That makes me laugh so much, I slap my knee. "Are you comparing women and sex to Internet speed?"

"Hell yeah. Tell me that didn't make sense though."

I laugh again. "It made a lot of sense."

"Exactly."

95

TREY

We didn't establish if she was coming back this week. As I walked her to her car last week, I thought about asking but was too afraid to. Now I'm sitting under our tree with an open book in my lap, and I haven't read a single word.

It's seven thirty-five. *She's probably not coming.*

Seven forty-five. *She's not coming.*

Seven fifty-five. *She's definitely not—*A pair of footsteps thumps against the ground in the distance. *Is it her?*

A vision of perfection appears from the woods. She's got a blanket draped over one arm and her purse in the other. All the blood rushes to my face as my lips effortlessly curve into a smile.

"Hey, you," I say when she reaches me.

"Sorry, it took me a little longer to get here. I had to stop at the store for this." She pulls out a little box from her purse. "It's called the Little Box of Questions to Ask Your Friends."

I read the colorful print on the box, and that's exactly what it says. "You consider us friends?"

She shakes out her blanket and lays it over the grass. "What else would we be?"

Good point. I guess being her friend is better than being nothing at all. I'll take it.

Once we're sitting and facing each other on her blanket, she unwraps the box of question cards from the plastic. The way the light from the setting sun hits her face makes her look like she's a hallucination. Sometimes, I'm *still* not sure if she's real. It's only once she speaks that I'm positive I'm not hallucinating. It's just hard for me to believe that she's actually here in front of me and that she has come four weeks in a row. *What did I finally do right?*

"Is this a game?" I ask.

"Yeah, but better, because it's the type of game where we both win. All we do is take turns pulling a card from the box, then we both answer the question. Would you like to go first?"

"Sure." I slip a card out from the middle of the box and read it. "What is one of your biggest regrets?" I think about my answer, then I playfully glare at her. "Is this another one of your sneaky ways to get me to open up?"

Her mouth spreads into a guilty grin. "You caught me."

"Is that really why you bought this question-box thing?"

"Let's just say that one deep thought a week is not enough for me. I want more, and I figured this was a subtle not-so-subtle way of asking for it without actually asking for it."

If she wants more, I can give her more. Hell, I'll give her all of me if that's what she wants. I just expect the same back. "You answer this question first."

"Okay. One of my biggest regrets is staying with my ex for as long as I did. I should have left as soon as I saw the red flags. Instead, I made excuses for him over and over, until I was trapped."

I could have guessed she'd say that. We've had multiple conversations about Nathan before, and they all ended with the same conclusion: No matter what, she's never going to stay in a relationship where she's abused or feels unwanted ever again. She vowed to herself that as soon as she saw the signs, she'd get out, even if it means starting over. I'm proud of her for that.

"Your turn," she says, leaning in to me with an eager look.

"Okay. One of my biggest regrets is waiting too long to tell someone I love them." I keep it vague on purpose and hope she won't ask me to elaborate. If she does, I won't. This is already too much opening up for me, and we're only one question in.

She must read my mind, because her face tells me she wants to ask a follow-up question, but her hand pulls a card from the box instead. "What is the first thing you noticed about me? This time, you have to answer first."

I make a stank face. "I dunno if I like this question. Your answer will have a completely different vibe from mine."

"How so?"

"Because when you met me, I was a stranger at your door, saying things you thought were insane."

"But that's not the first thing I noticed about you."

Suddenly, I'm a fan of this question. "Then what was?"

"Nuh-uh. You have to answer first."

"All right, fine. The first thing I noticed about you was your captivating eyes. Sometimes they tell me things your mouth doesn't."

"Your eyes do the same."

So I've been told.

Arella shyly tucks some hair behind her ear. "The first thing I noticed about you is how protectively you wrapped your arms around me. It felt desperate and possessive."

Because it was. For as possessive as I am with her, I give myself an A-fucking-plus for staying away from her for as long as I have. This shit isn't easy.

"Are you that way with Liz too?"

I waggle my head from side to side. "Protective? Yes. Possessive? No." I pull another card from the box, ready to stop talking about the moment I heard her say *"Who are you?"* Those three words echo in my head constantly, eating me alive from the inside out. I hold the card up and read it. "If you had the option to live forever, would you?"

"I wouldn't," Arella says without putting any thought into it. "I'd hate to watch all the people I love die and to have to go on without them."

"Yep, that would be hard." It's basically what I've been doing with her. She's not exactly dead, but the part of her that remembers me is.

"What's your answer?" she asks.

I let out a scoff as I fling the card next to the box. "My answer is fuck no. I hate my life. Why the hell would I *choose* to do this shit forever?"

"You hate your life?"

The fact that she's surprised by that means she doesn't know anything about my past. "I haven't really been dealt a good hand of cards to play with in this game of survival."

"But you seem to have enough money to buy or experience whatever you want."

"Money isn't worth anything when you've got no one to share it with."

She creases her face together and slumps her shoulders. "Oh, Trey . . ."

"Please don't look at me like that. I don't want pity." *Nor do I deserve it.* I pick up the little game box and scowl at it. "Are there any questions in this damn thing that will solicit a positive answer? I'm done with this depressing shit."

"Let's see if I can find one." She pulls out a card and reads it to herself. Then she shoves it back in. "Nope." She slides out another card. "Definitely not." She pulls out a third card. "Um, maybe. Tell me if this is okay. The question is, Who has had the most positive influence on your life?"

"That's easy. My answer is Liz."

Arella adds the card to our pile of used ones. "Tell me more."

"Liz taught me that when life gets shitty, you can still make something of it. When we first met, I was a drug addict. She helped me clean up. Then two years ago, when I fell back into drugs, she helped me get sober again."

"You were an addict?" Arella says, her jaw dropped.

"Are you really that surprised?"

"Like, how bad?"

I don't want to go into deep details about this with her, so I say, "Pretty bad."

"Do you still struggle with it?"

"Sometimes." *All the time.* It's been easier to overcome my urges lately—for the last four weeks, to be exact. Whenever I feel the urge to silence my chaotic mind with a substance, I just imagine seeing her at this tree on Sunday evening, and the urge fades away.

"What did Liz do to help you sober up?"

"It's not what she *did*. It's what she *said*."

"Which is?"

I eye her playfully. "That's enough opening up for one night."

"What? You're gonna leave me hanging?"

"That question was supposed to elicit a positive answer. Talking about my past is not positive. Why don't you tell me who's had a good influence on your life? Maybe that'll lift the mood."

"Sure. Growing up, my answer would have been my grandparents. They love me more than I've ever seen two people love someone. As an adult, my answer is Javina. She's been there for me from the moment we met, and she's part of the reason why I'm stronger now. Plus, if it wasn't for her, we wouldn't have had that conversation on that bench. Did you know Javina had extra fuses the whole time?"

My face contorts. "What?"

"Yeah, she dumped out her box of fuses and pretended to need more because she wanted me to be able to talk to you without an audience."

I swear, Javina is one of my favorite people in the world, and she doesn't even know it. "Was her car even broken?"

"Yes. That, she didn't fake."

I let out a soft *hmm*. "Remind me to treat that woman to a spa day sometime."

"She'd like that. Did you know whenever we talk about you, she always refers to you as *pretty boy*?"

A wide smile spreads across my lips. "You guys talk about me?"

Arella glances away as her hair falls to cover her blushing cheeks. "Sometimes."

"What do you guys say?"

She laughs and shakes her head. "I'm not telling."

"What? I just confessed to you that I had a bad drug addiction. It's only fair that you confess something too."

"Okay, fine. Most of the time, we just talk about you coming from an alternate universe."

"Does she know about *this*?"

Arella doesn't need me to specify what *this* is to know what I'm referring to. "I haven't told her, and I don't plan to."

"Does your dude know?"

"No, and I think it's funny that you call him my *dude*."

Because it stings to have to call him her hus—Yeah, I can't even do it in my head. "Liz doesn't know about *this*, either."

"Why haven't you told her?"

Because I already know what Liz will say. She'll tell me this is a bad idea. She'll tell me that when this ends, because it eventually will, I'll be left with a larger gaping hole than before. I already know that, yet here I am, plunging headfirst. Whatever the consequences are, I'll deal with them later. Right now, I'm too happy to care.

96

TREY

"Hey, you."

It's exactly seven thirty. She didn't make me wait for her this time. I wasn't even sure if she was coming tonight. When I walked her to her car last week, I weaseled out of asking her because I'd rather live on the hope that she *might* be coming than go through a whole week knowing she won't.

"Do you greet me like that because you're trying to avoid calling me Ari but you can't call me Arella either?" My perceptive woman lays her blanket over the grass, then sits on it.

"How would you like me to greet you?"

"You could try saying, 'Hey, Ari,' or 'How's it going, Ari?'"

My face remains impassive as I plant myself next to her. "I think I prefer *Hey, you.*"

"Try calling me Ari, just once."

Fuck no. "Why?"

"Because I want to prove to you that it won't kill you."

Maybe not physically . . .

"Just say something simple like 'Hey, Ari. How's your day?'"

To appease her, I force it out. "Hey, *Ari.* How's your day?" That name sounds foreign coming from my lips. The only times I ever called her Ari was when I was introducing her to someone new. Even when I talked about her to my bandmates, I usually referred to her as *my girl.*

"You know what? That sounded awkward. You should just call me Arella."

"But you always correct me." *And it hurts like hell every time.*

"I won't correct you anymore. From now on, you have my full permission to call me Arella."

I lock eyes with her to check if she's serious. Her sweet smile doesn't falter, making my insides throw some balloons in the air. If she's going to allow me to call her Arella, that means she's letting her walls down around me. Is it because I've been letting mine down around her?

Last week, I was the most open with her since her memories were scrubbed. I told her about my biggest regret and my addictions. In turn, I got to hear that the first time she remembers meeting me, she could feel how protective I was of her. *I still am, baby.*

I also found out that no one knows she comes here to see me. I don't know why that makes me feel so good—it just does. It's almost like this place is something only she and I share and, without saying it out loud, we've agreed to keep it a secret.

That means she puts a lot of trust in me. If she thought I had intentions to hurt her, she wouldn't come here, and she especially wouldn't do it without telling *someone* where she is and who she's with. I plan to do everything in my power to keep her trust.

"Do you think you're up for some more questions today?" Arella pulls the box of deep-thought-revealing cards from her purse.

I sit up straighter. "Sure."

"Ooh. Is that enthusiasm I hear? I would have thought you'd dread this game because it makes you open up."

"It makes you open up too, so I'm okay with it. I don't think you would have told me about the way I made you feel when you first met me otherwise."

She purses her lips together and thinks. "Yeah, probably not."

"So the real question is, Do you think *you're* up for some more questions today?"

With a grin, she plucks a card from the box and reads it. "What's the hardest thing you've ever had to do?"

"Whoa!" I dramatically jerk my head back. *"This* is how we're gonna start tonight off?"

"I can pick a lighter question, and we can come back to this one?"

"Yeah, let's do that. I'm not ready to dive into something that heavy yet."

She sets the card aside and plucks out another one. "What do you think is your best quality?"

"Easy. I have none. Next question."

"What? You have lots of great qualities."

I scoff. "Name one."

"You can play lots of instruments."

"Those are skills, not qualities."

"Learning an instrument, especially as many as you have at the level you can play them, means you have patience, determination, and a good work ethic."

"Or it means I grew up without any friends, so I had nothing else better to do with my time."

She rolls her eyes at me. It's something I've missed in our time apart. "Fine. Here's another one: You're generous with your money."

"That's because I don't think I deserve it, so I'd rather give it away than spend it on myself."

"You're protective of Liz, which means you're caring."

"I'm protective of Liz because she's all I have. If anything happens to her, I'll have no one. My protection is selfish."

She rolls her eyes again. "The next time you see your therapist, you should ask her to psychoanalyze why you feel the need to downplay all your good qualities."

"Eh, anything good about me is because I'm self-preserving or it was forced upon me due to situations out of my control."

"Don't you think you have *some* good qualities if someone as amazing as Liz chooses to be best friends with you?"

"Nah. Liz is the type of person who thinks she can fix people. I'm an ongoing project for her."

The first and only time I ever said that to Liz, she got really offended. She claims we became best friends because we bonded over shared trauma. That may have been the surface reason, but deep down, there's a part of her who befriended me because she saw a broken man who needed fixing. I bet she didn't realize how much fixing I'd need.

"Why don't we list off your good qualities instead?" I say, desperate to talk about anything except me. "For example, you're strong, and kind, and you're really good at baking."

Arella slides the box of questions toward me. "According to you, being good at doing something is a *skill*, not a quality."

I pick up the box. "In that case, being good at baking means you're creative, and you're really good with your hands." If she was the Arella who remembers me, I'd make a dirty joke right now.

"Did you know I'm starting my own bakery soon?"

"Really?" Owning a bakery is one of the first things Arella told me she wanted in life. She used to talk my ear off about what colors she wanted the walls to be and what she was going to name it.

"I've already written out my business plan, and I hired a woman to help me create a logo and marketing plan. My next step is getting a loan for a location. I've got two places in mind. The first one is in a great area, but the space is smaller than I want and needs remodeling. The second spot is a little bigger. It only needs some minor cosmetic fixes, but the location is terrible."

"Why don't you find a place that's the size you want in a location you want that only needs the right paint color?"

"Because I've already been to six different banks and I don't qualify for enough financing to—"

"I'll pay for it." I already know she's gonna turn me down.

"No, and don't you dare show up next week with a check, either. This bakery is important to me. I want to do this on my own."

Of course she does. Arella used to tell me that Nathan only bought her things to be able to hold them against her later. I'd never do that to her, but because of him, she feels the need to make purchases without anyone's help. I respect that she sticks to that, even though it's frustrating for me.

"If you ever change your mind, my offer never expires." I slide my finger over the top of the cards and select one from the middle of the box. "What is one of your happiest memories?"

Arella tilts her head back as she thinks. "My happiest memory . . ."

I prepare to fake a smile in case her dude gets mentioned. She doesn't mention him often, or at all, really. I'm not sure if that's because she's not thinking of him while she's here or if it's for my benefit. Either way, I'm not complaining.

"My happiest memory is probably when I first moved to LA," she says. "My grandparents are super protective of me, so I had never been that far from them before. Moving was scary, but it also felt freeing. What about you?"

Almost all of my happiest memories were made with her. How do I pick just one? "Could I share two memories with you?"

Arella perks up like I'm giving her a gift wrapped in sparkly paper and fancy ribbons. "Please."

"It was hard for me to feel happy again after my parents died, but the first time I felt true joy after their death was the first time I performed for a crowd with my band. We were so new that we weren't even Flames in the Night yet. We just called ourselves the Five. We performed at a bar to people who weren't even listening to us, but I didn't care. It was the way we all worked together so seamlessly, and our harmonies just felt right. My second happiest memory was my first kiss with my first love."

Arella waits a second before she circles a hand in the air. "You're not going to give me details about that second one?"

"What details do you want?"

"Whatever you're willing to share. I just feel like I got a whole backstory with the first one and nothing with the second."

"There's not much to share. We were in my kitchen, and she was teaching me how to bake cookies. After we got them into the oven, we playfully threw flour at each other. It got so heated that we ended up kissing for the first time. That's it."

That's not it.

I could tell her so much more, but it feels weird to talk to her about *our* first kiss.

Arella's eyes go wide as her mouth opens slightly. A thought has crossed her mind, but I can't tell what. Even if I was a Mind Reader, I still wouldn't know.

"How many times have you been in love?" she asks before I can ask her what she's thinking.

"Just once."

"But you said *first* love. I assume that means there's a second."

"Nope. It's just been the one." I don't think I'll ever fall in love again, nor do I want to. According to the z-net, it's possible to fall in love with people who aren't your soul mate. It doesn't make the love any less real; it just means you're in love with someone who isn't a perfect match. I don't want that.

"I've been in love twice," she says.

Technically, she's been in love three times, but to her, I don't count. Is her love with Caleb even real if it's something a Scrubber forced into their minds? It must be real if they're still together.

For the rest of the evening, Arella and I take turns pulling out more cards and talking until the sun is gone and it's time for her to go.

Like I did the previous four weeks, I ask if I can walk her to her car. Like usual, she says yes.

Side by side, we head away from our tree, still talking, still laughing, and still enjoying each other's company. I think about asking her if she's planning to come back next week, but don't. I won't be able to handle it if she says *no*.

When we reach her car, I try not to let the sinking feeling in my stomach get to me. I feel this way whenever it's time to watch her leave. As an attempt to prolong the high, I always head back to our tree and replay every moment from that night in my mind before I leave for the airport. I plan to do that again tonight.

Arella stops at her car and turns to face me. "You know what I just realized? We never went back to that first card I pulled out."

I was hoping she'd forget about that. "What was the question again?"

"What's the hardest thing you've ever had to do?"

"Oh. Why don't you go first?"

"The hardest thing I've ever had to do was go through a three-year-long abusive relationship and have to find myself again and relearn that I'm strong."

"You've done it. You are strong." *One of the two strongest people I know.*

"Thank you. That means a lot. Now you answer."

"The hardest thing I've ever had to do is . . ." *let you go.* I've been keeping my answers to these cards pretty vague. Either that or I tell her a version of the truth and hope she doesn't ask for more. I'm not sure how to spin this one to avoid saying too much.

Arella stares up at me, patiently waiting for me to finish what I started.

It takes me another moment. "Um, the hardest thing I've ever had to do is what I'm doing now."

"Which is?"

I knew she wasn't gonna accept that answer. "Which is . . . ya know, living. Moving on. Letting go of the past and stepping into the future. Sometimes I feel like I gave up, but Liz tells me I did the right thing."

Arella cocks her head at me, trying to read between the lines and figure out the deeper meaning behind my words. "Liz seems to know what she's talking about, so I trust that she's right."

"Yeah, but," I say, staring at the gravel I'm standing on, "that doesn't make it any less hard."

She slides a tender hand up my chest and stops over my pec. "You're so strong, Trey. And I see your strength growing with each smile you make. Just keep going."

Every nerve in my body sparks to life. My skin tingles from where she trailed her hand up, and it's on fire where she's keeping her hand now.

I don't move. I *can't* move. I'm too afraid it'll make her pull away. I want her to keep her hand on me for the rest of my life. If she does, I'll die a happy man.

97

TREY

"Arella." It feels good to be able to say her name to her. She smiles when I do.

"Trey." It feels even better to hear her say my name, especially because she's not saying it like she's wondering who I am. She's saying it like she knows me and is happy to see me.

This is the sixth week in a row she's come to our tree. It's been a whole month and a half of breathing easier and feeling the weight on my shoulders slowly chip off. I try not to think about how much it's going to destroy me if I lose her again—*when* I lose her again.

I'm not trying to fool myself. I know this won't last forever. That's why I'm imprinting everything she says and does into my mind so I can replay it over and over when I inevitably return to hell.

"Were you meditating?" she asks as I put my earbuds back into their case.

"Yep. I had the volume on low so I could hear you coming."

"I could tell. I didn't have to scare you this time." She shakes out her blanket and lays it down for us. "Did you finish your session?"

"No, but I can finish it later."

"Let's do it together."

I'm about to return my earbuds to my backpack when I stop. "Really?"

"Yeah. I've got some thoughts that need calming."

I hand her one of my earbuds, then we lie on her blanket next to each other and I hand her my phone. "Pick out a session for us."

She scrolls through the app, then chooses a guided meditation that's ten minutes long. As the soft music plays into my ear, I close my eyes and steady my breaths.

The point of meditating is to release all the thoughts clouding my head. With Arella next to me, it's near impossible. All I can think about is how close our hands are and how easy it would be to grab hers and hold it. I resist the urge to open my eyes and stare at her.

Halfway through the meditation, I lose the fight. As the lady in my ear tells me to focus on breathing deeply, I steal a peek at Arella through half-closed eyelids. She still has her eyes shut as she draws in a deep breath and slowly lets it out as instructed. I wonder what thoughts are storming through her head that need calming. *Do any of them have to do with me?*

At the end of the meditation, I close my eyes and slowly flutter them open as if they hadn't already been open for the last five minutes.

"Thanks, Trey," she says as she offers the earbud back to me.

"Did that help calm your thoughts?"

"It did."

"Do you want to talk about them?" *Please say yes. Please say yes.*

"If you want me to open up, you'll have to open up about something too."

Am I willing to do that? "How deep do I have to go?"

"I'll give you the freedom to decide that."

"All right. Deal. You share first."

She takes some time to think, then says, "I think my husband has turned into my roommate."

Hearing her call someone else her husband feels like accidentally touching a hot pan. The burn won't kill me, but the sting will linger for days.

She continues, "Lately, I feel like we're two people who just happen to live in the same apartment. I only ever see him during dinner, and most of the time, he's just scrolling through his phone. Whenever we happen to have the same day off, he's usually got plans at the gym with Rakesh."

Her dude hasn't made love to her in *months*, and when they're together, he's not even *looking* at her? What the fuck is wrong with him? "Who's Rakesh?"

"Caleb's best friend. They work out together almost every day."

"So he makes time for his friend, but not you?"

"I don't mind that they go to the gym together. I'm at work whenever they do, anyway. However, it does bother me that he makes plans with Rakesh, even when he knows I've got the day off."

It's official: The dude is an idiot. He has everything I want, and he's not even appreciating it. "Have you tried talking to him about this?"

"A few times, but it hasn't changed anything."

"Maybe you could suggest a system. Like whenever you both get your work schedules, you can sit down together and block out time to spend with only each other. Then talk to him about staying off his phone."

"A system . . ." Her voice trails off as she thinks about that. "That's really good advice. Thank you. Have you ever thought about being a relationship counselor?"

I burst into a loud laugh because that's the funniest shit I've ever heard. "Me? A relationship counselor? I haven't been able to keep a girl around for more than three months. No one would hire me with that track record."

"I would, judging from that one piece of advice. It means a lot coming from you."

What she's saying is that it means a lot coming from someone who would love to take Caleb's place. Technically, he took *my* place. I'd just be taking it back.

I might've given her different advice if I was certain we could have a future together. With her memories gone, that diamond ring sparkling on her finger, and no solid plan of how I could keep an intimate relationship with an Ordinary off the zovernment's radar, a future together is not a possibility. That doesn't stop me from yearning for it though.

"It's your turn to share something deep," she says.

"What would you like to know?"

"There's a question you refused to answer before that's been on my mind." She pauses, silently asking me for permission to continue.

With that curious glint in her eyes and the way her entire body is turned toward me so attentively, I eagerly grant her the permission. "Let's hear it."

"You said that Liz said something that helped you get sober a second time. I'm curious what she said."

I suck in a deep breath then slowly let it out. "Liz said a lot of things, but the winning line was, Is this the man she'd want you to be?" I don't need to specify who *she* is for Arella to know.

"And that's it? You went sober, just like that?"

"Basically." I say that like it's been easy for me, when in reality, it's a battle I'm fighting every day that sometimes feels like accepting an L wouldn't be the worst thing.

"If Alterella thinks similar to the way I do, then Liz is right. That isn't the man she'd want you to be."

That dark place in my chest floods with light. Suddenly, all those lonely sober nights of miserably living through my zero sense of purpose feels worth it. Just being here with her is worth it.

Arella tilts her head to the side, then softens her tone. "What's something you would say to her if you could?"

There is so much I would say. Most of them are things I write on postcards that never get stamped. I guess if I had to summarize all those handwritten notes, there would be one central message.

My words come out barely above a whisper. "I'd tell her that I miss her."

"What do you miss about her?"

"Everything."

"Could you be more specific?"

A shorter list would be what I don't miss. "You already got one deep thought from me tonight. Are you saying you wanna trade one more?"

With a smirk, she digs through her purse and pulls out our little box of questions. She slides the lid off, then plucks out a card from the middle and reads it. "What is something you'd say to anyone in any universe if you could? And be specific."

I burst into a laugh. "That's not what that card says."

"That's *exactly* what this card says. Word for word."

I hold my palm out. "Lemme see it then."

She hugs the card to her chest. "Nuh-uh. You have to answer it first."

"Lemme see the card first."

"Nope." She shoves the card down her shirt as if that's a deterrent. If she was mine, I'd have my hand down there already.

I drop my outstretched hand. "Fine. My answer is that I miss this. I miss being with her. I miss her playfulness. I miss how we used to cuddle in bed and talk for hours. I even miss arguing with her over stupid things, like which way to correctly hang toilet paper and whether putting icing on a muffin makes it a cupcake."

"First off, putting icing on a muffin does *not* make it a cupcake. They're completely different recipes. And second, the correct way to hang toilet paper is going over, never under."

I can't hold back the smile that spreads across my face. "Alterella had the same strong opinions."

"What's your opinion?"

"That I don't care if you call it a muffin or a cupcake as long as I get to eat it. I also don't care which way the toilet paper gets hung as long as I get to use it." Because I know it'll get a reaction from her, I add, "I tend to just put the TP on the holder whichever way it happens to be facing."

She leans back with a gasp. "That's even worse than going under. It's never consistent."

I chuckle lightly. "I don't give a fuck which way it's facing. At the end of the day, it's just toilet paper."

She narrows her eyes at me. "Are you one of those people who thinks pineapple belongs on pizza?"

"I don't mind pineapple on my pizza, but I wouldn't go out of my way for it."

"Ew!" She makes an *ick* face. "That's gross."

"Hey. At least I'm not a weirdo who pours their milk in before the cereal."

She slaps an offended hand over her heart. "Excuse me. I don't like soggy cereal. If I pour the milk in first, I can add a little bit of cereal at a time, then eat it while it's still crunchy before pouring in more. That's smart, if you ask me."

I don't think I've ever been more in love with this woman. The level of happiness and comfort I feel right now is beyond measure. I just wish I could get rid of the feeling that this happiness is coming to an end soon.

98

ARELLA

"Caleb . . ."

"What?" He glances up at me from across our little kitchen table. He's got his phone in one hand and a fork in the other.

"Remember what we talked about on Monday?"

He thinks, then sets his phone down. "Right. Sorry."

I took Trey's advice and talked to Caleb about being more intentional about spending time together and staying off his phone. Caleb agreed, and tonight, we're having a date night. Unfortunately, it's a Sunday, but this was the only night Caleb could take off work.

Around this time, I'm usually on my way to see Trey. I hope he's not sitting under our tree right now, waiting for me. I wish I had a way of telling him that I'm not coming. I don't have his phone number or email, and neither of us use social media.

With my fork, I push some of the rice around on my plate. I need to get Trey out of my head so I can think of something to talk about with Caleb. "How was your workout today?"

"Fine." He takes a bite of his rice and beans, barely even looking at me.

"What do you want to do for date night?"

"Whatever you want."

I thought I asked *him* to plan something for us, but I suppose I can do it at the last minute. "Would you rather stay in or go out?"

"Either." He stares blankly at his water glass as he takes another bite of his dinner.

I set my fork onto my plate. "Caleb?"

"What?"

"Is everything okay?"

"Yeah, why?"

That's a lie. He's more distant tonight than most nights. "You're barely even looking at me."

"I'm just stressed about work. That's all." He says it so nonchalantly, I almost believe him. Even if his stress was only about work, it still doesn't make it okay that he's letting it affect our relationship.

We haven't been actively trying to have a baby for four months. Correction: *He* hasn't been actively trying. I've been actively getting rejected. It takes two for this baby thing to happen.

"I'm ovulating?" I meant for that to sound sexy, but it comes out more like a question.

"Sorry, muffin. I'm not feeling it tonight."

"You haven't felt it for four months."

"It's hard to feel it when I'm stressed out."

I'm beginning to think this stress thing is just an excuse. I get stressed out at work too, but I don't allow it to affect my sex drive. All he has to do is walk laps around a closed museum at night. What's so stressful about that?

Maybe he doesn't find me attractive anymore. I've gained a few pounds since we met. I wouldn't say I'm big, but I've definitely filled out. *Is that it?*

"Do you want to talk about what's going on at work?" I ask.

He finishes eating the last bite of his dinner. "Not really. I don't want to put that burden on you."

But you are—indirectly. "Do you want to cancel date night?"

"We haven't had one for a while, so we should have it."

We *should* have it. He sees this as something we *should* do, not something he *wants* to do. I'm beginning to question if this date-night thing is something *I* want anymore.

Caleb stands and brings his dirty plate to the sink. I push my half-eaten food away because suddenly, I'm not hungry anymore.

After the kitchen is cleaned up, Caleb and I sit on the couch to pick out a movie together. By that, I mean it's him scrolling through movie options in four different streaming services before finally deciding on something.

We are three streaming services in when Caleb's phone vibrates on the coffee table. I don't have to look to know it's Rakesh calling.

Caleb doesn't hesitate to pick up his phone. "Hey."

The phone is loud enough that everything Rakesh says goes straight into my ears. "It finally happened, man."

"What?" Caleb tosses the TV remote onto the coffee table. "Just now?"

"Yeah. I just got off the phone with my brother. He was with her when it happened."

"Oh, I'm sorry."

"It's okay," Rakesh says through a sniffle. "She's not in pain anymore, I guess."

"Do you need anything?"

"Could you come over? I'd really like some support right now."

"I'll be right over." Caleb ends the call, then turns to me. "Rakesh's grandma just died."

I've never met Rakesh's grandma, so I pretend to sound like I care. "What happened?"

"She's been in hospice for the past few weeks."

News to me.

"Her colon cancer got really bad."

I didn't even know she had cancer. Honestly, I didn't even know Rakesh had a grandma.

"Are you cool with me going over to see him?"

"Of course." It's not like I can say no. He already told Rakesh he was coming.

Within seconds, Caleb has his shoes on. As he grabs his keys, he says, "Don't wait up for me." Then he's gone.

As his car engine rumbles to life, my heart sinks. He didn't even say bye or give me a kiss before he left. Just "don't wait up" as if he plans to be out all night. *Does he?*

I suppose it wouldn't be out of the norm. Lately, Caleb has been having game nights with

Rakesh and a few other friends. On those evenings, he usually doesn't return home until almost two in the morning.

I press a button on the remote, and the TV goes black. Then I'm left alone in a dark living room, questioning all my life decisions. Being alone was not part of my plan tonight. I pictured this evening filled with fun and laughter. I even hoped for some baby making.

Now I'm not even sure if I want a child with Caleb anymore. If this is how he's going to act when we don't have kids, how is he going to act when we do have them? Will he be an absent father? Will he leave me to take care of them every night while he goes out with his friends? Will he even look at our children when they talk to him, or will he just scroll through his phone?

Caleb hasn't been physically present in our relationship for four months. Now that I think about it, he hasn't been mentally present for even longer. Is this how it's going to be for the rest of our lives? I can't live like this.

Within seconds, I've got my shoes on and I'm out the door.

99

ARELLA

The stars are shining by the time I park my car behind Trey's motorcycle. The entire drive here, I was worried he had left already. I'm thrilled to know he hasn't.

When I get up to the tree—*our* tree—he's not there. His backpack is though. *Where did he go?*

I lay out our blanket, then set my purse down.

"Trey?" I call, because maybe he's nearby.

The crickets are the only things that answer me.

I glance around the oak tree toward the woods that always stretch behind us, but there's no movement.

Since his backpack is here, he's gotta come back for it, right? With a sigh, I sit on the blanket and wait.

Thankfully, I don't have to wait long. Barely five minutes later, the sound of footsteps comes from behind the tree.

When Trey rounds the trunk, he stops and jumps back with a hand to his chest. "Fuck. You scared me."

"Sorry," I say through a giggle.

"How long have you been here?"

"Only a few minutes." I pat my blanket and gesture for him to sit. "Where did you go?"

He drops down next to me and crosses his legs together. "My therapist suggested that I go for walks whenever the meditations don't work. So that's what I did."

"How often do you go for walks?"

"I used to almost every day. Sometimes twice a day. I haven't been on a walk in . . . seven weeks."

It takes me a second to understand the significance of seven weeks. Then that same warmth I've been feeling lately around Trey eases through me, filling my stomach with little flutters. "Why did you walk tonight?"

He blinks at me, and his eyes tell me his answer: He went for a walk because he thought I wasn't coming. He waited for me and overthought it so much that even the meditations didn't calm his mind.

"Did the walk help?"

"Not really, but I'm good now." He offers me a tender smile that says, *I'm good now that you're here.*

"I'm sorry. I didn't know how to contact you to let you know I wasn't going to be here. Maybe we should exchange numbers."

He twirls his thumbs around each other. "I've thought about that, and I don't think it's a good idea."

I try not to look disappointed. "Why's that?"

"Do you want to guess, or do you want me to just say it?"

"Um, is it because you don't think you should have a married woman's number?"

"No. It's because I don't think I can handle it. If I have the ability to text you, I won't be able to do anything else. I'll just stare at my phone all day, waiting for you to text me back. If you don't right away, I'll obsess over it, and I don't think that's healthy for me."

I can see where he's coming from. If I had his number, I'd probably spend all day texting him too. We never seem to run out of things to talk about. I wouldn't be able to get anything else done.

"So," he says, "you weren't planning to be here tonight?"

"Not originally."

"What changed your mind?"

Nothing really *changed* my mind. I've wanted to be here all week. Even when Caleb told me he took tonight off, I asked him if there was any other night he could take off instead. "I took your advice from last week. I talked to Caleb about spending more time together and staying off his phone. Tonight was supposed to be date night. Then Rakesh called. His grandma died, so Caleb ditched me to go be with him."

"I see." Trey's eyes cast down with a somber look.

I hate seeing him like that. "Why do you look so sad?"

He blinks like he's trying to arrange the right words in his head, then he bails. "It's nothing."

"It's *not* nothing. It's probably deep if you're not openly sharing it with me."

"It is deep, but it's also an inappropriate thing to say to you, so I should just keep quiet."

Now I *have* to know. I dig my hand into my purse and pull out our questions box. Then I take the lid off and pull out a card. I barely even look at it as I say, "What deep thought crossed your mind just now?"

Trey shakes his head at me, chuckling. "This tactic again, huh?"

I smirk a little. "It worked last time."

"If I share this deep thought with you, you're gonna have to fork one out too."

"Deal. Now spill."

He focuses on his hands in his lap for a while before finally saying, "The thought that crossed my mind was that the only reason you came here tonight was because your other plan fell through. To you, I'm just a backup plan. But to me, you're . . . well, you're not a backup plan. That's for damn sure. I shouldn't take it too hard though. I'd rather be your backup plan than no plan at all. I should just take what I can get."

Each of his words is laced with a brokenness I can feel in the depths of my heart. I'm sure his thoughts run deeper than what he was willing to share. I'm grateful that he shared *something,* though, because I need to correct him.

I place a tender hand over his knee so he can *feel* how much I mean my next words. "Trey, you are *not* a backup plan. I wanted to be here tonight, but this was the only night Caleb could get off. The entire time I had dinner with him, I was thinking of you."

"You were?"

"Yeah. I didn't like the idea of you sitting here, waiting for me. That's why the second he left, I came straight here."

Trey places his hand over mine on his knee. His warmth sends a tingle up my arm. "I would wait forever for you, even when I don't know if you're coming. The possibility that you *might* is enough for me."

My heart melts into a little puddle. That's the most endearing thing anyone has ever said to me.

My eyes lock with his. I recognize that intense look between all the chaos and misery in his blue-grays. It's the way he looks at me in my dreams—right before he kisses me. My breath hitches at the idea. His gaze drops to my eager lips and lingers there. I can practically see all the wild thoughts racing through his head as he battles with himself. Eventually, he leans back, clears his throat, and takes his hand off mine.

My skin feels cold where his hand used to be. I retract my palm from his knee as my throat goes dry. *Maybe it's for the best.*

To lighten things up, I say, "Does confessing that I was thinking of you during dinner count as forking out a deep thought?"

"Hell no. I'm gonna need something more than that."

"What would you like to know?"

He takes a moment to think. "Tell me a secret of yours. Something no one else knows."

I try to think of something I haven't told anyone else, not even Javina. She knows almost everything about me. The only thing she doesn't know is anything that's happened here with Trey. Lately, it's been getting harder to keep this from her. "A secret just came to mind, but it's not really a secret. It's just something I'd like to clear up with you."

"I'm listening."

"I don't have any food allergies. Nor do I have a birthmark. I've never had a dog either."

"But . . . you . . . when I came to your apartment—"

I offer him an apologetic shrug. "They were trick questions."

"I feel bamboozled."

I giggle at his funny word choice. "I'm sorry. At least you know now."

"You know, I drove myself insane trying to remember if you had ever mentioned having a dog."

He didn't say if *Alterella* had ever mentioned having a dog. He's talking about *me*. Usually, when he brings up the past, he's pretty good about keeping Alterella and me separated. I do the same. That way, we can continue living in our own little world where alternate universes explain why I don't remember him. A world where we don't have to talk about this unexplainable and unbreakable connection we have.

It's easier that way. I like being able to pretend like he's just an old friend I'm reconnecting with—a friend who appears in my dreams all the time. Because of those dreams, I feel like I know him. I don't know many facts about him, but I know his mannerisms, his tells, and the many thoughts he doesn't say aloud—things that people only know about each other after spending enough time together. Technically, I haven't spent that much time with Trey, but I have in my mind.

Despite that we've barely touched each other, I know his body too. I know what it feels like to have his muscular arms wrapped around me after a hot make-out session that leaves us panting. I know what it feels like to run my fingertips up and down the ridges of his abs. I even know what it feels like to wrap my palms around his thick shaft. These aren't things I remember doing in real life. They're things I've done only in my dreams, which I suppose could have been real life. I'm not sure anymore.

Trey said he can't tell me how I lost my memories because the government would throw him back in prison. If I guess it right, would he tell me? I have theories. Some are plausible; others are downright insane.

My craziest theory is that Trey is from the future—a future where they visit the past like it's a fun recreational activity, as if it's the same as taking a little vacation or going on a road trip—and on one of Trey's visits to the past, we met and fell madly in love. Since people from the future are forbidden from getting personally involved with people from the past, the future government wiped my memories using a memory-zapping device like the one from *Men in Black*. Then the future government banished Trey from returning to the future and said if he ever told me what happened, they'd imprison him.

Their memory zapper must not be that powerful if my memories have been returning in my dreams. Trey must know it's possible to beat it, because he once said, "Whatever they did to you, you can fight it. Look into my eyes. Try to remember me."

I wish I could fully remember him. My dreams only give me a tiny snapshot of the full picture. Sometimes my dreams are clear. Other times, they're blurry, like I'm watching things happen through a dirty lens. Occasionally, I have dreams where everything sounds muffled like everyone is speaking into a voice distorter.

My worst dreams are the ones where I can hear everything clearly but all I can see is black. Those are typically my dreams where Trey is screaming like he's being attacked by vicious animals. I can't see that it's him, but I know in my heart that it is, from how much it kills me to hear him in pain like that. If my other dreams of us actually happened, does that mean my dreams of him screaming happened too? If so, why was he screaming?

"You okay?" Trey asks.

"Yeah. I'm just a little cold." It's the middle of July in California. My shivers have *nothing* to do with being cold. I just get chills whenever I think about my dreams of what I'm assuming is Trey getting tortured. Who or what was hurting him? And why do I get the feeling that they were torturing him because of me?

He takes off his leather jacket and drapes it over my shoulders. His manly scent surrounds me like a warm blanket of comfort and ease. "Better?"

"Kind of." I'm not sure if *better* is the right word. His jacket over me is only jumbling my thoughts more. Why is his scent so familiar to me? And why does it spark up a desire between my legs?

"I don't mind sitting in the grass. Why don't we wrap this blanket around you too?"

A thought pops into my head, and I say it before I can think about the consequences. "Actually, could you just hold me?"

He freezes and stares at me like he's trying to figure out if he heard me right. "Hold you?"

"Yeah. Penguins keep warm by cuddling. They live in snow, so it must work, right?"

"Right . . ." Slowly, as if not to scare me, he lies down and pats his chest. "Come here."

I don't hesitate. Keeping his jacket around my shoulders, I scoot toward him, then lay my head over his chest. His tattooed arm circles my back and rests over my hip.

I nuzzle my face into his shirt, taking in more of his sweet scent. This is the first time he's ever cuddled me—that I can remember—yet it feels so familiar.

At first, Trey just lies there with his body stiff. It's like he's afraid if he moves too much, I'll disappear. As an attempt to make him feel more comfortable, I rest my hand over his abs the way I always do in my dreams.

"Arella?" He says my name all breathily.

"Yeah?"

"Is it okay if I put both my arms around you?"

"Mm-hmm."

Without wasting another second, he wraps his firm arms around my back and crushes me against his chest. He does it so tight, the air leaves my lungs. This feels like it did the first time: desperate, possessive, protective.

I give him a moment, but when he doesn't release me right away, I let out a stifled, "Trey, you're suffocating me."

He relaxes his boa-constrictor arms a little. "Better?"

"Yeah."

His chest rises with a deep breath. When he exhales, it sounds ragged. He breathes in again, and on the exhale, his breath comes out shaky, like he's trying not to cry.

"Are you okay?" I ask into his chest.

"Mm-hmm." He sounds choked up. "I'm just—um, overwhelmed."

"By what?"

"Happiness. It's been so long since I've held you, I forgot what it felt like."

I've never felt so comfortable in someone's arms like this. I've never felt so safe and protected either. "When was the last time you held me?"

"That day you looked at me with recognition and said my name like you knew me. Then you asked if I could stay and hold you until you woke up."

"I don't remember that, but I know it happened." *Only because Caleb said so.*

"I know, and that's okay."

"Is it though?" I tilt my head back to look at him.

His eyes are glistening with surface tears. He blinks them away, then clears his throat. "There's nothing I can do to change the situation, so I *have to* be okay with it. Besides, it doesn't matter how I feel, as long as you're happy."

It bugs me that he doesn't see his happiness as something important. He matters just as much as anyone else. "How would you know if I'm happy or not?"

"You have to be. Otherwise, going through hell wasn't worth it."

Going through hell. Is he referring to when he was being tortured? Or maybe when people were attacking me? A few times, I've had dreams of people throwing flaming objects at my face or a knife at my arm. I've done a thorough check of my arms and haven't found any evidence of a knife wound. Then again, Caleb said I remembered Trey getting stabbed, and there's no evidence of that either. Did whatever healed him heal me too?

"Did you leave LA because of me?" That question has been burning on my mind for years. I already know the answer; I just want to hear it from him.

"I left LA so you could be happy."

For the most part, I am happy. I have amazing friends, I love my job, and I'm planning to open my dream bakery soon. The only thing is that when I'm with Trey, I feel like my life is complete. I don't feel that way with Caleb, and now that I think about it, I never have. Minus the past few months, Caleb makes me happy. However, there's a difference between feeling happy and feeling complete.

"I think you should move back to LA."

Trey pulls me in closer and breathes into my hair. "Why?"

"Because I don't like the idea of you living in New York just to stay away from me. You don't have to do that anymore. We're friends now." The word *friends* sounds wrong to describe this relationship I have with Trey—a relationship that exists only on Sunday evenings under this tree, where it feels right to be held by him.

"Thanks, Arella. I appreciate your friendship, but I think I've gotta stay in New York."

What he means is that being friends with me isn't enough of a reason to move back. He wants more. *Do I?* "Is New York where you see yourself in five years?"

"Probably not."

"Where do you see yourself then? Or maybe a better question is, What would you like to see?"

"Like, in terms of life?"

"Yeah. For example, in five years, I see myself as an established bakery owner. Maybe I'll have a second location. I see lots of fun employees who enjoy coming to work every day the way I do at the bakery I currently work at." I also see myself as a mother, but at the rate I'm going with the man I'm with, that'll never happen.

"Do you want my realistic or unrealistic answer?"

"Both."

"Realistically, I see myself still making music, whether that's with my band or not. I've been thinking about what you said last year—about writing and producing for other artists. I've been playing around with the idea of starting my own production company."

I lean back with a wide grin. "That's a wonderful idea! Now, what's your unrealistic answer?"

"To have a family."

That's what I want too. "Why is that unrealistic?"

"Because to have a wife and kids, I'd need to have a girlfriend first."

I make a *pfft* sound. "Have you looked into the mirror lately? Finding a girlfriend can't be hard for you."

"Finding the *right* girl is. I don't want to have a family with just anyone. What I want is to have a family with *the* one, but . . ." He lets out a deep sigh. "Anyway, it's just not in the cards for me."

But what? But she's already with a man who spends more time with his best friend than his wife? A man who barely looks at her while he eats the dinner she makes for him every night? A man who doesn't even know his wife's been hanging out with another man every Sunday for the past seven weeks?

Even if I told Caleb about Trey, he wouldn't care. He'd probably just go back to scrolling on his phone. What does it mean for my marriage if my husband doesn't care what I do or who I'm with?

100

ARELLA

By the time I get home from my thinking spot, it's well past two in the morning, and Caleb is still gone. I call him, but he doesn't pick up, so I fall asleep without him.

When I wake up around nine, I'm *still* without him. *Did he stay the night at Rakesh's?*

After I brush my teeth, I call him, but he doesn't answer.

Twenty minutes later, I ring him again. Same thing.

Due to being out late, I called in sick to work, so I'm home when Caleb finally returns around noon.

"Is everything okay?" I ask when he strolls through the door.

"Yeah," he says as he kicks off his shoes. "Why are you home? I thought you had work today."

"I got the day off."

"Oh." He barely looks at me as he rushes into our bedroom.

I follow him. "How's Rakesh doing?"

"He's all right." After unbuttoning the top three buttons of his pastel shirt, Caleb drags it over his head and tosses it into the hamper. "We took a trip up to Bakersfield to visit his family last night. He felt better after that."

I climb onto our bed and sit with my legs to the side. "Is that why you were out all night?"

"Yeah. We stayed at his mom's place."

It would have been nice if Caleb had told me that. I suppose it's not like I was up all night worrying about where he was though. "I called you a few times."

"I saw. Sorry I didn't pick up. I fell asleep in the car on the way back."

But you didn't pick up last night either. "Do you think we could look at our schedules today to see when we can reschedule our date night?"

"Uh, sure." His tone comes out somewhere between hesitant and forced. "Let me take a quick shower first. I feel gross right now."

I'm on the couch when Caleb comes out of the bathroom from his longer-than-usual shower. He doesn't look at me as he heads straight past me and into the kitchen.

He opens the fridge. "I'm going to head to the gym, then Rakesh wants me to come over after that. I'll probably get dinner with him before I head to work tonight, so don't worry about me for food, okay?"

He already spends more time with Rakesh than he does with me. Now he's getting dinner with Rakesh too? During the only time I ever get to see him? Seriously? Do I even know this man anymore? I wouldn't even consider us roommates at this point. He's like a stranger to me. More of a stranger to me than Trey the first time I saw him standing on my doorstep. There's always been a part of me that's felt connected to Trey. I thought I felt like that with Caleb, but now I don't feel connected to him at all.

I step into the kitchen to find the stranger I happen to live with munching on a granola bar. "Can you pull up your work schedule?"

"What for?" he asks through a mouthful.

"So we can compare schedules and plan our next date night?" *What we said we were going to do before you showered.*

"Oh, that's right. Could we do it later? I'm supposed to meet Rakesh at the gym soon."

I suck in a deep breath, resisting the urge to roll my eyes. "Fine. Whatever."

Turning on my heel, I storm away. I expect him to stop me or ask what's wrong, but he doesn't. This is what I mean when I say he doesn't care. He hasn't cared for a while, so I don't know why I keep trying.

After Caleb leaves, I try not to cry as I write down a list of the things I want to hash out with him. I vowed to myself after Nathan that I would not stay in a relationship where I felt abused or unwanted ever again. Caleb doesn't abuse me, but he doesn't want me either. And if he does, he's got a crappy way of showing it. I'll tell him he's got one month to make things better between us or I'm out.

THE NEXT DAY, I BRING OUT MY LIST DURING DINNER AND HAND IT TO CALEB.

"What's this?" he asks with his fork halfway to his lips.

I play with the mashed potatoes on my plate. "It's a list of all the things I think we should work on as a couple."

He stares at the piece of paper in his hand. "Make spending quality time together a priority. Actually look at each other when we're having a conversation. Have more conversations. Have monthly date nights. Be intimate again." He sets the paper down, then goes straight back to eating his steak.

I wait a moment before asking, "Sooo . . . ? What do you think?"

"I don't know."

"What do you mean, you don't know?"

"As in, I don't know," he says, clipped. "You keep saying you want to spend more time together, but it's hard to do that when you work days and I work nights."

"That's why I suggested that we make it a priority. Like yesterday, I had the day off, but you went to the gym with Rakesh."

"I always go to the gym with him on Mondays. It's our leg day."

"Yeah, but you had dinner with him too, which is supposed to be our time together."

"Because I was going to his place after the gym, and then I had to work after that. It just made more sense to get dinner with him so I wouldn't have to drive back and forth."

"You didn't have to go to his place after the gym. You could have come home if you wanted to." And that's the problem. He didn't want to.

"Rakesh wanted me to come over because he wanted to talk to me about going to the funeral with him this weekend."

"Are you?"

"Yeah. The wake is on Sunday, and the funeral is on Monday. We're going to leave Saturday morning and stay at his mom's place. I should be back Tuesday afternoon."

That seems like a long time to be gone for one funeral. "Are you going to be able to get the days off for that?"

"I already did. I asked my boss last night."

How was it that easy for him to get three nights off in a row at the last minute? Whenever I ask if he can take one night off for me, he always makes it seem like it's a hassle to even ask. "What about all the other stuff on my list?"

He cuts into his steak with a knife. "What about them?"

"Do you think we could try to work on them together?"

"How do you want to do that?"

"Well, I was thinking for the intimacy one, we could start with cuddling more." *Or at all would be nice.*

"Sure," he says halfheartedly.

I pretend like he said it with enthusiasm. "Do you want to cuddle after dinner?"

"Not for long. I've gotta go to work soon."

I suppose that's better than *no*.

After I get the kitchen cleaned up, I sit on the couch and wait for Caleb. He comes out of the bedroom in his security guard uniform and plops onto the cushion next to me. When he puts his arm around me, it feels forced, not eager. When I lay my head against his stiff chest, it feels awkward, not comforting.

We get about two silent minutes in before Caleb says, "I've gotta go before I'm late."

I push myself off him and try not to frown. "Okay. Have a good night at work."

He gets his shoes on and rushes out the door like he couldn't get away from me fast enough. For being held by a security guard, I didn't feel safe or protected once.

101

ARELLA

Since Caleb is out of town, I don't have to wait until after he's fed and off to work to head to my thinking spot. I don't know what time Trey usually gets there, but he's always already there when I arrive around seven thirty. Tonight, I want to spend as much time with him as possible, so I leave my apartment early with hopes that he'll already be there.

And he is.

When I emerge from the woods at the top of the hill, Trey's gaze flicks from the book in his lap up to me, then his expression brightens.

"Hi." I'm breathless from the way he's staring at me so intently.

"Arella." I'll never get sick of hearing him say my full name. He peels his eyes off me to glance at his phone. "You're two hours earlier than usual."

"Are you complaining?"

"Fuck no. I'm ecstatic." It's good to know that *someone* feels that way about seeing me.

I lay out our blanket as Trey shoves his book into his backpack. "How far did you get in your reading?"

"About halfway." He sits across from me on our blanket with his legs crossed. "I'll probably finish it on my flight home tonight."

"What time is your flight?" I hope it's not early, because I plan to stay here for as long as he stays.

"Whenever I get to the airport and purchase one."

"You don't have a flight booked yet?"

"Nah. They've got flights leaving LA to New York every few hours. I'm willing to pay whatever, and I don't care if I have to wait, so lately, I've been getting on whatever is available."

I'm flattered that he makes so many accommodations just to be with me. "Do you ever have to wait long for a flight?"

"Sometimes, but I don't mind. I'm never in a rush to get back to New York. The only thing I've got going on there are my Monday afternoons with my therapist. The rest of the days, I'm basically just killing time until I fly back to LA."

I imagine him in his big fancy penthouse all alone. The scene depresses me, so I imagine myself there with him. *That's better.*

"Do you still talk to your therapist about me?"

"Occasionally." In Trey speak, that means *all the time.*

"What's the last thing you told her about me?"

"That you let me hold you, and that it wasn't because you suddenly remembered me."

"Do you have any idea how that might have happened?" *Because I'd like to make it happen again.*

"Not a goddamn clue." The pang of sadness that crosses his eyes tells me he's speaking the truth. It also tells me he wishes he knew just as much as I do.

My guess is that seeing that spider triggered my traumatic memory of being attacked by spiders, which must have triggered my mind into remembering him. I've seen more spiders since then, but my mind has stayed the same.

Suddenly, Trey perks up with a smile. "Can I show you something?"

I return his smile and eagerness. "Sure."

He stands, then offers me his hand. I don't hesitate to take it. "Do you know how to climb a tree?"

"Not really."

He gestures toward the lowest branch of the oak tree. If I stick my arm up, I could touch it without having to step onto my tiptoes. "I'll give you a boost, okay?" he says.

"Why are we climbing this tree?"

"Because I wanna show you somethin'."

"And we have to climb a tree to see it?"

His smile drops as he gives me a *come on* look. "Put a little faith in me, will ya? You're gonna like it. I promise."

With his help, I hoist myself onto the lowest branch, then climb onto the next one.

"Don't go any farther. Wait for me." Trey makes climbing the tree look easy. With one swift motion, he's already up and next to me. His warm hand presses against the small of my back to steady me, but I don't need the support. I'm clinging onto this tree so tightly, a hit from Thor's hammer couldn't make me fall. "You good?"

I nod.

"Cool. Now climb up three more branches."

My eyes go wide. "Three? That's pretty high, Trey. If I fall, I'll break something."

He lets out a little scoff. "Do you really think *I* would let you fall?"

Good point. I reach for the next branch and climb up. Three branches later, I've got leaves in my face.

Trey climbs up next to me with a huge grin. I don't know why he's grinning like that. This branch we're standing on could break any second. I'm surprised it hasn't already.

I cling onto the branch next to me. "All right, mister. What's so cool that we had to climb a tree to see it?"

"Shh." He places a finger against his lips. Then he whispers, "Turn around."

I match his hushed tone, even though I don't know why he's whispering. "Um, I'm not sure if moving on this branch is a good idea."

He places a hand over my waist. "I won't let you fall, baby. Promise."

He just called me *baby.* And it felt so normal.

With his confidence in the sturdiness of this branch, I slowly turn around, then gasp. A plump bird is curled up in her little nest, sleeping.

"Oh my god," I whisper. "She's beautiful."

Trey keeps his voice low too. "She's got eggs beneath her. I saw 'em earlier."

"How did you know she was up here?"

"I noticed her flying in and out while I was reading, so I climbed up to check it out."

I resist the urge to pet the bird. "Aw. I can't wait to see when her little babies hatch."

"See? I told ya you'd like this."

"How did you know I would?"

"You find joy in the little things in life, and this is one of them."

We stay in the tree, watching the mama bird sleep for another minute before Trey helps me climb down.

Once my feet have returned to the ground where they belong, we sit on top of our blanket and talk as the sun sets. It's not until after the stars are twinkling that I realize I haven't needed to take out our questions box yet. There hasn't been a single lull in our conversation.

We've talked about nothing yet everything at the same time. Trey told me the story of how he met Liz. He shared stories about some funny things that happened while he was on tour with his band. I cried from laughing so hard. He even willingly told me about seeing his parents' death, which was a huge step for him.

Now he's telling me about the time he woke up in a hotel room with a naked bartender in his bed. "I left that hotel with my head spinning, feeling pretty disappointed in myself."

I gaze at him, admiring his perfectly trimmed stubble and the way he's so comfortably sharing things with me. "Why were you disappointed?"

"Because it shouldn't have happened, and I told her so. She assumed I was married."

"Why?"

"Probably because I didn't fuck her that night and was sober enough to ask her to leave the next morning."

I'm not complaining, but . . . "Why didn't you have sex with her?"

"According to her, I couldn't get it up."

My jaw drops with a laugh. "What?"

"I was so wasted, I don't even remember it. How do you expect me to perform under those circumstances? She said I was a good kisser though."

If he kisses anything like the way he does in my dreams, that woman is right. "Was she good?"

"Hell if I know."

For my benefit, I'm going to tell myself she was terrible. She probably used too much tongue and was sloppy about it.

My stomach rumbles so loudly, it makes Trey chuckle.

"You hungry?" he asks.

"A little." I tuck some hair behind my ear.

"Maybe you should go home and make something to eat." He pulls his phone out from his backpack to check the time. I don't miss how he hasn't taken out his device once since I arrived. "Shit. It's almost midnight. Shouldn't you be gone by now?"

Usually, I'm *looong* gone by now, but tonight is special. "I can stay as late as I want. I have tomorrow off." *Because I took it off with the intention of staying out late.*

"When does Caleb usually get home from work?"

"Around four in the morning."

"Shouldn't you be home before he gets there?" It's endearing that Trey cares enough about me to even *think* about making sure I'm home before Caleb is. I'm sure if it was up to Trey, he'd keep me here forever.

"You don't have to worry about Caleb. He's out of town."

"What for?'

"Rakesh's grandma's funeral." I found out yesterday that Caleb never even met Rakesh's grandma, so I don't understand why he felt the need to go to her funeral. Even if it was just to be supportive for Rakesh, taking three days off work to be at the funeral of someone he never met seems excessive.

Trey's eyes light up. "So what you're saying is that you're free to get some late-night pancakes with me?"

I nod eagerly. "That's exactly what I'm saying."

102

TREY

I can't believe my luck right now. First, she arrives two hours early. Then, she stays two hours later than usual. Now we're going to get pancakes together? Seriously? Is this real life, or have the last eight weeks just been a long hallucination?

When we step out of the woods and onto the gravel road, Arella unlocks her car and tosses her blanket onto the backseat.

"Do you want to drive separately?" I ask, because maybe she'll want to head home after we eat.

"Actually," she says, "could we take your bike?"

I can't hide my shock. "Really?"

"Yeah. I've never ridden on a motorcycle before. It looks fun."

I swallow because it's moments like this that remind me she doesn't remember me. Sometimes when we're together, I forget about what's happened to her memories, because things feel like we've picked up right where we left off. "I've only got one helmet, but there's a diner not too far from here. Are you cool with me riding without a helmet?"

"If you're okay with it, then I am."

After we stash my backpack in her car and stick her purse and my wallet under my bike seat, I help her get my helmet on. It's a little big on her, but it'll keep her alive if we crash, which I don't intend to. As extra protection, I take my leather jacket off and hold it out to her. "Put this on."

She doesn't ask why. She simply takes my jacket and slips into it like she's been wanting to all night.

I mount my bike and pat the empty spot behind me. She throws her leg over the seat and wraps her arms around my torso the way she has before. A rush of warmth and tingles races down my legs and lingers there.

"Ready?" I ask. I almost call her *babe* but stop myself. I slipped up earlier, and even though her eyes lit up, I don't want to overdo it.

"Ready."

I start the engine, then we're off.

Riding my motorcycle with Arella takes me back to the good ol' days, when we used to do this all the time. Arella rode with me to work plenty of times. We'd take my bike to get dinner, or I'd take her back to her apartment on it. I even bought her a helmet, which later became one of the many things that disappeared from my home after the Keepers scrubbed her.

A cute twenty-four-hour diner sits on a quiet main street in the town next to where our tree stands. I pull into a front parking spot and kill my engine. Then I wait for Arella to hop off before I do.

She yanks my helmet off and hands it to me with a grin. "That was so fun."

I'm glad she enjoyed that. Probably not as much as I did though. She didn't trace her fingertips in figure eights over my abs the way she used to, but that's okay. I can't expect her to do *everything* the same as before.

Inside the cozy diner, some '70s music plays over the speakers in the ceiling. Two of the tables are occupied. One has a couple sitting on the same side of the booth, speaking in low voices to each other while they eat their waffles. The other table has a gray-haired man downing a burger.

Arella and I get seated in a corner booth.

"I'll be back with some water," our waitress says as she hands us our menus.

Once she's gone, I glance at the menu, see something I want, then set it back down. Why look at a sticky laminated piece of paper when I can stare at the delicious snack sitting across from me?

It only takes another minute for Arella to set her menu down, which means I got a full minute of uninterrupted time to admire her.

Our waitress returns with two glasses of water. "Y'all ready?"

I order my pancakes with extra whipped cream, some sausages, and eggs over easy. Arella asks for pancakes with a side of bacon. *Shit.* I should have ordered bacon too, in case she wants mine, like she has in the past. I think about changing my order, but the waitress is already gone.

Arella takes a sip of her water with a far-off look in her eyes. She's thinking about something heavy, and I wish I knew what.

I'm too curious not to ask. "What are you thinking about?"

She stares out the window at my bike. "I've been on a motorcycle with you before, haven't I?"

"What?" I say, not because I didn't hear her, but because I can't believe she just said that. Our unspoken rule is that we pretend we don't have a history and that she and Alterella are two separate people.

"Earlier, when I said I've never ridden on a motorcycle before, you got this look in your eyes."

Damn my eyeballs for always giving me away. "What look?"

"The look you always get when I say something that contradicts what you know. You got that same look when I told you I've been in love twice and again when I mentioned my pregnancy loss." She stares at me to gauge my reaction.

I keep my face impassive as I play with my hands in my lap. "I dunno what you want me to say."

"Can you tell me if I've ever been on a motorcycle with you?"

A knot tightens in my chest. If we drive down this road, I have a bad feeling we'll crash and it'll break this magic between us. Pretending that I came from an alternate universe is what's keeping our weekly slivers of heaven from feeling tense and awkward. Is she going to keep coming if things get complicated? If I start confusing her with stories of the past? Or mentioning things I know about her she doesn't recall ever telling me?

"You know what?" she says. "I don't need to hear you say it for me to know the answer. The second I sat on your bike and put my arms around you, I knew it wasn't my first time. It felt too familiar."

We never should have left the solace of our secret tree. The second we did, it changed things. She and I exist in peace there. It's a place no one else knows about, where we can be together without acknowledging the rest of the world. How am I supposed to find peace with her out here when there are thousands of things threatening to tear us apart?

"Can you at least tell me why you got that look when I told you about my miscarriage? What do you know that I don't?"

That knot in my chest pulls tighter, threatening to suffocate me from the inside out. "I, um, I don't think we should talk about this."

"Like right now in this diner or at all?"

"At all."

"Don't you think I should know?"

Yes, she *deserves* to know. *Should she know?* is a different question. This knowledge won't change anything. She'll still be married to someone else, and I'll still be forbidden from being with her. It's better if she lives in ignorance. That way, she won't have to carry all the pain and burden that comes with knowing the truth. One person doing it is enough.

"Arella, I think we should keep pretending like—"

"It was *our* baby, wasn't it?"

My bubble of bliss cracks straight down the middle. I'm about to lose my perfect little world of paradise that exists on Sunday evenings with sunsets under a tree. I can't allow this to happen. I won't.

"Arella, I—"

She slides out of her booth, climbs into mine, then throws herself into my chest. I hold her close as she quietly cries into my shirt. Her shoulders shudder, and I tear up as I let out a deep breath into the top of her hair. I can't break down right now. If I do, I might not be able to crawl out of that hole for a while.

"I'm so sorry," she whispers into my pec.

I caress little circles into her back. "You have nothing to apologize for."

"Yes, I do. I left you to grieve the loss of our baby all on your own. That must have been so hard."

It was. I lost my baby, my dad, and then Arella, all in a matter of days. But none of that was her fault. The entire situation was something neither of us had control over.

Arella wipes her wet cheeks off with the bottom of her shirt, then tilts her head back to look up at me. "Did you want to have a baby?"

"With you, yes."

"Was it something we tried for?"

"It was an accident." An accident I wish I would have known the truth about sooner. If the zovernment didn't lie to the Zordi world, saying it's impossible for us to reproduce with Ordinaries when we actually can, I never would have questioned Arella's faithfulness.

"Did you know it was a girl?"

My body goes rigid. "What?"

"After my surgery, the doctors sent the embryo to pathology. When the test results came back, it included a note that stated the embryo had XX chromosomes. That means it was a girl."

An invisible hand grips my lungs and squeezes all the air from them. I chomp down on my bottom lip as a debilitating wave of agony takes over my body.

I could have had a baby girl. She would have been two by now. I could have known what it's like to hold my own child in my lap and kiss her forehead. I could have known what it's like to hear a little girl call me her daddy. I could have had a family.

Hearing that our baby was a girl makes the loss more real. It makes the pain more real too. I was so close to being a father, and then it was torn away from me in the worst way possible. This miscarriage didn't happen naturally like Mia Wang said probably would have happened. Someone drugged and dropped lightning balls onto Arella until our unborn baby couldn't take it anymore.

I will never forgive Jodi for that or anything else she took away from me in her diabolical scheme to get revenge on my dad for having an affair. My mom and dad were soul mates. I used to think the soul-mate thing was just a ploy to justify adultery, but now I think it's valid. My mom and dad were meant to be together. Why get in the way of that? Why take it out on their son? Jodi could have gone off to find her own soul mate. Instead, she swapped minds with my dad and locked him up with intentions to torture him. Then she pretended to be him for over twenty years. That decision destroyed many lives and ended countless others.

The waitress returns to our table to find Arella sniffling into my shirt. She flashes me an understanding look, then without a word, she places our plates onto the table and leaves.

It takes Arella a few minutes to gather herself. Once she does, she sits up but doesn't leave my side, giving me a tender smile. "I'm ready to go back to pretending now, if that's what you want."

I return her smile. "Yes, please."

103

TREY

"I can't believe they hatched already," Arella says, smiling at the baby birds sleeping in their nest.

"The incubation period for small birds is only ten to fourteen days."

"You seem to know a lot about everything. How are you so smart?"

"Google," I say simply, and it makes her laugh.

We stand in the tree, watching the beauty of Mother Nature do its thing for a while. Eventually, the mama bird returns and sits on her babies to keep them warm, and Arella and I take that as our cue to leave them alone.

When our feet return to the ground, we immediately go back to the position we were in before I suggested seeing the nest. I lie first, then Arella nuzzles into my side with her head in the crook of my shoulder and her hand over my stomach.

We started off week nine like this. Within a minute of her coming out of the woods, she had her blanket over the grass and asked if we could cuddle. I didn't hesitate to pat my shoulder and gesture for her to come to me.

I put my arm that's not wrapped around her back behind my head like a pillow. Then I close my eyes and bask in the euphoria that comes from feeling her body against mine. It's a high that no amount of drugs has ever given me. This high also lasts longer than jaderro. After my Sunday nights with Arella, I've found myself feeling light and full for at least three days. By the fourth day, I'm still in a good mood but I'm definitely ready for my next dose of Arella.

"Trey?"

"Hmm?"

She traces a figure eight over my abs, and I couldn't be more thrilled about it. "Do you think we're soul mates?"

I know we are. "Why do you ask?"

"Because I've been doing some research on it. Did you know that soul mates can feel a connection to each other that's stronger than any other force in the world?"

"Yep."

"Did you know that my body felt it when you got into that motorcycle accident?"

"Yeah, I know." When I decided to live in New York, there was a part of me that didn't want to, in case I ever felt the glimmer again. How was I supposed to protect her from all the way across the country?

"I also read online that if soul mates are torn apart, it feels like losing a part of yourself. Do you think that's true?"

"Yes." *That's how I feel whenever I'm apart from you.*

"Did you know that just because you're soul mates, it doesn't mean you end up together?"

"Yep." My dad spent more years trapped in darkness than he spent freely in the light with my mother.

"Did you know that whenever your soul mate misses you, they appear in your dreams?"

"That, I didn't know."

"Well, it's on the Internet, so it must be true."

That gets a chuckle out of me. "If that's true, then you must dream about me a lot."

"I do."

"You do?"

"Yeah." She tilts her head back to meet my eyes. "Multiple times a week."

"For real?"

"Yeah. For the past two and a half years."

My body freezes as I gape down at her. How can she say that so nonchalantly? "Wait. Wh —what do you dream about?"

"Sometimes we're just doing mundane things like cuddling in bed or driving in a car. Other times, I've dreamt of us hanging out with your band or hanging out here at this tree."

"What was the last dream you had of me?"

"I dreamt that you beat up Nathan so badly, he left my apartment with a bloody nose and a limp."

My eyes go wide. Did it happen the same way in her dream as it did in real life? "What else have you dreamt about?"

"A few days ago, I dreamt that we were in a dark basement with an older Chinese couple, looking through a photo album."

My breath gets caught in my throat as I try to understand what the hell is going on. Are her memories returning to her in her dreams?

Arella continues, "Sometimes, I see the same dream over and over. One that has recurred a few times is the one where I'm in a kitchen with you, baking cookies, when all of a sudden, we're throwing flour at each other."

"What kind of cookies were they?"

"Snickerdoodles."

I let out a sharp gasp. Has she dreamt about everything that's happened between us? If she has, what does that mean for us? If she *hasn't*, what does that mean for us?

She keeps her eyes trained on me. "They aren't just dreams, are they?"

I clear my throat as I try to pull myself together. "If you have to ask, then you already know the answer."

"I think I've known for a while."

I put my hand over hers on my stomach as I let this sink in. "Why didn't you tell me about your dreams sooner?"

"I was afraid it would ruin what we have."

I totally understand. That's the same reason why I don't say half the shit I want to say to her either. "Why are you telling me now?"

"Because you actually talked to me about losing our baby instead of keeping up this charade that we don't have a past together. I understand why, because I do it too, but I felt like you should know about my dreams."

"I'm glad you told me." *Even though I have no idea what to do with this information.* At the end of the day, this changes nothing.

She pushes herself up and sits with her legs to the side. "Can you tell me what happened to my memories?"

I sit up too, then cross my legs. "I can't."

"Because you'll be taken to prison by the government from the future?"

I let out a laugh. "You think I'm from the future?"

"It's a possibility."

This reminds me of the time she asked if I was a superhero or an alien. Is that moment something she's dreamt about too?

"You've been watching all the Disney canon movies with Liz, right?" she asks me.

"We finished that already." Like six months ago.

"You saw *Snow White and the Seven Dwarves*, then?"

"It wasn't a favorite, but yes."

"Do you remember how Prince Charming broke the spell that was cast on Snow White?"

Where is she going with this? "Yep. True love's kiss."

"What if that's what can bring back all my memories?"

I sigh a little. "It won't."

"How do you know?"

"Because you're not under a magic spell. Plus, that would be too easy, and I've had twenty-nine years to learn that nothing in my life ever comes easy."

She rubs the ends of her hair between her fingers. "Don't you think we should at least try?"

Try what? To break a magic spell she's not under? One that doesn't even exi— *Wait . . .* "Are you saying you want me to kiss you?"

She nods and whispers, "Desperately."

That's all the permission I need. I seize her face and crash my lips against hers. She clutches my shirt and pulls me into her as our lips dance with each other like they've been waiting to for their entire existence.

I claw at her to come closer, and she does. She climbs into my lap, straddling me as she plunges her tongue into my mouth. My need for her has never been so strong.

My hand slides up her back, then I yank her closer to me, desperate to feel her breasts against my chest. Her fingernails scratch up the back of my head, then she pulls my hair at the top.

I groan as my cock hardens in my jeans. "Arella . . ."

"The spell isn't broken yet," she says breathlessly against my mouth. "Let's keep trying."

I don't need to be asked twice.

With my lips attacking hers, I gently lower her back to the ground until I'm on top of her. Then I straddle her and kiss her like a starving beast as she moans beneath me.

My lips travel down her neck, and she arches her head back to give me more access. I nip and suck on her skin as she lets out breathy groans and claws at my back. I want to feel her skin against mine, and I hate that all this fabric is in the way.

As if reading my mind, she reaches under my shirt and slides her palms up my bare chest. That does it for me. I do a push-up over her, then hold myself up with one arm as I tear my shirt over my head. It goes flying somewhere behind me.

I'm about to go back to kissing her neck when she drags her shirt over her head too. Then she throws it in the general direction I threw mine. Two perfectly plump breasts peek out at me from behind a purple lace bra. My hands itch to grab her tits, but I don't. What if that's too far for her?

She must see my hesitation, because she makes the decision for me. Within seconds, she unhooks her bra and flings it to the side. "It's not like you've never seen them before."

She's right. It's not like I've never sucked on them before either. She lets out a gasp as I drop my mouth over her nipple and suck it in. My other hand cups her other breast, then I roll her nipple between my fingers.

If someone would have told the man I was two and a half years ago that this is what I'd be doing right now, it might have been easier for me to get sober. This moment is worth all the agony I felt as I forced myself to stay away from her. I never thought she'd ever be so willing to let me touch her like this again.

"Is the spell broken yet?" I ask as I switch to tasting her other nipple.

She clutches the back of my head and presses me to her chest harder. "No. Just keep going."

I can't disobey her, so I suck her nipple into my mouth even harder. She tastes as good as I remember—maybe even sweeter because I waited so long for this.

My hips grind against her body before I even realize they're doing it. As I go back to kissing her lips, she fights with the button of my jeans, wins, then yanks my zipper down. After I kick my shoes off, she shoves the denim down my legs. Then I yank my socks off and climb back on top of her in only my boxers.

I return to nipping at her neck as she slips out of her shorts. They thump onto the ground behind her head. I pepper kisses down her chest and stomach, then gasp. I didn't realize she took her panties off too. I didn't even get to see what color they are.

I'm about to ask for permission to lick her when she grips the back of my head and slams my face into her clit. *So. Fucking. Hot.* I suck her clit into my mouth as she moans my name.

"Trey. Oh, god. That feels so good."

I stick two fingers into her only to find she's already wet. *God, this woman. She's going to be the end of me.* I pound my fingers into her, making her writhe beneath me.

"Yes," she says all breathily. "Don't stop."

"I won't, baby. Not unless you beg me to."

I stare at her with utter admiration as my fingers slam in and out of her. She keeps her eyes closed and her head back as she accepts all the pleasure I'm giving her. I want to keep giving it to her. I want to see her satisfied and hear her scream my name.

"You like that, baby?"

She nods and slides her thumbs between the elastic of my boxers. I stop fingering her so she can wrench my boxers off. My thick cock bounces up, the tip already wet. She's about to grab it when I seize her wrist and slam it above her head.

My voice comes out husky. "If you touch me, I'm—"

"Own me, Trey."

Those are the same words she said to me the first time we ever made love to each other. "Are you sure?"

"Yes." A flame of desire spreads within her eyes. "I want you, Trey. I've wanted you for a long time."

"I've wanted you for even longer." I pull her legs up and place my tip at her damp opening, sliding it up and down. "Once we do this, there's no going back."

"I know."

I don't think she knows what I mean. If we do this, there won't be any more Sunday evenings here where I talk to her and only *pretend* she's mine. Once we do this, I'm going to *make* her mine. "Are you sure this is what you want?"

"Yes, Trey. I'm sure."

I lean down to kiss her lips until it turns into a frenzied act of desperate need again. I want this woman with every fiber of my being, and I'll never feel complete until I have her back. I need her to be a part of me, not apart from me. I need her to be my rock, my savior, my sun to shine bright on all my darkest days. In return, I'll be hers, and I'll never falter from the duties that come with that. Never.

She pulls away from my lips and pants. "Trey?"

"Yeah, baby?"

"Don't be gentle with me."

That's all I need to hear to stop hesitating. I plunge my cock into her, making her scream out. She wraps around me, all tight and wet. I gasp as the pleasure ripples through me, and my climax threatens to explode out of me.

"Oh, fuck. You feel amazing."

Her fingernails dig into my back as I pull back and thrust into her again. I take deep breaths to hold back my release. I can't come this soon. I've barely had her.

She moans my name, and it brings me to the brink.

Fuuuck. "I don't think I can last long, babe. It's been so long for me."

"That's okay. We'll just have to do it again."

"You're going to let me have you twice?" I can't believe my ears.

"Yes, Trey. I want you twice."

I'm gonna need to find out what I did to deserve this, because whatever it is, I need to keep doing it. I take her waist into my hands and hold her still, then I pound into her over and over. She screams as her body takes every inch of me slamming into her.

The orgasm builds inside me, and I try to hold it back, but I can't anymore. I need to get one out. After that, I'll be able to focus on her pleasure instead of mine.

I'm almost there. "Babe, where do you want me to come?"

"Inside me."

"But what if—"

"Trey, just come inside. Please."

Hearing her beg is what does it for me. I continue thrusting until the pleasure becomes too much and I groan as my orgasm consumes me. I know she can feel me pulsing, because she moans and clutches my arms the way she used to. I pour every drop of my load into her, then I collapse on top of her.

Our heavy breaths sync together as I spiral down from my orgasm. She holds my head against her chest as if she's not ready for me to go anywhere yet. I wouldn't, even if I could. I can barely feel my arms right now. I'm too high from being inside her to feel anything except her beating heart against the side of my face.

Once we catch our breaths, she asks, "Were you going to say, 'What if you get pregnant?' "

"Yeah." *Word for word.*

"You don't have to worry about that. I'm not ovulating."

I'm not worried about getting her pregnant. I'm more worried that I *won't* be able to again. Either way, that's not something I want to think about right now. I kiss her, then grin. "Does that mean I can come inside you again?"

Her face lights up with an eager smile. "Yes, please."

104

ARELLA

"Oh, Trey," I say through a moan. His face is buried between my legs while his fingers work their magic inside me. The way he licks me with the perfect amount of pressure is sending me to the edge. It's only been a few minutes, and I'm already about to burst.

My hands clench the back of his hair as I arch my head back against the blanket and let out a guttural moan. This is exactly how he pleasures me in my dreams, and I wouldn't have it any other way.

"I'm going to come," I pant toward the branches above us.

Trey peeks his head up as his fingers keep moving inside me. "Not yet, baby."

"What?" I open my eyes, just to gape at him. "Why?"

"Because I haven't gotten my fill of you yet."

"But I'm so close."

"Not yet, babe. Hold it back." His mouth dips to suck my clit again, and I writhe beneath him. The more the pleasure builds up inside me, the more I dig my fingernails into his shoulders.

I've imagined him doing this to me for weeks, and my imagination is *nothing* compared to the real thing. This man knows exactly how to touch me. He knows exactly where to put his fingers and exactly how hard to press. How many times have we done this for him to learn all that?

With his fingers still inside me, he pops up to take my nipple into his mouth. I shout his name toward the stars. My body tingles from head to toe, and I'm dripping wet. I feel it running down my butt cheeks.

I need to release. "Can I come now?"

"Not yet," he says, then reburies his face between my thighs.

I clench my hands in the blanket. "But I want to come so bad."

"Almost, baby. Just let me enjoy this a little longer."

"Oh, god. I can't hold it back any longer."

His fingers rub little circles over my clit in a steady rhythm. "Keep holding it, babe."

"Trey, please! I'm . . . Oh, god. I'm . . ."

"Okay, baby. Come for me." He rubs me a little faster, using the same pressure.

I moan his name and feel the pleasure rising inside me until I finally jump over the edge. I scream out as ripples of bliss take me over. My legs shake. My hands tug at the blanket. I'm panting like my lungs are fighting for their next breath.

When I open my eyes, I'm disoriented. I can't remember the last time I had such a powerful orgasm.

Trey stares at me with a look of satisfaction. Then he grips his hard cock and gives it a few strokes. "You ready for me again?"

Breathlessly, I nod.

Without another word, he pulls my legs over his shoulders, then plunges his cock back inside me. I let out a deep moan and arch my head back as he thrusts his thick erection in and out of me, over and over.

I'm still sensitive from my orgasm, so he feels even better this time. Our chests slide against each other as he grunts out his pleasure. I love being able to hear him like this. So raw and unfiltered.

"You feel amazing, baby," he pants into my neck.

I'm veering off the blanket and into the grass, but I don't care. I just don't want him to stop.

Trey kisses the soft spot behind my ear, then peppers his lips down to my collarbone. His breath sends tingles down my spine as he keeps a steady rhythm thrusting into me.

He's about to lean back when I seize the back of his hair and force him back down to me. He doesn't need me to ask before he returns his lips to my neck. I arch my head the other way to give him more skin to play with, and he takes it as permission to suck a little harder. I whimper from the pain that quickly turns into pleasure.

"Are you ready for more?" he asks into my collarbone.

"Mm-hmm."

He pushes himself up, then grabs my hips to keep me securely against him. Then he relentlessly slams his dick into me.

In, out, in, out.

Harder, faster, harder, faster.

I scream out his name over and over as he arches his head back, taking all the pleasure he can get from me.

"Fuck, baby," he growls. " You make me wanna come so bad."

"Come inside me, Trey. I want to feel you."

"Can you take me harder?"

"Yes."

With that, he positions my legs over his shoulders again and props himself up on his hands. Then he pulls his hips back and drives himself into me as hard as he can. His cock hits my back wall over and over until he groans to the stars and I feel him pulsate inside me again.

He cries out as he hammers every last drop of his orgasm into me. I wrap my legs around his back, making sure I get all of it.

Only once his cock stops throbbing does he slide out of me, then he falls onto his side, panting. I'm left in that dazed state again, feeling a large empty hole where his thick cock used to be.

He grabs me by the shoulders, wrenches me against his body, and breathes into my hair. I melt into his chest, feeling more protected by him than I would if I was surrounded by an army. With Trey, I feel peace. With Trey, I feel like I can be anything I want to be. Like I can accomplish anything. Like I can—

"Arella." With a finger, he tilts my chin up until our eyes connect. "Will you come home with me?"

My body stiffens. "What?"

"Come home with me, baby. Be mine again."

Something in my chest locks up, and suddenly, I can't breathe. His words sound like a question and a request all in one. Go home with him? Like, forever? "I . . . I can't."

"I promise I'll love you and take good care of you. I'll make sure that you're happy. I'll help you reach all your dreams and goals, and I'll encourage you whenever you're down. You'll never have to doubt my love for you because I'll show it to you every minute of the day."

That all sounds wonderful. Any other woman would love to hear those words come out of a man's mouth. But me, I want to hear them from my husband's mouth. *Don't I?*

Oh, god. My husband. Caleb. I forgot that he existed. It's easy to do that whenever I'm with Trey. Under this tree, I forget about the rest of the world and all my troubles that come with it. Here, I'm safe and I feel wanted. Out there, I feel like something's missing and—

"We could have a family." Trey clutches my face and plants his forehead against mine. "I want that more than anything, and I know you want it too. I'll work hard to be a good father. I'll take parenting classes and read lots of books. I'll protect you and our babies like—"

"Trey, stop." *Please.*

"Arella, we belong together."

"But . . ." The words get lost on their way out. I clear my throat and try again. "But I'm married."

"Leave him," he says like he's been wanting to for weeks.

I sit up, feeling more naked than ever. "I . . . I can't just leave him."

"Why not? He doesn't even appreciate you."

Trey's not wrong, but that doesn't mean I should give up on Caleb. "What am I supposed to tell him?" Or Javina? Or my grandparents? My friends from work? They all love Caleb. *I love Caleb . . . don't I?*

"Tell him you've found someone who wants to love you right. The way you deserve to be loved."

"I can't do that. It'll hurt him." I stand to search the grass for my clothes. I find my panties first and put them on, ignoring how damp my inner thighs are. Then I pick up my bra and hook it on.

Trey slips into his boxers with a hard look on his face. "You weren't ever supposed to marry him anyway. What happened to your memories only made you *think* you were in love with Caleb."

Again, he's not wrong, but that doesn't mean Caleb and I haven't built a life together. We love each other now, and we're partners. I know it hasn't looked that way recently, but it's just a phase we're working through. *Isn't it?* "That doesn't change that I still married him."

"Only because you don't remember being with me."

"For reasons you refuse to tell me," I snap and instantly regret it. I'm not angry at him. I'm angry at myself. At all these answers I don't have.

Trey hands me my shirt, and I slip into it. Somehow, he's able to keep his chill. In a gentle tone, he says, "I refuse to tell you because I can't. But you remember me in your dreams. Maybe that means you can try to remember what happened to your memories."

"Don't you think that if I could remember, I would have by now?"

The air goes silent as we finish getting dressed. I'm about to pick up my blanket when Trey takes my hands into his. "Maybe being together will help trigger more memories for you. And even if it doesn't, I don't care. I want to be with you whether you remember being with me or not. We can leave the past in the past and start from here."

"But what about Caleb?" More guilt eats at me with each second I spend here, talking about my husband with the man who isn't. "I can't just leave him, Trey."

He drops my hands and takes a step back, putting a whole arm's length of distance between us. "Then why did you seduce me?"

"I . . ." That's a good question. *What was I thinking?*

"If you didn't want to be with me, then why did you allow me to make love to you?"

"I'm sorry. I got caught up in the moment, but now that my head is clear, I'm realizing I shouldn't have done that."

This isn't like me. I'm not the type of person who does these types of things. Why did I tonight? Am I just frustrated about my relationship with Caleb feeling like a train wreck? Am I allowing his recent distance to dictate my actions?

Trey drags a palm through his hair, unintentionally showing me his veiny arm muscles. Those muscles were wrapped around me barely a minute ago as I moaned his name to the starry sky. How did I do all that and not once think about Caleb?

"I don't understand," Trey says with a huff. "If you don't want to be with me, then why did you—was that a test? Did you just want to see if I'd do it?"

"Of course not." *I think.* I'd like to say I'm a faithful woman, but if I can't say that anymore, then am I the type to play mind games too?

"Is it because you haven't had sex in a while and I was an easy target?"

"No." *I think.* I'm not sure anymore.

"I don't want to be used, Arella. I allowed someone to use me before, and I told myself I'd never allow that again."

"I wasn't trying to use you, Trey. I don't know why I did that or what I wanted from it. I just—it felt right in the moment."

"And now it doesn't?"

My eyes fall to the grass. "I . . . I don't know."

Trey takes my hands again and gives them a comforting squeeze. "Look, baby, I know you're confused, and that's okay. You've got two conflicting parts inside you: the part that thinks you're in love with Caleb, and the part that's actually in love with me. I understand that, and I've been patient about it. Hell, I let you go for almost three years without knowing if you'd ever come back to me. But you did, and I don't want to ever let you go again. You belong with me, Arella. I know you know that. You've said it yourself. We're soul mates."

I choke up because there's so much truth in those words. However, the other truth is that I've already made a commitment to someone else. Caleb's recent emotional absence and lack of physical attention don't mean I shouldn't honor the vows we made to each other. *Right?*

Or is that just my past self talking? Am I doing that thing again where I make up excuses to stay with a man who doesn't treat me the way I want to be treated? Am I doing that thing again where I convince myself to stay in a relationship because it's easier than getting out? Or because I have hopes that he will change?

Maybe it's *me* who needs to change. Maybe I should be a better wife to Caleb. I have been pretty naggy lately. I suppose I could lay off bringing up all the things that bother me about him.

Maybe he needs more space. I suppose I could spend more time alone or with my friends. I need to work on getting a loan for my bakery anyway. I could put more time into that.

I could stop asking him for intimacy too. It's not like I *need* to have sex with him to know he loves me. He still tells me enough. I don't remember the last time he did, but it's within the last week for sure.

The bottom line is that Caleb loves me, and I think I should give him more time to . . . well, I don't know. Figure out how to work through his stress without letting it affect our marriage?

Whatever it is, I don't want to hurt him. Unfortunately, someone in this situation is going to get hurt, and if it's not Caleb, that means it has to be Trey.

"Not all soul mates end up together," I say with a lump in my throat.

Trey's shoulders slump as he drops my hands. "That's the excuse you want to stand on?"

"It's not an excuse. It's true."

"But you're with someone who doesn't truly love you. He only *thinks* he loves you because he had his memories altered that way. But *me*, Arella, *I* love you. Deeply. I feel it every moment of the day. Please, baby. Come home with me. I know there are logistics we'll have to figure out, but I'm confident that as long as we're together, we can make it."

For a split second, I consider it. I picture myself running home, packing up what I own, and running off with Trey. Then I picture the conversation I'd have to have with Caleb. I imagine telling him that we need to get a divorce. That everything we have together no longer matters. I picture my sweet husband sobbing from the heartbreak, and it kills me. I can't do that to him.

I look into Trey's eyes and hope he can see how much it kills me to do this too. "I'm sorry, Trey. I just can't."

"So that's it then?" He throws his arms out, letting them drop back to his sides. "You're just gonna go home and pretend like *we* never happened?"

"I have to."

"But do you *want* to?"

Not really. "I don't have a choice. I made a vow to be with Caleb."

Trey scoffs like that's the most ridiculous thing he's ever heard. "Vows can be broken. Half the married people in this fucking country do it."

"That doesn't mean I want to be one of them."

He huffs and shakes his head. "So let me get this straight: When you asked me to kiss you, you did it knowing you wouldn't leave him for me, and not once did you stop to think about how that would affect me?"

I didn't, and now that he puts it that way, I feel even worse. This whole time, I've been so focused on feeling guilty about betraying Caleb, I didn't think about how I was betraying Trey too.

He continues, "You know how I feel about you. It's not a fucking secret. Didn't you think it was wrong to play with my heart like this?"

"I'm sorry, Trey. I made a mistake." The second that comes out of my mouth, I know it's a lie. Everything I just did with Trey didn't *feel* like a mistake. It felt right. This is the first moment it has ever felt wrong—and only because society would say so. Inside, I'm not entirely convinced. Being with Trey has always felt right. Letting him touch me feels right. Even picturing a life with him feels right. So why can't I bring myself to do it?

"You just slept with me *twice*, Arella. That's not a mistake. That's a choice."

"I won't let it happen again," I lie, because if he kissed me right now, I wouldn't stop him.

He takes a step back as if he needs more distance from me. "So that's all I am to you? A mistake?"

"No. That's not what I meant."

"Then what did you mean?"

"Just that I shouldn't have let things get that far."

"But you did." He gapes at me like he can't believe what's happening.

I'm with him on that because I can't believe what's happening either. What have I done? And why do I feel so conflicted? My head is telling me I should leave while my heart is begging me to stay.

Trey swallows hard, his breaths going ragged. "You wanna know something I've learned in my fucked-up life? It's that when other people make *mistakes*, somehow I'm always the one who ends up paying for them." In one swift motion, he scoops up his backpack and tosses a strap over his shoulder. Without another look at me, he marches away.

I run after him and stop in front of him with my hands up to his chest. "Where are you going?"

"The airport." He doesn't stop. He only swerves past me.

I stay where I am. "You can't just leave like this."

He twists around with his arms out to his sides. "How do you want me to leave? Do you want me to tell you that my heart's not broken? Do you want us to go back to the way things were when we were living in our own little world of make-believe? Do you want me to walk you to your car and die inside as I watch you drive back home to *him*? I can't do that, Arella. I told you once we went that far, there was no going back. So—this is me—not going back." He hurries toward the woods again.

I catch up to him and stop him with a hand to his chest. He feels hard under my palm. "I don't like ending things like this."

"How do you want to end things, then?"

I lower my hand because I don't like feeling how tense he is. "On a good note."

"There is no good note. At least not for me. You know what's stupid is that I've always known this was going to end badly. Right from the start, I knew that eventually, you would leave and I'd be left with nothing.

"Yet every single week, I showed up here, willing you to come out of those trees. You know why? Because I'm so fucking in love with you that even knowing I would get hurt in the end couldn't stop me from yearning to see you.

"The stupidest part is that even if someone had told me at the beginning that this is a thousand percent how it would end, I would have come here to see you anyway. Because these last nine weeks with you are worth all the pain I'll have to endure trying to let you go again."

For a second time, I consider taking the other path—the one where I choose Trey. I can vividly see us in my new bakery together. I can picture myself getting to know his friends and supporting him in his musical career. I can picture us growing old together. In a perfect world, that's how it'd be.

But we don't live in a perfect world, and things happen. What if it doesn't work out between us? What if our relationship turns toxic? What if he ends up changing his mind? What if he gets too busy for me, and we drift apart the way Caleb and I have? I would have left my marriage for nothing, and I'd be right back where I am now.

"Why don't we try to come up with a solution that will make us both happy?" I say.

"The only thing that's going to make me happy is you saying you'll be with me. So I'm going to ask you one last time, Arella. And if you say anything other than *yes*, I'm heading straight to the airport, and I'm not looking back." He sucks in a deep breath, then blows it out. "Will you, please, leave him for me?"

I can't believe he's trying to force me into a big decision like this on the spot. Even if I knew that everything would work out for us, that doesn't mean I can just drop my husband without even talking to him first. "I'm sorry, Trey. I just can't."

The light that's been shining in his eyes for the last nine weeks suddenly goes dark. He takes one long look at me as if he thinks it's the last time he'll ever be able to. Then, without a single word, he turns and disappears into the trees.

I'm left stunned and speechless.

By the time I've gathered myself enough to realize I should chase after him, it's too late. When I run out to the gravel road, his bike is gone.

105

TREY

She's not coming. I mean, why would she? She has no reason to. The way we left things last week didn't exactly cultivate the most welcoming environment to elicit her return.

I shouldn't have said some of the things I said. I shouldn't have walked away like that either. What I should have done is given her more time to think about it. After a whole week of brooding over this, I realized that I pushed her too far, too fast. I got too caught up in the moment and all the feels of having her back that I didn't stop to think about how I was making her feel by asking her to drop her husband for me. Just because I'd be willing to drop everything for her doesn't mean I should expect the same.

I confided in Liz about the whole situation. At first, she was ticked that I never told her about my Sundays with Arella. Then she told me I was an idiot for thinking Arella would up and leave her marriage in a snap. At the end of the conversation, Liz encouraged me to write a letter with all the things I'd like to say to Arella the next time I see her—*if* I ever get to see her.

Slumped against our oak tree, I take my earbuds out of my backpack and shove them into my ears. I need to calm my mind because it's eight thirty. If she was coming, she'd be here by now.

The sun has almost set for the evening. If she's not here by midnight, I'll head to the airport and accept that I'll never see her again. And if this meditation doesn't work, I'll go for a short walk through the woods. Short because I don't want to miss it if she does show up.

I find a meditation that's an hour long because that's how much time I'm gonna need to calm my mind.

"Focus on your breaths," the lady on the app says as I lie back on the grass and shut my eyes. "Breathe in deep. Breathe out slowly."

I do what she says as relaxing music plays in my ears. I've got the volume all the way up because I need it loud enough to block out the screams in my head telling me I'm not good enough. Maybe if I was, she'd be here.

I haven't gone a single second without thinking of her or regretting the way I stormed off. I was just hurt, and I didn't know what else to do. Staying there with her when I knew she wasn't leaving with me felt like torture. Even so, the second I mounted my bike and rode off, I wanted to go straight back.

But there was nothing to go back to. She told me I was a mistake. I stood there offering her my whole heart and soul, and she didn't want it. I still don't know what she wanted from me or why she would let me make love to her without any intention of staying with me. Maybe she just wanted to feel loved because she's not getting it at home. Maybe she wanted to see how easy it'd be to seduce me.

Turns out, I'm easy. All she had to do was ask, and I was all over her. She should have known that I'm a weak man—especially when it comes to her. She could ask me to do anything, and I'd—

"Ah!" I scream when something pokes my arm. I jolt upright and yank my earbuds out. What's left of my shattered heart thumps wildly in my chest. "Arella."

She offers me a tender smile. "Sorry."

I stand and stash my earbuds in my jeans pocket. "You came back."

"Yeah. I didn't want to leave things the way we did."

"I didn't either. That's why I wrote down a whole list of apologies and other things I want to say to you." From the inner pocket of my leather jacket, I pull out a folded sheet of paper and hold it up.

Arella smiles warmly as she slips a piece of paper out of her back shorts pocket. "I wrote down some things I want to say to you too."

I hope that's a good sign. I mentally prepare to hear what she has to say. "Would you like to go first?"

"No, you go first."

"Sure. Would you like to sit?"

She hesitates, making my eyes drift to her empty arms. *Where's her blanket?* Its absence makes all my hopes deflate. Before I can think about it too hard, she plops onto the grass, and I join her.

With shaky hands, I unfold my letter and read it aloud. "Arella, I'm sorry for what happened. I didn't mean to make you feel uncomfortable or push you to do something you didn't want to do. I'll never make you feel that way again, because I don't ever want to make you feel like you *have* to be with me. What I want is for you to *want* to be with me.

"That's why I'm going to give you time. It was wrong of me to try to force you into making a big decision that night. I should have simply told you how I felt about you, then let you make that decision yourself. So please, take as much time as you need. In the end, if you choose me, I promise I'll love you until my last breath. I promise I'll—"

I stop reading because Arella's face drops. That's not the reaction I was hoping for. I'm not even halfway through my letter yet, and I don't think I should continue. The rest of it includes all the reasons why she should choose me, but maybe it's too much to ask her to love me back this soon. I've been in love with her for years, but she's only gotten to know me within the last nine weeks. This might be moving too fast for her. I guess I don't *need* her to love me back right now. *I could settle for less . . .*

With a long sigh, I crumple up my letter and shove it back into my inner jacket pocket. "You know what? I just realized that I don't need much from you to be happy. I don't need you to choose me, if that's not what you want. Seeing you once a week is enough for me. Actually, even if you only come once a month or once a year, I'll be fine with that. Honestly, I'll take whatever you're willing to give me."

I pause for a moment to see if she'll say something. She doesn't, so I continue speaking from the heart. "Arella, you've made me feel so alive lately, because without you, I always feel like I'm missing something. I think you kept coming here because you felt like you were missing something too, and whatever that was, you were getting it from me.

"So tell me what you want from me, and I'll give it to you. If you want me to pretend like last week never happened, I can do that. If you want to go back to being friends and live in our little bubble where we just talk and answer question cards, I'll make it happen.

"Hell, I'll even let you use me, if that's what you want. Just tell me what you need me to be for you. Whether that's a big part of your life or a small one, I'll learn to accept it. I'll learn to be happy with it. Because the bottom line is, I just want *you*. However I can get that, I'll settle for it."

"Oh, Trey . . ." She rubs her hair between her fingers, barely looking at me. "Maybe I should have gone first."

That doesn't sound good.

She unfolds her paper and is about to read it when I push it into her lap.

I hold back the tears threatening to fall as I choke out, "I've got a feeling that your letter is your way of letting me down softly." I give her a moment to deny that. When she doesn't, the shattered pieces of my heart break more. "This gaping hole in my chest can only take so much, okay? Can you just skip the fluff and give it to me straight? Did you come here tonight to say goodbye to me?"

The way she creases her eyebrows together with sorrow is all the answer I need, but she verbalizes it to me anyway. "I came to give you a proper goodbye because I didn't want to leave things the way we did last week."

The world stops turning and fades to gray as Arella continues talking. She goes on for a while, but I don't catch it all. What I hear are snippets of her explanation as to why she can't see me anymore.

"I owe it to Caleb and our marriage to try to make things work." She says some other bull-shit about how she spoke to him last week, and how they've agreed to work harder on their relationship. She even gives me some examples, like how they're going to have more date nights and make an effort to actually converse with each other. The more she talks, the more I spiral into a deep hole I'm not sure I'll ever be able to crawl out of.

Since this is the last time I'm ever going to see her, I stare at her face as she continues explaining shit to me. I memorize the curve of her cheeks and the shape of her nose. I remi-nisce on how it felt to finally kiss her plump lips again. I try to ingrain every little detail of her into my head so that whenever I need it, I'll be able to conjure up an image of her at will within seconds.

During our years apart, I started to forget what she looked like because I never got the chance to memorize her face. Maybe doing so now will help me remember her ten, twenty, or even fifty years from now. *Fuck. Fifty years without her?* That sounds like hell. Can I make it that long? Probably not. At least, not without some self-medi—

She pats my forearm. "Trey?"

"Hmm?"

"Did you hear me?"

I nod slightly as an invisible snake slithers around my lungs, strangling me from the inside out.

"What did I just say?"

"You said that you're . . ." The words get caught in my dry throat. "That you're never coming back."

"Did you hear anything I said after that?"

Mostly, sorta, not really. "Yeah, I heard you."

"What did I say?"

I swallow thickly, then bite the inside of my mouth. *You said that you love Caleb and that . . .* My tone comes out broken. "Please don't make me repeat it out loud." I can't even do it in my head.

"Did you hear my question?"

I suck in a ragged breath. "What was your question again?"

"I asked if you understand why I made my decision this way."

I definitely was not listening when she asked that, nor do I understand. "Yeah, I understand."

"I'm really sorry."

My breathing turns shallow, and my head feels like gravity is pulling me toward the center of the earth. There, I'll get swallowed whole and die an agonizing death. That'd be better than staying up here, forced to live out the rest of my life in my own personal hell.

My hand trembles against my thigh, and it takes me a few seconds to realize what's happening. I can't allow this panic attack to take control of me right now. Not while she's still here.

If it's bad enough, like to the point where I feel like I'm having a heart attack, my powers will go wack. If Arella sees a tree catching fire out of nowhere and the zovernment finds out about it, she's going to get scrubbed again. I can't let that happen. We've made some great memories here together, and I want her to remember them.

I close my eyes and take in three long, deep breaths.

In . . . out . . .

In . . . out . . .

In . . . out . . .

Once my breathing is under control and my hands are less shaky, I ask, "Will you go on a walk with me?"

"I'd love to."

I stand and think about offering her my hand, but I don't. I won't be able to handle feeling her skin like that. Not even if it's for a second.

Arella stands on her own and offers me a sweet smile.

I don't return it. It's taking everything in me to keep from falling over right now. I don't have the capacity to steady my breaths and fake a smile at the same time.

I head toward the dark woods behind our tree with Arella at my side. The black sky hangs above us with a dirty yellow moon and no stars.

My throat feels muggy as I work on sucking in more air. I don't think my body is getting enough oxygen, because I'm feeling a little light-headed. Or maybe that's the panic attack? Who knows?

The trail going through the forest is just wide enough for Arella and me to hike side by side. I shove my hands into my jeans pockets in an attempt to keep them from accidentally touching her. Then I concentrate on my feet the way my zerapist told me to: *"Just focus on putting one foot in front of the other. And if it helps, you can count your steps."*

So I do. *One . . . two . . . three . . .*

Twenty-one . . . twenty-two . . . twenty-three . . .

Arella taps my arm. "Trey?"

I force my head up. "Hmm?"

"Did you hear me?"

"Sorry. What did you say?"

"I asked if there's anything you'd like to talk about."

I shake my head. "Is there anything you'd like to talk about?"

"I think I said everything I wanted to earlier."

"Okay." The air goes quiet as I start my unhelpful step-counting activity from the top. *One . . . two . . . three . . .*

"If there's nothing you want to talk about, then why'd you ask me to go on a walk with you?"

I think about coming up with a filtered answer, but that would require more effort than I have to give right now. My words come out slow and somber like I've just woken up from a deep sleep. "I just needed to walk because I felt a panic attack coming. I also wasn't ready for you to leave yet, and it felt like you were about to." *This was my way of getting you to stay longer.*

"You get panic attacks?"

"Occasionally." *All the time.* "Let's not talk about it though. The point of walking is to help me forget about it."

"Right." She ducks under a branch, then says, "Why don't we talk about what you're working on with your band?"

I appreciate her attempt at trying to lighten the mood, but . . . "I'm not really in a good mind-set to talk right now, but if you want to talk, I'm happy to listen."

"I was talking earlier, but it didn't seem like you were listening."

"Sorry." I swallow some pain, then let out an unsteady breath. "It's just a little hard for me to concentrate right now."

She stops in the middle of the trail, making me stop too. "Trey, you're scaring me."

"How so?"

"For starters, you're quiet, and that's not like you. The Trey I know is always keeping up a conversation with me."

That version of Trey is the alive one—the one who was living under a false pretense that he could handle the consequences of losing the love of his life again. When I told myself I could handle it, it was because at the time, I was too high off the joy to care.

Turns out, I was wrong. I can't handle this. I feel like I've got a searing-hot knife sticking out of my chest and the weight of the world on my shoulders.

She continues, "When you answer my questions, you say the bare minimum, and you're doing that thing again where you answer my questions with a version of the truth instead of the full truth."

I let out a huff as I toss my arms into the air. "What would you rather I do?"

"Be open with me."

"I've been open with you! Look what that got me. I've got a one-way ticket back to nothing." I don't mean to raise my voice at her, but, goddamn, is it hard not to. "I don't think you understand that before you came back, I was drowning. Sometimes, if I was lucky and if I swam hard enough, I was able to come up for a single breath of air—only to get pulled right back down. I was constantly fighting to live and to feel any sense of belonging or purpose.

"Then one night, you came out of those fucking trees like a goddamn lifesaver. I didn't have to fight for my next breath anymore. I was exactly where I needed to be, doing exactly what I needed to be doing.

"For a whole week after that, I felt like I was standing in the shallow end. I was able to breathe without fighting for air, but still headed toward the depths. Then you showed up a second time and—" I snap my fingers. "Just like that, I'm saved again."

I shove my hands through my messy hair, shaking my head at myself. "I'm quiet because I'm scared, okay? I'm scared of what it's gonna be like to fall back into the deep end. This time, it'll be like my feet are tied to bricks. I'm afraid of returning to the bad habits I've worked so hard to fight off. I'm afraid of the person I'll become when I finally lose that battle. But mostly, I'm fucking terrified of not submitting to the numbing remedies because it means suffering through the raw misery of every day I have to live without you."

Tears glisten in her eyes. "Oh, Trey . . ."

"No." I turn my head away and aim my gaze at a tree. "Don't look at me like that. I don't want pity."

"I never meant to hurt you."

"I know." I soften my stance, then sigh and lower my voice. "I'm sorry for raising my voice at you. I'm not mad at you; I'm mad at myself. Deep down, I always knew you'd leave and that once you did, it would destroy me. I made the choice to continue seeing you anyway, and that choice came with consequences I'm gonna have to live with."

My breathing sounds like I'm suffocating. The anxiety is consuming me again. I need it to stop, so I don't think about it as I seize Arella's hand and cup it against my cheek. She allows me to hold it there while I close my eyes and work on some deep breaths.

It takes me a minute to steady my heart rate and reopen my eyes. A pair of beautiful brown ones stare back at me.

"Did that help?" she asks.

"It always does."

For a moment, I imagine throwing her over my shoulder and taking her home with me. I'll convince her that she belongs with me, and after a while, she'll believe it. She'll fall madly in love with me like I am with her. She'll want to have my kids, we'll support each other in our careers, and then we'll live happily ever after.

I let out a long sigh as I mourn the loss of the life I want so badly. Maybe in an alternate universe somewhere, another version of me has all that. Sadly, I'm stuck here, where Arella can't be mine and I can't do anything about it.

I gesture toward the trail we're stopped on. "Let's keep walking."

For a while, we trudge through the woods with only the sounds of our breaths and the crickets wailing in the tall grass.

I stare at my feet and count my steps again because it gives my mind something to focus on other than the idea of masking this ache with the first illegal substance I can get my hands on.

One . . . two . . . three . . .

Arella keeps a steady pace next to me. "Do you regret it?"

"Regret what?"

"Any of it. Our time together."

"No," I say without missing a beat. "If given the choice, I'd do it all over again, even knowing what I know now."

"Why?"

"Because I didn't deserve a single moment of it, but you still gave me nine weeks of pure joy, which is better than none at all. I'm grateful for what I got." *Even if it means falling into a hole that's darker than before.* At least I got to experience what it's like to live in the light with her again.

How long is it going to take for me to get over this woman? Is it even possible to get over losing a soul mate—again? Honestly, this whole soul-mate thing is bullshit. Why tie two people together and not allow them to be together? What's the fucking point?

"Do you regret it?" I ask.

She doesn't hesitate. "No. I feel guilty sometimes, but it's not enough guilt to wish we never happened. The only reason I came here in the first place was because I wanted to sort through my thoughts about how Caleb was refusing to be intimate with me. If he actually paid attention to me, I don't think you and I would have gotten that close. We probably wouldn't have had this time together at all."

"Did you tell him about us?"

"No."

"Do you plan to?"

"No. What happened at our tree stays at our tree."

I didn't know she thinks of it as *our* tree. The idea makes me want to smile and sob at the same time. "I'm glad you didn't tell him. You don't need to give him a reason to not want you. He seems to have enough reasons already, and he doesn't need another. Whatever it is that fell apart between you two, I hope you two can fix it and move on to be happy together."

"What about you? Where are you going to find your happiness?"

I keep putting one foot in front of the other as I think about my answer. "I already have. I've got nine weeks of it to replay in my head whenever I feel down. Every Sunday, when I'm back at our tree, I'll just imagine that you're there with your little questions box. I'll answer the cards and imagine that I made you laugh so much that you slap your knee like you sometimes do. It'll be great."

She shakes her head, giving me a sorrowful look. "That doesn't sound great to me."

That's because it's not ideal, and it actually fucking sucks. "Well, that's all I've got, so . . ."

"You'll find someone someday."

"I don't want anyone else."

"What if there's someone out there who could make you as happy as I do? What if you're missing out on her because you're refusing to let anyone else in?"

I let out a scoff. "I'm done letting people in, but I appreciate that you care enough to—I dunno. Whatever it is you're trying to do."

"I'm trying to encourage you to move forward."

"I will." *Begrudgingly, but I will.* "It just won't include some random chick who won't make me feel even half as whole as you do. Besides, I'm fine with being alone. I've done it my whole life, so don't worry about me. I'm more concerned about your happiness than mine anyway."

"Why?"

Because you're the one who's running back to a man who doesn't love you. I don't say that. The last thing I want is to start a conversation about how I'm right for her and he isn't. It'll make things tense between us again, and I'd rather end this evening on a good note. "Let's just say that if you ever find yourself in a place where you feel like something's missing again, you know where to find me on Sunday nights."

She's quiet after that. I hope it's because I made her think about the possibility that she's making a mistake. Maybe the more she thinks about it, the more she'll convince herself to leave him. *A man can hope.*

When we return to our tree, Arella picks up her purse and slides it over her shoulder. Then she locks her eyes with mine in an unspoken request. I know what she wants from me, because I want it too.

"Can I walk you to your car?"

She perks up with a relieved smile. "Yes, please."

We get there together in silence. Normally, silence irks me; it reminds me that I'm lonely, and it encourages all the raging thoughts of my worthlessness to beat me up inside. But when I'm with Arella, the silence doesn't bother me. Even now, as I walk her to her car where she'll end up driving away from me forever, this silence with her still comes with a teeny-tiny sense of peace.

After she sets her purse in her car, she shuts the door and turns to me. "Do you want a goodbye hug?"

Do I want one? *Fuck yeah.*

Can I handle holding her knowing I'll have to let her go? *Absolutely not.*

"I'm not sure if that's a good idea."

"Right. I understand." Her face falls more than I expected it to. I thought she asked if I wanted a hug for my benefit. Now I think she might have asked for hers. "Take care of yourself, okay?" she says.

I won't. "You too."

"And stay sober."

"Sure." *No promises.*

"And stay out of prison."

That one gets a chuckle out of me. It's small, but it's something. "I'll try."

She smiles at me like she's grateful to hear my laugh one last time. I'd like to hear hers too.

The idea comes to me easily. "You know what else I'll do?"

"What?"

"I'll start putting the toilet paper on the correct way."

She rewards my quick thinking with a giggle. "Of all the things I just mentioned, that one is the most important."

I take a step backward, keeping my eyes trained on her. I want to look at her for as long as possible. She grabs the door handle and pulls the door open. I brand the shape of her body into my mind. The length of her hair. The curves of her waist. The way her legs look in those shorts. When I'm old and gray, I want to remember all these little details about her. When I'm on my deathbed, I want the last thing I picture to be her.

She's about to step into her car when I can't hold back anymore.

"Arella?" My voice comes out like shattered glass.

She freezes and looks up at me with wide and eager eyes. My feet make their way to her before I can stop them. They pause once I'm in front of her again. I clear my dry-as-fuck throat. This is a bad idea, but I'm gonna do it anyway.

"I, uh, changed my mind. I think I'd like a goodbye hug. You know, if you're still offering."

With glistening eyes, she nods. I don't need more permission than that. I yank her toward me so hard, she collides with my chest with a thump. Our arms clutch each other like we're a couple in the 1940s and I'm about to go off to war.

I want to ask her why she's doing this. Why she's torturing us both. Why she feels like she owes anything to a man who didn't fall in love with her of his own free will.

But I don't.

I can't.

She's made her decision.

Maybe this is for the best. I'd probably only have her for a few short months before the zovernment takes her away, anyway. Unfortunately, this is our fate. Two souls meant for each other but fated to be apart.

I fist her hair and squeeze her against me so tight, a strangled breath leaves her mouth. I don't care. I keep crushing her anyway. Apparently, she doesn't care either, because even though I'm probably suffocating her, she doesn't pull away.

I breathe in her sweet scent one last time, then my words come out through held-back tears. "Count down from three, and I'll let you go. Slowly, please."

She nods against my pec. "Three."

Fuck, why is she counting so fast? I wasn't ready for her to start yet.

She waits a few seconds before saying, "Two."

I hug her tighter. Since I can't say it out loud, I hope she can feel how much I love her through my body.

"One."

I release her and march toward the woods so she can't see the tears dripping from my eyes. I feel her gaze on my back as I order myself not to look at her. If I do, I might drop to my knees and beg her to stay.

106

TREY

I kick a rock on the ground. It tumbles across the top of the cliff and over it. Then it's gone forever.

The sky draped over the forest is a swirly mix of pinks and purples intertwining with the dusty blue behind the trees. The October sun is about to set for the evening. Tomorrow, it'll return to shine on another day of me just trying to make it through.

My zerapist says I need to focus more on living in the moment. Whenever I dwell on the maybe-I-should-haves and what-if-I-hads of the past, I get depressed. Whenever I think about having to do this bullshit for another day, week, or year, I get anxious.

I've spent every Sunday over the last two months at our tree, waiting for her to appear out of the woods.

She never does.

Tonight is the first night I've told myself I'd stop looking. That's why I went for a walk. I needed to stop staring at those damn trees like they hold the answer to all my troubles. What I really need is to stop living my life as if she'll come back into it. She's not, and it'll do me some good to accept that and move on.

On the outside, I've been trying to move on. I've been working on my new career goals. I've also been looking into getting more involved with my foundation for kids with deceased parents.

On the inside, though, I'm still with her. It's like I'm stuck in the mud there, and no tow truck on Earth is strong enough to drag me out. A part of me doesn't even want to get out, but I have to. It's not healthy for me to keep hoping for a life I'll never have.

Liz keeps telling me that time will heal and eventually, things will get easier. Time hasn't done anything except make me realize that even when I offered everything I had to the only person I can see a future with, she only saw me as a part of her past.

The only thing that's gotten easier is my ability to hide the pain. I came up with some systems because I got sick of people asking me if I'm okay.

Whenever a bandmate catches me staring off into space, instead of apologizing for it, I tell them I was thinking up lyrics for a new song. It's been working to get them to leave me alone because I'm "in the zone."

Whenever a crew member asks me how my week has been, instead of saying *fine* like I have been, I tell them it was fantastic. I even add a whole bunch of enthusiasm into it, then ask them a question to take the attention off me.

I've gotten better at faking smiles too. I learned that if I do it while squinting my eyes, it's more believable. Many nights of practicing in the mirror helped me figure that out.

My hope is that the more I can make people believe I'm okay, the more I'll be okay. I lied when I told Arella that my unrealistic want in five years is a wife and kids. Sure, having a family would be great, but what I truly want is inner peace.

I just want to be able to wake up without feeling this constant weight on my chest. I want to be able to brush my teeth and take a shower without it feeling like a chore. I want to be able to perform in front of a crowd without feeling like I don't deserve to.

I envy the people who can get through their day without second-guessing everything they do or what they have, or wonder why they're even here. I'm jealous of the people who can wake up every morning with genuine vigor to live. And the people who never question their worth. And the people who've got all their shit together. How can I be like them? What's their secret?

When I said all that to Liz, she told me that part of their secret is that they didn't witness their parents' murder in a mushroom of fire when they were seven. And they didn't grow up with their abusive uncle who was really their spiteful aunt. And they didn't lose the love of their life to memory scrubbing.

"Everyone has shit they've been through," Liz said. "You've got a little more shit than most, but that doesn't mean some inner peace isn't achievable."

So that's what I'm working toward: *some* inner peace, because *some* is better than none. However I can achieve that—without getting high—I'm willing to try it. I even went on a date last week. I'm pretty fucking proud of myself for it too.

It was with the thirty-two-year-old Zordi woman who owns the sandwich shop near my penthouse. I go there almost every day while I'm in New York. Usually, she makes conversation with me about food or Disney movies while she puts my sandwich together. Last week, she asked if I'd like to get dinner with her sometime.

I was about to politely decline when I stopped myself and said, "Why not?" Later that night, I took her to a nice Mediterranean place.

We had a fine conversation over chicken pitas and hummus. She told me the entire story of how she started her sandwich shop, and I told her about how I started my band. She laughed at my lame jokes, and I pretended to be interested in her cat. Overall, I'd say the date served the purpose I was going for: to do more in New York than sit around my apartment, waiting for my next flight back to LA.

I didn't feel that spark with her that I do with Arella, but I didn't expect to. Part of the reason why I haven't wanted to date other women is because I keep looking for my next Arella. Since there is no such thing, I'm setting my expectations lower, like someone I can hold a conversation with. Sandwich shop lady met that expectation.

We didn't make plans for another date, mostly because I told her I'm moving back to LA full-time. Once that's done, I plan to focus on my new career goals, and then maybe I'll work up to going out with another woman I can hold a conversation with. Who knows? Maybe one day, I'll even get to the point of being able to kiss someone—soberly.

No, I don't have plans to find my "compatible partner," but I might be able to handle a casual, friends-with-benefits, no-strings-attached type thing. There's gotta be *someone* out there who's looking for that too. And if not, that's okay. Being alone is my destiny, and I've accepted that.

The sun is gone, and a few dim stars are trying to peek out from the depths of the black sky. I think I've stood on this cliff, staring aimlessly at the trees below, for long enough. It's time to head to the airport.

With my hands in my jeans pockets, I turn toward the trail, then jump back and gasp.

"Sorry!" A woman of angelic beauty throws her hands up in surrender as she stumbles out of the tree line. "I didn't know if it was you. It looked like you from behind, but I didn't want to say something in case it wasn't you."

I probably wouldn't be this jumpy if I could sense her emotions. I always know when someone is near—unless that someone is her.

"What are you doing here?" I ask. Not that I'm unhappy to see her. My chest is thumpy all of a sudden.

"I sat under our tree for a really *looong* time, and when you didn't show, I thought I'd look for you."

The one fucking time I go for a longer walk . . . "I hope I didn't make you wait too long."

"That's okay. I made you wait two months, so we're even."

I close the distance between us to get a better look at her. Her wavy hair looks more wavy than usual, like she spent extra time curling it. She's wearing more makeup than she normally does too. Not that I mind. I'll take her any way I can have her.

"I was just about to head back to our tree," I say, specifically using the word *our*. "You wanna head back with me?"

"Of course."

We get about ten steps through the woods before she asks, "How have you been?"

"Fantastic," I say, coupled with enthusiasm and one of my smiles with the squinty eyes.

Her shoulders perk up. "That's great to hear."

All that practice in the mirror is paying off. "How have *you* been?"

"Good. I finally got a loan for my bakery, and I found a location that's a good size in a decent location."

"Congrats. What's the next step?"

She keeps a steady pace beside me. "I'm meeting with the landlord tomorrow to sign the lease."

"Wow. I'm excited for you."

"Me too. This is something I've wanted for a long time."

That peace I always feel when I'm with her eases into me like sweet honey. I wish I could capture this feeling and turn it on whenever I need it. "Can I tell you somethin' cool?"

"Of course."

"I bought a studio."

"What?" She stops in the middle of the trail. "Seriously?"

I stop too. "Yeah. I just signed for it on Thursday. My band is outgrowing the backstage area of the Soul House anyway, so it'll be a good space for us to write and record our third original album. It's also where I'll start my new production company."

"That's wonderful! Where is it?"

We continue down the trail as I say, "Pasadena. Pretty close to where Liz lives."

"So what you're saying is that you've been keeping busy?"

"Trying." I think about mentioning the first date I had in almost three years, but I don't want Arella to think I'm unavailable. To her, I'm as available as available can be. "How about you? Have you been keeping busy?"

"I have. Lots of life changes, but they're all good."

I'm about to ask her if things are better at home with Caleb, then I stop. I don't want to know. Most of me hopes everything is good because I want her to be happy, but I'd be lying if I said there isn't a part of me that wishes things aren't good so she'll come back to me. It's better to wonder than to know.

When we make it to our tree, her blanket is already draped underneath it, next to my backpack. Her purse is also here, next to our little box of questions.

"You came prepared." I take a seat on top of her blanket because fuck the consequences. She's here, and I'm ecstatic about it. I don't give two shits that it's going to rip me apart when she leaves tonight. I don't even care that I might have to start the healing process all over again. I just want to enjoy her company while I've got it.

She pretzels her legs together, then hands me the box. "Would you like to go first?"

"Sure." I pluck out a card and read it. "If you could go back in time and change one thing, what would it be?"

Arella does that cute thing where she squints at the sky as if the stars will give her the answer she's looking for. "I think I'd stop all those people from getting onto the *Titanic*."

"The Ti-what?"

She lets out a little *ha!* "Very funny, mister. I know you know what that is."

"Nope. In my universe, no one has heard of the *Titanic*."

"Ha. Ha. Ha," she says with a sarcastic tone. "What's your answer?"

"My answer is more selfish than yours."

"That's okay. No one said you couldn't use your one imaginary trip back in time on yourself."

"There are a lot of things I'd wanna change, but the biggest one is that I'd get my mom to marry my real dad."

She cocks her head to the side. "What?"

"Long story short, I found out that the man I thought was my dad wasn't actually my dad. My mother had an affair with my dad's older brother, who's actually my dad. So if I could, I'd go back to make sure they got married instead." Then again, changing that could mean I wouldn't have met Arella. I wouldn't trade never knowing her for a better childhood.

"Wait . . . your mom had an affair with your uncle?"

"Yep."

Her eyes go wide. "And she got pregnant with you?"

"Yep."

"But they told everyone that your father was—"

"Yep.

Her mouth falls open and she goes silent. It takes her a moment to gather herself. "How did you take that crazy news?"

"At the time, my life was too chaotic to think about it. I've had more time to reflect on it since, and I'd like to think I'm taking it well." Finding out that Victor is my dad wasn't the hard pill to swallow. Finding out that my aunt swapped minds with him for twenty years was.

"There's something I've been meaning to ask you, but I haven't because I figured if you wanted to talk about it, you would."

"Go ahead and ask," I tell her. "If I don't wanna talk about it, I'll just say so."

She straightens up. "Okay. When we had that conversation about your tattoo, you said that the V is in honor of your dad because he died saving your life. What's the story behind that?"

"My dad saw me getting attacked by my aunt. He saved me but died in the process." I left out every important detail, but that's as much as she should know.

"Interesting."

I want to ask what she means by that, but if we keep talking about this topic, we'll get into illegal territory, so I push the questions box toward her. "Your turn."

She pulls out a card. "If you could have any superpower, what would it be?"

"Easy. I'd like to be able to teleport wherever I want, whenever I want. I'd save so much money on plane tickets." If I actually had that power, I'd also need a lot of self-control to make sure I wouldn't keep appearing outside Arella's apartment every day.

"I'd like to have telekinesis."

Ironic. "That could be handy."

"I'd also want the ability to make fire come out of my hands."

My eyes flick up to meet hers. Does she know? Is she trying to tell me that she knows? What's next? Is she gonna tell me she wants to be able to sense people's emotions too? I can't tell what she's thinking from the impassive look on her face.

She hands me the box. "Your turn."

I clear my throat as I pluck out a card. "What are your relationship deal-breakers?"

"Abuse. Gaslighting. Manipulation."

"Damn," I say with a chuckle. "Take a moment to think about it, will ya?"

"I've had a lot of years of thinking to know what I never want again."

"I'm proud of you for that. As for me, I only have one deal-breaker."

She gives me a second to expand on that. When I don't, she says, "Are you going to leave me hanging, or . . . ?"

"I think you could guess it."

"You've mentioned that one of your exes is a lying bitch. Is that it?"

I chuckle because she used the word *bitch.* "Nope."

"You don't want someone who's after your money?"

"No." *I don't want someone who's not you.* "Let's talk about something else."

"Fine. How about we talk about the fact that you have yet to ask me why I came here tonight."

"I don't question miracles."

She giggles as her face lights up. "That's what you think this is? A miracle?"

"Why else would you be here? Honestly, a part of me is questioning if you're even real."

"I'm not. This is actually a simulation."

I let out a real laugh for the first time in two months. "If this isn't real, does that mean anything goes?"

"What would you do if you could?"

Take you home with me. Kiss you until you're breathless. Make you mine again. "Things I shouldn't."

"Aren't you even the least bit curious why I'm here?"

"Yes, but at the same time, I don't care *why* you're here. I'm just glad you are."

I'd like to think she came here tonight because she missed me. I'd also like to think she's going to keep coming on Sundays again, but that's probably wishful thinking. If she does, I'll do better about mentally preparing myself for the impending end. Maybe this time, it won't hurt as much.

"Whose turn is it?" she asks.

"Yours."

She lifts the box, picks out a card, and reads it. "Will you take me home with you?"

My body tenses. *Did I hear her right?* I'm not sure, so I say the most intelligent thing I can. "Huh?"

"I said, will you take me home with you?"

There is no way she just said what I think she said. "That's the question on the card?"

She slams the card against her chest with a grin. "Word for word."

"Lemme see."

With a laugh, she sticks the card down her shirt. "Answer the question first."

"I . . . I don't understand the question."

She pulls the card back out of her shirt and stares at it. "The card says, 'Will you, Trey Grant, take me, Arella Rance, home with you?' "

I blink at her as all the blood rushes from my head. "What?" I snatch the card from her and read it. What the card actually says is, What are your biggest strengths?

I'm about to ask her what's going on when something hits me. She just called herself Arella *Rance.* Isn't her last name . . . ? My attention flicks to her left hand.

No ring.

My breath gets lost on its way out as my eyes lock with hers. Where's her ring? What does this mean? Did she leave him? *When? Why? How?*

She answers all my silent questions with "Our divorce was finalized on Wednesday. I'm officially—"

I launch myself at her, toss the card in my hand somewhere behind me, then pin her back to the blanket. She laughs beneath me as I straddle her.

"Are you coming back to me?" I can barely get the words out through my shaky breaths.

"If you'll have me."

I'm getting light-headed. "Are you planning to stay with me forever?"

"Forever," she says with so much conviction, it doesn't feel real. She wasn't lying earlier; this really is a simulation, and I don't give a fuck. I'd rather live in whatever this fake world is than the real one.

"Yes, baby, I'll have you." I lean down and plant a hard kiss over her lips. She kisses me back with a breathless sigh as she claws at my shirt to pull me closer. I snake my arm around her back and hold her tight against my chest.

I must be hallucinating, or I'm dead and somehow made it to heaven. She's kissing me. She's letting me touch her. She said she's going to stay with me forever. I don't deserve this. I don't deserve her, but I'm taking her anyway.

It takes me a minute to gather enough willpower to pull away. "Tell me you're mine."

"I'm yours," she says with dazed eyes.

"Tell me you're going home with me."

She doesn't hesitate. "I'm going home with you."

"Tell me you're never leaving me again."

"I'm never leaving you again."

An overwhelming wave of tears takes over my body. I lean back down to kiss her as they drip from my eyes.

"I love you so much, Arella." I trail kisses down her throat.

She arches her head back. "I love you too, Trey."

I suck on her neck, pulling moans from her that make my dick ache. I'm throbbing to be inside her, but I won't make that mistake again. There's no way I'm going to make love to her until she's got all her shit in my house and is lying in a bed that's *ours*. I need some sort of guarantee that *this* is it.

Panting, I flop onto my side and tug her against me. "How did this happen?"

107

ARELLA

It's been a month since Caleb agreed to make spending time together a priority. This is our second date night since, which is more than what we've had in the past six months.

Tonight's date night feels as bland as the last one. During dinner, neither of us could stay focused on the conversation. The silences between us felt awkward, and the way he kept staring off into the distance bothered me.

I wasn't much better. My mind kept wandering toward a man with dark hair and a sadness in his eyes that's been haunting me since the moment he stormed off and left for the airport.

I thought that after four weeks, I'd be able to forget about the way I saw his soul die when I said I wasn't coming back. I haven't forgotten. I also haven't forgotten about how for the rest of that evening, Trey got lost in his own thoughts and barely heard anything I said. I wanted to take it all back and ask him to whisk me away with him as if Caleb had never existed.

But Caleb does exist, and now we're on our couch, watching a movie.

Correction: Caleb is snoozing like he has been for the last twenty minutes. I'm staring blankly at the movie we were *supposed* to watch together, wondering what the heck I'm doing.

Why am I forcing my husband to spend time with me when he clearly doesn't want to? Why am I putting so much effort into fixing something I'm not even sure can be fixed? I have no idea why we fell apart or why he's been so distant, but I can't live like this anymore.

I told myself after leaving Nathan that I'd never subject myself to another relationship where I was abused or felt unwanted. Caleb wouldn't lay a finger on me that way, but I don't feel wanted by him either. Lately, I've also been questioning what I want.

I spend more time thinking about Trey than I do thinking about Caleb. I spend more time wishing Caleb was Trey than I do wishing this marriage will work. Caleb and I still have yet to have sex again, and even if we did, I'd probably imagine he's Trey the whole time.

What am I doing? This marriage is over, and now that I think about it, it's been over for a while—long before I even saw Trey at our tree.

Before I can talk myself out of it, I shake Caleb's arm.

He startles awake and upright. "Sorry. I didn't mean to fall asleep."

My heart thrashes in my chest—in a good way. "I need to talk to you about something."

He rubs his eyes, then straightens his back. "Okay?"

I try not to think about how this is going to hurt him. If I think about it too much, I'll chicken out. Yes, this is going to burn, but it's for the best. Our relationship isn't healthy anymore. I don't think Caleb has the courage to leave me, which means I have to be the one to leave him.

I suck in a deep breath, then let the words out. "I'm in love with someone else."

Caleb's body freezes. "What?"

"I said, I'm in love with someone else."

I expect him to freak out and ask me who. Instead, he says, "Me too."

"What?"

"I said, me too." From the way his face remains impassive, I don't question the validity of those two little words.

"Who are you in love with?"

"Rakesh." He stares at me for my reaction.

"But he's—oh . . ." It all clicks together: Caleb's late nights out with Rakesh. His lack of physical intimacy with me. His eagerness to drop me to be with Rakesh. It all makes sense now. "Is Rakesh gay too?"

"Yes."

"Does he also have feelings for you?"

"Yes."

"Have you guys . . . um, done stuff?"

Caleb sighs and picks up the TV remote, then turns the movie off. The room goes silent as he stands to flip the light on. When he returns to the couch, he folds his hands together in his lap. "How much do you want to know?"

"Everything."

"Are you sure? I don't want to hurt you." This is why I don't think he'd have the courage to leave me. He's too nonconfrontational for that.

I give him a firm nod. "I'm sure, Caleb. Just tell me everything."

He stares at his hands, trying to figure out how to start. "Um, it wasn't until after our wedding when I began developing feelings for him. I always chalked it up to how close of friends we are. Eventually, I couldn't ignore the feelings anymore. The more time I spent with him, the more I didn't want to leave him. The more I saw him shirtless at the gym, the more I wanted to touch him.

"It scared me at first because I've never looked at a man like that before. I also didn't know he was gay, so I suppressed my urges. I told myself I was just being ridiculous. I mean, I was already married to a woman, and he was my best friend, who I assumed was straight.

"As time went on, it got harder to suppress my urges. It also got harder for me to be with you because the idea of touching a woman just didn't appeal to me anymore. That's why I pulled away, and I'm sorry for that. You've been trying so hard to make this work, and I've been an asshole."

I lean in to him and lower my voice. "Caleb, you could have told me. You know how I feel about stuff like this."

"I was scared though. When I finally admitted to myself that I'm gay, I spent months keeping it to myself."

"When did you finally tell Rakesh?"

"When his grandma died. You remember how I went over to his apartment that night? I found him crying, so I gave him a hug that was meant to be consoling, but once our bodies connected like that, it was like something sparked between us. The next thing I know, we're making out in his kitchen."

In any other situation, I might feel betrayed to find out that my husband kissed someone else, but all I feel is happiness for Caleb. That kiss was a long time coming for him and Rakesh. It must have been a huge relief.

"Rakesh has known he's gay since middle school, but he never explored it because his very traditional Indian family won't accept it. He never came out to his friends either, because with his siblings at the same school, he didn't want it to get back to his parents. As for me, he's the only person I've told. And now you."

I place a gentle hand over his forearm. "I'm really glad you told me. That was really brave of you."

"Brave? No, Ari. I've been a coward. You're an amazing wife to me. You're everything a man wishes for in a woman. You're caring, loving, attentive, and you're an amazing cook. You deserve better than this. I should have told you much sooner, but I was too afraid of hurting you."

Obviously, I wasn't *that* attentive, because I missed seeing that my husband is gay. "Hurting me is better than killing yourself on the inside for being untrue to who you are."

He lets out a breath as he rubs his sweaty palms off on his pants. "Jeez, you're taking this way better than I thought you would. I suppose whoever you're in love with has something to do with that."

"A little."

"Can I guess who it is?"

Caleb is never going to get it right, so I say, "Sure."

"It's that Trey guy, isn't it?"

"What? How did you know?"

"You didn't see the way he looked at you, Ari. I mean, maybe you did, but you don't remember it. That man looked at you like you were his entire reason for existing."

I wish I could see the way Trey looks at me from the outside. If it's anything like the way Gramps looks at Grammy, then I'm making the right decision.

Caleb continues, "I still don't know what happened that day you acted like you knew him and tried to kick me out of our apartment. What I do know is that you looked at him like you loved him. At the time, I was freaked out by it, but I also loved you so much that I just wanted to forget it ever happened."

"I think I'm supposed to be with him."

"I think you are too, and despite how weird this may sound, I think you were with him before." Caleb stands and waves for me to join him. "Come on. I need to give you something."

I follow him into the bedroom, where he stops at his nightstand. He pulls out the second drawer, then grabs a little black box that used to hold a watch. He flips open the lid, then pulls out a shiny diamond necklace with gold angel wings.

He drops it into my open palm. "Read the back."

I gasp as I stare at the engraving. *Paris? T.G.* "Where did you get this?"

Caleb snaps the old watch box shut, then tosses it back into his drawer. "Do you remember the day of your surgery, when the nurses in the pre-op room asked you to change into a hospital gown?"

"Yeah?"

"After you changed, the nurses handed me a bag with all your clothes and personal belongings to hang on to. When you got out of surgery, I pulled your clothes out for you and found this necklace. I meant to give it to one of the nurses, thinking they must have accidentally put someone else's jewelry into your bag, but I forgot to.

"Later, we got home and were eating burgers when Trey showed up. The second he said his name, I thought about the initials on the back of this necklace and found it strange that some guy appeared at our door with the same initials as what's engraved onto a necklace that appeared in your personal-belongings bag from the hospital."

I run my thumb over the diamond. This is the same necklace I wore in that picture I gave back to Trey. It's also the same necklace I keep seeing in my dreams. How did this end up in my bag from the hospital?

"Why didn't you give this to me a long time ago?" I ask.

"Because I was weirded out by it. I mean, seriously, Ari? The whole situation is a little freaky, don't you think?"

It felt freakier to me three years ago. Thanks to my dreams, now I have a better grasp on the full picture. While it's still a little weird, I've accepted it.

"What do we do now?" Caleb asks.

"Now," I say, "we move forward."

"After I told him that I'm supposed to be with you, he agreed, then said he needed to give me something. From his drawer, he pulled out this." I drag the necklace out of my pocket.

The loudest gasp I've ever heard comes out of Trey's mouth. "He had it this whole time?"

"Yeah."

Trey gapes at me with his mouth fully open. "And he's gay?"

"Yeah, and Rakesh is moving into our apartment next week. That means I've got a week to pack up and move out."

"Give me one day, baby. That's all I need. I'll call the movers first thing in the morning."

"Most of my stuff is packed already. I started getting my things into boxes while Caleb and I worked out our divorce. It'll be expensive to get all my stuff shipped to New York."

Trey's face crinkles into hard lines. "New York? No way. You don't belong in New York. You belong here."

"But isn't that where you live?"

"Yes, but I've also got a house in Pasadena."

What? "When did you get a house in Pasadena?"

"Two days ago. With starting a new production company here, I figured I was ready to be back in California full-time. I was planning to go back to New York tonight to pack up."

"Is there room for me at your house in Pasadena?"

"Hell yeah. And if you need more space, I'll buy us a new house. Whatever you want, wherever you want."

I had already mentally prepared myself to move to New York with him during the week and work on getting my new bakery going over the weekends. Living in Pasadena sounds way better. "I'm sure the house you bought will be just fine."

"It's only got two bedrooms. I wasn't expecting to need more. We can use one as ours and share the other one as our office. You can have a desk where you do all your bakery business stuff. I can have my guitars on the other side."

"That sounds perfect."

He takes my hands into his, giving me a short kiss on the knuckles. "I can't believe this is happening."

"I can. I've been waiting for this moment for four weeks."

He shoots me a hard scowl. "Why did you wait so long?"

"I wanted to start our lives together without taking a single thing from the past with me. That included my marriage. Plus, I needed time to sort things out. This is a big transition for me. I had to tell people that Caleb and I were getting divorced, which was really scary."

"How did everybody take the news?"

"My friends at work were shocked. Javina wasn't surprised at all. I've been keeping her in the loop about Caleb, so she saw this coming. What she didn't see was that he's gay and that I'd been seeing you on Sundays. When I told her my plan to come straight here after the divorce was finalized, she was thrilled. Her first question was, Do you think he'll give me free tickets to see his band's shows?"

Trey throws his head back with a laugh. "Tell Javina that pretty boy is happy to give her free tickets for life—with spa days included."

"She'll love that."

"How did your grandparents take the news?"

I let out a long sigh as I recall the rough conversation I had with my grandparents. Rough is putting it lightly. They went on and on about how Caleb and I needed to try harder to make the marriage work, even though I explained multiple times that Caleb isn't interested in women anymore. "They didn't know that Caleb and I were having problems, so this came as a shock to them."

"Can I assume they don't know about me either?"

"Nope. My plan is that in a few months, I'll introduce you to them as if we just met."

Trey nods his approval. "That sounds like a good plan."

"Wonderful. Now before we get too ahead of ourselves, I need to ask you an important question."

"Before you do that, can I, please, put that necklace around you?"

I perk up and hold out the diamond. He takes it from me, then I gather all my hair to one side. Our eyes lock as he hooks the jewelry around my neck. Once it drapes down from my collarbones, he plants a tender kiss against my forehead, then my lips, then my nose.

I giggle as he continues pecking me all over my face. I don't stop him.

"Okay, I've had my fill for now." He straightens his back as if he's ready for anything I'm about to say. "You may ask your important question now."

I come straight out with it. "How are we going to keep the zovernment from finding out about us?"

As expected, his eyes go wide. "H—how do you . . . What?"

"For the past two months, I've been having dreams of us flying on a floating tire. On it, you tell me things that don't make sense but make everything else make sense. I've had that dream three times now. The last two times, I woke up and wrote as much of it down in my dream journal as possible."

"You have a dream journal?"

I adjust to sit with my legs to the side. "Yeah, to record all the dreams I have about you. I feel like my dreams are pieces of a puzzle, and I've been trying to put it together without most of the middle and only half the edges. Once I had this dream of us on a flying tire, everything finally came together. I'm still missing a lot of puzzle pieces, but I think I can see the main picture."

"Which is?"

"That we live in a world with two kinds of people: ones with powers and ones without. That you're one of the people who has powers and I'm not, and for some reason, I'm immune to everyone's powers. I know that you can create fireballs with your hands and move things without touching them. I know I was kidnapped and that you saved me. I even know that after the Enforcers captured us, I was interrogated for three days about everything I know about your world."

With every piece of information I say out loud, Trey seems to lose more air in his lungs. "Holy shit."

I place a gentle hand over his forearm. "Trey, if all my dreams over the past three years are things that actually happened, then I want you to know that I fought them when they tried to scrub me. I begged them to give me an exception. I even punched someone in the nose and made them bleed as they dragged me to the procedure room. I'm going to assume that's how I woke up in the hospital and that's the first time Caleb and I ever saw each other.

"I think I'm going to continue seeing the past in my sleep and eventually, I'll remember everything. Every few months, I see something new instead of a repeat, and it gives me more pieces of the puzzle." I hope that, through being with Trey, I'll be able to learn everything I used to know, and then some.

Trey lets out a long breath, taking this all in. "So what do we do now?"

"Now," I say with a grin, "we move forward."

"But what about staying off the zovernment's radar?"

"We'll figure that out along the way."

108

TREY

"**P**lease behave," Arella says as I pull her car into the driveway of a corner house—one that looks *waaay* too nice for a former mechanic and a stay-at-home grandma.

The large property is surrounded by blooming flower gardens and lawn gnomes. Thank fuck they're the cute cartoony gnomes and not the creepy grinning ones that look like they come alive at night. Some of the gnomes are even wearing Santa hats.

Christmas lights hang from the edges of the roof. A decorated tree with an angel on top sits just inside the living room window. I admire the cozy family-friendly vibes this house is giving. I could see myself raising kids with Arella in a house like this. Our current house is too small for that.

I turn the car off, unbuckle my seatbelt, then turn to face my girl for the last twelve weeks. "You don't trust me to charm your grandparents into liking me?"

"Honey, you're not about to meet Javina for the first time. My grandparents will need a little more convincing than some free spa days. They figured it out that I left Caleb for you, and when they asked me about it, I didn't want to lie. To them, you're what ruined my marriage."

I scoff. "Did you tell them that I moved across the country for three years just so I wouldn't ruin what you had with Caleb?"

"No. They think we met recently, remember?"

"Shit. You're gonna have to help me keep our story straight."

"Just go in with the knowledge that they think Caleb and I could have made things work but I gave up on him because I met you."

"Didn't you tell them Caleb's gay? Unless you're going to magically grow a beard and a penis, that man is not interested in you anymore."

The last I heard, Caleb and Rakesh told their families about each other. Unfortunately, neither family took the news well. Caleb's parents even called Arella, asking her to take him back.

I overheard the conversation and felt so proud of my girl for kindly explaining to Caleb's parents how they could be more supportive of their son instead of attacking him for something he can't control. Love is love, no matter the gender or lack of powers. Maybe if Caleb's parents can see it that way, the zovernment can too. More wishful thinking, I know.

Arella and Caleb have been keeping in touch, which I don't mind. Not just because I'm confident that he won't ever try to steal her back, but because they really do care about each other, and not because their minds were altered to care.

"My grandparents don't think Caleb is actually gay," Arella says. "They think it's 'just a phase,' which really rubs me the wrong way. But I'll work on getting them to understand that another time. For now, let's just focus on having a good Christmas dinner and getting them to like you."

I slash a nonchalant hand through the air. "Don't worry, babe. They'll like me."

"Okay. Remember that Grandma Roxy likes it when people compliment her garden and Grandpa Phil likes to talk about baseball."

"Garden. Baseball. Got it." I flash her a thumbs-up.

"And above all else, do *not* swear."

"Damn, babe. You didn't tell me your grandparents are prudes."

She slumps her shoulders and scolds me. "Trey, please. Just behave, okay?"

I throw my hands up in surrender. "All right. Don't say *fuck*. Got it."

Together, we exit her car. I don't need my powers to know my girl is nervous. She's rubbing the ends of her hair between her fingers and biting her lip. She's got nothing to worry about though. From what she told me, it seems like her grandparents are mostly concerned that what we have is a fling. They're concerned about whether Arella is going to be loved and treated right. I have every intention of loving and treating this woman right, so getting her grandparents to like me is gonna be a piece of cake.

Arella is about to knock on the front door when it opens. Her grandma is on the other side, wearing a huge smile on her face.

"Ari, dear! I'm so happy to see you."

Arella gives her grandma a tight bear hug. "Merry Christmas, Grammy."

The seventy-something-year-old woman drops her smile when her eyes land on me. I drop my friendly smile too, because all of a sudden, the zense in my chest is tingling.

109

TREY

"Is this your new boyfriend?" Roxy eyes me up and down. Her panic spreads through my body like wildfire.

If Arella notices Roxy's clenched jaw, she probably thinks it's just because her grandma is tense over the Caleb situation. I know better; that prickling in her chest is freaking her out. It's freaking me out too. The last thing I expected to find on the other side of this door was a Zordinary.

"How about I introduce Trey inside?" Arella says. "With Gramps."

"Um, sure . . ." Roxy hesitantly steps aside to allow us in. "Grandpa is in the living room."

As I step into the large entryway, I offer up one of my many charming smiles. Roxy's expression remains stony. She slams the door shut, then races down the wide hallway ahead of Arella and me.

"Phil! Ari's here."

A deep voice replies from the next room. "Wonderful. Let's meet the bastard who convinced our grandbaby to leave a perfectly good marriage."

Damn. He sounds like a fucking delight.

Arella gives my hand a reassuring squeeze as we enter the living room. The Christmas tree by the window is slightly smaller than the one Arella and I picked out for our place. Red stockings hang over the mantel, where a gaslit fire sits. Christmas-themed blankets are neatly folded and draped over the back of the couch and chairs. Every surface is covered in picture frames.

In a recliner sits an old man, who sets his book down on a side table and stands. He plasters a fake smile over his lips as if he didn't just say a rude comment he very much wanted me to hear.

His fake smile remains on his lips until the second I get within two steps of him. As the zense activates in my chest, his face falls, his back straightens, and his shoulders square. A rush of horror radiates off him. Just like me, he also expected to meet an Ordinary today.

As an attempt to ease the tension, Arella fakes a smile of her own. "Grammy, Gramps, this is the *amazing* guy I've been telling you about."

I play along, sticking my hand out to the gray-haired man. "Nice to meet you. I'm Trey."

The man takes my hand, shaking it like he's trying to squeeze my hand to death. Next, I offer my hand to Roxy. She shakes my hand a little gentler, yet still stony-faced.

Arella doesn't acknowledge their rough demeanors. "Trey, these are my grandparents, Phil and Roxy."

I almost scoff out loud. *Her grandparents?* What a joke. I've got half a mind to hoist Arella over my shoulder and run her out the front door. Save her first, ask questions later.

I don't do that because, based on the many loving photos surrounding me, this couple hasn't done any harm to my girl. From the many stories Arella has told me about them, they took good care of her after her parents died. I'm not leaving here until I find out why two Zordis would bring an Ordinary girl into their lives like that.

A long silence fills the room as Phil and Roxy's frenzied energy swirls around me. I'm waiting for one of them to say something. Neither does. They just keep staring at me as if waiting for me to make the first move. What move? I'm not sure, but they look ready to hoist Arella over their shoulders too.

Arella is the first to break the silence. "Why don't we all sit down and get to know each other?"

In silence, Arella and I claim the love seat behind us. I feel the need to grab her hand and hold it in my lap, so I do. I don't miss the way Phil scowls at our conjoined hands as he stiffly returns his ass to his recliner. Roxy eyes her husband as she settles on the couch across from us. It's as if she has a feeling Phil is going to attack me and she needs to stop him before he does.

"Tell us how you two met," Roxy says with a forced friendly tone.

I'm not gonna win any points by telling them that Arella and I originally met on the side of a highway while I was working a top secret ZIRDA mission to find out what makes her immune to Zordi powers, so I keep quiet.

Thankfully, Arella has all the right words. "We met at the Soul House, a music bar in downtown LA. Trey's a musician, and his band plays there on the weekends."

Phil's hard glare flicks from Arella to me. His tone comes out displeased. "You're in a band?"

"Yes, sir." Calling the man *sir* doesn't seem to win me any points either.

He scowls at me so hard, his entire forehead creases into thick folds. "Do you happen to have a *real* job on top of that?"

"Grandpa," Arella scolds. "Trey's band does really well online. They've also released two original albums, and all their shows always sell out. Just because it's not a regular nine-to-five doesn't mean it's not a *real* job."

I don't care what this wrinkly fart thinks of my career choice. I have well beyond the means I need to take care of the woman beside me.

Phil narrows his gaze on Arella. "You left a hardworking cop for a man who sings songs on the Internet for money?"

Simply stated, that does make me sound bad.

"Grandpa," Arella scolds again. "First of all, Caleb isn't a cop. He's a security guard at a museum. Second, Trey doesn't sing songs on the Internet for money. Being in a band is like running a business. What he sells just happens to be the music he writes. And third, you promised you'd behave today."

It's good to know I wasn't the only one who received a behavior lecture before this meeting that's going *sooo fucking well.*

Arella continues, "How about you give Trey a chance?"

Phil sighs and rubs the back of his neck. "All right, boy. Tell us. When you met Ari and she told you she was married, why did you still pursue her?"

"Phil . . ." Roxy says at the same time Arella drops her jaw.

"Grandpa!"

I really wish she'd stop calling him that. Everyone here knows this man isn't really her grandpa—except her.

Phil doesn't quit. "What kind of man steals a woman away from her husband?"

"Grandpa, stop."

"Not a real man, that's for sure. What made you think you had any right to dig yourself into a perfectly good marriage and—"

"Grandpa!" This time, Arella yells, and it shuts him up. "Stop saying my relationship with Caleb was *perfectly good*. It wasn't."

"He put a roof over your head, didn't he? He loved you, cooked for you, and made you happy. What about that wasn't good?"

"First of all, I had my apartment way before I even met Caleb. He's the one who moved in with me. Second, I did *all* the cooking. He's terrible at it. And third, I've explained it to you already: Caleb and I weren't good for a while. A woman needs more than just a roof and food."

Phil lets out a condescending *pfft*. "What else is there?"

Arella loses it. "Affection! Passion! Complete and utter devotion! Caleb stopped giving me any of that months before Trey and I started anything. There was absolutely no passion in our marriage, and neither of us were devoted to the other.

"For god's sake, Grandpa, the man is gay! And he's already dating his friend Rakesh. Now stop talking about Caleb. I came here today so you could meet Trey, the man who's sitting right here. The man who I'm passionate about. Who's devoted to me and has promised to take care of me better than anyone can."

Phil rolls his eyes. Now I know where Arella gets it from. He shoots me a skeptical glare. "If this band thing doesn't work out, how are you planning to take care of my grand-daughter?"

I'm so fucking close to aiming a fireball at him and accusing him of kidnapping an innocent three-year-old Ordinary girl. I almost do, until Roxy slaps her thighs.

"How's about we all take a break, huh?" Roxy grimaces at her husband. "Phil, how's about you and I meet in the kitchen?"

Phil stays where he is. "And leave her alone with *him*? Are you crazy?"

What the fuck? Does he think I'm gonna hurt Arella? Or is he more afraid I'll spill their secret? *It's definitely the latter.*

Roxy grits her teeth together. "If he wanted to hurt her, he would have already. Now come."

Okay? Maybe he *is* worried that I'll hurt her. If that's the case, this grumpy asshole knows nothing about me.

Roxy's words give me a little confidence that, on some level, we all want the same thing. These people don't want anything to happen to Arella any more than I do. Having *one* thing in common is good, I guess. Well, technically, we have two things in common, if I count having powers.

The second her "grandparents" stomp down the hall and disappear into another room,

Arella turns to me. "Oh my god, Trey. I'm so sorry. I don't know what's gotten into Gramps. He's not usually this mouthy. He promised me he'd try to like you."

Her "grandparents" liking me is no longer what I'm concerned about. "Um, babe, do you remember when your grandparents took you in, or is that just what they told you happened?"

"I was three. I don't remember anything that happened at that age."

My eyes scan the room, looking at every picture frame in sight. I don't see what I'm looking for. "Are there any pictures of your grandparents with you as a baby? Like from before your parents died?"

"Um, I dunno. Why does that matter right now?"

"Are there any pictures of your grandparents with your parents?"

"What does that have to do with anything?"

I stroke my stubbly chin as the gears turn in my head. "I dunno. Maybe nothing. Maybe everything."

I haven't told Arella what I know about her parents yet. Mostly because whenever I bring them up, it doesn't seem like she remembers our conversation about how her name was Hannah Calder at one point. I've been waiting for either her to dream about it or a good time to tell her. We've been too busy being happily in love for me to want to drop a bomb that big on her.

Arella throws her head into her hands and groans. "This is a disaster."

I'm still trying to piece things together as I drape an arm around her back. "Everything will be okay, babe."

"Nope. Gramps is still stuck on the fact that I left Caleb to be with you."

Actually, I think he's now stuck on the fact that she's with a Zordi, but I'm not gonna tell her that. Not yet. First, I need to figure out why and how two Zordis got their hands on an Ordinary girl and have pretended to be her grandparents for the past twenty-some years.

A pair of light feet shuffles down the hall until Roxy reappears in the living room. She locks her eyes on me. "Phil would like to speak to you in the kitchen, please. Just you."

"No!" Arella shouts. "I'm not going to allow Grandpa to keep talking to my boyfriend like that."

I love the sound of that. *My boyfriend.* I'd like the sound of *my fiancé* better, but boyfriend is acceptable for now.

Arella and I have been careful about only showing affection to each other in private. My band doesn't know about her yet, but Liz and Colton do. Basically, we're trying to keep the number of people who know about our relationship as low as possible. Hopefully, that will help keep us off the zovernment's radar. Introducing me to Arella's grandparents was something we debated for weeks.

When I get to my feet, Arella does too. "I'm coming with you," she says.

"No, Ari. Grandpa wants—" Roxy starts.

"Relax, babe." I place a gentle hand over her shoulder. "I can handle him. Just let us talk, man to man." *Zordi to Zordi.*

She stares at me for a long heartbeat before finally relenting. "The second he gives you *any* flak, you come straight back here, and we're leaving, okay? I don't care that it's Christmas. The way Grandpa's acting is unacceptable."

I plant a tender kiss against her forehead, and just because Roxy's watching, I make sure it's extra-long. When I finally draw back, I cup my girl's cheek. "I'll be fine, babe. Did you forget my childhood? Nothing he can say will break through my thick skin."

Roxy steps aside as I pass her to find the kitchen.

At the square table, Phil is seated in one of the four chairs. He points to the chair across from him, and I take it. For a few breaths, he doesn't say anything. His eyes never leave me either.

It's times like these when I wish I could read minds, not emotions. I want to know what he's thinking, not what he's feeling. I don't need my powers to know he's furious. The death glare he's shooting my way is evident enough.

"How much?" he asks.

I wait for him to finish, because is it just me, or is "how much" not a complete question? "How much what?"

From his lap, he lifts a checkbook and a pen. "How much will it take for you to walk away?"

Is he serious? The idea that anyone thinks it's possible to pay me to leave Arella is so ridiculous, I laugh.

"You think this is funny? I'm not joking, boy. Now tell me, how much? Name your price. I'll write you a check. You walk out this door"—he hooks a thumb toward the exit behind him —"and you never see or speak to my granddaughter ever again."

My granddaughter. Such audacious words.

I lean toward him over the table as my laughter dies. In a low tone, I say, "There's not enough money in this world to get me to walk away from her."

Phil doesn't hear a single word from my mouth. "How's ten thousand?"

I shake my head.

"Twenty?"

"No."

"A hundred?"

"Nope."

"Come on, boy. You're a good-for-nothin' musician. Imagine what a hundred grand could do for you."

I laugh deep in my chest. When I'm almost done laughing, I laugh some more, just to drill in my point of how fucking stupid this is. "Your money isn't worth anything to me. I make more than a hundred grand a month."

"Yeah, right!" Phil half sneers, half scoffs. "How the hell do you make that kind of living?"

"Royalties."

"From what? You're not the guy who invented the Internet."

"Nope. Better. My parents invented healing products."

Phil's entire face falls as his eyes turn to slits. "What did you say your last name was?"

I never said my last name earlier, but if he knows Zordi history, he should already know my last name. "It's Grant. Trey Grant. My parents are—"

Phil's chair tumbles behind him with a loud *crash!* He seizes me by my neck and pins me against the wall before I can take another breath. I gasp for air as he tightens his vise grip around my throat.

"How did you find her?" he growls into my face for only me to hear.

This man is lucky that Arella thinks he's her grandpa. Resisting the urge to punch the gray-haired motherfucker in the face, I claw at his fingers clenched around my neck.

"How did you find her?" he repeats louder.

"What . . . are . . . you . . . talking about?" I say through the little breathing space I have.

Arella bursts into the kitchen, screaming as she grabs Phil's arm. "Stop! Stop!"

Phil barely moves. He's strong for a guy in his late seventies.

"Grandpa, stop!" Arella punches at his arms, but it does nothing.

"Phil!" Roxy shouts. "Let the boy go!"

My relentless attacker finally releases me. I brace myself against the table, coughing as my lungs take in the precious air they were deprived of.

"What is wrong with you?" Arella scolds the man she thinks she's related to. She puts a hand over my shoulder. "Are you okay, honey?"

Nope. I'm still gasping for air as I force a nod. "I'm okay."

"Get away from him!" Phil grabs Arella by the arm and yanks her toward him. At least, he tries to.

She jerks her arm back and locks it and her other arm around my bicep. "What are you doing?"

"Protecting you! This man is dangerous!" Phil tries to grab her again, but she refuses to allow it.

I'm not dangerous—not to Arella—but I'm about to be pretty fucking dangerous to him if he keeps trying to touch her like that.

Arella stomps her foot. "Will you stop and tell me what's going on? Why are you acting like this?"

Phil turns to his wife. "Go make the call. We need to end this now."

"End what?" Arella shrieks so loudly, it hurts my ears.

Roxy doesn't move.

"Rox!" Phil's face is turning red. "I said, go make the call!"

Roxy looks at Phil, then at Arella, then at me, then back at Phil. I wish I knew what she was thinking, because it's definitely not about making a phone call. Who the hell does Phil want her to call, anyway? It's not the zovernment, because then, they'd be in just as much trouble as I'd be.

"Will someone tell me what the fuck is going on?" Arella screams to the ceiling.

Hold on. Did she just say *fuck*? After she warned *me* not to swear?

"I'll tell you what's going on," Phil says. "This man is not who you think he is. You need to get as far away from him as possible. He's using you."

"No, he's not!" Arella shouts with so much conviction, I don't feel the need to defend myself. "Trey loves me, and I love him."

"It's true," I add, intertwining my fingers with hers. "I love Arella—with all my heart."

The room goes silent as Phil and Roxy digest that. They gape at me with their mouths wide open. I think I've put them in shock.

Phil keeps his glare on me as if the second he looks away, I'll turn into a monster and eat Arella alive in front of him. "Rox?"

The old woman shakes her head. "I—I can't tell."

"What do you mean, you can't tell? Obviously, the boy is lying! I was only asking you for confirmation of what we already know."

"Well, my alarm didn't go off."

"What the hell are you talking about? Of course it did! You just missed it!"

A slow smile spreads across my cheeks as the realization dawns on me. Suddenly, a plan begins forming in my head.

Phil shoots a killer look my way. "Wipe that stupid grin off your face and get the hell out of my house."

Arella tugs on my arm. "Let's go, Trey."

"No!" Phil points a stern finger at her. "Not you."

"Seriously, Grandpa? Trey has done nothing wrong, and you're treating him like he's a rabies-infected wild animal."

"Wild animals are more humane than the Grant family."

Roxy gasps. "The Grant family?"

"Yes, Rox. They've finally found her. This boy is related to the Grants."

Roxy slaps a hand over her chest. "Oh no! Ari, please listen to your grandpa. Get away from that man."

"What?" Arella's face falls. "Just now, in the living room, you said you would give him a chance."

"That was before I knew who he was," Roxy says.

"He's manipulating you!" Phil yells. "That's what he does. That's what the entire Grant family does."

"Everybody shut up!" My yell silences them all. "I think I know how to clear this up. Well, some of it." I try to free my arm from Arella's grip, but she only hangs on tighter. "It's okay, babe. You can let me go."

"No."

"Trust me. It's okay."

Slowly, she releases me, and I take a step to the side to make sure our skin isn't touching and, more importantly, that her immunity isn't projecting onto me. Then I clear my throat, square my shoulders, and look straight into Roxy's eyes.

"I am *not* in love with Arella." I give Roxy a moment to process that before I continue. "I do *not* currently have a diamond ring in my pocket—one that I haven't been carrying around for the last two weeks."

"Honey, what are you doing?" Arella asks me.

I put my hand out to Arella, palm forward. "Just trust me." I lock my attention back onto Roxy. "Every day for the last two weeks, I have *not* been asking Arella to marry me because I do *not* have plans to spend the rest of my life with her."

"Trey," Arella says.

"Hold on. I've got one more. Arella is *not* currently pregnant with my baby, and I'm *not* thrilled out of my mind about starting a family with her."

Arella backhands my chest. "Trey!"

Last night, Arella and I agreed that we wouldn't mention the baby to her grandparents, but since we're letting everything air out, I made the split-second executive decision to air that one out too.

A huge grin spreads across my face. "Tell us, Grandma Roxy, how many of those were lies?"

Her eyes are watery. "All of them. Every single one."

"What?" Phil wheezes. "How is that possible?"

Keeping my grin wide, I close the gap between Arella and me, then I circle an arm around her waist. "Great! Now that that's settled, if you still wanna kick me out, I'll happily leave now. But I'm taking my girl with me, and if either of you try to stop me"—I drop my voice into a low growl—"I'll blast you with a fireball."

Arella's jaw drops. "Trey!"

"Oh, shit! I forgot one." I let go of Arella's hand and step away again. Looking back into Roxy's eyes, I say, "Arella does *not* already know about our kind."

Roxy gasps, slapping both hands against her chest. "Lie."

110

ARELLA

Minutes ago, my grandpa was choking my boyfriend against the wall. Now Trey is making a ton of backward statements, told my family I'm pregnant, and just threatened to blast them with a fireball. What is going on, and how did my life unravel so quickly?

The kitchen is silent. Gramps looks like he's about to strangle Trey again, and my man has a smug grin on his face like he's challenging Gramps to do it. I'm too confused to move.

Like usual, Grammy's the only one with her head on straight. She gestures toward the table before the men—excuse me, *boys*—can start fighting again. "Why don't we all sit down?"

Trey doesn't miss a beat. He twists on his heel to pull out a chair for me. I sit, then he pulls out another chair, moves it next to mine, and plants himself on it. He even makes a show of putting his arm around the back of my chair and resting his hand over my shoulder. Still smiling, he locks his gaze onto Gramps as if daring him to say something about it.

My grandparents take the seats across from us. Both of their expressions are like they've seen a baby get thrown off a skyscraper.

"I just made a bunch of confessions," Trey says, "all of which Roxy has confirmed are lies. I think it's time you two made some confessions of your own."

Gramps and Grammy swivel their heads to each other. They seem to say something with their eyes. What I gather from it is that neither of them know what to say and they're hoping the other will take the lead.

"No confessions?" Trey asks.

The room stays hushed.

"Not a single one?" He waits another moment. "All right. If you want, I could say my theories, but I think Arella would rather hear it from you."

Hear what? What am I missing?

Trey continues, "Let's see. I don't know the whole story, so I'll just have to fill in the blanks myself. What I don't know is how the fuck you came into her life and why. And what reason you two possibly have to think I'm dangerous to her."

Like a reflex, my arm flies to backhand him in the chest. "Trey!"

"Ow!" He rubs the spot I hit. "What?"

"No swearing, remember?"

His head jerks back. "Oh, *now* that rule is in effect? What about earlier when you swore?"

"Things were heated," I say defensively, straightening up. "It was necessary."

"What do you think, Phil?" Grammy asks in a soft tone, biting her lip.

"I think this boy is a good liar and has fooled you. I think I'm two seconds away from killing him. And while I'm dragging his body into a ditch, I think you should go make the call."

What call? And excuse me? Drag Trey's body into a ditch? I'd like to think Gramps is joking, but the daggers in his eyes tell me otherwise. "Grandpa! This is the father of my unborn child you're talking about murdering."

Gramps doesn't take his attention off Trey. "Ari, you are not pregnant with this man. It's impossible."

"What makes you think—" I gasp. He knows about Zordinaries. He thinks it's impossible for me to carry a Zordi child. But how does he know that?

"Phil," Grammy says calmly, "I think we've gotta tell her."

"We will do no such thing! We swore from day one that we would protect her. We won't stop just because some deceiving asshole has crashed into the picture. Now go make the call. They'll help us take care of this."

"But Phil . . . He loves her."

Bang! Gramps slams a fist against the table. "He's lying!"

"He's not," Grammy says with calm conviction.

"Seriously, Rox? He's already manipulated her. Now you're gonna let him manipulate you too?"

I've gotta hand it to Grammy, she doesn't allow Gramps's fury to affect her. Her voice stays even as she says, "My internal alarm went off as the boy made all those backward statements. You can't fool my gift."

Finally, it hits me. "Oh! You're a Detector."

Grammy nods. "Yes, dear. I am."

"But that means . . ."

"Yes, dear. We are."

My grandparents are . . . Zordis? How? Does that mean I am too? I don't have any powers though. Plus, my body functions like an Ordinary's body. Then that means . . . "You're not my grandparents."

Grammy's gaze falls to her lap. "No, dear. We aren't."

"Roxy!" Phil shouts, slamming both fists against the table. "What the hell are you doing? I did not agree to this."

Grammy isn't having it anymore. "Phillip, you need to exit the kitchen, and you are not to return until you have a handle on yourself. You're embarrassing me in front of Ari and her boyfriend."

Trey lifts a finger. "Actually, I'm not just her boyfriend. We're soul mates. Confirmed by the glimmer on multiple occasions."

Gramps grits his teeth together as he turns to Grammy. "Rox?"

"Truth," Grammy says.

"Jesus fucking Christ!" Gramps's chair squeals as he shoves himself away from the table. "I'm going for a walk."

"Good," Grammy says. "And don't come back until you've cooled down."

Gramps makes a grunt as he slips into a pair of shoes near the back door. He continues muttering swearwords to himself as he slams the door shut and stomps across the yard.

"I apologize for his rudeness," Grammy says. "I'll have a strict talking to him later tonight. Now, Ari, I owe you an explanation, and I'm happy to tell you everything, but first, I just realized I've been a bad host. Would either of you like something to drink? Or a snack? I've got Christmas cookies and milk."

"Milk and cookies would be great," Trey says with a sweet smile.

I only nod because I can't get any words out. My grandparents aren't really my grandparents? *What?*

Behind me, Grammy rummages around the kitchen. A moment later, three glasses of milk appear on the table. Trey grabs one of them. After he takes a long drink, Grammy tops off his glass, then returns to the table with a large Tupperware of home-baked cookies.

Trey grabs one from the box and pops the entire thing into his mouth. "Delicious."

"Thank you," Grammy says as she settles back into her chair. "I feel like there's so much to say. I don't know where to start."

My mouth is dry as I say, "I know where. Why don't you start with the part where you and Gramps aren't actually my grandparents?"

Trey places his hand over my thigh, offering me a small slice of comfort.

"Ari," Grammy says with a soft pouty look on her face. "I hope you can understand that while we aren't biologically your grandparents, it doesn't change that in every other way, we are. From the moment you were placed into our care, we vowed that we'd protect you with our lives and love you as if you were our own. If anything, you're more like a daughter to me. When you came to us, Grandpa and I were already in our fifties, so we had to claim to be your grandparents."

"Why did you have to claim to be my family at all? What happened to my real family?"

Grammy tears up a little, making me feel bad for what I said. She places a hand over her heart. "We *are* your real family, dear. Maybe not biologically, but Grandpa and I are the ones who raised you and made all the sacrifices we needed to for your safety."

"Safety from what?"

"Not what, dear. *Who.* And that who is the Grant family."

Trey's body stiffens. I put my palm over the top of his hand on my thigh, offering him my comfort in return. He doesn't ease into me the way he usually does, so I give his hand a little squeeze and shoot a scowl at my . . . well, the person I *thought* was my grandma.

"Don't lump Trey in with the rest of the Grants," I say. "Whatever happened back then, he had nothing to do with it."

"I suppose you're right." Grandma turns to Trey. "How old would you have been back then?"

"Seven," he says. "I was seven when my parents were killed. On the same day Arella's parents died."

Wait. What? It was on the same day?

Grammy furrows her eyebrows together as she thinks. "Ah, yes. It was the same night, wasn't it?"

Trey's body goes rigid. "Can you tell us what you know?"

"Are you sure you're ready for this, honey?" I ask, because this poor man has spent most of his life wondering what happened the night his parents were killed. I never thought it'd be my grandparents who might have the answers.

Trey closes his eyes, sucks in a deep breath, then slowly releases it. When he reopens his eyes, he nods with vigor. "I'm more than ready."

Grammy takes a drink of her milk, then begins. "Phil and I were living in San Diego. He was an Enforcer. I also worked for the zovernment, but in foreign affairs. We had been married for quite some time and had no children. We'd had a child at one point—a daughter. She died when she was fifteen from a severe case of zmonia. It's like the Ordinary pneumonia, but for Zordis, and worse. The mortality rate is about forty percent, and our little Cassie didn't make it."

Grammy locks her watery eyes on me. There's nothing but pain on her face. "Your grandpa and I were devastated. We only had one child, so when we lost Cassie, it felt like we'd lost our entire world. That's why when our longtime friend Rita came to us with a child who had just lost her parents and needed protection, we didn't hesitate to say yes.

"Rita had told us she was a graphic designer until she showed up that night on our doorstep with you in hand. She explained that she was really a ZIRDA agent and that she was working on this mission to discover what made some rare Ordinaries immune to Zordi powers.

"You were the youngest of the Ordinaries they were studying. Your parents were told that you were part of a top secret medical study led by the government. Your parents were assured that the research would cause you no harm. As you can guess, they were lied to. The tests were not safe whatsoever. ZIRDA was doing everything from cutting the Immunes open to pumping them with drugs and raping them."

I gasp with a hand covering my mouth. "No."

"Yes, dear. I would never make up something that vile. ZIRDA thought that if an Immune could block Zordi powers, then maybe they could also block our inability to mate. If it was possible to mate with an Immune, they figured they could create some of the most powerful Zordis on the planet. Could you imagine a Zordi immune to other Zordis' powers? That person would be unstoppable.

"Naturally, once the Immunes realized that the tests were unsafe, they tried to back out— your parents included. However, ZIRDA wasn't about to let the youngest Immune in their research pool go that easily. They offered your parents millions of dollars to give you up.

"When your parents still refused, like any good parent would, ZIRDA killed them. More specifically, Victor Grant killed them. He also killed another little Ordinary girl who looked just like you. Then his agents strapped all three of them into a car and rolled it off a cliff. The police were none the wiser. They ruled it as an accident and quickly moved on to their next case like it was nothing."

I glance at my man, who seems to be processing this information the same way I am: in shock.

Grammy continues, "When the other ZIRDA agents found out what Victor had done, the organization split into two groups. One half agreed with Victor that the Immunes project needed to continue as it was, involuntary surgeries, nonconsensual drug tests, rapes, and all. The other half believed that the project needed to end. Rita—and Suzie and Andy Grant—led that second group. On the same evening your parents' bodies were shoved off that cliff, Rita, Suzie, and Andy, with a number of other agents, made plans to save you.

"While some of the agents distracted Victor and his group, the others snuck you away. What Rita didn't know was that Suzie and Andy weren't actually on her side. Secretly, they wanted the Immunes project to continue, just in a more humane fashion. So they double-crossed her."

"No!" Trey shouts so loudly, his voice booms against the kitchen walls. "They wouldn't have done that."

"Oh, I can assure you," Grammy says, "they did. The original plan was that Rita would sneak Ari away to a location only Rita knew of. The less everyone else knew, the better. That place was with your grandpa and me," Grammy says, looking back at me.

"We didn't even know she had plans to bring you here until she showed up. At the time, we hadn't seen her in almost a year. We were friends, but we weren't *that* close. However, she knew us well enough to know that if she showed up with a precious little girl in need of care, we wouldn't say no. And she was right. Once she finished telling us everything that happened, we didn't hesitate to make you some food and a place to sleep."

"Can you tell us more about the part where my parents apparently double-crossed Rita?" Trey asks. "How did that all go down?"

"After Victor killed Ari's parents," Grammy says, "he locked her up in his ZIRDA hideout. While Rita and her team worked to sneak Ari out of there, that's when your parents tried to take her for themselves. I don't know everything that happened, but according to Rita, it sounded like a bloodbath. Some lives were lost."

Grammy locks her gaze on me. "In the end, Rita was able to get you out and away from the Grants, unharmed. While she made her way to us, Victor's team assumed it was Suzie and Andy who took you, so he ordered his people to the Grants' home, which was what allowed Rita to disappear without anyone stopping her."

Trey's hand trembles against my thigh. "That's why those men came crashing into my house that night. They were looking for Arella. When my parents realized that, they probably rushed home to save me and ended up getting killed instead."

Tears roll from my eyes. "Oh god, Trey. I'm so sorry."

"Rita told me about the explosion," Grammy says. "I have to admit, at the time, I was pretty dang happy about it. With Suzie and Andy gone, there were two fewer people in this world who wanted to hurt the innocent little girl who had just been dropped into our laps. The only people left that we needed to keep her away from were Victor and the people on his side."

"How did you do it for so long?" I ask.

"Well, within a week of having you, Grandpa and I quit our jobs and got new identities. We gave you one too. Your birth name was Hannah Calder. Your parents were Stanley and Robyn Calder, two very brave and loving people. Of course, I never met them, but I can only assume that of them for refusing to give you up for any amount of money.

"We named you Arella because Arella means *angel*. To us, you were our little angel. Our second chance at having a daughter or, since we were already in our fifties, a granddaughter. We gave up so much to keep you safe, dear: our careers, our names, our friends, and any connections we had to the Zordi world. We did everything and anything necessary to protect you. No expense was too big."

Trey raises his hand like we're in a school. "I have a question."

"Hopefully," Grammy says, offering him a sweet smile, "I have an answer."

"If you were trying to keep Arella safe from Victor, why would you stay in California? Why not move to the other side of the country or a different continent?"

"Good question. It's one that Phil and I have debated a lot over the years. We've lost countless nights of sleep over the many reasons why we had to get Ari away from California, but the answer was simple: Uprooting seventeen people's lives and tearing them away from their families was where we drew the line.

"Unless we were going to raise this little girl out in the middle of nowhere, there was always a chance that Victor or *someone* would come around knocking. We considered the isolation method, but that's not the life we wanted for you. Therefore, Rita and the other sixteen people on her team vowed to protect you for the rest of your life. Together, we agreed to remain in California so everyone could stay with their families. Then, if the day ever came, they'd only be one phone call away."

Things are starting to come together now. "That's the call Gramps kept asking you to make."

"Sure is. There are only twelve of them left. Some have passed. Some ended up moving away. The people who remain have named themselves Ari's Guardians. We moved around the state every year to be closer to each one, because every year, they rotated being your main guardian—from a distance, of course. We've been careful to ensure that if Victor's people ever tracked them down, they'd have no relationship with us to track back to you. Moving around the state also helped make you harder to find."

"Somebody somewhere was slacking," Trey says with a scoff, "because somehow, Victor found her, and that's how I came into her life."

That's not the way I would have said that, but okay . . .

"It sounds like you two have a story to tell as well. Maybe you can explain how this"—Grammy wiggles a finger between Trey and me—"happened."

"Yes," I say, "but I want Gramps to hear it too. Maybe once he does, he'll be more willing to accept Trey."

"You still want his acceptance? Even after finding out he's not really your grandpa?"

I nod firmly. "Of course, Grammy. Like you said, biological or not, you are still my grandparents. I still love you as much as I did before. Actually, I think I love you more now, knowing you took in a little girl you'd never met and sacrificed so much to give her a good life."

That does it for Grammy. She loses it, bursting into tears. I slide off my chair to wrap my arms around her. She stands to meet me, and we embrace in a long, tearful hug. After we step back, I wipe the salty water from my eyes.

We chat about lighter things as we wait for Gramps to return. Trey enjoys more of Grammy's cookies while she tells us some funny stories of the things I did growing up.

Eventually, Gramps steps back into the house and kicks off his shoes. He doesn't look like he's fuming anymore, but his expression is still hard.

"I told them the truth," Grammy says gently. "The kids have a story to tell us too. Are you ready to hear it?"

Gramps responds by sitting in his chair and giving Trey and me a nod.

Together, we tell my grandparents everything.

Trey starts by telling them that he was a ZIRDA agent. Big mistake. The way Gramps's face turns to stone makes me think he's going to start a war, but he keeps his cool and doesn't say a word. He relaxes once Trey gets to the part where he felt the glimmer and realized he was in love with me.

By the time I talk about how I was kidnapped by Victor's people, Gramps is back to fuming. He doesn't shout, but his hands turn to fists over the table. Those hands slowly unclench as Trey tells the details of how he rescued me.

When we get to the part where we were running to Las Vegas to hide from the Royals, Grammy's on the edge of her seat.

"You *know* we made it out okay," I say, trying to ease her. "I'm sitting right in front of you."

"That doesn't change that the Royals were right above your heads while you were crouched in an underground crawl space in a ginseng store. What happened after that?"

"Actually," Trey says, "I think we should go back a little. We skipped the part where I find out that Victor's not my uncle and is actually my dad."

Trey tells a shortened version of that part, and then we get to the part where we found out that his aunt Jodi had swapped minds with Victor for twenty years.

"You've got to be kidding me," Gramps says. "All those things Victor did to those Immunes . . . it was Jodi the whole time?"

Trey nods. "Yep. Everything from the brutality of the Immunes project, to killing Arella's parents and mine, to abusing me as a child, to running ZIRDA as a Royals camp, to kidnapping Arella, and everything else in between. It was all Jodi."

We give my grandparents a moment to digest that before I tell them about the zovernment erasing my memory and planting Caleb into my life.

"How is that possible when you're immune?" Grammy asks.

"According to the Executive Keeper I spoke to," Trey says, "they have a way of turning off her immunity by pumping her with a bunch of drugs and hormones to shut down her fear."

Thankfully, Trey doesn't mention how my immunity walls come down whenever he makes me orgasm. I don't need my grandparents knowing that.

"I swear," Gramps says, "the zovernment is full of corrupt bastards. They keep so much information hidden from the general public, and they—"

Ding-dong!

All four of us straighten up like rods as we glance at one another.

"Are you expecting anyone?" I ask.

Grammy shakes her head. "Nope."

Gramps is the first to rise from his chair. "Stay here. I'll go see who it is."

"I'll come with," Trey says, squaring his shoulders like he's ready for battle.

Gramps doesn't protest as the two of them disappear down the hall.

"It's probably just a package," Grammy says, rubbing the back of her neck. Judging by the way we all snapped into alert mode, I don't think it's just a package.

We listen intently as the door opens and Gramps says, "Can I help you?"

"Hello," a sweet voice says. "My name is Mia Wang. I'm a Keeper here to speak with Mr. Ward, Mrs. Ward, Miss Rance, and Mr. Grant. May I come in?"

111

TREY

This day cannot get any more insane.

At the sight of Mia Wang, I almost bolt back into the kitchen to rush Arella out of here. I don't, only because if a Keeper is here, that means the zovernment already knows about Arella and me. Now I've got the feeling they've known for a while.

Phil's back stiffens as he narrows his gaze on the woman on his doorstep. "Can I see your badge?"

I'm surprised he can think clearly enough to ask for credentials. Phil has been on information overload since the moment I started my and Arella's story with *So, I used to be a ZIRDA agent.*

Mia unbuttons the top button of her silky blouse, then drags the fabric to the side.

"Oh, you're not just *any* Keeper," Phil says as he glances at the branded crest over her heart. "You're one of the top dogs."

"Yes, Mr. Ward, I am. And no, I'm not here to take her away, nor am I here to arrest you. I'm just here to talk."

Phil goes silent as he thinks. He must come to the conclusion that he has no choice, because with a sigh, he steps aside and waves for the Keeper to enter.

"She claims she's not here to take away our little girl," Phil says as we return to the kitchen.

"I heard that claim," Roxy says, standing in front of Arella like she's guarding precious artwork. "I don't believe it."

"You can relax, Mrs. Ward. I promise you, if we wanted to take Miss Rance away from you, we would have three years ago when we found out you had kept an Ordinary hidden in your home for most of her life." Mia turns to me. "You can relax too, Mr. Grant. If we wanted to take her away from you, we would have the first night you two met at your oak tree."

My eyes have never been wider. How much does the zovernment know? Right now, it seems like they know everything.

Mia smiles warmly. "It's nice to officially meet you all, and you again, Mr. Grant."

I keep my expression tight. "Don't know if I can say the same. Not until I know why you're here."

"May I sit?" Mia asks, pointing to one of the kitchen chairs. She doesn't wait for permission before taking a seat and glancing around the room. "Your home is lovely. I've been admiring the gardens outside."

Dammit. I haven't had a chance to compliment Roxy's gardens yet. Every moment in this house has been wild. I'll be sure to mention her flowers before we leave—assuming I *can* leave, because I'm not stepping a foot outside this house without my girl.

Like Roxy, I don't trust that Mia is simply here to *talk*. I think that's just a ploy to get our guard down. When Mia gets the chance, she's going to snatch Arella away from us and scrub our minds before we can stop them. I won't go down without a fight, and I've got a feeling Arella's grandparents won't either.

As impatient as ever, Phil grumbles, "How's about we cut the small talk and get straight to the point? Tell us why there's an Executive Keeper in my kitchen."

"I advise you to keep your emotions in check, Mr. Ward." Mia's tone is tender yet firm. "I have no problem leaving without explaining anything. To be frank, fifty of the Keepers voted to leave this situation be and to not intervene this early. The other fifty-one believed it would be in everyone's best interest, especially Miss Rance's, that we stepped in. You're currently looking at the person who made that swing vote. So why don't you all sit down so we can have a nice chat?"

Arella is the first to move. She's either brave as fuck or just doesn't realize that having a Keeper here isn't good. She takes the chair straight across from Mia. I sit down too, only because I need to be as close to my girl as possible. If anyone tries to take her, I'll be right there with a fireball.

Roxy takes a moment to weigh her options before finally settling onto the last open chair. With a huff, Phil leaves the room. He comes back seconds later with a clanky folding chair and sticks it at the end of the table, next to his wife. Then he plops into the chair with another huff as if he needs to make it clear that he hates all of this.

"Do you need to take another walk, Phillip?" Roxy asks.

"No," he grumbles. "I'll keep it together."

The tension shooting at me from Arella's grandparents makes me a tiny bit more confident that they'll fight alongside me if this Keeper tries anything. When I first got here, I felt like it was me against them. Now it's us against this Keeper—except I highly doubt Mia came here alone. I'll bet there are other Keepers and Enforcers stationed outside this house right now, waiting for us to make a move. I expand my empathy power to check. Everything seems normal. Does that mean Mia is actually here to talk?

Mia flashes us an overly sugary smile. It makes me trust her even less. "Where should I start? I'm thinking this situation calls for a little Zordi history lesson. How does that sound?"

We all look at each other, then back at the Keeper and nod.

"Miss Rance, my understanding is that you can recall bits and pieces of the things that happened before you were scrubbed, is that right?"

Arella flicks her eyes to me with a look: *Do I lie?*

I give her a look back that says I have no idea.

Arella is smarter than I am, so I trust whatever decision she wants to make. She turns back to Mia. "Yes, that's right."

"Do you remember if Mr. Grant ever explained what caused the Grand Separation in 1326?"

"Not really."

"Great. Let's start there. The Grand Separation is what divided our kind from Ordinaries. What Zordi schools teach their students is that the separation was started by Ordinaries poisoning our alcohol, causing two million people to die within a year. Zordi schools also teach that we cannot reproduce with Ordinaries. While there are truths to both statements, neither is completely true. Yes, Ordinaries tried to eradicate us, but for a valid reason: We were killing their women." Mia stops there, letting us process that last statement.

"You're lying," Phil says, breaking the silence. "Our kind would never do that."

Mia flashes a smile toward Roxy. "Have I lied, Mrs. Ward?"

Roxy lets out a little sigh. "No. Not once."

Since Roxy has no reason to lie about this, I believe her.

"I should add that the killings were unintentional," Mia says.

"What does that mean?" I ask. "How did our kind *unintentionally* kill Ordinary women?"

"I'm so glad you asked." Mia straightens her back. "Let me explain. You've been taught that Zordi sperm does not recognize an Ordinary egg as a suitable host for reproduction. In addition, you're taught that Ordinary sperm is not strong enough to penetrate a Zordi's egg to conceive. While that is mostly true, it doesn't mean it's impossible. Occasionally, there are Zordi sperm that are less picky. There are also some Ordinary sperm strong enough to fertilize the Zordi egg.

"Back before the Grand Separation, the chances of conception were much higher than they are now. About one in every ten pregnancies between our kinds successfully produced a healthy child. Due to our separation over the centuries, the gap between our biological makeups has grown even farther apart, making one in every hundred pregnancies between our kinds viable. Again, difficult, but not impossible."

Roxy's jaw falls. "Are you saying there are people out there who are half and half?"

"No," Mia says. "The children are always born as one or the other—Zordinary or Ordinary —never both. As soon as the embryo is implanted, it has already determined for itself whether it's going to be a Zordi or an Ordi."

"Can we get to the part where you explain how our kind was unintentionally killing Ordinary women?" Phil asks.

"Yes. When a Zordi female becomes pregnant with an Ordinary male, there are usually no complications. The Zordi body can handle growing either type of fetus. The problems only arise when it's an Ordinary who becomes pregnant with a Zordi fetus. It's too hard on the Ordinary mother's body. If the mother doesn't die during the pregnancy, she usually doesn't make it very long after the birth. The chances of survival are about fifty percent."

Everyone at the table snaps their gaze to Arella, who has suddenly gone pale. I take her hand into mine, but it does nothing to ease the panic in her eyes. I don't blame her. Inside, I'm panicking too.

We've been trying to get pregnant since we got back together. Both of us are more than eager to start a family. Because it didn't happen right away like the first time, I was beginning to think it wasn't going to happen at all.

Yesterday morning, Arella's test came back positive, which I remember from prior experience means she's *positively pregnant*, not positively *not* pregnant. We've barely had time to celebrate it, and now I'm being told this could kill her? Having a baby is not worth losing her again.

Mia continues as if the rest of the table isn't losing their goddamn minds. "Before the Grand Separation, there were already plenty of Ordinaries who believed that Zordis didn't have a place in this world. Can you imagine how much deeper that belief became whenever an Ordinary woman died from giving birth to more of our kind? The worst of them was Sir William Knight. Do you remember learning about him in your Zordi history classes?"

"Yes," I say. "He was an Ordinary supremacist who believed all people with powers must be eradicated at all costs."

"Correct," Mia says, "and anyone who agreed with his beliefs joined his anti-Zordi cult. Unfortunately, when enough racist people unite, cloaking their bigoted message behind Christianity, they gain enough followers to become a problem.

"Their crusade began with refusing to give Zordis access to basic needs until they eventually graduated to murdering innocent Zordis, starting with the children. The young ones were easy targets, and they believed if they eliminated the kids first, then there would be fewer Zordis in the future to create more of our kind. It goes without saying that the Zordi community was not fond of Sir William Knight or his people.

"Now the person you aren't taught about in Zordi history class is Richard Taylor. He was the Zordi who raped William's wife, his two sisters, and his mother. Some say Richard did it as revenge for all the dead children. Others say he was hoping for one of the women to fall pregnant with hopes that if William had a Zordi in his family, he'd stop the killings.

"If that was Richard's intent, it failed, because he only made things worse. One of the four women did fall pregnant and carried the baby to term. That woman was William's oldest daughter, and she did not survive the birth. This was the event that caused William and his followers to produce the poison that triggered the Grand Separation."

No wonder I never learned about Richard Taylor in my Zordi history classes. His actions were no better than what the Ordinaries did to us. But come on. Murdering innocent, defenseless children? Really?

Mia continues, "When the zovernment made the decision to hide our world and scrub all the Ordinaries, they also altered all Zordi minds to believe that procreation between our kinds is impossible. We were also taught to start calling the regular people Ordinaries. Before then, everyone was considered to be either a human or a gifted human. The people who hated us called us *freaks*. The zovernment hoped that the new language would foster natural distance, while at the same time, not separate our worlds too much that a future reintegration would be impossible."

I shoot Mia a dirty look. "That's some bullshit. The zovernment is keeping people away from their potential soul mates."

My glare does nothing to faze Mia. "While there is some truth to your statement, Mr. Grant, it's not completely true. With our kinds being separated for so long, we've naturally found soul mates in our own kind more often than outside of it."

"So why are you here?" Phil asks. "I've got a feeling you have more of an agenda than to give us all a history lesson."

"Correct, Mr. Ward. I'm here because Miss Rance is pregnant." Mia flashes Arella a soft smile. "Despite how hard the zovernment works to keep our world hidden, our goal is to eventually bring our worlds back together. That's why when these pregnancies happen, we fully support them. The more Zordis there are in the world, the better. Our belief is that if we can get the Zordi population equal to the Ordinary population, then Ordinaries will be more likely to accept us again. We're currently nowhere near that, but it's a work in progress.

"Typically, we Keepers wait until the second trimester before we offer support, guidance, and medications to ensure the health and growth of your child to term. Because you're a rare Immune, it's our priority to do everything we can to increase your chances of survival."

I don't like the word *survival*. Arella shouldn't have to fight to *survive* the birth of our child. Especially not if the chances are fifty percent. With the way my life has gone, I can almost guarantee she won't make it. *Am I cursed? Is it my fate to see everyone I love die?*

"What about Trey and me?" Arella asks. "I'm not going to have this baby if the zovernment separates us again."

"Ah, right. Maybe I should have addressed that first. Have you heard of Augustine Island?"

"Yes," I say. "It's a hidden island where the entire population is Zordis."

"Correct. That island is common knowledge for our people. The hidden island that isn't common knowledge is the one called Jetty Island. It's where all the crossbreeding couples go to live with their children. Many generations of crossbred people live there now. It's a pretty nice place, in my opinion. There, our kind is free to be with whoever they want. Zordis can freely use their powers too. It runs like its own little country."

Arella tilts her head to the side. "Are you saying that if Trey and I want to be together, we have to move to this island?"

"Yes. In addition, the choice is permanent and there is no contact with the outside world. This is how we're able to keep this place hidden. Your current friends and family will have their minds altered to believe you're dead. If you don't choose this, your other option is to terminate your pregnancy, and we'll have to scrub you again."

"No!" Arella and I shout at the same time.

"I predicted you'd say that," Mia says with a chuckle, even though there's nothing to be chuckling about. "That's why I've come with a secret third option. With Miss Rance being immune, you have the ability to fool the Zordi world by claiming you're one of us. You can say your mind power is the ability to block powers and the zense. If you choose this option, my team can begin the process of getting Miss Rance added to our Zordi systems as one of us."

"What are the downsides to that?" I ask, because this sounds way too good to be true. There's gotta be a catch.

"The downside is that if this secret third option becomes a problem for the Keepers, we will force option two onto you without discussion. You'll both forget that any of this ever happened. As for any children you might have, they will also be scrubbed and placed into someone else's care."

Arella and I glance at each other. It only takes us a second for us to silently agree on which option we want.

Mia nods her approval as if she heard the conversation we just had with our eyes. "That's wonderful. As soon as I leave, I'll have my team begin the paperwork."

"Wait," I say. "Does this mean Arella and I have full permission to be together now?"

"There are certain rules you'll have to follow. For example, with Miss Rance pretending to be a Zordi, all Zordi laws will apply to her. Otherwise, yes, you are free to be together."

"Does that mean I can legally marry her too?"

"On paper, Miss Rance will appear as a Zordi, so, yes, you may legally marry each other."

I jump out of my chair with both arms in the air. "Fuck yeah!" I seize Arella's face and plant a long, hard kiss against her lips. I don't even care that everyone's watching. Neither does she, because she kisses me back just as hard.

Every day for the last two weeks, I've asked Arella to marry me. She's been rejecting me because we wouldn't be able to have a "real wedding" or be "legally married." I didn't care. I just wanted to see a ring on her finger. I wanted us to at least *pretend* to be engaged.

Now she has zero excuses to deny my proposals. I'm going to make the next one so special, she'll want nothing more than to say yes.

Arella has a giant smile on her face as I sit back down and take her hand into my lap. I can't stop smiling either. I never thought I'd see the day when a zovernment official told me I have permission to be with an Ordinary. I want to take Arella home and make love to her right now. After that, I want to show her off to my bandmates, then the rest of the world.

"Do the Keepers know what makes Ari immune?" Phil asks.

"It's as much of a mystery to the Keepers as it is to you," Mia says. "I can share our theories with you; however, nothing has been scientifically confirmed."

"Please share," Roxy says eagerly.

"Sure. Theory one is that while Ordinaries were developing the poison to kill us, they were also developing a drug that could make them immune to Zordi powers. It's possible that they succeeded and the drug altered the DNA of those people before the worldwide scrub. Now that gene has been passed down this far to Miss Rance. We don't have confirmation of this theory because we have yet to create an immunity drug ourselves, so we're unsure how a bunch of Ordinaries could have done it back in the 1300s.

"Our second theory is that Miss Rance and the other Immunes are merely an anomaly. There's no pattern to it, and it happens so rarely that we haven't been able to gather enough data about Immunes to make any firm conclusions."

"What data do you have?" I ask.

"We know about as much as you know," Mia says, and I don't believe her one bit. "The only thing I know more than you is the data involving Immunes and soul mates.

"Within the system of Keepers, my official title is Soul Mate Specialist. I lead a team of other Keepers who research and study how the soul mate connection is built, how it affects people, and how the glimmer works, especially when it's between a Zordi and an Ordinary.

"As you can imagine, with Zordis believing that our kind should stick to our own kind, that type of connection is pretty rare. Being immune is even rarer, which means being an Immune who has built a soul mate connection to a Zordi is the most rare. To this day, you are the third couple in history who fits that criteria, and the first to happen in my lifetime. That's why I, along with our Immunes specialist, have been keeping a special eye on you two over the past three years.

"When you were arrested by the Enforcers outside Shadow Ridge, word spread that they had found an Ordinary woman who seemed to be immune to Zordi powers. Once that word spread up to the Keepers, Grace, our Immunes specialist, went to check it out. You both might remember her. She has blonde hair with a strip of purple going down the front."

At first, I shake my head, and then it hits me: That's the woman I hallucinated the last time I got high. Was that woman actually real? Was the man with the goatee real too?

As if she can hear my thoughts, Mia says, "Yes, Mr. Grant, they were real."

"I saw that woman in my dreams once," Arella says. "All I remember is that she kept asking me a bunch of questions."

"Yes," Mia says. "You were in the middle of being interrogated by an Enforcer when Grace figured out through your informative answers that you and Mr. Grant were soul mates. And that's when I got called.

"Ordinaries who get scrubbed are never able to regain their memories. Immunes who get scrubbed are the same. However, when an Immune with a soul mate connection to a Zordi gets scrubbed, their memories return in their dreams. At least, that's what I gathered from the data from the two previous couples like you. Since this hasn't happened for over two hundred years, Grace and I weren't sure how accurate that data was.

"That's why we allowed you to keep your memories, Mr. Grant. That's why I allowed you to keep your photo with Miss Rance's writing on the back. That's also why I slipped that angel-wings necklace into her hospital bag. I hoped that leaving you two with those items would help keep your connection alive so we could see if Miss Rance would regain her memories or not."

I shoot Mia a nasty look. "So this whole time, we've just been a part of your little experiment?"

"I can understand why that might make you angry," Mia says calmly. "However, I have good news for you. Three Immunes with a soul mate connection to a Zordi is a small sample size, but it's a big enough pattern for me to conclude that permanently scrubbing an Immune who has made a soul-mate connection with a Zordi is impossible. That means the next time this happens, the zovernment will proceed differently. I suspect that Miss Rance will regain all of her memories over time and it'll be like she was never scrubbed at all. At least, that's how it was for the other two like her."

"But she *was* scrubbed," I say. "I went through three years of hell without her."

Mia doesn't look like she cares. "At the end of the day, Miss Rance was still an Ordinary who found out about the Zordi world. She would have been scrubbed regardless. Grace and I simply kept an eye on you two afterward."

"But you let it go on for three years. Why not just tell us your plan? Then Arella and I could have worked on getting her to remember me faster."

"That's not the way Keepers work. We intervene as little as possible. Also, we wanted to see how long it would take for Miss Rance's memories to return and at what capacity. We also wanted to discover what factors might play into her memories returning. That's all valuable data we wouldn't have been able to collect if we intervened. Letting you keep that photo and the necklace was already intervening too much. Saving your life after you tried to kill yourself was pushing it too."

"What?" Arella gapes at me. "You . . . what?"

I never told Arella that I used to purposely overdose. I also never told her about the many times I contemplated jumping out the window of my penthouse or the times I thought about tying bricks to my ankles and *accidentally* falling into the Hudson River. I've kept that information from her because I don't need to share the darkest parts of my past with the lightest parts of my future.

"Mixing alcohol with jaderro is a deadly recreational activity," Mia says. "Not only did you do that multiple times a week, but it went on for months. We tried diluting your supply a few times, but it only made you take larger quantities."

That explains why I kept having to up my dosage.

Phil's tone turns to ice as he glares at Arella. "You're dating a drunk musician with a jaderro addiction?"

I'm about to open my mouth to defend myself, but Arella beats me to it. "Trey has been sober for a long time now."

"I can confirm that," Mia says. "And please apologize to Liz for me. A Scrubber altered her memories to make her think she flew to New York and found you in a bad state on the floor of your apartment. In reality, we had already brought you to the hospital and pumped the drugs out of your system. Then we knocked her out and flew her there ourselves. We needed her to talk you out of doing it again. I'm pretty impressed by you, Mr. Grant. You quit cold turkey, and you haven't relapsed once."

"It's really fucking creepy that you know that," I say.

"I wish we knew more. Even with the information we have now, it's still unclear how Miss Rance is able to reverse the scrubbing." Mia smiles at Arella. "We can only assume it has to do with whatever makes you immune and the unique way our bodies function after building a soul-mate connection."

"How did you gather your information?" I ask. "How can the Keepers watch us without me knowing it? My empathy power would have been able to detect whenever someone was nearby."

"Your empathy power can't sense Astral Projectors."

Arella glances around the room, then at the ceiling. "Is there someone watching us now?"

"Yes," Mia says. "It's a normal practice. How else do you think the zovernment knows anything?"

Roxy gives Mia a motherly shake of her head. "Just because it's normal doesn't make it right."

I couldn't agree more.

"It's done with the intent of our kind's protection, Mrs. Ward. And obviously, things do slip through the cracks. For example, it's hard for us to keep up with all Royal crimes when there are more of them than there are of us. I mean, you raised an Ordinary child in your home without us knowing it. Our limited number of Astral Projectors can only see so much."

Mia glances at her watch. "I need to wrap this up, so I'll end with this: Over the centuries, we've learned that it's easier for our kinds to produce a healthy child together if the couple are soul mates. Since you've already gotten pregnant once before and that fetus was using her mind power in the womb, I've got a good feeling your current pregnancy will grow to term. Most pregnancies between our kinds don't even get that far. That's why it's crucial that we stepped in early. With our zoctors handling your prenatal care, we expect your survival rate to rise to almost seventy-five percent."

Almost? "That's it?"

"Seventy-five is much better than fifty, don't you think, Mr. Grant?"

I scoff. "But that means Arella still has a twenty-five percent chance of dying in the next nine months."

Mia ignores me and turns to Arella. "Why don't we start your prenatal visits as soon as the holiday is over? I'll have our medical team get in contact with you. If it gives you any hope, your chances of surviving this pregnancy and the birth are much higher if your child is an Ordinary. Around week ten, we will do a genetic test. If those test results come back with an elemental chromosome, that'll mean your baby is a Zordi."

Arella lets out a long breath. "I guess we'll find out in six weeks."

112

TREY

Arella's groans of pain echo against the walls of our kitchen. Last month, we turned this room into a birthing station in anticipation of our Ordinary child coming into the world. We don't know what gender we're having yet. Arella wanted it to be a surprise. I don't care what gender our baby is. I'm just excited to become a dad.

My girl has been in labor for almost fifteen hours. Four highly trained medical zoctors have been coming in and out of our house all day, doing everything they can to help ease Arella's pain. They're now surrounding her feet, ready to catch our baby when he or she pops out. Arella's midwife and two nurses are also at her side, coaching her through what looks and sounds like a goddamn horror movie.

I'm near Arella's head. She's crushing my hand in hers as I try to stay strong for her. I hate seeing her in misery, especially knowing there's nothing I can do to stop it.

"You're doing great!" the main zoctor says. "Your baby is almost here. Can you give me another hard push?"

Arella sucks in a deep breath, then pushes again. She squeezes my hand so hard, I internally yelp. The zoctors at her feet smile as an infant's cries fill the room.

My heart swells as my eyes fill with happy tears. That's my baby crying. *My* baby. *My* little boy or girl. I lean down to give Arella a kiss on her forehead. "You did it, babe! I'm so proud of—"

She lets go of my hand as her head drops against the bed. The machine she's hooked up to goes off with a loud siren.

"She's passed out!" a nurse shouts. "She's not breathing either."

"She's losing a lot of blood!" says a zoctor.

A nurse pushes me out of her way, and I stumble backward into the wall. *Passed out? Not breathing? Losing a lot of blood?*

We've had multiple conversations about this being a possibility. When Arella and I debated whether or not to continue her pregnancy, we decided to put trust in the zovernment to keep her and our baby safe and healthy. Now I'm thinking we might have made the wrong decision.

My vision blurs as muffled shouting and an infant's cries consume me. All the people in my kitchen yell things at each other I can't make out. They surround Arella with machines and cords I have no idea what to do with.

The head zoctor hooks an oxygen mask over Arella's face. At least, I *think* it's an oxygen mask. If it's not, what is it for?

If Arella doesn't make it through this, what does that mean for me? For our baby? I haven't thought much about that because I haven't wanted to consider it as an option. I've been living off the hope that seventy-five percent is enough.

Someone shakes my arm. "Mr. Grant?"

I glance up at the nurse from the kitchen counter I'm bracing myself over. "Huh?"

"Did you hear me?"

"I'm sorry." My voice comes out as shaky as my hands. "What did you say?"

"I asked if you could do skin-to-skin with your daughter? It's important that the baby gets it immediately. We typically do that with the mother, but . . ."

My daughter?

The nurse holds up a tiny human who's crying at the top of her lungs. She's so loud, I can barely hear the nurse ask me to take my shirt off.

Get yourself together, Grant. Your baby needs you. After sucking in a deep breath, I tear my shirt over my head, then the nurse hands me my daughter. I erupt into tears as I hold her against my chest and feel her skin against mine.

I'm a dad now. I'm a fucking dad.

I bounce my baby girl in my arms as the nurse rushes back to Arella's bedside. My hands tremble against my daughter's back while I wait for someone to tell me whether my wife is okay or not.

I stare at the canvas print of Arella and me hanging on the wall near the fridge, hoping it'll give me some peace. Arella looks like an angel in her long lacy white dress. At the time, she wasn't showing yet, which was why we had our wedding barely a month after Christmas. In the photo, I'm dipping her back, making her laugh so hard, she squints her eyes and drops the bouquet of flowers in her hand.

That was one of my favorite moments from our wedding because it was right after I was told I could kiss my bride. We had a small wedding at our oak tree at sunset with our closest friends, Arella's grandparents, my bandmates, and Li and Tao. Javina's maid-of-honor speech made people laugh so hard, they cried. Liz's best-woman speech was so heartfelt, I cried.

Now Arella and I have our wedding photos plastered all over our house—the house we moved into two months ago. It's much bigger than the previous one, and we chose it because the second we stepped into it, Arella said she could see us raising our kids here.

I can't live here without her. Correction: I can't live without her. We've had the most amazing eleven months together. I can't lose her. Especially not today. It's September fifth, the anniversary of my parents' death, which is now also the birthdate of my first child. It's crazy how the world works this way. Is the world crazy and cruel enough to give me my daughter and take away my wife on the same day it took away my parents?

My baby's cries mellow out the longer I rock her against my chest. "You're okay, baby girl. Daddy's got you."

Holding her is calming me just as much as it's calming her. I wish I could tell her that her mother is gonna be okay. I don't want my baby to grow up without—

Wait a second . . . I'm at least five steps away from all the other people in this kitchen. Why am I feeling the zense?

I glance down at my baby. It's her. The zense is coming from *her*. But how? Throughout Arella's pregnancy, she never felt the baby use any mind powers. Also, the genetic test came back confirming that our baby was an Ordinary. The test looked for the chromosome that determines what elemental power the baby will develop by the age of one. Our baby didn't have that chromosome at all. How am I feeling the zense from her?

"Mr. Grant?" the main zoctor says.

I turn to find her with bloody gloves and a pale expression. *That can't be good.*

"She's stable."

"What does that mean?"

"It means we've sedated her." The zoctor puts her bloody hands up in surrender. "It's okay. It's just to help with pain relief. Her body went into shock after the birth and she had a postpartum hemorrhage, but she's going to be okay."

A postpartum what? I don't recall hearing that term during any of our prenatal visits.

The zoctor must see the confusion on my face, because she says, "It just means she had heavy bleeding after birth. Remember, we planned for anything to happen. Therefore, we already had the right things in place to give her a blood transfusion if we needed to. The other zoctors are working on that now. She'll be fine."

I let out a long breath as I force myself to nod. If the head zoctor is saying Arella's going to be fine, I'm going to believe her. That's all I can do right now.

"May we take your daughter to get her cleaned up?"

Silently, I hand my baby off. The second I let her go, her cries fill the kitchen again.

I keep an eye on my baby as I make my way back to Arella's side and take her hand. As if she can hear me, I speak softly into her ear. "She's beautiful, Arella. I can't wait for you to meet her."

113

TREY

"Liz?" I say when she answers my call. I'm lying on the couch with my baby sleeping on my chest. I hope she won't wake up again.

"Hey, T-Bear."

"Can you come over?" I ask softly.

"Um, sure. Is everything—Oh my god. Is Ari in labor?"

"No."

"Damn. I thought for sure that's why you called. She's like, what, three days overdue?"

"Liz, she's not in labor because . . . well, she's done."

"What?" Liz shrieks so loudly, I have to pull the phone away from my ear. "Since when?"

"About two hours ago."

"Oh my god!" She switches to shouting. "Colton! I'm going to Trey's! Be back later!"

In the background, Colton shouts back, "Cool. Send me pics!"

A door slams shut, then Liz says, "Okay, T. I'm getting in my car now."

"Good," I say, "because I really need you."

"What for?"

I stare at my daughter, who looks just like her mother. "You know how to change a diaper, right?"

"Yeah, but don't you?"

"Arella and I took some parenting classes together. I practiced once on one of those fake dolls, but I can't really remember it right now. I don't wanna fuck it up. I'd ask one of the nurses here, but I'm too embarrassed to admit I don't know how to change my own baby's diaper. It's not urgent because the diaper's not full yet. Honestly, I just really need you here. Arella is . . ." I hear Liz's car engine start up in the background as I work up the courage to tell her what happened.

"Just take a deep breath."

I do, then let it out. "Arella is currently sedated."

"What?"

As Liz makes her way here, I tell her everything that happened, from the start of Arella's contractions to all the chaos during and after the birth.

"They said she's gonna be okay, so I'm trying my damnedest to believe them."

"Just hang in there, T. I'll be there soon."

When Liz arrives, she uses her key to get in so I don't have to move.

"In here," I say from the living room. My voice startles my baby so much, she wakes up with a wail. *Fuck.*

Liz drops her purse onto the floor as she enters the living room.

"Please help me," I beg as I sit up, holding my crying baby against my chest. "Tell me you know how to do baby shit."

"Oh, T. I'm sure you're doing just fine."

"I'm not. She keeps waking up and crying every ten minutes. Earlier, when I tried to feed her, one of the nurses had to step in because I couldn't get her to latch on to the bottle."

"That's pretty normal."

I hold my daughter out. "Just take her, and tell me what I'm doing wrong."

"Um . . ." Liz lets out a chuckle. "First off, that's not how you hold an infant."

"What? The nurse said I need to keep her neck supported. That's what I'm doing."

Liz offers me a gentle smile. "Here. Lemme help."

Five minutes later, Liz is on the couch with my baby calmly drinking from a bottle.

"I swear, you're a baby whisperer."

Liz giggles, never taking her eyes off my daughter. I don't blame her. It's been hard for me to look anywhere else too. "Becoming a parent isn't easy, T. Just be patient with yourself. It's a big learning curve."

"I don't think you realize how big my curve is. Until that nurse handed me my daughter, I'd never even held a baby."

"Seriously?" She gapes up at me from the couch. "Actually, now that I think about it, that checks out."

With the lightest plop I can manage, I settle onto the couch too. For a while, neither of us says anything. We just admire my daughter with light smiles on our faces.

Eventually, Liz breaks the silence. "What's her name?"

"I don't know. Since Arella did all the work to grow our baby, I wanted her to come up with a name. She told me she had some in mind but wanted to surprise me. The nurses and I have just been calling her *baby girl.*"

"That's cute."

I bite my lip before asking, "Liz, do you notice anything strange about her?"

"Strange? Like what?"

"Like this." I head across the room, standing well over an arm's length away.

At first, Liz crumples her eyebrows together with a *what the hell are you doing?* face. Then she gasps and stares down at my baby. "Oh my god. She's one of us!"

"Yep." I return to the couch.

"But—"

"I know."

Liz pauses to think, then says, "Do you think the genetic test came back wrong?"

"I dunno, but—"

Ding-dong!

"Who the hell is here?" I pop up to answer the door.

On my front stoop is Mia Wang wearing another silky blouse tucked into her black skirt. "The test was not wrong, Mr. Grant."

"Jeez. Remind me to never talk shit about the zovernment. Not even under my breath."

"We've heard it all. Trust me." She lets out a light chuckle. "May I come in?"

Back in the living room, I offer Mia the recliner. She accepts it with a smile toward Liz. "It's nice to officially meet you, Miss Hart."

I've told Liz all about how the zovernment watches us through Astral Projectors.

While the smile Liz flashes toward Mia is friendly, it's not her friendliest. "I'm guessing you're Mia Wang?"

"Correct."

"Are you here to tell me that my child is Dormant?" I settle back down next to Liz, who's still feeding my daughter like a pro. The milk in the bottle is almost gone, and my baby hasn't gotten fussy once. Seriously, what was I doing wrong earlier?

"Even Dormant Zordis have an elemental chromosome," Mia says. "They have the genetics to produce mind and body powers as well. They just have a condition that prevents them from doing so. Most Dormant children will develop their powers later in life. Unfortunately, being Dormant is not the case with your daughter."

"How long have you known that my daughter is a Zordi?" I ask, because even though the zovernment has been taking amazing care of my wife throughout her pregnancy, I still don't fully trust them.

"I got a message from your main zoctor about thirty minutes ago."

From what I can tell, Mia's speaking the truth. It's good to know this wasn't something the zovernment knew about and chose to keep from us. "So if my daughter isn't Dormant, what is she?"

"Since we've only had thirty minutes to theorize, we aren't a hundred percent sure, but we suspect your daughter might be the Helio."

"The what?"

"The Helio. It's a rare Zordi who does not have a mind, body, or elemental power. Instead, they *are* a power."

Liz perks up. "Oh! I read about this in Zordi school when we were learning about Zordinary myths and legends. Isn't the Helio like the sun or something?"

"Correct, Miss Hart. And just like the sun, there is only one. Think of the Helio as the sun in human form with the power to give energy to others. The Helio was once a living, breathing Zordi, just like us. When they died, they turned into an invisible wisp with its own thoughts and feelings. Because it takes its energy from the sun, it never fully dies. It just floats around the world until it finds its next suitable human host to latch onto. Once it does, it gives that host all of its powers, turning that host into the Helio. Once that host dies, the wisp moves on to find their next host."

I take a moment to process that. "So, um, you're saying there's a wispy thing inside my daughter?"

"If our theory is correct, then yes."

"How can we know for sure?"

"Like our limited knowledge about Immunes, we don't have much knowledge about this either. The legend says that because the Helio draws its powers directly from the sun, the host's skin will glow slightly when under sunlight."

I glance at Liz, then at the bit of sunshine coming through the living room window between the curtains. As if reading my mind, Liz stands and strides across the living room. I wave a hand at the curtains, and they slide apart all the way.

As soon as the sunlight hits my daughter's face, I gasp. Her skin instantly brightens and gives off a subtle glow.

"That's enough proof for me," Liz says.

"During the quick five-minute briefing session I got about the Helio before arriving here," Mia says, "I was told that the Helio used to be the most powerful Zordi to ever live. They had the power to do things like control the weather and bring people back to life."

I imagine my daughter growing up, running around gravesites, raising zombies out of the dirt. The scene doesn't sit right with me.

Mia continues, "However, there haven't been signs that the Helio has been active for centuries, so it's most likely that your daughter may never develop any Helio powers at all."

"Is there a way to get this wispy thing out of my baby?" I ask.

"Not that we know of."

"What does this mean for her then?"

"That depends entirely on if she develops any Helio powers or not. If she does, we'll have to make sure she's safe and under control. If she doesn't, she'll simply live out her life as if she's Dormant. Over time, her skin brightening under the sun should lessen, but it won't ever fully disappear. It shouldn't be noticeable unless someone's really looking for it."

None of that sounds ideal. I was thrilled about having an Ordinary child. This Helio thing sounds like a whole lot of chaos I wasn't prepared for. Not only do I have to learn how to be a father who can correctly hold an infant, but now I have to learn how to handle having the one and only sun wisp inside my daughter?

I really need my wife right now. She'd know what to do.

A NURSE KNOCKS ON THE DOORFRAME OF MY BEDROOM. "MR. GRANT?"

I finish swaddling my baby girl, then pick her up and support her against my chest. "Yes?"

"Your wife is awake and asking for you."

Thank fuck! I've been sitting at Arella's bedside for hours upon hours, waiting for her to wake up. Of course it's when I'm upstairs, changing our baby's clothes, that she rises.

I race down the steps and into the kitchen to find my wife sitting up in her medical bed. The nurses and our midwife are gone, but they haven't gone far. Their low murmurs of conversation and light emotions are floating into me from the living room.

When Arella sees me, her face lights up. "Is that our baby?"

"No, ours is upstairs. This one is a simulation."

She bursts into a laugh that instantly lifts my mood. "I'm glad you still have a sense of humor. The nurses just told me I've been out for a while."

"Yeah, and I've needed my sense of humor to be able to get through it." I choke up a little, grateful that she's okay. "Would you like to hold our daughter?"

"Daughter?" Arella takes our baby from me, cradles her, then tears up. "She's beautiful."

Seeing the person I love the most in the world hold a child we created together—there aren't enough words in the dictionary to describe all the joy rushing through me.

"Liz said she looks just like you," I say as I gently tuck some of Arella's hair behind her ear.

"Is Liz here? Tell her to come in."

"No, she left a while ago. Earlier, she taught me how to properly strap on a diaper."

"Did she teach you how to properly hold a baby too?"

I let out a laugh. "Yes, she did."

"Thank god. I saw the way you were doing it in our parenting class with a fake baby. The whole time, I told myself you'd come into it naturally with a real one."

"I got some good tips from Professor Google too. I'm like a pro now."

Arella cups the side of my face, and I lean into her palm. Her touch erases all my anxiety. "I'm so proud of you, honey. Thank you for taking care of our baby while I couldn't."

"Don't give me all the credit. Without Google, Liz, and all these trained women around, I might have poked at you until you woke up to help me."

She gives me a knowing smile. "Did you think you were going to lose me?"

"Yep."

"Did you think you were cursed for almost losing your wife on the same day you lost your parents?"

"Abso-fucking-lutely."

She chuckles and rolls her eyes. "Come here, honey."

I lean over our baby to give Arella a kiss. The second our mouths collide, every swarm of nerve-wracking thoughts from the past gut-wrenching day disappears. *My wife is alive, she's awake, and she's going to be okay.*

I only stop kissing her once our daughter gets a little fussy. I call our midwife back in to help Arella breastfeed for the first time—another sight I never imagined could give me so much fulfillment.

The entire time she feeds, I stand back in awe of everything my woman is. I hope that every morning she woke up nauseous, the constant lower back pain, and those fifteen hours of labor she went through are worth it for her. Everything I had to go through to get here is already worth it, just to see my wife looking at our daughter like she's the most precious thing in the world.

Once our baby falls asleep in Arella's arms, the midwife returns to the living room. I take the time to fill Arella in on finding out that our daughter is a Zordi, and not just any Zordi, but possibly the most powerful Zordi on the planet.

When I get to the part where our daughter could have the power to bring people back to life, Arella makes the same *ick* face I did.

"Are you saying our daughter can make zombies?"

It's nice to know her mind went there too. "Mia said the Helio hasn't shown signs of being active for centuries. She said our daughter is merely a host for it to exist."

"Aren't you a lucky man? You've got two of the rarest humans in the world under one roof."

I'm not sure if *lucky* is the right word, because I don't *feel* lucky. Mostly, I just feel the need to enclose my wife and daughter inside an impenetrable dome. Since they are so rare, they must be protected.

That's when it hits me: I know what my purpose is now. This is why I survived the explosion that killed my parents. This is also why I survived all the other shit I went through, especially those three years I spent without Arella. The world kept me around to protect my wife and our little girl.

I take a moment to let that realization sink in. My eyes close, and I bask in the rush of warmth that spreads through me. I imagine the rest of my life with my little family and silently vow that I will do everything in my power to give them the best and protect them at all costs. It feels good to know I was meant for something all along.

"Would you like to know our baby's name?" Arella asks.

I open my eyes, blinking away the happy tears. "You have a name picked out already?"

"Yeah. I had a name picked out for both genders. If our baby was a boy, I was going to name him Victor."

My heart swells up as I think about the loving man who deserved so much better than what he got. "That would have been a great way to honor my dad with more than just a letter in my tattoo."

"Yeah, but since she's a girl, her name is Katie." Arella has been seeing a lot of Katie in her dreams lately. Like many of her dreams, they don't give her the full picture, so I've been filling in the blanks as much as possible. Together, we have cried and mourned over the loss of the brave young woman who's a huge reason why we are here today.

"Do you like the name?" Arella asks.

I place a tender kiss against her forehead. "Yes, baby. Katie is perfect."

ACKNOWLEDGMENTS

*To my **husband, Joe**:*
Thank you for believing in me and being my biggest fan. I'm so lucky to be the "naughty girl"
you bend over tables and whisper dirty things to in public.

*To my **beta readers** who read this entire trilogy:*
Kaycee Racer, Priscillah Bancy, Kelsey Davis, Whitney Tanner, Mads Arlow, and Annie.
Thank you for being the first people to give me confidence that my stories were worth
publishing.

*To my **readers**:*
I'll never get sick of your messages and reviews saying how much my books emotionally
destroyed you. *takes a sip* Thanks for all your delicious tears.

*To **Enchanted Ink Publishing**:*
Natalia, Stephanie, Christian, Lisa, and Greg.
A team like this is hard to find. Your caliber of excellence is unmatched! May your traffic
lights always be green, your coffees warm, and your pillows fluffed.

*To my **Secret Keepers**:*
It still amazes me that a bunch of book-loving hotties on the internet chose *me* as an author
they want to promote in their spare time. Not only that, but some of y'all even traveled to
come hang out with me! I'm so thankful I didn't give up on writing. Otherwise, I never would
have known this amazingly supportive street team.

*To **the three babies I lost in the womb trying to have my first baby**:*
Your little brother made it, and he's happily thriving in the world.

*To **anyone who has ever lost a pregnancy or child**:*
You are not alone, and it was not your fault.

*To **anyone who wants to write a book**:*
Just do it and see where it takes you. :)

ABOUT THE AUTHOR

Melissa Lam loves reading and writing romance books that take the reader on an emotional roller coaster full of mystery, suspense, and heartache.

As an extroverted introvert who doesn't like to leave the house (because it requires wearing pants), Melissa enjoys playing strategic board games and taking long showers. When she does find the will to put pants on, she can be found traveling, enjoying bubble tea, or experiencing the world through food.

TL;DR I like to eat and write about heartbreaking shit.

Website: authormelissalam.com
Instagram: instagram.com/authormelissalam
Facebook: facebook.com/authormelissalam
Newsletter: authormelissalam.com/newsletter

SUPPORT INDIE AUTHORS

The best way to support indie authors is to leave reviews, because it helps other readers discover us! If you enjoyed this book, please consider leaving your feedback on Amazon, Goodreads, and anywhere else readers hang out.

Grab Melissa's other books on
www.authormelissalam.com

www.ingramcontent.com/pod-product-compliance
Lightning Source LLC
Chambersburg PA
CBHW081102300726
48976CB00011B/2698